THE KNIGHT'S BANE TRILOGY

OMNIBUS EDITION

BRYAN DONIHUE

Edited by
LAURA "L-WRAY" HEWITT

Edited by
DAVID "SPOOKY" CASSIDAY

Section 28 Publishing

DEDICATION

It may seem unusual for a paranormal action book, but this book is first and foremost dedicated to Jesus, the Christ - the only true Savior who can save us from evil. He is the real source of Hope.

This book is dedicated to my wife, Christina, and my brood of kids. You've put up with many months of my unavailability while I was writing and many weekends where I am traveling to comic cons. Thank you for putting up with me and my obsession with telling stories.

INCURSION: Knightmare Dedication

I have three wonderful editors on this project:

- Kathryn Gerard was my first editor. She helped me get this into shape for the original printing.
- Laura Hewitt is my General Editor. She is the one who truly refined my work to make me sound better, and she pushed me to produce the best story possible.
- David Cassiday is my Continuity Editor. He makes sure that I don't screw up all the little details, while also making sure that the story makes sense.

Any and all of the mistakes that are left in this book are solely mine, usually because I didn't listen to Kat or David.

Thank you to my Grand Rapids gaming group, Incursion: Hidden Worlds. They brought this story to life. They are:

- Ryan DeBoer - Burt "Six" Holstein
- David Cassiday - John "Spooky" Smith
- Zachariah Watkins - Jesús "God" Rivera
- Amanda Watkins - Rebekah "Boomer" Callahan
- Eulene Freeland - Noelle "Doc" Sorenson
- Simon Verburg - Jonas "Ghost" Vanhof
- Nate Miller - Arthur "Heavy" Murphy
- Scott Coles - Christian "Do-Right" Folsom
- Matt Poferl - William "Scout" Buckhorn

INCURSION: Faeblade Dedication

I have a wonderful editor on this project, David Cassiday. He worked diligently with continuity and style to make sure that this story is the best that I can tell it. He made sure that I didn't screw up all the little details, while also making sure that the plot makes sense.

Any and all of the mistakes that are left in this book are solely mine, usually because I didn't listen to David.

Thank you to my Beta Readers:
David "Spooky" Cassiday
Zachariah "God" Watkins
Amanda "Boomer" Watkins

Thank you to my Grand Rapids gaming group, Incursion: Hidden Worlds. They continue to bring these characters to life. They are:

- David Cassiday - John "Spooky" Smith
- Zachariah Watkins - Jesús "God" Rivera
- Amanda Watkins - Rebekah "Boomer" Callahan
- Eulene Freeland - Noelle "Doc" Sorenson
- Simon Verburg - Jonas "Ghost" Vanhof

- Nate Miller - Arthur "Heavy" Murphy
- Scott Coles - Christian "Do-Right" Folsom
- Matt Poferl - William "Scout" Buckhorn

INCURSION: Dragonfire Dedication

I had a wonderful editor on this project, David "Spooky" Cassiday. He worked diligently with continuity and style to make sure that this story is the best that I can tell it. He made sure that I didn't screw up all the little details, while also making sure that the plot makes sense. He is also a great friend who is not afraid to tell me when I screw things up. Any and all of the mistakes that are left in this book are solely mine, usually because I didn't listen to David.

Thank you to my Beta Readers. Not only is having an editor really important, having other people read your drafts before they get released is even more so.

- Simon "Ghost" Verburg
- Laura "L Wray" Hewitt
- Rick "Deacon" Stratton

Thank you to my Grand Rapids gaming group, Incursion: Hidden Worlds. They continue to bring these characters to life. They are:

- David Cassiday - John "Spooky" Smith
- Ryan DeBoer - John "Six" Black
- Eulene Freeland - Noelle "Doc" Sorenson
- Nate Miller - Arthur "Heavy" Murphy
- Simon Verburg - Jonas "Ghost" Vanhof
- Amanda Watkins - Rebekah "Boomer" Callahan
- Zachariah Watkins - Jesús "Little G" Rivera

I want to offer a thank you and a dedication to Heather Kalafut. In books one and two (Knightmare and Faeblade), she provided an awesome sounding board for parts of the story. You can thank her for the awesome "sparkly" vampire in Faeblade. Once again in Dragonfire, she has been a great sounding board for ideas. Heather, I missed crediting you in Knightmare and Faeblade. I hope your scenes here make up for it. You are an awesome Special Agent and friend.

I also want to offer a thank you and a special dedication to Applebee's

Restaurant on Alpine Avenue in Grand Rapids. Michigan. A surprising amount of this book was written at the restaurant, and I have to thank Angie Dawson, the manager, and Jessica, my usual waitress, and all the other waitstaff for keeping me fed and letting me write in peace. If you are in the area, stop by and tell them I said, "Hi."

This story is based on an original world created by Bryan Donihue, and an original roleplaying game created by Bryan Donihue, with David Cassiday and Troye Gerard. The "Section 28" name idea was from Troye, and he graciously allowed me to twist it to my own particular flavor.

BRYAN DONIHUE

INCURSION: KNIGHTMARE

THE KNIGHT'S BANE TRILOGY—BOOK 1

INDIEGOGO SUPPORTERS

For this novel, I ran a crowdfunding campaign to pay for some of the (rather minor) expenses incurred in self-publishing. I ran the campaign on Indiegogo (indiegogo.com), and can't say enough good things about their service.

I had a group of incredible backers in the campaign. Their support made the campaign successful, and I cannot thank them enough!

Campaign Contributors

Esoteric Research
Jeff Jackson
Jeremy Sampsell

Field Agent
David Cassiday
Ryan DeBoer
Paul Donihue

Veteran Hunter
Matthew Eastman
Eulene Freeland

Troye Gerard
Nate Miller

Support Staff
Jeff Donihue

PROLOGUE

Hunger. Pain. Cruel hunger gnawed away at the creature. Forced to hunt. Searching for prey to feed the growing hunger. Cold, dead eyes saw the world around it. Even though it was a dark, moonless night, the creature saw the path and the surrounding woods as if the sun were overhead.

Sounds. The rhythmic pounding of footsteps on the path. As the creature turned toward the sounds, it caught sight of a young woman. Even though the girl was still fifty yards away, the noise of the music on her headphones was apparent to the creature's newly heightened senses.

Blood. Smell the blood. Nostrils flaring, the creature could almost taste the blood pumping through the veins of the girl. Forcing itself to wait for the prey to come closer, the hunger drove the creature to the edge of madness. As the prey neared, the creature hunched into the dark shadows.

Running. The prey noticed the creature and screamed in alarm. She stumbled to a halt, turned, and ran away in a blind panic. Like prey was supposed to do. The creature leapt toward the girl and snarled as it quickly ran down its prey. One hand reached out and savagely grabbed the girl by the scruff of the neck. A heavy jerk and the prey was dangling from the creature's hand. The prey's screams grew more frantic as she came face to face with the creature. Reaching up, the creature hissed at the girl, and then hit her in the head with a mighty swing of its free hand. The girl shuddered, and her screaming abruptly stopped.

Alive. The prey was still breathing. Her head lolled in unconsciousness, and the creature grinned. Sharp fangs glistened in the darkness as the creature salivated at the thought of feeding. The creature threw its prize over its shoulder and ran into the shadows.

* * * *

THE EYES ARE the windows to the soul. When the soul leaves, eyes that were once capable of driving men wild lose their spark and grow cold. Her eyes were a bright blue. And lifeless.

The flashing light of a camera. The red and blue strobe patterns of the police cruiser. The portable work lights around the crime scene. The bright flashlights shone by the detectives. But none of them were bright enough to bring light back to those eyes.

A short, overweight man leaned over the body of the girl in the alley. His identification badge carelessly clipped to his scrubs proclaimed that he was the Medical Examiner. Careful to not disturb the scene, he reached out a gloved hand and gently closed the girl's eyes. "What gorgeous eyes you had," he murmured.

"What did you say, Bill?" The man in the sheriff's uniform leaned closer to the M.E. and peered at the body surrounded by the detritus in the alley.

Bill Stewart looked up at the sheriff. "Sorry, John. Was just muttering to myself. OK. White female. Approximate age... late teens? Maybe twenty? Did you find any ID?"

John Klooster, the sheriff responsible for the safety of nearly 10,000 residents of Trinidad, Colorado, wearily ran a hand through his short, salt-and-peppered hair. "No personal effects. No purse. No phone. We will go through this alley with a fine-toothed comb when we move the body out, but, if it's like the others..." John trailed off and shrugged.

Bill nodded slowly and looked back at the girl. Laid in the middle of the alley under a broken streetlamp, she was clad only in her undergarments. Studying her hands and body, Bill continued his examination. "No apparent defensive wounds. No visible signs of rape, but I'll test her when we get her back to the morgue. No blood, no bodily fluids." Looking up at the sheriff, he said, "Did your guys find any sign of the attack in this alley?"

John slowly shook his head, and Bill continued with his observations. "I'd say she was dumped here, like the others. Weird, though... It looks like she has the same post-mortem animal marks on her that the others had."

A deputy approaching the sheriff interrupted Bill's train of thought. Noticing the deputy, John looked up and said, "What do you have, Morris?"

Deputy Morris handed a copy of a missing persons report to the sheriff. "I thought I recognized the victim. She was reported missing about a week ago by her parents. They had a recent picture, and it looks just like her."

The sheriff turned toward the body and compared the picture on the report to the lifeless body on the ground. It sure looked like her. He bowed his head and sighed. Looking up, he handed the copy of the report to the Medical Examiner and looked back at the waiting deputy. "Good work, Morris. See if Shane needs any help with the evidence."

As the deputy walked toward one of the detectives at the other end of the alley, the sheriff looked at the M.E., "Well, Bill, she's all yours. When can you get to her?"

Bill thought for a moment and replied, "I'll get to her first thing in the morning. I should have a preliminary for you by tomorrow afternoon."

Thinking through his next several hours' worth of work, the sheriff said, "That'll work fine. The detectives will be at this all night anyway, and I've got to start the paperwork."

* * * * *

BY LATE AFTERNOON the next day, the girl's parents had identified their daughter, and the M.E. had filed his preliminary report with the sheriff. The sheriff had entered the initial report into his department's computer system, which was integrated with the Federal Law Enforcement Information Network.

Hidden in the Law Enforcement Information Network, or LEIN, was a small program that reported traffic back to the NSA. Part of ECHELON, the NSA's domestic electronic spying program, this small subroutine forwarded a copy of the information to the data center.

In the ECHELON data center, a tiny data worm sifted through

incoming information, looking for a specific set of parameters. The programmers who created and maintained the ECHELON data center did not know that this little data worm was in their system. Even if the legions of technical wizards had any idea that this little worm were present, they would have to torch the whole system to root this little worm out. But the technical wizards running the most secret software in the nation were unaware that their ultra-secure system was infected. It wasn't their fault—the ECHELON system, and every United States Government system like it, had been built with the worm installed.

This little worm found the report from the sheriff of a small town called Trinidad, Colorado. Recognizing specific keywords from a very long and eclectic list, it looked for more reports from this sheriff in Colorado. Then it moved away from the LEIN reports and searched for archived news reports with similar parameters. Gathering enough data to satisfy its programming, it hijacked a small portion of the system and forwarded its findings to a specific secure server, in a specific secure data center just outside Langley, Virginia.

And then it looked for other "interesting" things.

I

ORIGIN

1

SMITH

Section 28, Outside Langley, Virginia.

There was nothing remarkable about the building complex located just outside Langley, Virginia. A high chain-link fence surrounded the property and modest parking lot. Most people supposed it was a commercial or industrial park full of warehouses or service businesses. No signs hung on any of the buildings to indicate the names of the businesses, and the landscaping was minimal. With a simple brick facade and concrete block construction, the squat exterior did little to attract visitors. The only distinguishing feature about the complex was its private hanger and airstrip, though that was often unnoticed by passersby since it was safely hidden in the rear of the complex.

If someone happened to notice that the complex was even there, they would likely pass on by. If anyone stopped at the building, they would be stopped at the gated entrance outside the parking area. With a gated entrance large enough to accommodate tractor trailers, the guard shack at the gate housed one uniformed guard.

If a visitor is welcome and had permission to be on site, the guard would open the steel gates, and the visitor would pull forward and park in the small main lot. Approaching the building's only visible entrance, a visitor would see an electronic key-card access panel, a small push-button call system, and the words "Authorized Personnel Only" on a thick glass door.

If the visitor is expected, they would be buzzed through the door. Inside, they would wait in a small atrium until the second set of doors were unlocked from inside, then they would enter a typical reception area with a receptionist perched behind a high desk. There, the visitor would wait for their party to come and retrieve him or her, getting an RFID encoded "Visitor" badge from the receptionist.

If a visitor is unwelcome, they would not be allowed past the steel gates. At any attempt of forcefully gaining admittance to the facility, the guard would push an alarm button. This would trigger several events. First, the signal would reach the guard room inside the complex, and an armed rapid response team would be activated. That same signal immediately would be transmitted to the FBI Hostage Rescue Team at the FBI Training Academy on nearby Marine Corps Base Quantico, letting them know a high-value government installation needs their assistance.

Next, the steel gates would lock, and pop-up barriers hidden beneath the asphalt would spring out of the surface behind the gates in a rush of pneumatic air. Designed to stop a run-away armored vehicle, these barriers would be capable of ripping through the underside of most vehicles.

Inside the guard shack, a hidden panel on the wall would open, and the guard would have immediate access to an M4 carbine with a supply of armor piercing 5.56mm ammunition. After loading the rifle, the guard would defend the gates behind bullet-resistant windows and walls of the shack.

If this were not enough to deter an unwelcome guest, the similarly armed group of security officers pouring out of the building would deal with the threat. They would arrest this unlucky visitor for trespassing on government property and would spend a long time in a federal penitentiary all the while trying to determine what sort of building it was that he or she found.

For those unwelcome guests with malicious intent: the armed security team carried automatic rifles and are backed up by hidden machine-gun nests and missile launchers on the roof. Any survivors would then be sent to Guantanamo Bay for interrogation.

* * * * *

. . .

IN ONE BUILDING in the complex, a man sat at a nondescript desk in a sparsely furnished office. The man had close-cropped black hair and black eyes hidden behind small reading glasses. His dark gray pinstripe suit, white shirt, and black tie marked him as a middle manager, while his office, battle-scarred surplus desk, and less-than-comfortable visitors' chairs revealed that he was a government functionary.

The man in the office was pouring over intelligence reports from other agencies and situation reports from the teams of agents he supervised. Hearing a knock on his door, he did not even bother to look up as he said, "Come."

A young man opened the office door and leaned in. "The Director wants to see you, when you get free, boss."

"Fine, Timothy. Let me secure these files, and I'll head upstairs. Would you let him know I'm coming?"

Timothy agreed and returned to his desk outside the man's office. The man in the gray suit collected his files into stacks and reached over to put them in his personal safe. As the safe door closed, he placed his hand on the top of the safe, fingers splayed wide. Around the edges of the safe door, a series of odd looking characters appeared, glowing with a soft green light. The characters disappeared when the man removed his hand from the top of the safe.

Securing the files, he reached for a mug of coffee that was cooling rapidly on his desk. The man drained the last few swallows of coffee and left his office, nodding to his secretary as he passed.

He walked down a long, wide corridor, marked only occasionally with other office doors. None of the other doors had administrators in front of them, and the man mused that it was nice to have a secretary. As he got to the elevator, he pushed a button and waited for a chime to indicate the elevator's arrival. When the doors opened, he pressed the button for the Director's office suite. A small panel slid aside, and a fingerprint scanner levered out. Placing his right thumb on the scanner, a small retina-reading device emerged from behind another small panel at eye level. The man obediently removed his glasses and placed his eye over the device.

Three floors below, the server dedicated to internal security compared the RFID tag in the man's ID to the fingerprint and retinal scan on file. Upon receiving a positive match, the server then compared the biometrics to a list of those that had access to the Director's Suite. Confirming again that the man had special access clearance, the elevator gave an almost imperceptible shudder and ascended.

When the elevator stopped, the doors opened onto a plush reception area with an older woman sitting behind a welcoming mahogany desk that had a rich, warm patina that only comes with age and care. Seeing the man, she smiled warmly and picked up the phone and hit a button. "Sir, Agent Smith is here to see you. Shall I send him in?" A brief pause. "Yes, sir."

Motioning toward the man, she said, "He'll see you now, Agent Smith. Coffee today? Your usual?"

The man she called "Agent Smith" graciously smiled as he strode past her. "Thank you, Mary. I'd love some of your coffee. You really do have the best blends in the building."

Mary smiled and said, "Thanks. Go on in, I'll bring it to you." She turned and headed for the small alcove with the coffeemaker.

Agent Smith reflexively glanced at the red "classified meeting" light. Trained long ago to never interrupt a meeting in progress, he was relieved to see that the red light was not illuminated. Opening the heavy wooden door, he walked in to an office that was a stark contrast to his own.

Plush carpet covered the floor and the mahogany from the reception area carried through to the bookshelves, baseboards, and crown molding. A large and uncluttered mahogany desk was bare of a computer monitor or laptop. What little paper on the desk was meticulously arranged in a series of neat piles and file folders. The glow of a monitor through the glass top of the desk was the only concession to the need for a computer. The only piece of electronic equipment sitting on the desk was his office phone.

The two visitor chairs in front of the desk were stuffed-leather extravagance, and a small conference table with four chairs around it was staged for a meeting. At a gesture from the Director, Smith settled into one of the visitor chairs, turning as Mary brought coffee for both men. Mary closed the door on her way out of the room, pausing momentarily to reach over and turn on the meeting light.

Smith smiled as he inhaled the savory aroma wafting from the warm cup in his hands. "I don't know how she does it, but Mary makes the best coffee I've ever had."

Section 28 Director Clifton Day nodded and agreed with Smith. Several years ago, Director Day found Mary working as an administrator for another department, and she impressed him immensely. After pulling a few strings and threatening another Assistant Director, he orchestrated Mary's transfer to his office. After discussing her new benefits and the substantial raise in pay, she readily agreed to work for him. His life was much easier after that. Director Day knew he was a hard taskmaster and often ignored the social niceties when running his department, but Mary seemed to thrive on the job.

"James, I've read your reports and had Esoteric Analysis run your numbers as confirmation." Director Day's voice came out in a low growl. "Frankly, they scare the hell out of me. They couldn't find any fault in your work and came up with the same recommendation that you did. As of today, I've opened Operation Orbweaver, and I'm approving the formation of your third team, Knightmare. Have you selected any candidates?"

Supervising Agent in Charge James Smith thought for a moment and nodded slowly. His cultured voice had a hint of a southern accent. "Yes, sir. I have pre-screened several candidates. I'm only waiting for your approval to recruit and train. I've still got a couple holes in the team, but I should have the rest recruited by next week."

"Good," Director Day's deep voice rumbled. "Let Mary know if you need anything. Go get your new team spun up. If you are right, we will need them soon."

SAC Smith stood and smoothed imaginary wrinkles in his suit pants. Reaching out, he shook the proffered hand from Director Day and headed towards the door. As he walked towards the elevator, he heard Day shout through the open door to his office, "Mary, get DSS Andrews on the line. Schedule a working lunch here."

2

SIX

Baghdad, Iraq.

Commander Burt Holstein rolled up to the U.S. Embassy doors in one of his company's armored Humvee vehicles. His driver was his second-in-command, Robert Guzman. The trip to the embassy was a relatively short one, but it pulled him away from his current assignment, and it grated on him to be called to the embassy like an errant puppy while his team was out protecting some State Department VIPs.

Both he and Guzman had been contacted by his direct boss, the Regional Security Officer for Diplomatic Security Services. Told to grab his second-in-command and report to the embassy "ASAP," his arguments were cut off before they could form. Leaving the VIPs in the hands of his two squad leaders, Burt snagged a Humvee from the motor pool and tossed the keys to Guzman. The short ride to the embassy was filled with questions as neither he nor Guzman could figure out why they were summoned to the RSO's office.

Climbing out of the oversized SUV, the baking heat of Baghdad crashed into him with physical force, the normally oppressive heat compounded by the fifty pounds of armor, gear, and weapons worn by Burt and his driver. Normally, a civilian wearing that much gear and firepower approaching a U.S. Embassy would set alarm bells ringing and precipitate a violent response from local law enforcement.

Fortunately for Burt, he was not a normal citizen, in a normal city, in a normal country. Burt Holstein was the commanding officer of a team of contractors hired by the State Department to provide security for diplomatic VIPs and their families. Holstein was a senior team leader from the company that used to be known as "Blackwater." Now known as "Academi," the company had a multi-million dollar, multi-year contract to provide private security contractors to augment the Diplomatic Security Services agents in Iraq and Afghanistan. And Holstein was one of Academi's best team leaders.

Burt currently led a team of twenty contractors that worked for DSS. Most often, he and his team were charged with guarding high-value VIPs as they traveled around the city and countryside. He and his team were working guard duty for a small contingent of State Department "fact-finders" that were investigating an incident that fortunately did not happen on his watch.

He had his team split into two separate squads of ten, each one shadowing two of the staffers. Burt was leading one squad, while Guzman led the other. When they got the call over their secure radios, both squads were together as all four staffers were meeting with the mayor of one of the outlying villages. Since the command had been to report "ASAP," they did not have the time to go back to their apartments and change or clean up. Burt figured that the RSO would just have to put up with the sour smells and layers of dust on a man who was working in this sandbox.

As he and Guzman approached the building, they slung the M4 carbines on their backs. Drawing official State Department identification from their pockets, they presented the identification to the Marines at the entrance. Carefully studying the identification and comparing the pictures to the men before them, the Marines eventually handed the wallets back, waving them through the doors. As they entered the lobby of the building, both men took off their gloves and hats, storing them in their voluminous cargo pant pockets. As they handed their wallets to the guards working the metal detectors, the contractors were told to disarm.

Holstein looked hard at the guard in question. The contractor growled a terse, "RSO Hernandez just called us in from the field. 'ASAP' was the word he used. Call his office and clear us through,"

The guard muttered something unkind about Holstein's genetic relationship to monkeys and the anatomically impossible act of procreating with himself. He reached for a phone and dialed an internal extension. Keeping his voice low, he read the names and information from Holstein and Guzman's IDs and appeared to argue with someone on the other end. With a sullen "Fine," the guard hung up the phone and handed the IDs back to Holstein and Guzman.

He waived to the guard standing by the metal detector.

"Go on up. Third floor, RSO's office," the guard said as he motioned to the other guard. "Let 'em go, Mike. They're cleared, as is."

Holstein smiled at Guzman and led his partner through the metal detectors, setting off a cacophony of buzzers and sirens. Walking towards the elevators, Holstein watched the guard pick up the phone and report to the security office. With a smirk on his face, Holstein boarded with Guzman only a few steps behind. As the elevator doors were closing, Holstein smiled at the sullen-looking guard and was rewarded with a raised middle finger salute.

Disembarking the elevator on the third floor, Holstein turned right, walking towards an office he had only visited once before. Walking up to the reception desk in front of the RSO's office, Holstein smiled politely and said, "Burt Holstein and Robert Guzman to see RSO Hernandez. I apologize about the commotion."

The raven-haired beauty behind the desk smiled warmly. Her warm Georgian accent rolled over the men.

"No problem. Mr. Hernandez is expecting you gentlemen. Go on in. Would you like something to drink? Water? Iced tea?" asked the receptionist.

Holstein deferred to Guzman first who replied, "Water, thanks!"

"I hate to be a bother, but the iced tea, is it sweetened?" Holstein asked.

Laughing, the receptionist said, "Of course! What other way is there for proper iced tea?"

Smiling, Holstein laughed, too.

"As a west coast boy, I've tasted the non-sweetened variety, but, if forced to choose, I prefer it sweetened. The tea sounds delicious, ma'am," said Holstein.

He turned and walked into the office with Guzman on his heels.

RSO Hernandez was not behind his desk. Instead, a man in a gray pinstripe suit that screamed "Fed" sat behind Hernandez' desk, and the RSO stood beside him. Holstein took all this information in with a quick glance, unconsciously shifted into parade rest, and nodded to Hernandez.

"Holstein and Guzman, reporting as requested, sir."

"Thanks for coming so quickly," Hernandez said as he looked at both men. "Burt Holstein and Robert Guzman, I'd like to introduce you to Agent James Smith. Agent Smith is from Homeland Security and has requested a meeting with you, Holstein. Guzman, if you'd join me outside."

Hernandez motioned and followed Guzman back out the door, leaving Holstein and the federal agent in the room, closing the door as they left.

Smith stood and reached out to shake Holstein's hand. "Mr. Holstein, I appreciate your coming in today. Please have a seat," the Homeland Security agent said as he pointed to one of the visitor's chairs. "I'd like to discuss a job offer with you."

Holstein shook his head and relaxed slightly.

"What kind of job are you talking about?" Holstein continued, "I'm on contract with Academi for three more years. Most likely, I'll be here for that time. I can probably talk to you more as I get closer, but, if I leave my team now, I will lose my bonus. I'm not walking away from all that cash in my bank account."

Smith let a small smile show on his face. "I understand perfectly, and I've already been in touch with your home office in McLean, Virginia. I'm forming a new team at Homeland Security to... deal with a particular kind of domestic threat and would like to have you lead the team."

Smith consulted a thin file in front of him. He read from the file. "Los Angeles native, born to moderately wealthy parents. Father owned a high-end electronics store where your mother helped until a gang shooting took both of their lives."

The federal agent looked directly at Holstein. "Joined LAPD as soon as you could and excelled at the hard stuff. Appointed to SWAT at age 23. Served two years with merit. Left LAPD to join the Marines. Again, excelled at what you do best, and joined Force Recon, serving with distinction in Iraq.

"When your term was up, you left the service to make some real money. Simple security or police work did not cut it for you... you wanted to make real bank. Academi heard you were available, and you scored a contract that gives you the money you want. Working as a contractor here in the sandbox got you exactly what you wanted: you get to play with guns and make a lot of money doing so."

"When you were 12 years old, you saw a UFO while you were camping in the desert. You've been a conspiracy theory nut ever since, convinced that the government is hiding the aliens from the public." Smith looked up at Holstein. Looking the contractor in the eyes, he continued. "It wasn't a UFO that time, not in the classic sense. It was something... something else."

Leafing through the contents of the file once again, Smith continued, "When you have free time, you spend a lot of it searching for proof that what you saw was real. Your contractor's salary allows you to search for answers in areas and places that most folks couldn't afford."

Holstein sat and tried to absorb the dry retelling of his professional and personal life. "What do you mean 'something else'? How do you know so much about me?"

Smith just smiled and ignored the questions. "I know that your contract still has three years left on it. I am authorized to buy out your contract from Academi completely, including your bonus from this posting, and pay you a salary level somewhat higher than you are currently making here in the sandbox. You would become a full Homeland Security agent, with government service accumulation, and time towards your retirement."

The actual job offer sank in past the shock of having his background laid out so openly. Holstein asked a barrage of questions, "What do you mean 'somewhat higher'? Do you have any idea what I make here? And I still get my bonus? I've never seen the Feds throw around this much money. Only the private contractors can afford that kind of salary. What kind of threat do you need me for?"

Smith's smile widened as he realized that Holstein was taking the bait. "Yes, I know exactly what you make here, and we're going to start you at an even higher salary." Smith set the hook as he offered a number that caused Burt's eyes to widen in shock. The contractor thought about how that much money could help him find the answers he was looking for.

Smith continued, "As to your other questions, everything is classified Top Secret, and I cannot tell you any more until after you come on board. So what do you think?"

Holstein was still trying to process the information. And the job offer. And the salary. He wanted the job. He was hooked by the money, and the fact that he might be able to find answers. He asked the Homeland Security Agent, "What about my team? What happens to them? When would I leave and where am I going?"

Smith slowly stood and walked around the desk. "RSO Hernandez is currently telling Guzman that he is now in charge of the team until Academi sends a replacement. We leave immediately. A quick stop by your office and quarters to get any personal items, and then to the airport. I have a jet on standby, and we'll be wheels up in less than an hour. As to the where? You'll just have to wait and see. This is the only time I'm going to offer this job to you. Do you want it?"

Holstein looked down briefly. Looking back up, he reached out to grasp the proffered hand. "I'm glad to be on your team, sir. Where do I sign?"

Smith chuckled dryly. "I've given RSO Hernandez your transfer paperwork from Academi. You'll sign the official government contracts in a few days. For now, let's get moving. I have a schedule to keep. I need to get you back to headquarters so you can get settled. Once we get you settled, I'll need to go collect your new team."

3

SPOOKY

Fort Meade, Maryland.

Rows of numbers and letters filled all six monitors in front him. Formed in two curved rows of three, each monitor was a twenty-three-inch widescreen display with the whole stack wrapping around almost one hundred forty degrees of his vision. Each was filled with multiple windows of text and data, and anyone watching him work would see him shift his eyes and head in an-almost-neurotic way. Looking bird-like, his focus constantly shifted between the monitors, and his fingers rapidly flew between three different keyboards and two customized pointing devices.

John Q. Smith, or "Q," to his geeky friends, sat in his cubicle buried deep in the heart of the server farm for the NSA. Cropped in a short spiky cut, his red hair framed his face, and his brilliant green eyes hid behind small horn-rimmed glasses. Eschewing the standard shirt and tie demanded by the employee handbook, the young man wore geek-interest-related t-shirts and blue jeans. His boss had long ago figured out that Smith would never dress up regularly and only made sure that he was at least dressed in standard attire when management wandered through the cube farm.

Wrapping up for the day, John finished typing the final few lines of his report. He made a couple more references, read it one more time, and sent it to his boss. As the lead analyst for PRISM and

ECHELON, the NSA's domestic electronic spying programs, his report would be the first thing his boss would read on Monday morning. The strange reports and seemingly credible intell about "monsters" kept occurring enough that it made John curious. The deeper he dug, the more he found that confused and confounded his searches.

One name kept popping up over the last couple weeks, "Section 28." There were no hints about what or who they were. They seemed to be a governmental agency, but there was no record he could find—and he had clearance to find anything. Using the vast resources of the NSA, as well as CIA, FBI, and Homeland Security sources, he searched every crack in the internet for information. What few references he found were either sketchy "evidence" on conspiracy theory websites or occasional signals intelligence (SIG-INT) that pointed to some shadowy group that dealt with... monsters?

Finding this odd, he began compiling the information a couple weeks ago, and finally completed his report for his boss today. John was not only the lead analyst for PRISM and ECHELON, but he was also one of the key liaisons with Homeland Security for those programs. He thought about it for a few seconds and sent a second copy to his DHS supervisor as well. *In for a penny, in for a pound,* he thought to himself.

Making his way out of the labyrinth that was the NSA server farm, he passed all the checkpoints and emerged into the sun for the first time that day. Blinking painfully against the bright sun, he walked to the parking lot and climbed into his "Ghostmobile."

Growing up in Boston, Massachusetts, his Irish blue-collar heritage was painfully clear in his accent. In older Boston, there were plenty of houses that were rumored to be haunted, and he and his friends used to spend their time wandering those halls. As a budding electronics genius, he often made "ghost hunting" gear for himself and his friends.

At the top of his high-school class, he had scored high enough on SATs and ACTs to receive a full-ride scholarship to MIT. There his computer prowess and electronic savvy had served him well as he moved to the top of his class in crypto-analysis. While in college, the only distraction for "Q" and his friends was his ghost hunting hobby. He and several friends had often spent their off-time searching out the haunted locations and trying their newest custom equipment, searching for the proof they were so desperate to find.

Once he graduated, he received job offers from several government alphabet-soup intelligence agencies, and even more private firms and banks. With his cryptanalysis background, the two most interesting offers came from a bank on the west coast and the NSA in Maryland. With several of his geek friends taking jobs in D.C. and the surrounding area, John opted to work for the National Security Agency in Fort Meade, Maryland. Because he stayed in the area, he was able to continue "ghost hunting" with his friends from college, and that's where he was headed now.

He rolled down the highway towards a farm outside Manassas, Virginia. This farm was on the edge of one of the Revolutionary War battlefields and was supposed to be pretty active with ghost and poltergeist activity. As members of the D.C. Ghost Hunting Society, he and his team had arranged to spend the night inside the farmhouse. "Q" had several new pieces of equipment that he wanted to test tonight, and his teammates were bringing their new equipment as well. His best friend from high school, Billy, was supposed to be bringing their new equipment trailer/mobile base camp as well. As John drove towards the farmhouse, he slowly relaxed and let his mind forget about the report he sent his bosses.

* * * * *

WHEN MONDAY MORNING ROLLED AROUND, John was in a great mood. He and his DCGHS team scored lots of good evidence on Friday night, including what is called a "Class A" EVP in the paranormal world. This Electronic Voice Phenomena is a sound that is recorded on a digital recorder and is not heard by anyone actually present during the recording. Often, these sounds are recorded at a different frequency than normal human voices, yet they seem to have voice patterns and offer recognizable words. To be a "Class A" EVP, the voice must be clear and distinguishable. Their recording had a deep male voice growling, "Soon you will see." Coupled with some other interesting readings, it had been a fairly successful hunt. Before leaving for work, he uploaded the evidence collected to the DCGHS server, where the video and audio would be available for streaming.

John arrived a bit earlier than usual but still parked in his normal spot, on the edge of the lot, about a third of the way down the outer row. As John approached the large black, ominous looking building, he whistled the theme to his favorite ghost-hunting movie. John was in such a good mood that the onerous security procedures for entering the building and then the SIGINT area didn't bother him as much as they usually did.

But John's mood soured quickly when he got to his cubicle. A note posted on his primary monitor said, "See me ASAP. Kenneth." The "Kenneth" was his direct line supervisor, Kenneth McAllister. John's secure mobile phone then received a text, also from his boss, "Come to my office. NOW."

John swore under his breath. Grabbing the spare shirt and tie hanging in his cube for just such an occasion, he hurriedly drew it on, slipped the pre-tied tie over his head, and scurried down the corridor as he tucked in his shirt and straightened his tie.

Arriving at his boss' office, he knocked on the door and heard an immediate, "Come!" Kenneth McAllister looked like John felt. McAllister's tie was askew, his perfectly pressed shirt was stained with sweat, and he looked as if he got caught with his hand in the proverbial cookie jar.

When he got excited or angry, McAllister's original Texan accent crept back into his voice. The accent was almost overbearing as McAllister continued, "Get your butt in here, John. What in the hell were you thinking, sending that report? It's bad enough that you sent it to me, but you decided to send it to Homeland Security? I just had our Director chew me out. Your supervisor at DHS called *HIS* boss. His boss called the Director of Homeland Security, who called *OUR* Director. And he called me. It was strongly suggested to me that I reconsider the idea of putting someone who sees 'monsters and ghosts' in charge of the PRISM and ECHELON programs. Is he right?"

John's high spirits visibly deflated, and he collapsed into one of the visitor chairs. He had a sudden vision of being reassigned to the IT maintenance department. John tried to defend his work. "Did you even read the report? All I did was correlate data from the programs. It all got flagged, and I just analyzed the data. It's not my fault that these programs compiled this data. And I don't 'see' ghosts. Ghost hunting is a hobby, but it has never interfered with my job here. What's going to happen, Ken?"

McAllister stared at John with a probing look. He seemed to find the genuine innocence that he was searching for. "Listen, John," he began. His voice became much softer and the Texas 'twang dropped away. "This will blow over pretty soon, but you need to step back for a few days. Go hide under a rock. Keep your head down. I'm going to give you a couple of days off work, paid, of course. Heck, take a week. Take some time to relax. Get this out of your system. Come back in next Monday. We'll see what happens then."

John looked defeated. "So am I gonna' be pulled from my current job? What about Liaison to DHS? Am I even going to have a job when I come back?"

McAllister smiled wistfully. "You'll have a job. You're a great analyst. You're a freakin' genius with ECHELON. I'll do everything I can to keep you on this assignment, but you need to keep your head down for the rest of the week. Officially, your report never happened. This so-called 'Section 28' doesn't exist. And the only monsters out there are the ones that bomb malls and hijack airplanes... the human kind of monsters. Got it?"

John absorbed the keywords and nodded slowly. "Got it." He stood and walked out of the office. As he reached his cubicle, he grabbed his messenger bag with his laptop and left the facility.

It was a long ride home. His thoughts kept mulling all the data over in his head. *Section 28 has to exist, doesn't it? There's too much data.* Distracted, he drove past his exit on the highway and had to backtrack. Pulling into the driveway of his small rental, he grabbed his bag and walked up to the front door. It wasn't until he began to put his key into the lock that he realized the front door was cracked open. Looking around, he belatedly realized that there was a black sedan parked in front of his house that might as well have had a sign posted on it stating, "I am a federal agent." Fear filtered quickly through his mind. *What had he done wrong? Who was waiting for him?* The fear slowly changed to anger. This was his house that they busted into. It didn't matter that they were Feds. They broke into HIS house. With the stress of the morning, this was the last straw. Not caring if the "men in black" were in his living room, he threw open the door, spoiling for a fight.

Sitting in his favorite recliner was an average-sized man in a gray pinstripe suit. His black hair and eyes gave a hint to Native American or Latino descent, but his cultured voice spoke of a gentrified southern upbringing.

"Good morning, Mr. Smith. I am Agent James Smith from Homeland Security. And I'd like to discuss a report that you filed with your boss on Friday."

John was livid. "Get *OUT*," he roared. "Get out of my house. My boss already read me the riot act. I got the message. 'Section 28' doesn't exist. There are no monsters. This conversation never 'officially' happened, and I don't frakkin' know *YOU*! Now, get out!"

Agent Smith raised his hands as if to deflect the words, "I'm not here to, as you say, 'read you the riot act'. I'm here to offer you a job." Agent Smith withdrew his credentials from his inside pocket. "You see, I'm from Section 28. The monsters are real, and we could use your help."

4

GOD

Grand Rapids, Michigan.

The sniper carefully extended the bipod on the front of his rifle. Setting the bipod on the rest in front of him, the man visually inspected the five-round magazine for his rifle then inserted it into the receiver. Grasping the bolt handle, he twisted and shoved it forward, feeling the secure "click" as it locked into place with a round in the chamber. The sniper lifted the cap from his head, brushed his black hair out of his eyes, and put the hat back on backwards.

Next to the sniper, his spotter carefully unfolded the tripod that supported his spotting scope and placed the scope on the ground. With his gear set up, he reached over and tapped the sniper on the shoulder twice in a pre-arranged signal. He then reached to his side and withdrew a pair of binoculars to survey the scene just over a hundred yards in front of him.

Having spotted his target, the spotter carefully placed his binoculars in their case, laid back down, and switched to the spotting scope. He looked in through the windows of the large building in front of him. Keeping his voice low, he began a running commentary for his partner.

"Primary target, one hundred twenty-five yards. Wind speed..." he said as he glanced at the small instrument package set up in front of him. "Fifteen knots, three-two-zero degrees. Gusting to twenty-five."

The spotter performed the necessary calculations on a small computer attached to his wrist. Next to him, the sniper was doing the same calculations in his head. It was a private test to see if his instincts were still sharp.

The spotter received his answers from the computer, and murmured, "One and a quarter clicks up, three and a quarter left should put you spot on. You're good to go, Rivera."

Jesús Rivera made the adjustments to the scope, smiling because he was correct again, and he had the corrections planned before his spotter ever spoke. He brought his eye to the scope in front of him. Caressing the stock of his M24-A3 rifle subconsciously, Rivera looked through the scope and sighted in on the top floor of the Gerald R. Ford Federal Building in Grand Rapids, Michigan.

Home to many federal offices and a U.S. District Court, gunmen had barged past security checkpoints, shooting people and causing terror all the way to the top floor, taking a judge and several court workers hostage. They coldly shot the guards at the entrance on the way into the building and had fired at and wounded or killed every federal law enforcement officer they encountered. Early reports from witnesses said there were three of them. Claiming to be from the Islamic State of Iraq and Syria (ISIS), the jihadists were making demands that certain prisoners be released from Guantanamo Bay and that Sharia Law be officially adopted in the state of Michigan, as it had virtually been in Dearborn, Michigan.

As soon as local law enforcement knew who was holding the hostages, the FBI's Hostage Rescue Team was immediately deployed. They were on the plane and in the air from the FBI Academy in Quantico in twenty minutes and on the scene in Grand Rapids in three hours. Once on site, the local law enforcement responders deferred to the HRT for the resolution.

As the team arrived, their on-site liaison told them that the ISIS jihadists had killed one of their hostages. One of the gunmen stated that if their demands were not met, and if they did not have a helicopter on the roof within an hour, another hostage would be executed.

Thirty minutes before the deadline, the takedown order had been given. Rivera and his spotter, Stuart Duncan, were quickly ordered to post on top of one of the buildings close to the federal building. A position on the roof of the Grand Rapids City Hall would put them on the same level as the hostage takers, and they would be in a great position to guide the entry team.

Rivera activated the microphone around his throat. "Alpha lead, Overwatch. Eyes on target."

The HRT team leader replied, "Overwatch, Alpha lead. Sit Rep."

Rivera counted bodies through the scope, then heard his spotter mutter, "Three bad guys. Eleven hostages."

Since the count agreed with his, he relayed it to the team leader. "Three tangos. Eleven civilians. Tango one, by the entry door, with a mirror to see the corridor. Tango two, five feet from tango one, along north wall. Tango three, looking out the windows."

"Copy Overwatch. Alpha lead to all Alpha. We will execute in three minutes... mark," answered the leader.

Rivera heard Duncan mutter a curse under his breath. "Tango three has eyes. Looks like we're spotted."

Rivera switched to look at the terrorist by the window and watched as he scanned the city hall roofline with a pair of binoculars. He seemed to be directly looking at them and started waving his hands, gesturing wildly.

Rivera uttered the same curse and keyed his mic. "Alpha lead, Overwatch. Caution! Caution! Caution! Tango three has eyes and has spotted our position."

The team leader responded immediately. "Overwatch, Alpha lead. Priority target, Tango one. Take the shot. Alpha team, execute in 15 seconds."

Jesús agreed with the team leader. If the sniper shot the target by the door with the mirror, the other bad guys would have no idea when the entry team would come through the door, or where. Shifting the crosshairs back to the designated tango one, he paused, inhaled his breath, and then exhaled slowly. When he let about half of it out, his trigger finger moved just under a half inch. Easily taking up the slack and breaking at a crisp one-and-a-half pounds of pressure, the rifle fired.

The firing pin struck the primer on the .338 Lapua Magnum round in the chamber. The primer ignited and lit the gunpowder inside the casing, propelling the projectile down the barrel and out towards the target. Approximately twelve hundredths of a second later, the bullet ripped through the window glass, missing one terrorist by six inches. The large projectile slammed into the head of the terrorist by the door approximately five thousandths of a second later. The explosive force of almost 4,900 ft/lbs of energy imparted on the skull of the terrorist, and the head virtually vanished.

As the terrorist by the window heard the crack of the high-powered rifle, Rivera had already cycled the bolt-action and switched targets, centering his sights on the forehead of the trouble-some third terrorist. Another breath, another twitch, and another twelve-thousandths of a second later, this bullet did not miss the terrorist at the window. As Rivera cycled the bolt-action again, he shifted the crosshairs again, this time covering the second terrorist, the only one still standing. As the sniper stabilized, he watched the rest of Alpha team break through the door. The first agent through the door pointed his M4 carbine at the terrorist and pulled the trig-ger. Twice. Six rounds stitched through the terrorist, and he jerked and dropped.

After a few seconds, Rivera watched the all-clear hand signal being given across the team. Alpha lead rasped in his ear, "Alpha lead, Overwatch. All Clear. Good shooting. Wrap it up."

Rivera cleared his rifle and put it away.

Rivera and Duncan sat up, carefully putting their gear in the various pouches and cases. They stood, grabbed their gear, and headed toward the roof access door. This time around, they relaxed and took the elevator to the ground floor. Walking through the building and out the doors, they had stowed most of their gear when the rest of the team returned to the mobile command center.

A giant of an African American named Alton Lynch strode up to Rivera and Duncan. The leader of the FBI's HRT Team Alpha gave a thumb's up to the pair.

"Great shooting, Rivera," Lynch said as he turned to the rest of the team. "All right. Great outcome. Let's get everything stowed. I want to be wheels up in one hour."

* * * * *

AFTER A GOOD NIGHT'S REST, Rivera arrived at the Quantico Marine Corps Base training facility for debrief and training. Rivera thought the debrief went well enough, and Lynch only handed out minor criticism about being spotted by the lookout. Walking out of the debriefing room, the team headed towards the mess hall for lunch before their afternoon training. Rivera walked out, deep in discussion with Lynch about other tactics they could have used. They were stopped by one of the administrators for the group.

"SSA Lynch? Special Agent Rivera? There is a visitor here from Homeland Security. He is requesting a meeting with both of you directly. I have him in Conference Room 201, but he requested that I contact you as soon as you finished your debrief. Shall I let him know you are coming?" The administrator waited for an answer.

"Thanks, Krista. Rivera and I can walk with you," Lynch responded.

As they walked, Lynch turned to Rivera. "Any idea why Homeland Security wants you? Did you apply for a new job without telling me?"

"No, sir," Rivera said as he shook his head. "I'm happy here. Did we screw something up in Michigan?"

Lynch just shrugged. "Not to my knowledge. If this guy is recruiting, just say no. Any time one of these interdepartmental headhunters show up, it's never good for the head they are hunting."

Rivera agreed as they reached the conference room. Opening the door, he let Lynch go in first, and followed closely on his heels. Sitting in the room at the head of the conference table was a rather average sized man in a gray pinstripe suit. He had two folders in front of him, both closed. Rivera could see that the front of one folder displayed the FBI agency seal. The other folder was emblazoned with the Department of Homeland Security seal, and Rivera could just make out his name on the tab.

Without standing up, the man greeted the two agents. In a softly cultured voice he said, "Good morning, gentlemen. My name is Agent James Smith, and I work for Homeland Security."

Picking up the folder with the FBI seal on it, he opened the folder and continued. "Great job in Michigan yesterday. Sounds like it was a bad one. Do we have a final casualty count yet?"

Neither man sat down. Rivera could see Lynch stiffen and clench his jaw out of the corner of his eye. The sniper knew that meant his commander was about to shout. Lynch roared at the Homeland Security agent, "How did you get a copy of that preliminary report? That is HRT Eyes Only until the final report is ready. No one outside the Director or the Attorney General in cleared for that file. How did you get it?"

Agent Smith held up his hands as if to ward off the attack. "Relax, Agent Lynch. I have access to far more information than even the AG. Well-written report... really backs up your sniper here. It's good to see that you are watching out for your people."

But Lynch refused to be placated. "Who are you? Where is your ID? Why are you here? Did we trample on DHS' private playground in Michigan?"

Agent Smith reached into his jacket for his credentials, and opening them, he slid them across the table towards Lynch. "As much as I'd like to answer all your questions, Agent Lynch, I don't have the time, and, more importantly, you don't have the clearance for that. Instead, I'd like to spend a few minutes talking with Agent Rivera here. Alone. Don't worry, I won't keep him from lunch." Smith smiled and nodded towards the door.

Lynch carefully scrutinized the credentials and grudgingly concluded they were genuine. He looked at Rivera knowingly. "Remember what I told you. I'll wait outside for you." He then looked at Agent Smith and warned him, "Leave him alone. I back my team, AND I protect my team. He's mine." Lynch left and closed the door.

Agent Smith looked at Rivera and said, "Sit down, Jesús. I'm going to get a crick in my neck staring up at you like that." He glanced down and reached for the file with Rivera's name on it.

Opening the file, he summarized what was there.

"You grew up just outside Denver, Colorado, in a good Hispanic home to first-generation immigrants. Mother Maria and father Ramon, you were their only child. Your father started taking you hunting around the age of eight, and, from all accounts you were pretty good. You originally wanted to be a Catholic Priest, having grown up in the church."

As he read, the agent flipped through the pages, picking out the highlights. Smith continued, "Your family loved the outdoors life. You went camping, fishing, and hunting with your family all the time. During the summer of the year you turned fifteen, your family went camping in the remote wilderness. About two days in, there was a bright full moon. Unfortunately, for you, there was also a rabid wolf in the area. While you were down by the creek doing some midnight fishing, your parents were horrifically killed, torn apart by a wolf according to the local medical examiner."

"Being the good Catholic, you turned to the church to help you with answers. Unfortunately, the priest in your parish was more interested in the altar boys than in helping you find answers. So you ran from the church, never to return."

"You lived well with your aunt and uncle, and your inheritance paid for your admittance to Harvard. Graduated in the top two percent in Pre-Law and had a spot waiting for you at Harvard Law

School. You chose the FBI, instead. You are a standout agent. Quickly making the selection for the HRT. Your hunting days in Colorado really helped you become a sniper. And now I want you to come work for me. I am building a highly specialized team that will deal with rather... unique threats."

Rivera felt like he had been sucker punched. Hearing his life story laid out in front of him like a deer on the butcher block, he could barely think. Smith's delivery was perfectly dry, with no emotion. He simply read out of the personnel file. *Wait... How do they have my personnel file?*

Rivera was in such a state of shock that he almost missed the job offer. In fact, it was a few moments later when he finally figured out how to talk again. "What do you mean job offer? I'm happy here at HRT, despite you dragging my past back to me. What could you offer me that I don't have here?"

"I'm offering answers and a chance to make a difference," Smith said with a smile. "There is a threat facing this country that even your elite HRT is not prepared for. That's why you joined the FBI— to make a difference. You wanted to protect families. I'm offering you an opportunity to do that on a scale you have not seen before."

Rivera asked, "So... Terrorists? Islamists? Nukes? What is the threat?"

Smith paused. "I cannot tell you the threat—it's classified higher than you're cleared for. But I can answer a question that you've had for a long time. It was not a rabid wolf that killed your parents. It was a werewolf. She was pack-less, and had recently been turned. We put her down when we caught her, but she killed your parents and several others before we got her."

Rivera looked at Smith and thought for a few seconds. *Did he really say 'werewolf'? What else is he hiding? Lynch is gonna' think I'm insane!*

"Now, I am behind schedule already, and my next interview is on the other side of the world," said Smith. "I'm only going to ask you this question once. Do you want the job?"

Rivera looked up at Smith and extended his hand across the table. "When do I start?"

5

BOOMER

Pacific Ocean, Off the Coast of Japan.

"What do you mean I've 'been transferred'?" The angry woman wearing standard issue Navy working coveralls was standing in her Division Office on the USS Ronald Reagan, a U.S. Navy aircraft carrier in the Pacific Ocean. The woman with close-cropped hair cursed enough that some of the shipmates hanging around were learning new, creative combinations.

Chief Warrant Officer Harold Goodwin stood and let the young sailor vent for a little bit. He was being a little indulgent, realizing that this transfer would probably kill the career of a very promising sailor.

Having let her rant enough, he cleared his throat.

"Petty Officer Callahan." Goodwin's voice was cold and quiet.

Callahan stopped ranting. Realizing that she had just yelled at, and then cussed out, her boss, she quickly composed herself. "I apologize for my outburst, sir. I was caught totally off guard."

Chief Warrant Officer Goodwin nodded and then said, "I understand. Did you get that out of your system?"

"Yes, sir," Callahan said as she blushed. "Permission to speak freely?"

Goodwin nodded. "As if I could stop you, Callahan."

Callahan continued, "Any idea why I was transferred out, sir? Have I... screwed up lately?"

Smiling at her restraint, Goodwin replied, "No, Callahan. You've been great out in the field... But you probably should not have reported seeing the Loch Ness Monster while diving in Scotland. And then giving your account to that reality TV show was just stupid."

He looked at her shocked face. "You're a Petty Officer. Training other sailors how to blow stuff up. Do you really think Command wants to have one of their senior non-comms in EOD spouting off about monsters? You should have seen this coming."

"But I never claimed to see the Loch Ness Monster, sir!" The sailor pleaded her case. "I simply claimed to have seen what seemed to be a big creature down there. I never mentioned Loch Ness. How am I gonna' get out of this, sir?"

Goodwin liked the young Petty Officer. She was a fantastic EOD, and he knew her old man as a Chief Petty Officer a long time ago.

"I'm sorry, Callahan. This order came from Norfolk. They want you transferred immediately. You are to report to the mail flight for transport to Yokosuka Naval Base. From there, you fly out to San Diego NAS, and then on to Norfolk. You'll catch your new assignment there."

Rebekah Callahan fought back tears as she made her way to her rack. Taking a few moments to change into her dress uniform, she gathered her uniforms, gear, and personal items, which she stuffed into a canvas sea bag. She had just enough time to tell her teammates goodbye, and then she ran to get on the delivery airplane.

Goodwin met her on the stairs up to the flight deck. He looked her up and down with pride as she saluted him—ramrod straight, a perfect salute from the Academy. He returned her salute and caught her eye.

"Callahan, you're great at what you do. I'll see what I can find out, I will try to get you back here. Your father would be proud of you, even with 'Nessie.' You'll come out of this on top."

Callahan fought harder to hold back her tears.

"Thank you, sir," Callahan said, her voice choking with emotion. "I'll make them realize what kind of crappy mistake they made when they sent me to the beach."

Goodwin laughed. "That's the Callahan that I know. You'd better hurry to catch the COD. Dismissed."

Callahan threw one last salute and ran up the final stairs to the flight deck. As she appeared on deck, one crewman escorted her to the large, unusual looking plane. Having just begun service in Carrier Onboard Delivery services, the V-22 Osprey tilt-rotor aircraft had the nose, body, and wings of an airplane, but it also had two huge propellers, one on the end of each wing. These engines rotated through a full ninety degrees. This allowed the plane to take off vertically, like a helicopter. Once it reached the proper altitude, it transitioned and rotated the propellers forward, using the turboprops to act as a normal airplane propeller. This unique method of propulsion made the aircraft a perfect replacement for the aging C-2 aircraft the Navy had been using since the 1960s.

Once she stowed her seabag and strapped herself in, she was told they had a couple minutes while they waited for another passenger. Callahan waited impatiently, fidgeting and trying not to cry until the other passenger finally arrived and boarded.

As he was strapping in to the webbed jump seats, she realized he was not in uniform. Instead, he was in a gray pinstripe suit that looked out of place on the military aircraft. Nodding politely, any greeting was abruptly cutoff as the rear cargo hydraulics whined as the ramp drew back up into the fuselage.

The whine of the ramp was replaced by a louder, deeper whine of the propellers beginning to rotate. This quickly turned into a roar as the first one, then the other engine started and began rotating. Callahan gave up any thought of conversation as the engines roared and watched out the window as they slowly lifted into the air. The noise only slightly diminished as they reached altitude and the engines transitioned to forward flight. Rebekah became lost in her thoughts.

Rebekah's thoughts drifted as she thought about her father who had passed away five, no six, years ago. He was a Chief Petty Officer in the Navy and had been stationed in Norfolk for most of her life. She had grown up on base, and she had fallen in love with the Navy. The only activity that drew her away from the base was racing.

Rebekah Callahan had always loved speed. She loved to be behind the wheel, melting the rubber off her tires on track and off. When her widowed father realized that his little girl was going to go fast whether or not he liked it, he connected her with a local racing club. Sponsoring her first go-kart, Rebekah's father had watched her win her first-ever race. She had never looked back. Gradually working up to dirt-track racing, while dabbling in speedboats, the only thing that made Rebekah Callahan quit racing was joining the Navy.

As soon as she had graduated from high school, Rebekah had been in the recruiter's office to sign the paperwork. With her grades, background, and enthusiasm, Rebekah was one of the few women accepted to the Explosive Ordinance Disposal. She excelled at the training, earning her diving certifications, passing the EOD training, and even earning her jump wings. After five years of service, she earned her Senior EOD badge when she made Petty Officer First Class. Then she took that trip to Scotland.

The changing pitch of the engines brought Rebekah out of her reverie. Shaking her head slightly, she realized they were landing on the helicopter pad at Yokosuka Naval Base. As the V-22 landed, the crew chief came back and dropped the cargo ramp. He yelled loud enough to be heard over the noise. "All right, you passengers, this is your stop. Up and out. The sailor at the end of the ramp will direct you."

Rebekah grabbed her duffle and walked down the ramp. She was followed closely by the civilian. They both walked away from the plane and followed the E-5 into the building at the end of the pier. As they walked through the doors, the V-22 lifted off, heading inland toward the air base.

Rebekah asked the E-5 where processing was, and he gave her directions. As she walked toward the office, she realized the civilian was following her. She slowed her pace then stopped and looked at him. "Excuse me, sir. Are you lost?"

He smiled and replied, "No, Petty Officer Callahan. Actually, I'm headed to the same office that you are."

She frowned as she realized he must have read her name and service rank off her uniform during the flight. "Are you sure you need the processing offices, sir? Transportation is the other direction."

He smiled and a hint of southern charm was in his voice. "No, Petty Officer. I'm definitely headed to the correct office. Shall we?" And he gestured with his arm toward the offices.

When they reached the office doors, the strange man opened the door for Rebekah and let her enter first. Somehow, she expected no less—he had that "gentleman" vibe to him. As she walked up to the desk, Rebekah presented her orders to the clerk. "Petty Officer First Class Rebekah Callahan. Reporting as ordered to arrange trans-portation to NAS North Island, with an eventual destination of Naval Station Norfolk."

The clerk read through the orders before responding. "If you'll have a seat, Petty Officer, I'll begin working on your transportation. I should have something for you soon." The clerk then looked at the gentleman behind Rebekah, and she knew that she had been dismissed.

The strange man smiled wide for the clerk. "Hello, Cheryl. Back from the Reagan. She's a beautiful ship. Do you have a conference room I can use?"

The clerk returned the smile. "Certainly, Agent Smith. I've held Conference Room 1, as you requested. Commander Douglas is waiting for you in his office."

"Thank you, Cheryl. I'll be using that conference room when I'm done meeting with Commander Douglas."

Thirty minutes later, Rebekah watched the apparently important "Agent Smith" emerge from the Commander's office with a brief-case in his hand, and the Commander followed him out to the waiting area. As they approached her, Rebekah jumped to her feet and threw a smart salute.

Answering the salute, the Commander looked at Agent Smith then at Rebekah. "Petty Officer Callahan. I'll be talking to you in a little bit. In the meantime, please accompany Agent Smith to the conference room. He'd like to talk to you about an important matter."

Agent Smith smiled at Rebekah and then turned back to Commander Douglas and shook his hand. The Commander gestured for Rebekah to follow Smith, and she numbly followed the federal agent. As they entered the conference room, Smith took the seat farthest from the door, with his back to a wall. He motioned for Rebekah to sit down, and Smith opened his case, removing a rather thick file folder with the Department of Homeland Security seal on it. Rebekah was close enough to see her name on the tab.

The man then withdrew a set of credentials from his inner pocket and opened it, handing it across the table to Rebekah. "We got off on the wrong foot. I'm Agent James Smith from Homeland Security, and I came all the way here to talk to you specifically."

Smith opened the file and read the highlights. "Petty Officer First Class Rebekah Callahan. Senior EOD Technician. Raised in Norfolk, Virginia. Race car and race boat driver. You chose EOD because you got to blow stuff up, jump from airplanes, dive in the ocean, and work with Special Forces. But mostly to blow things up."

"You recently took a trip to Scotland to dive in Loch Ness. On the dive, you saw some sort of large underwater creature, and you decided to tell others." He looked up and caught her eye. "Oh, you did actually see Nessie, well, one of her descendants anyway. But that doesn't change the fact that CWO Goodwin thinks you were suffering from hypoxia. The skipper of the Reagan was worried about having a senior EOD tech that sees monsters. And your Command doesn't like that you went on TV."

Smith made sure that she was paying attention. "If you stay in the Navy, you are currently as high up the ladder as you'll go. You've been scheduled to begin training new EOD recruits. You're going to be stuck teaching new puppies how not to crap on the carpet. If you keep your nose clean and stick it out, you will retire with your twenty years in as a Petty Officer First Class. No more adventures for you."

The federal agent closed and began to put the personnel folder back into his briefcase. "On the other hand, you can come work for me. I'm putting together a rather special team to handle a rather special kind of threat to the United States. You have the skills I am looking for, and I don't care that you saw Nessie. At least she doesn't bother people too much. But I will need an answer. What do you say?"

6

DOC

Vatican City.

The middle-aged woman in a rather severe business pantsuit with her light brown hair pulled back into a tight bun was walking among the ancient stacks of books and scrolls in the Vatican Library. The section of the library that she was in was normally off-limits. Only a select few were ever given access, and this woman had received her unlimited clearance earlier that day.

As she carefully re-shelved the book, she glanced over and saw a title that caught her eye, *Monstra et Animalia, Of Monsters and Creatures*. Her gloved hands carefully drew the book from its resting place, and she examined the cover. Gold leaf inlay on what felt like leather. As she opened the front cover, she saw the author's name and smiled. Of course, this would be Gustaf Van Helsing's work.

She turned and walked toward the exit. The library itself was in a climate-controlled series of sub-basements with sections like this one having their own specially carved out rooms. As she passed through the archway, she nodded at the Vatican Guard standing at attention. Speaking Italian, she said, "I'm finished, Martin. I'm only removing this one item for study. Go ahead and close the gate."

The guard smiled at her and then closed and locked the gate securely. As she watched the gate close and lock, Doctor Noelle Sorenson, newly minted priest in the Catholic Church, signed her name on the entry log and noted which manuscript she had in her possession. She also noted that she would be taking it for an extended period, in her personal possession. She then turned and left, heading for the small apartment in Vatican City that she had called home for the last year.

Doctor Sorenson had never intended to work for the Catholic Church and had never expected to be ordained into the priesthood, especially since the church officially only ordains men into the Priesthood. How she had ended up in the Vatican was a long and unusual tale.

* * * * *

NOELLE HAD GROWN up in the United Methodist Church in Grand Rapids, Michigan. Raised as a "good Christian girl," she had been active in her local church and youth group. As she left to attend an out-of-state university, she had opted for Notre Dame for their history program.

At Notre Dame, she had started learning about the Catholic Church and attending Mass on campus. All of her professors were Priests or lay leaders, and they seemed to have the answers to her questions. After months of attending campus mass, she had begun attending and getting involved in a local parish. Noelle graduated with honors in European History and searched for a Master's program. After completing her degree, she had decided that she wanted to work with people. This had led her back into school where she had started her new major, Sociology. Again graduating with honors, she had once again looked at the job market and did not like her prospects in her chosen field.

Her wealthy parents had offered to support one more degree, and Noelle chose pre-med. The medical field had suited Noelle well, and she had thrived in the classwork. After she had graduated at the top of her class, she had applied and was accepted to the University of Michigan Medical School. With glowing recommendations from her professors, she had moved to Ann Arbor and quickly found a local parish to attend. Her graduation with honors and her completion of the Rite of Christian Initiation of Adults to become a full member of the Catholic Church had been celebrated the same week. Noelle had soon interned and quickly found a residency at a hospital in the Emergency/Trauma center.

The newly minted Doctor Sorenson had found that she thrived

in the trauma environment. Where most doctors tried to avoid the ER, she had gladly worked with the emergency cases. During her residency, she had explored other options and had thought about Doctors Without Borders, an organization that brought trained medical staff to third world countries where they were needed. When her residency was finished, she had applied for a position. Seeking extra funds to support her service, her local parish had raised support money to allow her to go help in third world countries.

While posted in Nigeria, Noelle had begun to see an interesting pattern in certain wounds on the people she was treating. Being told that they were so-called-monster attacks, she had grown more curious. When she had asked her supervisor, she had been told that the translator had mistakenly translated the Nigerian word for "animal" or "creature" into "monster." Not satisfied, she relayed the strange stories to her bishop back in Ann Arbor in her weekly correspondence.

When her tour was up and she moved back to Michigan, her bishop had asked more questions about the strange "monster" wounds. What she had thought was going to be a light conversation about an interesting story turned into a very surreal conversation.

The bishop had told Noelle that the wounds she saw and treated were caused by a form of shapeshifter, similar to a werewolf. During her care, she had inadvertently cured one patient from getting the "disease." Furthermore, the Vatican was interested in her story, and in her specifically. The bishop wondered if she would take time and fly to the Vatican to talk to one of the Cardinals there. The bishop had assured her that the Church would pay for the entire trip to Rome. Having always wanted to visit Rome and the Vatican, she gladly agreed.

When she had arrived in Rome, she was ushered into a meeting with two Cardinals and her bishop. Noelle was introduced to the Prefect, Cardinal Gerhard Ludwig Müller, and the Secretary, Archbishop Luis Ladaria Ferrer of the Congregation for the Doctrine of the Faith. After making introductions all around, Cardinal Müller began in a heavily accented English.

"Doctor Sorenson, we asked you to travel thousands of miles because we would like to hear first-hand your stories from Nigeria about the wounds from these monsters."

Noelle nodded and had begun to re-tell the now familiar story. Not embellishing, and not leaving any detail out, she had recounted all of her impressions and actions. As she was talking, the two

Cardinals would occasionally mutter back and forth in what sounded like Italian, and one or the other would ask a question to clarify her story. When she had finished, the Cardinals began talking amongst themselves in low Italian again, often switching to what sounded like Latin.

After what had seemed like an eternity, Cardinal Müller had turned to Noelle and said, "As Bishop Roberts has already informed you, you were actually seeing the results of shapeshifter attacks. Not quite what you would call 'werewolves', but close enough for your story. When a person bitten by these creatures survives the initial attack, they are infected with the virus that causes the affliction. You have seemingly done the impossible. Three out of the twenty, or so, victims you treated were somehow cured of their disease."

The Cardinal then seemed to shift the direction of the conversation. "Doctor Sorenson, do you happen to know the history of the Congregation of for the Doctrine of the Faith? No? I didn't think so. Our main purpose is to oversee and help facilitate Church Doctrine. We are here to help His Holiness in the task of making sure that Church Doctrine withstands the tests of time and scrutiny."

The Cardinal continued, "Originally, we were founded as the Supreme Sacred Congregation of the Roman and Universal Inquisition. I see by your response that you recognize the name of the Holy Inquisition. We were originally established with two missions. First to oversee the creation and implementation of Church Doctrine. Secondly, we were created to help oversee the enforcement of Church Doctrine. The Crusades and the Inquisition were part of that mission."

"One of the... hidden... missions of this Congregation is to search out, and destroy, monsters that threaten the Church. Even most of the Cardinals and Ordained do not realized that we are Monster Hunters. We have a special order called the '*Protectionem Dei Adversus Malum.*' Roughly translated, this order's name is 'God's Protection From Evil.' I would like to formally invite you to join this order."

"Before you give an answer, I would advise you that this order is staffed only by the ordained, or those who are in the process of being raised up. Full members of the order are always ordained Priests with missions to various countries.

"Yes, I can see your question before you even ask it. 'How can you be ordained if you are a woman?' Yes? This order, and this order alone, has a special dispensation from the Holy See to ordain women into this priesthood. With special stipulations, you would train and be raised up as a Priest to fight monsters. Would you serve God by joining the Priesthood?"

Noelle had been stunned. She had looked at Cardinal Müller, then at her bishop, Bishop Roberts, who had nodded solemnly. She had looked back at the Cardinals and took a deep breath, "Cardinal Müller, Archbishop Ferrer, I do believe that I will have to search out God's Will on this matter. May I have some time to think about it and pray for some guidance?"

"Absolutely," Cardinal Müller had responded. "I shifted your worldview. Certainly, take some time to decide. If you have any questions about what the service or training entails, please feel free to ask Bishop Roberts, who is an inactive member of the order."

He had continued, "Your room is reserved for you through the end of this week. If you need more time, we can give that to you as well. We do ask that the information we provided be kept in the strictest confidence."

"Certainly, Cardinal Müller. It was... interesting talking to you today," said Noelle. "I do believe I need to retire to my room to consider this matter."

As she had stood, the Cardinals and the Bishop stood as well. She had been led out of the labyrinth of corridors and back to her lavishly appointed room.

The very next day, Doctor Noelle Sorenson had informed the Cardinal that she was glad to accept appointment and training into the order. The following two weeks in Ann Arbor had been a whirlwind as she packed for a year-long training in the Vatican. Unable to take everything with her to the Vatican, she had arranged for a storage locker maintained by the local parish. Saying her goodbyes, Noelle had flown out of Detroit and into her new life.

* * * * *

THE YEAR HAD BEEN a frenetic blur of training and study. Between intensive courses in Italian and Latin, Noelle had spent time learning the Church Doctrine, and how to apply and interpret it. She had also spent time on physical training, including basic hand-to-hand combat and work with sharp and pointed weapons. Her favorite courses were those dedicated to the discussion of monsters and the special tools used to fight them effectively.

Noelle had become an expert in banishing the classic forms of the undead such as vampires and zombies. While she learned about other monster types that the church had a history with, her faith and skills fighting the undead quickly brought her to the attention of her instructors.

After about a year of training, Noelle was brought before the Prefect, the Secretary, and several other Bishops and Priests of the Order. The assembled men openly evaluated Noelle's performance and discussed whether her faith and training made her worthy of being lifted up into the priesthood. Throughout the discussion, Noelle knelt on the small cushion placed before the vaunted assembly and kept her face calm and down turned. Even while her thoughts raced, and she reacted internally to the discussion about some of her failures and shortcomings, she was very careful to use her training to keep all of her emotions from showing on her face.

The discussion took well over an hour, and Noelle was beginning to worry, as her legs were starting to cramp. Finally, Cardinal Müller raised a hand to end the discussion. As the conversation stopped, the Cardinal began speaking in Italian, "Rise, my child."

Noelle slowly rose to her feet, and the Cardinal continued, "Doctor Noelle Sorenson. It is the will of this Congregation, and the desire of this Order that you be raised and ordained into the Priest-hood. Please step forward and kneel."

Noelle reverently stepped forward to the spot just in front of the Prefect. The Cardinal stepped forward and laid his hand on her head briefly, offering a silent consecration. Then, one-by-one, the other officials present stepped in front of the woman and followed the Prefect's lead. After the last priest had stepped away, Cardinal Müller again stepped toward Noelle and began the traditional consecratory prayer. He then took a stole from a waiting priest and draped it over the back of her neck. It would fall almost to her knees while she stood.

Made of deep black silk and inlaid with spun silver thread, the stole was decorated with a large cross on each end with a very pecu-liar design connecting the crosses. As she looked closer, she recog-nized a few Latin phrases in the design. She had also noticed what appeared to be another, even older language woven throughout. As this stole was placed over her head and shoulders, it emitted a faint blue glow from parts of the design. Cardinal Müller muttered a few phrases in a language that Noelle did not recognize.

As the glow had faded, Cardinal Müller reached for a chasuble. Looking like a cross between a renaissance jerkin and a poncho, the vestment had a hole for the priest's head, and then loosely hung over the shoulders and back, with no fastenings at the sides. This particular design had originated in the 16th century and had much shorter sleeves, and the garment ended just below the shoulders on the side, leaving the priest's arms free.

This chasuble was a white, heavy silk with a spun gold thread inlay. A large cross was embroidered on the front and back of the garment, and the design that connected the two was very similar to the one on the stole. As the chasuble was laid on her shoulders, Noelle again noticed a faint blue glow originating from the threads. Cardinal Müller again muttered an invocation in a strange language.

The Prefect stepped back and said, "Rise child." Noelle rose to her feet, and Cardinal Müller continued, "I would like to congratulate the newest member of the *Protectionem Dei Adversus Malum*, Doctor Noelle Sorenson." The assembled men clapped and shook her hand.

As the convocation ended, Archbishop Ferrer, the Secretary for the Congregation, approached Noelle and asked to meet with her afterwards in his office. A short time later, Noelle accompanied the Archbishop to his office just outside the training quarters for her Order. As she was instructed prior to the ordination, she removed her vestments and hung them carefully in her quarters before she walked with the aging Archbishop.

Sitting behind his desk, the Archbishop gestured for Noelle to sit as well. Sitting in the comfortable chair, Noelle leaned back and patiently waited.

The Archbishop began, "Doctor Sorenson, I want to congratulate you again, and welcome you to our order. I have high hopes for you as you go fight the evil in the world. I wanted to meet with you to cover some final matters before you leave the Vatican."

"As you know, the Holy Church does not officially ordain women. Our order has a special, secret dispensation for the practice because there are certain rites that must be performed by an ordained priest for them to work. As such, you are only the third woman, and the only one currently serving, in the history of the order."

"Because of this, you will work to keep your status as an ordained Priest of the Holy Church confidential. While it is acceptable for the people to know that you work for the Church, very rarely will they ever know that you are ordained." The Archbishop looked at Noelle.

"To this end, you will be issued identification and paperwork that shows the Papal Seal. These credentials will gain you access to any of the Church's activities or locations in the United States. They will also enforce cooperation with you from those who also work for the Church."

Archbishop Ferrer drew an identification folder from his desk drawer. Bound in black leather, it was about four inches by five inches, and opened to show a strange identification card inside. The Vatican Special Services ID had Noelle's picture on it, along with her name, and the name and address of the diocese in Ann Arbor. In Latin and English, the card directed that Noelle was a direct representative of the Vatican and, as such, was expected the full cooperation of the person reading the card. Underneath that verbiage was more of the weird unknown script that was on her vestments.

As she accepted the folio, the script and ID had both glowed a faint blue, and then the glow faded. As she examined the folio, the other half contained a document that showed Noelle was a direct representative of Vatican City and was a registered Diplomat and qualified for immunity under the host nation's laws.

Noelle was stunned. *Diplomatic immunity? And what was that strange language?* "Archbishop Ferrer? What is this strange script that is on the credentials and my vestments?"

Archbishop Ferrer chuckled drily. "I wondered when you would get to that. God is all powerful, and your faith in him will help you battle the monsters. The Church also knows that there is other, less powerful authority out there. Sometimes it is useful to invoke that authority when a specific application of Faith does not work as specifically desired. As you will soon learn anyway, the language is an ancient tongue called Enochian, believed last spoken by Enoch. I will let you research and find out where it is from."

The Archbishop made sure to catch her eye as he continued, "One last thing. You are being assigned immediately. You will report to a specific office in the United States Homeland Security, no later than Sunday. There, you will be reporting to an Agent James Smith. You will work on one of his teams to fight these monsters and protect the flock. You will have a dual role. You will be under Agent Smith's authority, operating on his team. You will also continue working for the Vatican. You will report to my office directly. If you have any trouble with any American Church, have them call my office.

"For now, pack your personal belongings for this trip. It is a long-term assignment. Then see Cardinal Giancarlo in the travel office. He will arrange your travel as well as have your contact information and a secure smartphone for you. Go with God."

Noelle stood, shook the Archbishop's hand and went to pack her gear. Next stop, America.

7

WAITING

Section 28, Langley, Virginia.

I t had been two days of waiting for Burt Holstein. He had been brought to the Section 28 complex and admitted to the barracks that would be home to him and his new team. Attached to the barracks was a full gym with an Olympic-size swimming pool and a mess hall. The main living area of the barracks had a fully equipped galley, a dining area, and a large recreation area. The recreation area contained a pool table and ping pong table, a massive ultra-high definition screen with theater seating and access to any television channel imaginable, and a server full of movies and television shows to stream at will. One wall was lined with books ranging from popular fiction to classic literature, and reference and non-fiction works. Around the barracks facilities, there seemed to be ten different apartments with adjoining doors to the main living area.

When Burt Holstein had arrived, Agent Smith had handed him the keycard to one of the small apartments and had then explained to him that he was still assembling the team. Burt had been told that he had full access to the current building, but that his keycard would not allow him to exit the building or enter any of the other apartments. Smith had then told Burt that the meals and grocery stocks would be provided but that the delivery staff would not be able to answer any questions. When Burt had asked how long he would be confined to these quarters, Smith had shrugged and said, "I hope less than a week. As it is Saturday, the offices are closed, except for support staff. "

Entering his apartment, Burt had found that it was fully furnished with a small living space, a large bedroom, a small kitch-enette, and his own private full bathroom with shower. In the living area, there was a small high-definition television mounted on the wall, a leather loveseat, and an elegant metal and glass desk with a videophone and network cabling ready for a computer or laptop. Finding ample space for his personal effects in the bedroom, Burt had lain back on the bed and just sighed. He stared at the white institutional ceiling. *Great. I'm a thirty-six-year-old man who's just been sent to my room. Indefinitely.* Burt had closed his eyes and had fallen asleep almost instantly, sleeping for nine hours before waking up refreshed.

On Monday morning, Agent Smith brought another gentleman into the living quarters and handed him a keycard for one of the apartments. "Burt Holstein, this is John Smith. John has signed on to work SIGINT and electronics for your team," said Smith as he introduced the two men.

Burt surveyed the man in front of him. Looking about thirty, the six-foot-tall man was skinny to the point of gaunt. His disheveled red hair and green eyes betrayed the man's Irish heritage as much as his pasty white complexion, his boyish-looks, and thin, circular glasses were the epitome of geek chic. The man wore a t-shirt that announced, "There are 10 kinds of people. Those who get Binary, and those who don't." Burt didn't understand the shirt.

Turning to John, Agent Smith said, "Burt is going to be the team leader in the field."

John took his time as he studied his new team leader. Burt was older than John and in his mid-thirties. At five feet nine inches tall, Burt was shorter than John, but he was much stockier. His buzz-cut brown hair matched his brown eyes, and the deep tan told of some time spent in the sun. Looking at the tight t-shirt and cargo pants, John could see that all the weight was muscle. The rugged face, marred by scars, and hard looks told John that Burt was a warrior, and he was used to combat.

Smith turned toward each of them and said, "Well, I'm off to collect your next team member."

After Agent Smith left, Burt showed John the facilities, and John took his personal effects into his apartment. As the mess hall staff dropped off the food for the galley, Burt and John put together cold cut sandwiches and grabbed bags of potato chips and sat at the large table in the middle of the dining area. As John took his first bite, he chuckled to himself. "This sandwich is incredible. I'll have to admit, when I saw that we had a mess hall and galley, I figured we were getting government food. I was starting to regret signing up."

Gradually, Burt and John got to know each other. While they were both very guarded about their youth, they talked about their backgrounds before coming to Section 28 and about their hobbies. They discovered that they both enjoyed really bad sci-fi movies. Realizing that they shared some common ground, each man dropped his guard little by little. They sat back to watch a couple favorite movies in ultra-high definition splendor.

Late Tuesday afternoon, Agent Smith brought another gentleman to what Burt was beginning to call "the barracks." As Jesús Rivera was introduced as the team's sniper, Burt looked over his new teammate.

Jesús was a tall Latino man in his late twenties. His black hair and brown eyes showed his heritage, and the lean, muscular body told of a man who worked out and ate right. Wearing a black tactical shirt and black BDUs usually showed that someone was a "wannabe" or "tacti-cool" operator. On this man, however, the BDUs looked natural and hinted that this man was authentic... the kind of operator that Burt had worked with and got along well with.

The three men sat in the lounge area and slowly began to talk together. Reluctance and wariness stifled conversation. When Burt pointed out that they needed to begin to trust each other as they would soon be working as a team, both men became a little more forthcoming.

Jesús was the first one to cautiously bring up monsters. Recounting what Agent Smith had said about the lone werewolf, he asked the others if they had any similar stories. Burt admitted that he had seen what he thought was a UFO, although Agent Smith had said it was something else. And then John talked about ghosts. When Burt snorted in disbelief, John just looked at him.

John's voice dripped with sarcasm. "Sure. Werewolves and UFOs exist, but ghosts are crazy? Think about this. Just what the heck is Section 28 hiding? If I had my laptop, I could start climbing inside this network."

Jesús and Burt looked at each other and burst out laughing. Burt clapped John on the back, almost bending him over and said, "Point taken, John. Save the hacking for after we're officially sworn in. I'm sure we'll get a chance then."

It was three days later, on Friday afternoon, when Agent Smith brought in their final team members. "Rebekah Callahan, Explosives, and Doctor Noelle Sorenson, Vampire Hunter," said Agent Smith as he introduced the two women to the team.

Everyone gave a slight start at the word "Vampire," wondering if it was a joke. As the team members exchanged bewildered stares, Doctor Sorenson knowingly smiled and said, "I hunt all monsters. But vampires are my specialty."

Agent Smith said, "All right, team. Take the weekend to get to know each other." The DHS agent looked around at the new team. "Monday morning, you'll get sworn in and begin training together. Team meeting is at 0800 Monday. I'll have a staff member come for you then." He then walked out the door.

Burt looked at the two newcomers. Rebekah was a pretty 26-year-old with close-cropped black hair and piercing, bright blue eyes. She was about five inches shorter than his five-foot-nine-inch frame and had a slim, athletic frame. She was a beautiful young woman with a very pretty, pixie-like face. The way she carried herself and the Navy BDUs and white t-shirt told Burt that she was fresh from the Navy.

Doctor Sorenson, on the other hand, did not look like the someone who was used to active field work. Likely in her early forties, she wore a gray pantsuit and was very prim and proper. Her light brown hair was wrapped in a very tight bun, setting off her unusual gray eyes. Just a couple inches shorter than Burt's own five feet and nine inches, she looked more like a manager or business owner, not like the combat-trained "operator" Burt normally worked with. She did not look like someone who could fight a monster. *So how did she hunt vampires?* Burt asked himself. *Wait! Now I'm supposed to believe in vampires? What in the heck did I get myself into?*

Later, the newly formed team gathered their meals and sat at a long table together. Conversation ranged from personal backgrounds to speculation about what they were doing there and soon shifted to a raging debate about whether they were watching a sci-fi movie or the latest romantic comedy. The argument was finally settled by watching a reality TV show about storage locker auctions.

* * * * *

AS AGENT SMITH walked through the complex toward his own living quarters, he received a message on his secure phone. Looking at the message, Smith turned and walked briskly toward the operations room.

As he walked through the doors, the analyst who had sent him the message waived him over to her station. After a brief glance at her data, Smith motioned to the analyst to follow him to the planning center. He unlocked his phone and sent a pre-coded message to both Timothy, his secretary, and his boss, Director Day. The message to Timothy was simple: it instructed Timothy to call a list of staff and have them assembled in the planning center. Timothy was also to arrange with the kitchen staff for delivery of food, coffee, and other snacks.

The message to Director Day told his boss that there was a developing Incursion, and that the planning staff was being assembled. Smith knew Director Day would want a report first thing on Monday morning.

Smith reached the planning center to find that Timothy was already there, deciding which food the kitchen staff would bring to the planning center. As Smith reached his seat at the head of the table, the other staffers trickled in. A mix of analysts, planning strategists, and logistics experts, this staff was trained and assembled for this kind of meeting.

The lead analyst showed Smith a thumb drive, and he plugged it into a receptacle built into the table in front of Smith. As the computer spooled up the drive, the analyst grabbed the remote, and the last staffer came through the door. Closing the soundproof door and engaging the red meeting light, the final staffer took her seat. Smith nodded to the analyst and said, "Go ahead, Joan. What do you have for us?"

Joan looked around the room and made sure that every staff person in the room was ready. Seeing the staff staring at her, she fumbled with the remote. The analyst took a breath to calm her nerves and began the presentation.

Joan began by displaying a map of Colorado with a dot fixed near the southern border of the state, almost directly south of Pueblo. "Trinidad, Colorado. Population, just under eighty-five hundred. An hour and a half south of Pueblo. The search algorithms popped a hit, with an Incursion probability of eighty-nine percent."

"According to the data, there have been five deaths in the last month and a half. Last one happened a couple days ago. Average murder rate prior to this? Zero. The algorithms have also found ten missing people in the area in the last two months." Joan referred to some handwritten notes.

"Every death has shown signs of feeding at the normal locations. Local M.E. is signing off as post-mortem animal activity, but that's only because he isn't that good. The bad news is that the FBI has been alerted, and they are trying to decide if they want to send the BAU."

Smith frowned. He knew the FBI's Behavioral Analysis Unit would impede whichever team they sent. He asked the analyst, "Sounds like Incursion activity. Recommendations?"

Joan looked at her notes. "Team Alpha believes that this is likely a single creature. Most likely a vampire. Team Beta concurs on vampire activity but believes that there may be two. Both Alpha and Beta recommend priority Red."

Section 28 had a priority system set up to triage Incursion events. The highest priority is Black. Next is Ultra-Red, and then Red, Orange, Yellow, White, and Blue, in descending order.

Smith agreed with the Red priority. Vampires needed attention, but one or two fresh ones were not enough to classify and event as Ultra-Red.

Smith looked around the room. "OK. Priority Red in Trinidad, Colorado. Who do we have available to handle this?"

A woman next to Smith spoke up. "Knightfall is closest, but they're still recovering from their Priority Black," she said. "They are down to twenty percent capable, and their team leader is in rehab for her leg for another month. We also need to replace the casualties from that team."

Another analyst consulted his notes and spoke up. "Knights-dawn is still on location with their Ultra-Red. They are hunting down the 'fae' that came through in Oregon."

Smith thought for a moment and then began, "As most of you know, I've recently recruited the new team, Knightmare. They will swear in Monday morning. They are brand new, but there is a vampire specialist from the Vatican on the team, and most of them are from some sort of federal service. They should be able to handle one or two new vamps. This will be a great field test for them."

Having made his decision, Smith started issuing directions. "Logistics, prepare for the team's departure at 1000, Monday morning. Make sure you have proper ground transport available at the airport for them. Let the Armory know that they will be coming. Oh, and let Norbert know that the new team is coming to him. Send him their files."

"Intel, get everything you can on the town of... Trinidad, Colorado. We need to know who the local government and law enforcement is. Also, find out who is currently the SAC in the Denver office. We may need to give them a 'head's up.'"

"Operations, get the ball rolling. Good catch on the Incursion. Let's make sure this new team has all the support they need. Dismissed."

8

GEAS

By seven o'clock Monday morning, the block of apartments was frenetic with activity as the new teammates prepared themselves for the day. Each person performed their morning routine with a touch of nervous energy as no one had any idea what to expect that day. As the dining crew delivered breakfast at seven thirty in the morning, everyone was out in the lounge area waiting, except for John. He came stumbling out of his apartment about five minutes later with large, dark rings under his eyes attesting to another late night of watching bad science fiction movies.

As the dining crew was leaving, several staffers wheeled large wardrobes through the halls of the apartment block. As the team gathered round, one of the staff said, "All right guys. Welcome aboard. I am Agent Timothy Wilson, but you folks can call me 'Tim.' I am Agent Smith's assistant, so we'll be talking quite a bit." Wilson shook each team member's hand.

Burt appraised the assistant. Timothy Wilson was in his late twenties and looked like the stereotypical "preppy" college frat boy. Standing at five feet eight inches, Tim was blond with blue eyes and very fit and looked like he weighed in just over one hundred fifty pounds. Dressed in an immaculately pressed shirt and tie, Tim looked like he could be on the recruiting poster for any of the federal law enforcement agencies. Burt noticed that Tim was the first staffer that he had seen in the complex who was carrying a pistol. The agent had what looked like one of the Glock handgun models carried in a shoulder holster under his left arm.

Burt realized that Tim had continued speaking. "Today was scheduled to be an orientation day for you guys; however, your team will be going to work earlier than expected. I'll let Agent Smith handle all the details with you, but I wanted to stop by this morning for two reasons. First, I wanted to help drop off your training gear and your official tactical uniforms to be used while on a mission. There are multiple sets of each outfit in here for each of you. If you haven't discovered it yet, we do offer a complete laundry service for you. Just use the bags in your closets, put any special instructions on the form, and drop it off in the laundry area just inside the doorway to your team quarters. They will be returned, folded and pressed, to your individual rooms within twenty-four hours."

"Other than that, I really wanted to introduce myself. I know a lot of details from your file, but that does not mean I know you. When you receive your phones today, my contact information will be pre-programmed. You ladies and gentlemen can feel free to contact me about anything your team liaison cannot handle. Anyone have any questions?"

Burt cleared his throat, "So, we'll be able to leave our quarters today?"

Tim nodded, offering a good-natured smile. "I really apologize about that. Unfortunately, until you have officially been sworn in and signed your contracts, the vast majority of this complex is classified way above any of your former clearance levels. When we brought you here, we didn't anticipate having you in here this long. We really appreciate how patient you have been, especially you, Mr. Holstein."

"We ask that you not stray at all between here and the conference room where you will swear in. Once you are sworn in, you will have access to the vast majority of this complex, and your room keys will act as your access cards to the complex. Any other questions?"

When no one spoke up, Tim made a final request. "Agent Smith would like you to finish your preparations and then be ready at oh seven fifty-five. Your new team liaison will be coming down here to take you to the conference room then. I'll see you guys later."

After Tim left, Burt reached into the wardrobe marked "Training" and grabbed a large bundle of hung clothes wrapped in plastic. Reading the name on the tag, he said, "Rebekah," and handed her the bundle. He then repeated the process until the wardrobe was clean, and everyone had a bundle in his or her arms.

While Burt was passing out the training gear, Jesús opened the wardrobe labeled as "Duty." He continued the process started by Burt and passed out similarly marked bundles to almost everyone on the team. Looking in the now empty wardrobe, he looked puzzled. Jesús turned to Noelle and said, "Sorry, Doc. It looks like they forgot to add a bundle of clothes for you."

Noelle laughed lightly. "I'm sure they didn't forget me, Jesús. My action gear is a little more specialized. And customized. Trust me, I won't look like one of you guys when we go into action."

Jesús thought about it for a moment, nodded, and smiled. "I never thought about it like that."

"I recommend that we put our new gear away before we have to leave," Burt said as he looked at his teammates. "It sounds like we won't be needing the training gear today."

The others nodded their assent and took their clothing into their respective apartments to change.

As they met in the lounge a few minutes later, they all remarked that the training BDU uniforms seemed to be the perfect size. It was almost as if each set were tailored for each person. While they were speculating, there was a slight knock on the door, and a staffer opened the door to the apartment block.

Standing at the door was a young African American woman. She was just over five feet tall, her naturally curly black hair was gathered loosely in the back to form a ponytail, giving her a very youthful appearance. Her brown eyes perfectly complemented her mocha skin. The business pantsuit she wore accented her athletic build. As Burt welcomed her, he spotted a tell-tale bulge as her loose suit jacket flipped open slightly, revealing the butt of a handgun. *Another DHS agent?*

"Ladies and gentlemen, I am Agent Gretchen Massey. Please call me Gretchen. I am your team's direct administrative assistant; my official title is Team Liaison. It is my job to coordinate your life here at the Complex." Burt could almost hear the capital letter she placed on the word. She continued her introduction. "I help coordinate everything from meals to laundry, to entertainment so that you can concentrate on our mission. If you have any issues with the quarters, with your apartment block, or any services we're providing, please let me know. My number will be programmed into your SSP. That's the official designation of the secure smart phone equipment that you will be assigned."

She made a gesture. "Now, if you will follow me, I'll take you to the conference room. Agent Smith is waiting for you."

As the team walked through the warren of hallways and buildings, Burt noticed that there were several identifying marks at every corner that he could not decipher. While there were never any maps he could see, Burt guessed that a simple glance at a corner to read the markings would tell a knowledgeable employee exactly where they were in the complex. As they turned down a corridor mysteriously labeled "Ex1.3.NE," there was a subtle shift in atmosphere. The hall got quieter, as if the very sounds were dampened, and the staffers seemed to be in less of a hurry to move along. Burt noticed that the carpeting in the hallway went from standard industrial to a higher quality carpeting, and the plain metal doors became interspersed with wood doors and the occasional set of windows in the hallway. None of these windows ever showed an outside view. Instead, they always showed the interior of an office or conference room.

Gretchen led them to a door marked "Conference Room Ex.1.A." She opened the door and ushered the team into a large, beautifully furnished conference room. With wood paneling, a large wooden table, and comfortable seating, this room would have been fit for a boardroom for a Fortune 500 company. The large plasma screen at the end of the room nearest the door and the recessed speakers in the ceiling bespoke of fully integrated media. The only thing missing was an executive speakerphone in the middle of the table. At the far end of the table stood Agent Smith.

As the team filed in, Agent Smith motioned for them to sit down. This morning he was wearing the same gray pinstripe suit, immaculately pressed, with the jacket fastened. Agent Smith opened his arms in an expansive gesture and said, "Good morning, ladies and gentlemen. I am so glad we can finally get all of you officially sworn in to Section 28. I know that some of you have been puttering around in your apartment complex for several days now, and I thank you for your patience. As Timothy explained earlier, after this morning, you will not be confined to the apartment complex. In fact, you will not even be confined to this operations complex. Although you will be busy with training and missions, your downtime is your own to do with as you please. Timothy will arrange for any transportation needs that you might have. We'll talk about a lot of that later. I'd like to begin with the formal contracts and swearing in."

Agent Smith reached over and put on a pair of white gloves, the same ones that art and antiquities dealers use to handle rare or fragile items. He then reached over to a closed file lockbox at his right side and opened the lid. One by one, he reached into the lockbox and withdrew a heavy, white envelope. Each one looked like it was made of leather and had a wax seal over the flap on the back. Reading the name embossed on each envelope, he walked around the table, handing out the appropriate envelope to each team member. After watching intently, Burt realized that Agent Smith was careful to never make contact with the person to whom he handed the envelope and that he distributed each envelope individually, never holding more than one at a time.

As John took his pouch, he noticed a weird language written on the seal. As he looked closer, he realized that it looked like the Enochian language he had read about. Called "Celestial" or "Angel-ical" by the sixteenth century mathematician and occult philosopher John Dee, it was said to be the first language spoken, and the language of angels. They later called it Enochian because the last person on earth to speak it was the biblical figure Enoch.

Pulling a glasses case out of his pocket, John opened the case and replaced his normal glasses with the ones found in the case. The "glasses" that he put on looked like a weird mechanical contraption with multiple spindly arms that held different lenses and could be flipped up and down as needed. John flipped a particular set of lenses down and observed that the wax seal itself had a faint blue glow to it. Pushing that set of lenses out of the way and flipping another one down, he detected a faint green energy glow on the envelope itself.

Whistling softly, John looked at Agent Smith who was once again standing at the head of the conference table and remarked, "Can I get one without the glowing letters and spooky green glow?"

Agent Smith smiled. "No, Mr. Smith. I'm afraid that the paper-work comes standard with that 'spooky green glow' that you mentioned." Addressing the rest of the team, he continued. "Before you open the pouches in front of you, I want you to be very clear about a couple things that will happen when you do so. You might experience a wave of energy or a slight tingling sensation on your fingertips and in your hair. Some have also reported other strange sensory phenomena. I assure you: that is normal.

"This is your last and final chance to not join this team. If you choose to stop now, you will go back to where you were when I recruited you. No harm. No foul. No Take-backs. Does anyone want to exercise that option now?" Smith paused to see if anyone would take the deal.

When no one responded, he continued. "If you would now open your envelopes, taking care not to touch any of the materials from another teammate. Inside you will find a contract and a pen. Please pull both of those items out and begin reading the contract. This spells out your terms of service, and it details our agreement with you. A large part of this contract explains that this agreement will bar you from mentioning Section 28, what you do, or what you are hunting, except under certain, very explicit, circumstances. Even the existence of Section 28 is classified as 'Top Secret - Black,' and is on a need-to-know basis."

"On the back page, there is a spot to sign your name and date it. When you pick up the pen and begin to write with it, you may feel a slight pinch in one of your fingers. This is supposed to happen. At that time, your blood will be taken and mixed with the ink when you sign the contract. Each of your contract agreements is exactly the same, except for Doctor Sorenson's. Hers is slightly different due to her position with the Vatican. At this time, please read through the agreement and sign where indicated."

The teammates all opened their envelopes and began to read their contracts. As John read through the contract, certain phrases seemed to leap out and implant themselves in his brain: "...Secrecy *Geas* will be enforced...." "...Limited license to kill paranormal...." "...Incursion-level events...." "Housing, weapons, and esoteric research..."

More of these phrases rattled through his vision, and John was filled with a mixture of fear and excitement. Along the edges of the agreement, John noticed more of the Enochian markings, both along the sides and across the top and bottom of each page. The further along he read in the contract, he realized that the lettering on the sides of the agreement actually started to glow a faint neon green. For every page he turned, the markings became a bit more prominent and the glow went a bit lower on the next page. When he reached the end, all of the ancient script except the bottom of the page glowed. John held the pen and put the old-fashioned nib to the line to sign his name. As he signed, he felt a pinch and a tingle in his fingers, and the black ink from the pen changed to a deep maroon. As he placed the final stroke and dated the agreement, the script across the bottom of the page flared to life, and then the glow on the entire agreement faded.

John put down the pen and looked at his hands. He could not

see any wounds caused by the pen. As he looked up, he noticed everyone else examining their hands as well. One by one, they looked around at each other as they exchanged deeply disturbed expressions. The questions and surprise floating around the room were almost tangible, and Agent Smith cleared his throat to get everyone's attention.

"Now that you have signed your agreements, please place the contract back into the carrier pouch with the pen. Then simply press the flap to the seal and it will close."

A series of blue flashes around the table confirmed that all of the team members' pouches were sealed. In an orderly and meticulous fashion, Agent Smith walked to each team member, one at a time, to retrieve the pouches. After he had gathered all the pouches with the same care that he had shown when he handed them out, he placed the pouches inside the box, closed the lid of the file carrier, and muttered a few words in a strange language. A small blue flash from the locking mechanism indicated that the box was sealed with the same energy as the pouches. At this, Agent Smith peeled his gloves off and turned back to the assembled team.

"Ladies and gentlemen, I would like to formally welcome you to the Department of Homeland Security, Section 28. As of now, you are officially agents assigned to Team Knightmare."

9

KNIGHTMARE

Section 28 Conference Room , Langley, Virginia.

Agent Smith reached to his left and grabbed a stack of identification holders that was sitting on the table. Opening the top set of credentials, he read the name and began passing them out. "Special Agent Burt Holstein. Your new radio call sign will be 'Six.' As team leader, you will coordinate and lead the team while on assignment."

Turning to John, Agent Smith handed him his credentials. "Special Agent John Q. Smith," Agent Smith said with a smile. "Your new call sign is 'Spooky.' Use your electronics wizardry to find the monsters for your team to kill."

As he handed out the next set of credentials, he said, "Special Agent Rebekah Callahan. You like to blow things up, I think 'Boomer' is rather appropriate for your call sign."

The next set of credentials went to Jesús. "Special Agent Jesús H. Rivera. Your job will be sniper and overwatch, making sure your team doesn't get bushwhacked. I do believe that tradition says you should be called 'God.'"

Noelle smiled at Jesús and said, "Little 'g.' Don't forget it."

Agent Smith turned to Noelle. "And, Doctor Sorenson, that leaves us with you. Special Agent Noelle Sorenson. Not only are you the team's resident vampire hunter and esoteric specialist with

Vatican training, you are also a trained trauma doctor. I do believe that 'Doc' would suit you well on the radio."

"The credentials I just gave you prove your identity with Homeland Security," said Smith as he addressed the whole team. "If anyone questions the validity or authority of your credentials, have them call Homeland Security with your badge/ID number. They will be transferred to this office, and we will let them know that they are stepping into a pile of crap. Also, tucked into the credential wallet is a government credit card with your name on it. Use it for anything you need. Just make sure you bring back receipts for the Auditors.

"When you are on assignment, your authority trumps local law enforcement, the local FBI field office, and even the Secret Service, if it escalates to that point. You have the full authority to do your job and to protect America, and humanity, from the scary monsters that others simply cannot deal with. When you are not on assignment, you are to use your discretion on exercising that authority. If you suspect that we have a monster around, then use your authority to get the help you need. Do not abuse the authority just because you can. If you do, the 'geas' that you just signed in blood will make your life miserable if you abuse it."

John spoke up, a smile forming as he talked. "So, this is kinda like psychic paper, only it actually has something on it? Cool."

Agent Smith returned the smile, a bit bemused at the reference. "With the exception that you are not, nor will you ever be, a Time Lord. And you, John, would not look nearly as good in a trench coat and scarf."

Rebekah and Burt started laughing, and John sheepishly turned red. Noelle and Jesús looked at the team, and then at each other and shrugged, clearly not getting the reference.

After several moments, Agent Smith cleared his throat to regain the focus of the group. "Now that you all know who you are, I'd like to tell you why you are here." He paused briefly, looking at each team member, and then continued. "All of this briefing is classified."

Smith began as if he was addressing a college lecture hall. "Throughout history, there have been stories and reports of strange animals, evil creatures, and unexplained phenomena. While most people believe these are just tales, we have found out that the tales have at least some basis in fact. As best we can tell, there are certain locations where the boundary between our reality and another reality, another plane of existence, or another place, grows thin and weak. This weakening is rarely permanent and often appears in locations where it has not previously occurred. Sometimes, this makes the boundary thin enough that something from the other side can pass through the barrier. At other times, the barrier thins, and the fears and dreams of the people nearby allow their deepest fears to manifest in our reality. We call these crossings 'Incursions.'"

Smith could tell that he had his agents' attention. Their expressions ranged from rapt concentration to disbelief to an amused nodding. The one nodding and smiling was John, and Smith knew that he would have his hands full trying to keep John in check. Smith would have to keep the young intel specialist busy.

Smith continued with his explanation. "It is a relatively well-known fact that Adolf Hitler had a fascination with the paranormal. From collecting religious artifacts believed useful for gaining power, trying to communicate with the dead, or somehow using this thinning reality to help conquer the world, Hitler was a growing threat on the esoteric and paranormal front."

"On June 13, 1942, the Office of Strategic Services was formed as an intelligence agency during World War II. One of the smaller, but still substantial, concerns that affected the formation of this new agency was the threat represented by Hitler's esoteric research. Between Section 27 and Section 29 of the Presidential military order that formed the OSS was a small redacted notation labeled 'Section 28 - Top Secret (Black)'. Only a handful of people knew about the formation of Section 28 and to even reveal the existence of this program was considered High Treason. During wartime, a treason charge like this would have meant a swift trial and execution."

"In that original Section 28, this office and complex was formed and began hiring agents and training those agents to fight monsters. When the OSS was dissolved in 1945 for the creation of the CIA, the small redacted notation about Section 28 was again added to the charter. While it was technically no longer 'Section 28' of the new charter, the name and reference remained."

"When the Homeland Security Act of 2002 was passed on November 25, 2002, there was once again a redacted Top Secret (Black) notation that reassigned the offices and personnel of Section 28 to the Department of Homeland Security. Our credentials switched from the CIA to DHS, but nothing else really changed."

"Our mission is to hunt down and either manage these incursion monsters, destroy the incursion monsters, or send them back through the Incursion. There are some creatures who come through, with whom we, and other governments, have certain agreements. Those we work with to protect our citizens. Other creatures come through, we call them monsters. These are the ones that we have to hunt down. We either kill them, or we send them back through the Incursion. This is now your mission."

"To that end, you have virtually carte blanche access to equipment, tools, weapons, and research. Each Incursion is assigned a priority color, from no priority 'Blue,' then 'White,' 'Yellow,' 'Orange,' 'Red,' 'Ultra-Red,' and 'Black,' in ascending order. A priority Black means that the world is actually going to end if we don't get the call right."

Smith paused to catch the eye of every team member around the table. He wanted to make sure that they understood this next part very clearly.

The senior agent continued, "To help protect America from the very teams designed to save her, the contract you signed has a *geas* on it that will tear you apart from the inside out if you intentionally betray your team or Section 28. I watched one former agent turn a gun on the team as soon as he learned the truth. The fire that immolated him after he pulled that trigger for the first shot left nothing except ash."

Agent Smith was melancholy for a moment, and then seemed to visibly shake himself out of it. "As much as I'd like to begin your training this morning, I'm afraid that you are going to have to do some on-the-job training. Last night, we received a Priority Red Incursion. The target area is Trinidad, Colorado. With a population of just under nine thousand, this small town sits about an hour and a half south of Pueblo."

"They have had five murders in the last month and a half. No commonality among the victims except they were drained of fluids and had 'animal marks' on their ankles, wrists, neck, and inner thighs. There have also been ten people reported missing within that same timeframe. The local sheriff has not connected the murders to the disappearances yet, but he has called in the FBI Behavior Analysis Unit to profile the killer. Thoughts?"

Noelle immediately spoke up. "You obviously think that it's vampires. Any idea how many?" she questioned.

Agent Smith smiled and then answered, "Frankly, Doctor Sorenson, I would have been disappointed if you had not come up with that option. Yes, we are thinking vampires, and the analyst team believes that there are only one or two vamps, and that they are fairly new vamps, possibly turned by an Incursion."

"You will have access to records and Section 28 information on your flight to Trinidad. I really want to give you more time to train and prepare for this job, but I cannot let a Priority Red go while you guys are active. Your fire team has all seen combat of one sort or another. This should be a fairly simple run for you. Watch your backs, take care of these monsters, and try not to get your face on TV."

Smith motioned for the team to rise.

"OK, first stop is back to your quarters to grab your tactical BDUs and pack a small bag for clothing and essentials. We've provided duffle bags for your deployments. This should only last a couple days. When you have your bags, drop them in the area outside the entrance to your barracks marked 'Deployment' and head to the warehouse for outfitting."

"Once you have your gear, head to the airfield out back. The jet should be fueled and waiting for you. You need to be 'wheels up' in one hour. Gretchen is waiting outside to guide you back to your quarters and then on to the plane. Any questions?"

The abrupt reality of their impending deployment stifled any questions that were forming from the briefing. Seeing no questions, Smith dismissed them. "All right then, welcome to Section 28. Go kill some monsters."

The walk back was quiet as each team member tried to absorb his or her new reality. When the team returned to their barracks, they found several boxes waiting for them. Stacked in the commons area, each box had a name on it. Burt stepped forward and started passing them out to the team members.

When John opened his box, he found all the customized electronics that had been confiscated from him when he had first arrived. Sitting in the carefully packed box was his laptop, all of his electronics tools, several thumb drives, and a special wristband. Handcrafted over the course of a year, John's wristband covered most of his forearm and looked similar to plastic sleeves that college quarterbacks wear to keep track of plays and strategy. Inspired by those wristbands, John had designed and built the wristband as a full-capability touch-screen computer. And it was faster and more powerful than the desktops sitting in most homes. Gathering his gear, he ran into his room to pack a bag.

Jesús opened his rather long box to find a rifle case inside. Opening the case and checking the serial numbers, he confirmed that this was, in fact, his heavily customized personal M24-A3 rifle. Checking the action, he realized that it had been thoroughly and professionally cleaned. Although there was no ammunition or magazines with it, he felt like he had just found a long-lost friend. He packed the rifle back in her case and strode to his apartment to put on his tactical gear.

Rebekah's box contained a small assortment of personal electronics and a small necklace-sized velvet box. Rebekah opened the box and blinked away the tears. There was a small note from her former commanding officer, Chief Warrant Officer Harold Goodwin. The note read, "I fought for this. Orders came through the day after you left. Good luck." Underneath the note was a small collar pin of an eagle clutching a fouled anchor. A certificate inside the box announced that she was (then) Chief Petty Officer Rebekah Callahan. She placed the items back in her box and went into her room to pack.

Noelle opened her small box and found a package addressed to her from the Vatican. Opening the small package, she found a note from the Prefect. "Dr. Sorenson, I've enclosed one of the books from the Library. I believe that this will help you in your assignment. Go with God." Looking at the book, she felt the worn leather binding and saw the title *Cum Praeliorum Creaturae*. Noelle translated the title, *Of Battles with Creatures*. Noelle said a silent prayer of thanks, for the book she was holding was written by one of the Order's most prolific monster hunters. It was his battle diary. Noelle wandered toward her room lost in thought.

When Burt was finally able to open his box, he immediately smiled. Sitting inside was a complex holster rig and two pistol boxes. Opening the boxes, Burt caressed the gun inside each box. While they appeared to be normal Beretta 92FS series pistols, Burt knew these were his. A quick check of the serial numbers verified that they were his, and a function inspection verified that the custom-tuned guns were immaculately cleaned. Grabbing the gear, he headed toward his room.

The team met together in the commons area when they were finished dressing and packing. Gretchen led them out the door and to the warehouse. As they were leaving the block of apartments, Gretchen pointed out the spot reserved for "go bags" for assignments. As the team members dropped their go bags, a series of lights lit up along the wall. Gretchen explained that this summoned the staff to take care of their bags.

Walking to the warehouse, they went through another warren of corridors. Eventually the corridors widened out, and the team came to a large vault door that stood open and towered over twenty feet tall. It was about three feet thick. A small sign stenciled on the wall said "Logistics." When Burt remarked about the thickness of the door, Gretchen quietly pointed out that the weapons, gear, and equipment stored in the warehouse could actually affect the course of a nation.

The warehouse was impossibly large inside. Easily thirty feet high, the large space opened up into three distinct areas. Gretchen offered a running commentary for the introduction. "On your right is 'Equipment.' All of your tactical equipment and gear is here... secure radios, armor, electronics, and virtually anything you could want for the mission. If they don't currently have it, they can procure it within twenty-four hours. Normally, you are given more prep time for a mission and can have a list ready for the Equipment team."

Standing behind the equipment staffer was an enormous series of racks and bins. All of which was neatly labeled and ready to supply a mission deployment.

Gretchen continued her tour. "On your left is the 'Armory.' We stole Master Sergeant Russell Garner from the Army, and he is the one who will give you anything that goes bang or boom and anything that makes critters dead. Almost any type of weapon or ammunition is available, and what he doesn't have, he can get. Russell is also a master armorer. If your gun is broken or needs tuned, he can make it shoot better than it ever has. Once you've decided on a normal load out, Russell will have it ready for you on deployment."

Russell Garner was a large, burly man with a rough, blocky face and a salt-and-pepper buzzcut. Looking every inch the former Army sergeant, Russell was wearing a polo shirt and cargo pants, and the distinctive grip of a Colt M1911 stuck out of the holster on his waist. The man appeared to be old enough to have used the same type of weapon while in the military before they switched to a smaller 9mm round. Behind the armorer was a cage of steel that contained a series of racks that held everything from pistols to rifles and shotguns. There were sections where bins of grenades were stacked, and even a section that contained anti-tank rockets. Along the wall to the armorer's right was a series of bins with names, including the names of the team members.

Gretchen led the team to the final area, straight ahead. "And last, but certainly not least, is 'Esoteric Research and Logistics.' Because of what you do, we have an entire staff dedicated to researching how to effectively find, track, and kill monsters. Think of them as the Section 28 'Q' branch. And the head of this rather eccentric group is Norbert Guffy. If you look up 'mad scientist' in the dictionary, I do believe Norbert's picture is shown. On the other hand, if you need to figure out how to kill a particular incursion monster, Norbert will have the equipment for you. From holy water to silver ammunition, and stakes to wolfsbane, if you know what you are hunting, Norbert probably has something to kill it."

Norbert Guffy was a wiry little man around five feet tall. Seated behind a simple wooden desk, his unkempt hair and stained, disheveled shirt suggested a distinct lack of sleep and hygiene. The shirt was barely covered by the worn and frayed lab coat that used to be white, but now tinged gray. His thick, black-framed glasses gave him a slightly bug-eyed appearance. The strange, mechanical keyboard on a metal stand to Norbert's right was connected to a vast machine behind him. The machine was composed of large racks separated and entangled with a confusing nest of rails. Both large and small containers traveled along rails to be stored on the racks. Manipulating the boxes was a complex series of mechanical arms, using pulleys, wires, and bits of copper. John was fascinated by the complex mechanism in front of him and stared in wonder.

Gretchen turned to the team and watched them gaze in amazement as they looked around the Logistics warehouse. She cleared her throat to get their attention. "I know this is short notice, but requisition your gear, weapons, and any esoteric gear. We have about fifteen minutes to get to the plane outside." She then stepped back as the team members dispersed to gather their equipment.

10

LOGISTICS

Burt, Jesús, and Rebekah immediately headed for the Armory. Nodding to the armorer, Burt reached out his hand and grasped the former sergeant's. "Mr. Garner, it's nice to meet you. I'm guessing it was you who cleaned up my Berettas."

"Yes, Agent Holstein," Russell responded. "And please, call me Russell. I think you'll like shooting them even more now. Would you like ammo for them for the mission? What else can I get for you?"

Burt laughed and responded, "Ok, Russell, I'm Burt. Let's go with four magazines for the Berettas and two boxes of additional ammo. I'd like to make the Beretta M9 the standard load out for each member of the team, unless they have a different preference, except for our priest. Also, I'd like an M4, select-fire, with a foregrip and an ACOG on top for the sights. I'll trust your judgement for the setup. Four full magazines and a hundred rounds of extra ammo."

The Beretta M9 was a classic semi-automatic handgun chambered in 9mm. The pistol had been the standard U.S. military sidearm since 1985, and the civilian variants were often used in law enforcement from the mid-1980s through the 1990s. The M4 carbine was the shorter, adjustable stock variation of the venerable M16 rifle that had been in service since the Vietnam Conflict. Updated for modern usage, the M4 had an adjustable stock for individual shooters, a shorter sixteen-inch barrel, and was capable of semi-automatic shots or firing three-round bursts, selectable with the flick of a switch.

Burt turned to Rebekah and asked, "Any experience with a rifle?"

"Some. But I'm better with a shotgun," Rebekah said. "I preferred the Mossberg we used on the ship."

Burt turned back to the waiting armorer. "So, Mossberg twelve gauge. Thirty rounds, split between buckshot, slug, breeching round, dragon fire, and rubber."

Russell went to a rack and grabbed a black Mossberg 590A1 Tactical shotgun. The jet black, pump-action shotgun held five rounds in the tube, a pistol grip, and a collapsible stock like the M4 carbine. By racking the pump, the shotgun would strip out an expended shell and replace it with a fresh round that was nearly a half an inch in diameter. While not great for long distance targets, the shotgun was devastating at shorter ranges.

Rebekah spoke up. "Nice to meet you Russell; I'm Rebekah. What do you have that will make stuff go bang?"

Russell smiled and accepted her handshake. "You must be the EOD Tech. I like how you think. I have everything from Semtex to C4, and even dynamite, available. Anything more exotic will have to meet you on-site. What do you want?"

Both Semtex and C4 were considered "plastic explosives." Unlike dynamite, plastic explosives are an inert, moldable clay-like material that will only explode when the proper trigger is used. Safe to transport and mold, this type of explosive needs the concussive shock of a detonator or blasting cap to start the explosive reaction. Due to its energy potential, it only takes a little to generate the explosive energy of the kinetically slower dynamite.

"I might just fall in love with you, Sarge," Rebekah said as she smiled. "How about two pounds of C4. And an assortment of detonators, you know… motion, timed, remote? The fun stuff. I'll also take four flashbang grenades and four fragmentation, if you've got them."

Russell nodded, and Burt chimed in, "I'll take the same grenade load."

Russell said, "OK, give me five minutes to gather and crate it. I'll send it out to the plane for you."

As Burt and Rebekah walked toward the area marked, "Equipment," Jesús stepped up, placed his rifle kit on the bench, and shook Russell's hand, "I'm Jesús. Great job on my rifle. She hasn't been that smooth in a while."

Russell grinned. "I'm glad you liked it. I was going to leave it for you, but we got notice you were being assigned immediately, so I thought I'd help. Can I ask you something? Why did you choose .338 Lapua? I would think that a .308 would allow for a more selective application. Your magnum is going to shoot through a lot of things a .308 wouldn't."

Jesús nodded. "It might seem that way, but I was on the HRT. Most of the time, if I was pulling the trigger, I was shooting through glass, a wall, or even a car door. I had to have the long distance and heavy penetration. Besides, if you hit a bad guy with the magnum round, they don't survive for trial."

Russell nodded again. "You'll need that penetration for some of the critters that you guys are going to tackle. By the way, I tweaked the scope mount and mounted a new scope of my own design. With a simple click, your scope goes from regular to night vision to thermal. I sighted it in at one hundred yards, but you'll want to verify in the field." Russell reached down and grabbed a small hand-held electronic device that looked like a calculator. "Here's a new ballistics computer. I've pre-programmed it for all the commercially available rounds, as well as the custom rounds we make here. I've even included the fun rounds that the guys in Esoteric come up with. Since you don't have a spotter, you'll need the computer."

The sniper nodded. He paused to consider, and continued, "Instead of the M9, I'd like a good 1911," Jesús said. "It's what I carried for the HRT, and I know the gun inside and out."

Russell's grin grew wide. "Damn. I'm glad at least one of you likes to play with the 1911. I've got a custom built one that you can use, decked out with all the bells and whistles. She shoots through one ragged hole at 25 yards."

"That sounds great. At least four extra magazines, if you will," said Jesús.

Jesús thanked Russell and wandered toward the Equipment section. There, Burt had already ordered Level III flak jacket armor for all the team except the priest and the whiz kid. For those team members, he had requisitioned level IIIA armor they could wear under their clothing. Full battle helmets, night vision and thermal goggles, and secure radios with self-activating throat mikes rounded out the tactical requisitions. The three teammates wandered toward the other team members at Esoteric Research.

When the three combat specialists walked toward the armory, Noelle and John looked at each other and immediately went to talk to the man behind the Esoteric desk. On the plain wooden desk sat a nameplate that read "Esoteric Research–Guffy." Behind the desk the man looked at them quizzically. Realizing that they were waiting for him, he started enthusiastically talking in a running stream-of-consciousness.

"Oooh, you must be the new team. It's nice to finally meet you. I've been waiting hours or maybe minutes." Looking at Noelle, he glanced at her collar and clothing and said, "You must be the priest. Of course you are the priest. Only the priest would wear that collar. Right? Let's see. I know I had a box for you." Bending over his keyboard, he began hesitantly typing letters. "Let's see, that was 'P' for priest, no... 'V' for Vatican? No... Ah. 'B' for box. B-01-DF-6."

Behind the desk, the worrisome contraption of arms, pulleys, tracks, and boxes whirred into life. After a few minutes, a pair of arms brought a medium-sized box right to the desk. Opening the lid, Norbert pulled out a small box, what looked like a cross and a rather full pouch. "OK. Let's see. You have a crucifix, silver, with a wooden stake carved into the end... a box of, hmmm, what was that... something your Vatican recommended... oh, a dead man's blood. And a full pouch of consecrated salt. You guys must be going after vampires! Sounds like fun!"

Noelle accepted the items and asked, "Do you have anything else that might help? Like a way to deliver the blood?"

Norbert's face lit up, and he furiously pecked away at the keyboard, muttering to himself. A few moments later, the same arms whisked the box away and brought another one. Opening the lid, Norbert lifted out a rather strange looking handgun. He smiled and proffered it to Noelle. "Tranquilizer gun. My design." His face fell momentarily, and he began digging in the box again. Crying out triumphantly, he handed a small box to Noelle. "And here are the darts. Hypodermic. You should be able to figure it out. I hope so anyway... I lost the instruction book. Anything else?"

Noelle shook her head and stepped aside for John. John looked at Norbert and said, "OK, so what kind of gear do you have for me?"

Norbert looked him up and down and suddenly gasped. Muttering and punching furiously at the keys, he had another box brought to him. Inside were two small black pouches. Unrolling one, Norbert looked at John and said, "Let me see your glasses. Come on, come on, you don't have all day."

Reluctantly, John handed Norbert his glasses and cringed as Norbert's deft fingers disassembled his prized glasses effortlessly. The researcher's fingers moved way too fast for John to follow, and it seemed like the glasses almost reassembled themselves. Handing them back to John, Norbert smiled. "Try 'em on. I think you'll like them!"

John placed his glasses back on the bridge of his nose and was instantly amazed. Not only was the world around him sharper and crisper, but he noticed that by simply scrunching his nose a certain way he could switch between the various lenses. John started laughing and thanking Norbert.

Norbert handed John one of the tool pouches that was before him. "Amazing creatures, gremlins. Their stuff is always fun to play with." Norbert's eyes got wide as a thought struck him. He turned back to his keyboard and started muttering again. "Oooooh. One more thing. Let's see, was that 'B' for bullet? No... 'P' for pistol? No... Aha! 'G' for ghoul. GX-3-D-414-Z."

Again the boxes whirled around, and the mechanical arms brought a small but armored box down from the racks. The excitable Norbert gingerly pulled out a small padded carrying case with an explosives symbol on the side. Setting it on his desk, Norbert opened the airtight case. Inside the case, John could see a small box of ammunition nestled deep into thick foam padding. Norbert smiled at John while he closed the lid and secured the box.

Handing the box to John, Norbert said, "OK, a special surprise for you. Use on a vampire. Be VERY careful. Don't shoot anything you want to keep around. Have fun!"

Norbert turned to the team members coming up behind John. "And what can I get for you?"

Burt, Rebekah, and Jesús had walked over to the Esoteric Research area and were listening to the conversation between Norbert and John. Burt smiled at Norbert's greeting and said, "Do you have anything that we can use? It looks like we're vampire hunting this trip."

Norbert nodded and smiled, and then said, "Yes, yes. Let me see what I have here. What calibers are you carrying?"

As Norbert started typing on the keyboard, Burt answered, "Nine millimeter, and five-five-six. And Rebekah has a twelve gauge. And Jesús has three-three-eight Lapua, and apparently a forty-five auto." Burt looked at the holstered pistol strapped to Jesús's waist.

A fair amount of clicking and clacking sent the arms scurrying through the racks. Norbert muttered, "Only two vampires. Newbies. Calculate one hundred rounds of nine. Ninety rounds of rifle ammo. Twenty for the pretty girl with the shotgun. Thirty for the scary sniper..."

Eventually, the arms retrieved four of the containers, and the researcher dug into them. He began placing boxes of ammunition on the desk. "Two hundred rounds of nine millimeter. One hundred rounds of forty-five. Ninety rounds for the rifle. Twenty shotgun rounds. And thirty for the sniper. My own design. Brand new. Should work." Norbert shrugged. "Should, anyway."

Burt and Jesús opened their respective boxes and compared rounds. The rounds inside looked like a standard jacketed hollow-point design with a couple major distinctions. The outer coating of the jacket appeared to be silver, and Burt expected that it would test as silver as well. Inside this actual hollow cavity sat a piece of wood. Noelle leaned over and looked at the round. Nodding appreciatively, she turned back to Norbert. "You've combined silver shot with a wooden stake in a form that can be delivered from a distance. How ingenious. I'm going to enjoy working with you."

The researcher blushed crimson. "Thank you. It just sounded like it should work," Norbert said as he shrugged. The researcher looked up and saw Gretchen pointing to her watch across the hall. He said, "You guys need to get going. Vampires waiting. Have fun hunting!" And he began sending the cargo boxes back to their proper places.

The team turned and saw Gretchen waiving them forward. As they reached her, she said, "Your gear is on the plane. It's time to get 'wheels up.'"

The team followed their administrator through a couple short corridors and out into the bright Virginia sunlight. On the tarmac before them was a beautiful white jet. As the engines began to spool up, John emitted a sound that was very close to a squeal. "That's a Cessna Citation X. They are super rare, way expensive, and we get to fly in one?"

Noelle turned to the young computer wizard and said, "So? It's a plane. What's so special about this one?"

The pure fanboy adulation instantly made Noelle regret her question. John began speaking rapidly, "It is literally the fastest private jet in existence. It has a top speed of over point-nine Mach, or nine-tenths the speed of sound. We should be in Colorado in less than three hours with this thing cranking up..."

John continued excitedly pointing out technical details, but Noelle tuned him out. Instead, she walked a bit closer to Gretchen and asked her a question. "So, Gretchen. How does a government agency afford all these nifty toys and privileges? I can't imagine Congress approving this budget extravagance."

Gretchen smiled at Noelle as they approached the stairs into the plane. She replied, "Because of our classification, we cannot really be expected to publish a budget now, can we? As part of Homeland Security, we have certain discretionary funds available, and you are all correctly identified as Special Agents of Homeland Security. But we also hold the patent on several items through dummy corporations and holding companies. Add those lucrative royalties to the appropriations, and we can fund you enough to do your job.

"Very few agents ever retire from active service. You guys will live a rough life, so the Director believes that you should be taken care of while you are here. He looks out for everyone in Section 28, but he pampers the Incursion teams, and those of us who look out for you."

One by one, the team members climbed the stairs and boarded the jet. Each one gazed in amazement at the plush leather seating and chrome and glass furnishings inside the plane. Each found a leather recliner and sank into its comfort. As Gretchen climbed aboard last, she leaned into the cockpit and said, "All right Captain. We're all aboard, and the gear is stowed. Take off, please."

As Gretchen sat in her seat and fastened her seatbelt, the noise from the engines shifted from a high-pitched whine to a roar, and the plane began to move. As it taxied to the end of the runway, the sleek jet paused momentarily as the captain received clearance from air traffic control. Given the priority code, the air controller cleared the traffic around the field and gave permission to the captain to take off. Both the captain and the copilot placed their hands on the throttle controls, and the captain pushed the throttle forward to its limit. Holding the brakes for a short second as the engines built thrust, the pilot released the brakes, and the jet leapt forward, clawing for the sky.

The jet lifted off the runway. The pilot pulled the stick back toward him, and the plane climbed rapidly in a steep ascent. The copilot picked up his microphone and announced to their passengers that they would land in Pueblo, Colorado, in just under two-and-a-half hours.

Agent Smith watched the jet until it disappeared from his sight. The senior agent turned from the bay windows in the mess hall and walked back to his office. Before he got there, his aide approached him and handed him a folder. Looking at the name on the folder, Smith looked at his assistant. "Has this been verified, Timothy? Do they really have him locked up?"

"Yes, sir. Norfolk Police Department has him in jail awaiting trial. I don't know how we missed it, but he's been there for two months. I've had Logistics get a vehicle, and it's waiting outside. I've also arranged to have him transferred to a holding cell at the sheriff's office so you can talk to him."

Smith smiled at Timothy. "Do you have anything stopping you from being my driver today?" Timothy shook his head, and Smith continued, "Then let's go catch a ghost."

11

GHOST

J onas Vanhof sat in the holding cell at the Norfolk Sheriff's Office. He had been in custody for over two months and expected to spend the rest of his relatively short life in prison, at least until the Commonwealth of Virginia could execute him. It was all his fault that he had been caught. He had forgotten the first rule: don't be a hero. He should have left at the first screams, but he didn't. He had to play the hero.

The police officers and sheriff deputies had found him with a body, freshly murdered. Jonas had been cleaning up his gear and getting ready to leave when the officers kicked in the door to the couple's house. As Jonas had run for the backyard, the sound of crashing glass announced more officers were waiting for him there. Trapped like a rat, he had fought back, using his considerable hand-to-hand combat skills. While no officers had been permanently disabled, several had to go to the hospital. It had taken three tasers to finally drop Jonas to the ground.

Having been quickly denied bail, Jonas had waited to be assigned a public defender. His public defender had been frustrated when Jonas would not give her any answers about why he was there or give her any defense that she could use. She could not even get Jonas to plead temporary insanity as a defense. They were now just waiting for the trial.

After two months in a jail cell, Jonas was dragged out, put in shackles and leg irons, and transported to the sheriff's office. There he was placed in a holding cell and told to wait. None of his guards would give him any explanation, and Jonas just accepted it as his life. Sitting with his head down on his knees, Jonas heard the guard approach his cell, and then he heard the electronic lock disengage.

At twenty-seven years old, this was not his first time in a cell. While awaiting trial, many of his fellow prisoners had thought his six-foot-four-inch lanky frame meant he was weak and vulnerable. He didn't have mass, or obvious muscle tone; Jonas looked scrawny, as any easy target should. He only had to give a severe beating to two other prisoners for the rest to leave him alone. His long blond hair was usually up in a loose ponytail, and his blue eyes told those who looked that he was far older than his years.

"Hey, inmate. Wake up, or I'll wake you up." Jonas felt the tip of a baton touch the back of his head. He looked up into the guard's face. The guard continued, "Get up, scumbag. Someone wants to talk to you."

As they walked out of the jail cell, the guard leaned in close and whispered, "I know the guys you hurt. They're good guys." When they approached the edge of the cell, the guard shoved Jonas face first into the edge of the doorframe. "Oops, you should be more careful there, pal."

Jonas felt a small trickle of blood run down his forehead and blinked to keep it out of his eyes. The guard at the gate blatantly ignored the cut on Jonas' forehead and let them through. His guard led him to a room with only one door, no windows, and cameras in two of the corners. The table in the center of the room was bolted down and had a steel ring in the middle of it and a large red button on one side. The guard took him into the room and unshackled his hands long enough to run the chain through the loop in the table.

The guard said, "Sit down. Your visitor will be with you in a moment."

Jonas did not have to wait long. A medium-sized gentleman in an impeccably tailored gray pinstripe suit walked through the door, closing it behind him. Jonas could see that the man was carrying a file folder with the Homeland Security Seal on the jacket. As the gentleman walked in, he withdrew a small cylindrical object from his inner pocket and walked toward the camera closest to him. He pressed a button built into the base of the object and waived the cylinder within a couple feet of the camera. He then walked over to the other camera in the room and waived it near that one as well.

Replacing the object in his suit pocket, he walked around to sit down across from Jonas. The man smiled, and Jonas could think of nothing other than a shark circling its prey.

"Now we can actually talk," said the man in the suit. He opened the file in front of him and began skimming through the contents. As he worked his way through, he began speaking calmly, in a tone that suggested he was reading out of a dry history report. "Jonas Vanhof. Twenty-seven years old. You were caught in the house of a middle-aged bank manager, having recently killed the banker and his wife.

"The evidence gathered by the police shows that you were in the process of cleaning up after yourself. They found customized knives covered in the couple's blood. The wife was found upstairs in the bedroom, naked. There were vicious bite marks on her arms, and her head was found three feet away from her body. The man was found on the first floor, in the living room, naked. While there were no bite marks on this one, the man's head was found behind a chair across the room, approximately eight feet away. And there were signs that you had struggled with both of them pretty violently."

"Forensics also determined that it was you who kicked in the front door. Your boots matched the prints around the house, as well as the large impression left on the door itself. All in all, the evidence left around the house and all over the scene point to you as some sort of sick, sadistic killer." The man looked up at Jonas over the rims of his glasses. "Are you, Jonas Vanhof, a 'sick sadistic serial killer?'"

Jonas thought the man sounded like he was asking something as casual as what flavor of ice cream he wanted. Jonas leaned back and shook his head.

Jonas began counting off facts awkwardly on the fingers of his manacled hands. "Your suit is way too nice for the detectives around here. You disabled the cameras. And you didn't threaten to beat me up. Are you a Fed? A spook?"

The man smiled and responded with a question of his own. "What actually happened in that house, Mr. Vanhof?"

Jonas considered the options. Believing the man may be from the secret government agency his uncle had told him about, he decided to lay it all out. Jonas sat up and said, "You want to know what happened? I'll tell you, but you won't believe me." He recounted the tale.

. . .

* * * * *

NORFOLK, **Virginia. Two months ago.**

It was a dark night. Jonas specifically chose tonight because it was a new moon. The moon was nowhere in the night sky. The night was darker, the shadows were deeper, and things that relied on the moon for part of their power would have just a little less.

Jonas parked his car three blocks away from his target's house and walked casually until he was about three houses away. Because of his earlier recon, Jonas knew that the next couple houses would be quiet and the inhabitants asleep long before his two-o'clock-in-the-morning activity. *Got to love the suburbs,* Jonas thought to himself. *At least everyone goes to bed at a decent hour.*

As Jonas approached the front porch, he looked around one last time to make sure that he was not being watched. Carefully moving as silently as possible, he was worried that the monster he was hunting would hear him coming. Intimately aware of the heightened hearing and sense of smell, Jonas was careful to walk only on the soft grass. To avoid alerting the monster with his scent, he was in freshly laundered and bleached clothing that had been rolled on the yard outside the target's house.

Tonight's target was a rather surly bank manager. This manager had a reputation for being short with customers and outright hostile with his employees. Treating everyone else as if they were simply not worthy of his time, he had callously rejected a customer's loan application and made inappropriate derogatory comments comparing the customer's manhood to his creditworthiness. The desperate customer had lost control, attacking the manager viciously. Before the security guards could pull the irate customer off him, the manager had suffered severe bruising, a broken collarbone, and even some bites on his arms.

That was a month ago. The recovering bank manager had never realized anything was wrong until that first full moon. Fortunately for his wife, the manager had been out of the house the first time he changed. When the new werewolf had changed that first time, his instincts had pulled him to the forest to run and hunt. The following morning, a local farmer had found three of his cattle slaughtered and half-eaten in the field. The manager had woken up, naked, alone, and cover in dried, congealed blood.

Putting two and two together to get an impossible four, the manager had figured out that, against all the odds, he was a werewolf, a mythological creature. He had hidden his new affliction from his family, but he could not hide the reports from the eyes of Jonas. When his sources had traced the wolf to the bank manager, Jonas had traveled to Virginia to kill the wolf before he could kill a human.

Jonas stepped up on the porch, carefully avoiding the loose step his earlier reconnaissance had discovered. Approaching the door, he withdrew a lock-pick set from his inner coat pocket. He reached for the knob to unlock the door and heard a loud, terrified scream from inside the residence.

Jonas had two options: leave now, before the neighborhood woke up, or go help whoever was shrieking. Even as lights in the surrounding houses lit up, the monster hunter drew back his leg and kicked hard at the door, landing a solid blow right beside the lock and breaking the frame. The door swung open, and Jonas moved inside. Hearing the shrieks turn to moans, he raced up the stairs, his long overcoat trailing behind him.

Rounding the corner on the landing, he was met by a large furry mass that crashed into him. The collision was enough to shake them both, and they tumbled over the side of the railing onto the floor below. Vicious snarls and growls sounded from the large wolf-like creature as it tried desperately to sink its teeth into Jonas' face. Jonas could see the gleaming fangs and smell the fetid breath of the creature as its jaws snapped closed mere inches from his nose.

As the creature drew back again to bite, Jonas brought his forearm up into the path of those powerful jaws. The teeth clenched shut on his limb, and he cried out as his arm was crushed. The specially prepared abilities of his overcoat worked with the thick leather of the sleeves to stop the razor-sharp canine teeth from penetrating. In a small corner in the back of his mind, Jonas realized he'd be lucky if his arm was not broken from the bite.

While the creature gnawed on the monster hunter's forearm, Jonas slipped his free hand down and grabbed the hilt of a knife sheathed on his side. With the creature on top, the hunter was just able to draw the knife and thrust upward toward the heart of the wolf. The honed blade sunk in to the hilt, parting the skin and slipping between ribs in its quest for the heart. The creature howled in sudden, overwhelming pain as it was forced to release his forearm and to try to scramble away from Jonas.

Wrapping his legs around the creature, the wiry hunter heaved and flipped over, putting the wolf on its back on the ground. Jonas continued to drive the knife inwards, working the blade back and forth to wreak havoc on the creature. His other arm was now free of the wolf's mouth, and, with that one, he reached behind his back to withdraw the large machete from its sheath.

Raising the machete in a high swing, he abruptly brought it down on the neck of the creature. On the first swing, he made it most of the way through the neck, but stopped against the spine itself. The wolf suddenly went rigid and began reaching for its throat. With paws that were changing into human hands as he watched, the wolf creature tried to stem the flow of its lifeblood from its severed arteries.

The second swing of the machete cleaved through the spinal column and severed the head from the body. As it rolled away, the shape changed and the facial features became human. Jonas reached down and pulled his knife from the now-human torso it was buried in. Standing, he glanced up the stairs and heard small movements.

Covered in the creature's blood, Jonas climbed the stairs. Walking into the bedroom, he saw the wife of the banker in bed. She was nude and lying on the bed with her hands covering her face. The massive bite marks on her shoulder were no longer bleeding, and she appeared to have fainted.

Knowing that it was too late for her, the weary hunter grimly walked to the side of the bed and raised the machete. When he moved her arms away from her face and neck, the woman stirred. Incoherent, she saw a man with a large machete in his hand standing over her bed where her husband had just attacked her. She began sobbing and repeating the words, "No, please, no," as she begged for her life.

Jonas looked down at her and raised the machete to deliver a blow. "I'm sorry," he whispered as he brought the machete down.

* * * * *

"THE POLICE SHOWED up as I was cleaning up trace from the house. When they busted in, I tried to go out the back. There were four of them out there, and I guess I put a couple of them in the hospital. Sometimes I forget to pull my punches with mere humans. And for the past two months, I've been dealing with a public defender that is clueless and wants me to take a plea bargain, a jail crew that wants to make me suffer for beating up those cops, and fellow inmates that finally have learned not to pick on me, or else they suffer a beating." Jonas finished his story and looked at the man in front of him.

The man consulted the file he held and looked at Jonas over his glasses. "As strange as it may seem, Mr. Vanhof, I believe your story. That is why I'm here.

"You are originally from the Pacific Northwest, and you believe that you are the last in your family's bloodline. You were trained to hunt monsters since you were little. And you've been on your own since your uncle was killed. You are good at what you do. Unfortunately, you got caught this time."

Jonas smiled wearily. "So which secret government organization are you from? CIA? NSA? Ghostbusters?"

The man chuckled. "Mr. Vanhof, my name is Agent Smith, and I work for the Department of Homeland Security. I have a team that could use your particular... expertise. This is a onetime offer. If you come to work for me, this little problem goes away."

"As you know, Virginia is a death penalty state, and I hear that the prosecutor is going to try to make you dance that chemical dance. Your prosecutor has political aspirations, and he's been waiting for a juicy case like yours to come along. If you choose to work for me, the prosecutor will have to find another case to hang his political hat on. So what do you say? Do you want to take my 'Get out of jail free' card?"

Jonas started laughing at the absurdity of Smith's offer. Tears flowed down his face as the stress and fear of the last couple months fed the near-hysteria. After he had composed himself, he was wiping away the tears when he spoke again. "So let me get this straight. I can either come with you, and get paid to do what I was doing before, or I can rot and wait to die. I think that's a pretty easy choice to make for me. Where do I sign?"

"We'll get you signed up as soon as we get out of here," Agent Smith said as he smiled and shook the proffered hand. As Agent Smith stood and walked to the door he said, "The paperwork is waiting for my signature. You will be out in less than an hour." Agent Smith knocked on the door to let the guard know that he was done. "By the way, it's good to have a member of your family on one of my teams again."

12

HEAVY

Norfolk, Virginia.

It was closer to two hours later when Jonas and Agent Smith walked out the front of the Norfolk Correctional Facility. It had taken less than an hour to get Jonas released into Agent Smith's custody. The sheriff had complained to the prosecutor, and the prosecutor had called a local judge to get the transfer halted. Before the ink was dry on the injunction, he had received a call from the Virginia Attorney General and from the Governor's office, letting the judge know that enforcing the injunction would start an avalanche of trouble. The judge nullified his own injunction.

With that roadblock out of the way, the prosecutor could not stop the prisoner custody transfer. But when Agent Smith had demanded the personal effects, including the murder weapons, the sheriff had thrown every obstacle he had into the fray. From administrative "delays" to "missing documents," it had taken Agent Smith over an hour to retrieve the personal effects from the sheriff's office. In the end, it had required a threat from Agent Smith to bring in a team from both the Attorney General's office and the Department of Homeland Security to perform a complete audit and civil rights check on the sheriff's department, all the members of the department, and the correctional facility.

When Jonas finally received his clothing and gear, he stepped into a restroom to change. As he emerged fully clothed and equipped, Agent Smith was forced to calm the sheriff again just to avoid a near riot from the law enforcement present. As they stepped outside, the local press moved en masse toward them, shouting a cacophony of questions. Both Agent Smith and Jonas stayed silent as they moved through the crowd. The reporters quickly lost interest on the pair as the sheriff and prosecutor stepped out of the doors and announced a press conference.

Agent Smith and Jonas climbed into the back of the blacked-out Chevy Suburban. Timothy turned around and smiled at the two men, extending his hand to Jonas. "It's good to meet you, Mr. Vanhof. My name is Timothy." He turned toward his boss and said, "Sir, we have a developing situation in D.C. I forwarded a summary to your phone, but it is something we should move on quickly. I do believe you'll be interested."

Agent Smith nodded at Timothy and said, "I'll trust your judgement. I'll read up as we head that direction. Mr. Vanhof, I fear we may be a little delayed before we get you started in your new life."

Timothy nodded and turned around. He put the truck in drive and pulled out. Reaching down, he flipped a series of switches on the dashboard. At the front and back of the truck, red and blue emergency lights strobed. Under the hood, a very special box sent out a signal ahead of the vehicle. As the modified truck neared an intersection, the box changed the lights at the intersection to green as they were about to cross through it, clearing the path for the vehicle. As traffic began to clear out of their way, Timothy sped up. As they reached the top of the entrance ramp on I-64, the roar of the big V-8 filled the air as Timothy reached a cruising speed well above the posted limits.

* * * * *

IN A NEIGHBORHOOD just outside Georgetown University stood a historic brownstone. Outside that brownstone a line of police cars and a SWAT van blocked the street. Both ends of the block were cordoned off with police barricades and officers, and media crews waited impatiently just outside the barricades.

The blacked out SUV rolled to a stop, the vehicle's lights still flashing, and Agent Smith and Jonas both got out of the truck, leaving Timothy to wait. The pair walked up to the nearest officer, and Agent Smith drew out his credentials.

"Excuse me, officer. Department of Homeland Security. Who is the officer in charge right now?"

The officer glanced at the badge and then at Agent Smith. "What do you guys want with this one? Just some nut job that whacked his parents." When he received no answer, the officer nodded, "Lieutenant Porter is in charge; he's over there by the SWAT van."

Agent Smith thanked him and strode purposefully toward the SWAT van. On the trip from Norfolk, Agent Smith had called up the initial reports and found something very interesting. A direct Incursion alarm had tripped the sensors in D.C., indicating that at least one creature had stepped directly through into the heart of the city. Signature types had indicated that it was some form of a vampire. The alert had been quickly corroborated with a 911 call from the location in question. The massive array of sensors in the area noted shortly after the arrival that the creature or creatures had been terminated. That level of prowess had interested Agent Smith immensely.

Arriving at the SWAT van, Agent Smith again flashed his credentials. "Agents Smith and Vanhof, Department of Homeland Security. What happened, Lieutenant?"

The lieutenant looked long and hard at Smith. "This has nothing to do with Homeland Security. This was a Vet who went nuts and killed his parents. Caught him with those freaky looking knives in his hands, just sitting and sobbing on the couch. I had to call SWAT in to talk him down."

"This guy is a Vet, Spec Ops. According to his jacket, he's a staff sergeant in the Eighty-Second Airborne. It sounds like he was home visiting his family, and he just kinda went nuts. He'll probably claim some sort of PTSD. Sick son-of-a-bitch killed his parents, his little sister, and apparently a couple other guys whose heads we found. He then starts spewing some BS cockamamie crap about monsters and bodies disappearing. I think he got a hold of some bad drugs and just lost it. I went ahead and notified the Army, but like I said, this isn't Homeland Security's business here."

Agent Smith listened intently, thought for a moment, and calmly and politely said, "I'll be the judge of that. Where is the suspect now?"

The lieutenant shook his head. "You Feds are all the same. The guy's still inside, but it's an active crime scene. You guys can talk to him at the precinct."

Agent Smith frowned, and his words turned quiet and cold. "No, lieutenant. As I explained, we'll speak to him here. We will maintain the integrity of your scene, but we will talk to him."

Agent Smith walked toward the house, and Jonas quickly followed. The lieutenant waived to the officer standing in front of the door, "It's OK, Sam. Let them through." The lieutenant muttered under his breath, questioning the human parentage of the agents as they walked out of earshot.

Agent Smith and Jonas walked into the house. Noting the narrow rooms and corridors common to brownstone houses, they walked to the living room, breaking up a cluster of officers and medics, all hovering around an African American man that was handcuffed and sitting on the couch. Even sitting down, the man's bulk was imposing, and the handcuffs seemed tiny and fragile around his wrists.

Flashing his badge again, Smith announced, "I'm Agent Smith, and this is Agent Vanhof. Department of Homeland Security. I need to speak with this suspect. Alone. Please clear the area."

Despite a buzz of murmuring in the room, the officers and medics slowly filed out of the room, with one of the SWAT members remaining behind to stand in the open doorway of the house. As they were leaving, Jonas noticed that one officer had an evidence bag containing two large curved knives. Reaching out, he said, "Excuse me, officer. Can I have those for a moment? Don't worry. Chain of Custody is still intact."

The officer handed Jonas the weapons, and Agent Smith nodded approvingly. Agent Smith turned back to the man on the couch and spoke while he consulted information on his phone.

"As you heard, I'm Agent Smith, and this is Agent Vanhof. Could you tell me what happened?"

"I think I'd like my lawyer now," the large man's voice rumbled.

As Smith was talking to the suspect, Jonas looked around the room. Noticing evidence markers laid out, he knelt by a severed head that was laying on its side. Jonas reached down and slowly lifted the lips apart, baring the teeth. Not surprised, he revealed a set of large, pointed teeth that would look more at home on an animal than on a human. Looking around, he saw a small pool of fluid that looked like it was disappearing as he watched. The thick black ichor seemed to be melting and drifting away like smoke. Nodding, he stood up and walked over to Smith. He leaned in close and whispered a few words in Smith's ear. Smith nodded and Jonas sat down and began to examine the knives.

Smith turned back to the suspect on the couch. "Are you Staff

Sergeant Arthur Murphy? Currently assigned to the Eighty-Second Airborne Division?" When the big man nodded, Smith continued. "Despite your troubled past, you excelled in the Army. You are a natural leader, and your CO thinks very highly of you."

"The police seem to think that you went stark-raving mad and that you will take the weasel way out and claim it was some sort of PTSD. They say you came home hopped up on drugs–probably crack. You then butchered your family and those two headless guys. Are they right? Are you just another lunatic Vet with PTSD?"

The man stared at Agent Smith intensely. The anger in the man's voice was palpable, and he appeared to barely keep it under control. Through gritted teeth, the man spat the words out, "No, sir. I am not suffering PTSD. Nor did I kill my family. In fact, I found these two guys attacking my family. I was so mad I guess I killed them. But I never killed my family."

Smith looked at the man as he tried desperately to hold himself together. He knelt down in front of the suspect and gently, quietly said, "I believe you. In fact, I have a different theory. I believe that the two headless men savagely attacked your family. You fought with them, one at a time. It looks like you sent one of them through the wall over there and somehow found those special knives. Once you had those knives in your hand, I would say that you got the first one and then the second one. In the end, I bet you had to decapitate them to stop them. In fact, I would bet that when you decapitated them, the bodies just sort of... dissolved into the goo that is over there. Since then, it's been slowly evaporating. Am I right?"

The man looked at Smith incredulously. "That's almost exactly how it happened. I don't know why I decapitated them... I just did. How did you know?"

Smith was about to answer when the other agent spoke up.

"Agent Smith, I think you should see this." Jonas held up the knives he had removed from the evidence bag.

Smith walked over and looked at each blade carefully. Jonas pointed out faded script that looked like it was a combination of Chinese and another, much more ancient script. He then handed them back to Jonas. "Great eyes," Smith said. "I'm not sure I would have seen that myself."

Smith walked back over to Arthur. "Sergeant Murphy, where did you get the knives?"

Arthur looked up, questions fluttering across his face. "They were given to me personally by a Nepalese tribal leader that we worked with. I filed all the correct import paperwork with the Army. In fact, I have the declarations around here somewhere."

"I believe you," Smith said. "You have no idea how lucky you were to have those blades today. I would bet that these khukuris are probably what helped you kill your parents' killers. Actually, if it was a tribal leader, chances are he knew that you would need to have the pair of blades available."

Smith stood and continued talking. "Staff Sergeant Murphy, I'm going to make this offer only once..."

* * * * *

LIEUTENANT PORTER WAS JUST WALKING up to the house to kick out the Feds when they began to leave. Between the two Feds walked the suspect who was not in handcuffs. Porter slammed to a halt and yelled at the men to stop where they were. Drawing his sidearm, Porter yelled for the tactical team. Jonas felt Staff Sergeant Murphy tense up.

Porter barked at Agent Smith, "Stop right there. That man is in the custody of the Metropolitan Police Department. You have no authority to release him or to remove him."

By now, the tactical team and several officers had come running to the lieutenant's aid. Smith, Jonas, and Arthur were quickly surrounded by officers with their sidearms drawn. While none were directly pointed at the Homeland Security Agents, the implied threat of the drawn weapons made the tension palpable.

Agent Smith held up a hand and calmly addressed Lieutenant Porter. "This man is now under the supervision and jurisdiction of the Department of Homeland Security. If you have any doubts about my authority in this matter, you can call Homeland Security with my badge number. Let's all calm down. Make the call, Lieutenant."

Porter reached out and took the agent's credentials. He grabbed his cellphone and called his Captain. Quickly and succinctly summarizing the situation, he asked his superior to contact his Homeland Security liaison. After what seemed like an eternity later for the lieutenant, he received a call on his cell from the Captain.

"Lieutenant Porter. This is Captain Meyers. Homeland Security has control and jurisdiction of that scene. Follow their lead. Agent

Smith is the SAC on this one. If Smith tells you the suspect is leaving with him, escort him to his car."

"But, Captain," the lieutenant stammered. "How can they get away with this? This isn't federal. It's a nutcase Vet. This one should be ours. Have we heard from the Army yet?"

The captain cut him off. "Listen, Bill. I hate this as much as you do, but I have the Chief breathing down my neck on this one. The Director of Homeland Security answered the call on this one directly. Just suck it up and deal with it… they're Feds."

Lieutenant Porter hung up from his call and holstered his sidearm. "All right, guys, stand down," he announced to all who were present. "It's official. Homeland Security is the lead on this one; we're just cleanup."

Approaching Smith, Porter continued, "Sorry about that, Agent Smith. This is just so… irregular."

"I understand, Lieutenant Porter," said Agent Smith as he smiled graciously. "I'd be just as upset as you are right now. If you would have your people continue processing the scene, I would appreciate it. Have your forensic people work the house. Also, if you would have your M.E. perform the initial autopsy, my office will be in touch with your department for the findings. Have all reports forwarded to my office at this number." Smith handed Porter a business card.

"I'll be taking charge of Staff Sergeant Murphy here, as well as taking the weapons into my possession. Is there anything else you need from me?"

"No, sir," Porter said as he shook his head. "I'll have the reports forwarded as soon as they get filed."

With Arthur and Jonas trailing, Agent Smith walked toward the Suburban. Jonas climbed into the front passenger seat by Timothy while Smith and Arthur took seats in the back. Porter watched with a mixture of disgust and relief as the truck left the scene. He was glad to be rid of the Feds. He hated it when they interfered; it always caused him more headaches and paperwork.

Signaling for the forensics team to join him, Porter began assigning tasks as he heard the roar of the big V8 engine take the Feds away.

II

MISSION

13

PIECES

Gretchen Massey, the Knightmare Team Liaison, grabbed a silver briefcase from the storage compartment in the back of the Citation X and returned to her seat at the small conference table. Flying just under the speed of sound, the plane was much faster than a larger commercial airliner, and the trip to Pueblo, Colorado, was nearly half-way over.

After the flight attendant had seen to meals and the comfort of the passengers, the team had gathered around the active surface conference table for the mission briefing and planning. John "Spooky" Smith brought up the maps of the area on the electronic surface of the table and pointed out various land features and points of reference. He then posted all the medical examiner's reports and police files alongside the maps.

Spooky looked across to the team leader and said, "All right, boss. What's the plan?"

Burt "Six" Holstein studied the maps and information laid out in front of the team. After paging quickly through the maps, he seemed to find what he was looking for. Looking at Gretchen, Six asked, "Gretchen, what kind of transportation will we have? Will it be equipped as a command post?"

Gretchen consulted the notes on her secure phone and said,

"Yes, sir. I have an armored command transport waiting for our arrival. Full mobile communications and control."

The team leader nodded at the information and looked at the rest of the team. "Ok, team. Here's what I'm thinking. We will stay at this little motel on the outskirts of town. Gretchen, can you arrange that?"

Gretchen nodded and drew out her phone to make the call. Six continued, "We'll set up our staging and command center at a building owned by a non-governmental community organization. We have the exclusive use of the building as we've asked that they close operations from that building while we are in town. The building should have enough rooms and is located across from the only hospital in town. From what I understand, the forensic labs and the M.E.'s office are in that hospital. This will be our 'ops center.'

"When we arrive, we'll meet with the sheriff and the mayor at the ops center. While there, I want you, God, up on the rooftop with your rifle. You are on overwatch until I need you on an entry team."

Jesús "God" Rivera smiled and nodded. Turning to the team priest, he asked, "Doc, any clue what the best way to spot these guys is? Will they show up on night vision? Or thermal?"

Noelle "Doc" Sorenson thought for a moment and consulted the leather-bound book in front of her. "I don't believe night vision will work. Thermal should work, instead. Vampires run colder than normal, and often colder than the surrounding climate. According to our records, the only time that they radiate any measurable heat is just after they have fed. This goes away quickly, and they soon return to their normal temps—usually around forty-five or fifty degrees."

Six smiled at the information and turned to his electronics specialist. "Spooky, when we are set, launch the UAV and use the thermal to search for cold spots as well. Maybe we'll get lucky."

Turning to Doc and Boomer, Six said, "Doc, I want you to go chat with the coroner. See if he's on the level and see what he has to say. Boomer, I want you with her as backup."

Doc nodded, and Rebekah "Boomer" Callahan asked a question, "Do you want me armed with the twelve gauge? Or with only my sidearm?"

"Take your shotgun," Six responded. "Better safe than sorry. Your badge should clear up any authority issues. That goes for all of you. Everyone carries their primary rifle with them. I would rather get nasty looks than be defenseless against the monsters."

Gretchen indicated that she had something to say, and Six nodded in her direction, "Gretchen?"

Gretchen glanced at her phone and then back up at the team. Addressing the entire team, she said, "Ground transportation is waiting, as is your block of rooms at the motel. I also just received word from headquarters that the FBI has dispatched a Behavioral Analysis Unit team to Trinidad to assist the locals with the case. The BAU knows DHS is en route, and they will be informed that you have jurisdiction. They are going to be focused on profiling the criminals based on human psychoses. You are not hunting humans, and their profiles don't apply. They should touch down just before we do."

The team leader nodded grimly. "It seems it's going to be up to me to meet with the sheriff, mayor, and this FBI team. I'll try to keep them distracted while gathering information from the locals," Six stated.

Gretchen pulled out the aluminum equipment briefcase and set it on the table. The latches responded to her thumbprints, and the airtight case hissed slightly as the top opened. When the case laid flat, the team could see five brand new smartphones. Each smartphone had a case and holster packed in the foam below it, and mounted above each was a team member's call sign.

As she handed them out, Gretchen turned on each device to let it go through its power process. As the little white fruit appeared on the screen, a grayed-out Department of Homeland Security seal replaced it, and she handed the phone to its new owner. She talked as she handed them out.

"These are your new Secure Smart Phones, or SSPs as they are called around the office. Each one is synced to its own user, and each one can only be operated by its owner, or someone on this team. As they fire up, you will see a list of somewhat standard apps, as well as a few new icons. There are several contacts already programmed into the phone, such as myself, Timothy, and Agent Smith, and you have full access to voice, video, text, or email—all secured.

"There is a folder of apps on your phone you really should not mess with until you get back from this mission. The apps are esoteric in nature, and you could do great harm to your teammates unless you know what you are doing. Other than that, have fun exploring. Also, you do not have access to the application store, as the software on the phones is somewhat... non-standard. And, Spooky, don't open it up until you get back to the labs at Section 28. I know you want to, but just trust me. The anti-tampering protections are a bit more vicious than your standard protocols. I wouldn't want you to be eaten. Questions?"

Spooky raised his hand. "Any way I can get this to sync with my wrist computer?"

Gretchen gave a soft laugh. "Actually, Norbert already synced the two devices. He asked me to tell you he was quite impressed by your, how did he put it, 'fun little device.' He said he would have recommendations when you get back. Any other questions?"

The various team members shook their heads, and Gretchen continued, "Ok. We should be about an hour out. Take the time to rest and relax. You won't have much time when you are on the ground." She turned her chair around and stood up, walking to the cockpit to talk to the pilots.

* * * * *

JUST UNDER AN HOUR LATER, Gretchen returned to the passenger compartment and said they would land soon. The team quickly stowed their loose equipment and buckled their safety belts.

In the cockpit, the pilot contacted the tower controller for Pueblo Memorial Airport. "Pueblo Memorial. This is DHS Special Zero Three. Requesting direct clearance."

The traffic controller looked at his displays and saw the special Homeland Security notes attached to the flight plan. Noting the flight time, he wondered what kind of plane they were on. It looked like a small business jet, but it had traveled just under the speed of sound. "DHS Special, Pueblo Tower. Direct clearance to runway Two-Six Left. Winds are west-northwest at five knots. Nearest traffic at ten miles, fifteen thousand feet and climbing."

"Pueblo Tower, DHS Special. Roger Two-Six Left."

The pilot concentrated on landing the plane gently on the assigned runway. Despite the slight crosswinds, the touchdown was textbook perfect. As the plane rolled out towards the end of the runway, ground control contacted the DHS pilot and guided him to his designated parking spot. He also informed ground control he needed fuel "ASAP" and clearance for a rapid departure.

As the plane came to a halt, the team members stood and stretched. Grabbing their gear, they approached the door, and waited for the attendant to drop the stairs.

Six stepped into the bright sunshine and immediately put his sunglasses on. The clear air and beautiful sunshine allowed him to see the mountains rising to the west, past the city of Pueblo. Stepping down onto the tarmac, he was met by a woman in sunglasses and a suit that announced "Fed." She stretched out her hand toward him.

"Agent Holstein? I'm Sonja Hart, the DHS SAC for this region. I've got your ground transportation waiting for you, as requested. Will you need any backup or assistance for your deployment?"

He shook Agent Hart's proffered hand and introduced himself. "Please, call me Burt. Except for transportation, I believe we have everything we need for the deployment. If I need anything, I'll let you know." He released her hand.

Agent Hart evaluated the rest of the unusual team as they filed off the plane. Her eyes widened as Doc stepped off the plane in her gray business suit, with a weird sidearm in a holster on her hip. She looked back at Six and asked, "What's the deployment about? I wasn't given any information other than to bring you the truck. What's going on out here?"

The team leader shook his head. "I'm sorry Agent Hart. You're not cleared for that information. We'll take it from here. Are the keys in the truck?"

Agent Hart nodded, and her voice grew cold. "The keys are in there. I don't like being in the dark about what's going on in my region. It usually means I have to clean up someone else's mess. Do not make me clean up your mess, Agent Holstein." With that statement, she spun on her heal and stormed off toward the waiting vehicles.

Six looked at the truck waiting for his team. *Subtlety is not on the menu,* he thought to himself. The truck was a jet-black Golan Mine Resistant Ambush Protected truck, called an MRAP, manufactured by an Israeli firm. Six was familiar with the truck, with the angled front end, and the steel cage surrounding the bullet resistant glass, having driven one while in Iraq. Unlike the MRAPs from Iraq, this one had emergency lights mounted on top and in the grill and was marked with "Police" and "Rescue" on the front and rear bumpers. The only other markings were the Homeland Security seals plastered across the sides. Sitting over two feet off the road, the truck stood over seven-and-a-half feet tall. Almost eight feet wide, the truck was an enormous nineteen feet long. There was not one detail about this truck that was subtle or understated. He loved it!

He turned to his team and barked, "All right team, let's get our gear. Our transportation awaits."

As the team lugged their bags toward the truck, a fuel service truck pulled up to the waiting Citation jet. Gretchen arranged for the fueling and then climbed back aboard. As the fuel truck departed, the attendant closed that hatch, and the pilot restarted the engines for the flight back to Langley.

Inside the truck, Boomer climbed up in the driver's seat. Six looked at her and raised his eyebrows.

"Trust me, boss. I'm the one you want driving this heap," she said in her most innocent voice as possible. The former racer car driver continued, "For the rest of you, I really recommend that you strap yourselves in. We'll be in Trinidad soon."

* * * * *

AFTER A BRIEF STOP at a storage facility outside Norfolk to retrieve the majority of Jonas' gear, Timothy had driven the agents back to Section 28. Once they had arrived, Agent Smith had left them in the care of Timothy, with a planned regrouping in three hours. Smith had a busy couple hours ahead of him. He had needed to prepare the contracts and credentials, remove Staff Sergeant Murphy from the Army, and clean up a few police reports. He would be busy.

Timothy had escorted Jonas and Arthur to the Knightmare apartment block and had taken the time to give them a brief tour of the facility on the way. As they had walked, Timothy had answered all the questions he could, and had explained more about the mission and drive of the team. Leaving out the "Incursion" background, Timothy had studiously given non-answers about that, and other classified information.

After a meal and a brief rest, Timothy finally arrived to escort Jonas and Arthur to the conference room. There Agent Smith greeted them and told them to sit down.

The DHS agent started, "Gentlemen, I'm glad that both of you chose to join our team. As Timothy informed you earlier, it is your job to kill monsters—something each of you has done before. You will be joining as a member of a larger team that is currently deployed. In fact, you will leave tonight to join them on their current deployment. But before we can do that, you need to sign some paperwork."

Jonas watched as Agent Smith put on a pair of white cotton gloves. He then reached over to a closed lockbox at his right side and opened the lid. Smith reached into the lockbox and withdrew two heavy envelopes, one at a time. Made of white leather, each envelope had a wax seal over the flap and a name embossed above the seal.

Jonas looked at the envelope in front of him and saw a weird script written on and around the edges. Although he could not read what the script said, he recognized the symbols of the ancient Enochian tongue. Agent Smith continued, "Before you open the pouches in front of you, I want you to be very clear about a couple things that will happen when you do so. You might experience a wave of energy or a slight tingling sensation on your fingertips and in your hair. Some have also reported other strange sensory phenomena. I assure you: that is normal."

"This is your last and final chance to step down from this team. If you choose to decline, you will go back to where you were when I recruited you. Granted, that would be police custody for both of you, but you certainly wouldn't be in nearly as much danger as I'm going to throw at you. Do either of you want to exercise that option now?" Smith paused to see if either would take the deal.

When it was clear that neither man wanted to leave, Smith continued, "If you would now open your envelopes, taking care not to touch any of the materials from your other teammate. Inside, you will find a contract and a pen. Please pull out both of the items and begin reading the contract. This contract shows that you are freely offering to join the team and will be bound by the terms of this contract. This contract is also your formal work contract for the Department of Homeland Security, assigned to Section 28. A large part of this contract explains that this agreement will bar you from mentioning Section 28, what you do, or what you are hunting, except under certain, very explicit circumstances. Even the existence of Section 28 is classified as Top Secret - Black and is on a need-to-know basis."

"On the back page, there is a spot to sign your name and then put the date. When you pick up the pen and begin to write, you may feel a slight pinch in one of your fingers. This is by design. At that time, your blood will be taken, and mixed with the ink when you sign the contract. Each of your contract agreements is exactly the same. At this time, please read through the agreement carefully and sign where indicated."

It took over an hour for both men to carefully read through the lengthy documents. Once Jonas and Arthur signed the contracts, Smith directed them to carefully place them into the envelopes, and then he collected and stored the files. Reaching for the two credential holders on his left, he smiled and said, "Welcome to the Department of Homeland Security, Section 28. Here are your credentials."

He handed the first folio to Jonas. "Special Agent Jonas Vanhof. Your new call sign is 'Ghost' while on missions. Your role on the team is two-fold. First, you are the second in command of the team. You will support your team leader, Burt Holstein, in that role, assisting with planning, as well as media relations and liaison with local law enforcement. Your secondary role will draw on your unique background. You are tasked with esoteric R&D in the field. You have the resources to know what it takes to kill most of the nasties you come across, and you have the experience to rig up any supplies or materials to be effective."

He handed the second folio to Arthur. "Special Agent Arthur Murphy. You are the heavy weapons specialist for the team. Primarily fire support, you will augment the standard firepower with something bigger. Your mission call sign is 'Heavy.'"

Agent Smith then said to both team members, "I would love to give you much more time to learn and work, but I need to fly you out tonight. So, I will have Timothy take you to the Section 28 Warehouse. Draw whatever gear you need. Gretchen, your Team Liaison, should be back in about an hour. I want you ready for your trip in two hours. You can sleep on the flight."

As the new agents left the conference room, Agent Smith compiled all the records and prepared the pertinent information to be sent to their new team leader, Six. He had now officially closed the recruiting for Team Knightmare.

Jonas and Arthur followed Timothy to the Warehouse. Jonas spent most of his time while in the Warehouse, talking with Norbert. Afterwards, he drew ammo for his revolver from the armorer and a Kevlar vest from the Equipment section. Arthur, however, spent a great deal of time talking with Russell. Reminiscing about their time in the service, Arthur eventually drew a sidearm and his favorite weapon of all time: the M249 Squad Automatic Weapon. The SAW was a belt-fed machine gun that used the same rifle cartridges as the M4 carbines that the rest of the team carried, and could even use M4 magazines in a pinch. Holding one in his hands again, Arthur couldn't wait to get to his new team. He then walked over to the Equipment section to draw a heavy flak vest and the rest of his kit.

As Jonas and Arthur were stowing their gear into their bags, Gretchen walked into the Warehouse and introduced herself. Looking a little frayed around the edges from the last seven hours of traveling, she held a travel mug of coffee in her left hand. As they talked, she led the two new agents toward the airfield where the Citation was again being fueled and prepped. The flight attendant greeted that agents on the ground and let them know they were still waiting for the replacement flight crew.

Within a few minutes, the fresh flight crew emerged from the complex and walked toward the plane. After a quick, but thorough, pre-flight inspection, they told the attendant and the team they could board the plane. Within moments, the plane was making its second flight that day to Pueblo, Colorado.

14

TRINIDAD

Trinidad, Colorado.

As the blacked-out MRAP screeched to a halt in the parking lot of a building owned by a community organization, the passengers inside all had different reactions. The monster Cummins turbo-diesel rumbled and died away. Boomer turned around from the driver's seat and smiled. "Everyone still alive?" she asked.

A general chorus of moans and groans greeted her query. Six managed to find his voice and asked, "Where on earth did you learn to drive like that? I thought we were going to die... several times!"

The driver smiled and blushed at the same time. "I used to race cars and boats growing up. That's why I'm the driver. Besides, we made it in record time."

God groaned from the back, "Yes, but that was normally a ninety-minute drive. I know. I grew up around here. I'm not sure I could have made it in an hour in my car, let alone an armored truck. I don't even want to know how fast you were going."

Boomer laughed. "That's good because I couldn't tell you. I buried the speedometer when we left Pueblo. The important thing is that we made it." As she finished, a sheriff's car came roaring up, lights and siren blazing. The siren abruptly shut off, and a man in a sport coat and Stetson hat stepped out of the passenger side.

The explosives expert looked sheepish and said, "Heads up, boss. Looks like the locals know we're here."

The team leader sighed and shakily climbed down out of the rear hatch. Pausing to catch his breath and calm his nerves, he straightened and walked toward the lawman. Drawing his badge from his pocket, Six held it up so the sheriff could see it. "Special Agent Burt Holstein, Department of Homeland Security. Are you Sheriff Klooster?"

The sheriff nodded and looked the Fed up and down. He reached out his own hand. "Yes, Agent Holstein. Sheriff John Klooster. I didn't expect you guys for another hour. They told me your plane only landed an hour ago."

The man laughed weakly. "If you get any reports of low-flying aircraft shaped like a truck, or possibly UFOs, you might want to talk to our driver." Boomer smiled and waved as she climbed out of the truck.

Sheriff Klooster shook his head. "Well, that's a first for Feds, actually admitting to something. So, what brings Homeland Security to our humble little town?"

Six looked at the sheriff and said, "Can we find someplace to talk privately? And you may want to get the mayor involved."

Thirty minutes later, the mayor, the sheriff and undersheriff, and the Trinidad police chief and assistant chief were assembled in a conference room in the team's ops building. While the rest of the team was checking the gear and preparing to hunt the creatures, their team leader was holding the initial briefing.

As the assistant police chief walked in, Six began his prepared speech. "Good afternoon, ladies and gentlemen. For those of you I have not met, I am Special Agent Burt Holstein from the Department of Homeland Security. I would introduce the rest of my team, but they are preparing for our deployment. Everything I tell you in this meeting is Confidential and Need-to-Know. You do not have the authority to determine who needs to know."

Ignoring the questioning looks, Six continued, "We are the advanced team for a unit that specializes in a particular kind of terrorism campaign. We have very specific, credible intelligence that the five murders you experienced over the last month and a half are tied to a very specific type of foreign operative. I know that the FBI is sending a Behavioral Analysis Unit to help profile what you, and they, believe is a serial killer. They will work the situation from that angle while we work it from our own direction. At this time, that is all that I can tell you; however, I will expect full cooperation while we are here. I expect to wrap up this in a couple days at the most. Does anyone have questions?"

The police chief slightly raised his hand. "I believe your victim intel is wrong. We had another body show up this morning, same 'M.O.,' same weird animal marks. I believe the coroner's got the body now, doesn't he John?"

The sheriff nodded slowly and looked at Six. "Bill, our M.E., should be opening the victim up now."

Six nodded his thanks to the sheriff and looked around the room. "All right, does anyone else have any questions?"

When he realized that no one was going to ask another question, he dismissed the impromptu meeting and walked out to the MRAP. As the rest of the town's officials filed out, he asked the sheriff to wait for a moment.

"Sheriff? Any chance I can get an escort out to the latest crime scene? I'd like my team to look at it. I will have a few of them head over to the hospital to talk to your coroner, as well."

The sheriff nodded and radioed for a deputy to come to the building. "I've got one of our rookies on the way over here to escort you guys," he explained to Six. "Bill, our coroner, is over in the hospital. The morgue is in the basement."

The sheriff's eyes narrowed and became serious. "Are you going to level with us, or will you just piss all over this town and wait for the next victim to be snatched and killed?"

Six paused for a moment and looked at the sheriff, carefully considering what he could say. "Sheriff, I cannot divulge any classified information about the threat; however, my team is here to handle it. I do honestly expect to wrap up this in just a couple days." Six reassured the sheriff.

The sheriff looked at the crew in and around the truck. He then looked back at the DHS agent and asked, "Just what kind of special team are you running? I don't believe I've ever seen a stranger advanced team."

The leader of this rather odd crew followed his gaze. "Officially? We are here to investigate and verify the threat and resolve the matter to keep the community safe. Unofficially? Our team is tasked with neutralizing a very particular terrorist subset. And as per our charter, we expect to file this case under 'Case Closed. Suspect Deceased.'"

A patrol car pulled up in the parking lot, and a young deputy got out. The rookie walked over to the sheriff and said, "Sheriff? Dispatch said you wanted me for escort duty?"

The sheriff nodded and replied, "Deputy Folsom, I want you to escort this Homeland Security team to the last crime scene. I'm sure they'll take their truck. Guide them over and make sure that our folks help them out." The sheriff turned to Six and continued, "Agent Holstein, this is Deputy Folsom. He'll be your guide today."

Six nodded and shook the young deputy's hand. Slightly taller than the DHS agent, the deputy was very young and had that clean cut, all-American, blond-hair-and-blue-eyed look that was made for a recruiting poster. He looked the deputy up and down before he spoke. "Good to meet you, Deputy. I need to talk to my team briefly, and then we can get going. If you want to get your car ready?"

The deputy was smart enough to take the hint and walked over to his car. Six spun on his heel and walked toward the truck. Upon reaching the truck, Six gathered everyone around into a small group to discuss his new information. The rest of the team had already checked their equipment, put on their armor, and donned the throat microphones and secure radios.

Six began his briefing. "All right. New intel. Yet another victim last night. The feedings are getting closer together, so we need to set up shop and take care of this thing quick. God, I want you on the roof of the hospital, as we discussed in the briefing. It's the tallest building in this area, and you'll be able to see most of town, and provide overwatch for this location. This building is our new command post."

The team leader turned to address everyone else as he continued, "Spooky, I want you to launch the drone. Look for cold spots. Help God with overwatch duties. Doc, Boomer, go talk to the coroner. His name is Bill. Doc, it's your specialty. Find out what we're hunting."

"Spooky, once you launch the drone, you and I will follow the deputy in this war wagon to the latest crime scene."

Spooky grinned and started laughing. "Ooh. I like that. This big bad MRAP is now officially 'The War Wagon.'" The others chuckled along as they could hear the capital letters that Spooky used.

"Everyone clear on their job?" Six saw nods all around. "Ok. We all have radio communications. If anything pops up, call it out. Don't worry about using 'military' language or 'tactical' signals. Use plain English. These are scrambled and secure enough to use."

God grabbed his rifle bag, Boomer slung her shotgun over her shoulder, and the two accompanied Doc as they walked across the parking lot toward the hospital's main entrance.

As they walked away, Spooky climbed back into the newly christened War Wagon and emerged with a large remote controlled drone. The young analyst started the small engine and threw it in the air, and the drone took off, climbing into the sky. Reaching down, Spooky grabbed a controller and piloted it in a perimeter over the town. The electronics expert climbed back into the truck, sitting in front of two screens set up where he could monitor the drone's flight. The team leader climbed into the driver's seat, started the engine, and waived the waiting deputy onward. As the deputy pulled out, Six pulled out behind him, the War Wagon dwarfing the police cruiser like a hunter on horseback following a hound.

The vehicles rolled away while the three remaining agents all walked toward the hospital. Walking through the main entrance, they made quite an imposing sight: two figures wearing SWAT armor and a woman wearing a cassock and a clerical collar. The older security guard at the main desk stared in shock for a couple seconds, then rose to his feet as he stammered, "Can I help you?"

Doc opened her credentials and showed them to the guard. "Homeland Security. Can you please point us in the direction of the morgue?"

The guard shakily pointed in the proper direction and then weakly raised a hand in protest when the two women went in that direction. The larger gentleman in armor and toting a rifle case looked around, seemed to find what he was looking for, and headed for the stairs. The guard reached down and grabbed the phone. He knew the sheriff's cell phone number, and he was sure he should probably check on the strange trio.

After a couple of rings, the sheriff answered his phone. "What is it, Uncle Ron? I'm kind of in the middle of something here."

The security guard's reply was bemused. "I think part of whatever you stepped in just walked in my doors, heading for the morgue. What's going on, John? Have we been invaded?"

"I'm sorry, Ron," the sheriff began. He sounded slightly abashed. "I forgot to call you and warn you. We're stuck with Homeland Security for a couple days while they figure out that our murders aren't terrorist related. Just let them go about their business."

"All right," the older man conceded. "Heck, I only have a few minutes 'till I go home, anyway. I'll let the kid deal with them tonight."

The two women walked down the hall to the bank of elevators. Seeing the signage that declared the morgue was in the basement, they boarded the elevator and descended. When the doors opened, they followed the hall until they were in a cold, sterile entryway.

With cold remains storage, two autopsy bays, and a viewing area, the morgue occupied almost the entire basement. Walking through the first set of doors, the two women found an office door that proclaimed, "William Stewart, M.D., Chief Medical Examiner." Doc knocked on the door and heard a muffled "Come!" from inside.

The priest entered first, while Boomer followed, closing the door behind her. Before them was a short, overweight man who was balding on top and smelled like cigarette smoke. An unlit cigarette was perched between his lips as he bent over paperwork behind his clean, orderly desk.

"Doctor Stewart?" Doc spoke up first.

"Yes? What do you want? You can tell the sheriff that he'll get the paperwork as soon as I get it done," the annoyed man snarled without looking up from his handwritten notes and partially filled forms.

Doc looked at her partner and frowned. "Doctor Stewart, I'm Doctor Noelle Sorenson from the Department of Homeland Security. This is my partner, Special Agent Rebekah Callahan. We have some questions we would like you to answer."

Stiffening, the rude retort on Doctor Stewart's lips died out when he looked up at the two agents darkening his doorway. Seeing one in a collar and cassock, and the other carrying a shotgun and dressed in a flak jacket, made him lose track of what he was going to say. The pause became uncomfortable, and the coroner recovered his voice. "I'm sorry about that. What can I do for you ladies today?"

"We're here investigating the recent series of deaths," the priest said. "I understand you had one last night as well? Have you already performed the autopsy?"

Doctor Stewart switched to an ingratiating smile. "Yes, I've done the post-mortem. I believe the sheriff has all the files, except for the one I'm literally finishing right now."

Doc nodded. "I've read the reports. I would still like to see the remains myself. I'm not questioning your work, Doctor, but I am a medical doctor and would like to see the bodies and evidence first-hand." Doc's voice seemed to chill the air. "Do you have a problem with me looking at the remains?"

Dr. Stewart visibly blanched. "No. Of course I don't have any problem with that. However, all but the last two have been buried or cremated, according to family wishes. We'll have to get a court order to disinter the bodies..."

"That's fine," Doc said as she nodded. "If we need to see the other bodies, I'll get the order. In the meantime, let's pull out the other two." She and Boomer turned to leave the office. The doctor quickly followed them.

The three people walked into the cold storage room. They prepared two gurneys, and then Doc and Dr. Stewart moved the two bodies on to the gurneys, one by one. As they wheeled the bodies into the autopsy room, Boomer shivered in the cool temperatures. Watching from the other side of the room, the explosives expert winced as each body was laid bare on an autopsy table.

The priest grabbed a mask and face shield and bent over the first body. This was the newest victim. A male, in his early twenties. He looked empty. Glancing at the incision on the chest, she turned to the doctor. "So, you've completed post-mortem. What was the cause of death?"

The doctor looked at her and said, "Organ failure, due to exsanguination. I have no real cause for the blood loss. The wounds on the arms, thighs, and throat all are from predators indigenous to the area—probably wolf or mountain lion. All the wounds are post-mortem."

Doc looked even closer at the wounds. She pulled out a small spiral-bound notepad and began recording her findings. Seeing the doctor trying to interfere with her partner, Boomer walked over to the doctor and asked him some basic questions.

She noticed that the doctor was glancing back and forth between the clock and Doc. She saw beads of sweat form on the man's forehead, despite the chilly room temperature. She wondered what he was hiding.

Boomer sought his attention. "So, Doctor... Stewart, was it? Did all the bodies have these kinds of markings?"

Dr. Stewart turned to face Boomer, who was encroaching on his personal space. Putting on his best clinical voice, he said, "Of course. All the markings were the same. Wherever they are hiding the bodies, there are some pretty fierce predators. Some have come in chewed up worse than this kid."

The demolitions expert looked straight at the M.E. "What's got you so nervous, doc? Anything else we should know?"

Boomer saw a momentary flash of panic in the man's eyes. "No, Agent Callahan. Why would I have to hide anything? Why am I nervous? On top of some crazy killer running around town, I have two Homeland Security agents on my doorstop, questioning my work. I'm about done for the day, and I would like to finish up."

Doc suddenly looked up from the second corpse. "That's ok, doctor. I'm done here. I thank you for your time, and I look forward to helping you out on this case." The priest peeled off her gown, mask, and gloves and strode toward the door. "Come on, Rebekah. Let's go tell the boss what we saw."

As they walked out, the doctor stood there glaring at the backs of the ladies' heads. He wondered who was going to help him put away these bodies. Then he wondered what he would tell Zachariah.

15

CONTACT

The deputy's cruiser and the large black truck pulled up to the curb in downtown Trinidad. Police cars lined both sides of the street, and a forensics van sat at the end of an alley that was blocked off with crime scene tape. Six nodded to Spooky and jumped out, following the deputy toward the alley. The DHS agent pulled his credentials from his inner pocket and showed them to the officers near the edge of the tape.

The team leader spoke up. "Special Agent Burt Holstein, Department of Homeland Security. Who's in charge here?"

A man and a woman, both wearing suits, came to the edge of the crime scene tape. The man was tall and thin, dressed in a wrinkled suit, with a stained tie and mussed hair. The bags under his eyes and the stubble on his face told the agent that it had been some time since he had seen a shower or a bed. His partner was about six inches shorter than the man, despite her two-inch heels. As a contrast, her suit looked pressed and clean, and she looked more composed. "Detectives Young and Toursier," she said as she introduced herself and her partner. "What is Homeland Security doing down here?" she quickly inquired.

Six ducked under the crime scene tape and extended his hand to shake hers. "Detective Young, we're here to make sure that this isn't some case of a deeper threat against the nation. What can you tell me about this scene?"

Eyeing the large black armored truck and eschewing the proffered hand, Young stepped in front of him and looked him over. "Since when is DHS interested in serial killers? We've got the FBI's BAU on the way to help us. Frankly, it looks like you will screw things up."

Six smiled and said, "Hey look, we're all on the same team. I promise: we're not going to interfere with your investigation. Our job is to help solve the problem." The agent stepped around the detective and continued toward the alley.

Young's frosty tone drove the warmth from the area. She began rattling off facts from her notes. "Same routine as last time. Pick an alley without cameras, knock out the street lamps, and then drop off the body. In. Out. Done. Clean and simple."

Six looked up at the detective and asked, "So they are not killed here? Hmm. Any clues about who might be going a little nuts in your town?"

The detective looked at the brusque agent with a mixture of hostility and disgust. "I'm sorry we're not omniscient. This is my sixth crime scene in as many weeks. Of course we don't have any idea who is doing this. Do you and your mighty DHS?"

Six looked a bit chastened. He softened his tone as he replied, "We have a couple good guesses, but nothing I can point you to. But that's what we're here for." He turned as he heard another large vehicle pull up behind him.

Climbing out of a black Suburban were three men and a woman. With nearly identical dark gray "power" suits, sunglasses, and attitudes, the FBI had arrived. The leader of the team walked up to Six and held up his badge. "Special Agent Grant Taylor, FBI. Who are you and why is Homeland Security here?"

Six smiled and pulled out his own badge. He could see the hostility on the agent's face and tried to calm the situation. "Special Agent Burt Holstein. We're here because we believe this is one of our cases. Although you and your team are working the serial killer angle, we'll be working another. And before you ask—it's classified above your pay grade."

Agent Taylor angrily shook his head and stalked past the agent and toward the detectives. Six approached the War Wagon; he glanced back and saw the BAU team congregating around the lead detectives. Keying his secure radio, he subvocalized, "God, this is

Six. Any signs of our targets?" The radio attached around his throat picked up the minute vibrations and sent them out over the radio.

A few seconds later, there was a reply. "Six, God. Negative on targets."

The team leader climbed up into the truck and glanced back at the young man who was mesmerized by the screens in front of him. "Any signs of our targets, Spooky?" Six's voice was hopeful.

Without looking up, the young man shook his head as his gaze passed from screen to screen.

The older gentleman sighed and keyed his radio again. "Knight-mare, this is Six. Let's regroup at ops center in ten minutes. I'll run and get us some food on the way back. I want to figure out our next move." Six received a chorus of affirmatives.

The team leader climbed into the driver's seat and glanced back at his electronics specialist. "Spooky, contact the mayor, and the sheriff. Have them meet us at the ops center in an hour. And have them contact the press. We'll have a press conference in two hours." Spooky gave him a thumbs up as his other hand reached for his phone.

* * * * *

ELEVEN MINUTES LATER, Six pulled the War Wagon into a parking spot in front of the building they were using as an operations center. As he climbed out, he saw the same three agents who had been at the hospital walking across the parking lot, the two women in a very animated conversation. His hands full with the bags of food, he told Spooky to grab the city map and walked inside the community center and into the conference room he had appropriated.

Laying out the fast food, Six accepted the map from Spooky and tacked it up on the large corkboard. He then grabbed a sandwich and coffee and started to eat. As the rest of the team filed in, they each took their food and drinks and began to eat.

"All right. Let's get this party started," Six said as soon as he finished swallowing his last mouthful. "Quick review. I visited the crime scene and talked to the lead detectives. Basically, it's the same M.O. every time. Killed somewhere else and dumped in an alley with broken lights and no cameras. These newbies are being smarter than the average killer. Doc?"

Doc nodded and finished chewing the bite she had just taken. She cleared her throat and began, "The coroner was... off. There were two bodies that hadn't been buried or cremated yet, and they were both the same. Feeding marks on the thighs, wrists, and necks. It looks like a garden variety vampire feeding."

The DHS team leader looked at the priest and asked, "What are some of the characteristics of this 'garden variety' vampire? Is there more than one kind?"

The team's priest nodded and took a breath. "In a short–answer: yes. But if you want to know what you are fighting, you need to understand a little more background. First off, forget almost every-thing you have ever seen from movies, TV, or books. Very few points are correct and most of the big 'facts' are wrong."

"The traditional vampire, what I referred to as the 'garden variety vampire,' is not a suave, debonair creature of the night who seduces by looks. They do not have the gothic sense of dress. And they absolutely do not sparkle. Unless you roast them with a flamethrower, then their ashes glow a little." The chuckles around the table rose to nervous laughter.

Doc continued, "When a vampire is created or appears from an incursion event, they are monstrous in shape and form. Very animalistic with sharp teeth, not just the canines, filling their mouths. They can quickly grow long, razor sharp fingernails and use their enormous strength and speed to hunt, capture, and feed on their prey."

"When they feed, they do not poke two little holes in the neck. Instead, they rip open places where the major arteries are closest to the skin. They will rip open the throat, gnaw on the wrists, and shred the inner thighs. They need the oxygen-rich living blood to circulate in their bodies. Their own blood is cold, black, and slug-gish. They can survive off animals, but most prefer the taste of human." The slightly queasy expressions around the table offset Doc's calm, cool delivery. Boomer, in particular, was really regretting her choice of hamburger.

"So how do we stop or kill them? Garlic? A cross? What?" Six questioned.

The priest shook her head. "Again, ignore Hollywood. Garlic does absolutely nothing against a traditional vampire… except give it bad breath. A cross that is wielded by someone who has faith in that cross will drive a vampire away or make them cower on the ground. And that applies to any religious symbol. As long as the symbol represents the faith of the bearer and the bearer believes in the faith, it will be effective. I've read reports of the Star of David being wielded by Jews and even pentacles wielded by Wiccans."

"The most effective way to kill a vampire is to stop blood flow to its head. This stops the regeneration from happening, and the creature will die. Either separate the head from the shoulders or do enough damage to the heart that it can no longer function—although this takes far longer for the vamp to stop attacking you."

Boomer looked up and asked, "What about stakes? What does a wooden stake do?"

Doc shrugged. "The stake has a very weird effect. As best as we can determine, the most effective use of the stake is to use it as a 'grounding rod.' A wooden stake to the body, other than the heart or head, has no effect. A stake to the brainpan will interrupt the function of the brain and end the vampire's life—as long as the stake stays in there long enough to effect true brain death. If you stake a vamp through the heart, it seems to basically interrupt the function of the heart, as long as the stake is there. However, if you can stake the vampire through the heart and into the ground, it completely paralyzes them."

Spooky spoke up, "Can they be cured?"

"Great question!" Doc responded. "A vampire that was recently turned can be cured by killing its sire, the creature that made it. Although it's never a guaranteed cure, we have reports of two victims from the same sire, one being cured upon the death of the sire, and the other staying inflicted with the virus. The death of the sire must occur sometime within the couple days after it was turned, and the timing is different for every turned creature. I've never seen any reports for a successful cure after three sunrises."

God looked thoughtful. He thought about the vampire movies he'd seen and asked, "What about sunlight or ultraviolet light? Does that hurt them?"

The priest answered him, "This is one that Hollywood gets partially right, Little G. The ultraviolet rays in natural sunlight and artificial UV rays will burn and blister a vampire. Their skin is about a hundred times more sensitive than ours is, and they have a built-in psychological condition. The net effect is that if they could build up the willpower to completely cover themselves, and if they wore some really strong sunblock, they might be able to walk around during the day, but if sunlight hits their skin, they receive a third-degree burn within a few seconds."

"Silver is also really effective at slowing down the regeneration rates of vampires, and it physically causes a severe allergic reaction when it touches a vampire's open wound. This causes them to feel a severe burning sensation. It's not quite as strong as the lycanthrope's reaction to silver, but it hurts them."

Doc opened the small, leather-bound book in front of her and flipped through a couple of pages, taking care with the parchment. She read a few of the notes from the book aloud: "This type of vampire gains power as it grows older and as it feeds. New vampires are fairly easy to kill, with the right equipment; however, some the older masters were notoriously difficult to dispatch. Most masters will have a place where they stay during the day, a 'nest,' if you will. Typically, they have their newbies guard the nest, occasionally having familiars or revenants standing guard."

Sensing that questions were coming, the vampire expert continued, "Familiars are humans who have willingly offered their service to the vampire. While they may occasionally be bled for food, typically, they are simply controlled through will, fear, or mind control. It is difficult to tell who a familiar is as they rarely wear any outer sign."

"Revenants are basically a cross between a zombie and a familiar. They are a ravenous beast that feeds on living flesh. They retain some of their intelligence when they are turned but are completely loyal to their master."

Doc looked around. "That pretty much sums up what we know about typical vampires. Headquarters believes we are facing a couple recently turned traditional vamps here. There are technically two other types, called the 'vampyre' and the 'dhampir.' The vampyre is a creature that is typically classed as a 'psychic vampire.' They feed on the emotional energy of the humans around them, thriving on intense emotions such as fear, hatred, and even love. They are very intense and have different weaknesses. In fact, this is probably where the legends of the vampire's power of seduction come from. Current records are fairly sparse as this type is very rare."

"The other type, called the 'dhampir,' is the offspring of a vampire and a human. While they do not inherit many of the more animalistic traits of their sire, they also are not affected by many of the same weapons. Dhampir are mortal and are not necessarily evil. In fact, there are records of some becoming great monster hunters."

The team sat in stunned silence at the wealth of information that Doc had provided. They looked around at each other, many of them again wondering why they had joined the team. Doc returned to her seat, and Six recovered from his momentary lapse.

Six looked around the table at his team. He cleared his throat and gave orders. "Now that we have intel on these critters, let's hunt them down and kill them. I will be meeting with the mayor, the city council, and the sheriff tonight, and I'm sure the FBI will be there. Because the activity is speeding up, we will be instituting a town-wide curfew. Hopefully, we'll be the only humans hunting tonight."

"As before, I want God up on the hospital roof on overwatch. Spooky, get the UAV up in the air. Doc and Boomer, I want you ready to respond here in the truck. I'm going to go meet with the mayor and then we'll have the press conference. After that, I'll be back out to the truck to be able to go hunting." As the team stood and headed for the War Wagon, the team leader went to meet with the mayor and sheriff.

* * * *

THE TEAM COMMANDER wrapped up the press conference and announcement of the impending curfew. Ignoring all the reporters' questions, he grabbed his notes and headed out to the MRAP. As he reached the truck, Boomer was coming out of the rear hatch.

"Hey, boss man. Spooky just got a couple of weird cold blobs moving down an alley about a block from here. I was coming to get you."

Six nodded, reached for his rifle, and activated his radio. "God, this is Six. Spooky picked up movement. We're going to go get this critter. You stay here and cover the VIPs in the city center. Doc, Boomer, you're with me. Spooky, you cover from above."

Spooky waved from inside the truck as Doc climbed out. Draped over her normally demure suit jacket, the Catholic Priest wore a pure white stole with many intricate designs woven throughout. Around her neck hung a cross on a long chain, and Doc carried a very large cross that was ornately inlaid with an intricate silver design and mounted on a sharpened piece of wood.

Six activated his radio as he closed and secured the truck doors. "Spooky. Direction and range to target. What do you have?"

Spooky came back quickly. "Northeast of this location. There is an access drive behind this building. It leads to a neighborhood. About two hundred and fifty yards. Satellite and directional sent to your phone."

Six responded. "Roger. Northwest, about two hundred and fifty yards. Access drive behind city center. God, watch the VIPs and Spooky."

The sniper replied with a simple, "Copy."

Six grabbed his rifle with both hands and then turned toward the two women. "Boomer. Doc. Let's go get a nightcrawler."

He then turned, and they walked at a relatively fast pace down the access road toward the area where Spooky had seen the suspicious cold spots.

Rounding a slight bend, they came to a road. Across the street was a row of houses, with a church across and to the right. Six looked at Doc.

She shook her head. "No way. They can't go on consecrated ground."

Six nodded and moved across the road, carefully walking down the cross street.

From three stories up, God tracked the team as they walked. He shifted and moved his gaze back to the command center. Picking up binoculars, he scanned the area around the buildings and the truck. As he swept past the unlit sides, a dark shadow caught his attention. Moving slowly, the shadow appeared to study the side of the truck and the front of the building. The sniper saw another dark shadow slink out of the brush and move toward the back of the building.

Clicking his binoculars into thermal mode, he saw that the moving shadows were colder than the surrounding areas. Subvocalizing into his radio, he called out, "Six, this is God."

"Go for Six."

"Six, I have three cold shadows back here at the ops center. One is going around the back, make that two going around the back. One is heading toward the War Wagon. Spooky, heads up. One is coming your way."

Six looked at the other two team members. "Copy, God. We're on our way. Once the target is verified, you are cleared to engage. Repeat. Weapons free."

Even as the sniper acknowledged his leader's orders, he was putting the binoculars down and shouldering the rifle. Calculating for wind and drop, and flipping the scope to a thermal setting, he looked for a target. He barely caught sight of one as it broke around the building. God soon heard the screams from inside the building.

Six and Boomer sprinted toward the building, hoping they were not too late. Doc was a touch slower; her modest flats were definitely not combat-ready.

Six waved to Boomer as they approached the building. The

screams inside were dying out as they reached the back door. Seeing the door already ajar, Six shouldered through the door, moving into the room and raising his rifle to his shoulder in a practiced move.

Outside, Spooky heard a terrible screech and howl as something slammed against the rear hatch to the War Wagon. The electronics wizard was quivering as the truck physically shook under the repeated blows of a creature trying to get to him. Raising the gun in one shaky hand, the young agent leaned over and waited for his opportunity.

Earlier, Spooky had carefully pulled the special ammunition that Norbert had given him from its padded case and cautiously loaded two of the bullets into the magazine for his Beretta. As the howling intensified, he could see that the thick armored door was moving against its frame. Spooky reached out and timed his actions with the pulls from whatever was trying to get to him.

As the creature gave a fantastic heave, the analyst popped the latch on the door. The creature flew back, stunned, and landed on its back in the parking lot. Spooky saw the terrible visage of a small girl turned feral animal. The rows of sharp teeth gleamed as she snarled and rose. The young agent pointed the gun and pulled the trigger twice.

The once-young girl howled in pain as a blinding flash lit the area. There was a thunderclap, and Spooky saw the monster's arm fly away from her body. Wrecked and in severe pain, the creature howled and bolted into the night. The electronics specialist slammed and locked the truck's back door. He then began to shake.

Dimly registering the gunshots from outside the building, the DHS leader paused at the carnage staining the walls and floor around him. Blood spatters stained the walls of the room and body parts were scattered around the space. That moment of shock wore off as he finally glimpsed a feral creature with a half-gnawed arm in its mouth. The creature paused a moment too long to stare at the agent's sudden entrance. As it turned to run out the front of the room, Six pulled the trigger on his rifle.

Calmly walking rounds up the creatures back, Six shot as fast as he could, while still maintaining control. As the fourth round hit the creature at the top of the spine, Boomer burst through the door and raised her shotgun.

The demolition expert's Mossberg roared, and the vampire fell to the ground with a large hole where its spine and heart once were. Cycling the action, her shotgun roared again, this time taking off the top half of the creature's deformed head.

As Six began shooting the vampire inside the building, God watched another creature burst out of the front door. The thing paused momentarily to look back into the building and howl. That pause was long enough to center the reticle on the creature's head and squeeze the trigger. Less than a tenth of a second later, the large silver hollow-point bullet with a pure wood core entered the forehead of the creature. The former HRT sniper had just enough time to register that the vampire used to be a teenage girl before the head disappeared in a spray of black goo. *Huh. I guess dipping them in Holy Water makes them even nastier,* God thought to himself. A grin worked its way across his face.

Inside the building, Six and Boomer quickly made sure the rest of the building was empty, and then Six announced, "Six to all team. Building is clear." He nodded as Doc crossed the threshold.

"God to Six. Exterior clear. One Tango. One Body."

"Spooky to Six. Truck is clear, although I might need to change my underwear."

16

COVER-UP

Community Building. Trinidad, Colorado.

Doc stood in the doorway and blanched at the carnage. Even her worst experiences working for Doctors Without Borders did not prepare her for this. The vampires had not tried to feed. They had simply slaughtered everyone inside. Using their tremendous strength and near-invulnerability as powerful weapons, they had butchered everyone in the main hall. The priest could see enough parts to piece together several bodies, and she estimated that there must have been ten or fifteen people here when they were massacred.

She walked toward a corpse that was quickly becoming a pile of what could only be described as goo. She looked at Six and asked, "So, is this what's left of the one you guys took down?"

Six looked up and said, "Yep. Is this a vampire?"

Doc knelt down and carefully turned what was left of the head around so she could see the mouth. Seeing the telltale rows of razor-sharp teeth, she nodded. "This one's a bloodsucker. Help me clear out the rest of this room. Where is the other one?"

The DHS leader nodded toward the front of the building. "God said he got one outside," he said, distracted by the gore and remains around him.

The vampire specialist stood and walked toward the front door. Stepping outside, she immediately saw the black slimy ooze that covered the area around the broken front door. She looked around but could not find any remains large enough to be a head. As she watched, the black slime evaporated into thin air, as if it was ectoplasm from a ghost.

Keying her radio, the priest called for the sniper on the roof, "Little 'G,' this is Doc. Where are the remains of the one you shot? Am I missing something?"

Doc could hear the smirk as God answered through the tactical radio, "Negative, Doc. Apparently, when you hit the head with one of these rounds doused in Holy Water, the critters do their best to explode into little pieces of goo."

Six cut in. "God, knock out the commentary. I need you to spot for us. We need to clean this one up. Spooky, keep the drone up. Let me know if any humans are coming. We should have law enforcement in moments. We'll keep them outside for now. Also, Spooky, prep a report so I can send it to Agent Smith. We're going to need more cleanup on this one. Doc, come back inside and make sure nothing will be found of the creature. Boomer will help."

A chorus of acknowledgements sounded over the radio while Doc walked back inside to collect the remaining vampire's head. Six passed the priest on his way out to greet the approaching sirens.

* * * * *

IT HAD BEEN a long night for the team. By the time the first law enforcement officers had arrived, all trace evidence of the vampires had evaporated like water droplets on a hot summer sidewalk. Doc had placed the head in an evidence bag, sealed it, and taken it to the truck. Six then arranged for the medical examiner to take care of the victims and had talked to the undersheriff and the deputy chief of the police department for a few hours. He had finally convinced them that his team was in charge of the operation and that all of the investigation would be handled by his the DHS agents.

The medical examiner had retrieved all of the body parts and was in the middle of the gruesome task of piecing together the bodies and accounting for any missing parts. It had taken threats of physical arrest and detention in Guantanamo Bay to get the coroner to ignore that there were no bodies of the attackers. Only repeated reminders that this was a national security matter had kept him from complaining to the press.

It was the press who had been the most difficult to handle. The DHS team leader had enlisted the help of the sheriff's department and the police department to set up a quarantine with a one hundred fifty foot perimeter from the building. The press had been relentless, hounding the police and the team about the deaths inside. It had driven them into a frenzy knowing that members of the press had been slaughtered at the same time.

While the press had been difficult to handle, the worst phone call Six had made was to Agent Smith at Section 28. Agent Smith had critiqued the actions of the team, pointing out where they had done well, and where they needed improvement. Smith had also informed him that there were two more new agents on the way and that one of them would handle media relations and function well as the team leader's second-in-command.

Smith had informed Six that he would send their dossiers to him electronically and that the new agents were already on the ground in Pueblo. Smith had then told the team leader that a DHS Black Hawk helicopter was being tasked to take the new agents to Trinidad within the hour. After confirming the landing spot, Smith had assured Six that he would have all the support he needed to go after the remaining vampire, the young girl who got away.

After ending his phone call with Smith, Six ordered God down from his perch on the roof of the hospital and call the team together, briefing them on the new team members. As they were stowing their gear in the War Wagon, they heard the distinctive sounds of an incoming helicopter. Six looked up as a jet black military helicopter slowed to a hover over the hospital helipad. The Sikorsky UH-60 Black Hawk touched down and two men climbed out of the open helicopter side door. As soon as their feet hit the pavement, four large duffel bags and two long gun cases were pulled from the open door and placed on the ground.

The larger man on the left from Six's point of view slung a rifle case over his back, reached down and grabbed two of the duffels, and walked toward the team as he hunched over to avoid a possible rotor mishap. The second man also placed a rifle bag over his back and visibly strained to lift the two remaining duffels. He did the same hunched duck-walk toward the team. The engine noise increased, and the helicopter lifted off with a roar from its twin turbines. Once the helicopter was in the air, the men straightened up and headed for the team. As they approached, Six was amazed when the mass of the man on the left seemed to keep getting larger and larger.

Arthur "Heavy" Murphy was a mountain of a man. His dossier said the man was six feet seven inches and weighed in just a hair under three hundred pounds. The DHS team leader could tell that all the weight was muscle. The width of his shoulders barely fit inside his armor, and he had ripped off the sleeves of his uniform. The large, bald African American man smiled as he dropped one of the bags and raised his hand in a crisp salute.

"Special Agent Art Murphy. Reporting for duty, sir. So, what do you want dead?" The large agent's deep voice boomed.

Dragging the two duffels behind Heavy, the other man stopped and dropped the handles of the bags. While not quite as tall as the walking giant, the slender Jonas "Ghost" Vanhof seemed to disappear inside his voluminous leather overcoat. Between the black leather duster and the worn, black gaucho hat perched atop his head, Ghost looked about as far from a DHS agent as Doc did. Slender to the point of gaunt, Six didn't believe the reported weight of 190 pounds, it must include the weight of the leather duster. Ghost reached inside his coat and withdrew his identification.

Flipping the ID open, Ghost grinned and announced, "Special Agent Jonas Vanhof. I hear you have a vampire problem?"

Six just shook his head at the levity as he introduced himself and the team. Reaching out his hand to shake the hands of both new team members, the team leader said, "Special Agent Burt Holstein. I'm your boss. And this is the rest of your team." Six pointed to each one as he introduced the team members by names and call signs. Turning to the new team members, he continued, "Team, this is Arthur 'Heavy' Murphy and Jonas 'Ghost' Vanhof. Heavy is our heavy weapons specialist, and Ghost is my second-in-command… and apparently he is an esoteric research prodigy."

Old and new team members exchanged handshakes and greetings. After a few minutes, Six quickly reigned the team back in. "Let's head back to the conference room. We don't want to give the press anything to waggle about."

Once the team had walked back into the building and settled around the conference table, the lead agent looked up and said, "Ok. We have a major situation here. We've got at least one vamp still on the loose. We have a media feeding frenzy because of the latest attack, which we need to address A-S-A-F'in-P. The national media is now paying attention, and our faces will probably be on the news, if they aren't already. We will hold a press conference shortly. What are our options?" Six briefly looked at his secure phone to read a message from Agent Smith. "As if things weren't complicated enough, the FBI has dispatched a Hostage Rescue Team to this area. We are still in charge... barely. We need answers."

Ghost spoke up almost immediately. "Simple: terrorism. Blame the attack on some crazy terrorists and say that there is still a danger to the public. The media will draw that conclusion anyway because of the arrival of the HRT. Hold the press conference and institute a curfew from sundown until sunup. During the day, we can sleep and prep, and we'll hunt tomorrow night. If you want me to, I can be the spokesperson for this conference. I even have a suit with me for the occasion."

The team leader thought for a bit and nodded his assent. He looked around the table and asked, "Are there any risks, or anything we're missing?"

The team's priest spoke up softly, "What if someone talks to the media? What is our contingency?"

Six looked at Ghost and then back at Doc. His face was grim when he spoke, "Our contingency is simple. We do what DHS does best. Stall. Obfuscate. And if nothing else works, ship 'em to Gitmo. This entire operation is classified as 'Top Secret, Need-To-Know.' We just need to remind the couple of players who know something that they face federal prison time. Will that work?"

The priest nodded and said, "That will have to do."

"All right. Ghost, you go do the press conference," said Six. "I'll go with you, but I won't answer any questions. I will take the time to talk to the locals. They will be in charge of the perimeter around this building. Absolutely no admittance to this. After Ghost does his song and dance, we'll catch some rack time. Any questions?"

When nobody raised any questions, the team leader stood up, signaling the end of the meeting. The lanky new second-in command stood up, grabbed one of his duffel bags, and headed for the bathroom to change. A few minutes later, a very different agent emerged from the restroom. Dressed in a suit and tie, he looked like a respectable bureaucrat, exactly like the public information officer he should look like.

Six and Ghost walked toward the waiting mob of reporters, more of whom were arriving by the minute. Ghost noted news vans from Denver and Pueblo, as well as the large national cable news outlets. Stepping forward, Ghost nodded to the undersheriff and raised his hands for quiet. He addressed the assembled crowd.

"I am Special Agent Jonas Vanhof. That is V-A-N-H-O-F for those of you who can't keep up. I am the press liaison for this operation, and I will be issuing a short statement tonight. I will not be taking questions during or after the statement."

"At approximately nine o'clock last night, a special Department of Homeland Security action team was notified of suspicious activity at on East Main Street. As the team responded to the reported activity, an unknown number of suspected terrorists entered the back door of this location. There they attacked and killed Sheriff John Klooster, Mayor Scott Jennings, four agents from the FBI's Behavioral Analysis Unit, and three members of the press. This attack was pre-planned, and the distraction was designed to draw the DHS team from the building."

Ghost ignored the rising murmurs from the crowd and continued, "When the DHS team realized that this building was the intended target, they responded as quickly as possible. When they responded, they were able to take down two of the terrorists. At least one of these terrorists got away. We do not know which group these terrorists represent, nor do we know how many remain in the area. Until we capture the rest of the terrorists, we will continue the curfew from sundown until sunup. This curfew applies to all citizens of Trinidad. The only exceptions are on-duty law enforcement personnel and on-duty emergency responders."

"If you notice someone who appears suspicious or who acts irregularly, please contact your local law enforcement agency. These suspects are considered heavily armed and very dangerous. Do NOT attempt to apprehend them by yourself."

"As I mentioned. I will not be taking questions today. Good day." Ghost walked away from the press to the wild cacophony of shouted questions and accusations—real and implied.

Six joined him as they walked back to the ops center. His admiration for his new second-in-command was evident in his voice, "Great statement. You're already worth your weight out here. So how did you become an expert in chasing monsters? Your file says you got busted for killing a werewolf. Just a hobby?"

The esoteric specialist shook his head. "That was not my first," he said in a low voice. "You could say that this is a family curse to hunt creatures."

When he realized that the gaunt man was not going to elaborate, Six looked questioningly at his second. "And?"

Ghost shook his head. "Let's leave it at that for now." His grim tone brooked no argument.

The lead agent slowly nodded. He could wait for a better time. As they approached the War Wagon, they could see the entire team lounging on, or in, the truck. Six climbed up into the truck and sat in the jump seat next to Boomer, and Ghost took a seat in the back. As soon as the back door was closed, Boomer fired up the engine and dropped it in gear.

The hotel arrangements were made at a small motel just off the interstate, close to the team's ops center. The exterior of the single-story motel was white against the glare of the sun. The motel was shaped in a right angle like the letter "L", roughly splitting the rooms along each axis, with access to the rooms along the outside from the parking lot. There were only a handful of rooms in this hotel, and they chose it for access to the interstate and its location close to town. Taking up one entire side of the motel, they quickly divided up into pairs for security on Six's order. The two female agents, Doc and Boomer, took one of the rooms. Six and God decided to share a room, which left Heavy and Ghost in the last room.

Directly outside the block of rooms, the War Wagon sat, occupying multiple parking spaces. Nestled inside the truck, Spooky had refused to sleep anywhere that was not surrounded by heavy armor. Six had only acquiesced when the young agent brought up that he was the only one who knew how to use all the sensors and defensive perimeter gear in the War Wagon. That made him the logical choice to sleep there.

The team had been up for over twenty-four hours by the time the lead DHS agent had requested a pair of officers in a patrol car to watch their rooms so they would be undisturbed. Other than running off the occasional reporter, the police officers had a very quiet day watching the sleeping DHS team.

17

HUNTING

Ave Maria Shrine, Trinidad, Colorado.

On a hill just south of the hospital stood a two-story white structure, a shrine. From its inception in 1934, the shrine had seen the ebb and flow of the area for nearly one hundred years. A black armored truck was parking in the shrine's parking lot. And around the back of that truck stood four gentlemen wearing black tactical armor and carrying military rifles.

Inside the truck, Six leaned over the projected landscape that Spooky was showing on his displays. "According to the UAV, we've got four cold spots just a half kilometer due south of here, on the other side of this ridge. We'll be silent from this point on."

He looked at each of the men as he assigned the marching order. "God, you're behind me. Heavy, you're behind God, and Ghost, you've got the rear guard."

All of them nodded, and Ghost pulled at the collar of his armor vest. "You know, boss, I'd rather be in my duster than this armor stuff. It's way too restrictive for my movements. And I guarantee that I'd be better armored."

Six shook his head and sighed. "Not tonight. Take the armor. We'll discuss it after this strike."

The team leader looked at his team. "Let's move out. Spooky, you've got eyes on the targets?"

Spooky looked back at him. "Yeah, boss. Still being stupid."

Six shook his head. It felt like a trap, but he had no other choice than to spring it. He flipped his night-vision goggles down and began to walk due south. One by one, the others followed him into the rapidly darkening night.

He made his way slowly and carefully through the scrub brush that carpeted the area. As team lead, Six was constantly scanning all around him, but he could not shake the feeling of walking into a trap. The men behind him were nearly silent, attesting to their care and training. Reaching the spot marked on his navigational display, Six raised a closed fist to halt the team and spoke softly into his throat mic, "Spooky, this is Six. Target status?"

The agent replied almost immediately. "They're still sitting dumb and happy. You're all clear."

"Copy." Six raised his hand and waived it forward. God moved up on his right, walking parallel and about two yards away from the team leader. Heavy moved forward to Six's left, opening up the same spacing to the team lead. Ghost drew closer to his leader, still on rear watch, constantly looking around the team for danger. As they got close to the summit of the ridge, Six raised his fist again and motioned for a halt. Stepping tentatively closer, his head just barely cleared the summit. Switching to his thermal optics, he scanned the area in front of him where the creatures should be, and came up empty.

Scanning all around on that side of the summit, his thermal optics failed to detect any unnatural thermal cold spots. Stepping back, Six again subvocalized, "Spooky, Six. Negative contact. Where are they?"

"They're right there, Six. I'm seeing them on the drone. Wait one second."

The wait seemed interminable for the team in the field. In the truck, Spooky was typing furiously and watching his screens. Suddenly, he saw five cold spots moving to surround the team on the ridge.

Spooky keyed his microphone to warn the team. "Alpha team, Spooky. Those were a decoy. Five, repeat five, cold spots closing rapidly. Look around you."

Six jerked and swept his gun all around him as he looked through his optics. He quickly picked up two cold spots almost directly to his left, and they were closing in fast. Bringing his sights up and on target, Six keyed his mic again. "Alpha team, weapons free. Kill the SOBs." He released the microphone and grabbed the forward grip on his carbine and squeezed the trigger twice.

The muzzle flash from his rifle lit the night as the high velocity rounds entered the chest of the creature. The two silver slugs with their wooden payload caused the vampire to stumble, and it let out a fierce cry. Six silenced the screams with two more 5.56mm tumblers between the eyes and out the back of the creature's skull, along with the rotting meat in the brainpan.

Six pivoted to the next creature on his left as he barely registered God's rifle barking on his right. Four quick rounds through the creature's chest caused it to stop in its tracks. Six again took advantage of the pause to pull the trigger three more times. At least one of the three entered the howling creature's head, exploding violently out the back of the creature's skull.

To the lead agent's right, his sniper's first two shots hit the creature in the elbow and shoulder. God noticed that the vampire now had a stump of an arm. It ended where the specialized rounds chewed through the flesh. Mentally cursing, God took careful aim and began pulling the trigger. He casually walked the rounds right up the torso and into the cranium of the vampire, instantly killing it. The former HRT operator swung to his right to seek out more targets.

On Six's left, Heavy opened up with the Squad Automatic Weapon. Holding and aiming the large machine gun as if it were a rifle, he centered the sights over one of the remaining vampires, and then he pulled the trigger for a relatively short burst. Using the same rifle rounds as the rest of the team, the heavy gunner smiled as the rounds seemed to make the vampire dance. With a final burst to the head, the vampire's body tumbled to the ground.

The vampire that ran toward Ghost was suddenly surprised to see his target drop to his knees in a crouch. Smiling a horrible smile with those razor-sharp teeth, the vampire lunged at Ghost. With a speed that belied his build, a wooden stake appeared in the hunter's left hand while he drew his Webley Mark IV service revolver with his right. As the vampire loomed over him, Ghost shoved the wooden stake right through the chest cavity and into the heart. As the vampire collapsed onto the esoteric hunter, the weight of the body made it difficult for him to get out from underneath the stunned, but still dangerous, creature.

Ghost found enough strength to grab his revolver and point it at the forehead of the vampire on top of him. He squeezed the heavy double action trigger and was rewarded with a loud "bang" from the revolver. The 200 grain .38 caliber bullet split the forehead of the vampire open. Feeling the creature go limp, he fired again for good measure.

Suddenly the weight was lifted off him. Looking up, Ghost saw Heavy holding the rapidly decomposing body over him and then fling it off into the brush. Heavy extended his hand. Accepting the hand up, the lanky agent thanked the big man profusely.

Six stood and surveyed the area for the firefight. "I knew this was a trap. Someone is setting us up. Notice we're up over eight vampires so far, not just the one or two they said there were. We need to talk to Smith." He barked out orders, "Tag and Bag anything that didn't disappear, and then back to the truck."

* * * * *

DOC AND BOOMER were again interviewing the medical examiner as he sorted through the remains from the prior night's attack. The pile of unidentifiable parts grew steadily, and the bodies that were pieced together were incomplete.

The explosives expert wandered around the lab and offices while her partner kept the coroner busy with questions and suggestions. Doc noticed that the local doctor was getting more and more distracted as her partner passed around the labs. She wondered if it was a territorial thing or if the doctor had something to hide. She looked for any signs that the doctor was a familiar for a vampire, but there was nothing outwardly noticeable.

The chatter of the other team members' conversations was background noise for the team's medic, and she was only half-listening to the transmissions. She wanted to see if this coroner caught the unusual wounds or if he was incompetent. So far, he had passed over the wounds, but he had not made any big deal out of them. So either he must be incompetent or he is dirty.

Boomer stormed back into the labs from the direction of the offices. "Did you hear that? We need to go. They will want us to meet them at the ops center. They may need your help."

Doc started to respond, but her team leader's voice spoke in her ear. "All team. Meet at ops center immediately. Six out."

Boomer keyed her mic. "Copy, Six. Beta Team en route. Do you require medical?"

"Negative," Six replied. "New critical intel."

"Copy, Six. On our way." Boomer looked at her partner. "Time to go."

Doc nodded and followed her partner out of the labs and out of the hospital. They walked across the parking lot and arrived barely before the War Wagon slammed to a halt, rocking on its formidable springs.

Six climbed out of the truck and said, "Conference room. One minute."

Forty-eight seconds later, the team was assembled in the conference room. The lead agent filled them in on the details of the ambush

"This means that we are fighting something more than a couple newbies. That's at least eight vampires, including the one that Spooky nearly blew up. I've talked to Agent Smith, and he is tasking greater resources our way. Officially, our mission has been upgraded to Ultra-Red. Any recommendations?"

At that moment, there was a knock on the conference room door. Opening the door, Six found a pale young female deputy almost in tears. She choked out, "There's been another attack... just now. It's at one of our deputy's houses. You can follow me."

Six looked at the team. They were already standing and heading toward the door. "Ok, deputy. We'll be right behind you. Just wait for us to mount up."

Thirty seconds later, the War Wagon was loaded and following behind the deputy's patrol car in a mad dash across town. Three minutes later, the War Wagon came to a halt on a residential block. Multiple cruisers and ambulances lined the road.

As the team climbed out of the truck, two black Chevy Suburbans squealed to a stop. Suddenly eight men wearing green tactical armor and carrying automatic weapons piled out of the new trucks. God recognized his former team. He leaned over to Six and pointed, "HRT is here. You better step up if you want to stop them from taking over," the sniper recommended.

The lead DHS agent told the rest of the team to enter the house where the attack had occurred and to begin the investigation while he went to talk to the HRT commander. As he walked, he noticed a distraught young deputy being consoled by his peers. He paused momentarily when he realized it was same deputy that had been their guide around town the day before. *Nice kid. Shame. What was his name, Fuller? Fulton?*

He stepped up to the commander of the FBI's Hostage Rescue Team and flashed his badge. "Special Agent Burt Holstein, Homeland Security. Did you get the message from Washington? We're primary on this case."

The commander looked at him coldly before he replied, "Believe me, I got the memo." The commander's gravely voice sounded harsh to the DHS agent's ears. "Where do you want us?"

Six put up a hand to shake the commander's hand. The HRT commander accepted Six's handshake and the DHS team leader spoke, "We're going to secure the scene. Canvas the neighborhood. This is supposed to be real fresh. It is possible that the bad guys are still in the area. We believe they're armed with blades and high on a new PCP variant."

The commander dispersed his men. When the senior DHS agent turned to walk toward the house, his radio sounded in his ear, "Six, God. House is clear. It's a freakin' slaughterhouse in here. Looks like a trail out the back."

Six keyed his mike as he quickened his pace. "Copy, God. On my way. Spooky, get our UAV up and out looking for cold spots. Let's see if this is more vamps."

Moving in through the front door, Six crashed to a halt. Someone had splashed what appeared to be dark red paint all over the inside of the living room. The walls and furniture were covered with the mess. The team leader surveyed the room and saw a crime scene technician's flag by a hunk of meat that looked like it could be part of an arm. And then Six realized the "paint" around him was the drying and congealing blood of the victims. The scene at the Government Center had rattled him, but this was even worse. This attack was more vicious, more terrible, and there seemed to be fewer body parts lying around.

Walking through the front room, he joined the rest of his team in the kitchen. Looking around, he realized that this calm, cool, professional fire team was on the verge of breaking down. They had all seen horrific death before, but this was a level they had never encountered. He saw fear and pain in the eyes around him, and he wondered what they saw in his.

"Ok, team. What do we know?" The team leader's voice was coarse.

God spoke first. "Looks like there were at least two creatures. The wife was in the living room; there are two little girls upstairs. At least what little remains of them. The deputy was the first on the scene at his own house. He didn't see anything other than the slaughter before he called for backup. Other members of his department found the girls upstairs."

Six turned to his team priest. "This doesn't look like the vampire scenes we've found before. Is this normal, or is this another creature?"

Doc shook her head, fighting to hold back her tears for the family. She choked out her words, "If I had to guess, I'd say this was a zombie. But they would still be here. They are actually pretty slow in real life. Messy and voracious, but slow."

Six looked around and swore. "Whatever they are, they die tonight. Ghost, can you follow their trail?"

Ghost looked at the back door and shrugged. "I think so."

Six nodded and keyed his radio. "Spooky, this is Six. Any sign of creatures?"

"Negative, boss," the electronics specialist was quick to respond.

The lead agent pointed to the door and continued, "All right. Let's head out. Ghost, you're up."

The tall, lanky agent led the way out of the back door of the house, following blood trails left behind by the other creatures. As they walked out the back, Ghost could see the trail of blood and guts leading them to the left and over a fence. The esoteric specialist led the way, and the rest of the team followed, rifles ready. Doc had a little trouble scaling the short fence and brought up the rear.

As they approached the house next to the crime scene, they all heard screaming and growls from the house just over the next fence. The team turned to Six, and he quickly made a decision. "God, Ghost, and Boomer, you are Team 'B' on the front door. I'll bring Heavy and Doc with me through the back. Team B, you come through when you hear the gunfire. Watch the exits. Go. Go. Go!"

God, Ghost, and Boomer raced around the front of the house, just two houses south of the original scene. Six, Heavy, and Doc ran toward the screened-in back porch of the target house. As they ran, the lead agent keyed his radio. "Spooky. Activity in the house two south of the scene. Focus the UAV here."

As Six heard the confirmation from Spooky, the trio slammed through the back door to the porch. The screams inside faded to a gurgle as Six paused at the threshold of the back door. He jerked his head to Heavy, and the large man raised his enormous boot. A single kick tore the door jamb off the wall, and Six rushed through with his rifle raised. The small kitchen was strewn with overturned furniture and ripped open cabinets, but the sounds were coming from the room ahead.

As he moved through the doorway, the lead agent saw two crea-tures ravenously ripping an older man and woman apart with their bare hands. The creatures used to be human, but no trace of humanity remained. Their pale gray skin had a rough texture and was drawn tight where it was visible. The ripped and shredded remains of clothing hung loosely from their gaunt frames. Their fingers ended in long, dagger-like claws, and rows of sharpened teeth filled mouths that seemed to open wider than was possible. Coal-black eyes stared from hollow faces at their prey.

The blood and carnage were sprayed everywhere in the feeding frenzy. Six didn't hesitate. He pulled the trigger, aiming at the creature closest to him. Round after round hit the creature, and it jerked from each impact. Six noticed quickly that the creature wasn't reacting to the silver bullets. Even as it howled in pain, it stayed on its feet. At his left elbow, Heavy stepped up and stroked the trigger on his machine gun. The creature jerked more as the bursts all landed on target—the creature's chest. With a final burst that climbed its way up to the creature's head, the final two rounds blew open the top half of the creature's head.

When they heard Six's team burst through the door, God raised a booted foot and kicked the front door. It shuddered but remained shut. Rearing back again with all of his might, he kicked the door just below the knob. The second kick sent the door crashing inward on its hinges.

Boomer stepped into the front hallway of the small house. Pivoting left, she had less than a second to realize that there was a creature coming at her, and that it was dripping with gore. Instead of raising her shotgun to her shoulder, she simply swiveled and pulled the trigger, firing the big 12GA from her hip. She was too close to miss.

The large silver and wooden slug entered creature's diaphragm. The shot was a powerful enough blow that the creature stopped its lunge. As the creature howled in rage and pain, the young woman racked the pump on her scattergun, and pulled the trigger again. And again. The third shot opened a very large hole in its chest, dissolving the heart and the edges of the lungs into a fine spray of black ichor. The creature fell backwards in shock, and Boomer raised the Mossberg to her shoulder and stroked the trigger, sending the one-inch diameter piece of silver and wood through the front of the skull. The kinetic energy from the slug removed the entire back half of the head, and the corpse slumped over.

God and Ghost rushed past, and the sniper called out, "Coming into the room."

The demolitions specialist rejoined the rest of her team just as

Six told his team, "Heavy, take the front door. God, take the back. HRT and SWAT will be coming quickly at the screams and gunfire. DO NOT let them see the bodies. Keep them outside. Boomer, help me clear the rest of the house."

The small, single-story house was confirmed clear of any other monsters thirty seconds later. As the team leader walked into the living room, his heavy weapons specialist motioned to him from the front door. Six walked up to the door and was greeted by an irate Las Animas County SWAT captain.

"If you don't let me and my men in here, I will arrest you and your team. This was our own. I want to see the bodies of the bastards who did this!" He was getting angrier by the minute.

Six held up his hands, palm out, to calm the captain. "Captain Jackson, it IS your own deputy's scene. If you and your men investigate, you will taint the evidence for anyone we missed. We are the perfect third party to investigate this one. You have to see reason. Just know this: two suspects down. And this is still our call. If you have any questions, please call my department. You have my badge number."

"In the meantime. I will have the HRT guard the scene until your lab techs get here. I'll talk to you in the morning when I have a better grasp of what's happening."

Six turned and walked back into the house. The lead agent found his sniper on the back porch talking with the HRT guys.

"No, seriously. I'm glad I joined this team," God was saying. "I know all the secrecy crap is annoying, but I'm doing important stuff. Even better, I'm finding answers to questions that I've had for a long time."

The HRT team leader clasped his former teammate on the shoulder. "If you ever want out of the 'secret club' and want to come back to the real world, give me a call. I'll have you back anytime. And if you ever need backup, we'll be there to pull your butts from the fire."

God laughed. He noticed Six standing there and motioned him closer. "Hey, Boss. This is Special Agent Alton Lynch, HRT command. He was my team leader before I joined this team."

Six nodded at the large man. "We've met. And I believe he's still a little mad that we are here. Agent Lynch, I can honestly say thank you for giving us Agent Rivera here. Even if it wasn't voluntary. Jesús is a great testament to you and your team. If I ever get done with him, I'll send him back." The team leader stretched out his hand.

Lynch took the proffered hand and squeezed. "You better treat him right and send him back whole. Or I'll hunt you down myself."

Six nodded solemnly. "I make sure all my guys and gals come home whole... if it's in my power."

Six looked at Lynch. "While I've got you here, I would like to have a couple of your team detailed for a few hours to guard this crime scene and the other one. Just until the techs get done. Not only is this part of our original case, but keeping this in our jurisdiction removes any potential conflict of interest from the sheriff. Can you do that?"

Lynch nodded and called four of his team over. "Pearson. Sanders. No one but DHS and the lab techs come in or out of this house. Williams. Jones. You guys cover the other house." The HRT commander ordered, "Stay outside. This is a DHS scene, and we are seconding to them for this duration."

Lynch turned to Six and asked, "Can we get a briefing in the morning?"

Six nodded. "Absolutely. I'll brief you when I brief Captain Jackson and the undersheriff. Unfortunately, I don't think we're done here yet."

18

DAYLIGHT

Ops Base, Trinidad, Colorado.

I t was a beautiful sunny afternoon in Trinidad, Colorado, when the black MRAP rumbled to a halt outside the building they were using as a base. The back hatch opened, and a weary group of individuals exited the vehicle. As they wandered into the conference room, the five men and two women sat heavily in their respective seats.

Six looked around the table. "Let's regroup what we know, and what we don't," said Six as he began the briefing. "I'm going to bring Agent Smith in on this meeting with a conference call."

The DHS team leader dialed a number on his SSP and hit the speaker toggle on the touchscreen. Agent Smith answered on the second ring. Six said, "Agent Smith, I've got you on speakerphone for this briefing. I think you need to be in on this one."

"Thank you for including me on this meeting, Agent Holstein." The cultured voice of the senior agent was clear over the phone speakers. "I've read through all your reports. Any mistakes so far are solely caused by your lack of specific training here at HQ. I'm noting those only so we can correct that deficiency when you and your team get back.

"Overall, though, I have to commend you on an excellent operation so far. You guys have handled way more than any of us thought you should be thrown into. This was supposed to be a fairly light training mission. We have upgraded this mission to 'Ultra-Red,' which means you will be granted access to virtually unlimited assets. Burt, this is your mission, so I'll turn it over to you."

Six smiled. "First up: Doc. You handled the autopsies last night? How did those go?"

Doc stood wearily. "We learned several things from the corpses themselves, and even more from the hospital," she said.

* * * * *

WHEN THE ASSISTANT coroner and crime scene technicians had arrived, Six had ordered Doc to ride with the corpses and had informed her that she would handle the autopsies herself. He had sent Boomer along as a backup, in case any was needed.

Doc had supervised the handling of the two deceased creatures and had stood with the bodies until they had been packed into the ambulance for the short ride to the morgue in the basement of the hospital. Boomer had climbed into the passenger seat with the driver while her partner had ridden with the techs in the back of the transport.

When they had reached the hospital, the body bags had been wheeled down into the morgue, and the bags had been placed on the exam tables in preparation of the coroner's autopsy. When Bill, dressed in an exam gown and a surgical mask, had approached the tables, Doc had held out a hand to stop him.

"Bill, I am officially relieving you of the autopsy of these remains," Doc had insisted. "Unfortunately, you don't have the Top Secret Clearance required to perform the autopsies. As you know, I'm a board-certified medical doctor, and I will handle the post-mortem. In fact, I cannot even have you in the room with me while I do the autopsies," she had said.

"Are you kidding me?" Doctor Stewart had let the outrage seep into his voice. "You can't keep me out of my own lab! State law says that you have to be a certified Medical Examiner to perform an autopsy. You don't have the qualifications."

Doc had withdrawn her credentials from an inner pocket. She had opened them up and shoved them into Stewart's face. Her voice was cold and calm as she had said, "This is my authorization. This is officially a Department of Homeland Security operation and is currently classified Top Secret. You do not have the clearance. Period. Now get out before I throw you out."

Doctor Stewart had sneered and stepped closer, his bulk menacing the agent. "You couldn't throw me out if you tried," he had growled.

There had been a loud mechanical "snick-snack" of the slide on a pump shotgun racking that had echoed in the room. Bill had turned to see Doc's partner. Her shotgun had been raised, but not quite pointed, in Stewart's direction.

"Doctor Stewart. You will leave the labs to Doctor Sorenson," Boomer's voice had come out cold and hard. "Right now you are treading on very thin ice. If I think that you are actually threatening my partner with physical violence, I will end you. Are we clear?"

Stewart had gulped audibly. He had nervously rung his hands and had started stuttering and stammering an apology. Turning quickly, he went to his office to grab his jacket and phone and then left the lab.

Doc had looked at her partner and said, "I do believe we no longer have a friend in this office. Thanks for the back-up."

Boomer had smiled and put the shotgun on safe, slinging it across her shoulder. "No problem. Guy was a creep before this started. I'm going to go wander through his office," she had replied.

He partner had nodded in agreement. "Before you go, can you help me drag the bodies out of these bags? I want to work on these creatures."

The two women had wrestled the cadavers out of their body bags and had prepped them on the exam tables. As Doc had begun to slice into them with her scalpel, her partner had wandered into the office to snoop around.

About four hours later, the weary priest had removed the mask from her face and called for Boomer. "Can you come help me?" She had asked. "I want to bag these things up and get them over to the crematorium before our good doctor gets wise."

They had placed the bodies back into the body bags, and each had grabbed a gurney, wheeling them around the corner to the crematory. As they had entered the section, there was a lone technician waiting behind a desk. He had looked up, puzzled at the unexpected intrusion.

Doc, still dressed in her surgical cover gown, had been the first to speak. "I've got two here that need your services ASAP."

The technician had shaken his head. "No ma'am. There is

nothing scheduled. Do you have the correct paperwork? I don't think I've ever seen you around here before."

Doc had shaken her head, and the two agents had pulled out their credentials. The team's priest had spoken up. "Special Agent Noelle Sorenson, Department of Homeland Security. This credential here is my authorization. I will sign any paperwork you need me to sign, but you will fire up the furnaces. Now."

The face of the technician had gone pale, and the eyes had become slightly glassy for a moment. Then his eyes cleared, and he had said, "I don't like it, and you will need to fill out all kinds of paperwork. But you can do that while the furnace is working."

As the technician had walked away, Doc had seen a faint blue glow rising from her credentials in the dimly lit lab. It was so faint that she would never have noticed it in a well-lit room, and the glow had faded to nothing as she watched. *I must ask Agent Smith about this later*, she thought.

The technician had sat behind his console and had typed a series of instructions into the computer. Doc and Boomer had stacked both bodies onto the conveyor belt that fed into the furnace and had closed the massive door.

They both had heard a "click" and a "whoosh" as the natural gas furnace inside lit fully. Soon the furnace itself was at 1800 degrees, and the inner chamber door had opened, allowing the bodies to be shifted into the furnace. Ninety minutes later, with the monstrous bodies turned to ash, the female agents had walked out of the hospital and had hitched a ride in a police cruiser to head back over to the hotel.

* * * * *

AS DOC FINISHED HER RECOUNTING, Ghost spoke up. "Revenants. They were revenants, weren't they?"

She nodded at Ghost, then turned to Six. "Ghost is right. They were revenants."

The team leader spoke up. "Ok, so, other than having to put a ton of bullets into them, how do we kill these... revenants?"

Doc sighed and opened up her small leather book. "As I mentioned before," she began. "Revenants are basically a cross between a familiar and a zombie with some vampire speed and strength built in. Revenants have been traditionally used to guard the vampire nests during the day as well as enforcers to keep those in its nest in line. They are fast, hungry, vicious, and fiercely loyal to their master."

"When a traditional vampire 'turns' or infects a human, they can either turn them into a vampire or into a revenant. When a recently infected vampire tries to turn someone else, the result is almost always a revenant. Newly minted bloodsuckers don't have the control and willpower to create a true vampire yet."

Spooky raised his hand, and the priest nodded at him. "Doc, if these things are as loyal and obedient as you say, then they were set loose by the vampire to purposely terrorize the town, correct?"

Doc wearily nodded, her exhaustion was evident. "That would be my guess. It is the explanation that makes the most sense."

"So again, Doc. How do we kill 'em?" Six chimed in. "And can they be cured?"

The vampire specialist consulted the pages of her book.

"No, they cannot be cured." Doc continued to read from the little book. "Unlike vampires, the changes are irreversible. As for killing them? They are designed to take a lot of punishment. Like zombies, hits to the head will work and explosives will work as well. Like zombies, they do not receive pain from the nerve endings in their skin, so burning them, or using a baseball bat, will not work."

"On the up side, they are not technically undead, so they are mortal. Do enough damage to the heart or brain, and they will die. Think of them as if they were doped up on extreme PCP. Hard to stop, but they still have to have a heart and brain to live. They are also not 'contagious;' a bite will hurt, but you will not become a revenant. Although their saliva tends to be teeming with filth and decay, so you will probably get a nasty infection. Any other questions?"

Heavy looked up. "Will the special ammo do anything to them?" he asked.

Doc shook her head. "No, Heavy. Other than normal bullet damage, the silver ammunition is designed specifically for vampires." The priest looked around.

Agent Smith's voice rose from the phone in the center of the table. "Thank you, Doctor Sorenson. We'll add this information to our database. Would you be so kind as to forward your autopsy notes when you get a chance?"

"I'll send them as soon as I can," Doc replied. "If you need any more information about revenants, you might want to contact the Vatican as well; they have better records available."

Agent Smith paused momentarily. "Thank you, Doctor," he continued. "I'll have Timothy make the call. Back to the problem at hand. It's obvious that there are at least a few more vampires and some of their minions in the area. I've sent a re-supply of ammo for you. The helicopter should be there shortly. So what is your next step, Agent Holstein?"

Six looked around the table. He sighed and said, "At this point, sir, we're going to be combing through our data for any patterns. I've got Spooky working on the UAV and any other sensors we've got. Can you task us a satellite or two for extra coverage? Is there any way we can get some reinforcements for this?"

Agent Smith paused and then spoke again. "I've already tasked one of the NSA's KH-12 satellites to you. Spooky, you... now have access to the satellite in real time. It should be in geosyncronous orbit overhead in about ninety minutes. Unfortunately, I don't have any reinforcements to send you. This is code-word Top Secret, and you need to do your best to keep your actual mission and targets under wraps. You've already raised a big enough stink that we're working overtime to keep the President from noticing. So you can't get any of the locals to help, either."

Spooky spoke up. "Agent Smith? Any response to the requested vehicle specs that I sent? Any chance we can get that before the op is over?" he asked.

Six looked at his youngest agent and mouthed, *Vehicle specs?*

"Yes, John," Smith replied. "I approved the load out. Norbert's currently working on the specs now, and we should have it ready in a couple of days. I'll have it flown out to you, if you are still there when it's done. If there's nothing else, I'll let you get back to work. Keep up the good work."

As Agent Smith broke the connection, Six looked at Spooky. "What did you order?" he asked.

The young agent looked too smug for anyone's comfort. He could not keep the mischievous tone out of his voice. "I thought about ways to upgrade the War Wagon. Sounds like version two will be here soon."

Six turned his head as someone knocked on the door, and the team leader asked them to enter.

The assistant police chief of Trinidad was standing in the doorway. "Agent Holstein? We have a really weird situation, and I think it should be brought to your attention."

The lead DHS agent nodded and motioned for the man to come into the room fully.. "Come on in. What's up?"

"Trinidad only has two pharmacies in town, one in the hospital, and one new chain across town," the assistant chief explained. "The head pharmacist at the hospital has not showed up for work for almost two weeks. I've known Virgil for twenty years, and he almost missed his kid's birth because he was at work."

"Originally, he asked for a week off for vacation. At the end of that week, he began calling in 'sick.' Every day, for the last six days, he has called in sick at 8:45am on the dot. Today, he failed to call in."

The agents exchanged questioning glances as Six took notes.

The assistant chief continued, "The hospital's HR gal said she called him today when he did not show up or call. She said he answered the phone, but when she asked him if he was coming in to work, he started 'giggling.' That was the word she used, 'giggling.' Virgil hasn't giggled since he was three. Instead of sending one of my men up to his house, I thought I might give this to you guys. Is this something you want to check out?"

Six looked around at the team, then back to the officer. "Absolutely. This sounds like something I'd rather have us handle. What's the doctor's name and address?"

The assistant chief consulted his notebook. "Virgil Templeton." He rattled off the address. "Virgil lives at the top of one of the low foothills. He's the only one on the crest. It's a large hacienda-style ranch with an inner courtyard. He's a shorter guy, about five foot two, and is real skinny. He is sixty-three, according to records, and is bald on top with a white mustache. Are you going to want any of my people or sheriff deputies to go with you?"

"No thanks, chief," Six shook his head and replied. "We'll handle this one solo. Just keep the perimeter to this building secure as we instructed. The HRT will check around here in town, and we'll follow up with Mr. Templeton. I'll let you know how it goes."

As the assistant chief left, Six looked at the team. "It looks like we've caught a break. Doc, any idea what's going on with the pharmacist?"

The priest thought for a moment and then said, "Either he's now a familiar or he's been turned. No telling until we see him."

"All right." Six was planning and making decisions on the fly. "We will assume that there is a nest up there. Full combat gear. Spooky, when we get satellite coverage, point it at the house. Until then, get the UAV up and overhead. We've got ninety minutes until satellite coverage, so Doc and Boomer, you guys hit the sack. Take a power nap."

They all turned as they heard the loud rotors of a very large helicopter. Six motioned for Heavy and God to go meet the chopper for the resupply. He then turned to Ghost. "All right, monster hunter. What else can you tell me to help us prepare?"

Heavy and God ran outside and looked up. Instead of a Black Hawk helicopter, they saw a large airplane with rotors on the wingtips and an extended ramp down the back. As the aircraft settled on its landing wheels, the two agents ducked and ran toward the plane. The cargo master was placing the last of four large duffels on the end of the ramp.

Each of the agents grabbed two and hurried back toward the ops center. As they walked, they both heard the roar of the propellers increasing. Turning, they watched the V-22 Osprey virtually leap into the air and climb quickly into the clouds. Walking toward the War Wagon, they saw that the rear hatch was down, and Spooky was inside at the controls of the ever-present drone.

The two men set the bags down and opened them. Inside were multiple cans of linked ammunition for Heavy's machine gun and forty loaded magazines for the team's M4s and multiple magazines for the team's pistols. Digging, God was happy to also find several magazines of ammunition for his sniper rifle and several boxes of Norbert's special 12GA ammunition for Boomer's shotgun.

The heavy gunner was grinning and laughing. "Gee, it seems like Christmas came early this year! Now we can go hunting!" he exclaimed.

"Seems more like Halloween to me, but whatever." The sniper flashed a grin.

Ninety-three minutes later, the team finally got complete satellite coverage over the area. They gathered around the electronics specialist's screens as the agent pointed out the layout of the house.

"Can you show us thermal on this thing?" Six asked.

"Not for this house," Spooky replied. "It has a clay tile roof. That clay has absorbed the sun all day and is radiating that heat right now."

Six studied the house and the surrounding area intently. "Ok, team, here is the plan..."

19

GIGGLES

Foothills East of Trinidad, Colorado.

T he War Wagon sat idling on the side of the road in the late afternoon sun. Just around the next hill was the half-mile long, winding driveway that led to the pharmacist's house. Six was reviewing the plan with his team.

The team leader pointed to the various members of his team. "Spooky, you are going to drive us up to the front drive. God, you're up through the roof hatch; I recommend the M4 this time... I want you in on close support with the team. Doc, you and Boomer are in the back, waiting to jump out as soon as Spooky stops. Heavy, Ghost, and I will be on the outside rails, hanging on and providing cover."

"When we get to the house, we are all going to rapidly dismount and go through the front doors. Heavy has the ram. God, you are still up on the MRAP until we're inside and then I want you on the roof."

"Once the doors are breached, Heavy, Boomer, and Doc cover right, Ghost and I cover left, and we assess what we have. Do not engage if it's just a crazy old man. If there are any creatures, weapons are hot. Anyone have questions?"

Everyone shook their heads. Six nodded and said, "All right then, let's mount up."

God popped the roof hatch and stood up through the hatch.

Six, Heavy, and Ghost all climbed out the rear hatch and up onto the side mounts of the massive truck. Boomer closed the back hatch and keyed her mic. "Six, Boomer. All set inside."

Six's reply was immediate: "Spooky, proceed."

As the War Wagon approached the pharmacist's driveway at the bottom of the hill, Spooky looked back and noticed one of the sheriff department's cruisers with no lights on following them at a distance..

Spooky keyed his mic. "Six, Spooky. We have a local sheriff following us. What do you want me to do?"

Six turned around and looked toward the road behind them and saw the cruiser hanging back about five hundred feet, traveling as slowly as the MRAP.

"Spooky, Six. Stop the truck in the driveway's entrance. I'll deal with the occupants. Heavy, Ghost, watch around us. This may be a distraction. God, you cover me as I approach."

Spooky stopped the truck at the end of the driveway. Six hopped off and waved the police car forward while God provided cover.

The sheriff's car pulled up, and a young deputy got out. The team leader realized it was the same young deputy whose family had been killed the night before. Even though it had been less than twelve hours since their investigation, the kid looked like he hadn't slept in days. The bags under his eyes and his rumpled uniform told the tale of his loss and suffering.

Raising his fist to halt everyone, Six carefully walked toward the deputy. In a low voice, the veteran leader growled, "What are you doing here, deputy? You need to leave right now. You are interfering with a federal investigation, and I'm not in the mood to deal with any shit."

The young deputy defiantly raised his chin. "If the SOBs that killed my wife are holed up here, I want in on the raid. I deserve that."

Six muttered under his breath about foolish sacrifices and shook his head. "Look, I'm sorry about your family, but you deserve to live. Let us handle this. Get out of here while you still can."

"I have nothing left. I'm going in there with you, or behind you. Your choice," the deputy said as he crossed his arms and stood tall.

Six changed tactics. The DHS leader looked at the deputy and glanced pointedly at his pistol. "What are you going to use? Just your sidearm?"

The deputy walked around and popped the trunk of his cruiser. He reached in and pulled out an AR-15, the civilian model of the

M4 carbine that Six was carrying. He loaded a magazine and pulled the charging handle to chamber a round.

Realizing the deputy would cause trouble on his own, Six reached into his pocket for his credentials. "I tried to warn you, kid." He flashed his credentials in the deputy's face. "I am Agent Burt Holstein from the Department of Homeland Security. This is a Top Secret-code word operation. You are hereby seconded to the operation and must forever keep your damn mouth shut. Do you understand?"

The deputy's eyes glazed over for a second, then cleared. "I understand," the deputy said. A look of confusion briefly crossed the deputy's face, and he shook his head slowly. "What did you just do to me?"

Six ignored the question, and instead, said, "Hand me your AR." The slightly confused deputy gave it to the federal agent.

The veteran agent released the magazine and pulled the charging chamber as he cycled the round out of the chamber. He reached into the pouch on his side and grabbed three magazines. One of them went into the magazine well of the deputy's AR. Six then pulled the handle again as he loaded a new round. He handed the two spare magazines to the deputy. "Your ammunition was worthless. This new ammo will actually work on the target."

Accepting the rifle back from the DHS leader, the deputy asked, "What are we doing at Virgil's house, sir?" The young deputy was curious about all the firepower needed to take down a kindly old pharmacist.

"We're actually not sure yet, Deputy... Folsom is it?" The deputy nodded. "In fact, I think I can use your help with this. I want you to knock on the doctor's door. See if you can get him to come to the front door so we don't have to kick it in."

"Now park your car across the driveway to block access. Once you are done, climb up next to Heavy there. You'll ride with us up the hill. You follow my orders. You do what you're told. And maybe, just maybe, you get to keep your soul."

The young deputy smiled at the words, then realized that the dour agent was not kidding. He quickly pulled his car forward to block the end of the driveway. The deputy turned on his overhead light bar, locked the patrol car, and clipped the keys to his belt.

Folsom looked shaken as he clambered up the side of the MRAP. He tightened his grip on his rifle. No matter what happened to him, as long as he took out the monsters that took his wife and children, he was sure he would find peace.

Six climbed aboard and told Spooky to move out. Spooky slowly maneuvered the massive armored vehicle up the winding drive. When they pulled to a halt at the house, they all dismounted and staged by the door.

Six keyed his mic again. "Spooky, Six. Any change in the house or courtyard?"

"Negative, bossman. Looks like we're clear," answered Spooky.

"Great. Launch the drone and keep an eye on the satellite feed. You're our eyes tonight, Spooky. Back us up."

Six motioned toward the front of the house, and the deputy nodded. He walked toward the front doors. The rest of the team looked at their leader as if he were stupid for letting the deputy, of all people, simply stroll up to the house. Six shrugged, "He's now one of us, at least temporarily. Try not to let him get killed."

The deputy rang the doorbell. A deep booming gong sounded throughout the house. He then knocked on the door and heard his loud raps echo throughout the seemingly empty house. Two more cycles of the doorbell and knocking finally brought a voice to the door.

An old man's weak and sickly voice spoke softly through the doors, and a short shadow of a man could be seen through the frosted glass inserts. "Yes? Who is it? What do you want?"

"Virgil? It's me, Christian Folsom," the deputy responded. "You've known me all my life. Can you come out here and talk to me please?"

The old man's voice seemed even shakier now. "Christian? Why are you up visiting me? Is something wrong at the hospital?"

"Yes, Virgil. It's Deputy Folsom. I would really appreciate it if you would come out to talk to me. Can you open the door a little so I can see that you are ok? Some of us are getting worried about you, Virgil."

But then the voice behind the door suddenly changed.

"Hee, hee." Virgil childishly giggled. "Why would I come out there? I don't think your 'friends' want to talk to me... I think they want to hurt me."

The voice erupted in a fit of giggles.

"Virgil! Open up," Folsom demanded as he pounded on the door. "I don't want to have to come in there! Just come out and talk to us. Please?"

The giggling grew maniacal and then slightly calmed.

When the voice spoke again, it was deeper than it had been in years. "Why don't you come in, boy? Invite your friends, too. I think they'll enjoy it here."

God looked down from the roof of the MRAP and spotted shadows moving behind the windows across the front of the house. "Six, God. I've got movement behind the doors. Multiple shadows. And I see movement in many of the windows. He's not alone in there."

Six reached out and grabbed the back of Deputy Folsom's vest, yanking him back off the porch. Six nodded to Heavy, and the big man lifted the battering ram. All the team members raised their weapons as Heavy brought the ram forward and smashed open the front doors, right at the jamb. Glass and wood splintered and flew inward, closely followed by the front doors themselves. Standing in the doorway was a creature who used to be Virgil Templeton, giggling hysterically and holding a beautiful, old, double-barrel shotgun whose barrels looked like cannons to Six as he stared straight down the bores.

Six and Virgil opened fire at the same time; the rest of the team followed closely their shots. Six placed two shots dead center of the chest, and the muzzle of his gun began to climb toward Virgil's head. The twin loads of double-ought buckshot scattered as they left the ends of the barrel. Unfortunately for Virgil, the old man's aim wasn't quite so perfect, sending both loads of shot right between Heavy and Six. One of the pellets hit the armor on Six's shoulder and bounced away, slightly rocking the DHS leader on his heels. The rest entirely missed their targets.

Behind Six, Ghost brought his rifle up to his shoulder and pulled the trigger twice. Both of the shots scored solid hits in the torso before his follow-up shots climbed over Virgil's head. Boomer stroked the trigger of her shotgun, sending the three-quarters-of-an-inch-wide slug of silver and wood into the heart cavity. All the metal flying through the chest of Virgil ripped through and tore larger holes out of his back. The second shot from Boomer's shotgun put the silver and wood slug through Virgil's face.

As Heavy brought his SAW up to aim ahead of him, Deputy Folsom stood there, open-mouthed, with shock while he tried to comprehend the violence he had just witnessed. The team moved past him, fanning out left and right to cover their entrance. The deputy gave a strangled cry when the body of the man he had known all his life began to dissolve into wisps of smoke.

"God, Six. Go to the roof," Six said after keying his mic.

The area to Six's left opened into a very large living area with a fireplace. He barely had time to notice the fine leather furniture as a revenant screamed around the corner. Following the screaming creature was what appeared to be a human wielding a fireplace poker.

Six and Ghost targeted the gray-skinned revenant at the same time, squeezing off rounds in the chaos. Multiple rounds walked up his torso with the final four missing their marks over the creature's shoulders. The creature stopped and looked down, screamed, and ran again. Boomer stepped between the two men and raised her shotgun. She stroked the trigger twice, pumping the slide on her shotgun between shots.

Her first shot hit the revenant in the upper chest, leaving a very large hole, and momentarily stunning the creature. The second hit the creature's nose. The corpse fell as if poleaxed as the contents of its skull hit the wall with a sickening "plop."

Six shifted his aim and squeezed the trigger. He fired two rounds into the chest of the familiar, causing the target to explode. Ghost squeezed the trigger once; his M4 shot a three-round burst of bullets. He watched as two of the rounds went wide with the third finally connecting with the man's head. The round exited the man's skull in a furious explosion as it plastered gore on the furniture scattered around the living room.

Deputy Folsom had watched in horror as the DHS agents calmly shot and killed an old pharmacist that he had known his entire life. He had watched a body disappear into thin air. And he had even watched the leader and two of the other team members open fire on a creature that seemed straight out of a horror movie. *It took two rifles and a shotgun to bring down just the one creature!* He marveled to himself. But when he tried to wrap his head around how the team had gunned down Stevie Nelson, a man whom he played football with in high school, it was too much to comprehend. Deputy Folsom froze, waiting for his brain to come up with a logical explanation of what his senses were telling him.

Six and Ghost moved toward the open living room area according to their plan, and Heavy, Boomer, and Doc shifted the opposite direction. They entered a modern marble and granite kitchen wrapped around the corner toward the back of the house. Scrambling over the island was another revenant with crazed hunger in its eyes and screams of defiance oozing from its mouth. Behind the creature, another revenant with the rough gray skin and a human familiar scrambled toward the team.

Heavy and Boomer pulled the trigger at the same time. The shotgun and the burp of the machine gun mingled in the air as the revenant was thrown back across the granite island, disappearing out of sight behind the island. Heavy shifted his aim toward the other revenant. Pulling the trigger twice, the heavy gunner braced himself as his machine gun spat two bursts of fire. Each burst chewed over the chest area, leaving many gaping wounds in the revenants shredded torso and causing it to stop momentarily. Before the beast could recover completely, Heavy twitched his finger twice more, sending two more bursts into the figure. The final burst climbed through the creature's shoulder, with the final two rounds striking the head and ending the creature's miserable life.

Boomer was suddenly aware that the human familiar running toward her was a young teenage girl, maybe fifteen or sixteen years old. Her black hair and olive skin spoke of her Native American heritage, but her wild eyes and unintelligible howls spoke of her status as their next target. She hesitated long enough to have the girl close the distance before Boomer could pull the trigger.

The demolitions expert regained her bearings in time to raise her shotgun across her body to stop the young girl's thrust with the carving knife she was wielding. As the girl tried to slash and stab Boomer, the agent was driven backwards. Boomer collided with the stainless steel doors of the refrigerator. While the teenager had the ferocity granted by her insanity and devotion to her master, Boomer had sheer physical muscle mass coupled with panic-driven reactions. Heaving forward, the explosives expert used her momentum and threw the girl across the kitchen to collide with the island in the middle. The familiar bounded to her feet, and as the girl came at her again, Boomer treated her shotgun as a short club and knocked the teenager across the head with the butt of the stock. The girl crashed to the floor, sliding into the cabinet base hard enough to elicit a "crack" as her head connected to the hardwoods. Judging from the angle of the girl's neck, Boomer was certain that the familiar would never fight again.

Doc approached the kitchen and knelt at the girl's side to feel for a pulse. Shaking her head at Boomer, her sorrow turned to surprise as she yelled out a warning. Boomer and Heavy spun around and watched the revenant they first shot climb up over the island and spring toward them again. Although the creature was much slower this time, it was still growling and angrily snapping at them. Boomer casually raised her shotgun and stroked the trigger. The three-quarter-inch slug took the creatures head off, with the fragmented skull disappearing just above the eye sockets. As Boomer reloaded her shotgun, the three agents looked at the ceiling. They heard footsteps running across the roof, and then they heard gunfire.

God leapt from the top of the War Wagon and landed on the roof, rolling with the jump and coming to his knees easily. He carefully looked across the flat, tiled roof, only detecting roof vents and tiles. He noticed an open-air courtyard in the middle. Walking to the edge, he looked down into an overgrown courtyard and spied a large pair of cellar doors in the middle. Across the courtyard, he could see windows and glass doors on the other three sides of the courtyard. Looking through one set of doors, he could see two men armed with shotguns standing and waiting in ambush for his teammates.

He quickly raised his rifle to his shoulder and aimed through the scope at the first one and paused to steady his aim. He settled the crosshairs over the front man's head and squeezed the trigger. His rifle barked, and the window's pane spidered from a neat hole near the gentleman's head. As the man crumpled, the sniper swung to the second man, who was looking at his partner and the large pool of blood forming around the body. God watched as the man began to turn toward the window, and the agent pulled the trigger again. Just like the hunter who leads the moving deer to make his shot, the sniper gave a brief lead on where he believed the target's head would end up, and he was correct. The man's head intersected with the trajectory of the bullet in mid-flight, and the second ambusher crumpled to the ground as the glass door exploded inward.

Six leaned around the corner just in time to see the glass door disintegrate and the second lifeless body crumple to the ground.

"Thanks, God. Good shooting," Six said after he keyed his mic.

"That's why I'm here," the sniper quipped back.

Six motioned for Ghost to move forward as they carefully walked through the living room toward a long hallway with several doors. He watched as his sniper dropped into the courtyard and then brought his attention back toward the hallway. Motioning for Ghost to cover him, Six opened the door and swung around the corner as he rapidly scanned the bedroom for hostile targets. "Clear" he muttered so that Ghost could hear him.

He moved to the next door. Again, the bedroom was clear.

Across from that bedroom was another room, used as an office, and it, too, was clear.

The next door revealed a very large and luxurious bathroom with a second exit door. Moving through the bathroom, the two federal agents approached the door. Throwing open the door, they moved into the very spacious master bedroom. When they heard a slight noise behind a door straight ahead, they both raised their guns. Six motioned for his second-in-command to open the door as he covered it with his rifle.

As Ghost reached for the knob, the door slammed outward and a piercing screech filled the room as a small creature virtually flew out of the closet. The little girl looked to be no more than ten or eleven, but the rows of vicious teeth and the blood red eyes said she was no longer human. Six pulled the trigger, catching the creature in mid-air as it leapt toward his face. The two rounds in the chest burned the creature severely as her face twisted into a contortion of pain. The third round ended the creature's suffering as it traveled through the bridge of her nose and into the creature's brain. Her body crashed to the ground just short of Six. Ghost stepped forward and drew his machete. The silver inlaid runes on the blade glowed a bright white as he brought the large knife down across the creature's neck and severed the head of the young vamp.

Ghost flicked the black ichor from the blade and sheathed his machete, grabbing his rifle again. Both men walked back through the bedroom and hallway and made their way carefully to the other side of the house to meet with their team.

Heavy, Boomer, and Doc worked their way toward the back of the house. As they walked through the dining room, they heard another howl. They quickly spun around in time to see a creature with bright red eyes leaping at them. The creature was faster than the revenants, and it was between the agents before they could fire. The vampire backhanded Boomer, and she flew across the dining room and crashed into the wall with a thud. The creature then grabbed Heavy's machine gun and smacked at it, ripping it from the agent's hands.

A bright blue glow suddenly lit the air as Doc spoke in Latin and held her cross in front of her. The light was blinding to the creature, and it cringed away from the priest, covering its eyes with its forearms. Heavy reached up and drew the massive fighting blades from the sheaths on his back. As they cleared the leather, both blades glowed a ghostly green along their razor-sharp edges. The heavy weapons specialist swung mightily, bringing the blades toward each other. Unerringly, the blades sought the vampire's neck. The blades came together in a mighty clash, cleaving through the upraised shoulders and arms meant to ward off the light from the cross, and completely severing the head of the vamp. The head dropped to the floor alongside the severed arms, which were already beginning to dissolve into mist.

Heavy stared down at the ancient khukuri as the glow began to fade from their clean edges. Transfixed, he muttered, "Huh. I didn't know they did that."

Doc looked up at his hulking form. "What, nobody ever told you they were enchanted? Come on. We've got the rest of the house to clear."

The priest walked over to Boomer as she slowly got to her feet. "Anything broken, any injuries? You good to move on?"

The demolitions specialist looked back. "No problem, Doc. Just knocked the wind out of me. Damn things are fast." Boomer bent down to pick up her shotgun.

The three agents worked together and cleared the bathroom and hallway leading to the back porch.

Heavy clicked his mic. "Six, Heavy. This side is clear, we're coming back to the front of the house."

"Roger, Heavy. We'll meet you on the porch," replied Six.

The team gathered at the front entrance where the deputy was still standing. He was finally coming to his senses and was realizing that he was in way over his head. Six walked up to him and said, "You ok? You just kind of freaked out on us. Are you sure you don't want out?"

Deputy Folsom shook his head. "Sorry. I'm still having trouble dealing with monsters in town. I knew these people." He pointed to the first familiar that the DHS leader and his second had killed. "I played football with Stevie in high school. What the hell do you people do?"

Six chuckled at the inadvertent joke. "Yeah. That about sums it up. We still have a cellar to clear, are you with us?"

The deputy nodded his agreement.

Six keyed his radio and said, "Spooky, we're all clear in here. Anything coming out of that cellar?"

20

UNDERGROUND

Templeton House, Trinidad, Colorado.

"Ok, guys, I have a little thermal leakage from around the doors. That means that they are not sealed tightly. Nothing else on the satellite." Spooky announced over the radio.

"Copy that, Spooky," Six replied. He turned to address the team. "Ok, we have myself and Ghost on one side. Heavy and Boomer, pull on the other door. God and Doc should be at the opening so that they can shoot, or dispel, anything that comes out."

"This should be just a cellar, but it would make a perfect hiding place for any creatures during the day. We have not found the master yet, so we should expect him to be here. Any questions?"

No one had any questions.

The team leader continued his impromptu planning session. "If we go down in there, I will be on point. Doc will be next, flanked by Heavy and Ghost. Boomer and God, bring up the rear. Let's move out."

The team assembled in their assigned positions around the massive set of double doors, and the members on either side reached out to grab the handles. Each door was about nine feet tall, just over three feet wide, and seemed to be about two inches thick and made of solid steel. On "three," the teams pulled their assigned doors, straining with the effort that the solid doors appeared to require. Both doors flew open and sent all four team members sprawling. As Six looked up from the ground, he saw a system of pulleys and counterweights for the doors, and it looked as if one person could have lifted the doors easily. *We probably should've tried the doors first.*

With the doors now open, the team could see stairs descending into a dark cellar. These were no ordinary stairs; they were stone stairs cut into the bedrock beneath the doors. These stairs were worn and extended down into the earth about fifteen feet before they curved around a corner and led out of sight.

"Stairs," God called out to his teammates. "They go down and around a corner. Visible light. Clear." He stood with his rifle poised at his shoulder, waiting for the others to get in position.

The rest of the team scrambled back to their feet, each of them nursing bumps and bruises from the fall. They shouldered their weapons, and Six led the fire team into the cellar. About fifteen feet down, the worn stone stairs became broken stone stairs and curved around the corner. At the corner, the leader leaned around the angle, letting his rifle barrel lead the way. The stone walls became rough-hewn stone. The stairs eventually ended at a well-worn dirt floor, and the walls of the stairwell opened up to reveal a dark cavern.

Strung across the ceiling of the cavern was a series of wires, with a bare bulb hanging down about every twenty feet. The rough cavern walls ended about five feet to the left of the stairs, and the wall across was just over twenty feet away. To Six's right, the cavern stretched about thirty feet before curving out of sight to the left. The floor was relatively even and free of obstacles or debris; however, thin stalactites tightly clung to the ceiling approximately ten feet overhead. The floor was packed hard from what could only be years of use, and bare bedrock rose up through the hard earth, creating small pockets of stone flooring.

As the team maneuvered through the cave, they spread out behind Six. They rounded the corner, and the corridor opened up into another cavern. Across from the team, Six noticed a smaller passage leading off into darkness. To the left the cavern was deep and had a large stone formation that blocked his view of the end of the cavern.

Six, Boomer, and the rest of the team heard melodic plops and drips of water at the other end of the dimly lit cavern. They froze when a growl interrupted their footsteps. With a raised fist, Six signaled the team to halt. The growling appeared to be coming from the other side of the rock formation. As Six stepped to his left, Ghost and Heavy stepped to the right and aimed around the large block of bedrock. The others stepped out from the passage and took their positions.

Around the formation roared three revenants, their jaws open in eager anticipation. The creatures had almost reached the agents when the team opened fire. Six fired at the creature on the far left, in between the rock formation and the wall of the cavern. Boomer joined in; she pulled the trigger on her shotgun and worked the pump as fast as she could. A combination of high-powered rifle rounds and shotgun slugs nearly tore the creature in two. The revenant was still vainly trying to crawl toward them when the team leader aimed and shot the creature between the eyes.

Ghost and God opened up on the revenant on the other side of the rock formation. As the sniper calmly and methodically walked his rounds up from chest to head, the esoteric hunter peppered the creature with rounds to its chest and abdomen. When God finally put his fourth round into the head of the creature, Ghost ran his rifle empty and switched to a full magazine. The lifeless creature fell at the feet of the two shooters.

The former HRT operator looked at the hunter and said, "Next time, try aiming."

Ghost sheepishly returned God's grin.

The remaining revenant leapt for the heavy gunner. Two bursts of machine gun fire drove the creature back and left it dazed. Deputy Folsom aimed his rifle at the creature and squeezed the trigger twice. The first shot took the creature in the chest; the second shot hit the creature between its eyes. In the back of his mind, he thought he recognized the contorted features of Mrs. Marshall, his high school English teacher. He could not help but to take in the crazed eyes and the mouthful of sharp teeth for later... he knew he'd see them again in his nightmares. He thought he saw the body stir one more time, and he resolutely walked over and shot a point-blank round through the Mrs. Marshall's forehead.

The cavern echoed with the sound of automatic gunfire.

"Well, they know we're coming now," Six said as the echoes subsided. "Everyone be prepared."

As they moved into the center of the cavern, they noticed a pool of water at the far. As they got closer to the pool, they could see that it was very shallow and crystal clear.

After studying the pool for a few moments, Six concluded that the pool of water must be coming from underneath the wall.

He looked at Doc curiously. "Do you think you could summon up enough prayer to make that puddle Holy Water?"

She pondered the small pond briefly and then shrugged. "I can try."

She walked forward, and the others moved to create a defensive perimeter around her. She bent down and slowly began a chant in Latin. Closing her eyes, Doc prayed, asking the Spirit of Christ to bless the water and to make it Holy.

"That should do it," she responded a short time later.

Six nodded and smiled. "Let's move on," he said.

The agent led the team toward the smaller passage Six spotted earlier. A short led them into another cavern. Approximately the same size as the previous cavern, the walls were rougher. They had almost a hand-carved look, and there were two other exits from this cavern. As the team entered, Six noticed a large misshapen hole in the cavern floor. Large enough to fit a compact car into, the hole was pitch black just below the surface of the hole, and all of them felt waves of malevolence coming from it.

God positioned himself over the small three-foot passage that led into the base of the cavern wall opposite from where they had entered. Heavy trained his machine gun on the passage at the other end of the cavern. Six, Doc, and Ghost walked closer to the dark hole in the floor. When Six shined his flashlight across the surface, he could not see any deeper than the edge as the light seemed to be absorbed at the very surface of the darkness. Ghost took a chemlight from his vest pocket and broke it to mix the chemicals. He tossed it into the middle of the darkness, and the inky black seemed to swallow the fluorescent tube whole. The darkness rippled where the chemstick had entered the surface.

Six looked at Doc and asked, "Is it me, or did that darkness actually... ripple?" The team leader was at a loss. "What the hell is that stuff?"

The priest calmly looked at her boss. "To paraphrase your answer to Deputy Folsom earlier, I believe you have answered your own question." After a pause, she continued, "It is Evil." The team heard the capital "E" in Doc's voice. "I believe this is a hellgate, and it is something that we do not have the ability or desire to deal with now."

Just then, the sniper behind them let out a yelp. They turned to look and saw him backing away from the hole he was guarding. A low growl could be heard coming from the hole.

Moments later, a large, bloated head and upper torso pulled itself out of the hole and clawed its way toward God. Trailing torn and bloody entrails behind as it crawled, the torso reached its desiccated hand for the team's sniper. God shook his head to clear it and aimed his rifle down at the creature's head. A single shot rang out, and the bloated head exploded, showering the area around the creature with gore. The agent wiped the tread of his boots on the rock to remove bits of brain matter from his shoes. He looked at the priest and raised an eyebrow.

Doc shrugged and said, "Zombie."

God shuddered. "Shall we toss a grenade in there to make sure nothing else is coming?"

Six shook his head. "We're in a cavern. It could collapse the whole thing. We'll let Boomer prep explosives and set a timer for our exit. All right, let's get moving."

At the far end of the cavern, the wide passageway sloped down and around to the right. There was a small pool of water on the left. Six looked at the water, and then at Doc, and cocked his eyebrows.

She leaned over the pool for a few seconds to study the water.

"It must be connected to the other," Doc announced. "This is already Holy."

Six nodded and led the team around the corner of the passageway. After a short passageway, they stepped out into a larger cavern. The wall across from them was almost thirty feet away, and the cavern stretched half again that from sidewall to sidewall. At the far end there was another pool of water, and this one looked deeper and murkier. It also ran through the passage that was the only other exit to the cavern. The team spread out and approached the shore of the pond. As the team leader looked through the narrow passageway across from him, Six noticed that the water continued through the passage and that he could see another cavern at the end of the passage.

In what had become her routine, Doc stepped up and prayed in Latin over the pond of water. The team spread out around her, making sure she stayed safe during the ritual. Six noticed that her garments began to glow blue, and he suddenly realized that they hadn't checked the water beforehand.

The water exploded outward, and two creatures leapt out from the water. The vampires were smoldering and smoking, with parts of their flesh melting away as the pool of Holy Water began to take its toll. A screaming vampire landed on each side of the priest.

As Six shouted a warning, one of the creatures struck Boomer, knocking her twenty feet away and into the cavern wall. The other creature struck Heavy and sent his bulk flying.

Both creatures turned to look at Doc and hissed, "Priesssssssssst!"

She grabbed her crucifix and thrust it toward the vampire on her left. The ornate cross flared to life, its pure light driving the shadows from the cavern and pinning the vampire to the cavern floor. She shouted in Latin at the vampires, and both screamed in agony and pure hatred.

Six, God, and Ghost opened fire on the vampire on Doc's right. Through the melting, acid-burned features, the creature snarled as the men poured a stream of silver and wood bullets into its flesh. The creature's torso nearly split in two, and the barely connected lower half landed in the Holy Water pool. New agony hit the vampire until rounds from Six and God found its misshapen skull to end its agony.

The other vampire was pinned in place with the power of Doc's faith while the Holy Water melted and desiccated its flesh.

Deputy Folsom stepped up and took aim at the creature. His first two shots hit the chest dead center, tearing through the vampire and knocking it flat. His final shot was a carefully aimed shot through the skull. Black blood and gore exploded out and fell into the Holy Water, sizzling and melting into nothingness.

Boomer and Heavy climbed to their feet.

The big man winced and held his right arm tight to his chest. "I think it dislocated my shoulder. I can't lift it at all."

The priest stepped up to the Heavy and said, "Take off your armor. I need to feel your shoulder."

The giant man stripped his armor off while the rest of the team took up positions around the two, with Six, God, and Ghost watching the cavern through the next passage, and Boomer and Folsom watching the area behind them.

The team leader tried his radio. "Spooky, Six. Do you copy?"

When there was no response from Spooky, he tried again, "Spooky, come in. This is Six. Do you copy?"

Again, no response.

"Must be this cavern mucking up the signal," Six muttered out loud.

Doc looked at Heavy and said, "Brace yourself. This is going to suck."

She gave a yank and a twist, sliding the shoulder back into its natural socket with an audible "pop."

The heavy gunner let out a string of curses.

"Sorry, Doc. I try not to curse around you," Heavy said after the pain had subsided. "Arm feels right. I should be good to go."

"Don't worry about it," replied Doc. "We'll x-ray your shoulder when we get back to town."

Six looked at his gunner and said, "You and I need to talk. You taught me a few new choice invectives I've never heard before. All set?"

Heavy flexed and moved his arm. "I'm a bit stiff, but I should be good." He picked up and cradled his machine gun to prove the point.

Everyone took the time to change their magazines and prep for the next passage.

"Alright, boys and girls, it looks like we have to get wet. God, you are up for point; Ghost will follow. You guys go through first and provide cover while we come through."

The sniper looked at the water in front of him. He tentatively stepped into the cold water and waded forward. As he got about six feet from the water's edge, the water level stopped rising, and the water leveled out to about thigh-deep. The monster hunter walked in after him, keeping his rifle up and out of the water. As they walked through the passage, the cavern on the other side seemed smaller.

God keyed his mic. "This cavern's about twenty-five by thirty. Has one other exit. Standby while we look around the corner."

The two men approached the bend and slowly moved around it. The passage narrowed and doubled back and opened into a small six-by-ten cavern. Looking around the small cavern, the men concluded that there were no other exits and that the cavern was obviously empty.

God keyed his mic again. "Dead end boss. Nothing back here but a small cavern. We're at the end."

"Copy that," Six responded. "Come on back through. We'll bug out."

He leaned over to his demolitions specialist. "Boomer, make a small charge on a timer that we can toss into the zombie hole. Key word: small."

Boomer pouted her lips and said, "Sure. I finally get to blow something up and you make me be reasonable." She grumbled as she assembled the charge.

The two agents waded back across to the vampire cavern. The team slowly walked back the way they had come. When they reached the zombie hole, Boomer set the timer for two minutes and tossed a small charge into the hole.

"Do you want me to toss a charge into the evil pit, boss?" The explosives expert looked pleadingly at her boss.

"How about we not pick a fight with a hellspawn right now," Doc interjected. "We have a bad enough time with vampires."

After a brief pause to really comprehend what the priest had said, Six nodded. "Good call. Negative on the bomb into the pit, Boomer. Alright, let's keep moving back up top."

The team cautiously wound their way back to the surface. Carefully maneuvering through the passages, each team member was alert and looking for trouble. They double checked every nook and hidden corner carefully to make sure they were not leaving any creatures alive down there—neither living nor unliving.

As they reached the first cavern, they all heard a frantic radio call from a rather panicked young agent.

"... Calling Six. Come in, Six. Repeat. Spooky calling Six. Come in, Six."

"Spooky, this is Six," the DHS leader broke in. "We're back. There is an underground cave system here, and we lost communication. We're all fine. We're coming back up now."

"Copy that, Six." The team could hear the relief in their electronics specialist's voice. "Everything is still clear up here."

Heavy was the last man to leave the cave system. As he mounted the last couple of stairs, he heard a rather loud muffled roar. The rumble came through his combat boots.

"Did you all feel that?" he asked as he looked at the others. "Just how much C4 did you use, Boomer?"

"I swear. I only used a small amount," Boomer promised. "Unless something else in there exploded, we should not have been able to hear it."

A waft of dust rose from the cavern stairs.

The heavy gunner pointed to it and said, "We might want to talk about how much is 'a little'." He chuckled as he climbed the stairs.

Six closed the doors and keyed his mic again. "Spooky, do we have any chain and locks in the War Wagon?"

There was a slight pause before Spooky responded. "Have a little chain. I also have a small welding torch. Would that work?"

Ten minutes later, the team met by the back hatch of the MRAP. Heavy returned from the house carrying a small torch in his hand. "That door is chained shut, boss. I also welded the doors to each other and tack welded the outside seams. It would take a lot of work to get back down that hole."

"Great, Heavy. Sit down and rest your arm." Six looked at everyone else, including Spooky. "Ok, we need to tear this house apart. If it looks like a pertinent record, grab it. Spooky, you're on electronics. Don't worry about figuring out what's on them tonight. Just take the whole device, computer, etcetera. Check the garage. Check every nook and cranny thoroughly. I want every record. We need to find out what's going on in town."

"We will not be coming back to this location. We will burn the house down, and then DHS is seizing the land and everything on it. So grab every scrap, every note, and every bit of information. Pile it in the truck, and we'll sort it tomorrow."

Just over one hour later, the team had gathered every electronic device and bit of information in the house. From the deceased familiars' cell phones to the pharmacist's computer and tablet, everything that contained a microchip was stored carefully in the back of the truck. All the doctor's paper files were sorted in stacks on the ground outside. By the time the team had collected all of the information, the contents filled the back of the MRAP. There was only room inside for the driver and one passenger.

Spooky climbed up into the driver's seat, and Doc rode shotgun in the passenger's seat. The sniper climbed through the turret hatch on top and sat in what was becoming his usual perch. Boomer spread accelerant around the house to ensure a hot and fierce burning. After she set a small detonator, she climbed up on the truck. The rest of the team climbed onto the running boards outside of the MRAP for the short trip down the winding driveway. Spooky drove to the bottom of the hill and parked across the driveway to completely block access to the property.

Boomer's face lit up when she pressed the detonator. The sparkle in her eyes was soon reflected from the hillside as flames lapped at the interior of the house on the hill. Within thirty seconds, the entire structure was ablaze and Six could hear sirens coming from town. When the fire engines arrived, the DHS agent waved his badge and informed the trucks that they were only allowed to go up the drive to make sure that a wildfire did not result from the intense flames that had set the house ablaze. They were not, under any circumstance, allowed to extinguish the house fire.

Six sent Heavy and God up to the house with the firemen just to make sure the emergency crews let the blaze fully consume the house.

By three o'clock in the morning, the flames were out. The team rode back to the hotel to get some sleep before they would begin to tackle the mountain of information that was in the back of their War Wagon.

21

DO-RIGHT

Hotel, Trinidad, Colorado.

It was a cold, foggy morning when Spooky woke up to pounding on the ramp door. He stiffly climbed out of his chair in the War Wagon and walked to the back. As he looked out the gun port, he saw Six holding two cups of coffee in a cardboard drink carrier. The young agent unlocked the ramp and dropped it to the parking lot, raising dust as the ramp hit the pavement.

The lead agent climbed up the ramp and handed the coffee to the junior analyst. "Have you started working on anything yet?" Six inquired.

Spooky took a long drink of coffee. He finally spoke, "Ahh, the nectar of the gods. Normally, I'm an energy drink guy, but this is perfect. No, I haven't worked on anything we got last night."

He looked down at his wrist computer and said, "It looks like we've got some other information, though. When we found out that the pharmacist was involved, I asked HQ to run a telephone records dump and to correlate it to major activity, known friends, and a couple other parameters. It looks like they sent me a file."

Spooky walked over and dropped into his workstation seat. After only a few moments of typing, he soon brought up a document and displayed it on his main screen. The analyst looked it over carefully and pointed out interesting facts.

"Look there," Spooky said as he pointed to a telephone number in his document. "Our giggling vamp had never contacted this particular phone number until after the slaughter of the sheriff, mayor, and FBI guys." He gestured to another number and continued, "He also kept frequent contact with this hospital number."

Spooky bent over and typed furiously, muttering as he went. "Let's see... If we cross populate here... What if we looked at it this way? Oh, that's interesting!" Six could not keep up with whatever his specialist was doing between his dual monitors. The team leader finally gave up and sat back to savor his coffee. He figured that Spooky would let him know when he found something interesting. Six closed his eyes.

"That's IT!" Spooky's shout startled Six, and he spilled now-cold coffee over his hand. The agent was looking at him expectantly.

Six looked back at his electronics genius and said, "What do you have, Spooky?"

He turned and pointed at three phone numbers buried amidst the multitude of screens and windows. "This top one is the deputy mayor's number—her private office line. He's been making several calls a day to her since the massacre. According to her private schedule, he's also been in to see the now-acting Mayor Desiree Marshall three times. There isn't any reason for him to be talking to her quite that much, especially with no other history within the last three years."

He pointed at the other two highlighted numbers on his screen. "This top one goes to a specific line in the hospital. It just so happens that this one is the private office line of the county coroner, Bill Stewart. They talked occasionally before, but it ramped up all of a sudden after we took out that ambush."

Spooky sipped his now-cold coffee and then looked at the cup in disgust. He set the cup down and continued. "This one was harder to run down. It seems to be one of those burn phones. Unfortunately, for our quisling coroner, he didn't, in fact, throw it away. In fact, it's on and still broadcasting. We've traced it to the hospital, and it's most likely in the morgue with him. How stupid can you be to buy a throwaway phone and keep it? It seems like these are the only two people that are connected to the drug guy's vamp side."

The lead agent nodded and smiled. He clasped Spooky on the shoulder hard enough to make him wince. "Great work, Spooky," Six said. "We still need to process the rest of the information just to make sure we don't miss anything. We'll do that at the base ops. Until then, go take a shower and wake up. We'll need you in top form, and it's been a while since you've left that seat. I'll stay put until someone else comes out."

"Will do, boss," Spooky replied with a sheepish grin.

The young agent peeled himself back out of his chair and grabbed his clothing bag and opened the ramp. He walked down the ramp and brushed past Boomer as she headed toward the War Wagon to speak to Six.

* * * * *

TWO HOURS LATER, most of the team was in the conference room sorting through the mountains of paper and electronic data they had collected the night before. Spooky had his forensic computer tools running overtime and was merrily mining all the electronic data he could retrieve from the former pharmacist's phone and computer. Ghost, assisted by Heavy and Boomer, led the effort to gather any usable data from the paper files. Doc was on the phone with her Vatican contacts in an effort to hunt down research of a more esoteric nature.

About a mile down the road, Six walked into the acting sheriff's office with Deputy Christian Folsom in tow. Six reached out to shake the sheriff's hand while the deputy stood at attention. The deputy looked like had not slept for two full days, and the two days' growth of beard and tousled hair was far from the clean, professional looks he normally wore. His wrinkled and smudged uniform attested to his sleepless night. The acting sheriff looked almost as bad as her deputy. The dark circles under her eyes and wrinkled uniform showed that her past couple days had been rough as well. She motioned for the two men to sit in the seats across from her as she sat behind her desk.

She looked at her deputy with care in her eyes. "How are you doing, Deputy?" she asked with a tone of concern in her voice. "I'm so sorry for your loss. We'll do everything we can to help you get through this... that's what your Trinidad family is here for."

Christian wearily nodded and then spoke. "Honestly? I'm numb. I don't think I've hit the full impact yet."

The sheriff nodded. She kept her voice smooth, but it grew cold and hard. "You should be off work now. What are you doing in uniform? What is this about you responding to the scene last night at Virgil's house? Have you completely lost it?"

The DHS agent took this opportunity to speak up, earning a grateful smile from Christian and a cold glare from the sheriff. "Sheriff Sweeney, I believe I can answer all of your questions. Your deputy was a great help to us last night as we ran down some local sources that seem to have been involved in the original murders that brought us here, as well as the murders of the sheriff, mayor, and FBI agents. Those sources were also involved in the murders of the deputy's family and the older couple that night. Deputy Folsom offered his services, and I made the choice to bring him on board in our investigation."

The sheriff turned her glare on her deputy and then returned to the agent. "You caught the suspects in the death of his family. In fact, you told me that you have been able to track down several of the people that are turning my city into a slaughterhouse. How can a junior deputy, just out of POST training help you?"

Six shook his head and said, "I'm sorry, sheriff. I cannot give you specific information, as it is classified way above your pay grade. But I am here to tell you that as of last night, and for the foreseeable future, he needs to be officially seconded to my team." Six continued, "Deputy Folsom will act on our authority, and I expect that he will be temporarily removed from his duty shifts until he is no longer working with my team. I realize that you would normally provide compassionate leave, but he is not currently taking it. He will be working for me."

The sheriff stood and shook her finger at Six. Her voice rose to a shout. "How dare you come into my town, into my office, and treat me and my department like this? You do NOT have the authority to unilaterally second one of my deputies. You sure as hell do not have the authority to keep him from compassionate leave after his family was slaughtered by the guys you are chasing. I'm about done with you and your team using my town for a shooting range. Get out of my office. And get out of my county."

The federal agent calmly stood and reached into the breast pocket of his fatigues. He withdrew his credentials and slowly opened them in the sheriff's line of sight. "I assure you, Sheriff Sweeney. I have the full authority to do what I am doing. You do not want the shit storm I can rain down on your county. I, Special Agent Burt Holstein, of the Department of Homeland Security, formally require you to assist me and my team to accomplish our mission. You are to help us within your legal and lawful power, and you will not interfere with, or retaliate for, the work that Deputy Christian Folsom will be performing for my team. Do you understand?"

Six was glad to see the faint greenish glow emanating from his credentials. He was getting a handle on this esoteric-hero stuff. The sheriff's eyes glazed over briefly, and then her face re-animated. The anger and resentment visibly drained from her. She was calm, but her posture still seemed tense.

The sheriff nodded and gritted her teeth. After a few moments, she responded, "I understand. And I can't wait until you are out of my county."

The agent's tight smile never reached his eyes. "Believe me, I can't wait either," he said. He motioned for the deputy to stand and then turned and walked toward the door.

As they walked out of her office, he looked at the deputy and said, "Let's stop by your supply room to get you a couple new uniforms, and then we'll drive by your house to pick up some clothes and toiletries."

* * * * *

AN HOUR LATER, the two men arrived at the base ops in the deputy's pickup truck. Six and Christian walked into the conference room and were met with a massive pile of paperwork that threatened to collapse and bury those around the table under old records. The lead agent looked around and said, "All right team, the good deputy is officially ours, at least for the time being. What do we have?"

Ghost spoke up first, "We've confirmed our earlier suspicions, bossman. Acting Mayor Desiree Marshall is one of the vampire's creatures, most likely a familiar. Spooky also traced down the other phone. It belongs to our twitchy friend, Bill Stewart, the coroner. He's likely another familiar. We confirmed both of these connections through the electronics we confiscated."

"Great job," Six said with a smile. "So what do we know about familiars? Doc? Ghost?"

The priest looked down as she read from her notes, "My researchers at the Vatican tell me that familiars are typically humans who are enthralled by the vampire through a psychic hold, or who willingly give themselves to the vamp. The stronger the vamp, the stronger the connection and hold. If this master is the one who made them familiars, then they should be well connected."

"Great, but how do we break them? Silver? Stake?" questioned Six.

Doc shook her head. "No. These are actual, unmodified humans. Their one weakness is that they get real twitchy and cannot help but react when someone presses too far about their master. Indirect questions make them act as if they are in the throes of drug withdrawal. They get nervous ticks and even have a hard time talking. Direct questions seem to just set them off, so ask them questions."

Ghost asked a question. "Can familiars be cured? Can the vampire's hold be broken?"

Again, the priest shook her head and continued, "No. The only way they can be 'cured' is to kill the master they are connected to. Unfortunately, this often drives them insane. This mental break has been permanent for every subject the Vatican has seen. But sometimes, it's the best way to make them talk."

Six looked at the team and said, "Let's get this party started. We can either wait until the vamps attack again, or we can have a chat with their pet familiars, and step up the action. Anyone favor waiting?" He looked around to see his team shaking their heads.

"Pre-emptive strike it is. We need a location and plan of attack for the two pets. We'll have to hit them simultaneously, or they will get spooked. Do we know where they currently are?"

Spooky waved to get the team leader's attention. "Yeah, boss. The mayor is in her office at city hall, and according to her calendar, she is scheduled to be there all day. The quisling coroner is also in his office. This should be a simple divide-and-conquer."

Six divided the team. "Ghost and Heavy, you guys and Do-Right are Alpha Team, with me. We'll be talking to the Mayor. Spooky, you'll be driving the War Wagon and monitoring status while we are inside." Spooky started laughing, trying to keep quiet, but failing.

Six tried to ignore the young genius and continued with his assignments. "Doc and Boomer, take God with you. You guys are Beta Team. You go have a chat with the creepy coroner. Everyone be on their guard. We need to find out where the master vampire is, and what he's planning."

"Be ready to move out quickly. We may have to act on information faster than we had planned. Questions?"

Ghost raised a hand. "Yeah, boss. What is our load out for this?" he asked. "I'm not sure the full tac gear is appropriate for these interviews."

Six nodded in agreement with Ghost. "Good call," Six said.

"Load out is the following: no rifles; no machine gun, Heavy; pistols only. This means no tactical armor. Simple fatigues. And make sure you take your credentials and your sidearm. Anything else?"

After not hearing a response, their leader continued. "Let's load 'em up, then. Stow your heavy gear in the 'Wagon, and Beta can head out across the parking lot."

The young agent was still laughing as tears streamed down his face. The senior agent glared at him. "What in the hell are you laughing at?" the agent demanded.

Spooky barely wheezed his answer: "Do-Right. The Canadian Mountie who rides his horse backwards." He devolved into even more laughter.

By this time, the rest of the team began to chuckle. Doc broke into outright laughter and exclaimed, "I used to love that show!"

Six looked at Christian. "Sorry, kid. I didn't think they'd catch the reference. Should've known Spooky would pick it up."

Christian smiled with everyone else. He knew that this laughter was not directed at him. The team needed something to laugh about, and a silly nickname seemed to fit the bill.

"That's ok, boss. I kind of like it," said Christian. "Frankly, it's how I feel right now."

The laughter eventually died down and the oppressive weight in the room seemed to have been lifted. With all the death and horror that the team had seen over the last couple of days, they needed a laugh. Christian felt himself give a small smile for the first time in what felt like days. He realized that he desperately wanted to be on this team when they left Trinidad. He only hoped that they saw his value.

Beta Team walked across the now familiar parking lot as they made their way to the hospital. Waving to the security guard as they passed, they walked down the stairs to the basement. Las Animas County Medical Examiner Bill Stewart was sitting behind his desk, writing notes and working on the unceasing paperwork that his job demanded.

Doc knocked on the frame of his door. Her voice was warm as she asked, "Hey, Doctor Stewart? Do you have a few minutes to talk?"

* * * * *

. . .

ACROSS TOWN, Spooky pulled the enormous War Wagon across three parking spaces in front of the city/county building. When he noticed his boss's questioning look, the agent smiled and said, "What are they going to do, to me? I'd like to see them try."

Six shook his head as the crew popped the hatch and scrambled out of the truck. When they had dismounted, Spooky closed the hatch from inside and sealed the vehicle so he could begin to monitor his electronics.

The rest of Alpha Team walked through the front doors of the building.

Six heard his electronics expert in his ear proclaim, "I'm into the camera system. I've got eyes on you."

The DHS agent subvocalized a brief "Copy" as the team walked toward the stairs to the second floor. As they approached the mayor's office, Six noticed the mayor's administrator at the desk and two plainclothes police officers wearing suits who were standing at attention outside the door to the mayor's inner sanctum.

The federal agent smiled his most polite smile and drew his badge. Flashing the credentials at the administrator, he said, "Special Agent Burt Holstein, Department of Homeland Security. I would like to meet with the mayor, please."

The raven-haired administrator seemed unfazed by the credentials. "I'm sorry, Agent Holstein," she replied. "The mayor is very busy right now and is getting ready to leave for a meeting in the next few minutes. I could maybe work you in... tomorrow?"

Six continued to smile, but his tone grew colder and harder. "You don't seem to understand. I'm being polite right now, but I'm losing my patience. I will need to see the mayor right now. Not tomorrow. Not later. Now. You can either clear us through the doors, or we will go through the doors, anyway. It is your choice."

The two bodyguards next to the door tensed and took a step toward the agent. Heavy calmly stepped in between the two officers and his boss. Smiling, he crossed his massive arms over his chest. His sleeveless t-shirt and BDU pants only accentuated the mountain of muscle that the bodybuilder was carrying. The big man's deep voice was soft and warning. "You fellas need to calm down right now. You know we're federal agents. Do not start something that you don't me want to finish."

The administrator swallowed nervously as she glanced back and forth between the stand-off in front of the door and the agent in front of her. Six made the decision for her and continued, "Listen,

Miss Adams. I'm going to go in there now. Please feel free to let her know I'm here."

Six, Ghost, and Christian all walked past the guards. The DHS agent opened the doors, and they filed into the inner office as the administrator frantically called her boss.

"I'm going to wait out here, boss," Heavy said as he stared at the two bodyguards. "Holler if you need me."

Ghost closed the double doors behind the trio as they entered, sealing out the noise of the building. It was a plush office with a large oak desk and comfortable furniture. The mayor was placing the phone on its receiver as Six approached her desk.

Desiree Marshall was a slim African American woman with classical features and long hair that she wore down her back. She had spent her entire life in Trinidad and Las Animas County and had worked her way up the political ladder with grit, determination, and a backbone of solid steel. Capable of listening to her constituents and verbally flaying her opponents, she was used to her enemies underestimating her exactly one time. As acting mayor, Ms. Marshall would not put up with these federal agents barging into her office uninvited.

Six did not get a chance to speak; Mayor Marshall verbally attacked him before he came to a stop.

"Just what do you think you are doing?" she demanded. "Bullying past my administrator and physically threatening my police officers? I don't care what kind of badge you have. I'll have it in my desk before this week is out. I have an entire collection of badges from sanctimonious law enforcement pricks that I've had fired over the years." She smiled a hungry grin. "It will be nice to add a DHS badge to the collection."

The agent held up his hands to ward off the tirade. "Madam Mayor, I'm sorry that I had to barge in on your busy schedule, but I had some very important information that I had to talk to you about. It's about our investigation here in Trinidad. I believe that we're almost wrapped up. Can you spare a couple of minutes?"

The mayor's demeanor changed visibly from overtly hostile to coldly calculating. "If it will get you out of my town faster, I will spare you three minutes—no more."

"Yes, ma'am," the agent replied. "I can honestly say that it won't take more than that. In fact, I actually have one quick question before I tell you what we discovered."

"Well?" the mayor demanded impatiently. "What's your question?"

"Are you a familiar for the vampire master?"

The mayor snapped. Her conservative, calf-length skirt tore as she leapt across the desk at Six. Her eyes were wide with insanity, and she growled as she rushed at him. He was not expecting the direct attack and barely warded off her fists as she aimed punches at his face and throat.

Six grabbed her arms in his powerful hands as he tried to keep the feral woman off of him, all the while yelling for the deputy to grab his handcuffs. The mayor surged, howled and ripped her arms out of the agent's hands. Six responded by with a solid punch that stunned the mayor and a wild haymaker that connected to her jaw. The mayor fell as if pole-axed, thumping to the floor as the doors burst open. The bodyguards ran inside with weapons drawn pointing them at the team.

"Freeze. Police!" yelled the officers.

Six drew his sidearm with lightning speed, countering with, "Federal Agents!"

It quickly became a standoff—until Heavy stepped into the room. The mountainous agent slammed a thick hand across the arms of each police officer hard enough to make them drop their pistols. Grabbing the police officers by the back of their tailored jackets, he hauled them off of their feet and turned them around to face him. He shook them until he was sure he had their attention.

Six paused to take a breath, and then said, "The mayor is under arrest for assaulting a federal agent: me. The deputy will handcuff her, and we will take her with us. Do you understand?"

When the two officers reluctantly nodded, the big agent slowly put them back on their feet. Six nodded to Heavy and motioned for Ghost to help Christian take the mayor out to the truck.

He keyed his radio. "Spooky, Six. Fire up the Wagon. We have a prisoner."

Heavy was the last to leave the office area. He remained behind to make sure that no one interfered. He turned and looked at the still stunned police officers. As he glanced around the posh office area, he muttered under his breath, "I hate politics..."

22

FAMILIARS

Mt. San Rafael Hospital, Trinidad, Colorado.

While the Beta Team talked with Medical Examiner Bill Stewart in his office, God waited outside the cramped office and watched the halls. He noted that the crematorium was shut down and empty.

"Doctor Stewart, do you have those files for the original group of deceased that brought us here?" asked Doc. "I'd like to take another look at the files... and at the bodies," she explained.

The doctor hesitated as he handed over his files. Boomer noticed his hands and forehead were sweaty despite the cool temperature of the lab. He looked guilty of something, and she knew what it was.

After Doc quickly reviewed several files, she looked up at Stewart and asked him for some help. "I want to take another look at the post-mortem wounds," she explained.

"Sure," replied Stewart. "Which one did you want to start with?"

After the priest looked at the folders she said, "Let's start with that last one. The remains will be freshest."

Stewart nodded, and they all left the office.

Doc and Stewart donned surgical gowns and gloves and retrieved the remains from the cooler. Boomer stood near Stewart, subtly boxing him in against a wall.

The DHS medic began pointing out the various slashing and tearing wounds.

"What did you determine did these wounds? Was it some sort of big cat?" Doc questioned as she poked and prodded the injuries.

Stewart nodded fitfully. "Y-Y-Yes," he stammered. "A big cat, maybe a mountain lion. Why do you ask?"

Doc looked at him and then back to the corpse. She continued, "Because these bites have the same characteristics as human bites, albeit bites made by sharper teeth. Where did you get your degree from, Doctor?"

"Princeton," the doctor angrily replied. "I graduated with honors forty-four years ago. What of it?"

The priest looked quizzically at the man before her. "Because I don't understand how someone with your experience and time can mistake an obviously human series of bites for big cat bites," she continued. "They look nothing alike. Can you explain that?"

The doctor raised his voice shrilly and caught the attention of the sniper in the hallway. "I've got more experience with big cat mauling than you ever will! I'm telling you, this is a big cat. Post mortem."

Hearing the rising voices, God approached the lab, and placed his hand lightly on his sidearm. He reached for the door leading into the lab.

Doc looked at Doctor Stewart and calmly explained, "That's another thing. These wounds were not post mortem. These wounds were the cause of death. I'm really not sure how you missed that. There are two choices: either you are hugely incompetent, or you are covering up something. Which is it?"

The doctor paled at her words. He tried to choke out an answer, but Doc cut him off again.

"If I had to guess, I'd guess that no one can be this incompetent and hold a Medical Examiner position in this day and age, which leaves me with one real option: you are covering up for someone... possibly the real murderers?"

The coroner was ashen and trembled at the accusation.

Doc's voice took on a light, conversational tone as she continued. "Although I do have to admit one thing: the monsters that did this to these victims are technically more creature than human."

She looked Dr. Stewart straight in the eye. Her voice grew quiet as she continued. "How long have you been a familiar, Bill?" she questioned.

The priest was not sure what to expect, but the suddenness and target of Dr. Stewart's attack took her off-guard. In one frantic movement, the coroner grabbed a scalpel from the instrument tray and swung wildly at Boomer who was standing next to him. The scalpel missed the explosives expert's throat by less than an inch. The doctor overbalanced on the swing, and the agent's instinctive kick caught him in the gut. The kick drove the air from his lungs, doubled him over, and left him struggling to breathe.

When he saw the attack, God burst through lab door, running to help his teammates. Doc stepped back out of the sniper's way as God barreled into the fray, knocking aside the scalpel still clutched in Dr. Stewart's hand. A hard punch to the forearm made the doctor's hand go numb, and he dropped the improvised weapon. Boomer delivered another kick to the M.E., and her combat boot connected squarely between the doctor's legs, driving the man to the floor in agony.

God grabbed and twisted the doctor's wrists behind his torso, roughly hauling him up from the floor, and planted him in a nearby chair. A quick search around the office produced some industrial strength zip-ties. The sniper secured the struggling coroner to his desk chair. The sniper leaned over the doctor and whispered, "Next time, don't attack a woman who is trained in combat. Especially if she's already pissed at you."

He patted the doctor on the head and walked over to where the rest of his team stood.

Doc looked at both of the other agents and chuckled. "Mental note, if you ask a familiar if they are, in fact, a familiar, they get violent. Good to know. So now what?"

God looked at her and said, "Let's see how the other team is doing. See what Six wants us to do." He keyed his radio. "Six, God. What's your status?"

"Six. We have one in custody for interrogation. You?"

The sniper answered, "We've got one as well. Why don't you come to the morgue? It's quiet, and there's a back entrance for privacy."

"That's a great idea, God. We'll be there in five. Six out." The team leader sounded stressed.

The stoic sniper looked at his teammates, "Well, seems like the party is coming to us."

* * * * *

. . .

FIVE MINUTES LATER, the MRAP backed up to the morgue's entrance. As the back hatch opened, two police cars and a sheriff's patrol car pulled in and blocked the MRAP.

Six looked at the officers and the sheriff as they got out of their respective vehicles, and he looked back at his team.

"Heavy, you're with me," Six said. "Spooky, stay in the truck. Ghost, Do-Right, you guys escort the mayor inside and secure her with the coroner. I'll take care of these guys."

The lead agent thought for a moment and made a snap decision.

"Spooky. Contact the HRT and get them deployed over here right away. I want about half of them here; the rest should go to the base ops and secure the files."

Six turned, and Heavy climbed down out of the back of the War Wagon to stand beside him. They walked calmly over to the officers who were gathering around the black MRAP. As they approached, the murmurs and talking grew louder and angrier.

Six keyed his radio and subvocalized so the gathering officers could not hear him. "Spooky, ETA on the HRT?"

"Two minutes, boss," Spooky replied.

Six raised his hands up to shoulder level in an effort to calm the growing voices. "Ladies and gentlemen, before you get too angry, let's talk about what's going on."

He nodded to a couple of the people in the group. "Chief. Sheriff. I'm glad you are here as well. Let me explain what happened."

"Your team kidnapped the mayor, Agent Holstein," Sheriff Sweeney interrupted in a voice as brittle as glass. "What are you doing to this town?"

The federal agent looked over the restless crowd of uniforms, stalling until he saw one of the FBI trucks pull around the corner. As the HRT agents climbed out of the truck, Six addressed the group.

"I understand that there are a lot of questions today. Mayor Marshall is currently in my custody. She is under arrest for attacking a federal law enforcement officer, namely me. Our investigation led us to the acting mayor and the coroner as potential leads in the case."

"As it turns out, both are in custody because we believe they have a connection with the terrorist cell that's been targeting this town. I will update you on our progress, as I can, without revealing classified information in an ongoing investigation. That is all I can tell you at this time."

The grumblings were cut short, and the crowd of officers

dispersed when the armed and armored HRT team took up station around the MRAP and in front of the hospital door.

"Thank you for moving so quickly, commander," Six said as he addressed the FBI's team lead. "I'll handle security inside. If we can have you guys on site here for the next couple of hours, and on site over at our ops base during that time as well, we would appreciate it. We are close to wrapping up this mess."

"I hope so, Agent Holstein," the commander said as he looked at Six. "I've done some checking. You and your team are brand new to federal service, and we don't work the same here in the states as you did in Iraq."

The DHS agent chuckled. "Believe me, I know that. I'm just doing the best job I can to take down these bad guys," he said.

Six and Heavy turned to walk through the loading dock doors and left Spooky enclosed in the War Wagon surrounded by HRT.

As the men walked into the morgue, Six observed that both familiars had been securely fastened to chairs and that the chairs were three or four feet apart and faced away from each other. As they sat back-to-back, the two snarling people in front of him could not see or take their cues from each other.

Six smiled and walked into the mayor's line of sight.

"Madam Mayor, this is how this session will go. You can either cooperate and answer my questions or cooperate after we torture you. It is completely your choice. What do you say... want to take the easy route?"

The mayor looked sullen and glared at the agent with her head bowed low and her hair covering part of her face.

"You will not get away with this. He will find you and rip your throat out," the mayor threatened.

"All right, mayor. I'll take that as the obvious 'F-U' that you intended it for. Let's see what the coroner has to say."

Six moved into Doctor Stewart's line of sight. "What do you say, Bill? Easy or hard? Your choice."

The coroner just spat. His phlegm hit the floor by the agent's foot. Six backed away and looked at the rest of the team in disgust.

"The hard way it is then. Let's break these fools."

Doc stepped forward and said, "May I try something first, boss? I have an idea that just might get us some information."

Six nodded to her, and she moved to stand in front of the coroner. The priest leafed through her leather-bound book again and found the page she wanted. She looked up and placed her hand on the coroner's forehead, and then she spoke in Latin.

The effect of her liturgy was instantaneous: Doctor Stewart looked like he had been electrocuted. The energy that ran through his body froze his muscles, and he began to convulse. The lead agent looked at Doc in alarm, but she never stopped reading from her book. Stewart rocked back and forth in his chair.

Drool ran out between his lips as he muttered, "Cannot betray master... Going north... Cannot betray north... Going master..."

The mayor hissed at the coroner. She craned her head around to see him and threatened, "Shut up, fool. Do not betray Zachariah."

The coroner hissed at the name. "No. Mustn't betray him. No."

Six looked between the two prisoners and then approached the mayor.

"So, Zachariah is your master, huh?" he questioned.

"You are not worthy to speak his name. Shut your mouth, interloper," the mayor hissed. "You cannot stop our master. Soon everyone will get their reward."

Six turned to Doc and asked, "Anything ring a bell with this Zachariah character?"

While the priest shook her head, Ghost nodded and said, "I can't believe it. The rumor is true."

The entire team turned to look at the esoteric hunter. He continued, "Look, there have been rumors of an ancient master out here somewhere. He's supposed to be at least a couple hundred years old. If so, he's powerful. Twice in my prior life, I came across a reference to this 'Zachariah.' If he's mixed up in this, he's been here for quite some time."

Ghost turned to the mayor. "How long have you known your master?" he inquired.

Mayor Marshall hissed and squirmed to get free. "I will not tell you anything more."

Doc approached the mayor and laid her hand on the mayor's forehead. Doc spoke in the same Latin that the team heard earlier.

But the mayor did not react as the doctor had—she laughed instead.

"Fool. I have been with the master for a long time, I am immune to your parlor tricks and beliefs in a dead god. That will not work on me."

Six knelt down to look her in the eye.

Calmly and coldly, the agent whispered, "I don't care if you are not afraid of God. You should be afraid of me. I have the authority to do with you as I please. If you do not help me, you will regret it when this is over. After I find and kill Zachariah, I will then personally take you to one of those secret little government holes designed specifically for terrorists. You will disappear. Forever."

The mayor blanched but attempted to put on a brave face. "You cannot. There are enough people in this town that know you took me. The news will be all over this story."

Six smiled coldly. "I have the authority. And you are part of the terrorists that were attacking this town. Your people won't care about you. But none of that matters. You will tell me what I want to know."

The mayor shook her head.

"Never. I would never betray the master."

The agent smiled and tilted his head at the coroner who was regaining some semblance of coherence.

The agent's voice dropped to a whisper as he leaned closer to the mayor's ear. "You don't have to betray Zachariah. Your fellow familiar will. He can't stand the pain. And when I'm done with him, you will be next."

Six pulled a roll of duct tape from his fatigues and placed a strip over the mayor's mouth. He stood, drew his gun, and aimed it at the corpse that was still laying on the examination table. He motioned Boomer out of the firing line and wordlessly cautioned everyone to protect their ears. When his team had all plugged their ears, he pulled the trigger twice. The shots echoed in the small lab, and the corpse twitched at the impact of each bullet.

Six walked around to face the coroner. Doctor Stewart's face was ashen, and he violently twisted his neck to see the mayor.

The lead agent knelt down and stared silently at the coroner. After a brief pause, Six spoke.

"The mayor decided not to cooperate," Six said in a casual, conversational tone. "Do you want the same fate? There is no vampire present, so you will not be coming back. Now, what information do you have for me?"

"Don't kill me, please!" the coroner pleaded almost immediately. "All I know is that Zachariah is the master. He's working with some scientist in some small town north of Trinidad. I swear, I don't know anything more."

Six looked at his second-in-command.

"Do you believe him? Does that sound like Zachariah?" questioned Six.

Ghost shrugged.

"He's always been a legend. It's hard to know which stories are true and which are ones that he made up to scare the humans," explained Ghost. "Best guess? Yeah. It sounds plausible. Although why he is working with a scientist kind of scares the crap out of me."

Six looked at the coroner again. "What do we do with him?" he asked. "We can't turn him loose."

Ghost looked at his boss. "We have two options," Ghost offered. "Take them to Gitmo or kill them. Your choice."

The lead agent nodded.

"Let me think about it," he said. "Tape up the doctor's mouth. I want to have a chat with the mayor again."

As Ghost taped up the doctor's mouth, Six walked out of the lab to retrieve another chair from the office. He placed the straight-backed chair directly in front of the Mayor and sat backwards on the chair, protecting his chest and groin with the chair back.

The agent reached out and roughly ripped off the tape from the mayor's mouth. She gasped as several layers of skin stuck to the tape. He balled up the sticky tape and leaned over.

"Which scientist is Zachariah working with?" he pointedly asked.

Her reply was immediate, "You are not fit to speak his name. I don't know which scientist."

Six smiled and drew his knife from its scabbard at his side. He gazed at the exquisite finish and razor-sharp edge on his favorite Marine Ka-Bar fighting knife. Balancing the heft of the blade on an open palm, he waved the blade in front of the mayor's eyes.

"What are you trying to do, threaten me? You can't touch me," she said with a sneer.

Six smiled, flipped the knife in the air, grabbed the hilt so that the blade was pointing down, and drove the blade into the mayor's left thigh. The razor edge easily sliced through the skirt covering her thigh, through the meat of her thigh, and into the bone itself.

The mayor screamed. A shrieking and wailing cry that was testament to her pain.

Six bore his weight down on the knife. Leaning over, he looked into the mayor's panicked gaze and said, "Do I have your attention yet, Mayor?"

The mayor nodded and stopped screaming. She whimpered in agony.

The agent calmly asked again, "Who is Zachariah working with? Where is this scientist's lab located?"

The mayor shook her head, refusing to speak through the pain.

He wiggled the knife back and forth. Excruciating agony flashed up the mayor's leg, and she let out a new series of howls.

"Feel like talking yet?" Six ask conversationally.

The mayor nodded.

"Doctor Kaine. He has a lab up north in Divide. For god's sake, just take the knife out already," she pleaded.

Six continued to pry. "See, now I'm starting to believe you. How long has he been in the area?"

With tears streaming down her face, she admitted, "About twenty years."

"What is he planning?" questioned Six.

The mayor stopped and shook her head. Six took that as a cue and once again leaned on the knife, grinding the tip into the mayor's femur and ensuring her cooperation.

"All right, I'll tell," she relented. "The doctor is turning the vampire virus into a weapon. That's all I know."

Six looked at the priest and said, "I hate to say this, Doc, but these guys weren't all that tough to break."

The priest calmly regarded her boss. "I'm pretty sure the Vatican would loathe to use that method of information extraction," she said.

Six smiled, "Except for that darn Inquisition." The team leader stood up out of his chair and called Ghost and Doc out of the exam lab and into the coroner's office. The three walked into the office, and the senior agent asked, "Doc, can these guys be restored? Can we break the spell that Zachariah has over them?"

The priest shook her head. "These two are far too gone for them to ever be cured," she said. "Either throw them into a psych ward somewhere dark and dirty or kill them. Those are the only two humane options available. Once we kill the master, they'll be completely insane."

Ghost knew that his boss would want to kill them, and he was becoming increasingly bothered by the growing human body count. He knew he had to say something.

"So let's use that to our advantage," the monster hunter suggested. "Once we kill this master, they should go crazy. Toss 'em in an institution where no one will talk to them. If we kill them, we have to explain how and why they died in our custody. If they go bat-crap crazy, who cares what they say about us, or vampires, or anything?"

Six's smile was cold.

"I like that solution," he said. "Saves the problems. We just need to get them locked up until we kill the bad guy."

He called for Do-Right.

"Deputy, can we drop these two into solitary cells, at least for a day or two?" asked Six.

Christian nodded. "Yes, I think the sheriff will cooperate. I'll contact some deputies that I know so they can keep an eye on them."

Six nodded and said, "Set it up. If you have any problems, let me know. I'll deal with it."

He walked over to the prisoners while the deputy made the phone calls.

The mayor was whimpering in agony as blood seeped slowly from the wound in her thigh. "So, do you believe us? We told you the truth. What are you going to do now?" she pleaded.

Six replied coldly, "Yes, I believe you. I also know that I need to keep you out of the way while we go kill your master. You're going to jail. We'll transport you to Gitmo when we get back."

The mayor screamed in rage and violently jerked at her bindings to get loose.

The senior agent leaned down and said, "Calm down, or I will knock you out. Your choice."

Six looked pointedly at the bleeding wound on the mayor's leg, and the mayor immediately calmed down.

Six looked at his team. "Doc, bandage up the mayor and the coroner so they can sit in a cell. Put the bodies of the original victims into the furnaces and fire up the crematorium. Let's clean up and figure out where we are going next."

Six keyed his radio and spoke, "Spooky, did you get all the particulars?"

"Got 'em, boss," Spooky responded. "In fact, I've got a location on this scientist, and you aren't going to believe where this guy is hiding."

III

INCURSION

23

PLANNING

Pueblo Memorial Airport, Pueblo, Colorado

At the west end of the airplane parking ramp, far away from the terminal of Pueblo Memorial Airport sat a building that looked like an aircraft hanger, its blue and gray exterior large enough to house a military cargo jet. Instead, it was the main fuel office and depot for the airport with rows of fuel pumps and a small office attached to the outside. A large black MRAP marked as "Police/Rescue" and "Department of Homeland Security" eased its way through the security gate mounted in the airport perimeter fence, and the vehicle came to a halt at the end of the parking ramp. After the engine was cut off, the engine tick, tick, ticked as the large Cummins diesel engine cooled. The rear door swung open, and a group of heavily armed agents dropped down out of the truck.

"Seriously, Boomer. Can we keep it under the speed of sound next time? I almost lost my lunch." The tall lanky agent wearing a long leather jacket and a brimmed hat stood shakily against the back of the truck as he tried to keep his knees from wobbling.

"What's your problem, Ghost?" the driver said as she dropped out of the back hatch and stretched her muscular arms. "We got here safely, and we even beat the plane."

A man who exuded command walked over and clasped the complaining agent on the shoulder.

"Forget about it, Ghost," he said. "You won't win this argument with her."

Six glanced down at his secure phone and said, "Gretchen just sent me a message. They're two minutes out."

A deputy sheriff, whose brown and tan uniform contrasted against the black tactical BDUs of the rest of the team, shakily climbed out of the back of the armored vehicle. "Agent Holstein? You never told me I needed to take out a life insurance policy for when Boomer drives. Monsters I can handle, but I'm not so sure about her driving."

Six started laughing, and the others joined in.

Moments later, the team turned toward the runway as they heard the large roar of an arriving jet. Six had expected to see the Citation X aircraft the team had used on their last flight, so when the team leader saw a monster of an aircraft coming in for a landing, he was shocked.

The two large jet engines under each wing roared as the monster cargo plane made a graceful landing at the end of Runway 26L. With a wingspan of almost one hundred seventy feet, the Boeing C-17 Globemaster III was enormous.

As the Air Force jet rolled out at the end of the runway nearest to the team, Ghost looked at Six and asked, "What did Gretchen say she was bringing us?"

The team leader shook his head and turned when he heard laughing behind him. He saw Spooky climb out of the MRAP they were using. Spooky lugged all of his electronic equipment out of the truck and struggled not to drop the precious gear onto the tarmac.

Six looked at the electronics specialist a little closer and asked, "Why are you laughing? Whenever you laugh like that, I have to do more paperwork. What's going on?"

Spooky's reply was drowned out as the mammoth plane reversed the engine thrust to slow down. As the aircraft passed their end of the tarmac, the team felt the roar of all four turbines. An airport pickup truck raced toward the team from the terminal and rocked to a halt beside the scattered agents. The team tensed in surprise and reached for their sidearms while the men in the truck ignored them. A three-man ground crew got out of the pickup truck and waited for the plane to taxi to its spot on the ramp.

As the massive jet taxied toward the tarmac, the three waiting ground crew members guided the giant plane to its waiting parking spot. The four turbines wound down, and the noise quickly became more bearable. Just as Six was about to ask Spooky about his laughter again, the door on the side of the fuselage cycled open and dropped, forming into a set of stairs. At the same time, they all could hear the whine of hydraulics as the rear ramp dropped down.

Agent Gretchen Massey stepped to the doorway of the plane. She saw the team and walked down the stairs, carrying a small suitcase. Behind her, a man dressed in an impeccable gray pin-stripe suit adjusted his lapels and followed her down the stairs. He joined Gretchen at the bottom of the stairs, and they walked toward the waiting team. As the new arrivals walked to the team, a shuttle bus from the airport approached across the tarmac. Gretchen waved to get the driver's attention, and he pulled to a stop right where the team was standing.

The man in the suit approached the sheriff's deputy who stood beside Six. He reached out his hand and introduced himself.

"Deputy Folsom? I am Agent Smith, of the Department of Homeland Security. I suppose you could say that I'm your new boss," he said. "I'm sorry to hear about your loss, and I do want to welcome you to the team. Mr. Holstein has had nothing but good things to report. Do not worry. I'll take care of things with the sheriff for you."

Deputy Folsom wondered just who his new boss was that he could "handle" the sheriff.

Agent Smith continued, "We will have to postpone the official swearing in until after this mission, but I wanted to greet you personally."

Smith looked at the rest of the team and said, "It will take a little while to get your new gear offloaded. This bus will take us to a conference room that I've reserved in the terminal. Ms. Massey has arranged food as well so we can go over the new equipment with you."

Agent Smith turned to look at Spooky while the rest of the team climbed aboard. "Grab your projector. I've got some intel for your mission," he told the electronics specialist. As they boarded the bus and pulled away from the giant aircraft and headed toward the terminal, Six watched a squad of heavily armed men in tactical uniforms assemble and surround the plane and the MRAP on the tarmac.

––––––––––––––

DURING THEIR CONFERENCE, Agent Smith explained that he had arrived with the team's new vehicle and that it was loaded out according to their specifications.

The team leader looked over at his electronics specialist and frowned. He turned back to Agent Smith. "Just what specs did Spooky send you?" he asked.

Smith smiled. "You'll have to ask him," he said. "I know Russell and Norbert were up for almost two days straight getting all the systems integrated. However, this... War Wagon, as you call it, should be outfitted for anything you need while in the field. It will go with you on most direct action missions from now on. And if you find it lacking, work with the warehouse to get it straight."

Spooky leaned over to Ghost and whispered, "We really do have our own 'Q' branch."

Ghost nodded his agreement.

Agent Smith looked right at him and gave a hint of a smile. "Trust me, Mr. Smith, the 'Q' branch isn't nearly as good as Norbert and Russell. Those Brits have been trying to recruit them for years."

Spooky's jaw fell open as he digested what Smith said. Before he could ask a follow-up question, Smith continued his briefing.

"As of right now, this mission has been classified as a Priority: Black. Working with the intel developed by your team, and especially by your very own Mr. Smith, we've come to believe this is far larger than we initially thought. That is why I decided to make the trip out with Ms. Massey.

"The intelligence you were able to recover led you to a Doctor Bishop Kaine."

An image of a thin, brooding scientist in a lab coat filled the screen.

Smith continued, "Doctor Kaine is a brilliant specialist in genetic engineering, and worked for the CDC in Atlanta until about ten years ago. At that point, the scientist's rough demeanor and elitist attitude finally rubbed the wrong person the wrong way, and he was fired. As he was escorted out of the building, he made several threats against the personnel at the facility.

"At that point, he stepped out of the public life and dropped off the grid. It turns out that he put together the funds and bought an abandoned Atlas 'F' ICBM missile silo just north of a town called Divide, Colorado. I'll update the exact GPS coordinates to your new truck."

Six looked at Smith and asked, "So why is this now classified as a Priority: Black?"

Agent Smith looked at the team leader, then looked around the table. "Before I answer that, I want to talk about the master that was named by the familiars. This is not a random master vampire who has happened to hang around for a long time. This particular 'Zachariah' is currently one of the oldest known vampires here on earth. He's also the only one who's been able to stay ahead of this office.

"We have no idea how old this evil creature is, but he has taken out some of our best people. He has caused a lot of havoc in America and around the world. He is powerful."

Ghost spoke up. "Sir, the last information I heard was that he was at least a couple hundred years old... possibly turned during the American Revolution. Our records go back at least that far for him, but my... researchers... couldn't find any more information for him."

Smith nodded. "Thank you Mr. Vanhof. I trust your research. So this master is at least two hundred years old. If he is working with a disgruntled genetic engineer, then he is probably planning something that will certainly qualify as a Priority: Black."

A series of blueprints and a three-dimensional walkthrough of a missile silo appeared on the screen in front of the team.

Agent Smith continued. "This is the last known configuration of the Atlas F missile silo that Doctor Kaine purchased. There is no telling what the scientist has changed, but this information may be helpful to you anyways."

After the team reviewed the walkthrough twice, Agent Smith outlined the course of action for the mission.

"Team Knightmare, here are your mission parameters," said Smith. "Priority One. Find out what Zachariah and Doctor Kaine have planned, and stop it. Priority Two: Avoid destroying any of the scientific equipment or computer equipment or any paper records that the doctor has on his experiments. If his research has released a new threat, we need to have that information to stop it. Priority Three: Destroy the bunker and lab facilities after you have cleaned out the equipment. Make this site go away."

Boomer smiled when she hear the word "destroy."

Smith looked even more serious than normal.

"As a Priority: Black mission, you have almost unlimited resources," he continued. "Unfortunately, the other two Incursion teams are down or busy. Due to the nature of the mission, you are not authorized to bring in more team members. However, your new War Wagon and the equipment I'm bringing you should help with that.

"This new MRAP will be your team's personal truck and will be transported to any site where it is needed. It has been customized and outfitted beyond the standard MRAP to help with your rather unique challenges. In it, we've also packed a large amount of ammunition and some other gadgets that should help you take down this fiend.

"Ladies and gentlemen, this master has haunted our organization for years. This creature is responsible for the deaths of many agents, including my first partner. It is up to you to send him to the hell he has eluded for so long."

Agent Smith looked up as Gretchen walked into the room. "I see that Ms. Massey has indeed brought a light lunch. Let's eat this and then get you on your way."

HALF AN HOUR LATER, the team walked to the waiting shuttle bus at the entrance of the airport. Before they could climb on, two SUVs with dark tinted windows pulled up. Special Agent Hart, the SAC from Denver, climbed out followed by a small team. She quickly walked around the truck but came to an abrupt halt when she saw Agent Smith and Gretchen.

"Agent Smith?" The surprise in Hart's voice was evident. "I didn't know this was one of your teams. I should have realized that when I got stonewalled in DC. Next time, if you want to give me some heads up, I won't give your team such a hard time."

"Don't worry about it, Sonja." Agent Smith let a hint of amusement show in his voice. "If it would have been necessary, I'd have had Timothy call you. As it is, I believe you can have your MRAP back today."

Agent Hart's SUV followed the shuttle out on the tarmac toward the hangar where they had parked the War Wagon.

As they approached, Six realized that there was an even bigger armored truck, all in black, parked next to their MRAP. He turned around to face his electronics specialist. "What the hell is that? Just what did you ask for, Spooky?" he asked.

Behind him, Spooky laughed. "Boss, I told you I was requisitioning a new War Wagon. Call it Version 2.0, but this thing should really rock and work for all of our missions. According to Norbert, if we like it, it will be sent wherever we go. She is not the most subtle beast, and she should be perfectly decked out inside."

A small contingent of armed DHS tactical agents surrounded the vehicles. Two of them also stood by the stairwell to the C-17.

The department's Citation X was parked next to the C-17, and it, too, had its own guard.

The shuttle driver dropped them off by the two large MRAPs. His mouth gaped open, but he was smart enough to leave before he asked anything that he would later regret.

Hart's SUV pulled up beside them, and she and her team got out of the vehicle as they stared at the second truck.

Hart stammered a little. "When I got the call to come get our truck, I thought you guys were leaving." She pointed to the new truck and asked, "What the hell is this monstrosity?"

The new truck was a larger, beefier, blockier version of their previous truck. Built on an International Harvester platform, the Navistar Maxxpro Plus was one of the most used MRAPs in Iraq and Afghanistan. This model stood ten feet tall and was painted a deep matte black. Outfitted with emergency lights in the grill and on the exterior, the top was also ringed with small lamps that pointed outward. A large floodlight that was capable of rotating 360 degrees was mounted in each corner of the roof. The only markings on it were small decals on each door with the DHS logo and the words "Department of Homeland Security." Perched on the roof was a small cluster of antennas that include radio, satellite, and a few whose use was only known to Spooky.

The front driver and passenger doors and the rear loading stairs made entry and exit easier than their previous truck. Boomer opened the driver's door and climbed up into the massive vehicle with ease. As she looked at the instrument cluster, she noticed a few switches that were cryptically marked, but a toggle switch on the control cluster between Boomer and the front passenger marked "Rear Hatch" caught her eye.

She flipped the switch to the "Down" position.

At the rear of the vehicle, a small hiss the pneumatic seal opening was barely audible. The rear hatch lowered with a hydraulic whine. A thin sliver of light from the back turned into daylight as the rear ramp lowered and turned into a short set of stairs.

Spooky was the first to climb the stairs, lugging his electronics behind him. He quickly walked over to the seat in front of the electronics station. As he sat down, the lights and panels lit up around him. Plugging his laptop into the waiting ports, the electronics specialist put on a headset. A voice prompt echoed in his ear and on the screen and told him to identify himself.

He pulled the microphone close and said, "Identify. Agent

Spooky. Alpha One."

The screens around him hummed to life. He glanced down and realized that his forearm computer had also synchronized with the system. He grinned began to type away as he whistled a theme that Boomer later recognized as belonging to a show about other federal agents that looked for monsters and aliens.

The team's sniper was the next one to board the new truck. Once he was in the MRAP, he popped the top hatch of the truck, just to get a feel for it. The hatch itself was slightly wider than the one in the roof of their previous truck, and this one added several features that would allow him to be a much more effective shooter from the top of the vehicle. He dropped back down and sat in the surprisingly comfortable seat. He noticed the five point harness attached to each seat and caught Spooky's eye.

God lifted the seat buckle and asked, "Was this your idea?"

Spooky just grinned.

God nodded and said, "Good thinking." He then reached up and clipped both his sniper rifle and his carbine to the interior of the roof by the turret hatch. The custom brackets would be perfect for his firearms for secure storage and easy access for the sniper.

Heavy climbed inside the cabin of the MRAP and grinned. It was marginally larger inside, and the big man didn't feel quite so compressed. He leaned over and popped the latches on a bin marked "Heavy - Weapons and Ammunition." Inside was his favorite machine gun, the SAW, and nestled next to it was a smaller, futuristic-looking rifle. Unlatching the gun, he pulled it out and laughed. His booming laughter made Ghost stick his head inside the back and look at the big gunner.

The hunter looked at Heavy and said, "What's up, big man?"

Heavy grinned and said, "Christmas came mighty early this year. Looks like I get a new toy."

Heavy held a black rifle that bore a slight resemblance to the other team members' M4 carbines. The black polymer stock and forearm of the Auto Assault-12 belied the weapon's roots as a hunting shotgun. Capable of feeding from an eight round magazine or a 32-round drum magazine, the fully automatic assault shotgun could spit out 12GA shotgun rounds at the rate of one round every 0.2 seconds, an effective cyclic rate of 300 rounds per minute. Advanced recoil reduction design meant that the recoil from the full-power shotgun was less than other modern rifles that shot far smaller rounds.

Boomer turned around and noticed the shotgun in Heavy's

hands.

"No fair!" she complained. "I want a new shotgun. That one probably has less recoil than my Mossburg."

Heavy looked over and flipped open the latches for the container marked with the name of the EOD specialist. He smiled back at the driver and said, "No worries, Boomer. You have a shiny new toy as well. It looks like Norbert's loaded us up with lots of mags and drums as well."

Boomer smiled and turned back around as Ghost began to climb up into the MRAP. He found a long bundle placed in his storage bin, . The bundle contained with a note from Norbert that read, "This might help you in your hunt this time. I believe it belonged to a relative of yours."

Inside the bundle was a cane that appeared to be made from very old wood. The years of handling had soaked oils deep into the gnarled cane and created a patina that only came from time. A silver head extended from the top of the well-worn shaft. There was a silver band on both sides of the joint where the head met the cane. As Ghost placed both of his hands upon the ancient gnarled wood, several runes appeared in glowing white along the cane's form.

Ghost grasped the handle in his right hand and the shaft in his left. With a slight twist and pull, he separated the head from the shaft. Inside this beautiful old cane was a slim, rapier-like blade attached to the handle to form a sword. As he drew the blade partially, the sword recognized that he was family and emitted a soft white glow before it faded to shiny metal.

Outside the new War Wagon, Six talked with the DHS SAC from the Denver office.

"Agent Hart, I hate to leave things for you to clean up, but you need to be aware of a couple of prisoners that we have down in the county jail in Trinidad," explained Six.

Hart looked from Six to Smith and back. "You arrested some-one? Who? What do I need to do about it?" Hart asked Six.

Six tried to figure out how much Hart should be told.

"We have the acting mayor and the county coroner in custody in a holding cell in the county jail," Six began. "They are currently charged with assault on a federal officer. If our mission is successful, we will take care of their final disposition. However, if our mission happens to fail, you will need to coordinate with Agent Smith's office for final disposition. If you could send a couple of agents that you trust down there today and relieve the deputies currently watching them, I would appreciate it.

"Your team will immediately know if we are successful, as the prisoners will likely be going absolutely batcrap crazy. If that's the case, we'll be back to take care of them as soon as we can," Six concluded.

Agent Hart looked at the commander of this weird mix of agents that now included a sheriff's deputy from the county they were just in. She nodded and managed to sound inconvenienced and obliging at the same time.

"Alright, I'll send some folks down there. You better deal with this. I don't want this to wash back on me or my team," said Hart.

Six smiled tightly and then agreed. "We will," he said. "There is currently a team from the FBI HRT in town as well. They know DHS is in charge. Have your agents use them if necessary."

Again Hart nodded. "Anything else I need to know?"

Six gave a small laugh. "One last thing. The top speed on your little MRAP is limited to just over ninety-five miles per hour. According to our pilot, er... driver, it gets a little dicey to handle at that speed."

Six turned away as the Denver agent's mouth opened while she processed that news. She couldn't believe anyone would be crazy or dumb enough to go ninety in an MRAP.

Six shook hands with Agent Smith and Gretchen as they walked toward their waiting Citation. Smith motioned for the captain of the airplane to begin the preflight check and turned to the team leader.

"The C-17 stays here until you guys are done. It will transport you and the truck back to the shop when you are done. Keep me appraised. Good luck, and kill that creature."

Six saluted as Smith and Gretchen climbed the stairs. He turned and quickly walked back over to the waiting War Wagon, v2. He opened the side door and climbed into the passenger seat. As he fastened his seat belt, he gazed at the laptop station and row of gauges and instruments in front of him. He turned and saw Doc and Do-Right climb into the truck through the rear ramp.

Boomer looked over her shoulder and asked if everyone was present. After she received a chorus of "Here" and "Present"—and a lone "I'm not here," from Spooky—she flipped the switch. The rear hatch whined up and closed with a solid thunk.

As Six closed his door, Boomer reached down and turned the key in the ignition. The massive 435 horsepower Cummins Diesel engine fired up smoothly. Engaging the transmission, she turned to Six and asked, "Alright, boss, where are we going?"

24

BREACH

Divide, Colorado.

Approximately twenty-five miles west of Colorado Springs on State Route 24 lies the little town of Divide, Colorado. Settled in the 1880s, the town sits on the north slope of Pike's Peak, and is home to 127 people. The beautiful mountain views and the unique geography that has water run-offs in all cardinal directions draw visitors to, and through, this quiet little town.

Almost an hour and twenty minutes after leaving the Pueblo Memorial Airport, a large black **MRAP** bearing **DHS** markings rolled into the parking lot of the lone grocery store in town. The driver found a spot toward the back of the lot and turned off the engine.

Furious typing and the opening of latches in the back broke the silence.

Six turned around from the front passenger's seat and said, "Spooky, do you have eyes on the target yet?"

Spooky nodded without glancing up. "Yeah, boss. The satellite came online about five minutes ago. I'm targeting the area now for visual recon. And mirroring to your laptop... now."

Six looked at the display in front of him and nodded.

"Alright folks," Six began. "It's just after 3pm so daylight will keep the vamps inside. And there are no signs of any guards outside.

We are about three and a half miles from the turn-off to the silo. This is an abandoned Atlas-F silo. We believe we can get in. You know our objectives. First, figure out what the master and the mad scientist are doing, then stop it. Then kill them. Second, save the equipment because we might need it. Third, take out the bunker and anything in it.

"That second priority means that we have to be very careful of where we shoot and what we shoot it with. Heavy and Boomer, that means try not to use the pretty little FRAG-12 grenades for your new toys. In fact, be extra careful with your new toys, period."

Ghost nodded at his boss and asked, "What's the protocol? How are we going in?"

Six looked at Spooky and said, "You're not going to like this." Spooky just stared as he began to get an idea of what his boss was going to say.

He looked at the rest of the team. "Everyone goes in. Ghost, you and I are on point, and Heavy will back us up. Doc and Do-Right will flank Spooky behind us, and Boomer and God will bring up the rear. You guys will watch our back."

Spooky was almost apoplectic when he said, "What the hell, boss? I'm not leaving this truck. I'm your electronics guy, not the shoot-em-up guy. That's your job."

Six looked directly at the young analyst. "I need you along for your electronics expertise," Six reassured Spooky. "There is no telling when we're going to come across a lock that needs a code or a computer that needs to be cracked. In this case, you are vital to this mission. I'm putting you in the middle to protect you."

Spooky's eyes were wide, and he shook his head, making his wild hair fly. "I don't know anything about breaking codes on locks or anything like that. I won't be of any help."

Six consulted his computer. "According to the stores listed on this truck, in your pouch is something called an 'Electronic Lock Kit' and a special set of cables to use for your wrist computer. Both of them were placed in your bin by Norbert."

Spooky opened the bin at his side. "Frak me. There is a kit in here. I don't know whether to thank Norbert or to kick his butt when we get back."

Six smiled and asked if everyone understood the mission. He received a chorus of nods.

"If we have to split up," Six continued, "the fire teams will be the following: Alpha Team will be myself, Ghost, Spooky, and Do-Right; Doc will lead Beta Team, consisting of Boomer, God, and Heavy.

Load up with plenty of ammo. Take some stun and frag grenades if you're comfortable with them. Keep in mind that this is a giant steel trap. Ricochets and fragments will suck, so watch your fire and choose carefully. Use the tactical throat microphones for your radios. That will allow you to talk at a lower voice and still be heard. They can be keyed just by touching the sensor at your throat.

"When we reach the end of the access road that leads back to the silo, Boomer will stop and everyone but Doc, God, and Spooky will bail out."

The team leader pointed at his sniper. "God, you are up through the turret for the approach. Heavy, Do-Right, Ghost, and I will ride on the outside for rapid deployment. Boomer will drive us up to the silo and will block the drive leading back to the main road."

The team leader received a round of upraised thumbs, and he nodded to his explosives expert. Boomer fired up the truck and moved down the road until she spotted the small over-grown trail that led off to the left where the GPS said it should. She pulled into the car path, and stopped. She flipped the switch to drop the rear hatch as Six climbed out the passenger door. The passenger door slammed shut as the rear ramp dropped fully. Sitting about a foot and a half off the ground, the bottom stair easily cleared the weeds.

God popped open the turret and sat up through the opening, shouldering his M4 carbine. On the passenger's side of the vehicle, Ghost jumped up and grabbed the handhold just behind the front door, his carbine held loosely in his right hand. Having shed the heavy outer armor and BDUs, Ghost had instead opted for his original hunting outfit, including his long black leather duster and hat. Heavy jumped up next to the lanky hunter. The big man grinned as he slammed a drum magazine into his new AA-12 and charged the bolt.

On the driver's side, Six mounted up next to the window, holding his carbine in his left hand. Do-Right climbed up behind his boss and held his own personal AR-15 in his hand. Six looked over the former deputy and noticed that the deputy had taken the time to change into the standard black tactical uniform and armor that Gretchen had brought from headquarters.

Six nodded his approval. "Those BDUs look good on you," he said to the deputy.

He turned and rapped on the glass, giving the signal to his driver to move forward.

Boomer flipped the switch to close the rear hatch as the big vehicle started to lumber forward. Careful to maintain an even track and relatively slow speed, the explosives expert was very mindful of her exterior passengers. About three hundred yards down the access path, there was a fenced off clearing amongst the trees to her right with a small, squat building marking the entrance to the silo. Pulling up and blocking the gated entrance, she brought the truck to a halt and shut it down, mindful of taking the keys with her. She flipped the ramp release, and the back ramp dropped, allowing God, Doc, and Spooky to exit the vehicle.

Boomer waited until they had exited, and then she raised the ramp again, sealing the back against intrusion. She climbed in the back and got her new AA-12 out of her weapons bin and grabbed several drums and a couple magazines of Norbert's special ammunition. She purposefully left the mini grenades in the truck. After reaching up to check that the top hatch was shut, the demolitions specialist grabbed her pack containing some explosives and grenades and climbed out the driver's door, locking it behind her.

The team moved into formation. They carefully watched all around them as they approached the seemingly abandoned silo entrance in front of them. Ghost opened the gates with a loud creak, and it was only then that he realized that the forest around them was absolutely still and quiet. It was unnatural and confirmed to the veteran hunter that there were monsters in this area.

The team cautiously approached the entrance to the silo. The heavy steel door showed some signs of use, but the gleaming oil on the hinges revealed a hint that the "rusty abandoned look" might be just for show.

Six motioned for Ghost to cover him as he gave a tug on the handle of the door. It was solidly locked from the inside.

Six looked at Boomer and said, "You're up. Quiet and small."

The demolitions expert nodded and grabbed a strip of detcord from her pack. Sometimes used to trigger other explosions, Boomer knew that the "detcord" was a small explosive itself, and figured it should be enough to open the armored hinge on the door.

Motioning for the team to stand clear, she attached the leads to the detonator in her hand.

"Fire in the hole," she warned.

A loud ripping sound came from the front of the bunker entrance, followed by the loud "clang" of a heavy metal door falling off of its hinges echoed. The team quickly assembled in the entrance, and they shined their lights down the darkened stairwell. Ghost grabbed two glowsticks and broke them to activate their phosphorescent glow. He tossed each glowstick down the stairwell.

The team could see that the stairs went down about two stories and ended on a landing. They could clearly see through the grating on the stairwell, and it looked clear. In formation, the team entered the bunker.

The team carefully made their way down the metal stairs. Each agent watched for signs of rusted or broken stairs before they stepped, and each was looking around them for cameras or hidden obstacles.

Ghost hit the bottom of the stairs first and raised his hand to bring everyone to a halt. Leading away was a long corridor of cement. At the end of the corridor, Ghost's light revealed a corner with a passageway to the left. Other than the weapon lights mounted on the carbines and the ghostly green glow of the chem-lights, the tunnel and entrance were pitch black. Ghost scanned the wall and saw that the ceiling was a maze of steel mesh-encased conduit about ten feet overhead. The corridor itself was clean and free of debris or dust.

Ghost motioned his hand forward and led the team down the long corridor as Spooky took one last look at the sunlight filtering through the open doorway. He noticed that he was not the only one to glance back at the sunlight fading away as they pressed forward into the silo.

When the team reached the end of the corridor, the Ghost stopped and covered his boss with his rifle as Six approached the corner cautiously. The team leader peered around and spied a large hardened steel blast door designed to withstand attack and invasion. He tried the door, but it was locked.

Stepping back, Six turned and spoke in a low voice, "Spooky. Locked blast door. You're up."

Spooky nervously stepped forward and pulled a small box with wire leads out of his pack. All the security doors, including this blast door, were originally equipped with 1960s-era electronic locks. As he approached the door, he noticed that the electronic locks had been upgraded to current standards by the new owner. He pushed a key card into the slot waiting for him. Several wire leads ran from the card back to the small computer in his hand. As he watched the digital display, he saw numbers spinning down into a five-digit sequence as the computer used a brute-force attack to hack and find the correct passcode. When it finally stopped, he looked at the team leader and nodded.

Six nodded back and raised his rifle toward the door. The electronics genius keyed 4-9-4-3-6 into the keypad. The blast door hissed as it released its vacuum seal and swung open. The area beyond the door was designed to be an airlock, with another blast door roughly seven feet away. Unfortunately for the mad scientist, he seemed to have forgotten to seal the inner door. When the heavy blast door finally came to a stop in the open position, Six stepped in front of the door, leaning against it to make sure it did not close until his team was past it.

"Ghost, go through to the other door... looks like another blind corner," Six whispered. "Heavy, you follow. Block the open door until we all get through this mantrap."

Ghost and Heavy nodded as they began to move past their leader. The area beyond the trap was lit with cold fluorescent light spilling from around the corner. As Heavy braced his back against the open blast door, Ghost cautiously peered around the corner. This corridor ran dead ended in a blast door that appeared to have been forcibly opened and then torn from its hinges. Distracted by the massive steel door laying on its side, the hunter almost overlooked the small camera mounted in the upper right corner of the corridor.

He eased back around the corner and walked back to Six. "The next corridor is about twenty-five feet long, with a busted blast door at the end," Ghost reported. "There is also a camera mounted up high. It looks to be a newer model and is probably active. Past that, there appears to be the final blast door that is partially open. I couldn't tell if it was damaged."

Six nodded. "Ideas?"

Ghost's grin turned mischievous. He handed his rifle to his boss and said, "I'm going to stroll down the corridor and kill the camera. Once it's dead, the rest of you can come around the corner without being seen. If he sees me coming, he might think I'm alone."

The team leader thought for a moment and nodded his approval. He said, "I like it. Go for it,"

Six turned to ready the rest of the team while the hunter pulled out the silver inlaid cane and strolled around the corridor as if he belonged there. Once he reached the end of the corridor, he made sure that the area was clear and calmly reached up with the cane tip and smashed the little plastic camera. As he pulled the cane back down, the hunter heard a loud curse echoing from somewhere beyond the partially opened blast door.

Ghost clicked open his mic and warned Six, "Time to move, boss. Someone knows we're here."

He moved back down the corridor to meet the team as they

rounded the corner. Grabbing his rifle from Six, Ghost tucked the cane away and raised his rifle to his shoulder. The team moved back toward the end of the hallway that Ghost had just vacated.

When they reached what should be the last blast door on the level according to the plans, Ghost found that the door was partially jammed and would open no wider than three feet. He motioned for Six to cover him, and, with his rifle raised, Ghost squeezed through the door. Crashing to a halt, he found himself on a stairwell landing with a flight of stairs leading down three levels to the entrance for the first level. Ghost stepped to his right as he tried to cover all three flights at once.

Six came through the blast door opening and realized that Ghost needed some help. He told Ghost that he would cover him and ordered him to proceed to the next landing. The team leader swung his rifle down to cover the flight below them. Ghost shifted slightly and began to cover the stairway in the middle and then slowly moved down the wire mesh stairs. Heavy stepped through the doorway and immediately covered the stairs below them with his shotgun.

The landing was getting a little crowded when Six spoke up. "Three stairways leading down to command level one," he said "Heavy, Spooky. When we hit the bottom landing, you guys stay there and cover the stairs down to command two. Everyone else, will clear command one. Watch your targets and look for Dr. Kaine."

Heavy pointed his shotgun down the stairs in the middle. Six and Ghost carefully descended the stairs and guarded the lower landings with their rifles. They paused on the last landing before the doorway to gather the rest of the team. Doc and Do-Right quickly stepped through and walked down, joining the two lead agents on the landing. Boomer and God squeezed through and quickly joined the rest of the team with Heavy and Spooky bringing up the rear. The team made their way down the relatively short flight of stairs and came to a landing across from a six-foot wide opening with a faded sign above the open doorway proclaiming "Command Level One." Nothing living was visible.

As the team knew from the blueprints, the command level was a large circular level, roughly forty feet across with a ceiling approximately fifteen to twenty feet tall. The level was separated into compartments. According to the original plans, the first two doors to the left should be a janitor's closet and restroom, respectively. Beyond the monolithic wiring and ducting conduit in the middle should sit a small kitchenette, and the back of the level should house a mechanical room for HVAC and potable water.

At a silent three-count, Six and Ghost simultaneously burst through the opening. Ghost swung right slightly to cover the open side of the room as his boss stepped forward and opened the janitor's closet. Behind the two men, Boomer and God moved into the room and covered the restroom and the kitchenette entrances. Doc and Do-Right stepped in and to the right. The former deputy concentrated his sights on the mechanical room.

Doc noticed her vestments begin to glow their etheric blue and shouted a warning just as the first vampire burst from the kitchenette, distended jaws open and brimming with teeth. As the vampire charged out of the kitchen, the door to the restroom was flung open, and a human familiar reached for God who stood closest to Doc.

When Six turned to fire on the familiar rushing his sniper, he noticed that two revenants were running out of the mechanical room. He concentrated on his target, but he did not pull the trigger as he realized that Boomer was standing just beyond his target. He mentally switched gears and swung the butt of his gun at the maddened familiar's head, dully noting that the familiar was another teenager. The butt of his rifle connected with the back of the girl's head just as the butt of God's rifle stroked into her jaw. The force of the two blows violently jerked the girl's head around, and Six heard the bones of her neck snap as the body of the girl collapsed to the floor.

Boomer opened up with her shotgun as the vampire reached for her. The full-auto shotgun spit out a round every fifth of a second, and each three-quarter-inch bullet was one of Norbert's special vampire hunting slugs. The twelve gauge shotgun roared, and four slugs hit the chest of the vampire, sending it sprawling backwards from shock and energy. The demolitions specialist grinned wildly at the lack of recoil in her new toy. She raised the gun to her shoulder and fired another short burst, thumping three rounds into head of the vampire before it could recover. The head of the vampire disappeared in a mist of ichor.

As she raised the muzzle of her shotgun, she spotted two more vampires coming from the kitchen around the corner. She centered her shotgun on the beast to the right. As she pulled the trigger, Boomer heard at least two rifles open up around her. Both vampires were soon overwhelmed by the firepower as it hit them. Both

Boomer and God scored head shots on their respective monsters, and Six contributed to the withering firestorm.

Do-Right and Ghost targeted the two revenants that came howling from the mechanical room. Ghost called, "Right," and began firing at the monster on the right. Do-Right switched targets to the left-most revenant and pulled the trigger on his rifle.

Four holes appeared in the revenant's chest right over its heart. This staggered the creature. The former deputy raised his aim slightly higher and put the reticle right on the bridge of the creature's nose. Do-Right squeezed the trigger three times. He smiled slightly as the rounds all struck, emptying the monster's skull and dropping the creature's body to the ground.

Ghost managed to hit his revenant several times in the chest, but the shots only slowed the creature down as it shook off the effects of the bullets. He pulled the trigger again and again and felt a "click" as the bolt locked open on his carbine. He dropped his rifle to let it swing freely on its sling, and he drew the cane sword from his belt. With a click and a twist, the blade sprang to life and glowed white as it rose out of its sheath. The remaining revenant suddenly forgot the wounds in its chest and cringed back in abject terror. In a classic fencing stance, Ghost advanced on the creature.

The monster overcame its momentary fear and lunged at the hunter. He blocked the creature's claw attack with his sword as sparks danced all along the blade where the beast's claws struck. Ghost smiled as he whirled in a classic riposte, and the blade seemed to leap forward of its own volition and skewered the creature. The beast began to scream in pain, and smoke poured from where the sword ran it through.

As he ripped the blade out of the creature, Ghost parried the next claw attack with the shaft of the cane and again swung a masterful riposte. This time the blade met the creature's face and plunged through the eye and into the brain. The creature immediately stopped and dropped to the ground as if it no longer had bones. As he pulled his blade from the creature's corpse, the hunter flicked the blade slightly to remove all of the black ichor off the blade.

Ghost sheathed the blade as its glow faded. As he turned around, he saw the rest of the team staring at him.

Six looked at him and said, "We really need to have a chat about your background. I have a feeling I'm being left in the dark."

Ghost shrugged. "I suppose we should talk about it soon," the hunter replied. "After this mission."

Six nodded.

"What was that blade?" questioned Doc. "I've never seen anything like it."

The hunter chuckled drily. "It's designed to burn and damage vampires, or any of their spawn," he said. "It's been in my family for generations. Now I think it's time we go, boss," he said as he turned to his leader.

Six nodded and sent Do-Right, God, and Boomer back to wait with Heavy and Spooky. The rest of the team quickly cleared the remainder of the small floor. In the kitchen, they discovered a young girl, barely alive and fading fast, with feeding marks all along her throat, wrists and thighs.

Doc looked at her boss. Her voice was filled with compassion, "If we don't take care of her, she'll become a revenant as she dies."

Six said, "Wait a minute. I thought they were supposed to be cured if we killed the master that turned them. Why isn't she cured?"

Doc shook her head. "She hadn't turned before her sire was killed. If she had already turned, she would have likely turned back. Unfortunately, if they're still alive but not fully turned when the master dies, then they turn into a revenant."

She raised her cross and stake. Doc looked at Ghost. "Use your machete," she said. "Take her head once I perform the rites. It's the only merciful option."

The priest prayed over the young girl. The Latin phrases caused the girl to cry out in agony until she mercifully passed out from the pain. With a sharp plunge, Doc drove the silver spiked end of her cross into the girl's chest and straight into her heart. Ghost quickly stepped up and swung his machete and ended her torment.

25

KAINE

T he three agents were in a more sober mood as they rejoined the rest of the team. Heavy and Boomer both covered the stairway leading down with their shotguns, and everyone exchanged their partially emptied magazines for full magazines for their firearms.

Again, the team moved down the first two landings, pausing before the final set of stairs. Because he knew that the command level two should be the same size and shape as the level one, Six made a decision and stood at the top of the stairway leading down. He called out in a loud voice, "Dr. Bishop Kaine. We are here to talk with you. Come out with your hands raised. I'm giving you ten seconds to surrender peacefully... starting now."

The group heard a howling scream that announced a revenant. Two of the creatures barreled out the doorway below the team and lunged for the agents. Alerted by the screams, Heavy and Boomer both aimed and opened fire with their AA-12s. The deafening roar of the fully automatic shotguns quickly drowned out the screams of the revenants. The creatures never realized what happened as their mangled and torn corpses collapsed on the stairs.

Not willing to wait any further, the team moved down the stairs. As they reached the bottom, Six and Ghost again went through the doors first with Ghost covering the right side and his boss the left.

Two human familiars, each holding an aluminum baseball bat, stood by the ancient control center equipment on the left side of the room. As the humans surged toward Six, he flipped the selector switch on his M4 to burst mode and pulled the trigger.

A three-round burst chattered from the rifle hitting the chest of the familiar on the right. Six shifted to the left and placed a second burst into the chest of the familiar and watched as both tumbled to the floor. Flipping the selector switch back to single, Six stroked the trigger twice, once into each familiar's head. He stopped to cover what appeared to be a bedroom to the back and an open sleeping quarters in the center of the room and then motioned for the rest of the team to protect him by watching the other half of the level.

Ghost shifted his aim to the right as another screaming revenant burst around the corner. His rifle fire was joined by the deafening clatter of the full-auto shotguns carried by Heavy and Boomer. The chest and head of the creature disappeared in a spray of ichor, allowing the bottom half of the body to crumple to the ground.

God and Do-Right stepped over to join their leader in covering and exploring the left half of the level. Protected by the two agents, Six walked toward an open doorway located where an office as originally located on the plans. Six spied an unmade bed and some standard bedroom furniture in the former office. As he approached the room, he scanned the room and paused. He barely restrained himself from pulling the trigger. Huddled in the corner was a young girl, no more than eleven or twelve years old. Her disheveled clothing and frightened face made the DHS leader pause. He quickly scanned around the room to make sure that no other monsters were in there, and he muttered over his headset that one victim was alive.

Meanwhile, in the other half of the command level, Ghost slung his rifle and pulled the cane from his belt as Doc's vestments began to glow blue once again. He and Heavy stepped forward, allowing the priest to protect the rear of the party, while Boomer watched out for Spooky.

Another revenant screamed and burst from its hiding place and met its end at the tip of Ghost's ancestral blade. Ghost didn't have time to pull the blade from the skull of his latest kill when yet another creature appeared and charged for the hunter. The full-auto burn of Heavy's AA-12 roared as the center torso of the revenant who was attacking Ghost disappeared in a spray of ichor. The hunter yanked his blade free of the skull of the dead revenant, and looked at the big machine gunner.

"Thanks, man," Ghost said to Heavy. "Stupid skull on these critters doesn't like releasing blades."

The trio of agents moved further around to see the rest of the level. Ghost, Heavy, and Doc entered what appeared to be a fully functional portable genetics laboratory. Centrifuges and Gene-tracing equipment sat on the counters, with racks of test tubes and computers set between them. At the far back wall, was a man who matched the file photo of Doctor Bishop Kaine. The scientist's white lab coat was absolutely pristine, and he was holding a couple of vials of an unknown liquid material. The tall, lanky scientist was graying around the temples and wore his long dark hair in a ponytail. A pair of glasses was perched on his head.

From his viewpoint, Ghost surveyed the back corner of the lab where three large chairs with straps for the hands and feet of the subjects were arranged. In one of the chairs, partially human remains were still strapped into the chair. Only half of the remains looked human; the other half looked like some form of a nightmare straight out of Hollywood.

In the only other occupied chair sat a vampire that was obviously straining to break the bonds that held its wrists and feet to the chair. As soon as the vampire saw the blade in the hunter's hands, it recoiled in fear. When Doc entered the room, her vestments glowed bright, and the vampire began to panic in its attempt to free itself.

Ghost watched one of the thick synthetic wrist straps stretch and then break, the incredibly dense materials no match for the panicked strength of a vampire. The hunter quickly stepped forward and rammed the blade straight through the creature's eye socket. The vampire's snarling and growling were cut off abruptly as the blade passed into the creature's brain. The smell of burning, rotting flesh filled the room. A quick yank and the blade came free enough for the hunter to swing and decapitate the fiend. All three agents turned to the human scientist as they heard Six's report of finding the victim.

"Six, this is Ghost. This side is clear. We have Kaine."

Ghost, flicked the blade to clean any remaining offal off the blade and sheathed his sword. The glow had left both the sword and Doc's vestments by the time the rest of the team arrived. Heavy remained where he was by the door and pointed his shotgun at the unmoving Doctor.

Ghost noticed Kaine smile when the other part of the team appeared with a survivor in tow. He had just begun to wonder about that satisfied grin when the little girl shrank back and tried to hide behind Boomer.

Later, Six would piece together that several things happened simultaneously. It was when Doc began walking toward the child to check her over for injury that Doc's vestments once again lit with a brilliant blue glow. The child let out a loud hiss and climbed his explosives expert's back, swiping its now-clawed hand at the back of Boomer's neck.

Boomer immediately bucked hard. The movement broke the child's grip and sent it flying toward the wall. The girl nimbly shifted in the air and gracefully landed on her feet about ten feet away as she hissed and spat. Six noticed that the girl now had extended claws for hands and a mouthful of sharp fangs that were not present before. Rapidly filing that information away for later, he raised his rifle but did not shoot because he was afraid of hitting the equipment behind the creature.

Loud chanting in Latin filled the room, and a power thrummed through the team. Doc's vestments were so bright that it was hard to look at her. She had raised her large wooden cross in front of her and was walking steadily toward the vampire.

The creature hissed and spat, occasionally taking an ineffectual swipe at the priest, but it could not move any further. The vampire was pinned to the spot where it stood by the will and power of God as called by the priest. The closer she got to the creature, the more it shrank toward the ground, almost crouching into a position to grovel.

As she stood over the creature, Doc noticed that the girl was wearing some sort of camp uniform. She wore a shirt and shorts embellished with the emblem of some place called Blue Mountain Camp. The vampire looked up with defiance in her eyes. The priest carefully knelt over the creature and forced it all the way down to the ground. A quick turn of the wrist, and the silver end of Doc's cross plunged into the young girl's chest and pinned her to the ground as she screamed in agony and with hatred.

Heavy stepped forward and drew his khukuri blades. The edges glowed green as he stepped up and chopped off the vampire's head. Tears rolled down his cheeks as he sheathed his blades. Doc noticed that the girl's body did not disappear into the ether like a normal vampire's body would. She supposed that this was a different type of vampire, and she made a mental note to record as much information as she could about this new breed.

The rest of the team turned to a still smiling Bishop Kaine.

"Doctor Kaine. You will be coming with us now," Six said as he stepped toward Kaine.

The scientist gave a slight chuckle. "I don't think so. In fact, if you don't stop killing my people and drop your weapons right now, you will face a nightmare that you never dreamed possible."

The DHS agent looked around at his team. Doc was applying bandages to Boomer's neck, a lot of bandages from the look of it. Heavy had stepped back and was now guarding the door to the command level with his shotgun raised and pointed out the door. The rest of the team stood in a loose semi-circle around the mad scientist.

Six looked back at Kaine and said, "From where I stand, you don't have any bargaining chips. It looks like we've won."

Kaine shook his head. The scientist's voice was smarmy as he laid his cards on the table.

"Commander. In my hands I hold two vials of my latest creation," he began. "In fact, you've just experienced the results of the first direct field tests. You see, I've weaponized the vampire virus.

"Not only that, but I've given our new master race back the daylight. This virus infects one in every five humans by turning them into vampires. For those who it turns, they retain their old face and demeanor, unless hunting. They also are able to ignore the effects of sunlight and UV light. In short, they become the master predator that they were destined to be."

"Why do that, Doctor?" began Doc, "Why work with the monsters to enslave the human race? What's in it for you?"

Kaine smiled as he answered, his voice smooth and light. "Money, of course. Power. Wealth. Control. Zachariah has assured me that I will have a place in his dominion over the Earth. I'm going to give him the power to walk in the sun. I'm going to give him an army to control. And I will be well rewarded.

"Unfortunately, I'm quite immune to the virus. One of the unlucky. However, Zachariah guaranteed my safety and position of power. So I have to settle for 'favorite pet.' I don't mind. At least I'm not going to be left outside to be hunted."

Doc continued her questioning, "How does the virus work? Airborne or fluid contact? Is it a typical pathogen, or is it something else?"

The scientist looked puzzled. "How would a priest know all that to ask the questions? What are you?"

Doc smiled and said, "I'm a board-certified physician. How did you get blood-sucker and human genes to mix?"

Kaine laughed. "Vampires start out human and are changed by the original virus. All I did was deconstruct that virus and made a few, select changes. Zachariah offered plenty of test subjects, and I certainly didn't have to get 'FDA approval.'"

Kaine smiled and continued. "To answer your question, priest. The initial virus is airborne; however, every one of my new, improved vampires passes on the virus to those they bite or scratch. Your unfortunate team member over there will have to wait a couple of days to find out if she's infected."

The scientist looked at the rest of the team and raised his hands, showing off the vials filled with liquid. "Now put your weapons down and surrender, or I'm going to drop these vials and see how many of you are turned." The scientist smiled and raised the vials. "What will it be? Do you want to chance becoming a vampire here? Or do you want to live another day?"

Six looked at the rest of the team, and then back to Kaine.

"What do you want, Kaine?" asked Six.

"It's simple," said Kaine. "I'm going to walk out of here. When I'm clear of the bunker, you can do whatever you want. Until then, you don't get to do anything. If you follow me, I'll drop one of these vials in here. If you follow me outside, I'll drop one outside, and we'll see what happens."

The scientist took a step forward, and the team made a small path. As he cautiously walked amongst the team, Kaine looked at Boomer and shook his head. "I really hope you turn, darling. You could be a fun little vampire for Zachariah."

Boomer's eyes filled with hatred, and she shook with rage. God had to lay a restraining hand on Do-Right's shoulder. He could sense that the deputy wanted to intervene.

Keeping the agents in his sight, Kaine slowly walked backwards and away from the team. His smile grew broader as he crossed the room. As he approached the doorway, he nodded his head at Six and said, "I'll be seeing you, commander..."

The scientist abruptly stopped. His smile turned to a puzzled look and then to anguish. Kaine opened his mouth as if to speak and blood poured out. He half-turned to look behind him and collapsed to the floor.

As the scientist fell, Heavy released his big Ka-Bar knife and reached out to scoop up the delicate vials of the virus. Once he was sure that he had the vials securely in his massive hands, he nodded at his team leader.

"Sorry, boss. I couldn't let that guy leave with this virus," Heavy said. "Where do we want to put them?"

Heavy walked toward the lab area as Six and Ghost scoured the area for a safe vial storage and transportation case. Once they found a suitable case, Heavy retrieved his knife. Yanking it free, he calmly wiped the blade off on the corpse's clothing.

"Next time you want to take over the world, watch your back, Moron," he muttered.

Before he stood, Heavy noticed a small card that had partially fallen out of the scientist's lab coat. He grabbed the card and realized it was the electronic access card for the large blast doors. The big man handed the card to Six.

Six nodded his thanks and looked at Spooky. Six waved the electronics specialist over. "Spooky, secure these electronics and download whatever data you can from them."

He continued, "Ghost, help Spooky collect as much of the data and experimental equipment as possible.

"God. Do-Right. You guys cover the doorway. We still have to clear that silo—and we haven't run into Zachariah yet."

The commander walked over to the chair where Boomer was sitting. He looked at Doc, but she answered his unasked question with a slight shrug.

Six leaned over his explosives expert. "How are you feeling, Boomer?" he asked.

The demolitions specialist shook her head. "Those damn claws hurt. Even the fairly shallow cuts that I have were bleeding like crazy," she explained. "What's going to happen, boss? What if I change?"

Doc laid her hand on Boomer's shoulder while Six pondered that very question. The team leader looked right into the scared young woman's eyes.

"I don't honestly know, Boomer. If you turn, we'll probably have to put you down. Unfortunately, we can't worry about that right now. We need to take down this silo, and we'll need you to do it. Are you up for the task?"

Boomer nodded her head slowly, wincing as the bandages pulled at her wounds. "I can do it, boss."

Six smiled and stood back up. "Alright, people. We have a silo to clean out, and some electronics to salvage. God. Do-Right. You stay here and guard the virus and Spooky while he does his thing. The rest of you: it's time to kill more monsters."

26

SILO

Decommissioned Atlas Missile Silo, Divide, Colorado.

S pooky quickly inventoried all of the computer and electronic equipment in the lab. As he sat down in front of the computer, he clicked the mouse to wake it up from hibernation. The computer sprang to life with no requests for a password or verification of any kind. *Smart enough to create a vampire virus, but dumb enough to leave his computer without a password,* Spooky thought to himself. Spooky shook his head and went to work digging through the system.

God and Do-Right took up positions at the doorway while Spooky mined for data. They watched as the rest of the team filed out the doorway and down the short set of stairs to the final landing. At the bottom of the landing was another blast door, and this one was closed and sealed.

Six swiped the card in the access lock. The electronic readout above the keypad blinked to life and then said, "Enter Code."

"Spooky, Six. What is the access code for the blast doors?" he called over the radio to his busy electronics specialist.

Spooky thought for a brief second and then replied, "If I remember right, it was '4-9-4-3-6.'"

The team leader punched in that code and the door hissed open.

"Thanks, Spooky," he said. "Spot on."

Ghost was the first to step through the open door. Having sheathed the cane-sword, he once again held his rifle, muzzle up, ready to shoot monsters. The hallway beyond the door was about six feet wide and almost ten feet tall with the same maze of conduits and cables running along the roof. The access tunnel itself was about thirty feet long and ended in another closed blast door at the far end. Other than that, it was empty.

Ghost waved everyone through and walked toward the other end of the hallway. When he finally reached the end, he approached the closed blast door with Six. The team leader looked at the rest of his team and asked if everyone was ready.

"We have no idea what's in the silo area, said Six. "It could be empty for storage, or it could be Kaine's failed experiments. Make sure you have a full magazine. Watch your cross fire.

"Remember from the blueprints that there is a giant fifteen-foot gap in the middle of each floor. It's the elevator access. If the platform isn't there, it's a long way down to the bottom. The Department of Defense should have cleared out most of the heavy equipment, but there's no telling what Kaine moved in. Everyone ready?"

Ghost said he was ready while Heavy and Boomer gave a thumbs up gesture. Doc just nodded as she mentally prepared herself for more monsters.

Six radioed the others. "God, Six. We're opening the other blast door. If anything comes out of that tunnel that isn't us, kill it."

"Copy," said God.

The DHS commander reached up and swiped the access card and then keyed in the passcode. The door hissed and began to swing open. Six gripped his rifle a little higher and thought, *Once more into the breach. Literally.*

SPOOKY SAT at the scientist's computer as he tried to understand the filing system that Dr. Kaine had used. All of the folders and documents had labels that contained a series of numbers and letters and were in no order that the electronics specialist could discern. Giving up momentarily, the DHS agent inserted a specially built USB key in the slot on the front of the desktop unit. Wires ran from the USB key back to a small box that contained a power supply, a solid-state hard drive, and a couple of circuit boards. When the

USB device was plugged in, a series of small lights flashed down the side of the device. When all of the lights were solid green, Spooky pushed the button on top of the device to initiate a process that would automatically copy every hard drive and storage device attached to the computer.

With the copy process underway, the specialist randomly opened files and folders to see what was available. What little he understood made Spooky realize that this computer likely contained all the data necessary to replicate the process and all of the methodology behind it. He idly wondered what new gadgets Norbert could come up with if he got his hands on the data.

One document caught his eye. Labeled "Bu68dk3-668DH," the file was a memo from a youth camp. The document explained their camp dates and fees and that the good doctor would be welcome to send his son to the camp during the session designed for middle-school-age children that summer.

Kaine's son? He doesn't have any kids, Spooky thought to himself.

The realization that he had seen the camp logo somewhere before suddenly struck him, but he could not quite remember where.

Spooky looked around the lab. His eyes fell on the body of the young vampire, the one created by Kaine's virus. The blue of her shirt and shorts matched the blue of the camp logo. *Was that it?* The agent stood and walked over to the corpse. He nudged her and rolled her onto her back. As he looked down at her body, he realized that the same camp logo as was on the letter was on her shirt. Spooky softly swore.

The specialist drew looks from the other two agents as he ran back over to the desk and rummaged through the paperwork scattered over its surface. He found what he was looking for only after a few seconds. Raising the document in the air, he turned to the other two agents.

"Uh, guys, I think I know where Kaine tested the virus," said Spooky. "This guy was pure evil."

THE DHS TEAM leader heard the squelch as his radio activated.

"Six, this is Spooky. I think I figured out where Kaine tested his virus."

Six was about to reply when Ghost keyed in the numbers on the keypad for the second blast door. Designed as an airlock at this end of the tunnel, both the outer door between the command bunker and the silo and the inner door leading into the silo itself were locked and sealed. But the team leader was a fraction of a second too late, and the door hissed its release and began to open.

Havoc.

Two distended hands with razor-sharp claws wrapped around the door frame and yanked it open. The vampire standing in the doorway disintegrated under the withering hail of vampire-killing rounds from two rifles and two shotguns. The body was already beginning to disappear into smoke before it hit the floor.

Six and Ghost immediately stepped through the doorway and stopped at the edge of the landing. A short span of steel grating led across the two-foot gap to the platform. An octagonal platform about thirty feet across hung over the open space and was supported by massive steel springs attached at points around the inside of the silo. In the center of this platform was a square hole, about fifteen feet across and surrounded by a waist-high railing. According to the plans, this was supposed to be the second level in this structure.

Six looked up and saw the steel mesh underside of the level above them, with an elevator waiting in the center of that level. The team leader looked down through the same steel mesh beneath his feet and saw at least one other floor below. The silo was a bit overwhelming. The massive size and construction made Six pause briefly.

When the gunfire echoes died away, the team heard a cacophony of growls and screams, both from above and below. Six looked up and saw the platform above and stairs leading up from across the platform. The team leader spotted the elevator call buttons next to the pit and made a quick decision. He motioned to Ghost to close and secure the blast door. When the door slammed shut and hissed closed, Ghost joined him.

The DHS commander looked around and summed up their predicament succinctly. "Shit," he said.

He pointed to the Doc's glowing vestments and said, "Let's do this, people. Ghost and I will call the elevator. Doc, you help keep my back clear of nasties. Heavy, while we wait for the elevator, you cover the stairs. Boomer, your head is on a swivel—watch all the sides. We clear this out right now."

He reached over and hit the call button for the elevator.

As the elevator began to groan and move toward them, the rumbling was overshadowed by a roar from above. Leaping around the edge of the platform, a vampire rebounded off the concrete walls and sprang toward the team. Boomer didn't hesitate as she stroked the trigger on her AA-12. The volley of rounds caught the vampire in midair and tumbled the young creature. The vampire looked like she was maybe fifteen or sixteen before she was turned, and the rounds shook her hard enough that she landed in a heap.

Doc stepped forward as she shouted her Latin blessings, and the creature shrank back. Shaken by the fall and stunned from the priest's incantations, the vampire was unable to defend itself against Ghost's ancestral blade. The hunter stabbed the creature through the chest, then reversed and swung, striking the creature's neck and shearing the head clean away.

Distracted by the vampire, Heavy almost failed to see the revenant throwing itself down the stairs. When the creature leapt from the stairs, Heavy's burst of shotgun slugs tore into its chest. Thrown off balance, the creature misjudged its landing. It crashed into the railing that surrounded the elevator shaft and bounced over the edge, screaming all the way down. The screams were abruptly cut off by a crash from far below that shook the elevator's frame.

Six watched the area above when the revenant dropped over the edge of the platform and nearly landed on him. As the creature tried to bite him, the commander shoved the barrel of his M4 into the creature's open mouth and pulled the trigger. Ichor sprayed out, and the lifeless body tumbled over the edge.

When the elevator reached eye level with Six, the waiting vampire leapt out. The small boy, maybe eleven or twelve years old, grew fangs and claws and reached for the leader's face. As he quickly backpedaled, Six gave a startled shout, and Ghost swung around. The vampire shied away from the hunter and the priest; instead, he leapt for Heavy.

Heavy dropped his shotgun on its sling to dangle and drew the pair of khukuri blades from the sheaths on his back. Meeting the leap head on, both Heavy and the boy vampire swung at each other. The glowing blades were again unerring and removed the creature's head in one graceful movement. As the glow faded from the blades, Doc pointed and gasped. Heavy looked down and realized that there was blood running down his arm from a long, thin scratch down his forearm.

"Damn. Thing must've scratched me," Heavy said as he flexed his arm and moved around, causing a thin trickle of blood to ooze down.

Doc pulled out a small first aid kit and did a very quick bandage wrap on the wound. She tied the bandage and asked, "How's that feel? Good to go?"

Heavy nodded and picked up his blessed blades. "I think I'm going with these while we're here," he said.

The team stepped onto the platform and pointed their weapons upwards. Six pushed the button marked "Level One," and the lift started to rise.

As they slowly rose above the floor of the top silo level, Six looked around and was glad that there was nothing waiting for them. The team leader locked the controls on the panel and looked around. Boomer swiveled to keep watch over the nearby stairs.

Level one was mostly storage boxes and trash. It looked as if the creatures had been actually living on this level. The stench from the garbage was vile and masked the odor of anything else that was up there.

Six looked at his team and paused while he looked at Heavy.

"Are we ready? We're going to go down, level by level," Six explained. "We'll lock off the elevator on each floor as we reach it. We clear this place out as we go down. Scorched earth. When we get down below, Boomer, you figure out how to bring the house down.

"As we lower, everybody stay as close to the center of the platform as possible. Form a box in the middle with Doc in the center. Boomer, you and I will be on opposite sides. Ghost and Heavy, you guys are on opposite sides. Doc, you stand in the center and keep us alive and keep the really evil stuff back. Questions?"

Everybody shook their heads, and Six reached out to unlock the lift controls. He pushed the button for the third level. The lift began to descend. As they passed the second level, the team all subconsciously moved closer and thought about what they might find.

As they dropped below the second level, the lift rattled and a pair of taloned hands grasped the edge. As a vampire poked its head over the lip of the lift, the creature found itself staring down the large barrel of Boomer's shotgun. The vampire snarled, and Boomer pulled the trigger. The regular vampire's body started to dissolve before it hit the platform below.

As the lift came to a stop on the third floor, Six stopped it and locked out the controls. There was a large stack of packing boxes in front of Heavy. A scream tore through the air as a form hurled itself over the boxes and at the team. As the second creature bounced over the boxes, the machine gunner realized that they were revenants and shifted his stance for the fight.

Boomer shifted to face the screaming creatures when she was startled by hissing from directly above her. She looked up and saw a vampire release its grip on the ceiling of the level and begin to drop to the floor. The fiend pushed off the ceiling and was headed straight for the explosives expert. Boomer knew she wasn't fast enough and prepared herself for the attack.

The glow around the team intensified as the vampire got very close to Doc's vestments. An outstretched hand and a shouted phrase actually drove the creature away, to make it land in a heap in front of Heavy.

The stunned vampire landed right in front of the revenants caused the lead creature to trip and land sprawling across the vampire's back. Startled momentarily by the fallen vampire, the second one paused.

Heavy spotted the opening and took it. As he stepped forward, both blades whistled through the air and bit deeply. One blade took off the top of the sprawled out revenant's skull, and the other swiped clean through the neck of the vampire.

Boomer recovered quickly and sighted her shotgun down the barrel at the one remaining revenant. She stroked the trigger twice and sent two short bursts into the chest and face of the creature that killed it instantly. Boomer switched out her drum magazine for a fresh one and turned to look for more targets.

Six was watching the stairs when the young child vampire bounded up and over the top. Screaming in defiance, it rushed at the agents. The team leader pulled the trigger and sent a three-round burst of Norbert's ammunition into the chest of the young girl. The blast staggered the creature, but she quickly regained her footing and snarled. With bloodlust in her eyes, she again leapt at the DHS leader.

Ghost lunged forward. He timed his thrust to place the tip of his weapon right through the ribcage and pierce the heart. The vampire screamed in agony and rage as the blade burned its flesh from the inside. The creature raked its claws toward the hunter, raking them across the leather-clad arms and chest of Ghost's duster.

That one act of defiance was to be the creature's last. With the vampire pinned by the sword, Six aimed at the head of the small creature and pulled the trigger. Twice. Ghost pulled the blade free, and the body slumped to the ground.

Six quickly checked on his team. When each member of the team confirmed they were ok, Six engaged the lift. As they passed below the lip of the third level, the team scanned every nook and cranny of the walls and floor. This level was completely empty and was without even boxes or trash. Six didn't even pause the lift.

The fifth and sixth levels were also clear of monsters and debris, but that changed as the lift dropped toward the seventh level. Three sets of talon-tipped hands grasped the edge of the lift on different sides. The coordinated vampire attack struck with precision and speed, and the three vampires were on the platform before the team could react.

One of the vampires struck at Six directly. It reached up and knocked his rifle aside, avoiding the burst of bullets. As the vampire leapt onto the DHS leader, the vampire overbalanced its prey. Six crashed to the lift floor, and he fought for his life underneath the vampire.

Ghost's blade struck the vampire and ran it through the back and into its chest. The vampire howled in pain and reached up to swipe at the hunter. Six used the hunter's distraction to draw one of his M9s from the thigh holster. As he pointed the muzzle into the belly of the beast, the leader pulled the trigger.

By the fourth shot, the vampire rolled off Six and was stunned on the platform. Ghost yanked his blade free and swung it hard. In one swift movement, he cleanly removed the head of the creature. Six looked at the rest of the team to see how they were doing.

One of the vampires had landed in front of Heavy. Prepared for the attack, the big machine gunner raised the blessed blades he still carried and swung to decapitate the creature before him. The blades carried through the vampire's upraised arms and decapitated the creature. The heavy weapons specialist looked to his right and saw the vampire, cowering as it shrank away from the holy wrath of the priest. Boomer lined up the barrel of her shotgun and pulled the trigger, and the head of the cowering vampire exploded.

The team had no time to rest as four revenants attacked the platform. Six paused the platform at the floor of the seventh level, and the revenants leapt out of hiding. This time a concentrated roar of firepower quickly knocked out two of the creatures. Ghost and Heavy danced around the other two creatures as the teammates used their blades to wound the creatures while holding them out of striking distance.

Heavy was the first to get his kill. The two blessed blades bit deep into the neck of the revenant who proved too slow to avoid the big agent. With a simple yank and strike, the head of the revenant dropped to the platform as its body followed behind.

Ghost's revenant got desperate as its only remaining partner was killed. The revenant lunged in in an attempt to try to wrap up the hunter in a fatal embrace. Ghost's family blade burned right through the revenant's chest, but, unfortunately for the hunter, the creature used its last remaining strength and smashed its fists into the hunter's shoulder. Ghost felt a "pop" as the revenant died. Sheer agony blinded the hunter with red, and he passed out.

27

MONSTERS

Decommissioned Atlas Missile Silo, Divide, Colorado

Doc rushed over to the fallen hunter. As Six saw the priest bend over and start working on Ghost, he called out, "Cover Doc. Everyone pick an angle."

The medic-turned-priest gently, but quickly. assessed the passed-out hunter. She noticed that his shoulder was in a very odd angle, but she did not find any other wounds on his body. She rummaged through her field kit and found some smelling salts. She wafted the aromatic spirits of ammonia under his nose. Ghost awoke with a start and then cried out in pain as he clutched his shoulder.

Doc looked down at him and said, "Your shoulder has popped out of socket. This is going to hurt."

Ghost nodded and grasped her arm as she pulled and twisted. The pain flared and threatened to drag him unconscious again until the joint popped back into place. The pain dulled to a low ache, and Ghost flexed his hand and arm. He seemed to have most of his mobility back.

It was a long ninety seconds before Doc called out to Six. "We're good here. Let's get this over with," said Doc.

The team commander looked over and said, "We have no idea what's down there. Whatever it is, we kill it. Hopefully the master vamp is down here. Watch your targets, and watch the ricochets."

He reached out and pushed a button. The elevator began descending again.

. The farther they ventured down the shaft, the darker it became. Even though there were lights on around them, they somehow seemed dimmer. The normally brilliant lights turned to a low twilight as they descended. It was as if the very air surrounding them was dark and oppressive.

As the elevator dropped past the edge of the seventh level towards the bottom, there was a loud, terrifying roar from below. Moments later, it was followed by an answering call. The team gripped their weapons tighter, and Doc's vestments lit up and glowed blue.

Warned by her vestments, Doc looked up and watched as a vampire threw itself at the platform. It flailed in the air as it realized its momentum would take it near the priest. Doc raised the staked end of her cross and waited for the vampire to land. A loud thunder of gunfire disintegrated the head and upper torso of the vampire. Doc looked at the explosives expert and Boomer lowered her shotgun. The explosives expert smiled and swung back to face toward the walls of the elevator shaft while the glow faded on Doc's vestments.

The elevator stopped at the bottom of level eight a few seconds later. Here, the distance between the floor and the ceiling averaged about fifty feet instead of the usual twenty. The elevator platform was surrounded by several clusters of old storage tanks that previously housed liquid missile propellants such as liquid oxygen and hydrogen and a large mountain of crates. An inky blackness seemed to ooze from behind the crates, edging into the light and swallowing what it touched.

Out of the darkness stepped a large creature that none of the team had ever seen before. Standing eight or nine feet tall the massive creature made Heavy look like a small man. The bipedal creature stood upright and had dark gray and blue mottled skin. The large sloping forehead led down to an oversized mouth with two large canine tusks sprouting from the lower jaw. The creature wore a strange type of cloth for its clothing; the garments seemed to be made of a modern fabric, but both the top and bottoms were seamless and hung loosely, draping over the creature.

This creature was not carrying anything that remotely resembled a firearm. Instead, it held a large warhammer that looked like it weighed several hundred pounds. With short spikes on its face, the hammer looked more like a meat tenderizer than a weapon, if you discounted the three-foot-long blade that was opposite the hammer face. Holding this massive hammer in hands that spanned a foot and a half, the creature raised the weapon to parade rest, as if waiting to see what the team would do. As the creature stepped fully into the light, the inky darkness quickly curled in on itself and vanished with an audible "pop." The creature and the team stood as they stared at each other.

Six studied the creature for a brief moment and asked a simple question: "Doc? Ghost? What the hell is that thing?"

Doc and Ghost both shrugged.

"I don't know," Doc replied. "It is like nothing I ever studied in the Vatican."

The veteran monster hunter chimed in, "I've got nothing, boss. Some kind of troll, maybe? It's nothing like I've seen before."

The creature in front of them snarled in a bass rumble that the warriors felt in the soles of their shoes.

"How dare you call me a troll! I am Thoktaller, warrior of clan Urkantos, mightiest of all the Chikara," the thick, gravelly voice rumbled from the creature. "I was prepared to accept your surrender, but now I shall destroy you."

"Where do you come from, and how do you speak English?" Doc demanded.

The creature's chuckle dislodged some of the loose debris scattered around the team. "Ignorant human. I do not speak this 'English' that you prattle on about. The nexus translates for me, as it does for all travelers."

The creature then growled. "Enough stalling. It is a good day for you to die. Let us get on with it."

All of the team members already had their weapons drawn and pointed at the creature. Six squeezed the trigger and let loose two short bursts of fire. The team leader watched as most of his rounds impacted with the upper chest of the creature, but not one of them even penetrated the creature's clothing. The creature staggered slightly under the assault, but it never went down.

A fraction of a second after their commander had opened fire, the rest of the team did as well. Heavy and Boomer each unleashed a long string of automatic shotgun fire. The rattle of their shotguns was punctuated by the crack of Ghost's rifle. The combination of multiple hits from the automatic shotguns and the hunter's rifle was enough to make the creature reel and stumble.

Roaring in agony, the creature looked down and saw its thick purple blood running down and beginning to pool on the floor. It took a huge step forward and swung the massive warhammer at the team. All of the team members scattered like bowling pins as they tried to get out of the way of the enraged death.

Six and Ghost dove to the creature's left, and both of the agents ended up tumbled among the small crates and dross that surrounded the bottom of the silo. Six landed on top of a partially eaten animal carcass. Ghost landed a couple of feet away, ramming his still-painful shoulder into a small wooden crate that splintered on impact. The shipping materials in the crate spilled out and covered his face momentarily.

Boomer and Doc dove to the creature's right. They landed in a small pile of crates, and the impact jarred the cross from the priest's hands. As she reached for her sidearm, Doc realized that it, too, had fallen out during her dive. She quickly looked around the debris. Boomer landed and rolled onto her back about five feet away from Doc. She was somehow able to keep her hands on her shotgun. As she sat up to take aim at the creature, she realized she was sitting in a small pool of liquid. She really hoped that it was water.

Heavy leapt straight at the creature as he hoped to get inside the creature's reach. Dropping his AA-12, he rolled over and drew his blades. As they cleared the sheaths, he could see that they were again glowing their reassuring green. He crouched in front of the large creature and swung his blades. Hoping that the legs of this creature shared some of the same weak points that plagued human legs, he tried to swipe at the leg. The machine gunner's backhanded slash caught one of the giant creature's heels and bit deep, causing the creature to crash down on one knee as that leg gave out. Heavy rolled to the left and out of the way as he tried to stay out of range of those massive arms and giant fists.

Thoktaller had never felt such pain. His left leg refused to work, and he was angry that the insignificant humans had so far bested him. His rage was building inside him and threatened to tear itself out. But even with his rising rage, he realized that he could not take them all on in this condition.

"Matokar!" the creature roared.

The large stack of wooden crates directly behind Doc and Boomer exploded toward the team as another creature swung through the obstacles. Pieces of broken crates flew around the room. One of them struck Six in the head and shoulder and stunned him.

This new foe was of the same type and look as the first creature, but it was slightly larger and more muscular.

"My brother!" the creature roared back.

Matokar whirled his large warhammer above his head as he looked for his first target.

Doc scrambled to get out of the creature's way by backing toward the outer wall of the silo on her hands and knees. Here she was out of her element and out of the fight—her training never covered extra-dimensional beings.

Although Doc was fast, the movement caught Matokar's eye. Matokar looked at the small human nearly at his feet. Recognizing easy prey, he stepped toward her and prepared to strike. The giant creature grinned, its lips split showing rotting teeth and large yellowed tusks.

Doc began to pray.

Boomer had pivoted when the second creature burst through the stack of crates. Boomer quickly realized that this creature was targeting the priest, and the explosives expert dropped the drum from her shotgun and slammed a shorter magazine back into the receiver. She cycled the bolt, brought the automatic shotgun to her shoulder, and pulled the trigger. Twice.

The creature was about twelve feet away when Boomer's shotgun roared two short bursts of fire and the bolt locked back on an empty magazine. The first burst hit the creature in its right shoulder, and the miniature FRAG-12 grenade rounds detonated. Designed to explode and penetrate up to a half-inch steel plate, the miniature grenades detonated and tore apart the creature's shoulder; the damage severed the arm at the joint. The giant monster was only beginning to realize that it was in pain when the second burst hit the center of its chest. All four rounds impacted in a dinner-plate-sized area.

Matokar stood still for a second. As he looked down, it occurred to him that there was a hole where his chest and lungs were supposed to be. Even the natural bone plating that protected the heart of every member of his race was cracked. He fell to his knees, and then gave in to the embrace of death.

After seeing his brother killed so violently, Thoktaller roared in rage and grief. He ignored the human at his side and scrambled forward as he reached for the one who had just slaughtered his kin. He was brought up short when a human stood in front of him and drew a sword that glowed white in the dim light.

Angry that this insignificant human would dare challenge a warrior such as him, he struck at the human. The man dodged the creature's feeble attack and countered with an attack of his own. The tip of his sword pierced the creature's chest, and Thoktaller felt it lodge into the bone structure that grew around his heart. His rage blocked his pain, and he swung again at this swordsman. The man barely dodged his attack, and the swordsman countered with a thrust that struck bone. Each thrust injured the creature, drawing blood, and Thoktaller could feel his life-force ebbing away.

Ghost yanked his sword from the chest of the creature. He settled into his dueling stance as he prepared to dodge another attack from the massive creature. He was still perplexed that he seemed to be hitting some sort of boney substance inside the creature's chest. The creature feebly swung at him again. Ghost drove his blade into the creature's chest. This time, the creature seemed to give a final heave and collapsed, nearly trapping the hunter's ancestral blade underneath its great bulk. On the back of the now-dead monster clung Heavy. Both of his blessed blades were buried to the hilt in creature's back.

"I thought I'd give you a hand. I wasn't sure this damn thing was ever going to die," Heavy said as he wearily smiled.

Ghost smiled and agreed, "I wonder what it is."

Six stood up and shook his head as he felt a gash on his forehead. "Everyone ok? Make sure there's nothing else hiding down here," the leader said.

The team slowly rose from the wreckage around them. Each team member brushed at the debris on their clothing, and then scoured the level. They made sure that they were truly alone in the bottom of the silo. When they found no other creatures, the team leader gathered everyone together.

"Ok, Doc, Ghost. Either of you know anything about these creatures? Why didn't your robes light up, Doc?" questioned Six.

Doc shook her head. "They must not be vampires. My vestments only warn of hostile undead nearby, and these creature were clearly living," she explained. "What did it say it was? Chikata? Chikara?"

Ghost clarified that the beast called itself a Chikara. "I have never heard of that type of monster," he added. "I wonder if Section 28 has any records."

"We'll have to ask later," said Six. "Everybody make sure they have everything with them. Make sure you didn't drop anything. If you did, ask for help to find it."

Six activated his mic as he attempted to contact Spooky. "Spooky, Six. What's your progress there?"

"I'm about wrapped up here, boss. Maybe ten more minutes," Spooky replied. "You should see some of the stuff this dude had. I think I know where he released this virus. And you are not going to like it."

"Alright. We'll discuss it when we get up there. You have your ten minutes," Six said as he answered his electronics specialist. "Prep everything that we need to take with us. Anything left behind is going to be buried."

The team leader looked at his team to make sure they were ok. Doc had found and retrieved her cross, and everyone else was verifying that they still had all the gear they came in with.

"Ten minutes 'till we move out," said Six. "Doc, take some tissue samples of these critters, in case Agent Smith wants them. Ghost, take all the photos you can on your SSP. Take a video walk around as well. That should get us enough visual evidence. Heavy, I want to take one of the heads with us. You've got the blades; find a bag or box for transport. Boomer, bring this silo down, and don't let it be recoverable. I want to fill in this silo, the tunnel, and the command levels. Make your plans and start rigging. Set everything on a timer for, say, one hour."

Everyone acknowledged their assignments and got to work. Six walked around to see what exactly was in those crates that had been scattered about the silo. Most of them had contained basic necessities such as food, water, and clothing. A few of the crates had held what appeared to be items or knickknacks, whose manufacturer and style the agent had never seen before. Following a hunch, he grabbed several of the items to take them back to Section 28 for analysis.

Ten minutes later, everyone else had finished their duties, and they were waiting on Boomer to finish placing her last explosives. She walked toward the group and stared in shock at Heavy. The big machine gunner stood in the middle of the lift with a box under his arm and one of the large warhammers over his shoulder.

After Heavy had severed the head of one of the creatures, he had examined one of the dropped warhammers. Although he had expected to find it to be incredibly heavy, the massive hammer only weighed about eighty pounds. Because it was made of a metal that he had never seen before, he figured that Agent Smith would probably like to have one of these as well. When he carted it over to the elevator, Six had glanced at him and raised an eyebrow. The big man laughed and said, "Souvenir." The team leader could only shake his head trying to stifle a laugh at the big man's choice.

When all of his team was ready, Six pressed the button marked "Level Two" on the control panel, and the elevator slowly ground its way upwards toward the second level. Once the team had arrived at the second level, they all walked into the tunnel, pausing long enough to allow Boomer time to place another series of charges at the end of the tunnel nearest the silo.

The team walked toward the other end of the tunnel, and Six radioed ahead.

"We're coming up the tunnel now. Stand down," Six ordered.

"Copy," God replied. "We're all clear here. Come on in."

The silo team walked out of the tunnel and into the command level. The sniper and the former deputy both stared at their disheveled teammates, from their minor wounds to the torn jump-suits all around. When Do-Right saw the warhammer Heavy was carrying, he could only stare with a gaped mouth.

Six waived off any questions. "I'll fill everyone in on the way," Six said. "Are we set here?"

Spooky appeared around the corner and placed a small box on top of a small pile of similar boxes. He said, "I've got everything I need boss. We're ready to blow this sucker sky high." The electronics specialist caught sight of the giant warhammer. "What the heck is that thing, Heavy?"

The big man made a show of looking at the warhammer, then looked at Spooky and gave the same answer he had given his boss, "Souvenir."

Spooky thought for a moment and replied, "Remind me to never really piss you off."

Six scleared his throat to get his team's attention and started to direct them.

"Alright, let's start hauling all of this gear out. If you have a free hand, grab a bunch of stuff. If we have to make multiple trips, we stage everything in the entry corridor and then take everything out to the truck. God, you and Boomer have overwatch. Don't carry anything. Boomer's going to be laying charges behind us."

Boomer set several small explosives in the doorway and in the lab area of that command level. As the team carried all of the equipment and boxes past the first level, she stopped briefly to plant even more charges. With enough hands and help, the team did not have to make more than one trip, and Boomer placed charges at specific intervals throughout the tunnel behind them. When the team had left the tunnels and had moved to the waiting War Wagon, Boomer had Heavy prop the blown entry door back up and wedge it into the opening.

While they were able to store everything else inside the storage compartments of the truck, Heavy's giant souvenir wouldn't quite fit. He reluctantly consented to wrapping the massive warhammer in a tarp and strapping it securely to the top of the MRAP. After sternly warning Boomer about the consequences of losing or damaging his prize, he finally was able to secure it to his satisfaction.

As they waited for Boomer's explosions to seal the site, Spooky uploaded a report to Agent Smith about the excursion and included a query about the strange monsters encountered. While the report was being transmitted, the electronics specialist gave his team leader some troubling news.

"I think I figured out where the creepy Doctor Kaine unleashed and tested his virus," Spooky said as he began pulling up maps and charts on his terminal. "According to his notes, what he said about the virus spread appears true... only one in five typically contract the virus, and it takes a couple of days to incubate. He increased those odds dramatically, to fifty-fifty, when he used a series of direct injections. And according to this notation, the 'stability and manifest powers drop according to each generation of the host.' I think that means that every time a new vampire is created from a new breed, the powers that show up are a bit weaker than the generation before."

Doc leaned over Spooky's shoulders and read some of the technical areas of the document. "Spooky's correct. Each generation gets less powerful," Doc explained.

Spooky nodded his thanks and continued. "So where would you test this out? He needed someplace close, yet out of the way, and somewhere his subjects wouldn't be missed for weeks. I think he chose a youth summer camp."

Boomer swore, and Doc looked at Spooky in horror.

The electronics specialist continued, his voice flat and somber. "Every one of the new breed of vampires that you fought and killed was a young kid. I also confirmed that with the records. Two of the new breed that I saw both were wearing camp attire from this 'Blue Mountain Ranch.' It's a youth camp about sixteen miles from here. On his hard drive, I found a couple of letters to the camp, as well as an application for a youth to attend. That's the only proof I have at this point, but my gut says I'm right."

At that moment, the timer on Boomer's SSP went off. Boomer shook herself. "Thirty seconds until detonation."

While everyone found a porthole to look out, God reached up and shut the top hatch as a precaution. Seeing the move, Boomer reached over and toggled the switch to close the back ramp and sealed the vehicle.

As the rear hatch closed, a distinct rumble shook the MRAP on its massive springs. About a hundred yards away, the tunnel entrance collapsed with a shower of dust and debris.

Boomer looked at her team leader and said, "Alright. So what's next?"

28

HUNTING

It was late afternoon as the jet black **MRAP** marked with "Department of Homeland Security" rolled through the front gates of Blue Mountain Ranch. Thirty minutes earlier, the agent in charge of the team had contacted his boss in Langley. After a brief discussion, Six had received the approval to hit the youth camp hard, and with as much firepower as they needed.

With real-time satellite imagery to guide them, the team was able to form a rudimentary plan to assault the compact youth camp. Realizing that the age of the campers ranged from seven to sixteen, Six knew that they had to take extra care in planning this raid. Agent Smith told the team leader that they could not actually shoot unless they had positive proof that the camp was infected. They had to get a reaction from the campers and staffers and prove, to their satisfaction, that the camp was overrun.

In the end, the simplest plan was to roll up in the War Wagon with the story of an escaped convict on the loose. After Boomer pulled the truck to the front of the office building, they would all deploy quickly, having already geared up, and Doc would only climb out when they were relatively certain of infection. God would be up in the turret as soon as they established the presence of vampires.

Boomer pulled to a halt in front of the main office building and turned off the engine. As the big diesel cooled down, she flipped the switch for the back hatch. Six jumped out of his side door and walked around the front of the truck to meet the camp staff member who was coming out of the office.

The older gentleman introduced himself as the camp director, Frank Gould.

"What are you guys doing here? Is there some kind of problem?" the director asked.

Six gave the established cover story.

"I am Special Agent Burt Holstein, Department of Homeland Security. I hate to say this, but there is an escaped killer on the loose. His GPS tag last put him near this area. You need to enact whatever safety protocols you have in place. Every camper needs to be in his or her cabin, and we'll take one of your people with us on a quick look around the area to make sure he's not hiding out here."

The older gentleman turned and quickly walked into the office area. A moment later, the team heard a feedback squeal from the PA system, and then the director's voice came on.

"Attention campers and staff. This is a safety recall announcement. All campers and staff to their assigned cabins. Again, this is a safety recall announcement. All campers and staff report to your assigned cabins. I will provide more detail shortly."

As the director made his announcement, Six leaned over and activated his own mic.

"Doc, stay in the War Wagon with Spooky until I tell you to come out. We may be able to catch a break on this one," said Six.

The director walked out of his office and found a team of six DHS agents in a loose group, all facing different directions. The lead DHS agent introduced the rest of his team and asked the director if he had enough staff members not currently assigned to cabins to send one with each of his team members.

The camp director shook his head. "I can maybe rustle up three or four more but not enough."

"That's fine," Six said as he nodded. "The rest can find their way, and they can explain what they are doing to any cabin they meet. Can you get those people over here now?"

Gould reached for the walkie talkie radio on his hip. "Attention, auxiliary staff," he began. "I need you at the main office ASAP for briefing and assistance. Please come quickly."

The camp director looked up and saw three people already walking across the camp toward him. A fourth soon walked out of another outbuilding and jogged toward the growing group.

Six turned toward the truck and keyed his mic. In a low voice, he said, "Spooky, can you monitor their walkie channels? I want to know what they're saying."

He could hear the smile in Spooky's voice. "Way ahead of you, boss," Spooky explained. "I'm monitoring all CB band and digital 900Mz bands. If they say anything, we'll know about it."

Six keyed his radio to answer. "That's why you're the best. Six out," he said.

Frank introduced the agents to his staffers. "This is Cliff Legg; he's the rifle instructor. This is Lynn Powell. Lynn is our camp nurse. Yvette Shand is our arts director. And Dylan Blaney is our chef. Everyone else is either in town or with their assigned campers."

Six nodded and pointed to his team, pairing them off with the staffers. "Jesús, why don't you go with Mr. Legg? Rebekah, you work with Ms. Powell. Christian, why don't you accompany Ms. Shand, and Art, why don't you help Mr. Blaney."

The team commander paused as if pondering his last agent. "Jonas, you wander around and check on the outlying buildings. I'm going to stay here and coordinate with Frank. I'm waiting on the sheriff to call back anyway.

"Each team take a different set of buildings and cabins. Verify the adults and kids, number and names. You each know what this guy looks like, so keep your eyes open. Any questions?" Six asked. After pausing momentarily, he continued, "Alright then, let's get this show rolling."

All of the pairs split off. Boomer and the nurse headed toward the girls' cabins. Quickly moving across the grounds, the two women hurried across the tennis courts and approached the first cabin. The cabin was filled with the older girls. As the camp nurse explained why the DHS agents were there, the explosives expert carefully looked around, trying to determine if any of the girls were infected. The bunks and rooms were as neat as could be expected from young teenage girls. Almost every bed was filled, although there were a couple that stood empty or unmade dotted throughout the rooms.

Once the counselors in the cabin assured Ms. Powell and Boomer that everyone was accounted for, the two women and went to the cabin that housed the younger girls. After meeting the counselors there, Ms. Powell and Boomer were told the same story, that everyone was accounted for and that there had been no signs of strangers around camp. A few more empty beds dotted the rooms here, but no mention was made of them. While Boomer did not notice any outward signs of infection, the explosives expert's intuition told her that something was very wrong. As they stepped out of the second cabin, the nurse told Boomer that she needed to take care of some items in her office and asked if Boomer needed her help any longer. Boomer assured the nurse that she would be fine, and the nurse trotted across the expanse of grass and scrub that covered the grounds.

As she walked away, the nurse pulled out her walkie talkie and said, "This is Lynn. All of the girls are accounted for. Heading to my office next."

As Boomer explored the area around the cabins, an older teen girl, probably fifteen or sixteen years old, snuck out from behind a cabin. Boomer tensed and swung her rifle in the girl's direction. When she realized that the girl was not going to attack her, the explosives specialist asked, "What are you doing out here? It's not safe."

The young teen looked at her. "It isn't safe in there either," she whispered. "Last night, Tina was taken away. I think I'm next. I think I'm the only 'normal' one left."

Boomer knelt down and softly said, "Tell me what you know. I'll help you."

And the girl began to talk in soft, hushed tones.

ABOUT TWO HUNDRED yards away from Boomer, Heavy jogged with the camp cook toward one of the staff cabins and the mess hall. As he took a quick glance inside the staff cabin, the machine gunner noted that there were four made-up bunks in the men's side of the cabin. As he looked in the women's side, he noted that there were three made-up bunks and one that was completely bare.

He nodded at the chef, and they moved to the mess hall. The hall was cavernous, large enough to sit over a hundred campers and staff at the tables arranged in neat lines. Through an open doorway on the back wall, Heavy could see a large kitchen. As the pair walked around and through the large mess hall and kitchen, something seemed off. Heavy couldn't quite put his finger on what was wrong. He noticed that everything was put away neatly. It was all very clean.

As they were ready to leave the expansive mess hall, he suddenly realized what was wrong. It was *too* quiet. The chef should have been preparing food for the next day, and he should have had at least one other person helping him either prepare a meal or clean u from a meal. There should have been meals being prepped;

instead, the kitchen was spotless, and there was no one else in the building.

Turning to the chef, Heavy asked, "What time do you serve dinner here?"

The cook started stammering an answer. After several moments, he finally blurted out his response. "Five o'clock. Why?"

Heavy glanced down at his watch and realized that it was just after five. "Just wondering," he cautiously responded.

An odd look crossed the cook's face, and he said, "Will you excuse me a moment. I need to make a phone call. My office is back through there. I'll be right back out." The cook walked into his office and then shut the door.

Heavy began to look around, searching for evidence that the kitchen was actually being used. As he opened the refrigerators, the machine gunner found what seemed to be enough food to feed the entire camp. When he opened the walk-in cooler, he found a great deal of meat stacked on shelves as well as other cold storage food stacked away neatly. His cursory glance seemed enough and he turned to go, but then he spotted something in the back of the meats area. The big man reached back on the shelf and grasped a piece of meat that seemed out of place. Realizing what it was, he shuddered as he drew it out of the pile.

DO-RIGHT followed the older arts and crafts director as they headed north out of the office area. They first visited the offices for the staffers, including the nurse's office. Verifying that there were no intruders present in those areas, the two walked over to the large building that was just north of those offices and past the pool. As they trekked across the field, the former deputy marveled at the complete lack of local wildlife and nature sounds.

The wooded area surrounding the camp should be teeming with life, full of the sounds of birds and animals, but this area seemed almost unnaturally quiet. His hunter's instincts told him that this meant that there was, indeed, a major predator in the area.

The two reached the doors of the recreation hall. As they walked through the large set of wooden double doors, the young deputy looked around and whistled softly. The large building was elaborately decorated in the rustic charm of the west. The wood plank flooring matched the vaulted ceiling and exposed beams. The large exposed beam ceiling led his eye to the opposite end of the room to the massive fireplace that stood as the focal point of the room. Several long community tables were scattered throughout the expansive open area and, on one side of the room, an empty ping pong table and a foosball table awaited their players. Along one wall stood large cabinets and shelves filled with art and craft supplies.

"What a beautiful facility. You guys must be proud," the deputy commented to Ms. Shand.

"Thank you so much," she replied. "It makes a great place for the kids to be creative."

After verifying that no one else was in the facility, they closed the doors again and walked back toward the main office. Do-Right looked to their left and noticed a large building next to the small stables. Pointing to the building, he asked Ms. Shand, "What's that building?"

"That's one of the original lodges," the arts and crafts director explained. "They're currently trying to gather enough donations so they can renovate the building and make it usable, again. Right now, it's closed off because the structure is unsafe."

The deputy pointed to a lonely house up a short hill. "And that one?"

Ms. Shand smiled, "That's the head handyman's cabin, but I don't know if he's back yet. He went to town earlier today to pick up some supplies. "

Do-Right began walking toward the other buildings. "Let's go check those while we're out here," he said, not waiting for an argument.

The arts director nodded and grabbed her walkie talkie. "This is Yvette. Pavilion and offices are clear. We're heading up to Henry's cabin and the bunkhouse."

GOD AND MR. LEGG, the rifle instructor, walked toward the boys' cabins at the north end of the camp. The only building area further north was the archery and rifle range. Ghost wandered along with the two men and then left them to check out the outlying range.

The sniper and the rifle instructor approached the first of the boys cabins, which the rifle instructor informed him was for the youngest of campers, ages seven to nine. The two walked up to the cabin door, and the camp staffer introduced the DHS agent to the boys' counselor. After explaining what the DHS team was doing there, God walked around the cabin. He looked at the kids and talked to those who wanted to talk. He noticed that there were several empty bunks here and there, and there seemed to be no pattern or apparent reason for it. After he verified that all the counselor's kids were present, he and the camp rifle instructor left to check out the next cabin.

In both of the remaining boys' cabins, there were several empty bunks, much like the first. As God walked around the third cabin with the oldest boys, he noticed a small tear in one of the empty bunks, with a faint pinkish stain on the edges of the mattress. Feigning that he never saw the tear or stain, he kept his smile in place and walked right past it in stride.

The DHS sniper walked out the door with the camp rifle instructor, and God motioned to the bathroom and shower rooms that stood a short distance away.

"Let's check those out, then we can head back," said God.

The rifle instructor nodded and grabbed his walkie talkie off his belt. After keying the microphone, he said, "This is Cliff. All the boys are accounted for. We're on our way back soon."

GHOST PASSED THE BOYS' cabins and headed toward the boathouses that sat on the banks of a small lake. After quickly glancing around the structures, the hunter realized that they offered no place to hide, and he moved on toward the rifle range just around the bend in the access road.

As he walked, he keyed his microphone. "Spooky, Ghost. Any signs of life around the rifle range? Hot or cold?"

Spooky quickly replied, "Wait one... yes. I have one heat source in the bushes on the north side of the range, about twenty yards north. Looks like adult size. No other info."

Ghost replied, "Thanks, Spooky. Ghost out."

The hunter continued to stroll casually toward the range. As he approached shooting stations, he looked all around the range, including near the backstop. He then stood and faced the bushes Spooky told him about and cradled his rifle. Without directly pointing the rifle at the bushes, Ghost readied it enough so that he could bring it to bear before whatever was in the bushes had a chance to reach him.

"I know you're back there," he called out. "Come on out. I'm a Special Agent with the Department of Homeland Security. I will not harm you if you come out now."

A youthful sounding male voice rose from the bushes. "Don't shoot. I'm coming out. I'm unarmed."

Ghost watched as a young man in his mid-twenties stood slowly and raised his hands. He carefully stepped out of the brush and walked toward the agent.

Lowering the rifle a fraction, Ghost motioned for the man to come closer.

"Who are you, and what are you doing out here?" Ghost demanded.

The man nervously looked around them. Seemingly satisfied, he spoke.

"I'm Bill Buckhorn. I'm the archery instructor and assistant rifle instructor here. I'm so glad you guys are here. I've been hiding out here for two days. I think they've given up on finding me," the man explained.

Ghost looked the man over. "Why were you hiding out here?" he asked. "Who are you hiding from?"

The man looked around and gulped. He took a breath and began to explain.

"I think they're killing some of the kids. I noticed a few of the kids disappear over the last couple of days. And I think it had something to do with that doctor that was out here a few days ago. The director and the nurse said something about having everyone inoculated against a particularly nasty bug going around. After that, something changed."

There seemed to be a hitch in the young man's voice. "Yesterday, I was in the kitchen to get a snack during my break. I opened the cooler for some food, and I found... an arm! I thought it was a joke at first, but on the wrist was a craft bracelet that I recognized as belonging to one of my campers. I was told that she left camp early because she was sick. I freaked out and ran into the woods, and I haven't been back since." Tears slowly coursed their way down the man's dusty face.

Ghost reached down and pulled his cross out of his pocket. While not a Catholic, the hunter long ago learned how powerful faith was as a weapon against the undead. The hunter looked down. The cross did not give any hint of light, nor did the man shy away from it. He decided to break a few protocols and trust his instincts.

"I know this is going to seem strange, but would you reach out and touch this cross for me?" Ghost asked. "Just touch it."

The young camp staffer reached out tentatively and touched the cross. It stayed dark, and he was not burned.

The man looked at Ghost and asked, "What's the big deal about that cross? I'm wearing one here." And he reached into his shirt and pulled out his own plain gold cross.

Ghost nodded and held up his hand to the man. He keyed his radio and then spoke.

"Spooky, Ghost. Made contact. Check camp records for Bill Buckhorn. Archery instructor. And can you send a photo of Kaine to my phone?"

"Sending picture now," Spooky replied. "Confirm William Buckhorn listed as staff. Specialty is archery. Running search now. Twenty-six years old. Five-eight. Just over two hundred. Brown hair, brown eyes. Looks like possibly Navajo. Does that help?"

Ghost smiled. "Perfect," he replied. "Ghost out."

The hunter held up his phone with a picture of the late Dr. Bishop Kaine displayed on the screen. "Is this the doctor that was out here for the inoculations?"

"Yeah, that's the guy," Buckhorn said with a nod. "So who is he?"

Ghost smiled grimly. "Someone who keeps causing trouble. Even from the grave."

He held up his hand again to silence the archery instructor.

"Six, Ghost. Attention for all team. Confirmed sighting of Kaine here at the camp three days ago. Gave injections to staff and campers as 'viral inoculations.' Witness says kids are disappearing. Outbreak confirmed."

"This is Six. Copy report. Anyone else have confirmation?"

"Six, Boomer. Confirmed with another witness. Teen girl."

There was a long pause.

The team leader quickly thought created a battle plan. With his team spread all over the camp, he needed to get them back to the office area as quickly as possible. As he was thinking, he left the presence of the director and stepped outside to the War Wagon so that he could have some privacy from the camp director and his staff.

He made up his mind and let his team know. "This is Six. Everyone back to the main office to regroup. Meet at the Wagon. Ghost, Boomer, exercise caution. Keep your cargo safe."

Boomer grasped the hand of the teenager a little more tightly as she walked with her across the grass and toward the offices. The explosives expert found herself constantly looking around, waiting and watching for an attack. She saw God and the staffer with him appear from behind the boys' cabins, traveling at a jog. The sniper altered his course slightly so that he would be able to meet with Boomer and walk with her the rest of the way back to the truck.

Do-Right loped back down the hill from the empty groundskeeper's cabin toward the offices. As he looked to his right, he saw Ghost emerge from the wooded trails, his trench coat flapping and hat threatening to fly off with his movement. Beside the hunter trotted a young man who looked to be just older than the deputy. Their paths converged near the main pavilion, and they walked the rest of the way to the offices together. It soon became obvious to Do-Right that the man with Ghost stayed as far away as possible from the arts director who accompanied Do-Right. The young deputy was being as vague as possible when the arts director asked why they were returning.

Heavy had just started to pull the strange piece of meat out of the walk-in cooler in the main kitchen when Ghost called Six and confirmed the infestation. Looking at the child-sized human arm in his hands, with a sick feeling in the pit of his stomach, the big man realized that the cook had been turned as well.

The machine gunner looked up as the door to the cooler slowly opened. The cook stood in the doorway with a large cleaver in his hand. The man had a strange glint in his eye, and he flashed a grin filled with razor sharp teeth.

"I see you found my secret ingredient," the cook said. "Hey, it saves on the budget, and none of the non-enlightened kids ever knew."

"But don't worry," the cook added. "Your friends won't last long enough to tell anybody."

The man stepped toward Heavy.

"Catch!" said Heavy, and he tossed the arm to the unsuspecting cook.

The momentary pause and flinch of the cook gave the agent enough time to draw his khukuri. The blades once again glowed a faint green.

The cook lunged forward, and Heavy swung with the blades.

As he swung, Heavy tripped over some of the meat that had fallen on the floor of the cooler, and he fell face first, wildly swinging the blades. One of the khukuri went skittering across the floor and under one of the wire racks. The other one bit deeply into the lower leg of the creature, almost cutting clean through.

The creature stumbled and was unable to swing its own blade at the agent. Sitting back on his backside, Heavy fumbled with the shotgun that hung at his side. Bringing it to bear, he was only able to hold it with one hand. He pulled the trigger for a long pull. The fully automatic shotgun roared, sending ten rounds of silver and wood twelve gauge slugs through the torso and head of the vampire. The creature shuddered and dropped to the floor.

And then all hell broke loose.

29

CAMP

Blue Mountain Ranch, Florissant, Colorado

Six watched as his team approached the War Wagon. Boomer was holding the hand of her young witness while the rifle instructor was keeping pace with God. Do-Right and Ghost jogged across the field with the arts director and an adult, who Six did not recognize, in step. The roar of a full-auto shotgun filled the air.

Six heard the rear hatch of the truck begin to drop as he quickly keyed his mic and said, "Heavy, Six. What happened?"

The team heard the machine gunner's panting reply. "I'm good boss. The cook was a nightcrawler... must be the new kind."

Boomer raised her shotgun and pointed it at the arts director, but Boomer was hesitant to pull the trigger. The woman raised her hands and took a few steps back as she began to sob and nervously babble.

"What are you doing? Why are you pointing that big gun at me? I didn't do anything," the woman claimed.

Sensing something amiss, Doc stepped out of the truck, and her vestments began glowing a bright blue. As soon as she saw the priest, the arts director fell back and cowered as she hissed and spit at the priest. The team watched in fascination as the fangs extended from both the upper and lower jaws of the vampire. Her eyes turned totally black. She raised hands with long, sharp nails extruding from her fingers.

Doc stepped forward and began to speak in Latin. Before the first sentence was out of her mouth, Boomer pulled the trigger on her AA-12. The shotgun barked once, and the camp staffer collapsed. The top of the vampire's head was missing.

"No time for Latin. It's time to take out the predators," Boomer said as she looked at Doc.

The teen by Boomer's side crouched in fear and clung to her legs, hiding her face in the folds of the tactical BDUs. Boomer reached her left hand down and hugged the girl tightly. She knelt down so that she was eye-to-eye with the frightened girl.

"I'm going to put you somewhere safe until this is over," Boomer reassured the child. "I want you to sit in my big truck and wait for me to come get you."

The explosives expert led her gently around to the back of the War Wagon and up the steps.

"This is my friend, Spooky," Boomer said to the girl as she introduced her teammate. "He will make sure you're safe. Just don't touch any buttons or open any boxes. And don't look out the windows. It will be scary out there. Ok?"

The frightened girl nodded.

"Keep her safe. I'll be back for her," the explosives expert told Spooky.

Boomer reached in and grabbed several magazines of the FRAG-12 grenades, including a couple that Norbert had marked as "Experimental - Use Against Vampires." She then climbed down the steps, and Spooky keyed the switch to close and seal the hatch.

As she climbed out of the truck, Boomer saw that Heavy, who looked a little rattled, had re-joined the team. As she listened in on the conversation, she heard the big man exclaim, "And they were feeding the pieces to the rest of the camp, vamp and human! I found an honest-to-goodness arm—a child's arm—in the cooler."

Six cut in. "Estimates? Boomer, how many girls?"

"I saw forty-five or fifty girls. Unknown percentage not infected," the explosives expert said after quickly doing the math in her head.

Six pointed to God. "And you? Boys?"

The sniper paused and said, "About the same. Unknown number uninfected."

"Ok. God, up on the roof of the War Wagon," the team commander continued. "You are long distance line of defense. Start taking them out as far away as possible. Boomer, Do-Right, and I will cover from the ground. Ghost, Heavy, and Doc have close-in support. Engage from distance with your long guns but use your blades when they get close. Doc, anything you can drum up will help now.

"Call it eighty hostiles, with friendlies mixed in. Plus staff. My guess is the master is around here somewhere. Do not fire until you make sure of your target."

Six keyed his mic and said, "Spooky. If we go down, call in air support and level this camp. You cannot let any of these vampires get away."

Spooky placed the call directly to Agent Smith and provided him with Six's plan of action. Agent Smith asked his assistant where the closest air base was, and he was told that it was Ellsworth Air Force Base in South Dakota and that they flew the B1-B "Lancer" bombers. Agent Smith said he would call the base commander and request that he launch two of the bombers equipped with sufficient firepower. Smith explained to Spooky that the bombers were supersonic and capable of arriving within a short timeframe. They would be on station over the camp until the operation was over, one way or another.

The radio on the arts director's belt began to squawk. It was the camp director calling for his staff to check in. One-by-one, the staff radioed in, except for the cook and the arts director. Deducing the meaning of the gunfire and the lack of a response from two of his staff, the camp director gave a final chilling message over the radio.

"DHS agents who are listening to this radio: We are coming to get you," warned the camp director.

God scrambled onto the roof of the War Wagon and dropped to his knees for more stability. The rest of the team fanned out around the front and sides of the truck. Boomer and Heavy each stood on a different side of the massive vehicle. Six stood right in front of the truck, about equidistant from his long-range support. Ghost slipped in between Boomer and Six, while Heavy stepped between Six and Do-Right. Doc stood behind Six at the front of the truck, waiting to hold off vampires.

The doors to the main camp offices flung open and the camp director, the secretary, and the director's wife all came out the door in a rush. Boomer and Ghost immediately fired, sending shotgun slugs and rifle rounds through the body of the director's wife. As the creature fell under the fusillade of vampire rounds, the camp director howled in rage and launched himself at the two. Six turned slightly and placed the crosshairs over the man's head. After a quick squeeze of the trigger, a trio of rounds ripped into the vampire's chest. Screaming in agony, the camp director crashed to a halt and reeled from the blows. Regaining his senses, the director scrambled to his feet and flew at Six.

Boomer switched targets to the camp secretary. The explosives expert methodically squeezed the trigger on her shotgun and put three rounds into the chest of the creature. As the vampire fell, Boomer paused to carefully put one more round into the head of each vamp on the ground in front of her.

Ghost realized that Boomer could handle the last vamp and he turned to support his boss. The camp director had paused when being shot. As it again lunged for Six, the vampire found itself impaled on a silver blade that glowed white as it struck and then pierced through its chest. Surprise changed to pain, and the pain overwhelmed the motor functions of the monster. The creature watched in horror as the blade began to travel up its body and pierce its heart. Then its neck. The vamp did not understand its own mortality until the pain engulfed the creature, only to be relieved by darkness.

Six nodded his thanks at the hunter.

They both looked up in disbelief as the campers, led by their staff counselors, poured out of their cabins and savagely ran toward them. Many of the children ran across the grass much faster than should have been humanly possible. Every member of the DHS team opened fire.

The swarm of vampires ran in waves across the open ground. Ranks of infected kids and staff quickly covering the distance between the creatures and the DHS team. Even as the smaller children fell, the larger creatures jumped or ran over them, eager to tear into the agents.

Boomer felt the tears course down her face as she fired her shotgun. Her large vampire-hunting rounds ripped through the bodies as she shifted her aim and pulled the trigger. Concentrating on one vampire at a time, she would put two or three rounds into a creature, then shift her aim slightly to target another vamp beside the last. She numbly shot child after child as they charged toward the team. The bolt on her shotgun slammed open as the last round fired from her magazine, and she thumbed the magazine release button.

Realizing that her attackers were fast approaching, and with no end in sight, she grabbed one of Norbert's special magazines of FRAG-12 ammunition and slammed it into the receiver. She toggled the switch to automatic and squeezed the trigger, emptying the magazine in under four seconds. In front of her, a line of explosions rippled across the front of the charging mob. Eight explosions ripped the vampire children and staffers into pieces. Boomer saw a fine, silvery haze envelope the area where the explosions occurred, and those creatures who were merely wounded began screaming and writhing in agony as the cloud of atomized silver nitrate descended and coated their open wounds. The explosives expert had to blink away tears as she saw the contorted faces and heard the screams of these children-turned-creatures.

Six was busy on Boomer's left with his own wave of attacking creatures. Firing in short bursts, the team leader shifted targets between shots. As each vampire fell to the ground, Six would shift slightly, place the sights on a new target, and pull the trigger. His mind refused to see anything past targets on the battlefield. He realized that he would have to account for his actions later, but, until then, he would bury his feelings. As he switched magazines, he felt and heard the concussion as Boomer opened up with her mini grenades and watched as the mist of silver bit into the surviving monsters.

Slamming the bolt home to load a new round into the chamber, Six picked off more of the survivors of the initial rush. Concentrating on his wounded foes, who were slowly rising to their feet, he calmly and methodically chose his targets. If they recovered and stood, he would place a three-round burst into their head or chest. If the first burst did not kill the creature, a second one was usually enough to do so.

In between the Six and Boomer, Ghost held on to his sword with one hand. In his other, he drew the Webley revolver from his holster. Taking careful aim, the hunter pointed the revolver at a wounded vampire. He squeezed the trigger, sending the .38 caliber silver and wood slug through its brain. His next target took two shots before it fell; the vampire after that required three shots to put it down, leaving Ghost with an empty revolver. The hunter thumbed the lever to release the cylinder, and the entire cylinder and barrel rotated forward.

He dumped the spent shells on the ground and stuck the revolver under the crook of his sword arm. Ghost loaded six more shells into the revolver, grabbed his gun, and then flicked his wrist. The cylinder swung closed and latched. Ghost thumbed back the hammer again and set his sights on his next target. Two shots were required to put this creature down. Ghost moved on as he continued to shoot and reload, shoot and reload.

Heavy stood next to Six and waited as the first monsters came out of the cabins. He noticed that there was already blood on several of them. Narrowing his eyes, he began to methodically work the trigger on his shotgun, sending silver and wood slugs at the creatures. As the bolt locked back on the empty shotgun, the heavy gunner dropped the drum onto the ground. Palming one of Norbert's specialty FRAG-12 magazines, Heavy slammed it into the receiver and made the weapon ready. After moving the selector to single fire, Heavy walked the rounds across the front line of infected campers as they ran toward the DHS team.

The line of explosives tore up the monsters who were leading the attack. Those that weren't blown apart with a direct hit found themselves in agony as the clouds of silver nitrate filled the air. The grimace on Heavy's face exclaimed his pain in mowing down unarmed combatants, but he knew that he had no choice. He dropped the spent magazine from the AA-12, slammed another just like it into the receiver, and released the bolt forward. He lined up on a part of the attacking force that had not felt the effects of the shotgun and let fly.

At Heavy's side, Do-Right was doing his best to ignore every instinct he had so that he could fire on these unarmed children and adult counselors. Even the fang-filled mouths, animal growls, and black eyes only slightly alleviated his troubled conscience. Pushing past his training, he raised his AR-15 and pulled the trigger. With every pull of his trigger, a monster staggered or fell. The former deputy had grown up hunting wild game, but his prey today was making the hunt a lot easier by running straight toward him.

The deputy dropped the empty magazine out of his rifle and replaced it, then he let the bolt slide forward on a fresh round. Picking out more targets, he was startled when the ground erupted in explosions in front of the advancing horde. As he watched the silvery mist settle, he saw the heavy machine gunner to his left slam another magazine into his shotgun. When Heavy raised his shotgun again and started firing the fragmentation grenades, the deputy stopped targeting monsters in the same area. Instead, he began to finish off the monsters that had survived the initial explosions by doling out well-aimed shots to the head and torso.

Kneeling on top of the War Wagon, God used his rifle with a precision that few could match. The sniper constantly looked in all directions, paying close attention to the areas where the team's field of fire left area uncovered. Any time a vampire popped into an area that the team could not fire on, God's 5.56mm silver and wood core round would put an immediate stop to the threat and the life of the creature.

Living up to the "One shot, one kill" motto of snipers everywhere, the former HRT sniper was focused on the task at hand. The minor explosions from Boomer and Heavy only served to distract the vampires attacking the team, but they provided God with plenty of opportunity to capitalize on the distraction. He noticed quick movement to his right and swung in that direction. As he watched the camp archery instructor who Ghost had found flee the safety of the truck and run toward the staff offices, God could barely refrain from pulling the trigger.

Standing behind the DHS team as the vampires came out of their cabins and offices had been a real shock to the system for William Buckhorn, the camp's archery instructor. The volume of firepower was impressive, and the disciplined control had been incredible to watch. Bill had wanted to help, but he didn't have any weapons that he could use. After coming to the realization that these were actual vampires and that there was something he could do that might help, the archery pro took advantage of a pause for reloading and broke for the staff offices. When he had almost reached the building, it dawned on him that this could be a very bad idea for him. He knew he would have to be very careful on his way back to the truck... he didn't want to get mistaken as one of the creatures.

As he reached the staff building, he threw open the door and ran toward his office. He opened the door, glancing at the wall behind his small desk. Two bows hung on the wall. The first was a beautiful modern recurved bow. Even unstrung, the bow exuded power and quality. This bow was the one that almost took Bill to the Olympics five years prior, but he had never had a chance to compete. The other bow was a smaller, older, almost crude-looking longbow. Although this bow lacked the aesthetic appeal of the other, this bow was the reason he had made the dangerous dash back to his office.

The bow was originally handmade, and any repairs had been made with the same craftsmanship. As a full-blooded Navajo, Bill's grandfather was a Navajo Shaman and had hand-crafted this bow specifically for his grandson, Bill, before he died. While not as beautiful as the Olympic bow, this one held special meaning, and, if his grandfather was to be believed, special power for his grandson.

Bill reached up and lifted his grandfather's bow from the hang-ers. He quickly strung the bow as his grandfather had drilled into him He quietly spoke the ritual Navajo words he had been taught and felt better as the string neatly fell into place. Bill looked at the two quivers full of arrows that hung on the wall. One was of a modern material, with modern fiberglass target arrows neatly waiting to be slung and deployed. The second was a crude leather sling with a long single cross-body strap. The quiver contained authentic wooden arrows with feather fletchings and flint arrow heads. It was this quiver that Bill chose.

Bill slung the quiver over his shoulder and drew one of the arrows from the quiver. Nocking the arrow in the string, he turned to leave his office and head back to the DHS truck but, instead, found the camp nurse, Lynn Powell, standing in the doorway and blocking his escape. Her coal black eyes and mouthful of fangs told him that she had been infected. And his lack of vampire changes told her that he was her prey.

Before she could move toward him, he raised, drew, aimed, and fired in one smooth motion. One second the nurse was standing in the doorway looking hungrily at Bill; the next she was pinned to the wall behind her with an arrow jutting out from her forehead. The archery instructor looked down at the bow in his hands. He could barely make out a faint red glow as it faded quickly from the hieroglyphs carved into the shaft of the bow. Soon it was gone, and Bill didn't quite know if he had actually seen the glow.

As he stepped through the doorway, he could see that the DHS team was winning but that the battle was beginning to take its toll. Even with the tremendous firepower at their disposal, the team could not stop all of the vampires before they reached the truck. As Bill watched, the big mountain of a man they called "Heavy" drew two inward curved blades from the sheath on his back and began to attack those monsters that got too close for the others to shoot. Completely severing the arm of one vampire with a vicious backhand, the big man swung around as a follow-through and ran his khukuri through the neck of the creature and removed its head.

On the other side of the truck, Bill watched the tall agent who had earlier found him in the woods drive his glowing blade into the chest of an adult vampire. The creature screamed and writhed. The man they called "Ghost" withdrew the blade and made a swipe with the blade, severing the vampire's head from the body. Continuing that same movement, the hunter then stepped into another vampire that had gotten too close, drawing the blade across the creature's abdomen and chest. Moments later this creature was dispatched again by the blade.

As he stood next to Heavy, Six was startled as an infected staffer was able to slip past their defense. Six was unable to fire in time to stop the vampire from getting to him. Both Heavy and Ghost were engaged, and this one got inside the team leader's defenses. Six jammed his rifle sideways across the chest of the creature that was currently trying to eat his face. He could feel the hot, fetid breath of the vampire and see the gleaming of the razor-sharp teeth. As he struggled to get the creature away from him, the commander felt a the monster shudder as he watched an arrow with feather fletchings appear, sticking out of the temple of the monster's head.

The commander looked to his right and saw the archery instructor nocking another arrow in the string of an old bow. The bow was engraved or marked with some sort of writing or symbols on it, and they appeared to be faintly glowing red. Six watched as Bill took aim again and let fly another arrow, piercing the head of another vampire that was about to attack Do-Right. Six watched as the instructor drew and nocked another arrow before the archer ran back across to the truck.

The team was not able to kill every vampire before they came into close range. Those that were not killed from further away were killed by the blades of the hunter or the big man, or they were dispatched with a short-range shot by Bill. In scant minutes, the fight was over, and the silence was overwhelming. Blood and ichor soaked the grass all around the center of camp, and the small yard looked like a charnel house. After making sure that there were no more vampires in the vicinity, the team stopped to take stock of their condition.

Six wearily said, "Before we clear the remaining buildings, let's refresh our ammo and bandage up any wounds. Anyone get hurt?"

Heavy muttered a soft, "Damn." The big man looked at his team leader. "Looks like you caught a little piece yourself, boss," he said.

The team leader looked down at his shredded armor carrier and saw a small wound in his stomach. Shaking his head, he muttered a few curses.

"Well. Looks like I get to play the waiting game with Boomer and Heavy," Six reported. "Anyone else?"

Everyone else shook their head.

"Alright then, let's clear this place out," Six continued. "Non-vampires are screened for scratches. Vampires are killed. Questions?"

A deep, smooth voice emanated from around the corner of the staff office building. "I have one."

A monstrous figure, with its face obscured by the sunlight, presented itself to the team. Drawing closer, the figure inquired, "What will you do when you have to fight a real vampire?"

30

SHOWDOWN

Blue Mountain Ranch, Florissant, Colorado

Six did as best as he could to look unimpressed.

"Zachariah, I presume?" Six said to the creature.

The monster chuckled, his voice deep. "I am. And you must be Smith's latest team? How is Agent Smith getting along?" he asked. "I assume he told you that this was somewhat personal for him?"

The team leader nodded and said, "Yes. And that's why it ends today."

The vampire shook his head with an amused smile on his face. "Many before you have tried, and they have all failed," the monster said. "What makes you so special?"

Anticipating a fight, the team took their positions. God stayed perched on the War Wagon for his vantage point, but the rest of the DHS team spread out around the vampire. Boomer fanned out to the vampire's left and raised her shotgun. Ghost moved with her, making sure to stay in between the explosives expert and Six. The monster hunter held his now glowing sword at ready. Do-Right split off to the creature's right, and he raised his rifle and centered the sights on the vampire's forehead. After abandoning his shotgun for the green-glowing khukuri blades, Heavy positioned himself to the left of the former deputy. Doc stepped up next to Six and stood in the middle of the group as her vestments glowed blue.

"How are you out in the sunlight?" Ghost questioned. "You're a vampire."

The monster looked at the monster hunter. "So, the hunter speaks. You are the last of your line, correct? Too bad your line ends with you here.

"Alas, I *was* a proper vampire before the good Doctor Kaine was able to cure me of my terrible allergy. His virus made it possible for me to stand before you today. And I cannot wait to share this with my brethren."

Zachariah looked at the team spread around him. Raising his hands in mock surrender, he smiled. His fangs glistened with saliva in hungry anticipation.

"Now is the last chance that I will give to let you walk away from here," he said. "I have killed every team that dear Agent Smith has ever sent, and you will follow in their footsteps. It is your choice."

Even as Six pulled the trigger on his rifle to take his first shot, the vampire moved. Faster than any other vampire they had engaged, the creature danced to the side away from the reach of the team leader's rifle. Moving fluidly, and almost faster than the eye could follow, Zachariah struck at Boomer, knocking the shotgun from her grasp and spinning her around. She collapsed to the ground with a groan and cradled her arm.

Ghost was ready for the attack and struck, scoring a line across the vampire's chest. Howling in agony, the creature struck back at the hunter. The blow landed solidly on Ghost's ribs. Even through the protection of the blessed duster, Ghost felt a rib break as he flew backwards. The hunter landed hard on his back; he landed so hard that he felt as of the wind had been knocked out of his lungs. Ghost lay in agony, gasping as he tried to breath.

As Six shifted the aim of his rifle, he aimed at the vampire. He pulled the trigger and fired off another three-round burst. One of the rounds struck the vampire in the shoulder, spinning him slightly and it caused the creature to howl and swear. The monster leapt past Six and Doc and ducked under the blades in Heavy's hands. The vampire caught the big man's wrists in his hands and threw the machine gunner over his shoulder. The big man tumbled in the air until he crashed into one of the parked cars near them. Heavy dropped to the ground and lay still.

Do-Right stepped backwards as the vampire lunged at him. The creature grabbed the rifle and yanked, pulling the deputy off balance and whipping him around. Do-Right pulled the trigger on his rifle and sent a round through the hand of the vampire. The impact of the shot caused the vampire to let go. The deputy's momentum carried him toward the side of the War Wagon, and he bounced off the side of the truck and tumbled to the ground. Do-Right shook his head and tried to stand up.

A three-round burst hit Zachariah in the chest as he turned toward Six and Doc. The vampire looked up and seemed to notice God on the roof of the truck. The creature growled as he leapt for the sniper. In the same moment the creature left the ground, Six snapped his rifle up and pulled the trigger, sending another burst into the master vampire's torso.

The creature landed on the truck, and a thick black ichor dripped from the gunshot wounds on its chest and shoulder. Before the sniper could shoot again, the vampire grabbed the rifle barrel and dragged it and the agent off the roof and threw them to the ground. God felt a snap as his right leg hit the ground, and pure agony blackened his vision. He passed out.

With bloodlust in its eyes, the vampire turned and looked straight at Six and Doc.

"I'm going to enjoy killing you, priest," the vamp said in a harsh growl.

Doc closed her eyes and pulled her hands together. Chanting a high Latin liturgy, her hands began to glow with a blue light. Hoping to get to her before she finished her prayer, the vampire sprang at the priest.

Six leapt in front of the vampire. The agent collided with the monster and grabbed on, knocking it away from Doc as she finished her incantation. The two crashed to the ground, with Six hanging on in an attempt to keep the vampire busy. Six hoped his mangled armor would protect him.

Zachariah shoved Six with all of his might and broke the hold that the DHS agent had on the creature. Incensed that this human would dare physically attack him, the vampire quickly leaned down and opened his jaws. The razor sharp fangs pierced the throat of the team leader. Six went stiff when he felt the teeth take hold, but then all he felt was pain. Zachariah lifted his head, taking a large chunk of Six's throat in his mouth. Blood surrounded the vampire's mouth and dripped down his chin as the agent's life spilled out onto the ground. Zachariah grinned as the light left Six's eyes.

When the vampire looked up, his growled threat died in his throat as Doc opened her eyes and pointed at the vampire. Her eyes glowed with a blue light as she thundered, "*Creatura autem nox. Tu exterminantur. REVERTERE AD INFERNUM!*"

A blinding light seemed to envelope the master vampire. His screams and howls of agony reverberated throughout the camp. The vampire felt his body burning, and he looked down. Zachariah felt the heat rising from his body as flames appeared across his body. His skin began to blacken and peel away with flames filling the cracks.

Zachariah stood and took a desperate step toward the priest, but his agony drove him back to his knees. He stretched out a hand toward Doc as he tried desperately to reach her. The priest's hand was still outstretched, and she still glowed with righteous power. He gave one last effort to stand but collapsed back to his knees. The flames were rising faster now, and his agony burned brighter.

The monster looked in horror as a red, scaled claw reached out of the ground around him and grabbed him by the throat. Zachariah's screams were cut off abruptly as the massive hand wrapped around the vampire's throat and head and dragged the creature down into the earth. The last of the vampire's battered frame passed through the earth, and a small charred spot was the only evidence that it had been there.

The former camp archery instructor had watched the whole fight in horror. When the vampire had been dragged into the ground, he had watched as the priest let her hand drop and as the glow left her eyes and vestments. She sank wearily to the ground, once more looking like the middle-aged woman she was. The archery instructor rushed to Doc's side.

As Bill reached her side, he heard moans and groans from the rest of the team. He knelt down and asked if she was ok. She looked back up at him and offered a weary smile.

"That was worse than I thought. I'm ok," Doc responded. "I need to check on the rest of the team. We also need to make sure that we got them all. And check for other human survivors."

Bill looked at her with a no-nonsense look upon his face. "First things, first," he said. "I've got first aid training. I'll help you check on the others."

Doc nodded and stood to her feet.

The medic went to check on Six first. As soon as she saw that his throat had been ripped out, she blinked back tears and gave him last rites. Stepping back, she next walked over to Heavy who was unconscious and in a heap against a crumpled car. With the help of Doc's smelling salts, he woke with a start and groggily shook his head. Quickly checking him over, Doc realized the big man was probably lucky enough to walk away with a few simple bruises. Although he'd be sore for a while, he'd recover.

Next, she went to check on the former deputy that had joined their party in Trinidad. As she knelt next to him, she realized that he was groggy and that he couldn't focus on what she was saying. A few more field tests showed that he was possibly suffering a concussion and would certainly need medical care.

She then went to check on the sniper. By this time, Bill had already gotten around to him and was splinting his lower leg with supplies from the truck. As Doc checked the former camp staffer's work, she was impressed by the efficiency and scope of his work. The leg would be set temporarily—long enough to get him to a decent hospital in Colorado Springs.

Doc also checked over Bill's work on the other two team members. Bill had correctly diagnosed a fractured arm for Boomer and had applied another splint to the injured limb. He had also checked a possibly broken rib on Ghost and told the hunter that he would need to have it checked out at the hospital. As Doc examined Ghost, she told him the somber news about Six.

After resting for several minutes, Heavy was fully recovered and offered to check the rest of camp to make sure that there weren't any other survivors. Bill volunteered to go with him, just in case they came across a frightened camper. The two went south to start with the girls' cabins and work their way north.

As they walked off, Ghost pulled out his SSP and dialed Agent Smith's office. When Timothy answered, Ghost said in a flat, weary voice, "Timothy, it's Ghost. Is Smith in? I need to talk to him ASAP."

"Wait one," Timothy said as he placed the agent's call on hold.

"Agent Smith."

Ghost began, "Agent Smith, it's Ghost. This was a complete cluster. Zachariah is dead, but so is Six. There were at least eighty of the new vampires at the camp. It was an ugly battle. Only two known camp survivors, although Heavy is looking for more." Ghost paused to catch his breath.

The pause lasted a few seconds as Agent Smith absorbed the news. The supervising agent finally spoke, "Mr. Holstein was killed in action?"

Ghost nodded subconsciously. "Yes, sir. He sacrificed himself so that Doc had enough time to do her thing. She was the one who finally put the master down."

Agent Smith thought through the rest of the initial statement. "Was anyone else hurt? Does anyone need medical attention?"

Ghost began to run down the list of the wounded. "It looks like Boomer has a broken arm. God broke his leg. Doc thinks Do-Right has a concussion, and I probably have at least one broken rib. Heavy's going to be sore in the morning, but he seems to be ok."

"The best hospital for you guys is Evans Army Hospital just off base at Cheyenne Mountain Air Station. They'll be able to handle your wounds, and your ranks and credentials should keep them from asking too many questions. I'll have Timothy clear the way for you." Agent Smith paused some more as he looked at his notes.

"You found over eighty new vampires? Is there any chance that any got away?" Smith questioned.

Ghost thought for a moment. "It's not likely, sir," he responded. "They all seemed to have come to attack us. But Heavy is sweeping the camp with the help of the camp's former archery instructor."

"Who is this 'instructor,' Agent Vanhof?" asked Agent Smith.

Ghost backtracked a little. "Sir, I found him on our initial sweep. He seemed to be the only surviving adult staff that was not turned. He was hiding in the woods, but Spooky directed me to him. According to Spooky, he's a former world-class archer, almost made the last Olympics. He has an older, carved bow. And he took out several of the vampires during the final attack. I'll have Spooky forward his dossier."

Agent Smith paused and then said, "I'll trust your judgement. You said there was one other survivor. Who is it?"

Ghost recalled Boomer's tagalong. "Teen girl, fifteen or sixteen. She was not infected. Boomer found her and got her to us before the vamps attacked. I don't know if there are any other survivors yet, but I doubt it. These vamps were systematically slaughtering and eating those who weren't infected."

Agent Smith suddenly asked a very poignant question. "Has anyone on the team been infected?"

Ghost closed his eyes. He was wondering when that question would pop up. "Possibly, sir. Boomer and Heavy were both scratched in the silo. According to the doctor's paperwork, they each have a one-in-five chance of turning from the contact. The change takes several days, three to five, according to the doctor's notes."

Ghost heard a soft, "Damn," come from his boss. Ghost couldn't agree more.

The monster hunter asked his own question next. "Sir. What's next? As much ruckus as we raised, we're bound to get law enforcement out here eventually. And at some point, parents are going to want to come get their kids. These are new vamps. They don't dissolve in smoke. DHS just mowed down over eighty unarmed kids and adults. How do we cover this one up?"

Agent Smith was already thinking about the problem. He pulled up satellite maps of the area and saw that the camp area was actually a fairly small area. He made a snap decision.

"Agent Vanhof, your team has thirty minutes to vacate the camp. I'll have Timothy send the local law enforcement to the other end of the county. You are to get everyone clear. In precisely thirty minutes, an Air Force fuel tanker will crash into the hillside, precisely where you are currently sitting. It will, of course, have help from us. DHS will investigate. And the Air Force will compensate the families. There is nothing else we can do. Thirty minutes. Time starts now."

Ghost looked at his watch as he broke the connection. He keyed his mic and said, "Heavy, Ghost. We are leaving in twenty-five minutes. That is two-five minutes. No exceptions. Move your butt."

As each team member heard those words, they looked to the hunter for an explanation. They realized that no explanation was forthcoming.

Ghost quickly organized the team. Doc found a body bag in the truck's supplies, and she and Ghost carefully placed Six's body inside. They strapped the body to the roof of the truck so that it was mostly flat and would not show while they were driving. They cleared out other boxes and stacked them on the top of the MRAP as well, hiding the body even more.

Despite the pain, Boomer sat down to talk to the teenager that she had rescued.

"I don't know what's going to happen," she confided. "I can't have you talk to your parents right now, not until my boss gives me permission. Confidentially, I don't think he knows what to do with you. Until then, I'll keep you safe. I promise."

The teenager hugged Boomer, and slowly her tears dried up. After a few minutes, she wiped her eyes and thanked Boomer.

Boomer smiled and kept her arm around the girl's shoulder. "I don't think I ever caught your name, hon. Mine is Rebekah, but everyone calls me 'Boomer.'"

The girl smiled and replied, "Boomer? I like that. My name is Hannah."

After twenty-three minutes, Heavy and Bill jogged up to the truck.

"Nothing living out there, sir," Heavy reported to Ghost. "No other survivors. It looks like they slaughtered those who weren't infected before they came after us. Each cabin is a slaughterhouse. We checked out the old lodge, and it looks like Zachariah was living there. Found all kinds of crap from him... I grabbed a few journals and items and tossed them in my pack."

"Thanks, Heavy," Ghost said. "Bill," Heavy continued, "our thanks for helping. Unfortunately, it looks like you might be with us for a little while. At least until we can sort it out with our boss. You need to come with us. Anything you need to get from your office, or bunk?"

Bill shook his head and raised the bow still gripped tightly in his hand. "Honestly, this is the only thing I want to take with me. My grandfather was a Navajo Shaman. He carved it for me."

"Alright. Everyone mount up," Ghost said. "We're going to sit at the end of the camp driveway for a couple minutes and then we are leaving. This area won't exist in about three minutes."

A pained look crossed Boomer's face as she climbed into the passenger's chair—pained that she was too hurt to drive the Wagon. Ghost climbed up into the driver's seat and fired up the engine. He slowly moved the truck to the end of the drive, making sure to block any entrance to the camp. After two minutes, with just under a minute to spare, he put the truck in gear and drove back out toward town. As they were pulling around a curve, they all heard a very low roar and watched as a large Air Force jet trailing smoke dropped below the tree line. Moments later, the ground shook the truck violently, and a wave of wind and heat rocked the War Wagon.

Spooky was monitoring real-time satellite access and watched as an Air Force KC-135 Stratotanker flew with smoke pouring out of three engines. It pancaked into the ground right where the camp's driveway started and then fireballed, sending burning JP-8 throughout the camp and the surrounding forest. Spooky shuddered. There was no way anything was going to survive that inferno.

The resulting fire would incinerate everything within a quarter-mile of the crash site to ash and would leave a burn area that covered ten square miles before finally going out. It would soon be named the worst military and civilian accident in the history of the United States.

31

AFTERMATH

Pueblo Memorial Airport, Pueblo, Colorado

The War Wagon pulled into the Pueblo Memorial Airport the following afternoon. The evening before, the team had stayed at a hotel close to the base while Boomer, God, and Do-Right had their battle wounds treated at the base hospital.

God and Boomer both had their fractured bones set and were both told that they were lucky that they did not have to have surgery. Do-Right was put through a battery of tests, and the hospital staff concluded that he suffered a concussion. The team was also able to store the body of their leader in the hospital morgue for the night, and they made arrangements to get him to the airfield the next afternoon.

The next morning, a weary, bruised, and battered team set out for the small town of Trinidad in the War Wagon. Bill, the former archery instructor for the camp, and Hannah, the camper who Boomer rescued, both refused to stay and wait on base. Instead, they rode inside the cramped MRAP with the rest of the team. When they arrived, the team immediately went to the county jail to check on their prisoners. As Doc had predicted, the former acting mayor and the former coroner were little more than gibbering fools. They were shouting about monsters and blood and fire to any who would listen. A quick call to the Colorado Springs U.S. Attorney's Office yielded an involuntary commitment to a psychiatric facility for both of them.

At the urging of Ghost, Christian Folsom officially resigned from the Las Animas County Sheriff Department. Turning in his uniforms and service weapon, he walked out of the building with his head high. Do-Right's smile was bittersweet as he climbed up into the War Wagon, turning his back on his youth and his hometown. The memorial service for his wife and children, as well as all the other victims of the monsters, would take place in a week, and he promised that he would be back for the services.

The town of Trinidad had already started recovering and rebuilding from the tragedies of the recent monster scourge. The paranormal and conspiracy websites were working overtime due to the incoherent reports of monsters and secret government teams. The new acting mayor and sheriff were quick to stop any rumors that contradicted the official story of a deep ISIS cell buried in the small town. And they never, officially, deviated from those statements.

The team had one last stop to make before they could leave town. They traveled out to the old pharmacist's residence to make sure that the mouth of the hellgate was sealed. As they arrived at the top of the driveway, all but two of the team's passengers got out of the vehicle and wandered around the property. They individually kicked through the charred and scattered ruins of the house, making sure that there was nothing to link DHS to the house or to any monsters.

Heavy walked up to the big cellar doors that led down to the caverns. He gave several good tugs to make sure that the welds were solid and that the chains would hold. He jumped back when the doors started to rattle from the other side. As he stepped back and drew his sidearm, he yelled for his teammates.

As the others drew around, the large doors bulged and creaked outward, as if some immense force was pushing from the other side. Those who were armed quickly drew their sidearms, and Ghost drew his sword. The team took a collective step back as the doors groaned under the weight of the force. Suddenly, a weld seam ripped, and the doors crashed open as the chains that bound the doors shattered.

A roiling darkness waited just below the ledge of the doorway. Doc recognized that it was the same material that pooled in the pit from the caverns and the bottom of the silo. Her vestments began to glow a bright yellow as a form emerged from the inky blackness. As it rose smoothly, the darkness acted like liquid, as it dripped and ran in rivulets down the emerging figure.

The humanoid figure stood about five feet tall and was thin and dressed in all black. Its pale gray skin was visible on its hands as the figure held a small staff or cane, while the rest remained hidden beneath a voluminous robe with a cowl and hood that obscured the face. The figure threw back its cowl, revealing a pale gray face that was all at once terrifying and beautiful. Its blood red mouth was unadorned with fangs, however the creature's coal black eyes were lit with a faint red glow. Long violet hair was pulled back in a simple knot and revealed slightly pointed ears.

The figure smiled and spoke in a voice that was beautiful but cold. "You must be the humans causing me so much trouble. Not much to look at, are you?"

Ghost stepped forward and leveled his blade at the figure. "Who are you, and what do you want?" he asked.

The figure moved his hands and held them in a placating gesture. "Please, human. We will meet later, rest assured. I never forget an insult. As for who I am? Tell your Agent Smith that Demius Sayevuud sends his greetings."

With a small gesture, the inky darkness began enveloping the figure before them. In seconds, the figure was fully engulfed, and the darkness spread back down into the doorway. It then spiraled and folded in on itself until it vanished completely.

Heavy took the first step forward with his flashlight. The stair-well down was darker and a bit rougher after the Boomer's first explosion, but the corridor still angled out of sight at the bottom.

Boomer walked back over to the War Wagon and opened her kit. Working one-handedly, it took her a bit longer than was usual, but she came back to the hole holding a rather large chunk of plastic explosive fixed to a timer. She raised her eyebrow at Ghost, and he simply nodded.

Setting the time for ten minutes, she carefully double-checked her setup. Boomer walked down the stairs and leaned around the corner. The light filtering down showed her that the first cavern was still largely intact. The explosives expert calmly walked over to the center of the cavern and set the explosive package down. Looking around once more, she reached down and hit the start button to begin the countdown timer.

The War Wagon was parked at the bottom of the driveway when the explosive package detonated ten minutes later. The twenty-seven-ton truck rocked on its massive shocks as the top of the hill erupted in a geyser of rock and mud.

Heavy looked at the geyser and said, "I guess we call that Mount Saint Hellgate?"

The tension broke as laughter rolled throughout the truck. The team was still laughing minutes later as the fire trucks arrived on scene. Ghost wiped the tears from his eyes and stepped out of the truck. He waved his badge at the first responding truck and then at the fire chief when he arrived. By the time Ghost let the trucks through, there was nothing to clean up, except for a few small brush fires. Ghost put the War Wagon in gear and headed north to Pueblo Airport.

WHEN THE WAR Wagon pulled onto the airport parking lot, the team saw the waiting C-17 Globemaster. A small ambulance, surrounded by an armed troop of DHS agents, was parked next to the Air Force jet. Ghost parked the MRAP next to the waiting ambulance, and the team began to unload.

As the agents climbed out of the truck, the stairs to the passenger compartment came down, and Gretchen and Agent Smith walked slowly down the stairs. The supervising agent solemnly went to each team member and shook his or her hand as he offered his thanks and condolences. When he got to the two civilians, Ghost introduced them.

"Agent Smith, this is Hannah Cresswell. She was one of the senior girls at the camp. And this is Bill Buckhorn, former archery instructor at Blue Mountain."

Smith shook hands with both of them. "Ms. Cresswell. I'm sorry that we haven't been able to let you contact your parents yet. We have several questions that we need to answer before we can do so. Don't worry. I want to return you to your parents, if at all possible.

"Mr. Buckhorn. I understand you were instrumental in helping save my team. For that, I am grateful. We need to talk a little later about possible employment opportunities, now that your prior position is no longer available."

Smith looked at his team. "As Ghost requested, Mr. Holstein's body is still waiting to be loaded onto the plane. There is a special storage compartment for his remains, but I thought you would want to carry him aboard yourselves."

As one, the team moved to the back door of the ambulance. The paramedics brought out the body, still in the body bag they had orig-inally used, on a stretcher. Every team member took a handle, save for Doc. She stood behind the body and read last rites and funeral liturgies as the team carried the body solemnly up the ramp and into the waiting storage. They would again perform the somber duty when the plane touched down outside Langley.

The team grabbed their gear from the War Wagon and allowed one of the waiting cargo masters to drive the truck up the ramp and secure it in the plane. One-by-one, the team, their passengers, and the Section 28 staff filed up the stairs and into the waiting lounge. Unlike standard Globemaster aircraft, this one had been designed so that the passenger portion of the cargo bay was well appointed and comfortable to be in. Thick soundproofing muted the dull roar of the spooling engines, and comfortable chairs and tables were avail-able as well as fold-down bunks in the back. The team settled in, and Agent Smith lifted a handset attached to his chair.

"Tell the pilot we're ready to go when he is. Have him get clear-ance for a direct flight. Make this one as short as possible. Thank you."

The huge engines roared outside and the passengers felt the plane taxi and then take off. They would touchdown in Virginia in just under four hours.

———

BACK AT THE headquarters for Section 28, the team apartments somehow felt empty. Six's gear had already been collected and sent to storage. Agent Smith let the team know that memorial services would be held the following afternoon and that anyone needing a suit or other clothing should let him know so that the quartermaster could locate proper attire for him or her. The service would be a small memorial with only current on-site staff attending and Six would be interred in a plot consecrated specifically for Section 28 Agents.

The cold and dreary day fit the somber mood of those who attended the memorial. The light drizzle masked the tears of Boomer and Doc as they watched their fallen team leader lowered into the ground. The service was short with a few words from Agent Smith and final rites from Doc. The procession of black SUVs back to headquarters was silent as the other agents reflected on their own mortality.

The following day, Christian Folsom and William Buckhorn

were both sworn in as the newest members of team Knightmare. Do-Right had earned his new callsign in the field, and it became official. Buckhorn's experience and his Navajo heritage gave Agent Smith the perfect callsign for the new agent: "Scout."

That same day, Ghost was officially recognized as the new team leader for Knightmare.

Agent Smith talked with the new team leader. "You will need to pick a second, and soon," Smith advised. "I have full confidence in your leadership. Your skills with handling people will be a major asset as we move forward."

Do-Right flew back to Pueblo for the trip to Trinidad four days later. While he expected to make the journey alone, Agent Smith released the entire Knightmare team to attend with him for support. The Agency's Citation X flew the team to Colorado in style, and the multiple black SUVs waiting for the team at the airport added the perfect touch.

Instead of their tactical BDUs, all members of the team, except for Ghost and Doc, wore gray or black business suits the following day. Looking every inch the federal agents that they were, each member wore their suit well, while the team's sniper leaned on a cane with his leg in an air cast. Ghost showed up in a shirt and tie with dress pants instead of his normal jeans. Instead of a suit jacket and dress shoes, the new team leader wore cowboy boots, his blessed leather duster, and his hat, which he removed and held for the ceremony. Doc wore her full vestments and stole for the ceremony.

Once the memorial service was over with, Do-Right needed to see his family's home one more time. The former deputy entered through the front door, ducking under the police tape that was stretched all around. He went throughout the house and gathered some pictures and a few knickknacks that were of sentimental value to him. The new DHS agent wandered around his house for thirty minutes as he remembered his family and dried the tears from his eyes.

Do-right spent the rest of the next day sorting through his personal life and arranging for his departure from town. He met with a broker and put his house on the market. Agent Smith sent a discreet moving truck with additional help to clean out his house. Those possessions that he no longer wanted were cleaned and set aside for an estate sale.

While the former deputy sorted through his life prior to Section 28, the rest of the team split up and ran several errands. Doc led a team comprised of God, Heavy, and Spooky back to the recently nicknamed Mount Saint Hellgate. When they were there, they placed a small electronics package on the site. Burying the main box console about three feet deep, they extended two small antennas up through the ground so that they could sample the air and electromagnetic field emissions from the area around them. This specially designed instrument package was engineered to monitor the site for any incursion-related activity and to relay the activity to Section 28.

Boomer drove Ghost and Scout out of town the same afternoon. As they drove up to the former site of Blue Mountain Ranch, the agents were anxious to see the area firsthand. Two hours later, the government SUV arrived at the burnt-out wreckage that was the Ranch. Every building and most of the trees in the area directly surrounding the camp were flattened from the concussive blast and burned from the resulting fires.

The team was amazed at the destructive power that the tanker had unleashed when it crashed onto the field. They had read the reports of the mangled bodies and shredded remains, but they had not imagined what it would look, and smell, like in person. Ghost showed his credentials to the sheriff's deputy that was guarding the road. Moving forward, the team's SUV was forced to stop about a hundred yards from the actual site. After they exited their SUV, the team walked toward the main staging area for the National Transportation Safety Board and DHS teams charged with handling the crash.

Ghost walked up to the DHS agent in charge, Special Agent Hart, from the Denver office. Agent Hart recognized Ghost and Boomer, and her demeanor chilled. "Agent Vanhof, and Agent... Callahan. To what do I owe the pleasure? And who is this with you?"

"Special Agent Hart, this is Agent William Buckhorn," Ghost said as he turned to Scout and introduced him to the agent. "He recently joined our deployment team." Turning to Bill, Ghost continued, "This is Special Agent Sonja Hart. She's the SAC from Denver. If we're in this area, we're stomping on her backyard."

Scout reached out to shake Agent Hart's hand, and, as she took it, she paused. A look passed through her eyes as if she was putting pieces together. She suddenly rounded on Ghost and unleashed a torrent of questions.

"Isn't there a 'William Buckhorn' that's missing from this site? Is he of any relation?" she questioned.

Ghost smiled and replied, "You could say that. We got him out before the plane crashed. He's one of ours now."

The light dawned behind the senior agent's eyes. She let out an expletive, and her voice grew quiet and cold. "This was one of your operations? What happened? Did the little kids insult Agent Smith?"

Ghost's eyes narrowed. "Cheap shots don't become you, Agent Hart. I can neither confirm, nor deny, that we were here. If you need any further answers, you might want to contact Agent Smith's office.

"To that end, I do need a favor from you," Ghost said and then smiled his most disarming smile.

Hart spoke through gritted teeth. "What do you need?" she demanded.

Ghost set a small bag down on the table in the command center, and drew an incursion detection unit from the bag. Ghost set about showing Agent Hart how to bury and activate the device, a twin of the unit just placed in Trinidad.

At the end, the new team leader said, "Hopefully, this instrument package will help us make sure that there is not another incident like this in the future."

Hart looked at the device and then back at Ghost. "I'll make sure it gets done properly. Anything to get you out of my hair faster."

AT SECTION 28 HEADQUARTERS, outside Langley, Virginia, Agent Smith sat down to have a conversation with a sixteen year old survivor of Blue Mountain Ranch. The meeting was in the team's lounge area, outside the room where she was temporarily assigned.

A sixteen-year-old Latina girl with black hair and deep hazel eyes sat slouched in an overstuffed chair across from the prim and proper figure of Agent Smith. He had just sat down with the girl after bringing her a carbonated beverage. He paused a few moments to look over the girl. Satisfied, he began.

"Miss Cresswell. I sincerely apologize for making you wait this long to talk to your parents. I had to make sure that we had all the options sorted out before I could talk to you."

Hannah looked up, eagerly waiting to hear when she could call her folks. They must be going out of their minds. She leaned forward a little as she waited for the federal agent to go on.

"As I see it, we have two options for you. If we take the first option, you would be able to return to your parents' house almost immediately. With a little makeup and special effects, we can easily make it look like you were wandering in the woods for a long time." Smith saw the gleam in the girl's eyes. "Before you get all excited, this option requires certain... assurances.

"First, you will never be allowed to talk about what really happened at camp. You will have to forget that Section 28 even exists. This condition is absolutely required. What we do is a secret, and it has to stay that way. Other than a few crazy conspiracy theorists who might have seen our name somewhere, we don't really exist. We cannot officially exist.

"Second. If you ever do actually speak about what happened there, or who we are, there will be some unimaginable consequences. You'll be crucified in the media. We will sow the seeds of disbelief in your story. In the end, only the crackpot conspiracy theorists will believe you. Outside of them, you'll be a laughing stock." Smith saw that he had Hannah's attention.

"Not only will your reputation and presence be thoroughly trashed, but we'll go after your folks, too. Financially, we'll bankrupt them. Socially, we'll have them outcast. When they continue to believe you after your statements, they will grow to resent the effect you had on their life. Do not think that we won't do this. I crashed a multi-million dollar jet filled with jet fuel to cover for one of my teams. Crashing someone's financial future would be child's play."

Team Knightmare's supervising agent let the potential dire consequences sink in. "Of course, there is always the other option," he continued. "For this one, you stay here and eventually work for Section 28. I have a plan in place to form a new team, and I believe you would fit in very well. To stay here, you will officially die at Blue Mountain Ranch. We will provide you with a new identity and everything you need to live.

"Your marks in school were exceptional. You were also a track star and a rather formidable IDPA and three-gun competitor. We will continue your schooling at a local school that we can trust for the next two years. We'll also train you in hand-to-hand combat and monster fighting. When you graduate, you will be ready to fulfill our mission."

Hannah brightened a little. She asked a question, "So, I'd kinda be like that chick vampire slayer. Muffy? Betty? What was her name?"

Smith smiled a little knowing smile, "Ah... I think the name you are looking for is 'Buffy.'. And while you would attend school and train like the so-called 'slayer,' I am not British and you will likely not be killing vampires at your own school."

He paused and caught her eye, making sure that she understood the implications. "What do you want to do? Once you make a decision, there are no do-overs."

Hannah thought for a moment. She realized that she could eventually become like the woman who rescued her, Boomer. She thought about how great it would be to learn how to kill monsters, but she also thought about her family. She would be dead to them. Forever. She would, could, never see her friends again. Her life would be gone, and her parents would be devastated.

The sixteen-year-old girl took a huge breath, looked Smith right in the eye, and told him her decision.

EPILOGUE

It was 5:32am. The cool of the night was beginning to wane as the day prepared to spring forth. As was his routine, Garrett Malley pulled his gray BMW into the parking spot closest to the track. Climbing out of the car, he slipped his wallet and spare car key into his waist pouch, along with his cell phone. The rest of his keys, as well as the clothes that he would change into, went into the trunk of the luxury vehicle.

The man stretched through his normal routine. Jogging in place for a few minutes, he limbered up, his mind drifting as he began his routine. He stepped onto the running track that circled the baseball fields at the Williamsburg Recreational Center, in Kingstree, South Carolina. Setting off at his normal pace, his long strides began to eat up the distance. Garrett wanted to run a marathon in the fall, and he was training diligently.

As he rounded the final bend on his first, of many, laps, he noticed a form lying in the children's play area that was next to the track. Garrett slowed, and he looked closer at the form. It looked to be a man, and it seemed to be lying face down in the sand. His pace faltered, and he slowed to a walk, moving off the track and toward the body at the playground.

Hoping that the guy was decent when awakened, Garrett reach into his pouch and grabbed his cellphone. With his phone in hand, the jogger leaned down and gently poked then pushed the person as he tried to wake him.

Pushes turned into shoves, and eventually, the jogger gently rolled over the person. Wide, open eyes stared out into the early morning air. The man's face was frozen in his last terror. Looking up and down the body, the jogger noticed that the front of the shirt was soaked with blood. Startled, Garrett quickly stood up, and called 911 to report the body.

IN THE KINGSTREE, South Carolina, police department, Detective Melissa Chambers finished typing the report into the computer. This was the second body dumped in the last three weeks. Each body had a single puncture wound. The coroner's report showed a wide, triangular blade to the chest that was forced through to the heart. Each time, the body was at least a mile from where he or she was last seen.

The police department withheld one fact from the reporters: each body had strange markings drawn on the skin of their foreheads and chests. The detective shuddered. Although it seemed illogical, these bodies looked like they had been some part of a ritual sacrifice.

In a department with only fourteen full-time officers, Detective Chambers didn't think she had the right resources to handle this case. She looked up at the clock. It was too late now, but she'd call her friend over at the county sheriff's office to see if he could help her. This was going to take more than her small department had to offer.

IN THE LAW ENFORCEMENT INFORMATION NETWORK (LEIN), a tiny data worm was scrounging through all the materials being fed into the system, a country's worth of information and statistics. The data worm picked up on several characteristics of the case from Kingstree, South Carolina, and filed it in memory. It then snooped through the data for that city and the surrounding county. Finding another report with the same characteristics, it began to compile its findings. When it had enough information to trigger a response, the small program quietly transmitted the compiled report to its master.

The data worm bounced its findings to a server in Houston, Texas. From there, the report travelled to Los Angeles, New York,

Detroit, and finally back to a small building outside Langley, Virginia. Once the program sent out its report, it then resumed mining for more documentation.

AT A DESK LOCATED in Section 28 headquarters, Agent Timothy Wilson of the Department of Homeland Security received a small report from his worm in LEIN. Sifting through the compiled report and the raw data, Timothy made the same connections that the worm did.

Timothy keyed a very specific sequence on his computer. This, in turn, signaled Agent Smith's planning and analysis team and transmitted a copy of the report file as well as the raw data. This signal also informed each member that there was a potential incursion and that they needed to perform a quick analysis and assemble in the conference room within one hour.

Timothy then placed a call to his boss, Agent Smith.

The agent answered the phone immediately.

"Sir, we have a potential incursion event," Timothy informed his superior. "The planning team is assembling in the conference room as we speak."

Supervising Agent James Smith concluded the phone call with his assistant, and then he wrote the last few sentences of the report he was working on regarding the newest young field agent. Smith smiled and saved the paperwork. He grabbed his SSP and began the short walk to the conference room.

IT HAD BEEN TWO WEEKS, and Boomer was confused. According to the data from Dr. Kaine, the gestation period from exposure is about five days. Neither Boomer nor Heavy had turned to vampires because of the scratches they sustained while battling that new type of vampire. Earlier this evening at dinner, she couldn't tolerate much of the food. She normally had a healthy appetite, but her stomach was aching, and she was doubled over in pain. When Boomer looked at her reflection in the mirror in her bathroom, she was able to see how gaunt and hollow her cheeks had become.

Suddenly her fingers started to ache. The explosives expert began cursing as her knuckles and fingertips were suddenly on fire. She was in agony. Her bones felt fragile. Boomer looked down and watched as claws extruded from her left hand. She stared in horror at the newly-formed claws.

Boomer felt tremendous pain and pressure behind her eyes. It was almost as if she was having the most intense migraine of her life. She opened her eyes. Each eye turned a solid black, both the pupils and the whites. Suddenly, details became sharper and her vision shifted from color to black and white. Boomer noticed details on things that she had never been able to see before. She squeezed her eyes shut. Slowly, she blinked her eyes open, and the explosives expert found that she could concentrate and filter out some of the more garish sights.

While she was looking her new eyes, she felt a new, terrible pain in her jaw. She opened her mouth and examined her teeth and gums. She was watching when they first elongated and then sharpened. Through the mouthful of sudden fangs, she muttered a candidate for the Understatement of the Year, "Damn."

GRAND RAPIDS, Michigan. Saturday, 4/18/2015.

BRYAN DONIHUE

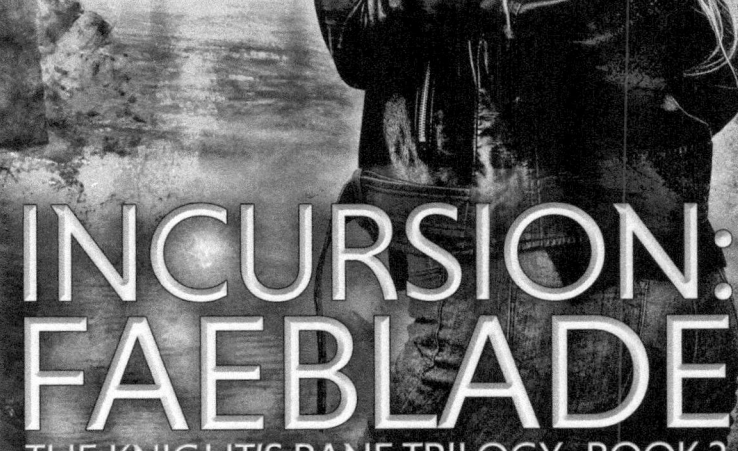

INCURSION: FAEBLADE

THE KNIGHT'S BANE TRILOGY—BOOK 2

KICKSTARTER SUPPORTERS

For this novel, I ran a crowdfunding campaign to pay for some of the (rather minor) expenses incurred in self-publishing. I ran the campaign on Kickstarter (kickstarter.com), and can't say enough good things about their service.

I had a group of incredible backers in the campaign. Their support made the campaign successful, and I cannot thank them enough!

Campaign Contributors

Esoteric Research
Jeremy Sampsell

Senior Field Agent
Amber Bibb
The Kalafut Family

Field Agent
David Cassiday
Danny Neimeyer
Jessie Stevenson

Experienced Monster Hunter
Eulene Freeland

Joel Wilkinson
Andrew Guastella
Troye Gerard

Apprentice Monster Hunter
Ben

PROLOGUE

A roiling mass of inky blackness rose from the worn concrete floor. To those in the room, the black seemed to writhe and move organically, as if it was a living thing. After a few seconds, the liquid darkness formed into the rough shape of a doorway anchored to the ground. As it finished forming the portal, a tall, well-groomed man appeared, stepping through the darkness. As he walked into reality, the liquid black appeared to run off of him, leaving no sign that the heavy darkness ever existed.

The man stood over six feet tall, had dark, almost a coal-black skin, and dark hair that was brushed back. His jet-black mane had scattered gray throughout, and his carefully groomed beard was short, almost a van dyke style, and it showed a great deal more of the salt and pepper look. His thin, angular face spoke of nobility, and his bright green eyes almost glowed with intelligence.

An expensive, tailored suit accented his fit and trim body, the dark suit offset by the pale blue shirt and royal blue tie. Anchoring the tie was a dazzling sapphire-crusted tie tack that matched the large sapphire in the ornate ring on his right hand. From his perfectly cut shoulders to the razor-sharp creases that brushed his black leather shoes, there was not a seam or crease out of place on his suit.

Plucking an imaginary piece of lint from his suit jacket, the man looked around the large warehouse floor. Nodding to those present, the man gave a slight grin. As his lips curled, the man standing in front of him could see a hint of a sharp, white tooth. The tall man spoke with a deep, warm voice that seemed to cover a harsh metallic undertone, "Mister Hammond. Report."

The man in front of him nervously adjusted his tie before he spoke. "Everything is as you commanded, my liege. Your court is waiting for your presence in the hall. I have personally verified the attendees, and even your Knight is waiting for your arrival."

The gentleman in the custom business suit nodded curtly and spoke. "And the other matter?" His voice was flat and cold.

The man called Mr. Hammond turned and looked at the woman to his right. She bowed her head slightly and purred, "The preparations have been laid, my lord. When you so order, my people will cause chaos for the other side. We'll keep them off balance while you strike them down. It will be your finest victory. They'll never see this coming."

The gentleman looked at the woman. Her ethereal beauty and diminutive size belied her warrior prowess. The ginger-haired woman had silver eyes, and was lithe, powerful without being heavily muscled. Her royal blue cocktail dress sparkled and shimmered. The effect was almost hypnotic as the dress clung to every curve on her perfect body. If there was any word that applied to this beautiful woman it was "sensual".

The gentleman's eyes glowed a deep red for a brief second, before returning to their natural green color. He turned back towards the liquid dark portal and made a small dismissive gesture with his hand. At the wave, the blackness started to fold in and consume itself, sinking to the floor, and quickly disappearing. Turning back around, the gentleman began walking towards the door on the opposite wall of the warehouse.

Around him, the men and women fell in step behind him. One of the larger men in a tailored suit had an earpiece in his ear. He raised his hand to his mouth and keyed the radio microphone he held in his hand. "This is Galen." The man spoke softly, "The King has arrived. We are en route to the Hall."

IN A LARGE CONTROL room just outside Langley, Virginia, an alarm was sounding, and one of the on-duty technicians was trying to silence it. After he figured out which alarm was sounding, a few simple keystrokes silenced the audible alarm.

Frederick Tremblay had worked for the agency for less than six months. After an intensive training period, this was his first shift without his trainer leaning over his shoulder. And this was the first time he had ever seen this alarm section come to life. Grabbing the action binder, he cross-referenced the alarm code, and found the proper response sequence. He keyed the sequence into the terminal in front of him and watched as the alarm location and activation type scrolled in front of him. At the bottom of the screen, a reference code flashed insistently.

Looking over his notes, Fred paled. He signaled the watch commander and told him about the alarm. The watch commander walked over to Fred's desk as he tapped out a series of messages on his mobile phone. The watch commander leaned down and read the summary of the alarm. Noticing the flashing code, he patted Fred on the shoulder and said, "Good catch. You did everything by the book. I'll note that in the after-action reports."

The commander's phone rang. Looking at the screen, he nodded and answered, "Yes, Agent Smith. This is Donaldson, I'm the watch commander tonight. We just got a new alarm that was code 'Zulu-Three'." There was a pause, and Donaldson continued, "Yes, sir. The Incursion alarm triggered for the Unseelie Court, sir." Another brief pause, and Donaldson began nodding absently to the person on the other end of the line. He assured the caller, "Yes, sir. I'll start the data collection. I'll have it ready for you by oh-eight-hundred. I'll have the new kid, Tremblay work with me. It'll give him some good experience. Yes, sir. I'll see you in the morning."

Donaldson looked down at the young rookie smiled. "Lucky break, Fred. You just caught a full-on Incursion alarm. You get to help me begin gathering data and then present it to Agent Smith and the planning team in the morning."

The color that had been returning to Fred's complexion was again lost as he realized that he was expected to present their findings to THE boss. Donaldson peered down at the screens in front of his young analyst, ignoring the look of horror on Fred's face.

The watch commander began muttering to himself, "Let's see where this alarm was located. Hmm. Looks like a city in western Michigan. Now, what the heck are the Unseelie doing in Grand Rapids?"

I

MISSION

1

WAREHOUSE

Industrial Park, Newport News, Virginia

D eep in the shadows of the alley squatted a large truck. Over eight feet wide and twenty-three feet long, the matte black truck hid in the darkness, only given away by a slight glint off of the thick bullet resistant windscreen. The roof of the vehicle rose over ten feet above the pavement, and an observant passerby might see several unusual antennas on the roof of the vehicle. If the passerby looked closely at the side doors, they would be able to make out a small decal on the otherwise blacked-out truck. This decal, no larger than the span of a small hand, proclaimed that the vehicle was part of the Department of Homeland Security.

Inside the truck affectionately nicknamed the "War Wagon," behind a blackout curtain separating the front cabin from the rear, a young man with wild red hair and black-rimmed glasses perched on his thin face sat in front of two computer monitors, both of them filled with multiple camera angles. The glow of the monitors lit his pale face as he looked from monitor to monitor, searching for his target.

John Q. "Spooky" Smith studied the monitors closely, watching the mass of people in and around the industrial warehouse. Spooky wore a pair of worn jeans, running shoes, and a faded black t-shirt announcing that the federal agent "Will Hack For Food." A light jacket that proclaimed "POLICE" hung on the back of his chair.

Spooky had been a top-tier analyst at the National Security Agency, and become the liaison with Homeland Security for the PRISM/ECHELON computer sniffing software. The young electronics specialist had been a rising star at the NSA, and had enjoyed being an amateur ghost investigator on his time off. During one of his routine data collection compiles, he saw references to Section 28 and monsters. Dutifully he had compiled the data references and forwarded a report up his command chain.

The following Monday, his supervisor had pulled him from the ECHELON project, and had threatened to fire him if he didn't back off. Awaiting the young NSA analyst at his house was senior agent from a secret group in Homeland Security, who offered the analyst a job that any paranormal investigator would want. Now the agent called "Spooky" found himself sitting outside a warehouse in Virginia

Frustrated in his fruitless search for his targets, he touched the switch on his microphone and contacted his team leader. "Ghost, this is Spooky. I've got eyes inside and out. No targets yet. But I can't distinguish much with these cameras. I wish the organizers had sprung for decent cameras."

A block away, a tall, thin man stood in the shadows of another alley, his long black leather duster and black bolero hiding him from the casual passerby. He did not feel the slight chill of the late autumn night as he waited. The man raised a hand to his throat to activate the mic there. "Copy, Spooky. You can tell them when we take them down." Jonas "Ghost" Vanhof paused momentarily, then clicked his mic again, "Ghost to Little G. What do things look like from up there?"

On the roof above him, a man in gray and black urban camouflage pattern fatigues knelt on one knee, looking over the edge of the rooftop. Slung across his chest was a bolt action M24-A3 rifle with an oversized scope mounted on the rail and a long, fat can of a suppressor attached to the barrel. The man scanned the building across the street and the alleys to the sides of the building with a bulky pair of binoculars.

With a touch of a button, Jesús "Little G" Rivera, switched his views from night-vision to infrared vision to standard vision. Looking for anything out of the ordinary, Little G was in position to watch the building that the team was about to enter. He had not seen any of the targets in the time he had been up there.

The sniper grew up in Colorado and then went to Harvard for Pre-Law. Out of college, he joined the FBI, and a short while later was asked to join the elite Hostage Rescue Team. As a sniper for the HRT, Jesús excelled at his job, and was instrumental at ending several hostage situations before innocent lives were lost.

After a particularly successful mission against terrorists, Jesús was recruited by Agent Smith for Section 28, the division of the Department of Homeland Security that hunts monsters. As the team sniper, he was given the callsign "God." Unfortunately for him, the team's resident priest refused to call him by that name, instead calling him "Little G". After the team's first mission, the new moniker stuck, and his official call sign changed. Now the former HRT sniper perched on a rooftop, in the dark, hunting vampires. He loved every minute of his job.

Little G reached up to key his mic and replied to his boss, "Ghost, this is Little G. Lots of foot traffic, but no sign of the targets. They should be here by now. How solid is our intel?"

After a brief pause, the sniper heard his team leader reply, "This is Ghost. Forecasting gave us eighty-nine percent probability."

The sniper was about to make a comment about the actual accuracy of the Forecasting Team when something strange caught his eye. Quickly changing back to infrared, he noticed that the three young people approaching the door of the warehouse were showing as colder than normal human body temperature. Gotcha, he thought. He keyed his mic permanently on and called his leader again as he placed the binoculars on the ground and took a hold of the rifle across his chest. He raised the scope on the rifle to his eye, switching the mode to infrared as he began talking.

"Ghost, this is Little G. Looks like three targets. Approaching the building from the east. Two female, one male." He tracked them down the street with the rifle and continued his commentary. "Seventy-five yards from the entrance. Am I weapons free?"

The team leader tracked the trio of people that his sniper was talking about. They appeared as a group of young partiers headed for the illegal rave like all the other teens that had passed the alley. He could not help but marvel as the three creatures looked perfectly at home among the crowd of teens. It was his neck on the line, but he trusted his sniper.

Just as he was about to pass the word to his sniper, Ghost paused. There is something wrong here. He looked over the street and alleys carefully. The veteran monster hunter's gut told him he was missing something. Suddenly he realized what it was. One of the creatures in front of the federal agent kept surreptitiously stealing glances his way. It was almost as if the creature knew they were there.

He keyed his mic for his sniper, "Little G, this is Ghost. Hold fire. Repeat, Hold fire." He knew the sniper was muttering under his breath right now. He continued talking, "Ghost to Knightmare. My cover is blown. Assume this is a trap. Switch to Plan Two. Repeat. Knightmare is switching to Plan Two. Advise when teams are ready and in position."

Behind him, the lanky team leader could hear a sharp intake of breath, and a rustle of cloth. The soft metallic "snick" told him that Boomer was cycling the bolt in her shotgun, and the whisper of clothing announced that Doc had drawn her cross from inside her robes. Ghost turned to look at the two agents behind him.

Rebekah "Boomer" Callahan stood with her back against the stained brick wall. She silently closed her eyes and slowed her breathing, making an effort to calm herself down. Her hands flowed over the bulky shotgun slung over her shoulder, checking the drum mechanism and safety with practiced movements, sight unseen. Finished checking the AA-12 full-auto 12ga shotgun, she checked the rest of her equipment. Her hand glided from her belt pouches full of explosives and detonators to the two grenades she had affixed to her belt. A final check on her body armor verified that she was ready.

As she felt her heart rate slow again, Boomer opened her eyes and found herself staring into her team leader's eyes. He saw her calm expression and raised one eyebrow. She gave an impish grin and assured him, "I'm all right, bossman. It's under control."

Ghost looked at his demolitions expert and said, "I know. Lets try to keep it that way. This is your first mission since...your change. Let's put all that training to use." Boomer nodded and gave a pensive smile. Ghost looked past her and spoke to the woman standing behind Boomer, "How about you, Doc? You ready for this?"

A slightly older woman stood next to Boomer, not quite leaning against the grungy brick wall. The middle-aged woman's brown hair was wound up in a tight bun, leaving her round face and gray eyes clear. A priest's stole and vestments draped over her shoulders, set off against the dark gray business suit with the black shirt and high white collar of a Catholic priest.

Noelle "Doc" Sorenson gripped the ornate silver and wood cross in her hands. Her face a mask of determination, she nodded at the team leader. Her voice was low and even, held tightly in check against the fear she was feeling, "I'm ready, Ghost. We need to end this before too many of these kids get hurt."

Ghost turned to look back out the end of the alley. As he did so, his earpiece crackled. "Bravo Team in position and standing by." Ghost watched as the trio of creatures walked through the front doors of the warehouse. His earpiece crackled again as Little G spoke up, "Overwatch is standing by." A brief pause and his earpiece spoke for the final time with Spooky's voice, "Eyes and Ears ready, bossman. Satellite is overhead for fifteen minutes. After that I lose coverage."

He reached up and touched his throat mic, "Alpha Team in position and standing by. Spooky, any sign of Heavy?"

The electronics specialist's voice crackled in his ear agin, "Negative boss. No sign of... Wait one. Yes. I've got him. He's, uh, actively engaged in his cover." In the darkened War Wagon, Spooky watched a very large African American man in a sleeveless t-shirt and BDU pants dance surrounded by a bevy of younger women gyrating to the music.

Ghost's hand tightened on the cloth-wrapped bundle he was holding. Inside the wrappings were two large curved blades called khukuris. These were Heavy's weapons, and he would need them once the team leader "rescued" his wayward team member from his reconnaissance job inside the rave. The DHS leader activated his throat mic, "Ghost to Knightmare. Sixty seconds."

In the alleyway behind the target warehouse, two figures hidden in shadows glanced at each other and prepared to go through the back door. The figure in the lead was the epitome of the clean-cut all-American country boy from the Midwest. His blond hair was cut into a military-style crew cut, and his features bespoke his youth. That youth did not reach his eyes as a closer look would reveal an age and a pain that belied his years. Christian "Do-Right" Folsom wore black fatigues and armor that fit well over his athletic build and proclaimed "POLICE" in block letters across his back.

Do-Right tightened his grip on the stubby submachine gun cradled in his hands. The short MP5K-PDW was just over eighteen inches long, and capable of firing 9mm rounds in short bursts or full auto through the attached suppressor. As he waited for the remaining countdown, the former deputy sheriff flipped the selector switch from "SAFE" to "BURST" with practiced ease. Do-Right kept the muzzle of the stubby sub-gun pointed at the pavement as he raised the stock to his shoulders. Waiting for the "go" signal, the young agent thought about how he got there.

Christian Folsom grew up in a small town called Trinidad, about two hours south of Denver, Colorado. He was a local high school football star, and spent his whole life in the Trinidad area. After high school, he got married and went through a string of jobs from factory work to EMT, looking for his future career.

He eventually got his law enforcement academy certification and applied with the sheriff's department in his home county. He was a rookie, just seven months out of training when a group of vampires descended on his town, quickly followed by the team from Section 28. Monsters created by those vampires killed his wife and two young children, driving him to despair and a hunger for revenge.

When the team realized that Christian was going to follow them, whether or not he was invited, he was quickly drafted, and eventually proved to be a valuable asset when killing monsters. With nothing to go back home for, Christian welcomed the opportunity to join the team. His classic boyish charm and naivete earned him the nickname "Do-Right," which became permanent when he was officially sworn in. Now he was standing at the back door to a warehouse, getting ready to once again confront vampires.

The young man standing behind Do-Right swallowed nervously and drew his pistol from the holster rig attached to his thigh. Dressed in the same black combat fatigues and heavy outer armor, the tall young man was visibly tense. His raven-black hair was pulled into a loose ponytail, accentuating his sharp, chiseled features and Indian heritage.

William "Scout" Buckhorn gripped the pistol with a strong, two-handed hold. The Beretta M9 was a large black semi-automatic that also had a fat black suppressor attached to the end of the barrel. Anticipating a crowd of young people inside, the former camp counselor had left his ancestral bow slung across his back. For the entry, he knew he could ready it quickly if he needed a long shot, but the cramped quarters dictated that the pistol and the large blessed hunting knife strapped to his hip would be better for the conditions. He inhaled and exhaled rhythmically, letting the breathing calm his thoughts and heart rate.

Across the road, Ghost mentally counted down the time, waiting until the last second to key his mic again, "Ghost to Spooky, tell the locals to move in. Ghost to Knightmare. Three. Two. One. Execute! Execute! Execute!"

On the last "Execute," Ghost leapt out of the alleyway, running across the wide abandoned street and up to the front door of the warehouse. Behind him, he could hear the pounding footsteps of his two fellow agents as they tried to keep up with their leader. His coat billowing behind him, he hit the sidewalk with a thump and slammed into the front door of the warehouse as it was being hastily closed. Crashing through the doorway, he dimly recognized the sirens in the streets outside as the local police department descended on the warehouse.

As their team leader crashed through the closing door, Boomer and Doc followed closely. There was a pair of large men, bouncers, who were trying to stop Ghost as he moved down the short hallway that led to the entrance. Ghost held his credentials up and announced loudly, "Homeland Security. Step aside. Now!" That last came out in a sort of growl.

The two men looked at each other and, as if they had rehearsed it, both took a step forward and swung a punch at the lead DHS agent. Ghost sidestepped both attacks as one and threw two quick rabbit punches into the side of the first bouncer. As the man doubled over in pain, the federal agent pivoted, whipping a back-hand strike against the bridge of the other bouncer's nose. Blood spurted from the man's nose as he howled in agony.

Ghost completed his spin and put his knee and thigh squarely into the face of the bent-over bouncer. The federal agent felt the bones of the man's nose crunch as the bouncer hurled backward and collapsed on the floor of the hallway out of the fight. The second bouncer was just now bringing his hands down from his face, and Ghost could see rage behind the bloody visage. Just as the bouncer reared back to throw another punch, the monster hunter planted his right leather cowboy boot squarely between the man's spread legs. The bouncer clutched his ruined manhood and dropped as if poleaxed where he lay retching on the floor.

A faint rattle and thrum shook the doors that the bouncers were guarding. Ghost laid one hand on the door and could feel the energy and music pulsing through the solid metal door. He reached up and keyed his mic, "Alpha Team is in position. Bravo Team —Execute!"

At the back loading doors of the warehouse, Do-Right had already set a small, specially prepared block of plastic explosives on the seam between the double doors, right where the locking mechanism would be. He and Scout leaned back and shielded their eyes when Ghost had given them the second signal. Do-Right pushed a button on a small transmitter that Boomer had given him with the explosives, and there was a loud "pop" and the doors shook and jarred open, leaving a gap of several inches between them.

The former deputy grabbed a door and held it open for his partner as Scout rushed in, looking up and down the long hallway that ran along the back of the warehouse. Scout led the way to the right and Do-Right followed, dimly noticing the sirens and lights that were starting to fill the alleyway they were in. The two federal agents moved deeper into the bowels of the building, feeling the bass line through the soles of their boots.

2

SPARKLES

Industrial Park, Newport News, Virginia

As Bravo blew the locks off the back loading doors and entered the building, Ghost opened the door and felt the wall of driving bass and noise cascade over him. The cacophony of sound and light exploded into his senses, and he paused to catch his bearings.

Shaking his head slightly in a visible effort to clear the cobwebs from his mind, he turned and looked at his two teammates. They had both paused upon being blasted by the noise and lights. They both quickly recovered and Boomer gave him a thumbs up to show she was ready.

He glanced back around and got his bearings. He touched his throat mic to transmit, "Spooky, this is Ghost. Where is Heavy?"

There was a momentary pause, and then the thin voice of his electronics specialist echoed in his earpiece over the din of noise. "Twenty degrees to your left." Spooky explained, "About fifty feet away. He's surrounded by a gaggle of girls. You can't miss him."

Ghost grunted a quick, "Copy," and motioned for Boomer and Doc to follow him. He set off through the mass of young people as they jumped and gyrated to the driving beat of the music. Glow sticks and drinks were tossed about casually, and each dancer had at least one of each in their grasp. Ghost pushed his way through the horde of horny teens and coeds.

Boomer had trouble keeping up with her boss, resorting to using the stock of the shotgun to club people out of the way with judicious jabs to the kidney or spleen. Doc followed in her wake, staring around her in wonder at the sea of humanity.

When Ghost reached the group of young women gathered around his heavy weapons specialist, he elbowed his way through the crowd of coeds, not caring who he jostled, or how hard they were hit. As he cleared the last ring of girls, he found that he was staring at the back of a massive bulk of a man, well over six feet tall, and gyrating to the heavy bass beat.

Stepping to the side of the mountain of muscle, Ghost realized that Arthur "Heavy" Murphy had his eyes closed as he danced and moved to the music, a look of sheer bliss on his face. Smiling cruelly, he reached up and slapped the giant on the back of the shoulder, hard enough to hear the slap over the music. The large man was startled out of his reverie and looked around wildly until his eyes met his team leader's.

A big sheepish grin flared across his face, and the man turned to the girl who was his dance partner. He leaned over close to the girl and spoke in her ear. Her smile turned into a frown, then into a pout as he lightly slapped her on the butt to move her along with her friends.

The heavy weapons specialist turned back to Ghost and rumbled, "Sorry, boss. I forgot where I was for a moment. Did you bring my blades?"

The lead DHS agent wordlessly handed the wrapped bundle over to his gunner. Heavy could read his Ghost's face—the big man would hear about this later.

The big man stood over six-and-a-half feet tall and looked like the bodybuilder he was. Thick, muscular arms emerged from the black sleeveless t-shirt, and barely contained his massive chest. He slipped a harness over his head, placing two large khukuri blades on his back in crossed scabbards. After securing the blade harness, he then strapped a holster equipped with a Beretta M9 to his thigh, securing it over the black combat BDU pants he wore. As he stood up again, he finished strapping the microphone around his throat and placed the earpiece in his right ear. The lights glinted off of his bald head as he completed the transformation from popular raver to elite federal agent.

Heavy straightened, waved for the team to follow him, and moved across the dance floor toward the back of the building. His wide bulk and ominous presence cleared the path in front of him, and the rest of the team followed in his wake. He angled left, walking toward a nondescript door on an inner wall marked "Private."

As they approached the door, the crowd thinned out, and the din from the rave was muted to a dull roar when they moved out of the direct line of the massive speaker banks. The team approached the door and Ghost activated his microphone, "Alpha at stage two. Holding for Bravo."

Raised in a long line of monster hunters, Jonas "Ghost" Vanhof trained from an early age to track down and kill creatures that bled through into reality. Jonas was very good at what he did. With few resources and a cobbled-together intelligence network made of paid informants and conspiracy theorists, he had hunted monsters that threatened humanity for years.

One fateful night, Jonas had made a mistake when he was hunting a werewolf, and had traced the beast back to its house. There the beast had changed and attacked its wife. Instead of leaving at the commotion, Jonas had barged in and fought the beast, eventually killing both the beast and his wife, who was also infected. He had been too slow, and the police had shown up before he could escape.

Agent Smith had found the monster hunter in jail, waiting trial for a vicious double murder. Smith had offered him a simple choice —join this secret government agency and fight monsters with government funding, or die by lethal injection. Jonas had truly been given a new lease on life, and his shadowy background earned him the call sign "Ghost." Now he led the team called Knightmare, and the burden of that mantle weighed heavily on him.

In the corridor along the back wall of the warehouse, Do-Right and Scout crept down a dimly lit hallway. The two men approached their target, an unmarked door at the end of the corridor. According to their intelligence, this door was the main staging area for all the sound and lighting equipment. They had encountered no resistance thus far, but they were prepared for that to change when they went through the office door.

Do-Right keyed his microphone. "Bravo team at stage two." The former deputy spoke in a low voice, "Holding for Ingress."

Just before Ghost responded with the "go" command, the DHS leader's earpiece crackled again and Spooky's voice came through, "Spooky to Ghost. The locals are ready to storm the rave. Holding for your command."

Ghost nodded to Heavy, who was ready to kick down the door.

The giant gave him a big thumbs up, and the DHS leader keyed his mic again.

"Ghost to Knightmare. Stage two — execute."

Heavy reared back his booted foot and slammed it into the door in front of him, landing the blow right next to the knob. The cheap wooden door splintered where his boot landed, and the door crashed inwards. The large man stepped back out of the way as Ghost stepped through the doorway.

Inside the room, pandemonium was reigning. Ghost saw six or eight people scattered around the room, most of them starting to panic as the team followed him through the doorway. Two of the people cowered at the sight of Doc as she walked through the opening, baring suddenly visible fangs and hissing. Ghost smiled and keyed his mic, "Looks like intel was correct — we have type-two vampires. Bravo, begin Ingress."

One of the now hissing creatures leapt at Ghost, hands outstretched as razor-sharp claws swiftly extended from the tips of its fingers. Ghost raised a beautiful cane between his hands and waited for the exact moment. Just before the claws reached his throat, he sidestepped, driving the cane up underneath the creature's upper arms and redirecting the creature's momentum away from himself, and into the wall behind him. The creature dove face first into the wall, punching a hole in the drywall and crashing to the floor in a heap.

Before the creature could recover, the DHS leader twisted the head of his cane slightly, and drew a rapier-like blade from the haft. As it cleared the haft, the lettering on the ancient blade began to glow, soon enveloping the blade with white light. Ghost pivoted and slashed the blade across the creature, cleanly severing the neck and causing the head to drop to the ground. The team leader noticed the body of the creature begin to dissolve as he turned to the rest of the room.

As Doc entered the room, her vestments glowed a radiant blue, alerting her to the presence of evil undead. Spotting a creature that was cowering away from her, she began chanting and held her cross up toward the creature as she walked over to it. The closer the priest got, the lower the creature seemed to cower, until it was prostrated on the floor, whimpering in pain and fear.

Noelle "Doc" Sorenson had grown up in Grand Rapids, Michigan, but had attended Notre Dame for Pre-Med, where she was also introduced to the Catholic Church. She had graduated Harvard Medical School with honors and had begun working at

Catholic-run clinics in the inner cities. Wishing to give more, she had soon joined with Doctors Without Borders. There she had excelled in trauma care and had even helped with animal attack wounds.

Her excellent work had brought her to the attention of the Vatican, which had recruited her into a special, secret priesthood dedicated to fighting monsters. After her training and ordination as one of only three female priests in the Catholic Church, she had been assigned as a Vatican representative to Section 28, where she had found a home on team Knightmare. Her first mission killing vampires had been a rousing success, and she has made a permanent home for herself on the team.

Finishing her incantation while staring down a creature of the night, the priest from the Vatican waved her hand with a flourish, and the creature screamed in agony. Knowing this creature was held down with supernatural force, Doc pulled the sheath off of the blade built into the base of her ornate cross. The blade glinted in the light, and she struck down with all her might, driving the blessed silver blade into the brainpan of the creature. The scream abruptly stopped, and the creature twitched and went still. The wound in the head belched smoke, and the body began to fade away.

As Boomer moved into the room, she was immediately attacked by two of the creatures' human thralls. These familiars were so lost to the control of their masters that they blindly dove at the federal agent holding the large automatic shotgun. Boomer raised her shotgun to her shoulder and squeezed the trigger. Riding the diminished recoil from the internal buffers on the AA-12, she shifted her aim slightly and squeezed once more.

Both humans withered under the hail of silver and wood slugs. Designed to penetrate and take down a full vampire, the large slugs hit each human in the chest, ripping through the ribcage, through the heart and left lung, and exiting out the back in a three-inch hole. One after the other, both humans staggered, then dropped, dead before they hit the dirty concrete floor.

Heavy stepped through the doorway last. As he did, he reached over his shoulders and drew his two ceremonial khukuris from the sheaths strapped to his back. As they cleared their sheathes, they began to glow a pale iridescent green. Grinning wildly, he stepped forward and pointed at the last two beings remaining. The two creatures bared their fangs and hissed. Then they sprang at the big federal agent.

The former Airborne special forces sergeant waited for a brief pause as the two vampires committed to their leap. As both flew through the air at him, the giant nimbly stepped aside and swung both of his ceremonial knives at the creature closest to him. The first blade swept through the outstretched arms of the vampire, severing them above the elbows. The second swing seemed to be drawn toward the neck of the attacker, slicing clean through and causing the head to drop and roll away from where the body landed and started to dissolve.

The second vampire landed and rolled, swiftly rising and slashing at the big agent. Heavy was ready for this attack and used one khukuri to fend off the attacks while he waited for his opportunity for a strike.

They sparred for a few long seconds, and the vampire finally made a mistake. It was used to attacking slower, weaker prey, and it overbalanced on a long swipe at Heavy's face. Heavy saw the opportunity and his arm was moving before his brain realized it. His right arm brought the khukuri in from the side, and the blade unerringly sought its target — the neck of this vampire. He barely felt the strike as the enchanted blade glided through the undead flesh encountering no resistance.

Heavy looked up as the head bounced away and the body began to dissolve into smoke. He looked around what used to be a lounge area, and then spoke to Ghost, "I count six, and only four were vamps. This can't be the main nest, can it?"

Ghost shook his head and gestured at the door in the back of the room. "We go through there," the team leader announced. "According to the intel, that hallway should lead us to the main nest, and the master. He now knows we're coming. Be ready."

The DHS leader moved over to the door he pointed to earlier and placed his ear against it. Leaning back, he said, "Sounds clear. Time to clean out the nest."

Heavy took point, trying the knob to see if it was locked. Finding the door unlocked, the big agent turned the handle, and then opened the door. Beyond the door was a short hallway, with two doors on each side, and a frosted glass door at the end with "PRIVATE" stenciled on it in gold paint.

Carefully checking each door on the way down the hallway, and finding each one locked, the team swiftly and silently made their way down the fifty foot corridor. As they got closer to the private suite, they could hear a different music than the one still pounding in the warehouse outside the offices. Somehow the classical strains of Bach meshed well with the driving music from the club.

Reaching the door, Heavy approached from the side, trying to minimize his shadow on the frosted pane of glass. The big gunner looked back at his boss, and Ghost gave a nod, signaling him to open the door. Heavy slowly turned the handle, and the door slowly swung open, revealing a decadent suite with a giant bed in the middle of the back wall, thick, lush carpeting on the floor, and heavy drapery all around the room.

Sitting on couches and chairs around the large room were several people. While most appeared to be vampire, Heavy could see several regular humans among them. On the bed in the center of the back wall crouched a vampire, hunched over as she ripped and tore the flesh off of the body in front of her. Her victim appeared to have been a teenager, dressed in club clothes, and now very dead, by the looks of her shredded wrists and thighs.

As the team strode in, the master vampire looked up from her feast. Heavy realized something was off. There was something about the scene that bothered him. Then he realized what it was. He could hear himself saying in his deep rumble, "It can't be. I didn't think they did that. Is that bloodsucker really...?"

Ghost finished his question, "Sparkling? It appears so."

Heavy could not tear his eyes away from the master vampire, his deep voice rising in plaintive denial, "No. They don't sparkle. You said so. Doc said so. Bloodsuckers don't really sparkle."

Ghost's voice was soft and thoughtful, "Well, I guess there's a first time for everything. Would you please go kill that sparkling vampire?"

Chaos erupted.

3

TAKEDOWN

Industrial Park, Newport News, Virginia

As Heavy let out a tremendous roar and leapt at the sparkling vampire crouching on the bed in the middle of the back wall, Ghost raised his cane sword and blocked a swipe of claws from the teenage vampire sitting by the door. The young vampire scrambled to its feet and the DHS agent recovered from his parry and performed a perfect riposte, shoving the glowing blade through the eye socket of the vampire and into its brain. The vampire jerked to a halt, and its considerable strength left the body as it quivered on the sword.

The vampire slowly slid off the tip of the sword, and Ghost took a quick swipe, drawing the blade across the neck of the creature. The creature's head slid free of its body and bounced out into the hallway. As its body slumped to the ground, it began dissolving into a greasy black vapor. Ghost looked up and searched for his next target.

Boomer almost tripped on the head of Ghost's first vampire as she strode into the room. She raised her shotgun to her shoulder and thumbed the selector switch to full-auto. The explosives expert centered her sights on a group of human bodyguards across the room that were reaching into their suit jackets. As the first guard drew his pistol, Boomer squeezed the trigger, firing a short burst of heavy 12ga slugs from her shotgun. The rounds hit the chest of the bodyguard and the trio of three-quarter-inch slugs ripped through his chest, shredding his heart and lungs.

The human guard started to fall and Boomer shifted to the guards around him. Squeezing the trigger for short bursts, the explosives expert placed perfectly aimed bursts of slugs into the three remaining human guards. All of them were hit and fell hard, and none of the bodyguards were able to return fire. Boomer quickly dropped the mostly empty drum magazine and rammed another home into the receiver. She raised the shotgun back up to her shoulder and scanned around the room for her next target.

Doc stepped into the room and her vestments lit with a bright blue glow. She looked carefully around and stepped cautiously toward the corner opposite where Boomer was working. She spotted two creatures as they noticed her movement. Abject terror crossed their faces as they froze in fear. She raised the cross in front of her and began chanting and intoning in Latin.

A blue glow enveloped the priest's cross, and she pulled a cap off the long end of the cross, revealing a silver dagger blade with symbols and latin etched along the edge. Doc waited, holding the two vampires with her faith as she waited for backup.

To the priest's left, Boomer had just put down another human thrall when she realized that Doc had cornered two vamps. She pivoted to the right and raised her shotgun to her shoulder. As she brought her shotgun up, she flipped the selector switch back to semi-auto. She carefully aimed through the red dot scope and placed the crosshairs over the chest of one of the vamps. She exhaled partly, and squeezed the trigger, sending the 12ga slug into the chest of the vamp.

Like the rounds she had been using all night, the large silver hollow point slug had a giant cavity in it, and that cavity was made from a special wood grown on sacred ground. As the slug hit the vampire in the chest, the pressure on the tip of the round forced the wood back into the solid silver cup. This started the expansion process, and the slug peeled back to create a one-inch wide mushroom of silver that bracketed a half-inch slug of pure sanctified wood.

This wooden payload traveled deep into the vampire's chest cavity, and the slug hit the creature's heart. As it was designed, the wooden part of the slug shattered as it neared the creature's heart. The slivers burst outward, and most of the fragments burrowed their way into the vampire's heart. Each sliver of wood acted as a miniature stake, paralyzing the vampire. Close behind the wood slivers, an inch-wide "mushroom" of silver slammed into the heart, turning the undead muscle into so much paste, and then exited out the back of the creature. As the first body was falling and starting to dissolve, Boomer again pulled the trigger, and the next slug shattered the heart of the second vampire, killing that threat as well.

Doc looked at Boomer and nodded her thanks, and then turned to survey the room, looking for more targets. The explosives expert was also looking around the room and saw Ghost attacking another creature. She saw them just in time to see the former independent monster hunter slice the head off of the vampire. She watched as Ghost flicked the ichor off of his blade with a quick hand motion and turned toward the giant bed.

Heavy had drawn the khukuris from their sheathes as he strode toward the raised bed. The blades began to glow a ghostly green that brightened as the big man got closer to the creature in front of him. The vampire on the bed raised its head, bloody maw gaping and lined with razor-sharp teeth. She let out a loud hiss that shifted to a growl.

The creature leapt at the big DHS agent, hands outstretched and claws glinting a muted red in the light. As it jumped, the vampire scattered her latest victim across the bed, and a small corner of Heavy's mind watched the torso and legs go in different directions with the force of the creature's leap.

The creature and Heavy collided in midair, both letting out savage roars. The vampire wrapped its arms around the big man, using its superior strength to pin the warrior's arms to his sides, and keep the blessed blades away. The two dropped heavily to the floor, with the big federal agent landing on top of the smaller vampire. The impact jarred the creature as several hundred pounds of weight landed on the monster; Sir Isaac Newton's physical laws playing out in real time.

As Heavy landed on the creature, he felt her arms loosen slightly. He drew his head back and brought his forehead down in a headbutt, slamming his hard forehead into the nose of the vampire. Crushed between the hard floor and the agent's hard forehead, the weaker bones in the nose and face shattered on impact. The creature howled in pain and she let go, throwing the big agent off of her.

Heavy briefly saw stars as his forehead broke the face of the creature. He shook his head and realized that he was free of the creature's embrace. He also realized that he still held both khukuris in his hand. He rolled to his knees, and saw the vampire four feet away from him, holding her face and howling as the ichor poured through her fingers. He seized the opportunity in her distraction and lunged forward, hoping to pin her on one of his blades.

The vampire raised her head at the last second, and her murderous gaze changed to fear as the glowing blade pierced her chest. The flesh around the blade began to sizzle, and the agony forced the creature to scream again.

With the creature pinned to the end of the khukuri, Heavy was able to draw a ragged breath, aim, and then swing his second blade around, severing the head of the vampire. He let the rapidly dissolving body drop from the end of his blade and looked at the room around him. Seeing the rest of his team staring, he dead-panned, "And all I had to worry about at the raves I attended were drugs."

"I wouldn't know. I never got invited," quipped Ghost. The team leader keyed his mic, "Ghost to Knightmare. The Master is gone, and the nest in clean. Begin mop up. Bravo, execute Insertion."

Standing outside the door, Do-Right nodded to Scout, and then raised a foot to kick in the locked door. As the door crashed open, two creatures stepped out of the darkness and rushed the agents. Do-Right pulled the trigger on his MP5. The small sub-gun chattered out a burst of silver and wood slugs that chewed into and dropped one of the charging vampires. Scout raised his suppressed pistol and squeezed off two rounds. One of them struck the vampire in the chest, with the second round entering the vampire's face and exiting out a large hole in the back of its head.

Scout dropped his aim slightly and pointed his pistol at the writhing creature on the floor. A single muted "clack" and the vampire stopped writhing in agony as a silver and wood slug opened the back of the creature's head and scattered the contents around the body.

William "Scout" Buckhorn was not yet used to using firearms to kill monsters. William had been an archery instructor at a camp in northern Colorado until just a couple months ago. A mad scientist under the thrall of a master vampire had infected a large majority of the children in the camp and most of the adult counselors with a genetically engineered version of the vampire virus. William had been fortunate to escape and hide in the woods.

When team Knightmare showed up to eradicate the vampires, they had found William and had attempted to rescue him. When the vampires attacked en masse, the team had been almost over-whelmed by the sheer numbers of the vampires. Seeing an opportunity to help, the former olympic alternate had grabbed his grandfather's old bow and started killing the monsters alongside the DHS agents. When the smoke cleared, William was conscripted to join Section 28, and he'd been given the nickname "Scout" to match his Navajo heritage.

Do-Right and Scout carefully explored the large room stuffed with electronics and made sure that there were no more surprises waiting in the crowded room. Scout found the back of a rack of computers, exactly as Spooky had described. He took a small USB thumb drive out of an inner pouch and stuck it in a slot in one of rack-mounted servers. When it was seated fully, he pushed the small green button on the drive.

A red light lit up on the specially designed thumb drive and Scout keyed his microphone, "Spooky, this is Scout. Package is uploaded. Scout to Ghost, Insertion complete. Will escort locals inside."

"Ghost to Scout. Affirmative. Ghost to Spooky. Patch us in to the local radio network."

In the blacked-out DHS truck, Spooky flipped a couple switches, and then began typing on his keyboard. After twenty seconds, he keyed his own mic, "Spooky to Ghost. You are live in... Five. Four. Three. Two. One."

As he checked all the bodies in the nest area, Ghost keyed his radio again, "Agent Vanhof to Captain Gerard. You are clear for entry. I have two agents waiting on the back side of the building, they will escort your men in. The rest of my team is in the main office area. I will post my people at the entrance. Consider the office area clear and off limits for your people."

Ghost's earpiece crackled and an older voice came back to him. "Affirmative, Vanhof. I'm sending my men in now."

As Spooky watched from the monitors in the truck, swarms of police officers in uniforms or riot gear approached and entered the building. As the first officer opened the outer door, the young electronics genius tapped out a pre-arranged key sequence.

In the electronics staging area, the light on the USB drive shifted from red to green. In the computer system, a series of random data was rapidly overwriting all the storage media attached to the network. At the same time, the data worm in the programming almost instantly infected the server, and then spread rapidly to the other servers. In less than a second, the specially designed worm transferred complete control of the servers to Spooky.

The electronics specialist keyed a macro sequence and hit "enter" on his command console. Inside the rave, the music died out and the lights came up as the police officers burst through the doors. Amid the sudden silence, the police officers shouted orders and pointed their firearms at the ravers. With the alcohol and drugs flowing through their systems, it took many of the partiers a long time to realize that their night of debauchery had suddenly, harshly, ended

At the rear entrance, the group of policemen followed the two federal agents inside the building. Scout led a small group of officers down a short corridor and onto the raised dais where the DJ was hurriedly gathering his equipment before he made a break for the exit. The DJ stopped and raised his hands as the trio of officers came through the back door, weapons raised and shouting orders.

Down the other hallway, Do-Right led the officers to the equipment room, and then the office area beyond the door. The agent and the officers with him didn't find anyone else in the area as they cleared the building room-by-room.

On the roof across from the warehouse, the DHS sniper watched the scene through a bulky pair of binoculars. Much like the scope on his rifle, Little G was able to cycle the view from infrared to low-light to normal light at will. He watched and counted sixteen police officers and tactical officers entered the front of the building. The sniper watched as the prisoner transport vans began to arrive, and then movement on the roof across from him drew his attention.

He shifted his aim and saw a second figure emerge out of a roof access hatch to stand next to the first. Both looked human, but were moving a little too fast to be normal. He carefully lowered the glasses and raised his scope, never moving more than a couple inches, lest he draw attention to himself. As his scope came to his eye, he thumbed the switch to infrared.

As he put his eye to the scope, he could distinctly see the colder body temperature of the figures on the rooftop. Too cold to be a living human. He grinned slightly and disengaged the safety on the rifle. He watched as one of the creatures looked over the front edge at the police cars and officers milling below it in the parking lot. The creature looked back over his shoulder and made a motion for the other creature to look over the back of the building.

As the second vampire turned away from the sniper and walked toward the back edge, the agent placed the crosshairs over the head of the first creature. Letting out his breath halfway, he paused, then his finger twitched slightly. The muffled "thump" of the high-powered round exiting the suppressed barrel was lost as the super-sonic bullet crossed the street in a fraction of a second and slammed into the head of the vampire. The head disappeared in a fine spray of ichor.

As the sniper cycled the bolt, the second creature turned around and looked to where its partner was crumpled and starting to melt away. Realization dawned for the creature as Little G's finger twitched again, and the head of the second vampire exploded. The sniper waited for a few more seconds for any signs of movement or any additional roof targets.

The sniper keyed his mic to report in, "Ghost, this is Little G. Two critters on the roof. Both neutralized. Holding position." The sniper heard his boss reply with, "Copy."

Inside the nest area, Doc and Ghost had begun the process of cleaning up the aftermath of their attack. Vampire heads were collected and bagged. Human familiars were tagged and recorded for later. And any trace of the unusual or illicit nature of the creatures was vigorously scrubbed from the scene.

Ghost told Do-Right to guard the door into the office area and sent Heavy to collect the heads and clean up the outer offices. Boomer glanced through paperwork and office decor, making sure that the nature of the creatures could not be found. She also spent a few moments opening each computer and ripping its drive right out of the casings. She knew that Spooky would enjoy digging through the information.

In the nest, Ghost reached the raised bed in the center. He gently searched the victim's body for identification and then looked at the master vampire. Puzzled, he looked closer, as it still seemed to sparkle. As he picked the head up, the tall fed started chuckling. After the stress and tension of the operation, the emotional trickle quickly became a flood, and the chuckles turned into laughs, and the laughs soon became great guffaws, only eventually running out of steam as the adrenaline dissipated.

Ghost looked up to see Doc staring at him. He wiped a tear from his eyes and grinned. As he held up the head of the vampire, he said, "Now we know why it sparkled."

Boomer and Heavy walked in to find the two agents trying to suppress another round of raucous laughter.

4

DEBRIEF

"And why was the vampire sparkling, Mister Vanhof?"

The speaker sat at a nondescript desk in a sparsely furnished office. The man was likely around forty years old and of Native American descent and had close-cropped black hair and black eyes hidden behind small reading glasses. His dark gray pinstripe suit, white shirt, and black tie marked him as a middle manager, while his office, battle-scarred surplus desk, and less-than-comfortable visitors' chairs revealed that he was a government functionary.

Supervising Agent James Smith looked at the tall, lanky man and the middle-aged woman sitting in the visitors chairs in front of him. Smith noticed a slight smile play over the lips of his senior agent. The man looked at the woman next to him and they both chuckled.

Ghost sat sprawled in one of the visitor's chairs. "Glitter. Plain old glitter." His grin hinted at the outright laughter inside him, and he continued, "It was a damn rave, after all. The master's victim had glitter all over her body, and the stuff must have rubbed off on its face."

Agent Smith let out a dry chuckle, "I'm sure Heavy had a few words to say about that."

Doc spoke up, her smile reaching her eyes, "He apologized afterward. I think he actually blushed when he realized I was there."

Smith nodded, then looked down at the file in front of him. He looked back at the duo in front of him, and his expression became serious. "What about Miss Callahan? How did she do? Was she able to maintain control?"

Doc answered him, reading from some notes as she did. "Yes, sir. Boomer kept it under control, with little sign of stress at all. She was just as efficient with her shotgun as she has been in the past. Frankly, I expected she would have trouble once we hit the nest. She kept it together the entire mission."

Smith changed subjects, "What about the follow-up? Any fallout from the locals or media?"

Ghost shook his head. "The locals are telling the media that the raid was an effort to take down one of the largest suppliers in Ecstasy in the area." The Knightmare team leader continued, "Any videos of us have been scrubbed or corrupted by Spooky, and even the conspiracy sites are silent on this one so far.

"On the plus side, this master actually was one of the biggest suppliers of 'Ex', so that worked out. We also helped expose two very dirty vice cops, and they should head to trial shortly. As far as we can tell, we were able to stop this master before she could spawn any more vamps that night, and only two victims were lost to the vamps before we arrived. The whole Norfolk area should be much safer now that she is gone."

Smith looked thoughtful. He nodded, as if deciding an important question. He looked at the file again and asked, "Anything else?" The two agents in front of him shook their heads, and Smith continued, "Good. We'll consider the mission successfully closed. If I or the Auditors have questions, I'll let you know."

The supervising agent steepled his fingers in front of his chest, a move that Ghost recognized meant that he was about to send them into harms way again. The team leader waited for his boss to brief him.

Smith set aside the previous mission file and picked up another one sitting in front of him. He opened it up and looked at the first page. He looked directly at Ghost and spoke, "We have just received word of another incursion-class event. This one is not something that your team has dealt with before, but we have to send someone to handle the incursion, and you guys are currently the only team available for active deployment. Is your team up for another one so soon?"

Ghost looked at Doc, his second-in-command. He turned back to his boss and cleared his throat, "I don't know boss. We haven't had time to really debrief from this mission, and I wanted Doc to work with Boomer some more before things got dicey. What about the other teams?"

"They are unavailable." Smith's tone was flat, and brooked no argument. "Mister Cassiday just brought Knightsdawn back from San Antonio, and they are down with four agents in the hospital and one in the morgue. Apparently this Chupacabra had pups. Knightfall is still in training. While Miss Watkins is bringing them along quite rapidly, they are not ready for a full mission yet. When you consider their rather unique makeup, I cannot afford to send them out on this mission. Frankly, you are the only agents I have available.

"I would love to give you time to debrief and decompress, but a situation has developed that will require Section 28 presence, and I trust your team will be able to accomplish the mission."

Ghost frowned and grew quiet. Doc spoke up, "What color is this mission classified as? Is there any way to postpone it?"

Smith shook his head as he answered, "I'm afraid not. This is currently classified as a Priority: Red mission, with the potential to bump to Ultra-Red if we wait too long. We are not in control over the timetable on this one. Certain... external forces control the timing. I need your team ready for briefing tomorrow morning at oh-eight-hundred. I've reserved Briefing Room E-1. You will have time after the brief to pack and prep."

Ghost frowned, but acquiesced. "We'll have them ready. I'll debrief them informally tonight. If there is anything raised, we'll get it sorted tomorrow." He and Doc stood to leave.

As they were leaving, Smith said, "Tell your team I said, 'Great job.' See you in the morning."

As Ghost and Doc walked back to the team's apartment block, they prepared a list of their discussion topics at debrief around the dinner table that night.

AT EIGHT O'CLOCK the next morning, team Knightmare walked into the briefing room. Ten plush chairs were arranged in rows of five, with the back row sitting higher than the front so those seated there could see the raised dais and large video screen behind the presenter. Each chair was a soft leather recliner with comfortable padding and a swivel out desk available for taking notes. Attached to the side of each chair were small stands with drink holders. In the front of the room, on the dais stood a clear lectern, with audio and video hookups in abundance. Two dark leather chairs sat off to the side of the dais, out of the way so they did not interfere with the presentation.

Sitting in the chairs were two men, only one of whom was familiar to the team. Agent Smith sat conversing with the man on his right. The other man was dressed in an olive green uniform with unfamiliar buttons and insignia adorning it. The man had a pale face that only hard living kept from being round. Alert emerald eyes tracked the team as they took their seats. His close-cropped military hair cut did nothing to hide the gray spread through the dark red hair, and his clean-shaven face was pale.

At precisely one minute after eight, Smith stood up and approached the lectern. He smiled and began, "Ladies and gentlemen, congratulations on a successful mission. We have received a thank-you note from the police chief of Newport News for our assistance in the overall mission. I really wish I could give you some time off, but we have a new mission you will begin this afternoon.

"At approximately ten o'clock last Friday night, a private club in Grand Rapids, Michigan, was attacked. The vicious attack lasted precisely six minutes and forty-three seconds and, despite a heavily armed response, killed everyone in the club. There were thirty-five victims in this attack, and the media has yet to be told about it."

Smith could tell that he had everyone's attention. He continued, "The victims in this brutal slaughter were shot or stabbed multiple times. The attackers were captured on video, and used automatic weapons and swords. They were dressed in full tactical gear with the word 'police' stenciled across the back, and the uniforms looked remarkably like ours."

By this time the murmurs were becoming audible. Smith raised his hands for silence. "Someone is pretending to be us, and that pisses me off. They are trying to set us up, and we need to find out why."

Spooky raised his hand slightly. "How has a slaughter like this not been in the media? It's not even on the usual conspiracy websites." The electronics specialist was pointing to the screen on his wrist computer as he spoke.

"Because the victims weren't human." Smith paused a moment to let that sink. "Yes. I said they were not human. None of the victims were human, strictly speaking. You are going in because the victims were *aes sídhe*." The DHS agent pronounced it as "ace sheeth-uh." He continued, "Better known as fairies, or the fae. This private club was one of their local hangouts, and someone slaughtered every last fae in the club. Whoever it was, knew that regular weapons aren't effective. The fae are susceptible to cold-forged iron or steel weapons. All the rounds recovered were specialized steel bullets, each inscribed with a special script of banishment. Each cut showed evidence of a cold-forged iron burn."

Heavy had been trying to listen to the briefing, but his mind was wandering, going back to how he joined the team. Arthur "Heavy" Murphy grew up in the Washington D.C. area and had been a gangbanger from his early years. Busted with a stolen vehicle at age eighteen, he had been given the choice of enlistment or jail.

Arthur had excelled at Army life, and had applied for airborne training. Once completed, he had been posted to the 82nd Airborne, and had quickly risen to squad leader, then eventually to Staff Sergeant. His natural leadership and easygoing demeanor had endeared him to his platoon, and to his CO.

On leave, he had returned home to discover a vampire attack in progress. The creatures were eating his older parents. Without thinking, he had grabbed a pair of khukuris that he had been given by a Nepalese tribal shaman and had attacked the creatures. The police had found him covered in blood, with his parents murdered and two more severed heads nearby.

It was only a swift intervention from Agent Smith that forestalled the investigation. Arthur was given a choice: join the agency or go to death row. It did not take him long to agree to join the team, and he was given the call sign "Heavy" for his affinity for heavier, belt-fed armaments.

What Agent Smith had said caused the big man to stop listening for a moment, and Heavy's voice boomed out, "Wait a second. Now there are fairies living here on earth? Sounds like these guys cleaned up the monsters for us."

Ghost shook his head as Smith spoke to Heavy. "I assure you, Mister Murphy, the fair folk are not the only incursion-related creatures to walk among humanity. In this case, we have a treaty with the *aes sídhe* courts that allows them, under certain circumstances, to live among us. These fae were living under the treaty and should not have been targeted."

Ghost raised his hand to get Smith's attention. "Was this club Seelie or Unseelie?"

Smith paused, a look of surprise flickered across his face. He gave a slight shake of his head and answered the question, "Sometimes Mister Vanhof, I forget what you did before we found you. To answer your question, this was a Seelie-aligned club."

He looked at the rest of the room and continued, "The *aes sídhe* are divided into three courts, or groups. The *Seelie* court is often considered the 'light' court, and traditionally have gotten along best with humanity. The *Unseelie* are the darker fae, and are often associated with the more malicious of the fairies. Keeping the peace and balancing the courts are the *Seanachaidh*, the gray court. Strictly speaking, none of the courts are truly an ally to humanity, but the Seelie are more overtly loyal to the treaty.

"Because the attack happened at one of her clubs, the Queen of the Seelie is requesting a delegation from humanity to answer for the attack. Because the attack happened on US soil, it is our mandate to come up with a delegation. To help you through the intricacies of the fae courts, we have brought in a consultant from another organization that works with the fair folk more often."

Smith gestured and the man he was sitting with earlier rose and walked toward the lectern. Smith continued his briefing, "On loan to us from the Directorate of Military Intelligence in Ireland is Captaen Callum O'Beirne. Not only is Captain O'Beirne an Army Ranger Wing commando, but he is also one of the team leaders for *Fóireann Gníomh Domhan i Bhfolach*, or FGDiB. The FGDiB is the covert agency, like Section 28, that deals with incursions in Ireland.

"Captaen O'Beirne will be our liaison for this mission, in a strict Observer capacity. Our mutual charter with his agency does not permit any direct action without prior authorization, and we do not have that authorization. This man is one of their most experienced team leaders. Learn from him." Smith gestured to the gentleman, "Captaen O'Beirne, they're all yours."

O'Beirne was short, around five and a half feet tall, but his presence filled the room. He began his briefing by turning to Smith, his thick Irish brogue marking his origins. "Thank you, Agent Smith."

The Irish Army Captaen turned back to the group and smiled, a twinkle in his eye. "I read the report about your recent mission. Great job killing the beasties. Unfortunately, this mission will not be quite so easy. You may be great at dealing with vampires, but you have not seen anything until you come face to face with a leprechaun who thinks you stole his gold."

5

FAE

Captaen Callum O'Beirne of the Irish FGDiB stood in the front of the briefing room and watched the rookie DHS team respond to his statement. He raised an eyebrow as a young man in the back sputtered around a mouthful of coffee. The sputtering turned into a hacking coughing fit as the young man tried to inhale the caffeinated beverage. When the coughing had subsided, the young man raised his hand.

"Yes, and you are?" The Irish intelligence agent asked.

"John Smith, sir. But you can call me 'Spooky.' Did you just say, 'leprechaun?' As in little guy with a green suit and bowler, always hiding his pot of gold?"

The Irish Captaen had a wry grin on his face. "Yes, Spooky. I said leprechaun. As in small faerie that is known for hiding gold and valuables and playing nasty little tricks. They don't typically wear perfect little green suits and bowlers, but they do often have patch-work green clothing on. It helps them blend into the forests better. And don't underestimate them. Those wee beasties caused the Great Famine in 1845, all because one got knackered and lost his pot o' gold. They got vindictive and introduced the potato blight to the crops. Millions starved because of one of these little arseholes."

The Irish agent gathered his thoughts and forged ahead, "But lets's not get too caught up on leprechauns. As far as we know, they aren't involved in this caper — on either side. In fact, they tend to stay more neutral. They don't like court politics. And they really don't like traveling across the pond because it's too far away from their gold. Instead, let's talk about this particular attack, and why you are being summoned to the Seelie court.

"The Seelie court is held by the Queen of the Fae. This is both a title of nobility and a position of rank in the fae realm. This queen is an *álfr*, an elf, who has held her throne for over three hundred years. As Agent Smith pointed out earlier, she tends toward the helpful side for humanity, as long as we don't make too much hassle for her. Her court is the same way."

O'Beirne paused to catch the eye of those in front of him. "You have been summoned to attend to Her Majesty Lishe ta Merunaré, the Queen of the Seelie. Because this attack happened on US soil, and because it appears the attackers were humans with faerie knowledge, your agency has been called to provide an explanation."

Agent Smith stepped up to the lectern again and addressed the team, "Your new mission is to go see the Queen and her court. Your job is to find out what happened in the attack. You will find out who initiated the attack, and if human, eliminate the problem. If the attack was coordinated by other fae, you are to help determine who those fae are, and then let the internal matter be solved by the court. Let me make this clear — you will be representing Section 28, and all of humanity by proxy to the fae. Act accordingly."

Ghost raised his hand, "What's the time frame on this op? When do we leave?"

"You will have a mission planning and background briefing this afternoon at fifteen hundred hours." Smith looked at a slim note that he had in his hand. "We'll meet back in this briefing room. You will finalize equipment load out tonight and leave for Michigan tomorrow morning. Take the rest of today to prep your kits. Any questions?"

Heavy spoke up from the back of the room, "Yeah, boss. What happens if this thing goes pear-shaped? What do we need to know to hurt fae?"

Smith frowned slightly. "I sincerely hope that things do not go... 'pear-shaped' as you say, Mister Murphy. If they do, however, then regular ammunition and weapons do not work nearly as well on the fae. As mentioned before, cold-forged iron or steel weapons will not only injure the faerie, it will allergically burn them as well, much like the reaction of werewolves and silver. Beyond that, I'm sure Norbert will be able to provide some new toys. Any further questions?"

The supervising agent looked around the room and found no raised hands. He looked at his watch and spoke, "Dismissed. I will see you at fifteen hundred hours, then."

As the team got up and started to leave, Smith spoke up again and said, "Mister Vanhof, Doctor Sorenson. Would you please stick around?"

ON HER WAY back to the team's quarters, Boomer decided to detour by the Knightfall training area. As she walked through the now-familiar corridors, she reflected on her journey to Section 28. Rebekah "Boomer" Callahan grew up in Norfolk, Virginia as a Navy brat. Her father retired as a Chief Petty Officer, and there was little he could do to slow down his daughter. She raced cars by the time she was tall enough to sit behind the wheel and moved to boats as she grew older.

When she graduated high school, Rebekah immediately joined the Navy. Fresh from high school, her enthusiasm and knowledge combined with her skills to propel her into demolitions. As a freshly minted female EOD tech, she worked her way up through the ranks for the next five years to become a Senior EOD technician. Then her life changed.

She was on the dive of a lifetime, diving in Scotland's Loch Ness when she had a close encounter with a large underwater creature. Even though she had no proof, her story made her fodder for the tabloids and conspiracy theorists. This soon caught the attention of headquarters staff, and Rebekah's promising career ended prematurely. Fortunately, her story caught the attention of Section 28, and Agent Smith soon recruited her to join Knightmare, where she was given the call sign "Boomer."

On their first mission as a team, they fought a large vampire incursion, and she was scratched by a new, genetically engineered breed of the creatures. She soon found out she was infected with the virus and had been learning to control her inner monster since then. It was on that same mission that she had rescued the person she was trying to find, a young Hannah Cresswell.

Boomer approached the Knightfall living quarters and talked to one of the new recruits. She found out that Hannah was undergoing her final field service qualification exercise in the training center, and the explosives expert went to watch.

THE DARKNESS no longer freaked her out. Hannah Sedano (née Cresswell) calmly closed her eyes and quieted her mind, listening for any telltale signs around her. There, off to the left, a dripping pipe. Slightly behind and to her right she heard a low hum from a computer power unit. Then she heard the scrape of a shoe across the concrete floor. About two yards away and slightly to the left. Remembering the layout of the room from the plans, she launched a kick in the direction of the footstep.

She felt a solid thud as her kick connected to someone's gut, and she heard a harsh exhale as the person dropped to the ground. She knelt and felt for the person's head. She felt a bulky night vision set, grabbed a hold of it, and yanked it off.

Hannah placed the goggles against her eyes and did a quick scan around the room and did not see anyone else sneaking up on her. She glanced down at her feet and saw one of her hand-to-hand instructors. He was still bent over, clutching his stomach, but he managed to flash a sign at her that showed he was "unconscious" for the scenario.

She kept the goggles against her forehead and walked quietly to the door against the far wall. Hannah knelt and placed her ear against the door, listening intently. She heard small sounds of movement behind the door.

The seventeen-year-old reached down and drew a small pistol from the holster on her thigh. The Walther P99 pistol was matte black, and Hannah loved the ergonomics of the grips. She raised the muzzle of the gun and gently turned the doorknob.

As the door moved a fraction of an inch away from her, light spilled around the frame, and she dropped the night vision goggles to the floor. She squatted and palmed open the door. Letting it swing fully open. The young trainee raised the muzzle of her handgun and pulled the trigger twice, sending the rounds into the chest of one man who was just turning toward the open door. She shifted her aim slightly and squeezed the trigger twice more. This time, both rounds missed and her new target began firing back.

The short burp of a suppressed MP5 sent rounds flying over the crouched girl's head. Before he could adjust his aim, Hannah corrected hers and two rounds found him in the chest. The young woman rose from her crouch and carefully walked into the room. She scanned all around her for threats as she edged toward the raised pedestal in the middle of the room.

A book with a wrinkled leather cover that almost looked like a face in horrible pain sat on a red velvet pillow atop the pedestal. The young woman paused momentarily before taking the familiar-looking book. She double checked pedestal and found a small, nearly invisible wire leading from the small pillow to the top of the stand. She carefully took her wire clippers and clipped that final wire, disabling the alarm.

As she stood back up, she grabbed the book and held it over her head. She smiled and said, "Klaatu... barada... necktie."

Lights came up all around the room as clapping and peals of laughter spread throughout. The men Hannah "shot" stood and rubbed their chests where the wax rounds had hit.

A middle-aged woman with a cane hobbled out from around a corner, surrounded by four other teenagers. The woman clapped and said, "Well done Hannah. Great thinking grabbing Scott's night vision gear, that was a great way to even the odds."

The young woman was still breathing heavily from the stress, and she had her "prize" tucked up underneath her arm. "Thanks, Amanda. So who's idea was it to make this the Necronomicon?"

A young African American boy shyly raised his hand, "I guess that would be me."

Hannah turned and gave him a thumbs up gesture. "I loved it! I just wish I had the shotgun and chainsaw to go with it."

"I'm sure Norbert can come up with something for you." A familiar voice came from behind the young woman.

Hannah spun around and rushed to hug Boomer, throwing both arms wide around her mentor and losing the prop in the process. The young woman finally released the explosives expert from the bear hug and stepped back, exclaiming, "I'm so glad you could make it. When did you get back? I haven't seen you for a couple weeks. Did you see the trial?"

Boomer nodded and said, "I caught everything from the dark-ened room on. Great move with the night vision headset. Way to think on your feet."

Hannah gushed with joy. She spoke up, "So, when did you get back? How did your last mission go? Can you stick around for the final selection? How long are you back in town"?

Boomer was almost overwhelmed by the sheer speed and mass of the questions from the young woman. She raised her hands in surrender and tried to break in, "Let's talk about that later. We ship out tomorrow on a new op, but I wanted to see you before that. When do you get final selection?"

Hannah spun to ask her team leader, "Amanda, when will Norbert and Russell be ready? Any way we can move it up to right after lunch?"

Special Agent Amanda "Bad Wolf" Watkins was nodding as she pulled out her phone and began to dial Logistics. She knew how close the young woman and the older agent had grown, and she would personally ensure that Hannah's Final Selection ceremony would take place after lunch.

Two hours later, Agent Smith and Agent Watkins both stood in front of Hannah. Smith began, "Hannah Sedano. You've success-fully completed your trials — the first among your team. And while your training is never done, you have come upon a special ceremony we call Final Selection.

"Here in Section 28, we sometimes acquire items that have a particular power. For some reason, these items seem to determine who their eventual wielder will be. New agents are offered the chance to peruse a selection of the items. Most new agents are never selected by any of the items, and they still go on to become phenom-enal agents, keeping the darkness at bay. Occasionally, an item will choose a new agent. That agent is entrusted with the care of that item until their service to Section 28 is done."

Agent Watkins spoke next, "Hannah, you passed your final field trial. It is time for you to go through Final Selection. Enter the room behind us. Feel free to touch the items located on the tables. You are able to pick any of them up. If something selects you, you will know about it, and your *geas* will react well. If not, come back out here."

Smith and Watkins stepped aside, and let Hannah enter the open doorway. Her eyes roamed up and down the tables, stopping occasionally on a small item here and there. Several bladed weapons, some firearms, and even a few items that Hannah could not identify were all laid out on thick black velvet, spread across several tables. As her eyes roamed over the items, she noticed a slight gleam of light.

The young woman walked over to a table about halfway around the large room. On the table, she saw a short sword with an intricate hilt and pommel and a slim blade. It lay next to a similarly ornate scabbard. The bright silver of the metal gleamed in the overhead lights, polished to a fine sheen. Etched into the blade near the base was a design of flowing lines and patterns. Nestled among the design were the words "*fion-fhuil*" in a beautiful flowing script. She felt drawn to this blade ,and she placed her right hand on the hilt. As she closed her hand around the hilt to lift the sword, she felt a small pinprick, and then energy flooded through her arm.

A deep rumble seemed to echo in her mind, *Who has awakened me?*

6

UNCORRUPTIBLE

In The Void

Hannah was standing on a small hill surrounded by rolling fields and meadows. The grass was almost two feet tall around here, and it was bowing with the wind that was sweeping her hair back out of her face. The sun was bright in the clear azure sky and warmed her face softly. She looked down at herself and jumped. Her standard blue jeans, t-shirt, and leather jacket were gone, as were her combat boots. Instead, she was in a light cotton peasant dress with soft leather boots that laced up to her knees. The young woman looked around frantically trying to figure out where she was, how she got there, and most importantly, how she would get back to Section 28.

A deep rumble seemed to echo in her mind, "Who has awakened me?"

Hannah whirled her head about frantically trying to locate the source of that voice. When she realized that no one else was around, she called out, "Who's there? This isn't funny anymore."

Again the deep bass voice sounded, this time like it was next to her.

"This is my home. Twelve hundred years ago, this was my domain. I believe you would call it 'England'." Hannah felt a hot puff of air over her right shoulder as the speaker continued, "Your kind was afraid of me and my kin. Your legends tell of your mighty heroes sallying forth to slay the monster. They don't tell you that the monster won most of the time." The voice took on an amused tone.

The young woman turned to her right and came nose to... snout with a very large reptilian head. That head was about the size of her torso, and was attached to a long, serpentine neck. The scales from the neck blended seamlessly into the large body at the base of the neck, and large wings grew from the creature's back.

"You're a dragon? How are you in the sword?"

The creature smiled, showing too many razor-sharp teeth. "Yes, I am what you would call a dragon. As to how I was trapped in the sword? I had a rather energetic disagreement with a wizard who had objected to me eating his apprentice. His final death curse trapped me in this sword. Thankfully, I still get to choose whom I serve."

Hannah studied the magnificent beast. Bronze metallic scales blended with deeper, copper colored scales to form a beautiful hide. The outspread wings and large tail of the creature were also the darker metallic scales, but the scales on the underside of the dragon were smaller and lighter. The dragon's deep black eyes seemed to glow a soft greenish glow.

"What do you mean you get to choose who you serve?" her voice rose with the question.

A low rumble began in the belly of the dragon, and small puffs of smoke began leaking out of the dragon's mouth. Hannah shrank back, but soon realized that the creature was laughing.

"What's so funny?" The young woman demanded. "Why do you get to choose who you will serve?"

The dragon stopped laughing when it realized that the young woman was serious. It spoke in a calming voice, as if to smooth over hurt feelings. "Please, young one. I meant no offense. Pardon my laughter. You must have been Called only a short time ago. You likely do not even know your heritage."

Hannah heard the capital "C" when the dragon called her "Called." She made a mental note to ask about that later, and then pressed on, "Seriously. You can simply choose not to be used by anyone? How would a sword keep from being used? Do you burn whoever holds you?"

It was the dragon's turn to study Hannah, and the pause made her nervous. The creature's deep black eyes were liquid pools of darkness and gave no hint of what it was thinking. It gave a small nod and spoke, "Yes, child. I choose the ones I serve. For those few, I let them perceive me. Those who are not worthy of me do not even know that I am here."

The dragon let that sink in for a moment and then continued, "And you, child, have been chosen to wield me. As long as you remain worthy, of course."

"Hannah. My name is Hannah Sedano, and I am not 'your child' or any other condescending term of endearment that you want to use. My name is Hannah. Do you have a name?"

The dragon's lips twitched in a semblance of a smile. Its tone was bemused as it responded, "Well met, Hannah Sedano. I am called Vellath. It is my pleasure to make your acquaintance. I must beg your pardon for my speech, as I have not chosen a warrior for over fifty of your years. The vernacular seems to have changed quite a bit since that time."

The creature moved, slowly, carefully positioning itself so that it stood in front of Hannah. The dragon made an elegant, if somewhat strained, bow, dipping its head below Hannah's shoulder height, and spreading its wings to lay the leading edge on the ground in front of her. "I, Vellath, Guardian of the Noa't, am humbly at your service, my lady. I shall remain to serve you until you are killed in battle, or choose to become unworthy of my service."

Hannah was unmoving. Having this large creature bow to her and tell her that he was in her service was very disconcerting. Before she could ask the creature what it was talking about, the dragon continued, "We will talk later, Hannah. But in the meantime, you should probably leave my world and go back to your own. We have much to do."

Abruptly, Hannah was back in the selection room, staring at the sword in her hand. She lifted the scabbard from the table and slid the blade home until there was a barely audible "click." She shook her head as she turned and walked back toward the door.

Outside the room, Smith, Watkins, and Boomer had all watched with Norbert as Hannah had walked among the tables. As she suddenly had walked toward one table, Smith had not seen any items on that table. He had turned to Norbert and had motioned him over. He had then leaned in close and had said, "What is on that table? I see nothing there."

Norbert had clicked a switch on his small glasses and the lenses had turned a pale blue. He had looked a little shocked when he turned back to Smith. "It looks like she's picked up *fion-fhuil*."

Smith looked at the young woman who was now walking toward them. She looked like she was carrying something about the correct size for a short sword, but her hands appeared empty. He muttered, "Interesting," and turned to talk quietly to Agent Watkins.

Hannah walked out the door and immediately asked, "How long was I in there? It felt like at least an hour. It must have happened when I picked up this." The young woman held her palms up as if balancing something across them. "What is this thing? I think it's possessed or something."

Just inside her head, Hannah heard a now-familiar deep rumble, *Of course it's possessed, young one. I possess it. We just talked about this.*

Hannah looked at the sword in her hands, and those around her saw her stare at her empty hands. She frowned and spoke to her empty hands, "Shut up. You can't be real. I can't start hearing voices."

Smith stepped toward Hannah and spoke softly, his calm tones reassuring. "None of us, except Norbert with his glasses, can see the object in your hands. It seems like you picked up *fion-fhuil*. Vellath introduced himself to you?"

The voice rumbled inside her head again, *If this Norbert fellow can see me, I may need to speak with him to ask precisely how he can accomplish that.*

Hannah did not think at all when she spoke, "Seriously, stop talking until I can figure this out." She then realized that she had answered the sword verbally again. She looked at Agent Smith with pleading eyes, and mouthed the word, "Help."

Hannah looked around the room and saw her mentor, her new team leader, and her boss staring at her. Her eyes widened and she slowly shook her head. "I'm not crazy—this thing is talking to me." She turned her frightened gaze to Smith and pleaded, "You believe me, right?"

Smith nodded. "I believe you, Miss Sedano. In fact, I have dealt with Vellath in the past, and have found him to be impossibly boorish at times. You are not crazy, but he has chosen you. You have the ability to... converse with him mentally through your bond."

The voice inside her head chuckled, *Boorish? I've never been called that before. Leave it to James to choose that word for me. Tell Agent Smith I said, 'Hello.'*

Hannah looked at her boss, "He's laughing. Inside my head. He said to say, 'Hello.'"

"Tell him to stop interrupting, Hannah. Tell him that it is impolite, and it does not befit him to act that way. That's why I called him a boor." Smith thought for a moment, "Just think it back at him. There is no need to speak verbally to him."

Hannah concentrated, and then thought at the sword, *Stop talking for a moment.* Not knowing what the limitations were, she put a lot of her effort and will into the thought.

The cry of anguish in her mind startled her, and she saw a brief mental image of the dragon in pain, with its front paws held tightly to the side of his head. The voice was a little shaky, *I got it. You don't have to yell at me. You could have just asked.* The voice pouted.

Hannah did not try as hard this time. *Is this better? I'm sorry. I didn't mean to yell at you. I didn't know how hard I'd have to try.*

The resonance of the voice shook slightly as Vellath tried to shake the loud thoughts. The dragon spoke again, *Proximity correlates to strength. The closer we are physically, the necessary requirement of energy in your voice drops. You just yelled at me as if I was half a continent away. If I had ears, I might have actually been hurt.*

I'm sorry. I didn't know.

My dear, how could you have known? The dragon sighed wistfully, *I apologize as well. I keep forgetting that you are newly Called. You have to merely beckon, and I will be summoned.* The voice seemed to fade away.

Hannah realized that Smith had begun talking again. She caught part of it, and said, "I'm sorry. I was talking with Vellath. Apparently I screamed at him the first time."

A smile touched Smith's lips. "Yes, he can be a bit touchy about loud voices. As I was saying, you will soon learn what *fion-fhuil* can do for you. I'm sure the dragon will teach you, as he has taught those who have wielded him in the past. And if he cannot, or will not, let me know. I will give you what insight I have."

Hannah nodded as she thought, then she asked, "So what does... '*fion-fhuil*' mean? Sounds almost Latin, or possibly an older pagan dialect."

Smith opened his mouth, but Norbert answered first, his voice animated with excitement. "It means 'Uncorruptible' in old Celtic. Or was that Gaelic? I can never remember. It doesn't matter. It apparently decided its own name when it was created, and has so informed every one who has wielded it.

"Also, good ear on the dialect. It's not often someone can pick up those subtleties. Sounds like you have an ear for languages." Norbert looked around as those around him tried to hide grins or snickered into their own hands. He must have said something funny. He didn't know what it was, but he was used to that.

Agent Smith cleared his throat and waited for those present to stop talking. "I'm sure there is a lot to discuss, but I believe that there is a graduation planned for a little while from now, and that the soon-to-be graduate must prepare a few things.

"Norbert, I expect that you will care for the weapons on the tables?" Smith received a nod and continued, "Then I will see you ladies in a short while." He turned and left the observation room.

Hannah grasped the scabbard that was clearly visible to her. And held the sword in her hand as she walked down the hall toward her apartment. Boomer and Agent Watkins followed her out the door, leaving Norbert alone with a cart and a rapidly growing pile of objects.

7

BRIEFING

Team Knightmare gathered in the briefing room by 2:55pm. Agent Smith and Captaen O'Beirne were waiting for them, seated in the chairs by the lectern. Ghost spotted a small table with a tray of snacks and a couple pots of coffee, and he knew that this would be a long briefing.

As three o'clock rolled around, Smith stood and walked over to the door. Just before he closed it, Hannah Sedano hurried through the doorway, slowing down as she saw the questioning glances from Knightmare. Smith gently closed the door and reached over to turn on the "Do Not Disturb" light.

He turned and strode over to the lectern, motioning Hannah to join him on the dais. The seventeen-year-old stood just over five feet tall. Her training and background in dance kept her fit, and Boomer could see that she was developing into a beautiful young woman. Her dark tan complexion and slightly round face told of her Latina heritage, and her long, raven-black hair was pulled back in a short ponytail that spoke of her youth.

Hannah had been attending the summer camp where Scout worked as the archery instructor just a few short months ago when a master vampire and a mad scientist under his control had infected almost the entire camp. If Boomer had not found her, she would have been devoured alongside all the other non-vampire campers.

When she rode back to Section 28 with the team, Agent Smith had given her a two options: She could either join Section 28, changing her identity and officially becoming a casualty of the horror, or she could go back to her adopted parents, swearing to never speak of the incident again, under penalty of treason. Hannah had chosen to follow her new hero, Boomer, and learn to fight the monsters that had screwed up her life.

Smith cleared his throat and began speaking to the team, "I believe all of you already know Hannah. As of today, Hannah has passed her trials, officially becoming a full agent of Section 28."

A round of applause and cheering broke out, with Heavy's bass rumble vying for volume with Boomer's raucous whoops. Smith waited a few seconds for the cheers to die down, and continued, "As I was saying, Miss Sedano passed her trials, and was taken through the rite of Final Choosing. There, my suspicions were confirmed as one of our most powerful, and most... selective artifacts chose to reveal itself to her."

Smith pushed on over the rising murmurs from the team, "It is for reasons I will discuss later that Miss Sedano will be temporarily joining Knightmare for this mission. While she will move to a permanent role on Knightfall, she will accompany you on this current mission. So I present, Special Agent Hannah Sedano, call sign 'Dancer.'"

More applause and whistles followed a blushing Dancer to her seat. Once the noise had died down, again, he cleared his throat. "Now that we have settled Miss Sedano's presence, we can begin the mission briefing. As usual, ask questions when you have them."

Smith clicked two small buttons recessed into the top of the lectern. The first button dimmed the lights to a pre-set value. The second button activated a projector with the mission briefing already loaded. Then the supervising agent began.

"As we talked about this morning, you are being sent to represent humanity while attending the Seelie court. You will be directly working with the Her Majesty Lishe ta Merunaré, the Queen of the Seelie." He pushed another button, and the screen showed a picture of what had to be an elf.

Spooky was mesmerized. It looked like the creature on the screen was even more ethereal than the elves in *The Lord of the Rings* movie adaptations. Her long golden hair was bound up in an intricate pattern that wove in and out of the small white-gold tiara perched on her head and did nothing to hide her delicately elongated and pointed ears. Her features were thin, without being sharp, and beautiful. She had piercing purple eyes and a pale, unblemished skin. Spooky would have believed that this was an artist's rendering, except that Agent Smith was standing across from her, bowing slightly at the waist and holding a small case outstretched toward her.

Now that he had all of their attention, Smith continued, "Her Majesty is of the *Lo'a*, or the Light Elves." Smith pronounced the name of the elves "low-HAAA" and then moved on with the briefing. "As we previously talked about, the Seelie court is typically considered the 'light' court. This generally means that they will not actively plot to trick or harm humans or humanity. Usually. However, they will defend their honor according to their laws and traditions, and this means that insults may be challenged with lethal combat. By ancient law and long tradition, Her Majesty is married to the King of the Unseelie court."

Smith again advanced the slide and a new picture of a different looking elf appeared on the screen. The man on the screen was very handsome and his strong, angled features complimented his dark, almost black complexion. His black hair was scattered with a distinguished gray and styled in a perfect mane fit for a Fortune 500 executive that fit his perfectly groomed van dyke-style beard. His piercing green eyes seemed to stare at the photographer. The only real distinguishing feature that set him apart from an executive on Wall Street was his rather tall, sharp pointed ears.

Smith motioned to the screen, "This is His Majesty Arkanai t'Nakaót. His Majesty is of the *Draukh*, or the Dark Elves." Smith carefully pronounced this word "droe-ka" and continued. "The *Draukh* hold the Unseelie court. In history and legend, the Unseelie are considered the 'dark' fae, and are typically blamed for all kinds of misfortune. The Unseelie traditionally work against the Seelie court in a contest for power and thus oppose most of humanity. As among the Seelie, honor is taken very seriously among His Majesty's court, and any real or perceived slight can demand satisfaction."

Spooky raised his hand from the back of the room. "Is it me, or do they kind of look like a dark elf race from a certain roleplaying game? I mean, add more silver hair and he could be a dead ringer for..."

Smith broke in, "Yes, Mister Smith. The resemblance is not accidental. An unsubstantiated rumor tells of that game's creator coming face to face with the *Draukh*. We've not been able to prove or disprove the rumor, but the resemblance lends credence to the rumor. Can we continue?

"The Seelie and the Unseelie courts are the fae courts you will be dealing with. We will provide a full briefing on the fae in your data packets before mission departure, but there is one other faction of fae you must be aware of." Smith clicked the controls again and a third picture showed on the screen, this one blurred as if from a hidden camera.

On the screen was the Queen of the Seelie and two other creatures. The two other creatures were both very short, likely around four feet tall, from the photo. Both looked to be humanoid, one male and one female. Both creatures had intricately designed tattoos running from the crown of their head down their necks. The one on the left had voluminous flowing robes that hung to the floor and a sash over his shoulder with an unfamiliar script on it. That particular being had a very round face and a large, bulbous nose. The eyes were squinted too tight to see through the large bushy eyebrows, and a long, full mustache and beard flowed down the creature's chest.

The being on the right had a long top-knot rising from the center of the tattoos on her head, with a slightly thinner and more muscular build. She was wearing a dark padded sleeveless vest that looked like modern armor, and a matching pair of pants and black boots. The extensive tattooing extended all the way down her arms. Strapped to the waist of the fae was a pair of short swords, both of them resting in sheaths next to each other. Slung over the back of the creature was a modern military-style rifle, either an M4 or the civilian equivalent.

After giving the team some time to study the picture, Smith went on, "The two shorter beings are dwarves. Yes, Spooky, just like those dwarves. The dwarves form the third court of the fae, called the *Seanachaidh* court." Smith pronounced this as "se-a-na-kaig."

He continued with the explanation, "*Seanachaidh* is the Celtic word for Keeper. This signifies that the dwarves are both the keepers of the libraries of the law volumes and the police officers making sure that the law is followed. They intervene in fae machinations whenever there is any challenge or suspicion of breaking fae law. The dwarf with the beard is Oracle Telacus Sturmwargh, and he is the Oracle, or leader, of the 'Keepers of Law' faction. The other dwarf is Praetorian Urteghat Dhorjachen. She is the Praetorian, or leader, of the 'Keepers of Peace' faction. The Keepers have almost unlimited power when they intervene. Do not make the mistake of underestimating the dwarves."

Ghost raised his hand to catch Smith's attention, "So, if these...

dwarves are supposed to keep everything in check, why are we going out?"

Smith motioned for Captaen O'Beirne to join him. As the Irish spec ops warrior was standing, Smith answered, "According to the *E'Tuatha* Accords, if either the Seelie or Unseelie courts are attacked by humanity, they have the right to call for an accounting by the host country where the attack happened. Those who go to the accounting will officially represent humanity before the courts and sue for peace."

O'Beirne broke in, "According to the treaty, if the attack is from an outside, non-official group that the signatories have no control over, the courts are free to exact their revenge to reclaim their honor. Unfortunately, the representatives of humanity must prove that it was not an officially sanctioned act."

Doc spoke up, raising her hand belatedly, "And if it actually was a sanctioned attack from an Accord signatory?"

O'Beirne's face grew somber as he answered. "Then the representatives from humanity will have to sue for peace. If the courts do not accept, humanity goes to war with the fae. None of the signatories want that to happen. The last time the faeries got involved in a human war, the Unseelie made a deal with the Japanese. An entire regiment of chikaran orcs was forming in Nagasaki before being integrated on the front lines. Regardless of what the history books say, this is why the city was targeted for the Fat Man bomb. And no, the bombardier did not actually miss his target, as the history books record. The bomb landed exactly where it needed to land. It neutralized the orcs and closed the gate, sending backwash throughout out *Alfheimr*, the realm of the fae."

Ghost thought for a moment and then asked, "So if it wasn't us, who was it? Who was it? Who is top of the list for suspects?"

Smith answered the team leader, "If it truly was humans, there are a couple options, and you probably know a couple of them, Mister Vanhof. There are several private organizations in America, and a few more scattered around the world, that also hunt 'monsters'. While most of them have little, or no, resources, there are always a couple that find the backing of a major patron, and have a few key members who can actually hunt. Most of them are dedicated to fighting whatever pet non-human type their patron doesn't particularly like, and they gather like-minded individuals.

"At the top of that list for this mission would be The Society for the Preservation of Humanity. Formed in the early 1900s by a rather eccentric millionaire, the SPH has the resources and knowledge to make this attack. They also operate heavily in the Midwest, and their headquarters is in Grand Rapids, Michigan. This attack would be very unusual for them, however, as they normally concentrate on elder god cultists and are more investigative in nature. There are a couple other groups, but the SPH should be at the top of your list."

Ghost was grim, "And if it was the SPH, or another human group?"

Smith looked just as grim, "Let the Seelie settle the accounts."

"You'd just let the fae kill humans?" Doc's anger was plain on her face and in her rising voice.

"Believe me, Doctor Sorenson. I do not relish letting the fae take any human lives. But the *E'Tuatha* Accords protect humanity and fae alike. It is their right, according to the treaty. And if we interfere, we jeopardize all of humanity." Smith paused for a moment. "You will need to be present to make sure that the retribution does not fall outside the Accords."

"What if the perps aren't human? Who could it be?" Boomer's voice covered Doc's not-so-quiet fuming.

Smith was grateful to deflect away from the previous train of thought, "If it was not a human organization, then you may be asked by the Seelie to stand with them and help settle their accounts. As for who it might be? The primary suspects would always be the Unseelie. This may be a power play, trying to separate the Seelie and humanity as allies."

The DHS supervisor looked at the Irishman next to him, "Then again, it may be Captaen O'Beirne's leprechauns. It's been a while since they messed with people, as only hopped up brownies snorting gold dust would."

O'Beirne chuckled, "Ah. You're right. It's been a while since those buggers have messed around with an elf. They'd think it's a grand sport."

Smith waited for the chuckles to die down. "You will have your briefing uploaded to your data packets for study, as well as dossiers and background on as many of the fae as we know about. Knightmare flies out tomorrow morning at oh-eight-hundred for Grand Rapids. You will not take the War Wagon with you as the oversized tank may give the wrong impression to the courts."

Seeing the crestfallen look on Boomer's face, Smith continued, "Don't worry Miss Callahan, Norbert and Russel have been specially modifying a new vehicle for you, with input from your Mister Smith, of course. This new truck will make the trip with you.

Eat your dinner, then make any final requests from Logistics. The C-17 will be loaded and waiting for you on the airstrip. Special Agent Stephen Lewis, the DHS Regional SAC, will meet you on the ground.

"He knows that you are coming to the area, and that your mission is classified well above his clearance. I have never personally met Agent Lewis, as he is a recent promotion from another office in Michigan. As always, if you have issues with the local authorities, Gretchen should be able to handle it, or have them call Timothy or myself. He knows that he is to provide full support at your whim.

"Captaen O'Beirne will accompany you as Observer and Advisor for dealing with the fae courts." Smith's lips curved into a small smile, "As I said earlier, Miss Sedano will also accompany you. Any further questions?"

Smith looked around the room and saw shaking heads. He said, "Ok. I'll see you in the morning before departure. Be ready by oh-seven-fifty. Dismissed."

As the team got up, Smith looked at Boomer and Dancer, motioning to them. "Miss Callahan and Miss Sedano. Would you stay for a few minutes?"

When the two women stood in front of him, Smith considered them thoughtfully. "Miss Callahan, I will be brutally frank with you. Are you ready for this mission? Your teammates' lives will depend on your control over the beast within you. If you need more time to train that's perfectly acceptable. I can hold you off of this mission if you need it. We just need to know before you get into the field."

Boomer hesitated. She believed that she had her affliction under control, didn't she? There was nothing else she could do until her control was tested under real stress and combat. She spoke, trying to keep her voice calm, "I'm ready, boss. There is absolutely nothing else that I can do to prepare. I need to return to active duty sometime."

Smith was nodding as she spoke. "I believe so, too. I needed you to believe that. Very well, you are returned to full active duty. I'm also giving you special duty. You will be the on-mission mentor for Miss Sedano. Your job is to teach her how to be a successful Section 28 agent, and to bring her home safely. She is your responsibility in the field. To that end, make sure you go with her to Logistics. I know that Norbert will have some gear specifically for her. Show her how to pre-load for a mission." Boomer nodded.

Agent Smith then turned to the younger woman. "Miss Callahan will not be your babysitter for this mission. You were selected for this mission due to your savant-like ability to learn languages. I expect you to learn the basics for *Álfein*, the fae language, by tomorrow evening. Use this knowledge carefully. Do not let the faeries know that you speak their language until you have to. It will provide you a great advantage. You also know eskrima, which is very similar to the martial art that the elven warriors train in called '*muir 'leeir*.' Do not forget about *fion-fhuil*, as Vellath will be a powerful ally."

Smith looked at his watch and back at Dancer. "Now, Miss Sedano, you need to get moving. I understand Miss Watkins and your teammates have prepared a celebration for you tonight. Do not forget to connect with Miss Callahan and go to Logistics. You are both dismissed."

Boomer and Dancer left the briefing room, parting ways at one of the branching corridors. They arranged to meet at Logistics later that evening. Dancer ran toward her team and celebration. Boomer walked toward her team's apartments, contemplating the heavy responsibility that Agent Smith had placed on her.

8

ARRIVAL

Gerald R. Ford International Airport

T he hulking C-17 Globemaster III touched down on runway 26-L at Gerald R. Ford International Airport in Grand Rapids, Michigan. Using the longer runway to roll out, the pilot reversed the thrust of all four of its engines to help slow the specially modified cargo plane to the point where the pilot and co-pilot could work the brakes.

At the end of the tarmac, the pilot turned the jet onto the taxi-way, rolling back toward the large plane parking ramp where private and corporate aircraft were parked. The jet was met by a white pickup truck with a sign that announced, "FOLLOW ME" in giant letters mounted to its roof in between two flashing yellow strobes. The truck guided the Air Force jet directly to a spot on the open parking ramp away from a row of corporate jets. Three ground crew personnel guided the plane to a stop on its assigned spot. As the four big turbines spooled down, the crew began working their post-flight check.

Down in the passenger section of the aircraft, the members of Section 28 Team Knightmare were gathering their personal bags and stowing any travel gear they were using. Special Agent Gretchen Massey gently shook the sleeping giant nicknamed Heavy. He never moved and his loud snores barely broke their rhythm. She looked exasperated and turned toward Ghost, "I tried. He's your heavy gunner — you wake him up."

Gretchen was the official team liaison and administrator for Knightmare. She often traveled with them, and she was responsible for arranging their travel and coordinating with Logistics when they were out on a mission. It was also her job to be available for them while they were in Langley. The team's girl Friday was twenty-four years old, and looked like the gymnast she had been in college. Her light brown skin and deep brown eyes were framed by black hair that was often pulled into a loose ponytail with tight curls escaping from the sides.

Before Ghost could reply to Gretchen, Spooky pushed past him and said, "I've got this."

The electronics specialist bent down until he was right next to his best friend's ear. He paused to take a deep breath, then he screamed at the top of his lungs, "OH MY GOD. IT'S VAMPIRES. VAMPIRES EVERYWHERE."

Spooky leapt back just in time as the big man flailed his arms around in a vain effort to wake up and protect himself. His gyrations dumped him on the cabin floor, on his knees, struggling to breathe. The big man worked to open his eyes.

Hearing his perpetual tormentor, and good friend, Spooky braying with laughter, the not-so-gentle giant turned to glare at the electronics specialist. His voice came out a barely coherent bass rumble, "Just you wait, little geek. I'll get my revenge."

Heavy slowly picked himself up from the floor to the chuckles of the team around him. The rest of the team continued to gather their bags and then followed Gretchen through the now-open main cabin door and down to the tarmac. As the team gathered next to the plane, a black SUV sporting tinted windows and a government license plate pulled to stop in front of them. Three men and one woman climbed out of the truck.

The man who climbed out of the passenger-side door drew a badge from his pocket and flashed it at the group. "Special Agent Stephen Lewis, Detroit SAC. Which one of you is Agent Vanhof?" Stephen Lewis was a tall African American gentleman who appeared to be in his late forties. Brown, close-cropped hair topped a thin, angular face and his brown eyes seemed to penetrate to the soul of his current focus.

Ghost gave a small wave and reached inside his omnipresent black leather duster for his credentials. He showed his identification to the Detroit-based Special-Agent-in-Charge, the regional supervisor, and said, "Special Agent Jonas Vanhof. Please, call me Jonas. It's great to meet you Agent Lewis." The tall monster hunter reached out to shake the Detroit agent's hand.

"It's good to meet you, as well, Jonas. Call me Steve. Although I'll admit, I was a little pissed when your boss called. I feel like a total mushroom on this one. Why are you guys here?"

Ghost paused for a moment. He gave a small grin while he replied. "I understand how you feel. The first time I met my boss, I felt much the same way. Unfortunately, I cannot tell you why we're here. This mission is so classified that we're not even here right now. All I can say is that we're just doing what you guys are doing—trying to stop bad people from doing bad things."

The monster hunter motioned back towards his team. "Let me introduce you to my second-in-command. Steve, this is Doctor Noelle Sorenson, and yes, she is a Special Agent with DHS as well." Doc put down her bags and shook the Detroit agent's hand.

As the rest of Knightmare dropped their bags in a small pile near the plane door, Ghost said, "I'll introduce you to the rest of the team after they unload their gear." At that time, the Irish observer made his way down the jet's stairs and approached Ghost. The Knightmare team leader introduced the Irishman, "This is Captaen O'Beirne. Captaen O'Beirne is from Irish Army Intelligence and has official observer status with us." This got a raised eyebrow from Agent Lewis.

Gretchen finished talking to the crew of the big Air Force jet and walked over to join Ghost and Doc as they talked to Agent Lewis. As she walked up, she stuck out her hand to shake Agent Lewis'. "SAC Lewis? I'm Special Agent Gretchen Massey. I'll be staying on site here with the transport and will be coordinating with your office. Did you get the request I forwarded for the uniformed security detail? I need DHS personnel to stand guard, not local police units."

Lewis shook her hand. "Yes, ma'am. I did get the request and have some local agents arranging their schedules now. How long will you need site security?"

"For as long as we're here—likely several days. I need two agents available around the clock. This aircraft must maintain its security because it acts as a mobile command center while we are in the field."

The Detroit SAC nodded and said, "The first two should arrive on site in about twenty-five minutes, depending on traffic. My staff and I will remain until they get here." As he said this, Lewis turned toward the other agents with him and made a motion. The local

DHS agents opened the back of the SUV and began pulling out their gear. Each of them removed their suit jackets and slid on bullet-resistant vests with the word POLICE stenciled across the back. Then each man reached in and grabbed an M4 carbine and loaded it. When they were loaded, they moved out to take stations at key points around the plane.

Spooky and Boomer had turned as they heard the rear ramp being lowered, and they started walking toward the rear of the cargo jet. As they walked, Boomer looked at Spooky and asked, "What are we saddled with this time? I really like the War Wagon."

The electronics specialist's grin was mischievous. "I think you'll like this one, once you get to know her. She's been designed for more covert urban ops, able to blend in better than the giant MRAP. I'm even going to let you name her—as long as it's not something goofy. Or girly."

As they walked around the corner, Boomer paused momentarily. She was staring at... a delivery truck? Painted a dull, flat black with no external markings that she could see, it looked like a standard delivery truck.

As the explosives expert looked closer, she noticed other small details. There was a peculiar refraction effect with the windshield that told her it was thick, bullet resistant glass. The grill guard was a much finer mesh weave than a standard grill cover over a radiator, and a push bar was mounted on the wide steel front bumper. The tires were larger, and the truck squatted a little lower than normal.

She looked at Spooky, who was waiting impatiently. "You got us an armored bread truck?" Her voice was rising in incredulity.

"Oh, trust me, it gets better." Spooky's grin got even wider. "Wait 'til you see the inside."

The two agents walked up the ramp and approached the truck as the cargo master finished removing all the straps and tie-downs. Spooky pressed a button on a key fob he pulled from his pocket and the interior lights came on as an audible "thunk" echoed from both the driver and passenger door. The electronics specialist handed the fob, and the attached keys to Boomer and quipped, "It's even got keyless entry."

Outside the plane, the rest of the team had gathered near the Detroit office's SUV. As they met and shook hands with the Detroit agents, they all heard a deep rumble as a large diesel engine roared to life. The exhaust roared for a moment and Boomer eased the new truck out of the back of the cargo jet and brought it around to where the team stood. The former race car driver let the engine idle in a low growl for a few moments before shutting down the massive engine.

As the engine died out, Boomer climbed out of the driver's side door, grinning like a cat that swallowed a canary. As she hopped down, the demolitions expert patted the hood of the truck, "What do you think of the new Wunder Buggy?"

Agent Lewis was the first to find his voice, "Did you guys just really drag a bread truck from Langley? We've got surveillance vans here you could have used."

Ghost turned to him, still trying to process the new truck. "I'm sure that whatever the department has added to this, er, truck is slightly different from one of your standard surveillance vans." The Knightmare leader turned to Boomer and said, "Just what did Logistics give us?"

Boomer was almost giddy as she answered, "The Wunder Buggy is pretty much equipped with everything like the War Wagon, but with a really cool new feature." She reached into her open jacket and grabbed a small radio. Depressing the transmit button, she said, "Pattern one, Spooky."

The truck shimmered. As the rest of the team watched, the matte black paint job on the truck shifted in a sweep. Starting with the front, the paint color changed to a light blue, and on the side appeared the logo of a local bread distribution company. In less than thirty seconds, the pristine black delivery truck changed to a light blue delivery truck with small rust stains and some faded paint.

Gretchen quickly stepped forward and glared at Boomer before turning back to the Detroit DHS agents. She held up her credentials to get their attention. "By order of Homeland Security and by the Signatory-status of Section Twenty-Eight of the *E'Tuatha* Accords, I hereby bind you from mentioning this aspect and technology to anyone who is not currently present or cleared to know."

She turned to Boomer and growled, "We need to talk. I need you as well, Jonas." She stalked toward the stairs leading up and into the jet. Boomer looked crestfallen as she followed Gretchen. Ghost locked at Agent Lewis and shrugged, then followed. Once inside, Gretchen rounded on Boomer.

"Just what do you think you are doing? That technology is classified. It cannot be made public, yet. And you just showed it off to the local agents and ground crew. Seriously. What were you thinking?"

Boomer shrank in on herself. Fear welled in her eyes, and her voice quavered. "I'm sorry. I didn't even think about it. I just wanted to show off the new truck's tech. What's going to happen to me?"

Ghost laid a hand on his young demolitions expert's shoulder. He spoke quietly and calmly, "Nothing is going to happen this time. Right, Gretchen?" He caught the agent's eye, and she nodded. He again addressed Boomer, "You need to be more cautious. When we change the paint job, make sure no one else is around. Fortunately, Gretchen caught it in time, and bound their voice under a *geas* so they literally cannot talk about the technology."

The team leader turned to Gretchen, "In fact, that seemed like a pretty nasty, yet handy, *geas* to have available. I'd like you to teach that to me, in case we need it later."

Gretchen nodded. She had visibly calmed down, and spoke again to Boomer, "Listen, I know I blew up at you. You made a mistake. Just don't do it again. Frankly, if you are too careless, your own *geas* will punish you. Are you good?" Boomer nodded. "Then let's go back out there and finish cleaning up the mess. Lewis will have questions, and I'm worried that I just screwed up any chance of having good relations with this office."

The trio walked back outside to hear a very loud and abrasive Agent Lewis demanding answers from Doc. She stood with placating hands raised and they could see her trying to calmly talk to the irate agent.

As Ghost hit the tarmac again, Lewis rounded on him, "What do you think you were doing? What is the meaning of that mumbo-jumbo with the badge? Who the hell are you people?"

Ghost hesitated for a second as he decided how he would handle the mess. He still wanted, really needed, the cooperation of the Detroit office, and especially that of SAC Lewis. Catching Gretchen's eye with a warning glance, he slowly raised his hands to calm the rising flood of questions and hostility.

When Lewis slowed to catch his breath, the monster hunter gestured to the open plane. He calmly said, "Listen, I know you have a lot of questions right now. I'm going to break protocol once with you. You will have to give certain assurances, but I believe that I can at least give you some background and explanations. I need you to understand something: everything I'm going to tell you is classified WAY above anything you are cleared for. If you let any of it slip, treason charges would be the least of your worries. Are you willing to listen under those constraints?"

Agent Lewis froze. Ghost's calm demeanor and matter-of-fact delivery had stopped the rant cold. The mention of treason sent a chill down Lewis' spine, and the calm threat of worse consequences made him reconsider, at least briefly. The Detroit-based agent nodded.

Ghost said, "Ok. Let's go have a chat in our transport. I know that the plane is secure. Gretchen, can I borrow you for a moment?" Gretchen nodded, and the three agents walked back toward the plane.

Thirty minutes later, a pale and visibly shaken Agent Lewis stepped down the stairs, followed by Ghost and Gretchen. The rest of the team had already loaded their gear onto the new "Wunder Buggy" and were waiting for their leader. Lewis shook hands with Ghost and walked over to his SUV to wait for his relief. Ghost and Gretchen walked toward the truck.

"I've booked you at a slightly nicer hotel this time around," Gretchen was saying. "It's about four miles from the airport. I've booked four ground-floor rooms, figuring Spooky will stay outside in the new truck. If you need more rooms, let me know, I'll procure them. Spooky has the coordinates of the Seelie court, and the head of the Queen's Guard will meet you there for an audience with Her Majesty."

Ghost motioned for everyone to climb on board. Boomer fired up the big diesel engine, and the innocent-looking bread delivery truck moved away from the big Air Force cargo jet and toward the exit.

9

AUDIENCE

The house was a large, sprawling ranch-style home with a wide expanse of lawn around it. The back lawn led to private access to a small lake, and the neighbors to the east were several hundred feet away, hidden behind their own trees. To the west lay the links of a local country club golf course, and the course was separated from the property by another treeline. The gray stucco exterior and weathered metal roof made it seem as if the house had just been teleported from somewhere in Pacific Northwest. Located in a wealthier Forest Hills area of Grand Rapids, the large house was well off the beaten path. Invisible from the road, the house also sat on a ley line—a line of mystical energy and power that the *Álfr*, the elves, can use to open gateways to and from their realm.

Boomer pulled up to the drive and entered. A large gentleman wearing a dark suit and sunglasses stepped out of the small shack near the road and motioned for her to stop. As she did, she noticed that his suit was just a little too large, leaving room for weapons with no tale-tell bulges. The explosives expert also noticed the radio earpiece in his slightly misshapen ear.

"This is a private driveway. You are not welcome here." The man's voice was soft, yet projected well.

Ghost reached into his duster and withdrew his credentials. Opening them up for the man to see, he told the guard, "Special Agent Jonas Vanhof, Section Twenty-Eight. We have an appointment to see Her Majesty Lishe ta Merunaré. We are expected."

A ripple passed over the guard's face as the DHS agent mentioned the Queen's name. The guard held his fist up to his face and muttered low enough that even Boomer couldn't hear what he said. He waited for a response and nodded when he got one.

"You are clear to drive up to the main house and follow the directions of the guard there for parking." The large man talked to Ghost, "You are officially granted honored visitor status for your appointment today. As honored visitors, you are expected to follow all protocols for that status. Do you require assistance at this time to comply with the status, or do you wish to decline the honored visitor status?"

Ghost looked back over his shoulder to see Captaen O'Beirne shake his head. He looked back at the hulking man standing by Boomer, "No thank you. We accept the status and require no assistance at this time."

The guard nodded and stepped back. He waved Boomer on through past him, and down the short driveway. As she neared the house, there was a circular round-about in front of the house. She pulled up around it slowly, coming to a halt mere inches away from another guard who was motioning for her to stop.

"You can leave your truck there," the guard said. "We will watch it for you."

Ghost leaned over, "There is no offense intended, but my driver and a couple of others will stay with the truck, as is their duty. There will be three of us attending Her Majesty."

The guard grunted. "No offense taken, Mr. Vanhof. As an honored visitor, of course, those of you attending will leave your weapons in your truck. None may enter the presence of Her Majesty armed, except for Her Guard and her Maidens."

Ghost nodded, "Of course. We would not dishonor Her Majesty. I and my entourage will exit from the back of the truck. Will you mind if my staff stretch their legs around the truck?"

The guard shook his head and walked toward the back of the Wunder Buggy. Ghost stood and stepped into the back of the truck. He unstrapped his pistol and removed several small, hidden knives from various locations about him. As he did so, he looked up and said, "Just as we discussed. Doc and Lucky are with me. Doc, your cross should be fine. I'm going to be walking with my cane. Lucky, do you have any weapons on you?"

"No, Agent Vanhof. I've been to her court before. Although I don't know if she will remember me. It's been twenty years."

Spooky reached out and handed all three leaders a small case. Inside was a small device that looked like a hearing aid. He said, "I requisitioned these from the CIA. They're not great for combat, but for covert communications, they do a great job. They are each activated. You will hear anything I send you, and anything you say, or is said around you, will be transmitted back here. I'll be recording from moment one. Questions?"

Ghost shook his head, then placed the tiny earpiece into his ear. Doc and Lucky did the same. Spooky leaned over and pushed a button on his console. He spoke into a microphone, "Testing. Testing. Are your hearing me?"

All three gave a thumbs up gesture, and then Ghost spoke up, "Time to get moving. Let's talk to the Queen of the Seelie."

His voice echoed with a slight delay as the transmitted sounds came out over the speakers next to Spooky's rig. He gave a big thumbs up and the trio climbed out the door.

Ghost stepped out and smoothed his leather duster around him. As he climbed out, he placed his hat upon his head and donned sunglasses. Under his duster, he was wearing blue jeans and a gray button-down shirt. Black cowboy boots rounded out his outfit. As he stepped aside for Doc, he shifted his cane from one hand to the other, making sure that the blade within was locked away.

Doc stepped down from the team's truck dressed in a conservative gray pantsuit. The white collar that symbolized her office was offset against her black blouse, and her stole was carefully draped over her shoulders. Clutched in her nervous fingers was her large crucifix on a silver chain, and her normal black loafers rounded out her wardrobe. The guard failed to hide his shock when the female priest stepped out of the truck, but he quickly regained his composure when the priest smiled at him.

Last out of the truck was Captaen O'Beirne. He was still wearing his Irish army uniform, and the medals and buttons flashed in the sunlight. He removed his cap from under his arm and placed it on his head, cocking the hat at the perfect angle proscribed by regulations. The Irish observer also put on a pair of sunglasses and looked around in earnest.

The waiting guard had called inside the house for an escort, and a massive creature headed toward the team. The creature stood over seven feet tall, and was broad shouldered, with muscles showing through the sleeveless uniform and a short gray and brown mottled fur covering all the exposed hide. While the creature was humanoid, with two arms and two legs, the head was an altogether different matter. With a long, drawn face that would be more correctly called a "snout" the creature had large eyes that homed in on the DHS agents.

A large bone plate wrapped around the top and sides of the massive head, and two large, curved horns emerged from either side of the creature's head. The horns extended sideways and almost curved like a ram's horns, except they only extended about a half circle, and the points almost touched the creature's jawline. The creature wore an ornate uniform, sleeveless, and carried a massive war hammer effortlessly in its left hand. Ghost did not recognize the make of the massive automatic pistols sitting in holsters on each hip. The creature stepped up to the trio of humans and raised a massive three-fingered hand in greeting.

"Welcome and well-met, honored visitors." The big creature spoke a deep, perfect English with a slight Eastern European accent. "My name is Tar Katel, and I am the head of Her Majesty's Elite Guard. It is my honor to be your escort today as you visit Her Majesty."

Ghost collected his thoughts. "Well-met, Tar Katel. My name is Jonas Vanhof, Special Agent from Section Twenty-Eight, and representative envoy to Her Majesty. My adjutant is Doctor Noelle Sorenson, also from Section Twenty-Eight, and our guest is Captaen Callum O'Beirne, representative from Ireland and the European contingents. We are honored to visit Her Majesty."

Lucky nodded slightly as Ghost was able to put together all the correct phrasing for this important initial meeting. They had spent several hours together as the Irish intel officer taught the monster hunter how to talk to the fae without insulting them. Ghost was an apt pupil, and he had not been flustered when the giant minotaur had appeared.

Tar Katel bowed slightly and spoke, "Would you please follow me. Her Majesty is expecting you." The trio of human agents followed the lumbering hulk of a creature.

Inside the truck, Boomer had let out a gasp when the minotaur had lumbered out of the house. Spooky had quickly run through the images of known fae on his screen, searching for a match. Even as they heard the thing introduce itself, the electronics specialist had stopped scrolling and pointed to his screen.

"Apparently, that thing is called a minotaur," the young man had spoken. He squinted as he read the fine print. "They look to be the Queen's elite guard, or something. They're like her secret service. Looks like tough SOB's."

Heavy had spoken up and pointed to the massive war hammer clutched in its hand. "That looks just like the one in my room. I hope we don't actually have to fight these guys."

As the creature led their teammates away, those still in the van had grown quiet, listening to the their leaders walk into the Queen's court.

The minotaur led the DHS agents into the well-appointed entryway of the home. Granite tiles and heavy wooden furniture bespoke an understated elegance that never went out of style. A wide staircase rose to the smaller second story, and the house continued in all the cardinal directions off of the entryway.

Inside the small mansion, several minotaur and elven guards stood motionless in strategic locations, and small creatures floated around on rapidly buzzing wings, flying close to the visitors, before buzzing away. Doc thought they looked like the classic pixies or fairies found in european fantasy. As the priest gazed in wonder, the group seemed to pick up a small entourage of the creatures, following around them as they walked.

Ghost was nervous. According to his family's archives, pixies were not nearly as nice or friendly as the fantasy made them out to be. Known as fierce warriors, their speed and deviousness more than matched their size disadvantage. As he watched, he noticed that the group now had at least six of the creatures fluttering around them in a constantly moving circle. His fingers clenched the head of his cane as he willed himself to relax. He forced himself to remember that he was representing humanity today.

The minotaur led them toward a large set of double doors that looked like they were cast from solid bronze. As they approached, the doors smoothly, silently glided open, drawn apart by two of the burly minotaur from inside the court. The room was likely the original great room or family room. All the modern family furniture had been stripped from it, and large floor-to-ceiling expanses of glass offered panoramic views of the grounds and the woods surrounding them. In the middle of the room was a large throne, made of blond and dark wood. The woods had been crafted so finely and with so many intricate curves that it was almost as if the monarch's throne had grown in place. Ghost mused that it might actually have been grown in place. The *Lo'a* are druids and forest creatures of the highest order after all.

Standing in front of the throne was a tall, slender elf, dressed in a finely tailored jerkin and clothing that looked as if it had come directly from the middle ages. A wide golden sash was slung across his left shoulder, and it was accented against the maroon of the elf's attire. The sash was attached to an ornate sheath that held a very slim, rapier-like blade. The hilt of the sword was golden, with small jewels worked into the hilt and crosspiece.

Seated on the throne was the Queen of the Seelie court. Radiant in the sunlight pouring from the strategically placed skylight above, Her Majesty Lishe ta Merenaré gracefully stood and glided down the small raised dais to stand by the elf in the golden sash. Her long, flowing gown billowed behind her, and made her look as if she was floating on a cushion of air toward them.

Ghost slowed to a halt and stood about six feet from the faerie Queen, his companions did the same. Ignoring the menacing minotaur close by and the pixies dancing in the air around him, the DHS agent bent and gave a small bow to the Queen.

"Your Majesty. May I present myself and my companions?" The monster hunter saw her give an almost imperceptible nod. "I am Jonas Vanhof, designated envoy and representative of the signatory Section Twenty-Eight, and by proxy, representing humanity. I am joined by my adjutant, Doctor Noelle Sorenson, and by formal observer and representative of Ireland and the European signatories, Captaen Callum O'Beirne. We thank you for granting this audience."

The Queen of the Seelie bowed slightly, acknowledging the introductions and the formal presence of signatories of the Accords. Her soft, lilting voice was musical, and she began. "Well-met, Jonas Vanhof. I recognize your honored visitor status and your presence as the designated signatory to the Accords."

The Queen turned slightly to address Doc, "Well-met, Noelle Sorenson. Is it not... unusual for your Church to have a woman priestess? I would wish to hear that story later if you are so inclined."

The monarch then turned slightly and gave a wider smile toward the Irishman. "Well-met, Callum O'Beirne. It is truly good to see you again. I am thankful for your presence."

The elf queen turned back to Ghost and smiled warmly, "I formally welcome the representatives of Section Twenty-Eight, the United States, Ireland and Europe to the Seelie court. I welcome you as signatories of the Accords, and all due honor is granted to you.

"My second for this audience is my Knight, Tó Coferal." The Queen of the Seelie gestured to the tall elf in maroon standing next to her. She made a small gesture towards a doorway, "Let us adjourn to the conference room for this audience. I have a room prepared and have light snacks available if you so desire."

10

ULTIMATUM

Seelie Court, Burton Street SE, Grand Rapids, Michigan

The Queen's Knight led the party through the doors leading away from the receiving hall and down a short hallway that was over ten feet wide. Gorgeous stone flooring accented the richly papered hallway. The furnishings continued the appearance of comfortable, unpretentious wealth. A plush red carpet was laid down the center of the hallway, and the Queen and her Knight seemed to glide over the floor.

As the group walked in silence, Ghost noticed that the sprites had taken up their circular station around the moving group, never straying within arms length of the humans, but always nearby. He followed one of the little creatures with his eyes, waiting for just the right light, and he finally saw what he thought he would see. The fluttering ball of light was a female sprite, wearing a perfect little uniform and tiny sword buckled to her waist.

His attention was drawn back to the Queen as she reached a large mahogany door that was guarded by another *Lo'a* elf. This elf's uniform was the same color of the Knight's clothing, however it was a slightly darker shade, and was overlaid with armor of the same color. The creature opened the door for his Queen, and then stood at stiff attention, warily regarding the humans as they passed him through the open door.

They group of humans was led into a large conference room that was dominated by a gigantic wooden table at least fifteen feet long and half as wide standing in the center. The rich wood adornments and furniture spoke of a Fortune 500 boardroom. Scattered around the enormous table were several plush leather chairs, and a tray with a selection of light snacks and hors d'oeuvres sat at one end of the table. Ghost realized that he could only identify about half of the food before him.

The Queen moved to the head of the table, and her Knight deftly held her chair as she sat. Her Majesty gestured for the human delegation to sit in several chairs as her Knight sat next to his Queen a couple of feet away. As they sat, Ghost noticed that two of the sprites had alighted on the back of the Queen's chair, sitting mere inches from her shoulders.

The Queen of the Seelie court noticed his gaze, and she gave a small laugh. "I see you have noticed my guardians, Jonas Vanhof. These folk, and the others you have seen around here, have been specially chosen to be my Handmaidens. They are my loyal guardians, and my last line of defense. They care for my heir and I. It is their sole purpose in this life."

Doc pursed her lips as if about to say something, but Ghost broke in, "I had heard that the pixies were fierce warriors, but have never seen them outside of my... research. Thank you for enlightening us, Your Majesty. And thank you for your hospitality in providing these delicacies for us." A small smile crept onto his face, "I'm sure my companions who wait in our vehicle will be jealous of your hospitality."

The Queen returned his warm smile, "Worry not, Jonas Vanhof. My guards are bringing some of the snacks to your companions as we speak. It is only befitting that they should eat as guests as well. As we begin our discussions, please feel free to eat and drink. This is what you would call a 'working lunch' for the court."

"Speaking of the business at hand," Doc spoke up as she reached for some small, interesting tidbits close to her. "Would you be able to give us information on the attack on your private club? I'm afraid that we have been tasked with this investigation and are woefully unprepared with information."

The Queen looked at her Knight and nodded for him to answer. He cleared his throat and his melodious voice rose, "The club is located downtown, just south and west of the interstate intersection. It is unmarked, and as proscribed by the Accords, closed to the public. Yesterday morning, just past dawn, one of my Knights went down to the club. When he walked in, there were bodies, or pieces of bodies, everywhere." As the Knight talked, his voice grew colder, and less alive, while his lips curled in a fierce growl.

"He quickly looked around for survivors, and found none. We reviewed the camera footage from inside the club, and we could clearly see humans in SWAT-style body armor enter the building and kill the fae that were present. Their weapons cut through them better than any normal human weapons would. Each attacker seemed to know how to kill each particular type of fae present.

"The group of butchers that committed this massacre then went back through to look for survivors. Any fae that they found with even the slightest light of life in them were quickly dispatched. They methodically killed every fae present in the club and did so remorselessly. They were trained in fighting those that come from a reality incursion."

Ghost thought for a moment. He looked back and forth between the Queen and her Knight, trying to figure out how to ask the hard questions he needed to ask. He looked at Doc and Captaen O'Beirne. The priest looked just as lost as he was. The Irishman, on the other hand, looked thoughtful and caught the monster hunter's eye. They had discussed several possibilities and questions on their trip to the court, working on a particular set of questions to ask. He gave a slight nod, telling Ghost to ask the questions.

"Your Majesty. Tó Coferal. I can provide complete assurance that Section Twenty-Eight had no part in the attack on your court. We are prepared to investigate this attack, and we will begin with several groups that are our main suspects. But before we begin, I have a few questions for you.

"Can you provide us with your records for which fae were present in the club during the attack?"

The Knight looked at his Queen and then nodded, "We can provide those records for you. Which groups do you think might have done this?"

Ghost shook his head, "I don't know who committed the attack. Will we have access to the video footage as well as the club itself? We want to see if your initial investigation missed some information that might point us toward the attackers."

"You will have access, as I stated." The Knight's voice grew cold again. "Which groups do you think attacked the court? We can assist with the investigation."

Doc spoke up, her softer voice barely audible as she realized she might tread on cultural taboos. "Tó Coferal, has anyone completed an autopsy on the victims? If it breaks none of your laws or customs, may I examine the bodies?"

The Knight focused his growing irritation on the priest, "It is not against our customs to do so, however, what do you think you will be able to learn that we weren't?"

"I might help by providing weapon data and other clues. While I am not a forensic pathologist, I have plenty of experience in trauma care." Doc never flinched from the elf's gaze.

Ghost cut in, "May I ask why you are so anxious for me to name our suspects, Tó Coferal?"

The Knight shifted back to the monster hunter. He paused for a moment, visibly trying to calm his rising rage. "I would like to interrogate these suspects. I believe that we have methods you are unable, or unwilling, to use. Those methods work well, and it is our right under the Accords to deal with any attacks on our court committed by a non-signatory."

Agent Smith had been afraid that this would be the fae response. Ghost realized that his fears were correct. "I understand, and agree that it is your prerogative under the Accords to confront those who attack your court," the federal monster hunter began. "However, you do have to make sure you are confronting the correct enemy. The Accords also spell out consequences to the court if you attack non-signatories without provocation."

Ghost continued, careful to keep his voice neutral as he chose his words carefully, "Frankly, I believe your emotions might be too close to this matter for you to objectively evaluate the evidence. Your honor demands satisfaction, and your desire for revenge might blind you to the real culprits.

"Is there any possible way this could be a fae attack? Could the Unseelie court be involved?"

The Knight was darkly fuming as he considered his next words. Before he could speak, the Queen laid a hand on his forearm and spoke up, "Jonas Vanhof, you do not understand the Unseelie court as well as you might believe. It is unlikely that this attack was perpetrated by the Unseelie. The weapons and tactics were human. The video from the attack bears this out."

The Queen's soft voice grew older and brittle, "Is it possible that your lack of... experience leads you to consider those that the evidence does not support? Is it possible that you are too close to case, and that you may be subconsciously biased against the fae?"

Ghost shook his head. Before he could respond, the Seelie

Queen spoke again. "I would remind you that, under the Accords, if a signatory interferes with another, grieved signatory in action against the grieved, that signatory forfeits all rights under the Accords, and can suffer severe sanctions."

O'Beirne let out a gasp as the Queen's words sunk in. He looked at Ghost, desperately trying to reign in the federal monster hunter. "Agent Vanhof," the Irish representative tried to make the DHS agent pause. "The Queen is right to have called on the Accords to remind everyone of the possible sanctions."

Ghost intentionally failed to take the hint. He was upset at the sanctimonious Knight, and the stiff-necked monarch. He was furious with the group of humans who had taken down the private club. And he was angry that he had just been surreptitiously threatened by the Seelie court.

Ghost tried to calm his voice and keep his expression neutral, but his words were sharp enough to cut paper. "Before we label a perpetrator, we will have to conduct a thorough investigation of all the suspects. We will find the correct perp, but we will not give you carte blanche to use your methods of extracting information. In this country, people are innocent until proven guilty."

The DHS hunter continued, barely pausing to breathe. "I will, however, ask the question again, aside from circumstantial evidence, why are the Unseelie excluded from consideration?"

The Queen replied, "We know this was not the Unseelie court because of the weapons used, and because the video shows a heavy human response. While the Unseelie might decide to try a power play, this was clearly orchestrated by humans."

Ghost raised the question again, "But what if we discover that it really was the Unseelie court behind the attack? How are you going to respond?"

The Queen's Knight shook his head angrily. "It was a filthy human group. The video and evidence bears that out. I do not understand your fixation on the Unseelie as suspects. Tell me who your primary suspects are, and I will get the truth from the perpetrators. And then we will show those who dare attack the Seelie what will happen to them." The Knight's eyes were wild with rage.

Ghost sat for a moment, stunned at the vitriol and accusations that had been bandied about. He slowly raised his empty hands in a placating gesture. The monster hunter cautiously chose his next words.

"Tó Coferal, I cannot, in good faith as a signatory to the

Accords provide the names of our primary suspects." Ghost licked his suddenly dry lips. "I assure you that we will conduct a thorough and speedy investigation. At the end, we will provide you with the identities of the perpetrators. Will that satisfy your honor, at least temporarily?"

The Knight was momentarily speechless. He had expected the humans to go along, and their persistent denial was making him enraged. His honor, his Queen's honor, and the honor of the Seelie court was at stake, and these humans were standing in the way.

The Queen raised her hand, calling for silence. The sound of heavy, angry breathing was the only sound that the group could hear. Her eyes grew as cold as ice, and her words chilled those in the room. "For the time being, my Knight's honor, my honor, and my court's honor shall be satisfied. You are to investigate this savage attack against my court. When you are done with your honest investigation, and have proof against the perpetrators, you will turn that information over to myself, or to my Knight, as is mandated by the Accords.

"To accomplish this, you shall be given great latitude in what or who you investigate. My Knight, and his fellow knights, will provide you with every detail and every amount of full cooperation possible. I personally guarantee, on my honor, that you will have our full cooperation. Does that satisfy your needs, Jonas Vanhof?"

Ghost looked up and bowed his head slightly in approval. He spoke, "As signatories of the Accords, I hereby offer acceptance of your conditions, as stated. I would, however, like to add one addendum. My team will, in all likelihood, require a representative from the court as we approach other fae while investigating this attack. Will you provide a representative and safe passage while we are among your fae?"

The Queen looked at her Knight and raised a single, perfect eyebrow. The Queen's Knight nodded and said, "I will furnish a minder for you, while you are investigating this attack."

The Queen addressed the humans gathered at the table, "As we conclude this audience, I will offer one more... statement. As Signatories, you are bound by the codes within the Accords. We are also bound by these Accords. I am giving you forty-eight hours to find the killers and report to myself or my Knight.

"If, at the end of the forty-eight hours, you have not provided the names of the perpetrators, I will consider your delay as deliberately trying to hide the perpetrators, and thus contributing to the attack on my court, and we shall consider the Accords, themselves, broken. If you are the cause for the broken Accords, we will regain our honor through battle with you.

"In forty-eight hours you will provide the identities of those who massacred my court, or you will start the next fae war."

II

INVESTIGATION

11

HUMANS

Seelie Court, Burton Street SE, Grand Rapids, Michigan

I t was over an hour before the human agents emerged from the house. By then, Heavy was getting antsy. The big man kept walking around and pacing, often looking at the house as if he was calculating how to assault the place. Their assigned court guards would have been very nervous if they knew that he was mentally planning an assault on their Queen's Court. Meanwhile, Spooky monitored the audience with the Seelie court, hunched over and typing away furiously, keeping notes on the conversation.

The big heavy weapons expert let out a sigh when his team leadership reappeared from inside the Court. His shoulders visibly slumped, and he waited a few seconds to make sure they were ok. Ghost raised his right hand and made a small whirling motion with his index finger, telling the big man to climb back up into the truck.

Doc and O'Beirne climbed up into the back of the truck as Ghost walked around to the front passenger side. The DHS team leader looked through the open side door and watched as Boomer clambered into the driver's seat. Ghost removed his duster and hat before he climbed up into the truck and stowed them in the compartment behind him before pulling the side door closed.

Boomer turned the key and the monster engine roared to life. She dropped the transmission into first gear and looked at her team leader, "Where to, boss?"

Ghost said, "MCC. I've got to make a few calls." The lanky agent pulled out his secure phone and placed a call to Gretchen. He had a lot to discuss.

THREE LONG HOURS LATER, two government-issue Chevy Suburbans rolled to a stop beside the C-17 on the parking ramp. SAC Lewis climbed out of one and walked over to the stairs leading up into the large plane. As he arrived at the bottom of the stairs, Ghost stepped out of the doorway and walked down to greet the senior agent. Lewis and Ghost spoke briefly, and then Lewis gave the veteran monster hunter a set of keys, turned, and walked over to the second black SUV.

As that other SUV pulled away, the rest of Knightmare assembled on the tarmac outside the plane. Ghost addressed them all, indicating each agent as he mentioned them.

"As we discussed. Heavy, Scout, and Do-Right are with me in the nice shiny SUV. We are team Alpha. We will go meet with the SPH to see if they kicked over this hornet's nest."

He looked at the others, "Doc, you take Boomer, Spooky, Dancer, and Captaen O'Beirne in the Wunder Buggy. You are team Bravo. Go check out the crime scene and any of the evidence the Seelie will let us have.

"You will meet Tó Coferal at the club. Nudge him hard, but stay within the boundaries of the Accords. Listen to the Captaen. He's our liaison for a reason."

He slowly met each agent's eyes. "Any questions?"

A chorus of negative disclaimers and shaking heads confirmed his thoughts. "All right, then. Mount up. Good hunting." The tall monster hunter walked toward the black Suburban with his kit-bag in his hand. Heavy already had the rear lift-gate open and was stowing his massive weapon cases inside. As the team leader dropped his kit into the back of the black truck, he heard the roar of the Wunder Buggy fire up. There was a slight "chirp" from the tires as Boomer dropped the truck into gear and raced for the club. *I didn't even know it was possible to bark the tires in an armored truck*, the hunter thought. He shook his head, bemused at his team's crazy driver.

His team was soon on the road, headed downtown to the heart of Grand Rapids. He pulled up outside an older office building that boasted various law firms and offices. Finding a parking spot in the attached lot, he and the other three agents climbed out of the SUV. It was early fall, and the wind had a chill running through it. Ghost wore his hat and duster, walking cane in his hand to complete his ensemble. Other than the that, he did not look out of place in this area.

Do-Right was wearing a jacket over his open-collar shirt and khaki pants. The jacket was there to cover his duty weapon, and he would easily pass as a local business man or even a police detective. Scout was dressed in a polo shirt and slacks and had found a light jacket to cover his sidearm. Scout fit in with the rest of the group, looking natural on the streets of the city in the early fall.

Heavy, on the other hand, would stand out wherever he was. A tight black t-shirt and black BDU pants were covered by a black jacket. The fabric on his sleeves looked as if it would burst from pressure if the giant man flexed at all. As the wind caught his jacket, it revealed his sidearm holstered. If anyone was looking, they would also see what appeared to be handles of two tools sticking up out of the collar of his jacket. The large black man got stares from several bystanders. He simply smiled with his eyes hidden behind his sunglasses.

Raised brass letters running down the side of the building proclaimed this the "Federal Square Bldg" in block script, with the address "29 Pearl Street NW" posted over the entrance. All four men walked through the lobby doors and walked inside the building. Built in the early 1900s, the lobby welcomed visitors with expanses of dark wood and brass. Marble tiles were underfoot, and a wide staircase rose up and to the right. A small sign made of black wood and accented in brass listed the building's tenants, and Ghost pointed to the one they were there to visit—Society for the Preservation of Humanity.

All four gentlemen walked across to the stairs and began the trek up to the fourth floor, the top floor of the building. As the walked, Ghost thought about his briefing on the SPH and its founder.

The Society for the Preservation of Humanity had been founded by William DeVoer, Jr. in 1922. The wealthy businessman grew up the youngest of three in his middle class family. While they were not rich, the DeVoer's never went hungry. The senior William worked to raise his own cattle and manage the small family farm, but always encouraged his children to gain an education and make their own lives better.

All that changed when young William's mother began attending strange religious meetings. Wanting to keep his wife happy, the elder

DeVoer encouraged his wife to study her new religion. Two years later, on the youngest DeVoer's birthday, his mother had invited several members of her religion into the house to help "convert" the rest of the family.

In his memoirs, the younger DeVoer remembered hearing his fathers screams of horror and pain as his mother drove the knife through the ribs and into his father's heart. Frozen in terror, he could only watch as two of her friends grabbed his sister, the eldest child, and held her for the child's mother to drive the same blade into her child's chest, driving the knife home multiple times.

His older brother had grabbed his arm and yelled for the youngster to run. He had given him a good shove and then reached up to the counter for a knife that was lying near the stove. His brother dove at his mother even as she drove her own knife down into his body. As the life was ripped out of his brother, William saw his mother clutch at the knife in her own breast. The two slumped to the floor, dead. William vaguely remembered the other cult members running away from the house.

In that moment, a deep-seated hatred for religion and the occult was born in young William. He was sent to live with his aunt and uncle, and there learned business and sales in his uncle's shops. At the age of seventeen, William left for college with an academic scholarship awaiting him.

After he graduated *magna cum laude*, William opened his own retail store. With a shrewd business sense and an almost preternatural luck, William was soon one of the wealthiest men in town. With the money and career he needed, DeVoer soon founded the Society for the Preservation of Humanity. The SPH was specifically chartered to hunt down and learn from or destroy the supernatural, specializing in the occult studies and eradication.

Over ninety years later, the man who was angry at cults had left a legacy of chasing down and eradicating any cults they found. William DeVoer left an impressive legacy of monster and occult hunting, and Ghost wondered if they hadn't overstepped their bounds.

Alpha team strode up to the secretary's desk, and she eyed the group warily. Ghost read the nameplate on her desk and flashed his biggest, most sincere smile and drew his badge. Opening the credentials, the DHS leader said, "Hello Betty, I am Special Agent Jonas Vanhof from the Department of Homeland Security. I need to see your boss. Is he busy now?"

At the mention of DHS, the secretary's smile faltered, and she cast about for what to say. "I'm sorry, Agent... Vanhof? Mister Lancaster is currently in a meeting and gave direction that he is not to be disturbed. May I tell him what this is regarding?"

Ghost still had his badge out and flashed it again, forcing a little willpower into it. His grin grew predatory. "I know that you think you are protecting your boss. This is not a game you want to play. I hold all the aces, and you don't even have a pair of twos. you can either announce us, or I will simply walk past you. If I have to go past you without being announced, you will not enjoy the consequences. Am I clear?"

Terror flashed in the older woman's eyes. She had never been threatened in such a calm and utterly terrifying manner. She quickly lifted the handset and buzzed her boss. Once he picked up, She quickly announced the federal agents, and winced at the string of cursing coming through the handset.

She nervously tittered as she hung up the phone. Her voice quavered as she told them to all go back through the office doors behind her. The tall fed smiled, thanked her, and strode onward. The other three agents walked past her without a word, although the giant black man flashed her a large, genuine smile as he strode past her.

Ghost opened the door into a spacious office space, richly appointed with soft, dark leather and wood. A massive mahogany desk sat before the door. The expanse of its top was covered with loose papers and files. They completely covered the top, and the only clear spot was around the large computer monitor. The brushed aluminum and black accents looked out of place on the old desk. A man was seated in an overstuffed executive chair that was again richly appointed.

Ghost broke the silence. "Mister Alistair Lancaster, I presume? I am Special Agent Jonas Vanhof from the Department of Homeland Security. We have a few questions for you." As he was talking, the DHS team leader drew and opened his credentials to show to the gentleman.

Alistair Lancaster was a rather portly gentleman. His dark gray suit jacket was draped over the back of his high-backed leather chair, and his tie was askew with the top button of his shirt undone. The current Director of the Society for the Preservation of Humanity was sweating profusely in the well air-conditioned office.

Lancaster's eyes grew wide as they read Ghost's credentials. When the strange runes around the wallet flashed a sickly green, the man's tan face flushed pale, and he stuttered. "You guys are from

Section Twenty-Eight? My investigators have only been gone two days, and I was going to call you guys later this week. How did you guys hear about it?"

Ghost paused, caught completely off guard. *What was this guy talking about? Is there something else?*

"What do you mean your investigators have been gone for two days? Where did they go? Are they the ones who committed the massacre?" Out of the corner of his eye, Ghost saw Heavy's hand drop to the butt of the handgun on his hip.

The man in front of him sputtered, "W-w-w-what massacre? My investigators were at the old Dawkins residence when they disappeared. What are you talking about?" He genuinely seemed confused.

The federal monster hunter stopped and realized that they were talking about two different events. Related? It would have to be something they checked on later. He decided to press on with his original purpose. Changing tactics, he abruptly sat down in one of the comfortable chairs arranged in front of the desk. Do-Right sat down next to him, and Heavy and Scout backed up and stood near the door.

Ghost was almost conversational, now. "We are not here to talk about any missing investigator team, we'll have to look into that later. We're here on Accord business. We know you are not signatories, but you seemed like someone who might have information.

"There was a massacre at a Seelie club in town a couple days ago. It seems like the perpetrators were human, and I'm here to find out if you have any information about who might have committed the hit. No humans were killed, so this is not a human enforcement issue. Since it was in our territory, we are the Signatory responsible for the investigation."

Lancaster relaxed slightly, then caught what Ghost was insinuating. He shook his head, "No, Agent... Vanhof. I hadn't even heard that something had happened to the club. None of my sources ever mentioned anything, and it certainly didn't hit the gossip rags here.

"I can guarantee it was not any of my people. We don't employ any kind of 'hit' team, or 'action' team like some of the other groups. You know us. We work against cults, especially Chthonian or Lovecraftian variants. We don't use violence. I've worked with your Agent Smith a couple times now to help him in this area. Why would we attack an Accord signatory?"

The fed nodded slowly. "I know that you have worked with us in the past. I honestly did not think one of your crews was behind this.

Do you know of anyone else operating in this area that might have serious firepower? Taking on a young vamp or a couple cultists is nothing, but these guys just took on a bunch of Seelie fae."

Lancaster leaned back in his chair, his brow creased in thought. He slowly shook his head. "I can't think of anyone with that kind of stupidity...." He trailed off, then said in a low tone, "No, they wouldn't be that crazy. Would they?"

Ghost raised a single eyebrow, questioning the man's not-so-inner monologue.

Lancaster looked at the federal hunter and said, "There may be someone. There's a new group in town that just formed up. The leader supposedly watched his kid brother get killed by a werewolf, although I couldn't ever validate that one. We interviewed him, but he was way too, I don't know, crazy? He just wanted to blast everything not human. I didn't want the liability of him on one of my investigator teams."

Ghost was interested. This sounded like someone with a grudge.

The SPH Director continued, "This guy started his own monster hunting group. He called it 'Zero Tolerance.' He calls it 'ZT' for short. He got a bunch of his militia buddies to join him, and now they make noise. They spend a lot of time up north, especially in the U.P., but I've seen them down here recently. His name is Nate Miller. I think I've got his original paperwork in the reject files. I'll have Betty get them for you. I think he's your best bet."

Ghost nodded. That really sounded like their suspects. "I guess it's time to find this Zero Tolerance and ask them a few pointed questions. Thank you for your time. You'll have to forgive me, but I need to reinforce the *geas*."

Lancaster seemed to slump, but agreed with the need for supernatural secrecy. After Ghost was done and Lancaster had told his assistant to find Miller's paperwork, he had one final warning for the federal agent. "Be careful, Agent Vanhof. Those ZT guys are a little off kilter anyway, and they already don't like the government. The fact that you are government monster hunters and may interfere may just push him over the edge. They are well equipped for battle against non-humans. And the same weapons work against humans as well."

Ghost thanked the man and the two men shook hands. Betty was waiting in the lobby with the requested paperwork, and the team filed down to their SUV. Once they were inside, Ghost leafed through the paperwork they had been given as Do-Right drove the black government Suburban. As they pulled up to a stop light,

Ghost read from the file, "This looks promising. Grand Rapids address is listed as primary address. He's in the suburbs." He entered the address into the on board GPS and Do-Right followed the directions to the northwest side of the city.

The DHS team leader placed a call to Spooky to see what kind of information he could dig up on this Nate Miller.

12

SUSPICIONS

Zero Tolerance, 8th Avenue, Marne, Michigan

The black Chevrolet Suburban with government license plates sat idling on side of the road about a mile away from the target house. The team had twice driven by the driveway of the address, but could not see the house because of the growth of trees and brush near the road. The early fall sun was still high in the air, but the late afternoon would quickly turn to twilight.

Alpha team had earlier stopped by the listed address of Miller in Walker, a suburb on the northwest side of Grand Rapids. His wife had answered the door with an infant in her arms. Once Ghost had flashed his badge, she had said that her husband was with his club just outside the city, at one of his friend's house. After getting the location from her, he had forced some willpower through his credentials and made sure she would not call and warn her husband they were coming.

Now they were sitting by the side of the road, a mile from that target house, while the DHS leader pulled up satellite images of the address on his tablet. Looking at the house from a satellite tasked for this mission, Ghost counted seven cars in the driveway, including one that looked like the late model red Chevy Impala that Miller drove. The six others were trucks and SUVs. He could see no activity outside the house now, but he had seen three gentlemen walk into the large connected outbuilding on the property.

"All right. These guys are suspects only, and have not injured or attacked humans, as far as we know. Paperwork shows that Miller owns several firearms, but does not have any run-ins with law enforcement. They may be a fringe group of nuts, or they may be something harmless. We are going into this one as investigators, not interrogators. A little intimidation is ok, outright threats will not help." The DHS lead looked at the large hulking agent taking up two-thirds of the back seat. "Heavy, this means you need to be nice."

"Aww, man." The big agent complained, "I was looking forward to this one, too."

"Save it for later. I will do most of the talking. Heavy, you are with me. Do-Right, you and Scout stay outside on the perimeter. Everyone got their radios set?" Nods all around. "Great. Do-Right, pull us up into the driveway, and leave room to maneuver."

The former deputy sheriff put the Suburban did as instructed, pulling into the driveway and coming to a stop, while leaving several feet of distance between Knightmare's truck and the others in the driveway. As Do-Right shut off the big V8, the door to the outbuilding ahead of them opened, and a man came out. As the DHS agents climbed out of the truck, the former deputy noticed the large pistol worn in the holster on the man's right side.

The man went back inside and closed the door. As Ghost nodded for Do-right and Scout to spread out a little, the door opened again. A different man stepped out and walked toward them, followed by two more.

The man in front was Nate Miller, according to the picture in the file. Just over six feet tall, the large man was in his late twenties and had a boyish grin on his face. Unkempt short brown hair and a thin mustache and goatee matched his large brown eyes. Dressed in a t-shirt and jeans, the unbuttoned flannel shirt failed to cover what looked like a Beretta 92-series handgun in a holster strapped to his right side.

Behind Miller, his two companions were both more serious-looking, and were both openly sporting large stainless-steel handguns in holsters, one a 1911-style automatic, and the other a large caliber revolver. Both men had their arms crossed and were definitely not pleased about being visited that day.

As Ghost drew his credentials from within his duster, Heavy stepped up beside, and a little behind him, his giant arms crossed over his chest. Before Ghost could introduce himself, Miller welcomed the agents.

"Gentlemen, to what do I owe the pleasure? I'm guessing you

are here to talk to me? From the looks of you, you are not locals, nor county. You are driving a blacked out Suburban. You must be feds. Secret Service or CIA?"

"Mister Nate Miller? I am Special Agent Jonas Vanhof, Department of Homeland Security. And these are my colleagues. Yes, we would like to ask you a few questions."

Miller's brow furrowed, "Homeland Security? What do you guys want? Normally, if you have questions about groups of guys with guns, you bring an entire SWAT team with you."

Ghost looked around and then spoke, "Is there any way we can talk in a more... private setting? I just have a few questions to ask you about some recent events."

Miller made a show of looking around, "It doesn't get much more private than this. Anything you have to ask me, you can do so in front of my friends. And frankly, I'd rather not invite you anywhere inside right now. You don't get to peek unless you have a warrant.

"Agent Jonas Vanhof?" The young man switched subjects, "Don't you come from a long line of rather famous monster hunters?" His eyes widened and his smile got even wider. With something approaching fawning admiration, he began babbling, "Oh my gosh! I knew the government had a special group for hunting monsters. Holy crap, I can't believe I'm meeting you. Are you the same group that works with the aliens?"

The federal agent was taken aback. The people he spoke with did not normally react like this. It took him a moment to regroup. When he did, he interrupted the torrent of words flowing from the gentlemen in front of him.

"Yes, Mister Miller, I am that Jonas Vanhof, but who may or may not be my family is not of concern today. I'm here to talk to you a recent incident in Grand Rapids. As you have deduced, part of our job is to deal with rather specific types of cases in America. This is where you can help us."

Miller was nodding emphatically while his two companions were very stoic in their response.

Ghost shifted subjects slightly, "I understand you tried to join the Society for the Preservation of Humanity a while ago. Why?"

Miller's face clouded with pain, "I wanted to fight back. I watched a werewolf, or some creature like it, take my kid sister. Once I knew that evil things like that existed, I wanted to kill them all." His voice grew soft, and a single tear found its way down his cheek.

"But they didn't want me." A flash of anger in his tone and eyes. "Some bullshit excuse about my mental state and not being the right kind of person." His eyes cleared up, "But I'm over that now. I found like-minded friends, and we have formed our own little group."

Ghost nodded. He had watched the rapid shifts in emotions with alarm. There was something manic in there. He casually began, "That's the group I want to talk to you about. What do you call it? 'ZT?'"

Miller nodded emphatically, "Short for Zero Tolerance. It's our way of saying that enough is enough, and humans are the only ones who matter."

The federal monster hunter looked at the man before him. "So have you and your boys been busy dispensing a little 'zero tolerance' justice lately? What have you been doing?"

The young man suddenly grew quiet and looked at Ghost and his companions shrewdly. "We've not done anything that concerns humans. As I said, we're strictly pro-human. Why do you ask? What happened?"

Ghost could not figure if the man was intentionally playing dumb, or really was that clueless. He decided to push a little further, just to see if he could draw the man out. "It seems that there was some activity dealing with a couple of the supernatural creatures in town. Someone hunted them, and we're here to find out who."

"Sorry. That doesn't sound familiar." He turned to the men behind him. "Jim? Scott? Anything in that sound familiar to you?" Both men shook their heads. Miller turned back to the federal agents, "Sorry. We didn't have anything active lately. Did you check with Lancaster at SPH? There's a couple of his 'investigators' that really don't like monsters and have no problem killing them."

Ghost decided he needed to take a more direct approach. "What was your group doing two nights ago in Grand Rapids?" The federal agent asked. "Are you sure you guys didn't happen to enforce a little of that 'zero tolerance' attitude?"

Ghost was expecting a reaction. He figured he would get a vehement denial, a loud diatribe justifying the action, or possibly even a gunfight once Miller realized that he had been caught. He was not prepared when Miller burst out laughing. It was a few seconds before the man could control his breath enough to talk.

"I'm sorry, Agent Vanhof. I didn't mean to laugh at you, but I couldn't help it. Two nights ago was the Big & Rich and Gretchen Wilson concert at the free fair. Hell, half the boys worked security for the show, and the rest of us got backstage passes because of them. We were all out enjoying great music and warm beer way too late. I know my wife chewed me a new one the next morning. You could check with the fair board for the guys working security, I guess."

"Listen," the ZT leader continued, "What happened? It wasn't us. I can vouch for all my guys, and the fair itself can vouch for at least half of them. If you are telling me a couple monsters got roughed up, I'd love to know who to thank."

Ghost grew serious. He was getting frustrated and starting to worry about the Queen's ultimatum. "I'd like to talk to your group. Even if you didn't authorize it personally, your group looks guilty. This is serious, and you are mucking around with matters that you have no conception of. This is not the simple matter of a lone lycanthrope, or a simple vampire staking. You are actually messing with signed treaties."

Miller was getting agitated. "Look, just because our government kisses a monster's ass instead of kicking it, it's not my problem. I know what these monsters can do. Hell, man, you know what these monsters can do. Why should I care about some stupid monster treaty?"

Ghost kept his voice low, his calm exterior desperately covering his building anger at the willful ignorance of this man. "Mister Miller. I assure you that such treaties do affect you, as they keep some of the nastier things away from humanity. My department is charged with maintaining those treaties. So I will need to speak to your group, just to make sure that none of them did something monumentally stupid two nights ago. I will have to insist on this, and you do not want to test me."

Miller stood there and Ghost watched the flickering of emotions across the man's face. Pride. Anger. Cunning? That last one made the federal agent pause. What was he thinking?

Miller's eyes cleared, and he gave a small nod, as if to himself. He then turned and shouted for a couple of his guys, "Jason. Alex. Go get the rest of the guys. Tell 'em meeting in five, in the workshop." He looked at one of the men with him and gave him directions as well. "Scott, go into the workshop. Make sure you clean up any of the trash and pizza boxes. Let Bill know that we'll be having guests, so he can put on some coffee. Make sure the place is ready for our esteemed visitors."

The DHS team leader knew that they were cleaning up anything they considered "secret", but it did not bother him. His instincts told him that this group had not committed the massacre.

Those same instincts told him they would definitely be addressing a hostile crowd.

The next ten minutes involved Miller trying to be defiant and threatening, while across from him, Heavy exuded confidence and the belief that he was invincible. Miller and the big fed were getting into staring contests, and the results were fairly even, until the leader of Zero Tolerance abruptly stopped his games, glanced at his watch, and said, "Well, they should have everything ready for you." Then the man and his escort turned toward the workshop door that he had exited earlier.

Ghost and Heavy immediately stepped forward to follow their host. As they stepped through the door and into the workshop, they saw a group of men and women sitting on chairs or standing, waiting for them. With ages ranging from the late teens to the late fifties or sixties, the men and women were a diverse group, and looked to be from all different walks of life and ethnic backgrounds. And every one of them was looking at the federal agents with a hard, hostile glare.

Ghost looked around at the headquarters of Zero Tolerance. The room was large, roughly thirty feet across and another ten feet longer. Part of it was arranged with various workbenches and equipment that would make some machine shop owners jealous. There was a full kitchen at the far end, and a lounge area next to that, complete with rugs and furniture surrounding the battered cast-iron potbelly stove with a fire blazing away. Ghost also noticed a large battered desk near the lounge area, but it was currently free of any paperwork or office supplies.

Miller stopped in front of his group and cleared his throat. The general noise died very quickly. "These gentlemen," Miller indicated the two Section 28 team members, "Are federal agents with Homeland Security. They are here to ask you all questions. They have not produced any warrants, so none of you have to answer. Agent Vanhof, they're all yours."

Ghost stepped forward and raised his credentials. "I am Special Agent Jonas Vanhof with the Department of Homeland Security. My partner is Special Agent Arthur Murphy. Mister Miller is correct that we do not have a warrant, but we have some questions about an incident that happened two nights ago. We are specifically looking for more information." He paused to let his statement sink in.

As he looked around the room to begin again, Ghost noticed Miller reach into his jacket pocket and pull out an older cell phone.

The man pushed a button and answered the phone, walking away from the group.

Ghost and Heavy spent the next several minutes asking about activity for the last three days. Each question was either met with stony silence or professed ignorance and innocence. Both federal agents were getting frustrated, and the team leader became convinced that this group had had no part in the massacre at the Seelie club.

As he and Heavy were wrapping up, Ghost looked for Miller. He spotted the man back in the lounge area, animatedly talking on that phone. He watched the man end the call, then do something really strange. The DHS agent watched Miller look around, then open the back of the phone. He pulled a small card out of the back of the phone and cracked it in half. This he threw in the potbelly stove's fire.

Ghost realized that the SIM card was just destroyed. The agent watched as the ZT leader broke the phone into several pieces with his hands, and each piece, save the battery, followed the SIM card into the fire in the stove. When Miller walked back toward the group, the anger on his face told Ghost that he might have trouble.

Miller shouted from the back of the group, "You are a bunch of damn traitors to the human race. You don't hunt monsters. You coddle them. Hell, you hire them." The group was beginning to grumble. Miller pressed on, spittle flying from his mouth as he really got going, "In fact, isn't it true that you have a vampire on your team currently? One of your team got infected, and instead of staking them, you kept them on the payroll. How can we trust you?"

The murmurs in the group were getting louder. It was getting dangerous for Ghost and Heavy. They were outnumbered and out-gunned. The federal monster hunter needed to wrap this up before it became violent. He held up a hand.

"The backgrounds of the members of my team are classified, and I will not confirm or deny any such request. I do think that we will be leaving now. Thank you for answering our questions. If you do have further information, please contact me."

Ghost looked at Heavy, nodded his head toward the ext, and the two agents walked back out to the driveway. Without running, Ghost and Heavy hastily walked back to the SUV, with Heavy telling Scout and Do-Right to meet them at the truck so they could leave before someone did something stupid.

Once they were a couple miles down the road, Heavy rumbled from the back seat, "What the hell just happened? We were doing ok, then that Miller character began spouting off. And just how in the hell does that piece of shit know that Boomer's a vamp?"

Ghost was wondering the same thing. As Heavy and Scout were talking, he remembered the phone call. Miller destroyed the phone. Could Section 28 recover the data? Does anyone else even know that Boomer exists? It had to be the phone call, and it had to be from within the organization. The lanky agent had two phone calls to make before they even met up with the other team. He pulled out his phone and placed the first secure call.

"Boss? It's Ghost. We have a mole."

13

MASSACRE

Club Ljós, Bond Ave NW, Grand Rapids, Michigan

The Wunder Buggy pulled up outside a brick building that had no external signage. The bricks were painted a brighter red than was natural, and the white trim highlighted the unique characteristics of the building. There were a few cars in the small parking lot adjacent to the building, and Tó Coferal was standing outside the solid-looking metal door chatting with another gentleman, possibly a bouncer or security guard.

The gentleman standing next to the Queen's night wore black pants, a tight black t-shirt with a high neck, and black designer shoes. A light gray sport coat completed his outfit, tailored well enough that it almost concealed the bulge of the handgun under his arm. The clear wire of his radio earpiece poked out of his left ear and ran down under his coat collar.

Doc watched as the two men were animatedly talking, gesturing with their hands. It was clear that the man in black was not happy with Tó Coferal, and Doc figured that it was probably the presence of the humans. Doc looked at the man in black a little closer. Then she realized what struck her as wrong. The man had pointed ears. They weren't the tall points of the *álfr*, instead they were shorter, flatter, with only a hint of a point on the back edge and top.

The leader of Bravo team looked over her shoulder at the

gentleman behind the monitors. "Any idea what that one is, Spooky? Captaen?"

O'Beirne looked through the window and said, "I believe that is a *Hugtandalfer*, they are relatives of the elves. Less magical than the elves, however they often appear to be human, aside from the slight point in the ears. The Seelie use them for short term, important security or bodyguard duties. They are a force to be reckoned with." After a second's pause the Irishman continued, "We call them elfkin, but never to their face. It would be an insult to their honor."

Spooky gave his approval, "Yup. According to our database, *Hugtandalfer* are often employed by the Seelie to work in positions where they need fae, but where most normal humans won't realize that the person isn't human. Sounds like the perfect bouncer or security position."

Doc thought for a moment. "Spooky, send a note to Agent Smith. Then start pouring over their video feed to figure out what happened. Also, see if there are any cameras close by that might have been shooting the outside of the building. Everyone else out of the truck. I want a full analysis, use everything you have to figure this out. If something seems odd, make a note of it.

"I'll work on any of the bodies that are left. Boomer, you and Dancer look around for bullets, shell casings, anything that is related to gunpowder or explosives. Wear gloves and bag everything you find, but take pictures of the area where you find it. I want to know what weapons they were using. Captaen O'Beirne, I would like you to talk to the security guard, or anyone else who has visited the site since the massacre. Any questions?"

Aside from Spooky, all the federal agents climbed out of the truck. They walked up to the Queen's Knight and waited to be acknowledged. The Knight turned and greeted them, "Doctor Noelle Sorenson, I would like to introduce you to Etan Kanak. He is the head of security at the club, but he happened to be off premises the night of the incident. Etan Kanak, I would like to introduce you to Doctor Noelle Sorenson, from Section Twenty-Eight. She and her team are investigating the massacre."

Doc looked up at the large fae towering over her, and greeted him formally, "Well met, Etan Kanak. I am sorry for your losses in this tragedy, and we hope to help you determine who the perpetrators were.

"This is my team." She motioned to each as she introduced them, "Special Agent Rebekah Callahan, Special Agent Hannah

Sedano, and Captaen Callum O'Beirne. I have another teammate in the truck, but he will not likely be joining us."

The Etan Kanak's voice was surprisingly soft and mild for such a large creature, "Well met agents of Section Twenty-Eight. Please, call me Kanak. I will help you in any way possible to bring the cowards who attacked our club to a swift justice. I understand that you want to examine the bodies *in situ*. We have moved none of the bodies that remain corporeal. As you know, there are certain fae whose corporeal existence fades and disappears after death. Those you obviously cannot examine."

"Do you have a list of those fae who were in the club at the time of the attack? I don't need names, but numbers and types would be helpful."

Kanak looked Doc, "Absolutely, Doctor Sorenson. I already have that list prepared. On it, I marked which fae corpses have faded, and which remain."

Doc smiled at the elfkin, "Thank you, Kanak. Of the fae that faded out, are there any that only dispel when a particular type of weapon is used against them. In other words, are there some who fade because a particular knife was used, where the body would have remained had they been killed with bullets?"

Kanak frowned, his handsome face creased in thought. "Now that you mention it, the *bean sidhe*, the banshees were kind of strange. There were two on premise that night, and only one corporeal body remains. If banshees are decapitated by cold-forged iron, then they fade, otherwise, you just have a dead banshee. That was how I figured that at least one person had a blade of cold-forged iron or steel. I wonder what else I missed."

Doc's soothing voice spoke of her best matronly attributes, "There is a reason that your Queen called and Section Twenty-Eight sent us. We are good at our job. Let us see what we can uncover. Do you have the footage from the internal cameras that night?" Kanak nodded. "Can you have someone give it to my agent in the van, he will run through the footage."

They reached the door of the club which was guarded by another elfkin. Kanak handed the elfkin a flash drive and asked the him to take it to the agent waiting in the truck. The elkin did so as Kanak opened the door to the club.

Doc involuntarily crossed herself when she got a look at the carnage inside the club. It was as bad as the scene in Colorado a few short months ago. There were bodies and pieces of bodies strewn about everywhere. Various dried patches of different colors were scattered on the floor, and there were sprays of the same colors along the walls. Greens, blacks, and silvers blended in with the dark crimson one expected from human blood. The sight alone was almost overwhelming.

Then there was the smell. The bodies had lain in their own pools of blood and ichor, for two full days, and the temperatures outside rose to the low 90's. Even though the building had air conditioning, it could not keep up with the heat. Most of the creatures killed had also evacuated their bowels, adding offal to the room. Rancid, pungent odors of rotting meat wafted over the room, mingling with the smell of fecal matter and other unrecognizable odors.

An eery silence hung over the large club. Other than the soft footfalls of the newcomers, the background hum of the struggling air conditioner were the only sounds in a room that would normally be bustling with activity and the loud pounding of club music. The silence was broken by a soft murmur of concern, then the rush of feet back to the door. Doc turned in time to see Dancer yank the door open and make it two steps out the door before she violently threw up. The door swung shut as the newest federal agent heaved and emptied her stomach a second time.

Doc muttered a small prayer under her breath for the young girl and then turned to survey the club further. Her trained emergency room eye noted details about injuries and probable causes of death. She noticed a lot of bullet holes in the bodies, accompanied by a lot of bladed-weapon damage. Those bodies suffered clean-edged incisions, slicing neatly and deeply into the skin. Over there, the victims sustained ragged lacerations, which looked hacked instead of sliced. Other hacking-type attacks were evident in the avulsions on that body—the attacker having flayed the skin of the victim. And there were minor and major amputations everywhere, with body parts being cut or ripped from the bodies.

She put on a pair of surgical gloves and walked through the sprawled remains. She motioned the *Hugtandalfer* over to where she was kneeling. "Kanak, what I'd like to do is for you and I to work together. I will choose a body, and have you identify the type of fae, and help me figure out if all of its pieces are present. Then mark that particular fae off on your list. This way we can make sure that we cover each and every victim and match it to the names on the chart. Does that sound ok?"

Kanak nodded with grim determination and grabbed a clipboard resting on the counter nearby. He came back to Doc and looked down. "This first one is one of the *álfr*. It looks like his left hand is missing. Anything else?"

"Write down that I see two lacerations and three bullets. Let's go on to the next one."

The pair worked their way around the room, going from body to body. Trying to identify and gather all the pieces, like a grim three-dimensional jigsaw puzzle designed in Hell. It took about fifteen minutes before they came across their first anomaly.

"That's not on here," announced Kanak. "I don't have any standard humans on the list of club goers. Maybe it's one of the attackers."

Doc frowned, then spoke, "Ok, mark it as 'Unknown Human' so we can still get the vitals. It's one large laceration across the back. Notice that she isn't wearing any of the body armor or police gear you said was on the footage. Is it possible she was a guest of a member?"

"There was no human female guest listed on the log that night. I guess it is possible, it is just unlikely that my entrance guards would let a human in without vetting or at least noting her arrival on the logs."

"Ok. Let's keep moving."

An hour later, they were working their way toward the back of the club where the victims were the most dense when they found something that shocked Kanak.

Doc rolled a corpse over, and the elfkin with her stiffened. She noticed his change in demeanor and asked, "What's wrong, Kanak? Do you know this one?"

Kanak shook his head, then his features began clouding over with anger. "Most assuredly not. That is trollkin. They are dark fae in the service of the King. It is not on this list, and it would not be granted access to the club. What is going on here?"

At that moment, Boomer called from across the room, "Doctor Sorenson? You might want to take a look at this."

Doc looked at Boomer, then back at the dark fae corpse. She spoke to Kanak, "write it down. 'Unknown Trollkin' with three bullet holes to skull. Then, let's go see what Agent Callahan found."

The big elfkin nodded, made the notations on his sheet, and helped the doctor to her feet. They walked gingerly over to Boomer and O'Beirne, avoiding the largest piles of body parts and waste.

When they got there, Boomer was pointing to a bright silver dagger laying on the ground. Covered in intricate etchings, the twelve inch blade was thin and sharp, and had a misshapen handle carved from what looked like bone. The demolitions expert looked at the big elfkin with Doc, "Does this look like anything your Seelie would have on them?"

Kanak looked at the blade carefully, then gingerly bent and picked it up by the handle. He examined it in the light, twisting it back and forth to see the etchings better. He slowly shook his head, his eyebrows furrowing into a scowl.

"This is an Unseelie weapon designed to harvest the *bith-bhrigh*, the lifeblood, really essence, of a creature. This etching calls upon the power of the *thional an duirche*, the gathered darkness or the forces of darkness, to slay in the name of the *Álfheimer*." He suddenly looked around, "Find the one who carried this. They will have an intricately carved red leather sheath on their belt."

They didn't have to look far, they found another elf, dressed in a dark robe that was intricately embroidered with a silver thread pattern. Tucked into the crimson sash was the rich red leather sheath for the dagger. Kanak hissed in fury, "Necromancer."

Doc glanced at the elfkin sharply and Captaen O'Beirne muttered a small curse. Dancer asked, "Necromancer? Is that what it sounds like, a dude who controls the dead?"

Kanak growled in his throat. His voice was harsh, "Necromancers are a pox on the Seelie. They commune with darkness and consume the essence of other creatures to power their foul magic. They are cancer willingly held by the Unseelie. Our druids kill them wherever they are found. There is a standing bounty for the Seelie on the head of any Necromancer."

Doc spoke up, "This is beginning to look less like a human attack. Unless, of course, humans recruited these dark fae. We still need to find some answers." The priest turned back to Boomer, "Did you find anything else?"

Boomer nodded. "We sure did. There were a scattering of nine millimeter and two-two-three casings from standard weapons, but we also found some casings I don't recognize in size or maker." She held up a baggie of large silver bullet casings, "Do these look familiar, Kanak?"

The big creature stepped over to Boomer and held out his hand, "Let me take a look at those, Agent Callahan. Hmm. Yes, I know what these are. These are from an Archon. It is a weapon designed and manufactured by the *khoztak Seanachaidh*—the enforcers for the Keepers. Their guns are not usually found outside their own ranks, however I know there is a small black market in used Archon revolvers. It's about a .80 caliber bullet that is susceptible to loading with various enchantments. It's a real nasty round in anyone's hands. I'm not sure a human could actually fire it safely."

Boomer got a twinkle in her eye, "Sounds like a fun gun to shoot. I may have to borrow one for some range time."

Kanak chuckled, "I doubt a small human like you could stand the recoil. It might be fun to watch you try, though. This is looking more like the dark *sídhe*. But what about the video? Why does it show humans, and not fae?"

Spooky chose this time to interrupt, transmitting through the radio earpiece that each agent wore. "I have an answer to that, Doc. You guys wanna come back out to the truck?"

Doc looked at the *Hugtandalfer* in front of her, "My technician in the truck says he may be able to answer your question. Would you like to join us back out to the truck?"

14

COVERUP

Club Ljós, Bond Ave NW, Grand Rapids, Michigan

The team trooped out of the club, squinting in the transition from darkened club to harsh sunlight. Doc saw Spooky leaning out of the truck side door with a wide grin splitting his face. She realized that he was so excited that he was actually vibrating.

"I had to dig at it," Spooky announced as they reached the truck, "But you're not going to believe what I recovered."

Doc pointed to Kanak and said, "Special Agent John Smith, this is Etan Kanak. He is the head of security at the club. Kanak, this is Special Agent Smith."

Kanak answered, "Well met" to Spooky's "Howdy." Then Spooky started talking, "So I reviewed the footage, but was not satisfied. I did a whole bunch of tests, then found something really interesting. Here is the attack footage that the security team saw, and that was found on the servers." Spooky began the footage.

The team watched in growing horror as they saw what were obviously humans in full tactical vests and helmets carrying M4-style rifles and pump-action shotguns. They stormed in past the entry cameras and begin indiscriminately shooting the people in the crowded club. Almost filled to capacity, the club patrons had nowhere to run. They were quickly surrounded and killed.

When the majority of the patrons were on the ground and

writhing or bleeding out, several of the humans wearing the vests with "POLICE" stenciled across the back drew knives and swords. Even as some patrons struggled and put up resistance, they went through the crowd stabbing, slashing, and hacking their way across the room. Dancer turned away and left the truck when the body parts began flying; her stomach was still upset from her trip inside the club.

While the crew with knives and swords went through the crowd in the main area, small groups of assailants wandered off to check the rest of the building, and occasional pops of gunfire and screams of survivors were heard. Within ten minutes, every Seelie in the club was dead, either lying in a pool of its own fluids or faded back to its original realm. As they were filing out, the last human in the building stopped, took off their helmet and goggles, and looked straight at the camera. The smile on the man's face was absolutely demonic.

When the video stopped, Doc let out a long breath, as she was trying to force her horror down so that she could process the video. She looked around at the team, and Boomer and O'Beirne were pale and shell-shocked. Kanak was openly weaping. Spooky looked puzzled. Puzzled?

Spooky cleared his throat. "Did you see it? Did you see where the video gave itself away? Don't you see how it was fake?"

Four pairs of eyes stared back at him, unblinking.

"Seriously, how could you miss it? Ok, you probably missed the really subtle ones, but how do you not see the obvious." Spooky was genuinely confused at this moment.

Doc was the first to speak, her voice trembling from witnessing the rage and violence, "Obviously we don't see it. How do you know this footage is fake?"

Spooky smiled, "Oh. Well, let me show you." He reached out to cue up the video again. He explained as he was working.

SPOOKY HAD BEEN GIVEN the hard drive pulled directly from the video recording deck. Once it was connected to his system, the electronics specialist rapidly duplicated the entire drive, consulted his notes, made a few mental calculations, and reviewed the footage. He watched the whole attack and aftermath twice before he began noticing anomalies.

The young agent couldn't figure out why the images were bothering him until he realized that the footage was an HD-quality signal before the attack, but it switched to a lower-resolution video during the attack. About two minutes after the last assailant walked out of the club, the feed inexplicably switched back to the standard HD-quality that it was before the attack. He began running algorithms and filters on the copied data, but he found no underlying reason for the degradation of the video.

Setting the copy aside, he grabbed the original hard drive and searched for forensic indications of digital tampering. The young man quickly found several traces of file deletion and insertion. Spooky smiled a predatory smile, grabbed an energy drink out of the mini-cooler by his workstation, and began recovering the missing data.

The former NSA specialist knew that simply erasing files on a computer never truly erased the data. A standard "delete" command would only erase the header information—the electronic bits that told the computer there was actual data on the drive. There were several commercial data recovery solutions available on the general market, but Spooky had long ago built his own specialized software.

Spooky muttered, "All right, Mr. Gopher. Go dig me up some data." He clicked his keyboard to launch the retrieval app. A small dancing gopher popped up on screen and cavorted around the screen. A couple minutes later, the little animated gopher waved goodbye and disappeared into a hole as a report popped up on the screen.

The young electronics specialist pushed his glasses up his nose and looked at the report. He quickly noticed where the files were originally deleted and sent his program to retrieve the data. As it worked, Spooky turned to another monitor and began searching for cameras on the street. He found out there were two cameras that would show the building from the outside at two different businesses.

The first was a small mom and pop convenience store about three stores down. He noticed the camera connected to the store's exterior was an IP-based camera, which meant the feed was available online. Not wanting to wait for official subpoenas, he went to work with a backdoor password that the NSA had already built into the system. Finding the right camera did not take long, and in a few minutes he was able to recover the footage from the night in question. He downloaded that footage while working on the other source.

The other source was a local bank branch. Spooky again decided to forego the official process and simply breached the network. Using other passwords available from the NSA, he was quickly through the firewalls and into the main surveillance servers. Searching for the correct time and location took scant minutes, and soon that video file was also being downloaded to his system.

The footage from the convenience store was downloaded first. The footage showed an almost empty street moments before the attack began. Then two black panel vans pulled up and stopped in front of the building. Spooky watched as the bouncer at the front door stepped forward, likely to tell the vans to move. He walked two steps and then reached for the gun tucked into his jacket. The bouncer was barely able to draw his gun when he began jerking from bullet impacts. Spooky watched as the man crumpled to the ground, then begin to fade from this plane of existence.

Suddenly, both vans disgorged two groups of creatures. The electronics specialist began paging through the files for fae as he noted which types were attacking the club. A selection of automatic rifles and shotguns were passed around while swords and daggers were sheathed on most of the creatures' hips. All the creatures went inside the club. Twelve minutes later, the last of the attacking fae walked out of the club, and it was laughing maniacally.

Spooky re-ran the footage. He counted as eighteen fae went into the club. Only thirteen fae left the club. Unfortunately the resolution and quality of the video did not allow him to see any license plate information, and he could only identify a handful of the fae.

As he was writing down some of his observations, the former NSA analyst noticed that the bank footage had downloaded. This view showed the front of the building from the opposite angle. This one was a higher resolution so he was able to make out partial plates as the vans pulled up to the club.

Spooky watched the scene unfold from a different angle, this time seeing what the bouncer originally reacted to in fear. He was able to identify a few more of the fae. He feverishly wrote notes about what he saw. He needed to be able to point these things out to the others.

Two minutes later, Spooky was slamming another energy drink down when his Mr. Gopher routine notified him that it had retrieved the data. Spooky settled back to watch the footage that was lost. He was soon regretting that he had drunk that last energy drink. It was souring in his stomach at the raw, unedited carnage.

Spooky watched the screen as all eighteen creatures burst through the front door and began randomly shooting, stabbing and slashing patrons. The inside door bouncer was the first to be dispatched. A full burst of rifle fire killed him outright, and a slash with a wielded sword lopped the poor bastard's head off.

By the time people realized that something was wrong, it was already too late for their escape. As the groups separated to cover more of the club, Spooky found the lack of defensive attacks from the patrons disturbing. It was almost as if the patrons had gotten so lax that they could not be bothered to defend themselves. Here and there, small pockets of resistance were forming, and the attackers were using those areas as target practice. In doing so, the attackers were killing some of their own.

There. A fae took an assailant's own rifle and shot the human with it. Over there, a man in dark robes and wielding a silver dagger was clubbed with a chair from behind by minotaur. The seething anger and strength of the massive beast made the blow powerful, Spooky saw the angle of robed-figure's neck as he slumped to the floor. Before the robed-figure settled to the floor, three large-caliber shots slammed into the minotaur. It was dead before the other figure stopped twitching.

The brutality of the attack seemed to last forever. When the rifle fire stopped, several of the attacking fae stepped forward and used their pistols to finish off those who were merely wounded. Some went through the crowd with their swords and daggers, slashing and stabbing those still living fae. The blade-bearing attackers were creative and cruel, often cutting off parts of their victims before finishing them, just to make them scream.

The attack ended and the only sounds in the club were labored breathing and the dripping of blood and ichor. One-by-one, the assailants filed out, leaving a last person standing to survey the carnage. He was a very tall black man. Spooky estimated his height at around seven feet tall, and his skin was the deep rich dark brown of an African tribesman in the jungles, not the lighter skin of those with different bloodlines. And he was naked. The naked man was laughing and reveling in the charnel house around him. As he walked out, he paused at the base of the security camera over the door. He looked up directly at the camera. His eyes glowed a deep, rich red, and the man grinned with an evil that Spooky felt come through the monitor.

The former NSA analyst was stunned. He could do nothing but sit there for a few minutes and stare at the last frame of the footage, the man with a sinister, predatory grin on his face. He finally snapped to and overheard the conversation that Doc was having with Kanak. He decided to butt in and let everyone know what he found.

THE TEAM and Kanak stood shocked, staring at the image on the monitor before them. Kanak was the first to speak.

"*Oude Rode Ogen.*" The elfkin said. "Old Red Eyes. Now we have proof that this is Unseelie, because that spawn of demons never works without their direction."

Spooky typed furiously on the keyboard in front of him as Doc spoke up, "How nasty is this thing? Are there any known weaknesses with this creature?"

Kanak turned to the priest. "He is literally the spawn of a demon and human pairing. If he has come out during this, what is his end game? The Queen must be told of this."

Doc responded before the elfkin could do anything rash, "The Queen will be informed. We were invited by Her Majesty to investigate the attack, and we will be bringing all of our findings to her at the same time. We have another team out tracking down other leads."

The priest looked around at the gathered monster hunters and Kanak, "We still need to process the rest of the scene. If I remember fae law well, the Keepers will want much more evidence than a tampered video. Continue collecting evidence so that we can present our findings tonight."

With a renewed sense of purpose, the team went back into the club to gather evidence, followed by Kanak. Knowing what to look for, the team was able to find many more instances of fae weapons being used, and other signs that pointed to fae warfare. They also found the other three Unseelie, all with weapons and armor supplied by the *khoztak* black market.

As they wrapped up their investigation, Etan Kanak directed his other security team members to clean up the site and dispose of the bodies properly. Within minutes, a fire restoration truck rolled up, and the crew got out to begin working. Moments later, a large refrigerated box truck rolled up to the front of the building. The back door rattled as it rose to the top of the frame, and two elfkin came down carrying large bundles of black plastic. Doc recognized the body bags and realized that this was the full cleanup crew.

After exchanging contact information with Kanak, the Section 28 crew loaded into the Wunder Buggy and drove out of the neighborhood. Doc called Ghost to relay their findings and get the results of his investigations. It was another half hour before they returned to the airport, pulling up beside the giant Air Force jet serving as their Mobile Command Center. As they climbed out, they were greeted by the fresh DHS guards.

Boomer was the last to climb out of the truck, and she had six pizzas from a local restaurant carried in one hand. She shut the door and chirped the lock. The demolitions expert smiled and handed one of the pizzas to the guards standing outside, "This job shouldn't be all bad. I hope you like pepperoni."

The guard's face lit with a wide grin as he thanked her. As she walked up into the MCC and closed the door, the second uniformed guard was joining the first for a slice of the pie.

15

TAKEN

Gerald R. Ford International Airport

As the team and Captaen O'Beirne devoured the pizzas placed before them, they discussed their investigations. Once they connected by videoconference to Agent Smith at S28 headquarters, Ghost began, "After we got the ultimatum from the Queen, we split the teams to investigate. Alpha was with me, and we went to talk to the Society for the Preservation of Humanity. SPH turned out to be a dead end, but led to a new group called Zero Tolerance."

Agent Smith broke in, "And how is Mister Lancaster doing, Mister Vanhof?"

Ghost smiled, "I figured you two had met. Lancaster is doing fine and honestly did not seem to know about the attack. He is the one that named another suspect, an incursion survivor by the name of Nate Miller." The team watched as Agent Smith typed on his computer terminal. After a second, their boss looked back at the camera. Ghost continued, "Miller started Zero Tolerance when he was rejected by SPH for being too militant. This guy gathered a bunch of his good-old-boy friends and they play monster hunter."

Ghost glanced at his notes, "We interrogated Miller and his friends, but that was also a dead end. He fingered SPH for the attack. There was one troubling aspect of this. When we were talking to the group, Miller received a call on a burner phone. After he hung up, he pulled the SIM and threw it in the fire. He then broke the phone in pieces and threw those in the fire. Before I could ask him about it, he announced that we couldn't be trusted because we had a vampire on our team. Spooky's been working on pinpointing the phone number to trace the records, but he's been unsuccessful so far."

Smith looked perturbed. "I'll look into that from our end. I doubt it is someone inside our group. It may be a congress critter's staff. We had some confidential reporting after your last mission."

Ghost nodded, "Ok. I'll let Doc tell you about her experiences."

Doc stepped forward into the camera frame. She looked at her notes and began, "My team was assigned to the crime scene. When we got there, we talked to the head of security, and get the video footage from that night. I gave it to Spooky for processing and asked him to see if there were any other cameras in view of the building. Then the rest of my team went inside."

Doc went on to discuss what they saw inside, including the extent of the massacre. "I don't think any of us were prepared for the amount of bodies and the sheer carnage in the room. It reminded me a lot of the slaughter of the town leaders in Colorado. Lots of weapons fire, and lots of missing pieces. We also found five corpses that were apparently Unseelie. That wasn't the only evidence we found against the dark court."

The priest nodded to Spooky, and the electronics specialist linked in parts of the video that they had recovered. The team's medical doctor spoke as the clips played, "This first clip is the one we received from the club security. It looks like a human police or SWAT team raiding the club and killing everyone in it. In fact, the video doesn't even show any injuries to the attackers. Spooky noticed several anomalies within the video, so he went digging. This is the video he recovered."

The former NSA analyst switched clips and showed the recovered footage. Doc began again, "This is the recovered footage. As you can see, this is not a human SWAT team. It's a fae assault team, positively linked to the dark court. What is most interesting is the last images... There, Spooky." The image frozen on the screen was the large man with glowing red eyes."Oude Rode Ogen."

Agent Smith blinked. He then typed furiously on his keyboard and stopped to read the surrounding monitors. He slowly looked back at the camera, "This is the first image I've ever seen of this fae. Old Red Eyes was always a myth, a legend. I've never seen any concrete evidence of this creature before. I'll put together a packet for you."

"Thank you, sir. Spooky was also able to find some corroborating video evidence from a local bank and a nearby convenience store. It is quite apparent that the Unseelie court is behind this attack. I believe we have all the evidence we need to convince the queen to not hold humanity culpable."

Smith was nodding as the priest was talking. He spoke up, "Thank you team. Great work. Spooky, send me the files you have, including the reports from your teams. You may have to stay out there a little while longer until the Queen gets this matter settled. As a reminder, you are Signatories representing humanity. You are not to get into internal Fae Court dramas. Observe. Represent. Call me for approval for anything else. I'll talk to you tomorrow."

The video conference winked out and Spooky transmitted the reports and packages to headquarters. As the team finished their meals, they walked out and climbed into the Wunder Buggy for the short ride back to the hotel. When they arrived, each team member broke off and wandered back to their rooms to get some sleep.

When they got to their suite, Boomer approached Doc and let the priest know that she was going for a walk. Doc asked her if she wanted company, and Boomer answered in the negative. The demolitions expert said she wanted to walk and think a little bit.

The young agent walked toward the lobby of the hotel. As she walked out of the suite, she was stopped by Dancer. The new agent said she wanted to talk to her mentor about something that was weighing on her mind and wondered if she could join the demolitions specialist.

The two young women walked out of the hotel together. Heading generally south, away from the busy main roads, the pair wandered back through a light industrial area. They walked past several businesses, including a gun range, all of which were closed for the evening. Walking further south, they talked about the current mission. Boomer asked her young protégé what was bothering her.

"I'm not sure. I'm worried I can't hack this gig. Heck, I puked my guts out at the crime scene earlier. I don't know if I'm right for this team."

Boomer looked at Dancer. The vulnerable young woman was staring at the ground as she walked. The explosives expert remembered the first time she pulled the trigger in combat. She remembered the scene at the slaughter in Colorado. She remembered that the only thing that stopped her from losing her lunch was the desperate need to kill the monsters. How could she convey all this to the girl who, until a few short months ago, was at a summer camp in the Rockies?

As she was thinking about this, her eyes were roaming all over the surrounding area. Flipping in and out of her vampiric vision was starting to give her a headache. That, combined with her worry for Hannah caused her to miss the faint metallic glint about a hundred yards to her right. The muted click of a well-oiled bolt locking into position was missed among the noise of the interstate about two hundred yards away.

Boomer finally turned to Dancer and opened her mouth to speak, "Hannah, you are right where you need to be. You are talented. You may be a bit squeamish now, but you haven't truly been in the middle of combat yet. What you are feeling is normal. You just feel overwhelmed and unsure of yourself."

Off to her left, the vampire demolitions expert heard a muted thump, and felt a sharp sting on her left shoulder. She said, "Oww...." and then collapsed in a heap.

Her exclamation and the sound of her mentor's body hitting the ground was enough to get Dancer's attention. She whirled, looking around, and noticing Boomer lying crumpled in a heap. The young woman felt something slap her shoulder, registered a sharp prick of pain, and the world went black even as she was reaching for her shoulder.

IT WAS eight o'clock in the morning when Doc walked out of her room in the suite she was sharing with Boomer and Dancer. Dressed and ready for the meeting with the Queen of the Seelie, the priest wondered where the other women. She hoped that they had not been out all night, the youngest team member would need her sleep for the next couple days.

Doc saw that Boomer's door was closed, and she knocked. "Boomer? Dancer? You guys up yet?"

Not getting any answer, Doc knocked again, then opened the door and looked around the room. Both beds were still tightly tucked in from the room service cleaning before their arrival. The bed on the left had Boomer's duffel and kit still lying on the foot of it, unopened. On the right, Dancer's smaller kit bag was lying open on the bed where the teenager had dumped it and dug for makeup earlier. Neither bed had been slept in.

Doc pulled out her SSP and called the team leader. Ghost answered gruffly. His voice betrayed his lack of morning coffee and patience, "Yeah, Doc. What do you need?"

"Is Boomer with you? Or Dancer?" The team's medic asked. "Neither one is in their room, and it looks like their beds have not been slept in. I wouldn't normally worry about Boomer—she doesn't need much sleep. But Dancer is human and should have slept at least some."

Ghost was fully awake now. "No. Neither are with me. Ask Spooky, see if he knows where they are. I'll gather the rest and meet you at the Wunder Buggy in a couple minutes."

Doc briskly walked out of the hotel and headed to the team's transportation. Banging on the outer door, she yelled for the electronics officer to unlock the vehicle. The young man inside eventually opened the door.

"Have you seen Boomer or Dancer since last night?" The priest could see that she had awakened the young electronics specialist from his sleep, and he appeared to be having trouble concentrating. "Do you know where they are?"

Spooky had been driven out of some particularly vivid dreams by the loud pounding on the truck's door. He could barely hear a muffled voice, but it sounded angry, and it wanted into the truck. It had taken him a few more seconds to realize that Doc was waking him. He had stumbled to the door and unlocked it. As he opened the door, he belatedly realized that he had forgotten to make sure he was wearing pants. A quick glance downward confirmed that he at least was dressed in front of the priest. He finally was able to register what the priest was saying.

No, he hadn't seen the two women all night long. The last he had seen, they were walking away from the main road late last night. What did she mean that they were gone? How could they be gone?

Spooky grabbed his phone and dialed Boomer's SSP. It rang several times, then went to voicemail. He hung up and tried Dancer's. Same results. He tried each number one more time. Tossing his phone down in annoyance, the former NSA analyst realized that he had realtime access to location data for the phones. The young computer tech's fingers flew on the keyboard in front of him.

As Ghost and the rest of the team arrived at the truck, Spooky was grinning madly. He looked up as the tall federal monster climbed up into the truck, "I got locations boss. Looks like about half a mile from here."

Ghost leaned out and told everyone to board the truck. The

team leader climbed into the driver's seat and fired up the big engine. Shifting the transmission into first gear, he yelled back over his shoulder, "Where to, Spooky?" Spooky gave him directions.

Less than half a mile later, the heavily modified surveillance truck braked to a halt in a rising cloud of dust. The team piled out of the still settling Wunder Buggy, fanning out in ever-widening directions. Spooky yelled from the interior, "About forty feet to the west."

Do-Right found the first SSP. Battered and scuffed, the screen had a small crack on one corner. He thumbed the button and recognized Boomer's wallpaper. "I've got Boomer's SSP," the young former deputy announced.

Moments later, Scout found the other missing SSP. It, too, was scuffed, and the screen was shattered. Looking around the area, the Navajo archer searched for signs that he could track. A careful examination found plenty of evidence for his experienced eyes. He began to point them out to Ghost.

"If you look here, there are tire tracks, including four deeper depressions where the vehicle sat for an extended period of time." The young tracker pointed to the depressions in the soft earth. "Here there are two sets of drag marks. It looks like two people were dragged. The drag marks end at the tire tracks, so they were likely loaded into the waiting vehicle."

The young Native American looked around some more, "I'm not seeing any type of blood, or ichor, trail. There are plenty of boot and shoe prints. It looks like the vehicle left in a pretty big hurry." The tire tracks ended at the paved road. "My guess is they realized that the phones could be tracked, so they dumped them."

Ghost thought for a moment, "The fact that they left the SIM cards tells me that we were meant to find the phones. This seems more like the fake human attack on the club. It would not be hard to cover their tracks—it's like they meant for us to find them. This is beginning to smell like a nighttime Unseelie raid."

"Why?" Doc's tone was genuinely curious.

"We were getting ready to present our findings to the Queen. This was an attempt to shut us up or distract us. They even tried to pin the blame on humans again." The monster hunter's eyes grew cold, "We need to settle this." His voice rose to be heard, "Everyone mount up! We're headed to the MCC."

Doc spoke up, "Speaking of the Queen, you need to call her Knight, let him know what is happening. We will soon be late for our audience."

As the others clambered aboard the truck, Ghost pulled out his SSP. He dialed a number from memory. "Tó Coferal. This is Special Agent Vanhof. I apologize for breaking protocol, but we are in the middle of a crisis." He listened for a moment, "Thank you for your understanding. We just found out that two of my team have been abducted. Evidence from the scene points to machinations by the Unseelie Court. We hope that Her Majesty will understand and forgive our absence. I will contact you when we have resolved the issue. I do not expect the matter to last more than a few hours."

Ghost listened impatiently as Doc drove the massive truck back to the airport. The guard almost did not get the gate open in time, and the priest thought she felt a scrape on the exterior of the van from the still opening bar as they flashed underneath the steel gate.

Ghost said, "Thank you, Sir Knight. You are a credit to your Queen. I will update you as I find out." The lanky fed hung up with one deft finger while he hung onto the seat and window frame to keep from being bounced around the cab.

The truck rocked on its heavy-duty springs when Doc brought it to a halt outside the large cargo plane. The team exploded out of the truck, all of them heading toward the opening plane door. Ghost was the last to exit, his SSP in his hand already dialing Agent Smith.

Gretchen came barreling out of the air force jet, sidearm held at low ready. Ghost held up his hand, "We have two missing team members," Ghost barked. "The goddamn Unseelie Court kidnapped Boomer and Dancer."

Gretchen stopped, holstered her firearm, and motioned for the team to join her in the plane. She shrugged, as if it really was a common occurrence. "Well, if that's the problem, then let's find the ladies and kill whichever fae decided this was a good idea."

16

HUNGER

In the Void

"Wake up, young one." The deep rumbling voice was familiar, but Dancer couldn't quite place it. "It's time you woke up, here, so you can wake up out there."

Wake up here? The young woman opened her eyes and saw horizontal blades of grass. *Why is the world sideways?* Then she felt the soft loam under her head, and realization struck her. She was sideways. Slowly sitting up, the world righted itself, and she realized she was again in a field, and this place was familiar. *Vellath?*

She looked up as the great bronze dragon walked into her view. The creature's head snaked into view at the end of its long serpentine neck. The creature seemed to smile and its voice rumbled a bass vibrato, "Of course, young one. Who else would bring you here? But you must wake up now little one. You are in grave danger if you do not wake up. No time for questions. Just concentrate on waking up."

She thought a quick, *Thanks,* as the world faded to black again.

———

DANCER FELT PAIN. The world was no longer the pure black of unconsciousness. It was becoming red with pain. Her right shoulder felt like it was on fire, like it needed to be itched. She tried to scratch it, but she could not move her hands or arms. The young woman opened her eyes. As she blinked away the mental cobwebs, she took stock of her own body.

The young federal agent was sitting upright in a chair. It seemed to be an older wooden chair, and it was uncomfortable. She could not feel any padding under her or on her back. Dancer could feel something wrapped tightly around her torso, pinning her arms to her sides and tying her to the straight back of the chair. Her hands were similarly lashed to the arms of the chair at the wrist. Trying to flex her legs, she realized that her ankles were tied to the chair legs as well pinning her in place.

Her back was uncomfortable as she felt the sharp edges of *fion-fhuil's* scabbard digging into her spine. Something about that bothered her. Then she realized that they had not seen or felt the weapon, so they had not removed it. She still possessed Vellath. That's probably why Vellath was able to contact her. Hope flared within her as she realized she could use this to her advantage.

The room around her was dimly lit with a bare bulb hanging from the ceiling. The walls and ceiling were bare concrete with years of dirt, grime, and neglect staining them a mottled black and brown. To her left there was a large doorway. The door itself was standing open and looked to be several inches thick and made of steel. She could only turn her head so far, and the solid back of her chair rose well above her head. She could see nothing past the chair on either side. The lack of light told her that if there were any windows in the room, they were boarded up or otherwise covered.

Dancer heard a low moan of someone in pain behind her. She looked around in a futile attempt to see beyond the edges of her chair. The young woman steadied her voice and called out, "Who's there?"

The groan sounded again, and a familiar woman's voice answered her, "Hannah? Is that you?"

"Rebekah! I'm here. What happened? Do you remember anything?"

"I don't know." The newest agent could hear the confusion in her mentor's voice. Boomer continued, "The last thing I remember was feeling something hit me in the shoulder. They must have tranquilized you, too."

"But who? Unseelie? This seems like an awful lot of trouble to kidnap us."

Boomer thought for a moment, "Not likely. My guess would be

those creeps at Zero Tolerance. The boss said they had a mole at headquarters."

Slow clapping sounded from the doorway. Dancer turned her head and saw a human being standing in the doorway of the holding cell. The large man was young, he had a boyish face and tousled brown hair. His mustache and short beard did nothing to hide the wide grin.

"Congratulations, you found me out." The man's booming voice echoed around the room and sent off crescendos of pain through Dancer's skull. "Let me introduce myself. I am Nate Miller. And yes, my group of monster hunters has decided to hunt monsters. You guys. Oh, I realize that you are federal agents, but at least one of you is a vampire. And if the other is human? It doesn't matter. You are still a traitor to the human race." He rubbed his hands together as if anticipating a fine meal. "So the question is, which of you is the monster? And which of you is the traitor?"

Dancer refused to speak. She simply glared at the man. He shrugged, "Your glares do not affect me—I'm a married man. Well, lets see what your identifications tell us."

Miller opened a battered leather credentials holder. Comparing the picture inside with the women in front of him, he walked over to stand in front of Boomer. "Special Agent Rebekah Callahan. Are you the infected one? Not answering?" A loud smack echoed off the walls, and Dancer heard her mentor grunt. "Fine. Let's see about your beautiful young partner."

Miller walked around and stood in front of Dancer. He opened a set of credentials that looked much newer and read, "Special Agent Hannah Sedano of the Department of Homeland Security. You look really young for this. Did they spring you from daycare? Or maybe you were infected young?" The young federal agent continued to glare at her captor. "I bet you are the vampire. You're too young to be a real agent. No answer? How about now?"

She saw the strike coming, but there was nothing she could do about it. She tried to roll with the blow, but her limited mobility stopped her from getting out of the way. Miller reared back and closed his fist. He launched a powerful haymaker at the seated girl. Dancer's face exploded with pain. She felt the crunch of broken nasal bones, and here eyes blurred with instant tears. She could feel what must be blood streaming down her face and her vision went a hazy red. The redness quickly faded to black as she gave up on remaining conscious.

Boomer heard the terrific thump of the haymaker and the shriek from her protégé. She cursed loudly, calling Miller every name she could think of, and questioning the ancestry of the man and his entire family. Her time in the military served her well as Miller's eyebrows raised slightly when he heard some of the combinations.

He casually walked over to her and looked at her. She was writhing and testing her bonds. The head of Zero Tolerance sounded as if he was discussing a pleasant evening. "I would guess from her fainting and your reaction that you are the vampire, and she is the traitor. Oh, don't worry. You will both end up dead. But I have a really fun game that I want to play."

He watched her face as she grew quiet. It was the quiet before a violent storm. "You see, I've been told that if you get really hungry, you tend to lose control over your appetite. I hear that's a pretty gruesome sight. I've also been told that the more damage you soak up, the sooner you have to feed. I do believe that this will be a fun experiment. Well, fun for us, anyway."

Boomer clenched her teeth. She was struggling to control her inner demon, and the strain showed. "You will pay for this," she hissed. "My team will find us. And I will make it my personal mission to kill you. Slowly. Painfully. Your last view of this world will be my face devouring your still-beating heart. I guarantee it."

Miller winced, "Nice visuals, but your mouth should not be writing checks your body can't cash." The man's eyes grew cold as ice. "You will never leave this room alive. Once I turn you into the beast that you hide, I will leave your precious teammate in here for you to feed on. When you are done, I will put you down myself."

He suddenly stood. "Unfortunately, I need to leave you right now. I have dinner plans with my wife, and I'm suddenly in the mood for steak. But don't worry, I'm going to leave you in very capable hands."

He shouted, "Boys!" Two very large men entered the room, one carrying a duffel, and the other a small table. "I'd introduce you, but it won't matter anyways. I'll leave you in their capable hands." To the newcomers, he said, "Have fun boys. Do not kill her, and for heaven's sake, don't let either one of them get up." Miller walked out of the room, humming a popular tune.

Boomer looked up at the two men. One was blond and one had black hair. Both were well over six feet tall and looked like offensive linesman from an NFL team. She also noticed the butcher's aprons and leather gloves that covered their ham-sized fists. The men looked at each other and grinned.

Boomer almost did not see the fist that jabbed out from the

torturer on the left. Her head snapped back, and she felt the bones in her nose break. Pain exploded between her eyes and she could not hold back the cry of agony. The bruiser chuckled as his partner hit her with another jab, and this time she felt her cheekbone snap. It hurt to cry out, and it hurt to hold her mouth closed. Boomer watched as the giant that hit her last held up a pair of brass knuckles and grinned.

She spat at them and hissed, "You've just sealed your fate, assholes. I'm going to rip your throats out."

They both laughed and wandered around, in and out of her vision. The blond bruiser stopped outside her view. His voice was deep and gravelly, "Wow. Look at that one. She's a hottie for sure. Are you certain we can't have a little fun with this one at least?"

His partner laughed. "Maybe." He pointed at Boomer. "We'll see what happens to this one first." He twirled the brass knuckles around his index finger, catching it deftly.

He suddenly put them on, reared back, and hammered Boomer again. The demolitions specialist was seeing stars as her head rocked again. She felt tearing and knew that her cheek was just torn open. The one not broken.

As she cried out in pain again, she felt her nose mend itself. It hurt almost as much as it being broken. This was going to be a long day. The dark-haired thug watched her nose heal and told his partner, "Hit her nose again. It just healed up." The blond obligingly reared back and swung a sap with which he had been toying. The weapon landed on the bridge of her nose, and she screamed, seeing red, then collapsing as the blackness consumed her.

BOOMER WOKE SLOWLY. Her skull was throbbing, and her ribs felt like they were on fire. *How long was I out?* She wondered at the pain in her ribs. She didn't remember taking my shots there. She wondered if the thugs had continued to work her over while she was unconscious. The federal agent listened intently around her. She heard her breathing, and a labored, even breathing behind her. No footsteps. No breath sounds from the thugs.

She tried to open her eyes and felt her lashes pull as dried, crusted fluids pulled at her skin and lashes. She was able to finally force them open and look around her. She was still in the same room, with the same grungy walls. The door was shut. She could see that the inside was smooth, no handle, no gaps. She assumed there were locking mechanisms on the outside of the door.

Just as she was getting her bearings, she heard a hiss as the door unsealed. Two sets of boots clumped toward her. She looked up defiantly, and saw the same two thugs, wide grins on their faces.

The blond bruiser spoke, "Well, well. Sunshine is awake again. How are you feeling sunshine? All healed up from round one? Are you getting hungry yet?"

"Just let me loose," she hissed. "I'll show you how hungry I am."

"Ooh. looks like we have us a feisty one here." The brunette thug laughed with his partner. "I don't think she's hungry enough. I think we need to soften her up some more. What do you think?"

His partner just grinned and moved in, swinging the sap.

BOOMER WAS AGAIN slow to wake. She did not remember much beyond the first couple swings of the sap. Vague flashes of memory filtered through her mind. Her jaw ached as if all of her teeth had been broken or pulled. Again her eyes were crusted shut with dried tears and blood, and again it hurt to force them open.

She was getting hungry. The demolitions expert knew that every time she healed, she drew more power and energy from her stores. This energy would have to be replaced with blood. If they kept beating her long enough, she might eventually go mad with hunger.

She rocked and strained at her bonds, putting all her might into breaking the ropes that were binding her to the chair. There. The ropes seemed to give a little. Not much, but enough for a glimmer of hope. Her right arm seemed to move a fraction of an inch. As she struggled, concentrating on that arm, she heard the door open and the two torturers stomped into the room.

Seeing she was awake, the blond one smiled. He looked at his brunette partner, "This time it's your turn."

Boomer could not duck the brass knuckles. Again the world went black.

THIS TIME WHEN SHE WOKE, she knew the hunger was beginning to affect her. The pain in her face and shoulders was agonizing, but she realized that her hands and feet ached as well. The bastards were literally breaking every bone in her body, simply to give her more to heal. Boomer was getting desperate. She had to break free if only to save herself.

What about Hannah? She hadn't heard from the young woman at all the last couple times she awakened. Did they kill her? If so, the assholes would die slow, terrible deaths. She had to get out of here.

The door opened, and the two thugs swaggered into her view. This time, the brunette spoke first. "So, are you hungry enough yet? I hope not. this is getting really fun." The leer on his face was truly terrifying. "Heck, we haven't had this much fun since we caught that little gnome. He lasted for ten whole days before he died. How long are you gonna last?"

The blond stepped up, slapping his sap on his palm. "The best part? We just got permission to start working over your partner here. We want her nice and bloody for you when your hunger takes over. That way, there is no way you can stop yourself. So I get to play with you a little more while my brother plays with your friend."

The thug leaned in close as if to impart some confidence, "I personally think he got the better deal. They put up less fight when they are knocked out cold. Lots of perks working her over. I hope I get my turn, too."

Boomer's angry retort was cut short by the sound of automatic fire. Somewhere else in the building, Boomer heard the distinctive thunder of an AA-12 shotgun told her that Knightmare was on site. Her grin was cold, "Too late. My friends are here."

The thugs both turned toward the door, giving the vampire the break she needed. Her vision shifted to the weird monochrome vision of her inner beast. Fangs extended into her mouth and she felt her claws extrude from her fingertips. Enraged and finally able to risk letting her inner demon out, the vampire fed tensed her arms and pulled. The wooden arms of the chair splintered.

17

STAGING

The team had gathered in the Mobile Command Center's conference room. The interior of the Air Force C-17 was well lit, and the coffee pots were working overtime. Gretchen had immediately contacted Agent Smith, and the video-conference was relatively short. Once appraised of the situation, Smith had told Gretchen that this was a "Code Gamma One" situation, and had instructed her to begin the preparations for the ritual.

Spooky disconnected the video conference, and Ghost looked at Gretchen pointedly, "What the hell is Code Gamma One? I've never heard that phrase before."

Gretchen shook her head, "You would not have heard of it. It is an emergency protocol in place if one of the team members goes missing. The ritual can be performed from headquarters, but it goes better when performed in the field. We get better results when we are closer to the subject of the ritual."

"Ok. But what is the ritual for?"

Gretchen rummaged through a storage chest in the conference room. She paused long enough to answer the team leader, "Each team member is under a *geas* for control and secrecy, right?" Ghost nodded. "But management wanted some way to control and track the team members in the field, some esoteric version of GPS before it was ever a thing." The team liaison went back to pulling items out of the storage chest.

She looked up, searching for someone. "Doc, do you have current, viable genetic samples of both Boomer and Dancer?" The team doctor nodded, standing to go get the requested samples from storage in the MCC.

Gretchen had studied the items placed on the table before her. She nodded and began setting up a magic circle. Sand was carefully measured and poured out to form the perimeter of a circle. As she was drawing the outline of the circle, the liaison said, "Built into the *geas* is a tracking element. It doesn't matter where you go on earth, We can track you, specifically for cases such as this." She considered the circle in front of her and placed several candles around the small circle, igniting each as she went.

Gretchen accepted the samples from Doc and put the samples inside the circle. A blank piece of parchment followed the samples into the circle. The team's adjutant then drew her own credentials from her jacket and held it up, with the identification and badge facing the circle. She then closed her eyes and muttered a phrase that Doc thought might have been Enochian, as it was not any Latin she had ever heard.

The runes along the inside and outside of the credentials glowed a soft, sickly green. For a few moments, nothing happened. Just as Doc was starting to worry about the spell failing, the priest saw writing appear on the parchment. Except that it was not writing. A closer examination revealed that a small map had appeared.

Gretchen gave a small sigh and relaxed. The glow around the runes on her credentials quickly dissipated, and the candles were suddenly extinguished, as if by a wind. Gretchen reached out and took hold of the parchment, handing it to Spooky. "While I clean up here, match this to satellite photos. They are still alive and located somewhere in that map."

Spooky accepted the parchment with something approaching awe and scanned it into his computer. It looked somewhat familiar, but the computer specialist could not figure it out. A quick algorithm search produced a match that surprised everyone. Spooky cursed softly, then announced the location, "You are not gonna believe this, boss. They are located somewhere at the Zero Tolerance compound. Those assholes were actually stupid enough to kidnap Boomer and Dancer."

Ghost let out a string of curses, then glanced at the priest. "Sorry, Doc." She nodded, and the team leader continued, "All right everyone, gear up. Stupid humans assaulted and kidnapped Boomer and Dancer. Spooky, tap their communications. See what you can do with surveillance."

He thought for a moment, "If these idiots were willing to kidnap federal agents, they will be stupid enough to fight back. Gretchen, contact SAC Lewis, I need four of his field agents available, and the tactical team from the local sheriff. Pick a spot to stage for the raid. Tell DHS and the locals that it's a terrorist cell, but they are to be there for peripheral duties only. We may end up with arrests tonight, but they are to be sequestered and removed immediately. I would like you on the mission with us as the liaison for DHS and the locals. You'll have a radio, but stay with them outside the raid area.

"Once you get DHS moving, contact a federal judge. We need the warrant ASAP. Let them know that we are moving on this in sixty minutes, so we'll need it before then. Send it to the Wunder Buggy. Doc, chances are, Boomer's going to need some blood. Do we have some fresh on tap for her?" The priest nodded. "Good. Let's take that with us." Gretchen made her calls.

The DHS leader looked around at his team. "Ok. Load up. This is a raid, not a slaughter. There may be children on the premises, and possibly other family members that do not know how monumentally stupid their husbands are. Arrest everyone. If anyone raises a weapon, kill them. The only exception is that asshole Miller. I want to interrogate that douche bag myself. Spooky, can you show us a current satellite view?"

The electronics specialist immediately entered a few commands, and the screen on the wall lit with a live view of the address. Ghost studied the area closely for a few minutes and then started pointing to various spots on the screen. "Ok. This is a daytime raid, so it could go pear-shaped in a hurry. The good news is that there will not be any other agencies in the raid, so we'll be able to do our work. Do-right, have the locals block off the road about a hundred yards away from the house on each side. Here. And here." Red marks appeared on the screen where he pointed. "Block these driveways. Once they are in position, you will join Alpha to begin the sweep."

Ghost pointed to some of the team. "Heavy and Do-Right, you are Alpha, with me. We will stage here, at this driveway south of the secondary target." A box appeared on the spot indicated. "Once the roads are blocked, we will sweep north. We will clear this garage and this house first, detaining anyone inside. There is a small shed to the east, and one of us will clear it. Once that is clear, we will call DHS to come secure the prisoners. At that point we start moving north toward the primary target."

Looking at the map more intently, Ghost continued. "My guess is that our teammates are being held in the outbuilding where the club was meeting before. Alpha will attempt to secure the main house first. Bravo will provide backup and watch the target building."

The team leader pointed to the sniper, the tracker, and the priest. "Little G, Scout, and Doc, you guys are Bravo. I want you to take up position in the woods north of the target here and here." Again, marks had appeared on the screen. "You will be responsible for surveillance and overwatch. I want both of you to use your suppressed M4s on this one. You'll want a rifle, but the M24 will do you no good on this one, Little G. You will sweep in when we reach the main house. Keep an eye on the target and assist if needed."

Ghost looked back at Alpha, "Once the house is secure, we will clear the target building. Bravo will provide overwatch. Be ready for anything. Once everything is clear, Doc, you are up for injuries and working with Boomer."

The team leader looked all around the room, "Questions?"

Captaen O'Bierne spoken up, "What about me?"

Ghost shook his head. "Sorry, Captaen. You are an official observer. If this was fae, I might include you. This is human stupidity. You can wait with the DHS folks. Anyone else?"

Heavy raised his hand. After receiving a nod from Ghost, the big man asked, "Boss, I don't wanna even think this, but what if she is... uncontrollable? If she is in full vampire mode, can we talk her down? Should we carry anti-vamp rounds just in case?"

Ghost shook his head. "According to Agent Smith, if Boomer loses control of her beast, her *geas* will burn her out. That's why she's been working so hard lately to fight for control. She will literally fry if she attacks one of us. Heck, I'm not sure your *geas* would allow you to attack her. Does that satisfy you?"

Heavy nodded, "Good enough for me."

"Ok, Spooky, print out this map on the wide format so the locals will have some clue. Armor for everyone and don't worry about any special rounds. We're only fighting humans. Alpha, we each need a couple CS grenades, and masks. Bravo, grab your air masks in case we have to smoke someone out. Let's get ready to move."

Other than Ghost and Doc, the team changed into all-black fatigues, and clambered into their body armor. Ghost was already wearing his standard attire and armored jacket, while Doc was wearing her vestments. The priest slid body armor underneath her clothes just in case.

As they filed down the stairs to the tarmac, Ghost said, "Spooky, standard DHS Urban Assault black for the Wunder Buggy please."

Spooky nodded before disappearing into the back of the truck. Ghost climbed into the driver's seat as Gretchen came down the stairs. She pushed a remote, activating the powered retraction of the stairs. The door to the MCC closed with a solid "thunk." She climbed aboard the truck to sit in the passenger seat, giving an address to Ghost. "DHS and SWAT will meet us at that location in fifteen minutes."

Ghost nodded and started the truck. The engine roared as the team leader dropped it into gear and goosed the accelerator.

THIRTY MINUTES LATER, the team was en route to the target house outside the town of Marne. Following the Wunder Buggy were two sheriff patrol cars and a black SUV with government plates. They would be approaching the target location from the south. Not far away, another black SUV and two more sheriff patrol cars were moving in on the location from the north.

When the Wunder Buggy had pulled into the library branch they were using for their staging spot, they had been met by two federal SUVs and the four patrol units. There were six DHS agents dressed in fatigues and body armor. Gretchen had asked for four of them and SAC Lewis had brought his driver as well. There were also eight members of the Kent County Tactical Apprehension and Confrontation Team. The eight members of the TAC team had worn their tactical uniforms and vests and were equipped with rifles and sidearms.

The teams had gathered and introduced themselves. Opening up the back of the truck, Ghost had displayed the map of the target, and had run down the various duties required of the individuals.

Ghost had also stressed that only his team was to engage the targets unless the others were actually fired upon. It was likely, the Knightmare leader had noted, that there would be a firefight. Gretchen would act as liaison, and it would be her call to send in the other teams.

Once the DHS agents and the sheriff's deputies had known what they were supposed to do, they had planned their approaches and mounted their various vehicles. Little G, Scout, and Doc had climbed into one of the SUVs. It and two of the patrol cars had driven north, while the rest had followed the Wunder Buggy.

Minutes later, Ghost pulled the Wunder Buggy up to the pre-determined spot on the side of the road and left the engine running. Spooky stayed in his seat and called up the live satellite view of the target. He quickly ran through several checks and zoomed in around the entire perimeter.

"I'm not seeing any indications of perimeter guards, boss." The electronics specialist spoke up, "Could be someone under the trees, but I'm not seeing them. There are two guards standing outside the target, both armed with rifles, either M4s or the civilian models. They are both just watching around the front of the building."

Ghost nodded and activated his radio throat mic, "Ghost to Bravo. Go for insertion."

"Roger."

The next five minutes were some of the longest he had to endure to that point. Finally, Little G's voice broke the silence, "Bravo in position. Two tangos watching target. No other guards."

Ghost lifted a different radio to his mouth. This was one of the sheriff deputy's spare radio, which was also being monitored by the DHS team. "This is Team Lead. Go for perimeter." He glanced outside the truck as the two patrol cars and a Black SUV moved just past the truck and blocked the road. Both cruisers lit their light bars, and the SUV's police lights started flashing. The sheriff's deputies climbed out of their cars and set up a perimeter. Two of the deputies walked up the driveway they were blocking and knocked on the door. They would keep the owners of the house busy during the raid.

Just down the road, to the north of the target house, Ghost watched the same thing happen, with the cruisers lighting up and blocking the road, and the deputies going up to the house where they were blocking the driveway. He raised the radio one more time to his lips, "This is Team Lead. Go for Sweep Alpha." He tossed the radio on seat.

He, Heavy, and Do-Right all climbed out of the truck, double checked their gear and weapons, and worked their way toward the secondary target.

18

RESCUE

Alpha team carefully approached the secondary target house. This house had a driveway that connected with the driveway from the min house, and it also had an outbuilding, a detached garage. Approaching from the south, Ghost motioned for Do-Right to check the windows on the garage. Shining a light inside, Do-Right could see it was used as storage, and there were boxes and crates and even pieces of furniture in the closed building. He shook his head and cautiously rejoined his team.

Both Ghost and Do-Right were carrying team-standard M4 select-fire rifles. They were both equipped with suppressers, which were designed to turn the loud roar of gunfire into a muted chatter. Do-Right was also equipped with his Glock 22 sidearm, riding in the tactical holster strapped to his thigh. Plenty of extra magazines for both firearms were secreted away in various pouches on his belt and armor.

Unlike Do-Right, Ghost carried an old Webley Mark VI revolver. The World War I-era revolver was a family heirloom and old friend from his monster hunting days. The old top-break revolver was not as fast as modern sidearms, but it was deadly in the monster hunters hands.

Heavy was behind the other two agents as they approached the house. Where Ghost and Do-Right carried modern assault rifles, the large black man carried a strange, almost futuristic cannon that had a huge muzzle and was fed from a large drum. This was the AA-12 full-auto shotgun, and was designed to clear a room within seconds, while inflicting maximum carnage. A Beretta M9 sidearm rested in his tactical thigh holster as backup.

The team leader motioned for Heavy to move out slightly and cover the house. He approached the front door and slung his rifle, motioning for Do-Right to step off to the side, out of sight of the main door. He knocked on the door and heard footsteps.

The door was opened by a middle-aged woman in a t-shirt and jeans. Her expression was one of disdain, and before she realized who was standing there, she groused, "I don't want any. I'm not buying any. And if you don't leave I'm calling the...."

Ghost flashed his badge and asked, "Cops?" He abruptly pulled her aside and opened the way for Do-Right. The former deputy pushed through the door, and into the living room. Ghost continued, "Homeland Security. Is there anyone in the house right now?"

The woman was speechless. She stared in horror at the man in the black leather duster and her eyes fixated on the badge he was holding up. The credentials flashed a greenish glow as Ghost willed more power into it. "I'm not going to ask again, is there anyone else in the house? We need to know so they won't get hurt."

The woman shook her head, her eyes still reflecting the green glow.

Ghost called softly, "She says it's clear. Verify it quickly. The clock is ticking."

"Got it, boss."

Two minutes later, Do-Right was back at the front of the house, standing just inside the door with Ghost and the woman. Her hands were zip-tied in her lap, and she was sitting on the overstuffed chair in front of the tv. She had recovered her voice and was cursing and threatening the federal agents with everything from kidnapping charges to civil rights lawsuits.

"The house is clear, sir." The former deputy looked at his boss. "Checked all three levels. Found some weed, but nothing worth worrying over."

Ghost nodded and keyed his mic, "Ghost to Gretchen. Send DHS to this location. One agent. One in custody."

"Affirmative," came the reply.

About a minute later, one of the DHS agents walked through the door. Ghost looked at the name tag on his vest. "Agent Verburg.

This subject is temporarily detained. We will release her when it's over. You stand watch until then."

The man nodded, "Yessir. I'll babysit your detainee until you release her."

Ghost clapped him on the shoulder as he and Do-Right exited the house to rejoin Heavy outside on the lawn.

As one, the three agents moved around to the rear of the house. They moved up to a tree line and looked through the line at the property beyond their position. Directly to their east was a small shed with tools and yard equipment around it. North was the primary target and the main house. Not seeing a way to approach the shed without being seen, Ghost decided that they would have to leave that unchecked until the end of the raid. That left the property to the North.

Ghost pulled out binoculars and looked over the target from deep inside the tree line. He could see the two guards at the main entrance of ZT's headquarters. Both were cradling their rifles, and both men looked like they knew how to use them. He looked back toward the house and saw a child playing on a swing set in the back yard about forty feet from the guards.

Ghost cursed softly. He keyed his mic. "Ghost to Knightmare. Alert. There is a child approximately forty feet away from the guards, on the south side of the primary target. Bravo, check fire."

The team was too professional to curse on the radio, but Ghost knew that several colorful words were being said at that moment. He knew his snipers could not see the child from their vantage point, and the swing set was covered, so Spooky would not have seen the kid either.

Spooky broke into the radio chatter. "Ghost, this is Spooky. Be advised I just intercepted a landline call from the target location. The caller was giving a status update to someone I might assume was Miller. The caller said that "the vampire had not broken yet.' Those were the words they used."

The team leader looked at the two agents with him. That was the confirmation he needed. "Ghost to Bravo, be advised Alpha is two hundred feet from target. Bravo will initiate. Bravo, tangos are the two sentries. Alpha will break cover five seconds after tango down. Bravo remains on overwatch."

Two simple clicks told the team leader that his other fire team understood their orders. The team leader again touched his mic. "Ghost to Gretchen. I need the two fastest guys you have. DHS or sheriff, doesn't matter, but tell them to leave their rifles behind to have both hands free. They need to make their way to our position at the back of the secondary target, in the tree line."

Gretchen figured out what he was doing and sent a DHS agent and a TAC team member to meet the team. They were instructed to leave their rifles in their vehicles because they were on rescue duty. They quickly, but cautiously, made their way to meet up with Alpha. Ghost told them that their job was to go get that child and pull him back to the secondary target, inside with the other DHS agent. Both men nodded their understanding.

Ghost keyed his mic again, "Ghost to Bravo. DHS and sheriff will rescue kid. Watch fire." Again two clicks acknowledged the message.

Ghost pointed to Heavy, "You've got overwatch this side. Stop anyone coming out of the workshop." He now pointed at Do-Right, "You and I have the main house. Quick sweep. Then we take down the target." Both men nodded.

Again activating his radio, the monster hunter said, "Bravo, cleared to engage. Weapons free."

In the tree line to the north of the target, Scout sighted in on one of the guards. He knew that Little G would take the other one. He held his breath for a moment. On the exhale, he held once again, steadying his shot. As his finger moved on the trigger, the Navajo archer heard a soft "thwack" from the rifle beside him. He twitched his finger, and his rifle made the same soft sound.

The guard on the right dropped to his knees, clutching at his heart. There a red stain was spreading, even as he collapsed in a heap. His partner on the left was only starting to realize that there was something wrong before the 5.56mm round entered the back of his head and exited the front, taking most of his brains with it.

Ghost waited five long seconds, then he, Alpha, and the rescue team burst from the tree line. When they were halfway across the lawn, a woman walked out of the back porch and stopped. She saw the two figures laying in growing pools of blood and froze. Movement in the corner of her eye made her turn her head, and she watched as five armed men ran across the lawn to the south. She wailed, but it quickly turned into a piercing scream.

Ghost reached her in another second. He introduced himself as he ran past with a quick swing of his rifle butt to her head. Her cries cut off abruptly, and she dropped to the ground. The lanky monster hunter took the stairs two at a time, reaching the top of the back porch in mere steps. A momentary pause as he nodded to Do-Right, who was right behind him. Do-Right flung open the screen on the back porch and ran inside the house. Ghost followed on his heels.

The men cleared the main floor very quickly, as the modern, open floor plan made sight-lines a breeze. The team leader pointed up the stairs and the former deputy raised his rifle and crept slowly, carefully up the stairs. Checking every bedroom and bathroom on the floor, they finished clearing the house in one minute.

As they were walking back down the stairs, Ghost heard the sound of a rifle firing. It was answered by the unmistakable thunder from Heavy's shotgun. He looked at Do-Right, nodded, and they both scrambled for the door. The former deputy led his boss out the door.

There was a small covered walkway that led from the house to the outbuilding. A man crouched in the walkway behind a column and fired a Russian-style rifle at their teammate. Heavy's return fire was slowly chipping away at the column where the man was hiding.

Do-Right raised his rifle and took careful aim. As the crosshairs settled over the man's head, he gently squeezed the trigger. The muted sounds of his rifle were lost in the cacophony from the shotgun. The man's head disappeared, and the headless corpse fell out from behind the column.

Heavy smiled and nodded at the two agents on the porch. As he started to join his companions, another rifle opened up from the club's outbuilding. The big man immediately dropped to the ground, rolling away from the bullets.

Ghost and Do-Right both knelt, raised their red-dot reticles to their eyes, and pulled the triggers. Six rounds hit the gunman targeting their comrade. Three of the 5.56mm bullets impacted the face of the gunman and exited out of the back of his skull. The other three rounds hit the already-dead gunman square in the chest, as the body fell to the ground.

Heavy rumbled, "Thanks," as he stood to his feet. With his two teammates already covering his approach, the big gunner approached the door cautiously, stopping to the right of the main door with his back against the wall,

Ghost tapped Do-Right on the shoulder, and the former deputy advanced to the other side of the door while Ghost covered the entrance. As the former deputy was moving, the team leader activated his microphone, "Ghost to Gretchen—shots fired. We're all ok. Remind DHS and SWAT to hold position unless called."

He heard Gretchen acknowledge his transmission, but the team leader was already preparing to move for the door. He waited to make sure that Do-Right was safely to the entry point, and then he followed.

Ghost and Do-Right covered the entryway from opposite sides. Heavy stepped back and slammed his foot into the door. The frame shook, and the door moved a little. Ghost nodded at Heavy and he slammed his size fifteen boot into the door again, right beside the knob. The frame shook again, and the door bowed inward, but did not give.

"Little G to Ghost. Suspects rabbiting from door in rear of building. Engaging."

Before the team leader could respond, a small hidden door swung open about five feet off the ground, about a foot in front of the agent. The eight-inch square opening was filled with the muzzle of a pistol. Ghost shoved the muzzle of his carbine into the opening and fired a burst. A scream of pain sounded, and the pistol fell from the opening.

Heavy saw the opening and his leader's attack and quickly yanked a grenade from his belt. Pulling the pin with his teeth, the big man reached into the hole and dropped the now-live grenade. Shouts and curses sounded thru the opening and were cut off by a loud "bang" and a brilliant white light.

Heavy returned to concentrate on the front door and gave one more solid kick to the battered portal. This time the door seemed to explode inward, bouncing off one dazed ZT member before slamming into the wall. There the knob stuck in the drywall, preventing a rebound. Heavy went through the door, followed by Ghost. Do-Right stayed outside to watch the compound.

Immediately to the right of the door lay a man writhing in a pool of blood. Ghost took a brief moment to look and realized that he had hit the man in the chest with his burst. The man might survive if he could get help soon enough. Heavy took one look and ignored the man.

As he followed the team leader, Heavy clubbed the dazed ZT member standing to the left of the doorway with the butt of his shotgun. The second blow dropped the man to the ground, out cold. Both he and his team leader scanned around the open building, looking for any armed resistance. Ghost motioned for Heavy to split left while he walked up the right side of the building.

Thirty seconds later, the duo had cleared the entire floor, including the small bathroom. Ghost looked for a door to a basement in earnest. As he did so, Heavy took up a station by the open back door, and said to his boss, "I've got three tangos out the back door. One is still moving."

Ghost nodded as he walked into the lounge area. He was carefully pacing off distances and realized that the lounge was about five feet shorter. He walked over to the wall of bookshelves. His eyes ran across the titles of the books. Fiction and nonfiction, they were haphazardly arranged, with a few surprising titles among them. He found one that caught his eye. *Secret Passages* by S. Terces was a large hardback volume that had a moderate amount of wear on the top of the spine.

The federal agent grinned and called out, "Heavy. Found our door. Back me up."

The big agent thundered over and pointed his fully automatic shotgun at the door. Heavy nodded at his boss, and Ghost pulled the spine of the book. There was a click as the book levered forward. Ghost pulled on the shelf next to the book, and the center section of the bookshelf levered open, showing steps leading down into gloom.

"Federal agents. Come out with your hands up."

WHEN SHE HAD HEARD the rattle of the automatic shotgun, Boomer had known that she would only get one opening. As the two torturers had turned toward the door, she had focused all her of anger at being kidnapped, all her rage at being tortured, and all of her fury at their torture of Hannah into a key that unlocked the demon living inside her.

The wooden arms and legs of the chair shattered as she strained to raise her arms. The young demolitions specialist did not feel the slivers of wood slice into her flesh. She did not feel her left radius snap like a twig. Boomer could feel nothing except for the rage and hunger that drove her demon.

The twin brutes realized how much trouble they were in when they both heard the wood snap like kindling. The blond man was a bit faster than his brother and turned to see the vampire that they had been torturing all day leaping at his throat.

Even as her demon demanded to be fed, Boomer was thinking about the tactical situation. *Cripple one, kill the other, then feed on both.* As she prepared to leap at the men, she saw the blond turn his head back first. *First target.* One moment she was crouched to jump, then she was in the air, and landing on the blond bruiser's chest. Her momentum caused the man to stagger back and crash to the ground. A quick blow to the man's exposed throat with the side of her hand incapacitated the man. She looked at her next target.

The brunette was stunned, slack-jawed as his brother was taken to the ground by the small vampire. He tried to recover and began to paw at his belt holster. The creature leapt at him.

Boomer watched the man reach for his gun. He would never make it. With a mighty scream and a powerful surge, she was airborne and crashed into the man's chest. This time, distance and momentum worked in her favor and the man was knocked several feet back, landing on his back and knocking the breath out of him. He would never be able to breathe easy again.

Boomer bent down and bit, ripping a large chunk of the man's throat out, and drinking all the warm lifeblood. Her third bite scraped along the man's spinal column in the back of his throat. Swallowing the large chunk of meat, she decided the rest could wait.

The vampire agent looked up as the blond man was trying to rise to his feet. She watched him get to his knees and then get one leg underneath him. She grinned. Springing forward, she swept through the man's legs, taking them out from underneath him and hearing both of his femurs shatters as she hit them.

The man landed on his face with a sickening crunch. Muted howls rose from his wounded throat, and the vampire agent grabbed the man's shoulders, rolling him over to face her.

"I told you I would make you pay," she hissed. Her black eyes were cold. She bent to whisper in his ear, "I'm going to enjoy this, a lot."

The man's eyes were wide in fear as Boomer took the first hunk out of his ruined throat. She was finishing off the man's throat when Ghost and Do-Right appeared in the doorway.

19

EVIDENCE

Gerald R. Ford International Airport

"**A**nd how is Miss Callahan now?" Concern showed on Agent Smith's face and in his tone. "Is she still mission capable? What about Miss Sedano? Is she going to make it through the mission?"

Ghost and Gretchen sat in front of the camera and monitor in the conference room while the rest of the team was sitting in the lounge area inside the MCC. Both Ghost and Gretchen decided that it was too dangerous to stay at the hotel that night and had asked the local SAC to provide two extra perimeter guards. Ghost did not think that Zero Tolerance would attempt anything else, but it was better to take the precautions.

"Boomer seems to be fine." Ghost responded to his boss, "According to Dancer, she held onto her temper and her creature until we were making the assault on the compound. Then she used it to break free and kill their tormenters. When we got there, Boomer recognized Do-right and myself right away. She slowly stood and stepped back away from the corpses. She wiped her face and neck off on her shirt until we could get a canteen and some towels down to her."

Gretchen chimed in, "I would consider both of them still mission capable. Agent Sedano may have a few nightmares, but

Agent Callahan took most of the torture. I think she purged most of it by... eating the problems."

Agent Smith winced, "Keep an eye on Miss Callahan. Both of you. Watch to make sure her creature isn't winning control."

Smith paused to look at the monitor in front of him. "What about Zero Tolerance? Are they going to cause more problems?"

Ghost shook his head, "Negative, boss. They had nine members killed today, three hospitalized, and waiting charges, and a one on life support. He probably won't make it."

"What about this Miller character? Was he among the wounded or dead?"

It was Gretchen's turn to shake her head. "No, sir. He was not there for the raid. We have initial testimony from two of the thugs that Miller was the one who gave the orders. Must have just missed him. We've got BOLO's out on his vehicle and the locals will pick him up for us. DHS will take custody as soon as the locals get him."

"Does Miller have any resources?"

Ghost shrugged. "Unknown, boss. ZT was new to us when we landed. We have no intel on current members or resources. Spooky is going through the computer drives, but they used good encryption. It will take some time, much to Spooky's chagrin."

Smith raised a quizzical eyebrow, "Anything else for me?" When he got negatives from both of them, he continued, "Ok. It's late, but within time limits. Go present your finding to the Queen. Let her know it was the Unseelie Court. Do not offer to help. If they ask for help, contact me, and we can get concessions. Good luck." Smith signed off the transmission.

Out in the lounge area, the rest of the team, plus Captaen O'Beirne, were sitting and talking about the events of the day. Both Boomer and Dancer had showered and changed, scrubbing the grime from their bodies. As much as she had fought it, the youngest member of the team had fallen asleep in one of the leather loungers. Boomer had gently put the feet up and laid her back, covering her with an available blanket.

Ghost and Gretchen walked out of the conference room as Boomer was tucking in Dancer. Ghost looked at the teenager and said, "I guess it all finally caught up with her. I hate to do this, but we will be leaving for an appointment at the Seelie Court in two hours. Let her sleep as long as possible, but she needs to go with us."

The Knightmare team leader addressed the rest of the room, "Good work, everyone. No casualties on our end, no innocents killed, and the locals get credit for taking down a terrorist cell. That works on all levels for me, and for our boss. It's good to have you back, Boomer."

He walked over to an empty chair and sat heavily. "Spooky, make sure you have all the electronic files tagged and ready. You'll be joining us inside, try to wear something halfway appropriate. Doc, you have the physical evidence from the club. O'Beirne, you will accompany as liaison for Europe. And then me. Any questions?"

"Yeah," Heavy's bass voice was weary. "Can those of us who don't get to meet the queen not actually go. I'd like some rest after the activities of the past couple hours."

Ghost shook his head, "Sorry, big man. We might need all hands if things go wrong. Anyone else?"

Heavy muttered under his breath about stupid duties and the distinct lack of monster killing.

Kicking his own feet up on the recliner, the team leader laid his head back and put his hat over his eyes. From underneath the hat came a muffled, "Someone wake me in an hour-and-a-half." Snoring soon followed.

The only Knightmare team members not sacked out shortly after that were Boomer and Spooky. Boomer caught Gretchen's eye, and the two walked into the conference room. Spooky started double-checking his files and footage for the right cues.

JUST OVER TWO HOURS LATER, the Wunder Buggy pulled into the driveway at the Queen's court. The truck was quickly waved through and directed up to the parking area. As arranged, Ghost, Doc, Spooky, and O'Beirne all climbed down from of the heavily modified bread truck. It was early evening, and the sun had begun its descent from the sky.

Although Captaen O'Beirne was wearing his dress uniform, every member of Knightmare was dressed and armed for battle. Even though Ghost's team was supposed to be unarmed, the DHS leader still had his cane sword, and the priest had her cross/dagger combo.

Inside the truck, Boomer sat in Spooky's seat, monitoring the radio earpieces worn by her teammates. Every team member left in the truck was fully dressed for battle and had their weapons within easy reach. There was a nervous energy in the truck as if the past several hours were merely the prelude to something bigger.

Ghost led the human representatives up to the front door once

again greeted by the big minotaur called Tar Katel. After pleas-
antries were exchanged, the creature led them in to the anteroom.
Here they met Tó Coferal, the Queen's Knight.

"Well met, Tó Coferal. I bring news and resolution of the
mission that her majesty has requested of my team."

The elf appraised the tall human, "Well met, Special Agent
Jonas Vanhof. I understand you had some delays in your
resolution?"

"None that related to the resolution of the mission directly. A
foolish group decided to kidnap one of my own. It did not work well
in their favor."

A thin smile brushed across the lips of the Knight, "With your
reputation, I would think it would go poorly for them. Her Majesty
is eager to review your findings."

Ghost bowed. "We are ready when she is ready to receive us."

The Queen's Knight turned and led the group of humans to the
receiving room. Outside the massive oak doors stood two more
elves, both standing ramrod straight. One of them opened one of
the massive doors and announced their presence. Her Majesty
offered a simple, "Come."

The Knight led the human group before the queen, and all the
ritual greetings were once again performed, this time adding
Spooky. With her Knight now standing beside her throne, the
Queen began, "Have you found the information that satisfies your
mission?"

Ghost bowed, "Yes, Your Majesty. We bring physical evidence
from the scene as well as video surveillance from the actual event. I
will now let my experts present their findings."

Doc stepped forward and described her physical findings. She
described, in detail, the physical evidence collected and conclusions she drew from such evidence. She included that she was
skeptical that there was any real evidence of a human-based
attack.

When Doc finished, Spooky began setting up his monitors and
screen, as well as his portable projector. He was nervous, so he took
an extra couple minutes to set up his projection equipment and
screen. When the electronics specialist was finally ready, the Queen
indicated that he should begin.

Over the next thirty minutes, Spooky explained his steps, his
theories, and his methodology to get the clear video before the
stunned Court. The Queen's Knight was outraged when he saw the
recovered camera footage from outside the club. The footage from

inside the club horrified all the fae present, and a couple of the attendants fainted before continuing to watch.

Ghost explained that the brutality and speed with which the Unseelie fae raided the club showed that they had been planning this for quite some time, possibly several years. The fae had seemed to know precisely where to strike, how many guards were on duty, and had been prepared with a fake video stream, which they had uploaded to the video surveillance system in the club.

Based on the weight of the gathered evidence, the human team had no choice but to conclude that the Unseelie Court was behind the major attack on the Seelie-held property. The Unseelie had likely intended to drive a wedge between the Seelie Court and the human representatives of the Accords.

When Ghost was done speaking, he waited for the Queen and her entourage to absorb his findings. It was a few tense minutes before the Queen spoke.

"We acknowledge the findings you have presented and agree with your conclusions." The Queen's voice was as melodious as ever, but there was a hint of anger buried in her tone. "We ask that you be available to present this evidence to the *Seanachaidh* on the morrow. I will call for them to convene as an urgent matter."

Ghost nodded, "We would be happy to assist you in calling for justice. Have your Knight contact me regarding the time and location of the meeting. Is there anything else for us to discuss at this time, Your Majesty?"

The Queen of the Seelie Courts shook her head as a loud explosion rocked the house.

NATE MILLER SAT in his red Chevy Impala in the parking lot of a large grocery store on 28th Street SE and waited for his soldiers to arrive.

He had been lucky enough to miss the raid on his ZT compound by just a couple minutes. He considered that as a sign of God's protection over him and his mission. He had pulled up to the end of the road leading to the compound and had seen the police cars blocking the road. He had quickly realized that they had been compromised and had left.

While driving, he had placed several calls to ZT members that had not been at the compound. It had been a call to arms. This federal agency had attacked his men and women, and they would get a surprise soon. He had known that they were based on their transport plane and had figured that they would no longer stay at the hotel where he and his men had kidnapped the vampire.

Miller had arranged for his remaining soldiers to gather what arms and explosives they had available, and to start toward the airport. The Zero Tolerance leader had then driven his car to a small industrial park outside the Grand Rapids airport and had simply waited for the their truck to leave the airport.

Being careful to maintain his distance, the young fanatic had followed the truck as it had made its way north and east into a much wealthier area of town. When the truck had turned off into the gated estate, Miller had slowed enough to get a look at the guard who had let the federal agents' truck pass. It had definitely not been human.

Knowing he finally had a location for the hit, he had placed a call to his second-in-command. Once he had set the location for the meeting, he had hung up and had driven slowly past the house once more. Miller had then parked at the corner of Burton Street and Candlewick Court and had pulled out a large pair of binoculars.

Four hundred yards away, Miler had watched the various non-human guards and escorts talk to the arriving federal agents, and then they had gone inside the house. He had then driven less than a mile to the rendezvous point for his soldiers, and that was where he still waited.

When the soldiers finally arrived, they were split between three vehicles. There were five men armed with rifles and pistols in a white panel van that advertised one of the Zero Tolerance soldier's electrician competitors. Two more rode in a white Ford Crown Victoria, and were armed with pistols. These two had several pipe bombs loaded and ready in the trunk of the sedan, and the sedan was painted in the livery of a local security company. It was also outfitted with and amber light bar on top. The final three were in a dark blue minivan. Armed with rifles and pistols, the men also had two satchel charges ready in the back of the minivan.

Miller climbed out of his car and shook hands with his crew. He quickly told the team in the Crown Vic and the minivan that they were to create massive diversions for the security of the monster's compound. They were to limit the casualties of humans to a bare minimum, and none would be preferable. They were to blow up several places around the monster's house, enough to get their attention.

Two of the men in the van were to drive up to the gate and

crash it. Shoot the guard at the gate and take several potshots at the compound. When the security guards responded, they were to resist a little, but drive away slowly. This would hopefully entice some of them to follow. Miller's job was to attack the compound when they were distracted. He and the remaining men from the van would be in his car. They would drive around to park in a small subdivision that sat in the midst of the golf course. There, they would trek across the golf course toward the woods that flanked the target house.

The men stowed their rifles in the duffle bag in the trunk of Miller's Impala, and the four teams checked the time. Miller told the explosives teams to set them for thirty minutes from that point. That would offer enough time for him to get into position. The teams separated, driving to their assigned tasks.

Thirty minutes later, Miller and his three companions were waiting in the woods to the west of the house. The first explosion went off to their south, just outside the property lines. The Zero Tolerance leader was pleased to see the activity in the parking area as guards and attendants began to look for the source. Then three more explosions shattered the air, all of those being to the east. A large fireball and a plume of black smoke rose from a building on the other side of the property. There would definitely be damage from this one.

Guns were suddenly drawn by many of the guards in the parking area. Miller watched as one particularly tall beast with a full set of horns unlocked a cabinet and grabbed a large rifle. The creature pointed in both directions and two guards ran, one toward each of the explosions. He raised his gigantic fist to his mouth and talked into it. The beast was obviously communicating by radio with others, likely his boss in the house.

Two minutes later, Miller heard an engine roar and the rending screech as the van tore through the gate. Automatic rifle fire chattered from down the driveway.

The creature in front of them with the rifle yelled and ran toward the gate. As the guards and attendants left the parking area, Miller looked at his three companions and pointed. "Frank, Smitty. You guys hit the house. Wipe 'em out. Bill, you and me will hit the truck. I want to kill that vamp once and for all. Kill everything you can, then bug out. Got me?" Three heads nodded.

"Go!"

20

REVENGE

W hen the first explosion had gone off, Heavy was chatting with Tar Katel, talking about the various weapons available to fae. It was actually a pleasant, if surreal, conversation to be having with a living minotaur. Both the human federal agent and the minotaur looked toward the blast, then at each other. Before either could speak, the second series of explosions rocked the estate to the east.

Heavy looked at the lead guard and said, "It looks like you have work. We'll stay put, but we will get ready. If you want us to help defend the Queen, just ask."

Tar Katel nodded and went to gather his exterior guards by the garage. Heavy watched him send a uniformed security person in each direction, and then the big fed heard the crash at the front gate.

Turning to see if it was part of this or just a coincidence, his question was answered by the rattle of heavy-caliber rifle fire. Recognizing the distinctive sound of an AK-74 variant on semi-auto, he climbed into the truck and told the others what was happening. Do-Right already had his armor on and was helping Scout into his own. Boomer was helping Dancer get into her custom made armor. Heavy grabbed his flak vest and was fastening all the straps and velcro as Tar Katel ran past the van carrying a very large rifle of an unfamiliar design. Several of the security detail followed the big creature.

His next step was to unlock the gun locker and draw out his AA-12. The big man caressed the big automatic shotgun lovingly, then reached back in and drew out several of the drum-shaped magazines for the big auto-loader.

Do-Right and Scout drew their rifles and loaded them, and Dancer grabbed a suppressed MP5K-PDW submachine gun. She rammed a magazine home and pulled the charging handle. Flicking the selector switch to "SAFE", the young woman slung the weapon over her shoulder and grabbed a couple extra magazines.

Heavy reached over an otherwise occupied Boomer and grabbed the microphone for the earpieces the inside team was wearing. "Ghost, this is Heavy. There is an attack on the compound. We are holding for direction from the Seelie guard force." He watched two figures with rifles dart into the open garage door and continued. "Update. Two bogies just entered Queen's residence. Humans with rifles. Keep your heads down."

Heavy looked out the front of the truck and flinched as sparks flew from the windshield in front of his face. There were two more men firing at the bullet-resistant glass of the Wunder Buggy.

Heavy yelled over his shoulder, "Two assholes trying to shoot us. Take one of them alive."

NATE MILLER and the three soldiers with him had burst from the edge of the woods. Two of the men had veered toward the open garage door with their rifles raised. Miller and his partner had run straight for the Wunder Buggy.

The men Miller called "Frank" and "Smitty" ran through the open garage door and stopped at the door leading into the main house. A silent three-count and Smitty pulled open the door.

Frank peered around the edge and saw a figure in the adjoining hallway. He quickly aimed and pulled the trigger on his rifle four times. The figure in the hallway was just turning around to see who had opened the door when the first round hit them in the right shoulder, spinning them around to face the intruders. Frank's second and third shots hit the female creature in the chest. His fourth bullet blew the top of her head off as she fell. She was dead before the empty shell case hit the floor.

He paused, hearing shouts further in the house. When no one

immediately appeared at the end of the short hallway, he waved Smitty into the house. As they reached the end of the entryway, they swung right, looking for the main rooms. They quickly glanced inside each open doorway they passed and moved on to the next. Looking up in the hallway, they saw two large creatures similar to the horned creature that was leading the guards. They both opened fire as the hulking guards at the same time.

The gunfire was deafening as multiple rounds struck each guard in the torso and head. Frank noticed that rounds would ricochet off their horns, but their bodies were certainly soaking up the bullets. The onslaught of incoming fire kept the guards from drawing their own sidearms and returning fire. Both rifles ran dry, and the two men dropped the empty magazines and slammed fresh ones into the magazine wells. The loud "clack" as the bolts slammed forward and loaded fresh rounds lost among the groan of pain from the two downed guards. Smitty smiled cruelly as he put one more round into each of their faces, ending the moans from these creatures.

Both men heard footsteps running down the halls toward them. Frank tried the handle on the double doors that the creatures were guarding. The handle moved. He quickly motioned to Smitty to get ready, then he threw open both doors.

MILLER and his partner Bill reached the federal agents' truck quickly. They stopped to aim at the windows and Miller saw an agent peer out from behind a partition. Both of the men opened up, firing multiple rounds at the federal agent in the truck.

Miller was shocked to watch the bullets spark and ricochet off the front windshield of the modified bread truck. He was not expecting armor or bullet-proof glass, and he was beginning to get a bad feeling about this attack.

Just as Miller motioned for Bill to go around the other side of the truck, both rear doors sprang open, and the ZT leader watched them swing wide to provide cover. He was trying to figure out what he would do when he heard a rattling roar of a full-auto shotgun. Bill disappeared in a spray of flesh and blood. Staring in horror, the shaken leader of Zero Tolerance almost missed the figure leaping over the truck.

The man tried to raise his rifle as a figure hurled straight up and over the tall DHS truck. He was too slow as the figure landed on the short angle of the hood and then leapt straight at him. He registered the wild flying hair and the diminutive stature as the creature slammed into his chest, driving him to the ground. He never recognized the small fist that hit him in the nose, breaking his nose and driving his head back into the driveway with a solid thump.

WHEN THE EXPLOSIONS had gone off outside the compound, the Queen and her guards had tensed and begun to look around her throne room. The Queen's Knight had quickly walked to the double doors of the receiving hall and had stood in front of them. The Queen's pixie Handmaidens had started flying in a much more randomized pattern, maintaining a menacing bubble about six feet around their Queen.

Ghost nodded to himself when he received the message from Heavy. He turned to the Seelie Queen and bowed, "Your Majesty, my team has informed me that intruders have entered your house. May we defend Your Majesty?"

Her smile seemed sincere, "Jonas Vanhof, we do not need human defense. We would request that your group stays to the side and let our Knight and our Handmaidens do what they will."

The federal agent shrugged and ushered the team over to the side of the room as the rattle of gunfire erupted outside the doors. The hail of gunfire died down, then two individual reports rang out. The handle of the door rattled, then both doors were pushed open.

The doors flew open mere inches from the Knight's nose, but he was already lunging forward with his sword drawn. The man who opened the doors took the blade through the chest as if he was a human kabob.

The Knight's lunge was a classic pose, and the elf held it for a few long seconds while his victim figured out that his life was draining away very quickly. The human on the end of the blade crumpled as the elf withdrew it. Two shots rang out, and the elven warrior stumbled and fell.

The human who shot the Knight rushed into the room and pointed his rifle at the Queen. A cruel smile played over his lips as his finger twitched.

Ghost was not sure what happened next. It would take some time to sort out exactly what he witnessed, and even then he was never really sure. He saw two light trails as the sprites in front of the Queen dove at the intruder. In the span of a thought, several small and large cuts appeared on the intruder's hands, neck and face, and the four fingers and the thumb holding the pistol grip of the rifle were suddenly falling to the ground.

The other four winged creatures blurred toward the intruder, and the attack was suddenly finished. Six light trails whirred briefly around the upper torso of the attacker known as Smitty, and hundreds of cuts opened up all over his face, neck, scalp, arms, and hands. One moment the attacker was pointing his rifle at the queen, and the next moment saw the rifle falling from fingerless hands and an amazing amount of blood flowing from the upper torso of the man called Smitty.

The lifeless body fell to the ground and the pixies once again took up their station around their Queen. The Seelie monarch was concerned with the blood spreading from her Knight, and she ignored the lifeless heap in front of her as she stepped to his side.

Doc quickly stepped out, "I'm a doctor, can I approach to help him, Your Majesty?" The queen nodded.

Realizing the sprites were still on edge, the priest carefully, deliberately went to look at the Knight. As she knelt, she saw the bullet wounds in the right arm and right shoulder of the tall elf. Both wounds were bleeding, and the Tó Coferal was becoming pale.

She quickly donned gloves and then broke out other parts of the first aid kit she was handed. She applied bandages to the elf's shoulder wound first. She placed pressure over the entrance wound and then lifted him slightly. The priest looked and felt for an exit wound. She found it. The bullet had passed clean through the elf's shoulder, and she could patch the holes.

Once the shoulder was bandaged, Doc looked at the arm wound. There was no exit wound that she could find. She realized that the bullet must have struck the bone, and likely broke or fractured the arm. This also absorbed the bullet's energy, not allowing the round to exit from the body. As she watched, the wound started smoking.

She gasped, "The bullet's still in there. His arm feels broken, and the wound is smoking. They must be using steel or iron bullets. You might want to warn the rest of your people, Your Majesty."

She pulled a small scalpel out of her kit and said, "I need several water bottles. If we don't get this soon, he will die."

The Queen pointed to one of the other elves in the room, and they went to fulfill the request. She then motioned for a sprite to approach and spoke to it in a low murmur. It flew off, a blur of light leading out of the door.

The elf attendant soon returned with a case of bottled water and set it down near Doc. Kneeling, the attendant opened the case, opened a bottle of water, and handed it to the priest. She smiled and thanked him. Doc poured the water over the wound to clean it. Finding the small hole, she opened it a bit wider, and stuck two gloved fingers into the small wound. After digging around in the wound for a few long seconds, she found the bullet, and pulled it out, dropping it on the ground beside her.

She dumped more water into the wound to clean it and then looked for any major bleeding. Finding none, she bound the wound, and finished by closing up the elf's arm with some rudimentary stitches. She then bowed her head and muttered a few words in Latin, made the signs of the cross over the wounded elf, and gave a quiet, "Amen." Doc sat up and stretched, sighing as her back and bones creaked. It had only been ten minutes, but it had been a stressful ten minutes.

She stood and turned to the Queen of the Seelie Court, "It is done, Your Majesty. I pulled out the bullet, and it appears to be steel. Your Knight should recover."

The Queen nodded, "Thank you, Doctor Sorenson, for saving my Knight."

"I hate to interrupt, Your Majesty." Ghost cleared his throat. "I need to contact my team outside, and our command center to let them know what is happening. By your leave?" The Queen nodded.

The federal agent slowly reached into his coat and pulled out his SSP. He dialed Heavy's phone first, and the big agent answered on the first ring, "Yea, boss?"

"Sitrep." Ghost heard gunfire in the background.

"Two tangos out here. One DOA, and the other is out cold and in custody. That one's Miller. Tar Katel is mopping up the idiots at the end of the driveway. That minotaur and his guys can sure as hell shoot. None of our guys are hurt, but a couple of the Seelie are down. What's your situation?"

"Much the same. Two tangos DOA. No casualties on our team. A couple Seelie down, and Tó Coferal has been wounded, but Doc patched him up." The DHS team leader began to think about the cleanup. "When the firefight is over, get the Wunder Buggy down to the end of the driveway and intercept any law enforcement. I'll call it in. I'll have the Queen let her people know what you are doing. Call me when the locals have arrived and are blocking off the area."

"Copy that, boss. Talk to you in a few." Heavy hung up.

Ghost looked to the Queen and raised his eyebrow in a silent question. She nodded, summoned another sprite, gave it some instructions, and sent it on its way. The sprite was blurring by him as he dialed Gretchen in the MCC.

Gretchen heard a brief summary and connected to Agent Smith in Langley, bringing him into the call. Ghost filled them in with as much as he knew and received a few instructions about the desired disposition of Mr. Nate Miller. The former monster hunter knew that Boomer would not be happy.

Five minutes later, a worn and dirty Tar Katel knocked and entered the receiving room, his large rifle slung over his shoulder. The big creature was frowning, and its scowl deepened when it saw the Knight propped up in a chair, with bandages around his shoulder and arm.

Following close behind the large creature was another pair of minotaur, dragging a man along between them. The minotaurs were dirty from the fighting and carried rifles slung over their backs. The man hung limp between them. His face was crusted with dried blood, and his eyes were already turning black and blue from bruising.

Boomer and Dancer brought up the rear of the procession. Boomer had no visible weapons on her, but her BDUs were filthy. Dancer had her submachine gun slung over her shoulder and both women had a grim, almost angry, look clouding their faces, and Boomer kept staring at the man being drug into the chambers.

Tar Katel bowed before his Queen. "My Liege. Our forces have defended the compound. The human Signatories helped us greatly and acquitted themselves well in battle. All the perpetrators have been found, and have been eliminated, except for this one we bring before you. He was the leader of this contemptible lot, and we bring him before you so that he may answer for this assault."

The Queen nodded and looked at the two women behind him. "Thank you, Tar Katel. Today you have brought honor among you and yours. And who are the guests behind you?"

Boomer stepped forward, with Dancer just half a step behind her. "Special Agent Rebekah Callahan, Your Majesty, and this is my protégé Special Agent Hannah Sedano. We work for Special Agent Vanhof, Your Majesty."

The Queen looked at Boomer closely. There was something that was just a little... off about the young agent. She opened herself up to the power of the earth, and she realized what she was sensing. Her eyes widened in shock, and she let out a small gasp.

The Queen turned to Ghost, "Special Agent Jonas Vanhof, you did not tell me that you had a member of your team who was infected and turned. How extraordinary. I am surprised that she is still on your team. You continue to amaze me, Special Agent Vanhof."

Ghost stepped forward, "We certainly did not mean to deceive you, Your Majesty. The subject was never raised, and we have had more pressing issues to work out."

"I agree, Agent Vanhof. And no offense was taken. It is unusual for humans to shock me, and the novelty is all I was commenting about.

"And what do we do with this person who dared to attack our Court?" The Queen wondered aloud. "Wake him up to see if he will answer."

One of the minotaur guards reached over and grabbed one of the full water bottles that Doc had been using to clean wounds. He ripped off the cap and emptied the whole bottle over the prisoner's head. The prisoner sputtered and looked around groggily.

The Queen straightened in her chair, looking more beautiful and regal than ever. "I am Lishe ta Merunaré, Queen of the Seelie Court, Ruler of the Light Fae, and Heiress to the Throne of Light on *Álfheimer*. You have attacked our sovereignty. How do you plead?"

Miller looked around at those standing around him. He looked at the assembled fae around him. He glared at the federal agents standing to his right. He then straightened and responded to the Queen, "I am Nate Miller. I am a citizen of the United States of America, and do not recognize your court, or your authority to exist in this country. And I denounce the cowardice of the federal government whose agents stand idly by while their citizens are killed by unnatural creatures."

The Queen's shifted. Cold as ice and hard as diamonds, she proclaimed, "As humanity is a recognized Signatory of the *E'Tuatha* Accords, the Accords provide for the full legality for our existence. They also provide for the legality for our method of handling attacks on our sovereignty. Therefore, with no defense given, I pronounce guilty. You will be summarily be executed for making war on the Seelie Court."

Doc gasped, and Boomer shouted, "No!"

The Queen looked at the demolitions expert, and she hastily amended her response. "Your Majesty, I do not disagree with your legality or verdict, but I have prior blood claim on this piece of trash. He tortured my protégé and I. He personally directed his goons to do so, and I swore an oath to repay the violence."

Boomer's thoughts raced as she continued, "Your Majesty, I

request two favors. First, I would like to be able to question the prisoner. He has knowledge about traitors in our own organization, and we would like to get that information from him. Second, I would like the honor of personally carrying out his sentence."

The Queen gave a small cold smile. She nodded and spoke, "As you have served our Court honorably in bringing this being before us, I will grant you this boon. You will be able to question the prisoner for the information he possesses. You will then personally carry out his sentence as you see fit, immediately."

"Thank you, Your Majesty." The vampire turned to Miller, who was staring at her in horror. "So Mister Miller, let's find out what you know."

The man's face blanched as Boomer grinned a mouthful of fangs.

III

TRIALS

21

ACCUSATIONS

Gerald R. Ford International Airport

Nine o'clock in the morning came early to team Knightmare. The team could not leave the Seelie Court until four o'clock that morning. Ghost and SAC Lewis had argued with the locals for two hours before Ghost had called Agent Smith. Agent Smith had then called the Chief of Police and the County Sheriff directly and had explained that DHS would investigate the events that transpired. Everything about that incident had been classified Top Secret, and the respective departments would receive appropriately redacted reports for their files.

Once the jurisdiction question had been settled, SAC Lewis had demanded that Ghost explain why there was a major operation in the city that involved explosions and gunfire, and why neither he nor his men could interview any of the witnesses.

"Do you remember the conversation that Gretchen had with you on the plane?" Ghost had asked.

"Of course. But how does that apply to a major terror incident here?"

"You don't have the clearance to even ask the right questions, let alone be told the truth." Ghost had paused. "Listen, you know the classifications for closing DHS cases, right? 'Case Closed: No Charges Recommended' and the others?"

Lewis had nodded his head, wondering where the conversation had been headed.

The federal monster hunter had continued, "We tend to focus on Top Secret cases that usually end with 'Case Closed: Suspect Detained, Guantanamo' or 'Case Closed: Suspect Deceased'."

The Detroit-based SAC had paused at that. Shaking his head, he had grunted an acknowledgment, "Fine. I'm really starting to feel like a mushroom on this one. What do you want my team to do?"

Ghost had directed the SAC to deploy his men to the perimeters and collect any evidence they stumbled across. He had also asked the SAC to coordinate with the locals to recover the bombers' vehicles and evidence. That had been around eight o'clock the prior evening.

By the time the team had been finished with the initial scene cleanup and sorting, it had been 4am. The team had wearily ridden back to the MCC to sleep for a few hours. Gretchen had awakened them just before nine and told them of a debrief conference call with Agent Smith at ten o'clock.

The timing gave the team an opportunity to clean themselves up and get ready for the new day. As he was dressing, Ghost looked at his SSP and realized that he had a text from the Queen's Knight. Tó Coferal said the council meeting was scheduled for 1pm that afternoon and then gave the address.

The team leader grunted and finished dressing. He arrived in the conference room in enough time to snag a couple of the provided donuts and a large mug of coffee. He looked around and noticed that only Spooky was missing. "Did anyone wake up Spooky?"

Gretchen shook her head, "I forgot. I'll go wake him up." She made as if to rise.

Heavy held out his hand, "Forget it, Gretchen. It will be my pleasure to wake him up." The mischievous grin on his face showed his intentions.

Heavy stood up and walked out of the conference room. He popped his head back in, "Hey, Boomer. Does that thing have a car alarm on it?" After receiving a shake of her head, he grinned and said, "Good."

The big heavy weapons specialist went to the extensive weapon locker on the MCC and opened it. He reached in and selected a specialty grenade that Norbert had designed for him to use in the field. This would be a perfect time to use it.

Heavy walked down the ramp and waved 'hello' to the DHS

guards watching the perimeter then raised a finger to his lips, urging them to be quiet. He casually strolled up to the passenger door of the Wunder Buggy and keyed the door locks on the fob. The big man carefully, silently opened the door and leaned in. At his console, Spooky was leaned back in his chair, noise-canceling head-phones on, and snoring loudly. Suppressing a giggle, Heavy pushed aside a cover and mashed a button on the top of the grenade. He set the grenade down gently at Spooky's feet and closed the door.

Stepping back, he waited the long seven seconds for the internal timer to countdown. A loud boom was muffled by the steel in the truck's armor and the interior started to fill with a white acrid smoke. Muffled cursing came from inside the truck, and Heavy started to laugh. The door was flung open, and a bedraggled, stunned, and coughing Spooky stumbled down. The tears of laughter streaming down Heavy's face matched the tears flowing from Spooky from the CS gas now billowing out of the open door. Heavy was doubled over with laughter, holding his stomach.

Spooky sputtered and cursed, his creative use of foul adjectives interrupted by hacking coughs. He looked up through tear-streaked eyes and saw the big gunner almost on his knees, laughing. Hearing more laughter, the electronics specialist looked at the surrounding tarmac. Both DHS guards were trying not to laugh, and both were failing. At the top of the stairs into the MCC stood the rest of Knightmare. Every one of his teammates were laughing, and even Gretchen was trying hard not to laugh.

A few minutes later, the laughter was mostly gone, and the mood had lightened considerably. Boomer braved the CS gas from the grenade and started up the internal air circulation. It would take some time, but eventually the air would be cleared from the gas. She coughed a bit as she came out of the truck, "Heavy, if there's CS crap all over, you get to clean it up."

"Hell, yeah," was his deep base reply. The big fed smiled, "Totally worth it."

At ten o'clock sharp, Agent Smith connected through the video conference system. All the team was in the conference room, with Spooky in clean, non-CS-covered BDUs. Everyone grew quiet as the face of their boss showed on the screen.

"Good morning, everyone. I understand it was a late night. Let's talk about what happened. Ghost?"

Ghost recounted the events of the previous day. Beginning with the Seelie Court presentation, the leader worked through the events leading up to the attack on the Court and the team. Through it all,

Smith gave noncommittal sounds, simply absorbing the story and asking very few questions. Ghost had given enough debriefings to know what information his boss was looking for. When the monster hunter recounted the Queen's judgement, however, Smith seemed to pay more attention.

"Mister Vanhof, what is the final disposition of this Nate Miller?"

Ghost paled slightly, remembering the scene. "Sir, Nate Miller will never bother another human or fae again. His judgement was carried out within minutes of the judgement."

"Were you able to question Miller about his source inside our organization?"

Ghost shrugged. "Some. I was able to ask a few questions during the early part of his...judgement. He told us that he never knew the actual person inside Section Twenty-Eight. Miller said that he had just been sent the burner phone, with instructions on how to dump it. He claimed he got the phone three months ago, right about the time he formed Zero Tolerance."

Agent Smith looked thoughtful and then began to work on the keyboard in front of him. After a few seconds, he looked up, "So, what did happen to Miller? What did the Seelie do?"

Ghost blanched and looked at Boomer. She straightened up and looked at the image of her boss, "I informed the Queen of his history with Hannah and I, and she took compassion on me. The last time I had seen him, I had promised that bastard that I would eat him slowly, causing him unimaginable pain. I was able to keep my promise to him."

Agent Smith blinked. Multiple times. Time seemed to slow to a crawl as the team waited for him to respond. "I see. And how are you this morning, Miss Callahan? You have now eaten three humans in less than twelve hours. Are you still with us?"

Boomer nodded, "I feel fine. In fact, I have more energy today than I've had in a long time. I'd say that eating bad guys agrees with my digestion. I know, you were asking about my *geas*. Still seems to be there. I don't want to go out and commit murder. I want to do the right thing, but sometimes that right thing is going to be to eat a bad guy."

Smith was nodding along and taking notes. He glanced up, "Mister Vanhof, has she maintained control over her monster?"

"Sure, boss. She was totally in control last night, and I told you that she stopped immediately when we rescued her from the first two. Last night, I watched specifically for any slip in control. She was perfectly aware last night—monster and all. She was brutal, but the guy did torture her. Hell, she probably let him die too quickly, but the Queen was getting impatient."

"Thank you, Mister Vanhof. Miss Callahan, I understand what you did last night, and why you did it. I'd rather not see torture fall into our repertoire, however, last night was an acceptable aberration."

"Yes, sir."

"Good. Captaen O'Beirne, do you have anything else to add to the events from last night?"

The man's Irish accent was thick, "No, Agent Smith. I do believe your Mister Vanhof covered the events well enough. Anything he left out is not worth mentioning."

"And your opinion of the treatment of Miller?"

The Irishman paused and thought. Taking a deep breath, he said, "I just don't know, Agent Smith. I could not tell how Her Majesty reacted to Miss Callahan's feeding. I know some of the attendants fainted, but I also know there were a few who looked on with perhaps a little too much attention."

"Her Majesty was impressed by your team overall, though. The way they acquitted themselves in the firefight only enhanced her feelings toward them from the investigation. As of right now, I'd say your team ranks higher than any other human team she's met. Except, maybe, for your own team."

Agent Smith nodded, "That is good, then. Mister Vanhof, when are you supposed to be meeting with the *Seanachaidh*?"

Ghost checked his watch. "In about two hours, boss. We are scheduled to meet at the Gray Court at one."

Smith looked at his computer monitor, "Ok. Let's talk about what's going to happen with the process."

———

THE SIGN out front read "Gray Arbitration" in small white letters on a black background. Boomer eased the Wunder Buggy into the parking lot and parked off to the north side of the building. Team Knightmare disembarked from the truck as a newer model Bentley Flying Spur sedan pulled into the lot. Already parked in the lot were two Porsche Cayenne SUVs.

Heavy let out a low whistle. The big man's voice barely rumbled, "Lotta money sitting in this parking lot. I'm not sure our truck is the most expensive one on the lot."

Ghost grunted his assent and looked to make sure everyone was present, and presentable. The summons had requested all the members of Knightmare be present, plus Captaen O'Beirne. With the monster hunter leading, the team walked up to the doors and entered the building.

The waiting area was very richly appointed, with expensive-looking leather chairs and rich hardwood flooring. A young woman occupied the receptionist desk in the far corner. Smiling, the woman said, "Welcome to Gray Arbitration. The arbitration specialists will be out to receive you soon. In the meantime, my name is Wendy. Is there anything I can get for you while you wait?"

The DHS team leader returned the woman's smile, "No thank you, Wendy. We'll be fine."

Four minutes later, the thick oak door set in the far wall opened and a very short man entered. Ghost noted that the man's suit was very expensive as it must have been custom tailored for the man's stature, and the large automatic in the shoulder holster under the jacket. A full beard was the only hair on the man's head, and Ghost finally noticed the slightly misshapen ears of a dwarf.

"Ladies and gentlemen, I welcome you to Gray Arbitration." The dwarf's voice was almost as deep as Heavy's, with more gravel in the throat and pronunciation. "If you would follow me, I will lead you back to the conference room."

The team followed the creature through the door and down a well-decorated corridor. A door was open at the far end of the corridor, and Tó Coferal stood waiting for the team to enter. The Queen's Knight greeted each of the members warmly, clasping forearms with the men and bowing slightly to Doc, Boomer, and Dancer.

Knightmare entered the large conference room dominated by a huge mahogany table. Already seated at the table were the Queen and her staff, minus her Knight. Standing at the far end of the room and conference table were four dwarves in custom-tailored Armani suits.

Two of the dwarves wore the ceremonial sash of the *khozten* across their torso. One of the *khozten* stepped forward and cleared his throat, "Welcome, guests. I am Oracle Telacus Sturmwargh, and my companion is Scholar Eraste Thrughar, who will act as Arbiter and Judge for today's meeting." The woman next to Oracle Sturmwargh bowed slightly and smiled, her bald head showing ritual tattooing.

Next to the Oracle of the *Khozten*, the other two dwarves had ornamental sword-pins on their lapels. The *khoztak* directly next to the Oracle stepped forward. The topknot in the middle of her head was the center for the intricate tattoo pattern over her skull. Ghost recognized the Praetorian as she began to talk.

"Welcome honored guests and honored warriors. I am Praetorian Urteghat Dhorjachen, of Clan Frostwind. My companion is Protector Dhaviha Chrechank, also of Clan Frostwind. He will be the Protector for this meeting."

Ghost bowed slightly to both, then gave a small bow to the Queen and muttered, "Your Majesty."

Ghost stood and gestured to his team behind him, introducing each member with their title and name. At each introduction, Both the Oracle and the Praetorian bowed slightly and said, "Well met."

As The DHS leader introduced Boomer, there was a sharp intake of breath and a frown from the Praetorian. "Special Agent Vanhof, I must protest. There was no mention of you having a tainted creature on your team. How can we trust you when you harbor such a creature?"

Ghost blinked, trying to comprehend. "Praetorian Dhorjachen, I personally apologize that we did not mention Special Agent Callahan's affliction. She was a valued member of my team before she was infected, and she is an invaluable member now. Her monster is under external controls that you likely know about. As a designated Representative of a Signatory nation, I personally vouch for her here at the *Seanachaidh*."

The Praetorian took a moment to look closely at the young demolitions expert, and Boomer was becoming embarrassed at the attention of the stern-looking dwarf. The Praetorian finally nodded. "I do know of those controls, as I helped your Agent Smith originally craft those controls. If she is truly still bound by the *geas* and you are willing to vouch for her, she will be accepted."

Ghost continued introducing the team, and was once again interrupted when he introduced their junior member, Dancer.

Again the Praetorian's eyes widened, and her voice quivered and softened, "My apologies, Special Agent Sedano. I had not realized that Vellath had chosen someone again. Would you tell him that Urteghat Dhorjachen bids him well?"

22

INQUIRY

Gray Court, Roger B. Chaffee Memorial Blvd SE, Grand Rapids, Michigan

A ll eyes turned to Dancer, and the young woman blushed self consciously. The Oracle gazed at her with an intense concentration, and the Queen did likewise. Dancer heard the deep rumble of her companion in her mind, *Thank her for me, dear.* He sounded pleased.

"Vellath thanks you," the young woman said with hesitation. "I'm sorry, was I not supposed to bring this?" She jerked a thumb at her empty shoulder.

All of her teammates were staring at her, and Boomer was hiding a small smile. She had been there when *fion-fhuil* had chosen her protégé.

Spooky reached up and clicked a button on his goggle-like glasses, and a series of lenses clicked down over his primary lenses. He saw the ghostly outline of a sword. "Damn," he muttered. "How did I miss that?"

Dancer ignored the electronics specialist and spoke to the Praetorian, "Is it all right if I have him with me? I never even thought about leaving him behind"

The dwarf shook her head, making her topknot fly. "It was perfectly fine for you to bring Uncorruptible. We never laid claim to an unarmed meeting. I apologize for embarrassing you, but I

was surprised that the dragon chose another champion, and more
so that it was one as young as you. Vellath must see something in
you."

Dancer blushed, the pink burning through her normally tan
skin.

Praetorian Dhorjachen nodded at Callum O'Beirne. "And we
are familiar with Captaen O'Beirne." She turned to Ghost, "Is that
your entire party?"

The DHS team leader nodded, and the Praetorian gestured for
them to take seats around the conference table. The Oracle then
stood and began the meeting.

"Honored guests, we are here to discuss a charge that Her
Majesty Lishe ta Merunaré, Queen of the Seelie Court, is bringing
against the Unseelie. We are here to determine if there is enough
evidence to call a formal Court Inquiry. And if there is enough
evidence for the Inquiry, to schedule the Court Inquiry with the
Unseelie. Your Majesty?"

The Queen's calm exterior was marred by the anger in her eyes.
"Oracle and Arbiter. We come to the Keepers to right a grave injus-
tice. Our people and our property were viciously attacked by
members of the Unseelie Court, and they then committed the
despicable act of trying to frame another *E'Tuatha* Accords Signatory to avoid detection and retaliation. Unanswered, this attack will
constitute an act of war between the Courts."

The Arbiter was studiously taking notes, and he looked up at the
end of her statement. "And you have proof of these accusations?
Who is the other Signatory?"

The Queen thoughtfully responded, "The other Signatory is
humanity, in this case, specifically represented by Special Agent
Vanhof and his team, as well as Captaen O'Beirne. They responded
and investigated the attack. It is their findings that direct blame at
the Unseelie Court."

The Arbiter looked at Ghost, "Is that true, Special Agent
Vanhof?" After receiving a nod from the man, he continued, "And
do you have this proof with you today, for this Inquiry?"

Ghost smiled and gestured toward Spooky and Doc, "Yes,
Arbiter. We have brought the evidence with us, and the Agents who
procured the evidence are present, as well."

The Arbiter wrote more notes and then looked up Ghost. "Call
your first witness, please."

Doc stood and walked to the empty head of the table. The
Arbiter held up a small yellow cord that had a loop with a slipknot

in it. He asked for the priest's right hand, but she held back and asked what it was.

The Arbiter looked offended. "Doctor... Sorenson, is it? This is the *Aidmheil*. Roughly translated, this is the Confession or Declaration. The *Aidmheil* will make sure that you tell the truth while you are talking. At least as you perceive it to be. If you tell a falsehood, it will flash or light up, with the brightness correlating to how far from the truth you stray. It does not influence your story, it merely ensures its veracity."

The priest nodded and held out her arm. The Arbiter gently looped the cord over her wrist and tightened it to a light contact. She looked at the cord and then began her presentation.

Doc worked her way through the evidence from start to finish as she had in front of the Queen. Covering her initial impressions of the scene, then presenting the physical evidence. Shell casings, photos of boot prints, and recovered bullets were all presented, and she offered explanations for her conclusions.

When she was finished, she looked at the Arbiter and the Oracle, "Do you have any questions for me?"

The Arbiter looked at her notes, conferred with the Oracle, and asked one question, "Have you been able to determine the manufacture of the weapons used in the attack?"

Doc looked at Ghost, and he nodded. She answered, "We have. Part of the weapons used were human in origin, including a nine millimeter semi-automatic or automatic, and a thirty-eight caliber revolver. Part of the shells collected were not of human origin. I believe they were identified by Tar Katel, as *khoztak* manufacture. I believe one was identified as a Forge Warblade Mark Two. The other one is of similar manufacture."

The priest took a breath and continued, "This is one of the reasons we believe that the perpetrators had to be of fae origin. Only the fae, and their close allies have access to those weapons. "

The Arbiter nodded, made a few more notes, and asked, "Is there anything else you want to tell us, Doctor Sorenson? No? Then will the next witness present their evidence?"

Doc sat down as Spooky stood and approached the end of the table. He placed his laptop on the table in front of him and connected it to the provided display wires. Once it was powered up and ready, he looked up at the rest of the room.

The Arbiter motioned for Spooky to come closer, and the dwarf placed the *Aidmheil* around his wrist. The analyst looked apprehensive, but he did not shrink away. Consciously leaving the cord alone, he looked at the Arbiter for permission to begin. The dwarf nodded at him, and Spooky recounted his evidence.

It took the former NSA analyst about forty minutes to walk the Gray Court through his findings. He first showed the damning video showing a human police unit brutally slaughtering the fae in the club. Spooky then described his search for exterior video, and the results of his search. He then showed the recovered, actual video from the attack that night. It clearly showed the fae attacking the club. Like Doc, Spooky ended his presentation and asked the Arbiter if he had questions.

The Arbiter looked at the *khoztak* dwarves. "Praetorian Dhor-jachen, is it possible to identify the fae in the second video? Are they truly from the Unseelie, or are they unaffiliated?"

The Praetorian asked Spooky to replay the video, pausing it several times. At the end she nodded, more to herself, than to anyone else. "Yes, I can identify at least five that are directly connected to the Unseelie Court. Three of the others are usually peripherally connected to the Court, and then there is Oude Rode Ogen. His presence is an ominous sign. If he has truly signed with the Unseelie...." The Praetorian shook her head as she trailed away.

"Special Agent Smith," the Arbiter shifted her focus to the analyst. "Are you convinced that the video you recovered is the true narrative, and that it was not planted by any other parties?"

Spooky thoughtfully considered for a moment, and then answered, "I am firmly convinced that this video that identifies the Unseelie Court is the correct video from that night."

"Thank you, Agent Smith. I believe that is all the information I will require." She looked around the room. "Is there any other relevant information regarding the initial charge? Does anyone have anything to add?" Heads shaking negatively all around the table met her questioning gaze.

"Then I will take a moment and confer with the Oracle and the Praetorian. I will be back with my decision momentarily." The Arbiter stood and walked out the door, followed closely by the Oracle and the Praetorian. The Protector folded his arms and blocked the door after them.

Spooky packed away his laptop and other electronics while they waited. Ghost talked to the Queen about her cleanup efforts from the previous night's attack, assuring Her Majesty that Section 28 would help with the matters outside the Seelie compound. They were discussing logistics with Tó Coferal, the Queen's Knight when someone knocked twice on the door into the conference room.

The Protector turned and opened the door, admitting the three who left to confer. The Arbiter once again sat in her seat, and the Oracle and the Praetorian stood behind her, the latter with a grim look on her face and her arms folded tightly across her chest.

"After listening to testimony and reviewing the evidence in question," the Arbiter began, "I have decided regarding this matter. As Arbiter of this Inquiry, under the authority of the Oracle of the *Seanachaidh*, I now declare judgement in this Inquiry." She looked at a sheaf of paperwork in her hands and read.

"I find there is sufficient evidence to call a Tribunal. The Tribunal will charge the Unseelie Court with participating and orchestrating this attack on Seelie grounds, in the territory of the Human Signatory Section Twenty-Eight. The Tribunal shall be held tomorrow night at midnight, at the *Seanachaidh* compound designated. The *Seanachaidh* will contact the Unseelie and inform them of the time and of their required attendance."

The Arbiter looked around the table, making sure to catch each participant's eye. "Each of you is charged to be at the Tribunal, as your testimony may be called on. Will this be a problem for anyone?"

Ghost looked at Captaen O'Beirne and raised a questioning eyebrow. O'Beirne spoke up, "No, Arbiter. I will vouch for Humanity. We will be present as required by the Tribunal as a Concerned Signatory."

The Queen echoed the Irishman's sentiments, "No, Arbiter. I will vouch for the Seelie. We, too, shall be present as required by the Tribunal as a Concerned Signatory."

"Then we shall convene the Tribunal tomorrow night at the appointed time and place. If you need any special accommodations, please inform myself or the Protector. Until tomorrow night."

The Arbiter stood and walked out. The Oracle and the Praetorian had a brief discussion with the Protector, then left the room as well. The Protector stood at the end of the table and announced, "Thank you for your presence at the Inquiry. For the Tribunal, you are advised to keep weaponry to a minimum. While the Tribunal will not take notice of blades or hand weapons, rifles or heavy weapons will be officially noticed, and may result in Official Sanction. For the safety of the Tribunal, I will have a team of Protectors present. Are there any questions?"

"No, Protector. Thank you for your service and for the warning." Ghost turned and raised an eyebrow at Heavy.

"What, boss? I got it. No boomstick." The others laughed at the big man's sheepish grin.

THAT NIGHT WAS a quiet night as the team strategized and planned for the coming Tribunal. Spooky, Boomer, and Heavy worked through the files of the known members of the Unseelie Court, concentrating on their weaknesses and suspected special abilities. Meanwhile, Ghost and Doc worked with Captaen O'Beirne and Gretchen on the protocols and customs of the Tribunal.

The next morning was another casual meeting and strategy session for that night. Agent Smith joined in a video conference with the team, talking some about his recent history with the courts, and what he personally knew of both the Queen of the Seelie and the King of the Unseelie.

The DHS supervisor warned his agents to be constantly aware of what was going on around them. Agent Smith told of experiences with both courts where the traditional enmities between them caused the courts to give up favorable terms to humanity, simply to spite the other court.

Agent Smith also reiterated that the team should listen to Captaen O'Beirne, as he had a great deal of experience working directly with the courts. O'Beirne would be an invaluable resource for protocol and custom, and a capable advisor during the Tribunal. Smith ended the call with "Good Luck, Knightmare. I trust you will represent Section Twenty-Eight and humanity well." The senior agent closed the video conference, and the team began to prep for the day.

At half-past eleven that evening, the Wunder Buggy pulled into the parking lot of a company that made fine art decorations for houses. When Spooky had done his research on the meeting place, he had simply grinned and had pointed out the company information to the others. What better way for fine craftsmen to hide their presence than to own a fine woodworking and metalworking plant in the industrial part of town.

The Wunder Buggy was in its base configuration, a flat black paint job with no external markings or anything to break up the metal. Boomer brought the truck to a halt just inside the parking lot to speak to the guard on duty. When Ghost showed his credentials to the guard, Boomer was directed around the back of the building, to a different parking lot. As they pulled away, the demolitions expert mused out loud, "Did you see the ears underneath that hat. Looks like the human guards have the night off."

Boomer was directed to park in a specific location by another, less-human-looking guard. As she shut down the big V-8, Knightmare piled out of the truck. On Smith and O'Beirne's recommendation everyone was in their assault BDUs, except for Doc, Ghost, and Captaen O'Beirne. Leaving their long-guns in the truck, each team member was wearing their handgun, and Heavy was wearing the harnesses with his two enchanted khukuri fighting knives. Dancer had *fion-fhuil* strapped to her back as well, although none of her team could see it.

Doc wore her typical suit, with her stole and vestments plainly visible over her shoulders. She carried her crucifix dagger on its chain around her neck and carried one of her books in her right hand. She was muttering prayers as she climbed out, and her vestments glowed a brief soft blue, then went dark.

Ghost stepped out just before Boomer. His scarred and worn leather duster covered his standard black button-down shirt and black jeans, and his bolero rode smartly upon his head. He clutched his ancestral cane in his right hand, and his old Webley rode low on his hip.

The Irish Captaen wore his full dress uniform, with medals polished and gleaming against the olive drab coat. The Captaen's peaked hat rested across his brows at regulation angle, and he wore his ceremonial saber at his side. Other than the saber, the Captaen was unarmed, enforcing his observer status. Ghost had argued that the Irish officer should have been armed with at least a handgun, but the Captaen had made clear that the protocol was for him to be unarmed.

The group walked to the doorway where a uniformed dwarf stood with a very large rifle slung over his shoulder. Ghost raised his credentials, "Special Agent Jonas Vanhof, and party, representing Section Twenty-Eight and Humanity as witnesses called before the Tribunal." He had rehearsed that line often with O'Beirne's coaching.

The *khoztak* stiffened and nodded. "Special Agent Vanhof. You and your party are expected and welcomed with *Seanachaidh* Hospitality. I am Protector Koragan, and I will be at your service this evening."

The Protector eyed the group and spotted the satchel slung over Spooky's shoulder. "I apologize for the inconvenience, but I must inspect your companion's bag. Tribunal orders."

Ghost nodded, and Spooky held the bag open. Once the Protector was satisfied that there was nothing dangerous in the bag, he turned and led them into the building.

The cramped hallway emptied into a large open warehouse area. In the center, a raised platform and podium had been built. There were four areas of seating in front of the platform, and one table with several seats off to the side.

A handful of dwarves walked around the assembled crowd of fae creatures. Some carried trays of small snacks or drinks while others carried paperwork back and forth. Ghost saw the Seelie Queen and her court placed in one of the seating areas, acknowledging Tó Coferal's wave with a nod. Another seating area had a group of *khoztak* and *khozten* milling around the waiting chairs. It was this group that drew the greatest concentration of the runners moving paperwork back and forth. Their Protector guided them to the section just to the right of the Seelie, and the team found seats.

As Ghost sat down, a resounding clang echoed throughout the building and the crowd murmured. The DHS leader looked up and watched as the Unseelie King strolled through a different entryway, followed by his retinue.

23

JUDGEMENT

Gray Court Hall, Broadway Ave SW, Grand Rapids, Michigan

His Majesty Arkanai t'Nakaót strode through the open doorway, followed closely by his retinue. The King of the Unseelie Court drew the attention of the room in a black William Westmancott suit. His black and gray hair was perfectly styled, and his eyes were hidden behind Bentley Platinum sunglasses. His presence spoke of modern royalty.

Another *draukh* elf followed his king through the doorway. While his suit was clearly not as expensive as his liege's attire, it was obviously tailored for the tall elf. With dark black skin and gray hair of his race, the creature was also wearing an ornate sash similar in design to Tó Coferal's. A saber hung in its scabbard where the sash connected to the elf's belt, Unlike the ornate design of the Seelie Knight's sword and sheath, the handle was leather-wrapped brass, and the scabbard was a plain brass sheath.

Trailing the Unseelie King, four large trolls rumbled into view. Each wore simple tribal clothing and carried a monstrous warhammer. A tall figure in a black ceremonial robe followed the trolls, remaining by the doorway as the others entered the great hall. A cowl cloaked the being's face in shadow, although two red embers seemed to appear in the darkness.

As the rest of his retinue made their way toward their traditional seating area, the King and his Knight strode to the Seelie Court.

There he stopped and made a slight bow, holding out his hand. The Queen took his hand lightly, and the King raised it to his lips for a soft kiss. He stood straight again.

"Good evening, my Queen. I'm glad to see that you are well after the terrible attack of the human scourge on your Court. Two attacks in one week?" He raised his voice enough to just be heard by the Section 28 team, "It is a shame those humans are starting to get delusions of grandeur. Maybe we ought to rid ourselves of them once and for all."

The King turned and looked at Ghost, "Present company excluded, of course." The elf's voice was syrupy-sweet and smooth as silk. A small smile briefly touched his lips as he turned back to the Queen.

Anger danced in the eyes of the Queen. She willed her voice to remain calm and light. "Well, my King, that is apparently why the *Seanachaidh* have called this Tribunal. I'm sure the parties responsible will be dealt with."

Worry crossed the King's face momentarily and his smile slipped. The Unseelie elf quickly regained his composure, "Of course, my dear Queen. It will be good to hold the humans responsible for once."

The King bowed and turned back to Ghost. "I apologize, we've never been properly introduced. I am Arkanai t'Nakaót, King of the Unseelie Court and *Àrd-`righ* of the *Draukh*. And this is my Knight, Ukonan Ortá."

Ghost bowed slightly, "Well met, your Majesty. I am Special Agent Jonas Vanhof, of Section Twenty-Eight. This is my second, Doctor Noelle Sorenson."

The King of the Unseelie nodded at Doc, who bowed slightly in response. "Well met, Agent Vanhof, Doctor Sorenson. I look forward to discussing your human response after the Tribunal." The condescending smile and tone was back for the King.

As the *draukh* walked away, Ghost muttered under his breath, "We'll see, you smarmy, self-righteous bastard."

A bell sounded, and the assembled representatives quickly found their seats. Once everyone was seated, an all-but-hidden door opened from the far wall, and four dwarves entered the hall. Telacus Sturmwargh, the *Khozten* Oracle, led the procession, his ornate robes and draped stole proclaiming his status. To the Oracle's right, and slightly behind him strode Urteghat Dhorjachen, Praetorian of the *Khoztak*. Her eyes were constantly roving the crowd, alert for any danger. The Praetorian's badge of office was attached to her ceremonial sash, and twin blades hung in scabbards from her belt.

Behind the Oracle and Praetorian, two more dwarves walked side-by-side. Ghost recognized The Protector and the Arbiter from their Inquiry the day before. The Arbiter wore the stole of her office, draped with both ends touching the floor. She also carried a small, ornate box between his hands. The Protector wore a similar badge and sash as the Praetorian, however he only had one blade attached to his belt.

The Praetorian stepped up to the podium in the center of the platform and paused. She took a breath and began. "According to the Law of *Álfheimer*, homeland of the Courts, and as is required by the *E'Tuatha* Accords, this Tribunal is convened at the order of the *Seanachaidh*. This Tribunal is in response to an Inquiry from yesterday afternoon. As Praetorian of the *Seanachaidh*, I hereby call this Tribunal to order." She walked back to her designated chair and sat.

The Oracle rose and stepped up to the podium. Both the Praetorian's voice and the Oracle's voice resonated around the hall, and Ghost could not tell if it was magic or hidden electronics. "As Oracle of the *Seanachaidh*, I agreed to bring an Inquiry yesterday afternoon at the request of Her Majesty, Queen of the Seelie Court. For that Inquiry, and subsequently for this Tribunal, I have appointed Eraste Thrughar, Scholar and Conclave Member as Arbiter of the proceedings. As required by the Accords, Praetorian Dhorjachen has appointed Dhaviha Chrechank as Protector for the proceedings." The Oracle turned and walked slowly, deliberately to his place on the platform.

The Arbiter rose and approached the podium. As she did, two *khoztak* assistants walked up the aisle with a small table held between them. The two dwarves placed the table next to the podium and retreated. The Arbiter carefully placed the ornate box on the table next to the podium and stood before the assembled creatures.

"Assembled Courts. Signatory Representatives. I am Arbiter Eraste Thrughar and attest that my statements during this Tribunal are factual and accurate." She leaned over and opened the lid of the box. She touched two hidden controls on the podium and the overhead lights dimmed to about half of their illumination.

"Yesterday, I convened an Inquiry at the behest of Her Majesty Lishe ta Merunaré, Queen of the Seelie Court. Signatory Representatives of Humanity were also present as material witnesses. The Inquiry was called to discuss an attack on fae and property under the control of the Seelie Court. The attack was particularly egregious, and was reported to be of human origin."

The Arbiter drew a small controller out of her robes and pushed a button. In the air, above the box, several beams of light shot out, angled toward the ceiling. The lines moved quickly around, rotated, and then became a blur. Above the box, a view appeared, the flat, two-dimensional view of a security camera in the club.

Spooky recognized the view from the footage that he recovered from the scene, the fake footage. He was more interested in the amazing holographic projection from the little box. The electronics specialist touched his wrist computer, opening the screen, and making a note to talk to the Arbiter once they had finished this current mission. He was already thinking about how he could use that technology, and what he could develop further with it.

The Arbiter touched another control, and the video began. The video showed the carnage as the group of human police and SWAT raided the club, killing the assembled fae with a ruthlessness and ferocity seldom witnessed on the battlefield. Automatic fire mixed with slashing blades to injure or kill the fae in the club. Then the perpetrators went back through the club, coldly killing any survivors.

As the video played through, Ghost could hear murmurs and menacing tones from those in the chamber who had not already seen the footage. Seeing it up on the platform, Ghost appreciated how this would have caused a war with the fae had it been real. He was just hoping that those assembled would wait long enough to let the Arbiter play the real footage taken that night. A quick glance around told him even the stoic Protectors were being affected.

As he glanced around, he noticed the King of the Unseelie. Knowing it was actually Unseelie killing the fae in the club, the *draukh* tried to hide his smile as the Seelie were killed. He leaned over to his Knight and said something, the latter trying to hide a chuckle in response. Ghost noted the behavior and wished he had more than his family's heirloom with him. He wanted to wipe the smile right off that face.

When the video ended, the murmurs turned into angry voices, rising as the energy built. The Arbiter raised her hands, and the noise subsided. The Unseelie King rose and shouted, "It is obvious that Humanity has broken the Accords." Ever the statesman, he looked around at all the assembled fae, "It is time that Humanity answered for crimes against the fae."

The Arbiter touched another control and a loud gong echoed

throughout the hall. Her face grave with warning, she continued, "Outbursts during a Tribunal will not be tolerated from any present, regardless of their rank or family. I will have any offenders removed, and issue summary Judgement about reparations on their case. Have I made myself clear?" She glared around the room, her gaze returning to the now-grinning Unseelie King. He sat back down, confident he would see his plan come to fruition.

"That was the original video recovered from the surveillance system of the Seelie property, and it shows abhorrent actions committed by human police. Her Majesty contacted the Signatory of record for this jurisdiction, and they sent Representatives immediately. The Tribunal recognizes that those Representatives are present today. The Queen asked the Representatives to investigate the events at the property, and they did so, with the full cooperation of the Seelie Court."

She clicked the button on her controller, and the holograph changed to an image of a collection of shell casings found at the scene. Each one was singled out, then magnified, and wire-framed, showing dimensions and caliber of the round. As each did so, firearms that used that particular ammunition flashed above the wireframe. They started out showing standard human calibers and firearms, but that quickly changed.

"As you can see, several of the casings found were not of human manufacture. In fact, the casings showed that fae-made rounds were used in the attack, along with human firearms. Even more strange, gunpowder that was formulated specifically for fae rounds was found on the contact wounds of the survivors who were mercilessly killed." A series of complex chemical formulas began to flash across the holographic projection. Doc nodded to herself, noticing the strange components she had found on the bodies.

"At that point, the electronic specialists employed by the Signatory Representatives discovered that the video itself had been tampered with, and that the video that was originally found, happened to be a fake video recorded over the actual video from that night. That specialist was able to recover the actual footage. He could then corroborate that footage with external cameras from the area, showing the real perpetrators of this heinous assault."

She toggled the controller again, and the footage recovered by Spooky began playing. It started with the view from outside the club, watching the vehicles arrive and disgorge their fae passengers. The view soon switched to the inside of the club as those same fae attacked and slaughtered the patrons inside. The attacks were even more horrific than the human-centric video, and the murmurs rose again.

Ghost looked at the King of the *Draukh* and smiled. The King's eyes were on the screen, and his brow was creased from anger. The King looked at Ghost and noticed the DHS leader's grin. His eyes narrowed and anger flared behind the lids. Ghost looked back up as the view switched back to the outside as the fae exited the building and left in their vehicles.

The Arbiter held up her hands in a gesture to quiet the angry voices among the Seelie and *Seanachaidh* onlookers. She touched the lighting controls and the lights came back up in the great hall. Many of the fae were staring at the Unseelie King with anger plain on their faces, and it was evident that his Knight was nervous. The Arbiter cleared her throat, drawing attention back to the podium.

"As you can see from the evidence brought before the Inquiry, it is clear that Humanity was not the perpetrator of this attack. Under expert witness and from multiple sources, I learned that many of the fae pictured in this video are confirmed to be aligned with the Unseelie Court of King Arkanai t'Nakaót. I suspect that those that could not be identified are also Unseelie Court-aligned, and that further Inquiry would bear that out." She looked directly at the King. "Does His Majesty have anything to add to this Tribunal?"

The King sat and regained his composure for a few seconds. He then stood and angrily glared at Ghost. He pointed an accusatory finger at the DHS leader. "That human and his team have obviously crafted false video to smear my Court with lies and insinuations." The anger crept into his voice, "I know their headquarters has access to the specific weaponry listed as fae origin. It would be expected that they might fabricate evidence to indict my Court." The King looked back at the Arbiter, "What guarantees do you have that your noble personage has not been lied to and given false evidence to make you an unwitting accessory to their vile attack?"

The Arbiter coolly returned the King's gaze. "Your Majesty. Under the Law, you do not have the right or ability to question my methods or facts. However, due to the seriousness of the charges, I will provide an answer. All witnesses that provided testimony were subject to *Aidmheil*." A small gasp ran through the crowd. "The veracity of their answers is unquestioned. In your defense, would Your Majesty and your Council consider submitting to the *Aidmheil*?"

The King suppressed a shudder. "I will not subject my Court to such an artifact. I simply deny that I and the Unseelie Court had anything to do with the attack on the Seelie vermin. It was either

Humanity, or the Queen herself who committed this foul act to trap my Court."

"As you offer no defense or mitigating evidence, I will pass judgement on Your Majesty and your Court."

The Arbiter stood stiffly as the Oracle, Praetorian, and Protector rose to their feet behind her. The Praetorian and the Protector walked down off the platform and stood in front of the platform while the Oracle approached to stand near the Arbiter.

The Arbiter began, "It is my finding that the Unseelie Court and King Arkanai t'Nakaót are guilty of using agents to attack the Seelie property and kill all the Seelie-aligned fae inside. It is my finding that the Unseelie Court, or its agents, then planted evidence and framed Humanity to misdirect the investigation and potentially start violence among Accord Signatories."

As the Arbiter spoke, Ghost watched the King tremble in fury. It had all gone wrong for the *draukh*, and he had been caught. The DHS leader knew the monarch would retaliate. He only hoped that the elf did so outside the hall when Knightmare would be better equipped.

"Due to the severity of the actions, I am forced to order the following reparations." The Arbiter took a deep breath and began again, "For impugning the Signatory known as Humanity, the Unseelie Court will turn over twenty-five percent of its liquid assets here on this plane to the Signatory Representative Section Twenty-Eight. This is both compensation for loss and punitive damages for the Court." There was a small gasp from the King's Knight.

"It is hereby ordered that the Unseelie Court must turn over ten percent of its current holdings of *geleafa* to the Seelie Court." There was an audible gasp from the crowd that time. Ghost knew the Courts collected this substance that they harvested here on earth to power their magic here and to ship back to their home realms. *Geleafa* was the theoretical substance that powered the faith or magic in this realm. It also could gather enough to draw other creatures from other planes of existence, the source for the incursions his team dealt with regularly. It was literally the substance that powered beliefs and faith.

The Arbiter raised her hand and toned, "This is my judgement. As Arbiter of this Tribunal, I consider this matter Adjudicated."

The King abruptly spun and strode for the exit, his startled Knight close on his heels.

24

SACRIFICE

Gray Court Hall, Broadway Ave SW, Grandville, Michigan

The King of the Unseelie Court angrily strode down the aisle toward the exit and his Knight bellowed for the way to clear. Ghost watched the King storm off, and muttered loud enough for Do-Right to hear, "I do believe that man is going to try to kill us."

The former Colorado deputy sheriff answered, "Yeah boss, and I think we'd better get our gear ready soon." As his boss turned to go talk to the Queen, the former deputy saw the King pause by the robed figure. The figure nodded, and the Unseelie monarch left the hall. Do-Right watched as the figure worked its way through the crowd toward the platform.

There was something off about the robed figure, and the former deputy's training and instincts screamed that the figure was dangerous. Trying not to be noticed, Do-Right started moving toward the hooded figure, aiming to intercept the figure just before it reached the platform. He could see that the figure was homing in on someone, and it looked to be the group of dwarves that were leading the Tribunal. As he looked around, the former deputy noticed that the King's retinue of trolls had remained behind as well, and were quietly standing near their seats.

Do-Right made a small wave and got Heavy's attention. He subtly pointed to the lingering trolls. It took the big man a few seconds, but he finally nodded. The heavy weapon specialist leaned over and tapped the diminutive Boomer on her shoulder and motioned for her to join him. The two began to make their way to cover the trolls, just in case something happened.

Do-Right was close to the hooded figure when it reached the group of dwarves. When he was within arms length of the being, it threw back its hood and hissed. The Praetorian turned and found herself face-to-face with a large, bald, black man. The former deputy realized he looked familiar just before he saw the glowing red eyes. Do-Right looked down at the creature's hands and saw a glint of polished metal as it drew a dagger from its sleeve.

Without thought or hesitation, the former deputy lunged forward grabbing for the knife as the creature swung it in an arc. The Praetorian's eyes widened as she realized what was happening, but her reflexes were not nearly fast enough. Just before the blade swung through her throat, Do-Right collided with the creature in a perfect open-field tackle. His old coach would have been proud.

Do-Right felt a cold, yet burning, sensation in his stomach as the two crashed to the ground. The robed creature growled a guttural curse, and the pair rolled for several feet, each trying to gain an advantage. Do-Right was fighting the creature with everything he had, but his arms and legs were getting weak. In some small corner of his mind, he realized that he had probably been stabbed by the creature. He pushed that thought away as he struggled to subdue the robed figure.

Sensing that it was beginning to lose the battle, the robed creature fought with a manic intensity, trying to tear itself away from this human who had tackled it. The being stopped trying to get at the deputy with its knife, and instead began to concentrate, pulling in power around him. After a particularly nasty elbow across the Do-Right's face, the former deputy momentarily lost his senses, and the creature seized its opportunity.

Hands turned into paws, and skin grew furry. The creature's face elongated and the bones in its body began to rearrange itself. Do-Right felt the change as he struggled to hold on to the creature. Suddenly, the former deputy was staring at the muzzle of a very large dog with glowing red eyes. As Do-Right struggled to hold the beast, the muzzle flashed toward him.

When the hooded figure had revealed itself, Heavy had been momentarily distracted. By the time turned around, the big agent had larger problems at hand. Four of them. All four trolls were standing with their tall warhammers, and they looked like they were spoiling for a fight.

"Alright, fellas." Heavy stepped up and placed one hand out in the universal stop motion. "I think that you are about to make a huge mistake. Listen, I understand that you are pissed, but don't make things worse than they are."

"Little human. How do you expect to stop us?" The troll at the front of the group spoke. He spun his warhammer in a careful arc, building up the crushing momentum that the weapon could then transfer to whatever, or whoever, its target was. "You are nothing."

"Aw hell, fellas. I was merely trying to distract you. She's your real problem." Heavy pointed at Boomer.

The DHS vampire demolitions specialist leapt at the troll closest to her. The big creature was just turned around when she struck, driving her razor-sharp claws through the big fae's body armor and between two ribs into its chest cavity. She felt the creature's heart beating. She grabbed the creature's heart and pulled, dragging it out through the small, fist-sized hole in its chest. Blackish-blue ichor spilled as she held the heart up in front of the creature's eyes. Comprehension dawned under the thick eye ridges of the creature as it realized that this small woman had ripped its heart from its chest. The life in its eyes faded, and the corpse collapsed to the floor.

The remaining trolls paused, watching this small woman rip their companion's heart from his body. One of them raised its warhammer and let out a war cry that echoed around the room. The other two joined in. As the first began to swing its heavy warhammer at the little woman, it faltered in its swing and missed the small human as it was splashed with the blood of the troll behind it. Boomer deftly dodged out of the way of the lumbering swing of a warhammer, and watched Heavy step away from the now-headless corpse. As Boomer's attacker raised its arms to swing the warhammer again, it was again distracted by a bellow of pain, and then a grunt from the troll next to it.

Boomer took advantage of its momentary confusion leapt at the creature, grasping for the creature's throat. It was not fast enough to block the DHS vampire. Boomer dug both of her taloned-hands into the throat of the troll and pulled. Large chunks of troll flesh and ichor sprayed as her hands ripped through the flesh like tissue paper. The troll looked into the inky black eyes of the vampire as it died. Boomer rolled free as it tumbled forward.

She stood at looked at her partner. Heavy held his two Nepalese khukuris in his hands and looked around the great hall. There were no other signs of battle around the hall although there was a cluster of his teammates by the platform. He noticed that all the *khoztak* Protectors were holding their rifles and guarding the doorways as if they were expecting a siege. The big man flicked his wrists and the troll ichor on his blades flew off to land on the floor. He slid them back into the scabbards on his back. He looked at Boomer and motioned for her to follow.

As they approached the platform, Heavy saw that Doc was kneeling down and working on someone who was sprawled out on the floor. He recognized the style of boots and pants and realized that the medic was working on one of his teammates. He pushed the crowded fae aside until he was towering over the medic and the person on the floor. As he looked, Doc reached one gloved hand up and closed Do-Right's open and staring eyes.

The big heavy machine-gunner looked at the body of his slain comrade. He could see that the throat was shredded. He also noticed the large bloodstain on his abdomen, and the incision in the clothing and armor that could only have been made by a bladed weapon. Heavy then looked at the man's face. The face would never laugh again. The eyes would no longer help share someone else's pain. Heavy saw red.

With a growl, the big DHS agent suddenly looked up at the assembled crowd. "Who did this?" His voice was a low rumble, the menacing growl of a predator ready to pounce.

The Praetorian spoke, her voice softer than it had been all day, "Oude Rode Ogen. Old Red Eyes attacked me while I was conversing with the Oracle. Your companion saw the attack, anticipated the strike, and grappled with the beast. He sacrificed himself to save my life. He will be honored."

There was a long silence as Heavy stared at his fallen companion.

"Fuck honor, I want revenge." The big man's cold, flat voice lowered and a dangerous note entered his tone. It was the calm in the eye of a hurricane, and his rage was just underneath the surface. "This bastard needs to die. Where do we find it?"

Ghost looked at his heavy weapons specialist. Face somber, he felt he had to speak, "Don't worry, big man. This thing will die."

Doc suddenly stood and looked Ghost in the eye, "Find this bastard. Christian deserved better." She blushed slightly, realizing what she said, but not correcting herself. The medic turned to Heavy, "Are you injured?"

Heavy shook his head. "No, Doc. Just some trolls. Rebekah took half, and I took the others."

Ghost looked at the Praetorian, "So what happens now? What's your protocol when the Unseelie Court directly attacks the *Seanachaidh* after an Accord-bound Tribunal? It seems to me that they think you and the Seelie Court are weak, and that you can't do anything about this shameless act."

The Praetorian looked at the body of Do-Right at her feet, "I'm not sure." She paused before she spoke again, "We have had nothing so egregious happen since the Accords were signed. I will have to confer with the Oracle and the Queen of the Seelie Court."

She looked up at the DHS team leader. Her voice grew firm, "As a Signatory party of the Accords, this matter does concern you. Because your Representative was killed by Oude Rode Ogen, you have the right to carry out a hunt of the creature. Because this happened at a Tribunal, my Protectors were supposed to protect the attendees and Representatives. Because they failed, they will help you in your quest to find Oude Rode Ogen."

She paused then looked Ghost in the eye, "You are not, on the other hand, authorized to attack the Unseelie Court, or the King himself. Until the Oracle passes judgement, they are still inviolate." Ghost frowned. The Praetorian continued, "However, should the Unseelie Court interfere with your hunt of the outlaw Oude Rode Ogen, or if there is resistance to your search, you are authorized to protect yourselves and to continue your search. But take care. Do not simply attack the Unseelie Court, or Humanity, too, will be held for judgement."

Ghost nodded slowly. "I believe that I understand you. When will the Oracle pass judgement on the Unseelie?"

"Likely yet this night. I expect that we will meet shortly, and work to find the answers for him."

"And the response to the Unseelie's attack?"

The Praetorian shook her head. "I genuinely do not know, Agent Vanhof. We will seek a peaceful resolution if possible, and we must contact some fae in *Álfheimer*. I will contact you when the Council has made their decision. In the meantime, I will have my Protectors available to help guard you as you walk to your vehicle. I believe that you will be sufficiently well equipped then to protect yourselves?"

Ghost let an empty smile touch his lips, "I believe we will be able to defend ourselves, then." As quick as it had appeared, the smile vanished. "I will assist Doctor Sorenson with Do-Right's body, and we will be ready to go out to the truck."

Doc was already laying out one of the body bags that she kept in her equipment. Ghost walked over and helped her place the deputy's body inside the black bag. After zipping the bag closed, Doc wiped a single tear away as she rose. Ghost, Heavy, Scout, and Boomer all grabbed a corner of the bag and lifted it together. Ghost nodded to the assembled Protectors, and they led the team out into the cool night air.

After they loaded Do-Right's body into the truck, they all mounted and it was a silent somber ride back to the MCC. A light drizzle began to fall as if the heavens themselves were mourning. Ghost called Gretchen and told her an abbreviated version of the night's events. He recommended that she contact Agent Smith, and that she have a video conference waiting when they return. He also told her to make sure that the body storage area was cooled to the right temperature for storage.

The Wunder Wagon pulled up next to the giant Air Force C-17 that was the Mobile Command Center. The somber team silently carried the body bag up the stairs and into the back of the jet. The DHS security team looked at each other as the body bag was carried past them. Once the door to the Air Force jet was closed, they looked at each other in bewilderment. The lead agent made a note to inform the SAC when he got off duty.

Gretchen touched Ghost's shoulder in sympathy after they had placed the body in the cold storage of the jet. His face tightened, and he shook his head. She removed her hand and led the DHS leader and Doc into the conference room.

The other members of the team peeled off their gear and sat in the couches and chairs. Grim faces stared around blankly. It was only a few moments later that Heavy let out a loud, "Dammit!"

This seemed to shake the team out of their reverie and they began to get busy. Heavy washed up, changed his clothes, and began to clean and oil his khukuris. Once done with that he methodically stripped, cleaned and reassembled all of his firearms. Finished, he caught some shuteye.

Spooky opened his wrist computer and activated the active and passive sensors in the Wunder Buggy. He chose a couple options and linked the Buggy's sensor net into the sensor suite in the C-17. While he would normally be working and sleeping in the Buggy, he wanted to be in the MCC that night after the attack at the Tribunal.

Boomer took a shower and changed her clothes, getting rid of the troll ichor. She and Dancer had a long discussion about hand-to-hand techniques, weapons and tactics, and the benefits and hazards of dating men. It was several hours later that both crashed from exhaustion.

Scout took his time cleaning his firearms and caring for his ancestor's bow. When he was done, he sat and meditated for some time, clearing his head and communicating with the Spirits to guide his friend, Do-Right to the other side.

Ghost and Doc had followed Gretchen into the conference, and both had been mildly surprised to see Agent Smith's face already present on the screen. It took the pair several hours to recall the night's events, from the Tribunal to the attacks afterwards. Agent Smith kept interrupting and asking pointed questions, clarifying details or questioning the pair's perceptions.

When they finished recounting the events for a third time, Smith finally ran out of questions to ask. He sat back, steepled his fingers and thought for a moment. He looked up and leaned back toward the camera. "Mr. Vanhof, Doctor Sorenson. It is time for you to go hunting."

25

MOURNING

At 9:30am, Gretchen closed the conference room door in the MCC. All the remaining team members of Knight-mare were present, as well as Captaen O'Beirne. As Gretchen sat, Ghost stood and motioned for Spooky. The electronics specialist turned on the projector and called up a picture of their target.

Ghost began, "Our target is hiding, but we are going to kill it. Oude Rode Ogen, or 'Old Red Eyes' as he is sometimes known is an Eastern European boogeyman. Large black-skinned male, usually seen naked. According to our records, he has glowing red eyes, and he has a really hard time hiding them. So look for the eyes. He can also shape-shift into a huge dog or wolf with black fur. He still can't hide the red eyes there."

The DHS leader nodded to Spooky who showed a satellite over-head of Grand Rapids. "We've got two possibilities for this target. The Unseelie Court is brazen, so he may be hanging out at one of the Unseelie strongholds. We have a limited authority to search them, and we have at least two in mind today."

The view zoomed in to show an industrial neighborhood. One building was circled. "This is the first stop for Alpha Team. We will go in, ask questions, and generally make it really uncomfortable to hide the creature. We will ALL be heavily armed, but we are not to start a fight. This is a fugitive hunt and a show of force, reminding the Unseelie that they are on our turf."

The view switched to a different neighborhood. This one was in a rundown section of town. Even from above, the neglect of the neighborhood was apparent. Ghost continued, "This is location two. This is a known troll safe house. It's also known for a lot of the nastier Unseelie who have a hard time blending with humans. Since Arthur and Rebekah took out four trolls last night, they may get a little pissy if we push too hard. I don't care. Push hard enough to find the target."

Yet another building flashed into view, this in a decidedly rural area. "And this is location three. This is the regional Unseelie Court. Much like the Queen's location, this is where the King and his entourage reside when they are in the area. This is our last stop, and we will have to walk this path very carefully."

Ghost looked at Spooky and the former NSA analyst switched to a satellite view of a park. "This is Aman Park. We have unconfirmed rumors that there is a shelter here for certain Unseelie who are being hunted. It is possible that our target is here. This will be the target for Bravo Team. Go into the park and track him down. Watch your backs. You will be on his home turf, and Alpha will be a long way away."

The team leader looked around the room and let out a sigh. He knew he would get pushback, but he had decided, and Smith and Doc had agreed that this was the best way to use his team. "Team assignments. Little G, Heavy, and Dancer will join Doc and I on Alpha. Scout will join Boomer on Bravo. Spooky, you will provide backup for them in the Wunder Buggy. We should be getting one of the Homeland Security Suburbans soon for Alpha. Questions?"

Spooky looked up, "What kind of assets do I have access to?"

"Agent Smith has given us full release to find this creature. It is now considered persona non grata here on our soil. So you have access to anything you want."

Spooky smiled and tapped out instructions on his wrist terminal. "Any other questions?"

Captaen O'Beirne raised his hand up to shoulder height to get Ghost's attention. "Yes, Jonas. To which team am I assigned?"

Ghost shook his head. "I'm sorry, Callum. This has gone from a diplomatic mission to a hostile target hunt. As of today, I can no longer have you in the field as an Official Observer. Agent Smith made the call last night. I'm to ask you to fly back to Section Twenty-Eight today. If you wish to remain as a guest of Section

Twenty-Eight, you can spend the time at headquarters. You can even consult from there if you want to be in on any of the conference calls. But right now, you are no longer authorized to ride with us. I'm sorry. I don't have any choice in this one—Agent Smith is calling this one."

The Irish intelligence officer was dumbfounded, and could not respond. He eventually pulled it together and mustered as much dignity as he could. "I will comply with your Agent Smith's wishes. I will have to ask him about this particular turn of events."

The Irishman stood. He shook hands and exchanged goodbyes with the team, leaving a lingering handshake and a heartfelt "good luck" for Ghost. Gretchen stood and walked him through the conference room door, already talking on her phone to arrange transportation.

Once everyone was settled, Ghost again got everyone's attention. "It sucks. I know. Does anyone have any other questions about the mission today? No? Then let's get ready to hunt this creature down."

They all stood and made their way out to the equipment and weapons lockers while Spooky headed straight out to the Wunder Buggy. Ghost was already wearing his Webley revolver in its custom holster slung low on his hip. He pulled on a soft armor vest over his casual button-down shirt and attached various bits of gear to the armor. Next was the custom communications gear that the team wore for battle. He then pulled on his long, worn leather duster and grabbed his bolero. Finally, he took his ancestral sword from its holder and held the cane in his hands.

Doc replaced her normal soft-soled shoes with a pair of black combat boots, her lone clothing choice dictated by Section 28. She grabbed a paddle holster from her kit and slid it into the waistband of her pants. She drew her Norbert-modified tranq pistol from its case, loaded it, and slid it securely into the leather. Her radio was next, and she carefully attached the microphone and earpiece. She then placed her stole over her shoulders, careful to make sure the ends were even. Her chasuble was next, the silver and gold threads glinting. Her long rosary and cross were her final pieces.

Little G seemed to live in his FBI tactical pants. While slightly different than the standard BDUs the rest of the team wore, he was simply used to them. He pulled on the heavy long-sleeve tactical shirt and then strapped his heavy armor plate-carrier on. His pistol belt was next, and his custom-tuned 1911 slid into the leather with a soft sigh. The former HRT sniper put his radio gear on, strapping the throat mic around his neck, and the earpiece went into his ear.

He drew his modified M4 out of the weapon locker and checked the action. He slid a magazine home and closed the bolt, loading a round. Six more magazines filled various pockets on the vest, and the final empty pocket got a flash-bang grenade.

Heavy was already wearing his black tactical BDU pants and a black t-shirt. His first layer was the heavy custom-tailored armor carrier, adding eighty pounds of weight to his broad shoulders. He drew his specially blessed khukuris out of their case and slid them into the specially designed slots in the back of the armor. Next was his pistol belt and standard-issue Beretta M9. His radio was next, followed by spare magazines filling the pouches mounted to the armor. With a grin, he unlocked his weapon locker and drew out the large AA-12 assault shotgun. Reaching into the ammo bin, he drew out five drum magazines filled with a combination of silver slugs and cold-iron 00-buckshot. He paused, then reached in and grabbed two eight-round magazines filled with miniature grenades. There was no telling what they would encounter.

Smallest of Alpha Team, like Heavy, Dancer was already wearing black tactical BDU pants and a black form-fitting turtle-neck. She reached out and grabbed her Norbert-custom body armor. Once she was safely wrapped in the armor, the young woman reached for *fion-fhuil*, sliding the sword carrying the spirit of a dragon into the built-in sheath on the back of the armor. Next was a pistol belt, and her custom Walther P99 pistol easily clicked into its holster on her hip. She slid the radio into its own holster and tested her microphone and earpiece. She then reached up into her locker and pulled out the suppressed MP5K-PDW, which had become her personal weapon of choice. One final check over her gear and a quick re-tying of her boots, and she was ready.

Like the others, Boomer wore her BDU pants. She was also wearing a black t-shirt, over which she slid a soft body armor vest. The vampire then pulled her black BDU shirt over the armor. She, too strapped on her pistol belt and loaded her Beretta M9. Once it was in the holster, she went put her radio on, and attached the microphone and earpiece. She then opened her weapons locker and drew out her own AA-12 shotgun. She reached in and grabbed four of the drum magazines and two of the mini-grenade box maga-zines. "Just in case he gets feisty," she muttered to herself.

Scout was wearing the black BDU pants and t-shirt that was the standard uniform for the team. He knelt and removed his combat boots. The world-class archer pulled a pair of authentic Indian moccasins out of his kit and slipped them on his feet. Although they were dyed black instead of brown, the moccasins were in every other way authentic. He wanted them for slipping through the woods. He then strapped on his pistol belt, loading the Beretta and sliding it into the Kydex holster. He then grabbed his soft body armor and strapped it in place—he wanted freedom of movement today, so the heavy plate carrier was out. The BDU long-sleeve shirt buttoned over the body armor, and a Navajo ceremonial headband was wrapped around his forehead. He then strung his grandfather's blessed-bow and finally grabbed a quiver full of hand-honed arrows. He turned and saw that everyone else was ready and waiting for him to finish.

As everyone filed past Gretchen to leave the MCC, Ghost stopped and spoke to her and Captaen O'Beirne. He wanted her to know their plans for tracking the target, so she could relay them to Agent Smith if he needed them. He wanted to thank the Captaen for his time, and to again apologize for having to send him back to Langley. The monster hunter was the last one out the door, and he closed exterior door firmly.

The DHS leader wished Bravo Team good luck as they clambered into the Wunder Buggy. Boomer shut her door with a solid thud, and the big engine roared to life. Boomer dropped the transmission into gear and the big truck roared toward the parking lot exit.

Ghost looked at the waiting SUV and realized that his team was ready. He quickly walked around to the other side of the truck and climbed into the driver's seat. After punching in the GPS location of the Unseelie club called Fade, he put the transmission into drive and put his foot on the accelerator. The huge V8 under the hood of the truck howled as it surged forward, following the quickly vanishing Wunder Buggy.

THE OUTSIDE of the Unseelie-aligned club was dirty and looked like it was abandoned. Only the poorly disguised camera over the exterior door showed that there was anything in the empty building. The parking lot was in the rear of the building, and it was impossible to tell if there was anyone in the club from the front. Ghost pulled the SUV up in front of the club and parked in a no-parking zone. If the government plates didn't give the official vehicle away, the red and blue strobes on the dash and in the grill should deter any ambitious meter maid.

Ghost flung open the driver's side door and Heavy flung open the passenger's door. As both men climbed out, the rear doors opened and Doc emerged from the driver's side, followed closely by Dancer. Little G hopped out of the passenger rear door and went around to the back of the truck. Once he opened the rear hatch, he reached in and pulled out his rifle and Heavy's shotgun, which he handed to the big fed. Dancer reached past him and pulled out her submachine gun, slinging it over her shoulder. After making sure that everyone was ready, Ghost led the team toward the front door.

The leader of Alpha Team pounded on the metal door and then held his credentials up to the camera. A gruff voice sounded from a small intercom next to the door. "Can I help you?"

"Special Agent Jonas Vanhof of Homeland Security and Signatory Representative of the Accords. Open the door now."

"And what is this regarding? This is a private club."

Ghost was getting angry, and it crept into his voice. "This is the Unseelie-aligned club called Fade. As I said, I am a Signatory Representative and I am demanding entry by the authority of the Accords, and by special dispensation from the *Seanachaidh*. Either open this door, now, or I will break it down and will assume that you have something to hide from the other Signatory parties, and I will tear your place apart looking for something. It is your choice. Five seconds."

As Ghost's internal voice reached the number one, he heard a buzzing sound coming from the door. He quickly reached out and grabbed the handle, yanking the door open. One by one, his team entered the darkened building.

As they entered, Ghost could see the inside of a modern nightclub. Even at this time in the morning, there were several patrons of varying shapes and races already, or still, in the club. The ever present club music was muted to a dull beat, likely in deference to the early hour. As his team spread out behind him, a small, rotund man walked toward them, almost waddling. As he closed the distance, Ghost could tell that he was a dwarf of some kind, likely *khozten*. The portly dwarf was agitated and waiving his arms, and Ghost tried to keep from laughing at the comical sight.

"What are you doing here? This is Unseelie-aligned. Your kind aren't welcomed here."

Heavy swung a one of his ham hock-sized fists and the rather portly dwarf and socked him in the jaw. The dwarf dropped to the ground.

26

TROLLS

The dwarf was only out for a couple seconds before his eyes fluttered open. He looked up from the floor in a dazed expression at the big fed who had just slugged him. He shook his head slightly as if clearing away any lingering effects. The dwarf propped himself up, and then slowly clambered to his feet.

When Heavy had knocked the dwarven manager out cold, Ghost had pushed a little of his willpower into his credentials and held them up. The sigils had glowed a sickly green as he had announced in a loud voice, "Special Agent Jonas Vanhof, Department of Homeland Security. This is an Accord matter. Your cooperation is appreciated."

Ghost reached down and helped the dwarf stand up, "I must apologize for my friend, here. He is a little testy since one of the Unseelie Court attacked and killed his friend last night at the Tribunal."

The DHS leader looked at Heavy, then back at the dwarf. His tone was overly friendly, "I'm sure you understand his frustration right now. I myself am a much more patient and forgiving man, but I need you to understand how serious we are. Do we have your attention, now?"

The dwarf nodded several times, his disheveled hair flying as his head bobbed rapidly. He looked at the two federal agents in front of him and then back around at the club. The manager of Fade realized that several of the fae in the bar had risen to their feet in his defense. The dwarf was desperately trying to figure out how to get out of this incident without tearing the nightclub apart.

In the far corner a large creature had risen and had taken several steps toward the conflict at the entrance. As it stepped out of the shadows, the light revealed a rock troll. Larger, and reportedly less intelligent than other troll types, Ghost knew the creatures were violent and hard to bring down. He just smiled.

The huge rock troll took one more step forward and found its way blocked by a small human female. It was puzzled. Normally small humans ran away from the troll, they did not normally interfere. This one was dressed as a warrior. Maybe she thought she could slow him down. His puzzlement turned to shock as the small human reached up and a large sword glowing a pale gold materialized in her hands.

"I would not do that," Dancer's young voice was sharpened steel. "We bring no intention of violence, but if you take one more step, it will be your last."

The troll looked at the blade, now pointed at his gut. It continued to glow a faint gold, and he grew afraid. Normal blades were hardly noticed as they could not usually penetrate the thick hide of the troll. Magic blades, though, they tended to cut clean through troll hide. He thought for a moment about testing the small warrior's skill, but he decided to save that for another time.

Dancer watched as the troll appeared to weigh her words. Apparently, it had decided that she was telling the truth, as it turned and lumbered back to its table. She silently thanked Vellath for his appearance and slid the enchanted sword back into its sheath. She then walked over to rejoin Ghost.

As she walked by, a small creature reached out and grabbed her ankle, causing her to stumble. In a flash, she was on the ground staring up at a grinning face and the point of a very sharp knife. The face was a craggily gray with a long, crooked nose, and a mouthful of sharp teeth. The creature's voice grated as it wheezed, "Not so strong now, huh little one. You need a lesson about choosing a fight with the Unseelie."

Keeping her eyes locked on the creature's black orbs, she slowly, carefully drew her Walther from the holster riding mid thigh. Once clear of its holster, she stuck the muzzle of the pistol into the creature's gut and pulled the trigger twice. The creature's body muffled the reports, but the pain on its face told the story.

Suddenly, the creature fell to the side, clutching the wounds in its stomach.

Dancer scrambled to her feet and kept the pistol pointed at the creature who was writhing in pain. She quickly glanced around her, and the rest of the patrons were frozen at the sudden reversal. She walked over to the creature and leaned over, "Thank you for the lesson. The next time, I won't be so nice." The youngest fed pulled back and kicked the creature in the head, knocking it unconscious.

As she calmly walked over to Ghost, she re-holstered her pistol and reached for the slung MP5 on her shoulder. Once she had a grip, she took a stance behind the DHS leader, overlooking the rest of the club. Ghost looked at her, then at the rest of the club. He raised his voice, "Now that the introductions are over, let's have a chat."

Two hours later, the team was finished interrogating everyone in the club, except for the unconscious goblin that had attacked Dancer. While everyone knew of, or knew their target, none of those present knew where the Oude Rode Ogen was hiding out. The team left the nightclub, piling into the government SUV to travel to the Unseelie safe house.

When they pulled up to the Unseelie safe house, it looked like another abandoned building in a neglected part of town. Once a wholesale auto parts store, the neglect and wear was evident. The only clue to its current occupation was the heavy steel door replacing the original retail glass. The few windows scattered on the facade were boarded up or covered with brick.

Ghost pulled the sleek black SUV into the small parking lot and parked beside a rusting panel van. As they climbed out, each member of the team was alert, looking around the neighborhood for those who might be watching. Once they retrieved their long guns from the truck, Ghost led the team to the front door. He sent Little G around to the back to watch the rear of the building. The sniper walked back and found a spot that gave him some cover and allowed him to watch the back door and side of the building.

Ghost again held up his credentials to the camouflaged camera and pounded on the heavy front door. This time, the speaker announced, "What do you want?"

"Federal Agents and Signatories of the Accords. We're here on *Seanachaidh* business. Open up or we will open it for you."

The door buzzed, and Ghost pulled it open. He walked in, followed by Heavy, Dancer, and Doc. They walked into what would have originally been a reception area of the business. It was now a lounge and had various couches and chairs placed around the room. The furniture was well worn and trended toward large and of the "overstuffed" variety. Lamps were placed around the room, and a large flat screen TV was mounted to the wall and playing a daytime soap opera. As they looked around waiting for someone to greet them, Ghost got nervous.

Doc's vestments began to glow the warning blue of an imminent evil attack and suddenly all the lights cut out. For two long seconds, there was absolutely no sounds or movement. Then the room was filled with growls and snarls of large, angry animals. Heavy and Dancer clicked the activation button on their weapon lights and scanned around the room. Two large trolls with brutal looking war axes in their hands stood in the opening that led to the rest of the building. Several more trolls stood behind the front two, and every one was armed. Ghost keyed his radio, "Ghost to Little G, it's an ambush."

The first troll charged and Heavy pulled the trigger. The burst of three 12GA rounds ripped into the chest cavity of the big creature, and the roar of the shotgun was deafening to those in the room. The troll stumbled, but still continued to raise its axe. Heavy shifted his aim and ripped another short burst into the creature's face. Its head disappeared in a spray of gore and ichor, and the lifeless body tumbled forward.

The troll on the right snarled and charged at the young agent holding the other light. Dancer raised her MP5 and pulled the trigger, aiming for the big creature's massive head. The first couple rounds glanced off the thick skull, but several entered through the massive eye sockets, burrowing back and scrambling the troll's brain. The creature toppled, it's axe falling from its lifeless fingers.

Doc took a small step back and chanted in Latin, praying a protective blessing on her team. Her hands glowed blue as the power began to build within her. Ghost took a step forward to protect his priest, and drew his ancestral sword. The blade glowed a bright white and it seemed eager to taste troll flesh.

A simple step forward and he plunged the blade deep into the chest of a troll coming through the opening. It stopped and screamed, its flesh burning and melting around the enchanted blade. The short sword it was carrying dropped from nerveless fingers, and the troll began to fall backwards. It managed to free itself from the blade, and then collapsed as its life ebbed away.

Heavy's shotgun ran silent as he emptied the magazine, three more trolls falling to the barrage of cold iron shot. He looked at the entryway and saw at least ten more trolls, plus a few goblins pouring up from what must be the basement. He grabbed one of the smaller box magazines and shouted, "Grenade." He slammed the magazine into the receiver, and dropped the bolt, loading the first of eight mini-grenades.

Switching the selector to single shot, he stroked the trigger at the group around the door. Two of the trolls exploded, and a third was thrown across the room, missing at least two of its limbs. He shifted aim and pulled the trigger again, this time knocking down two more trolls, and killing a troll and several goblins outright. He worked the process, aiming and firing, killing at least a few and mangling everyone and everything coming up from the basement.

Next to him, Dancer crouched and aimed her submachine gun at those who were merely wounded or knocked down by the grenades. Every downed monster got at least one burst to its head, sometimes two if their skull was particularly dense. She calmly switched magazines when hers ran dry, and was switching to her third new magazine when Heavy's shotgun ran dry. Two more bursts finished off the last two felled trolls, and the silence was deafening.

The smell of gunpowder and explosives lingered heavily in the air, and the team waited to see if any more creatures were coming up from the basement. Ghost keyed his radio, "Ghost to Little G. Clear in here. Status?"

"Two hostiles out here. Both neutralized. You were awful loud in there, I would expect local law enforcement soon." Little G's voice was as calm.

"Copy on the hostiles and locals. Contact Gretchen to roll local DHS support. You deal with the locals until they get here. Keep your eyes sharp. We're going to clear this building."

"Copy. I will contact Gretchen and keep the locals busy. Little G out."

Ghost re-focused on the building around him. "Dancer, cover the basement door. Heavy, spread out and verify we are alone up here. Doc, check for any computers or files." His team spread out to their tasks. Dancer covered the stairwell that led down into darkness. Ghost produced a flashlight and he and Heavy walked around the building, checking in corners and checking to make sure that any of the creature's that had attacked them were deceased. Doc produced a flashlight, and walked around the building as well, checking for computers or files they could take back to the MCC.

As they were searching, Ghost's radio crackled. "Little G to

Ghost. The locals are here and not so patient. Regional SAC is en route, and Gretchen said to tell you to be careful."

"Copy. We're getting ready to check out the lower chamber. We may lose radio contact. If you don't hear from us in thirty minutes, recall Bravo and send in the cavalry."

Little G responded with a simple "Copy."

Ghost and Heavy finished checking the bodies and met up with Dancer by the stairwell. Ghost shouted down into the darkness, "Federal Agents and Accord Signatories. If you are down there, now is your one chance to surrender."

After waiting for thirty seconds, he nodded for Heavy to lead. the big man walked carefully down the stairs, his light shining the way. The stairs emptied into a large living room, with more of the battered, overstuffed furniture scattered throughout the room. Several open doorways and arches led from this main area.

Signaling to the left, Heavy led the team to the first door. Once Dancer was covering the door, Heavy slipped inside and looked around the room. This was obviously a sleeping quarters for one or more of the goblins. The bunk beds against the wall were too small for large trolls and the clothing that was scattered around was obviously for the smaller creatures.

A thorough look around told the big fed that there were no creatures hiding in the room. Heavy walked about and said, "Goblin bunk room. All clear."

They cleared the next several rooms the same way, Dancer covering and Heavy clearing each room. They found three more goblin bunk rooms and a large barracks-style room with beds sized for trolls. All of this looked like a simple hostel-like lodging for the transient fae creatures.

They also found a large kitchen at one end of the underground complex. There was a large pot of stew with very questionable meat in it, and a torso of some animal that Ghost refused to think about sitting in the refrigerator. One large dorm-style bathroom facility rounded out the complex in the basement. The team found no other creatures hiding down in the basement.

Ghost looked at his watch and realized that they had been working for about twenty-five minutes, and he motioned for Heavy and the others to wrap it up and meet him upstairs. As he walked up the stairs, Ghost called on his radio, "Ghost to Little G. We're about done in here. No other hostiles. How are things out there?"

"DHS is on scene and dealing with the locals. Gretchen is calling in a cleanup crew for us. What's your status?"

"We're clear here. Let the locals and DHS know we're coming out the door."

As he opened the door, Ghost's SSP buzzed. Looking at the screen, Ghost realized that Spooky was calling. He answered the phone, "What's up, John?"

27

HUNTING

Boomer pulled the Wunder Buggy to a halt outside the main building at Indian Trails Camp. She climbed out of the driver's seat and went inside the office. She showed the on-site personnel her credentials and verified that there were no campers using the site that week. The vampire then ordered all the staff to remain in the main building until the park was cleared. As she walked out, the administrator was recalling the maintenance personnel back to the building.

Boomer watched a drone launch from the roof of the truck as she walked back to climb into the truck. She then pulled the truck a little further back into the camp area to set up Spooky's base camp.

She and Scout grabbed their gear, checked their radios, and looked at Spooky. The former NSA analyst was looking hard at real-time satellite imagery of the camp and comparing it to imagery coming in from his drone. He pointed to a spot in the park about half-a-mile back into the woods.

"There. There's a spot about four hundred yards across that the video goes all wonky. It starts half-a-mile back into the park, looks like bearing three-four-eight from here. I've got no video return signal from the satellite, and the drone starts to lose control if it gets too close."

He switched to another view, the commercially available view from an online mapping site, "There appears to be a stream in this area, maybe a hill. But there is nothing in that area that could interfere with a Keyhole satellite. I can only get within about five hundred yards of that spot with the drone. Something doesn't want to be seen. Seems like your first target area."

Boomer and Scout both nodded. Scout jumped lightly to the ground first, his moccasins making very little noise, even on the gravel of the parking lot. Bow in hand and arrow nocked, he took his bearing, and started for the edge of the trees. He barely heard a scratch of gravel behind him, and he realized that Boomer had also exited out of the truck. He paused and turned to look. He was surprised when he realized that she was a mere five feet behind him. Even the best hunters will make noise on a gravel parking lot while wearing combat boots. That she was silent spoke more of her vampiric powers than her spec ops training.

He also paused and realized that she was bare-handed. He glanced down at her hands and back up to her face, silently asking his question. She grinned and shrugged. *Whatever.* He shook his head and turned, leading the way into the woods.

They had walked about a quarter of a mile into the woods and the trees were getting older, and more densely packed together. Scout was very careful to make sure his footing was solid, and that he was making as little sound as necessary. He was also watching his bow and bow-string, making sure he did not snag it on an errant branch. He was nearly silent in the walking, slowly moving forward one step at a time. Twice he was able to get within mere feet of a deer or rabbit before it even knew he was there.

As quiet as he was, the vampire behind him was silent. He could not even hear her breath from a couple feet away. They were fortunate as the cool breeze blew toward them. It meant that they were already upwind of anything in their path. He could see a little daylight through the trees ahead and knew it must thin right about where they were going to be searching. He slowed to an imperceptible walk, and he felt Boomer do the same.

His earpiece crackled as Spooky came over the radio, "Two hundred yards straight ahead of you." Scout clicked his radio once in reply.

They reached the edge of the grove and looked out across a meadow in the middle of this forest. A lone oak tree stood in the middle of this meadow, and most of the branches were bare. He looked across the expanse of long grass and saw a large black man standing and talking into the tree.

Watching for a moment, he realized that the man was not talking to the tree, but to a large black crow sitting on the branch at eye level. They were too far away for him to hear the details of the conversation, but he could hear two distinct voices, a male and a female.

Boomer put a cautionary hand on his shoulder and leaned in to whisper, "Who is 'the Morrigan?' That's how he keeps addressing the big black bird."

Scout shook his head and whispered, "I don't know. Another fae? Either way, it doesn't matter."

Boomer continued, "She keeps saying that there will be death this afternoon, and he needs to pledge to her if he wants to be the one living at the end. He keeps asking about specifics and she's not answering."

"If she wants death nearby, let's oblige the big black bird." Scout stood still, feeling the minute shifts in the wind. He figured that their target was only about a hundred and fifty yards away. This was a shot he could make every day. He centered himself and slowly raised the bow. He pulled the string back to his jaw, his form perfect for the Navajo bow. The bow made the slightest sound as it stretched during the draw.

The crow turned its head and stared right at the Olympic archer. He saw the move and wondered what it meant. No time for worry. He concentrated on the big man's chest, then elevated his bow a few degrees. He relaxed his fingers and the string "twanged" out loud, loosing the arrow at his target.

Faster than his eye could follow, the crow shifted to human form, a beautiful woman with long, curly red hair. Her feathers and bird's body changed in the air as she jumped down. Suddenly, she looked as if she had stepped straight from an equestrian event. The athletic woman wore green leather vest over a white peasant blouse. Tan breeches tucked into brown leather riding boots rounded out her appearance.

One moment she was a raven on a low branch. The very next this ginger-haired woman was standing next to the Oude Rode Ogen clutching the Navajo arrow Scout had launched to kill the creature. Her eyes flashed with an inner fire.

Almost faster than even Boomer could follow, the archer drew and loosed two of his arrows. The runes on the side of the bow glowed a slight red each time an arrow was loosed. The strange fae near their target caught the first arrow that Scout aimed at her in her empty hand. The second magically enhanced arrow got through her defenses.

The arrow slammed into the woman's shoulder, the fletchings quivering. Everything stopped in that moment. The Oude Rode Ogen and the woman both looked at the shaft sticking out of her shoulder. Blood began to seep out of the wound to stain the shoulder of her blouse and vest.

She let out a howl of rage mixed with pain. The woman reached up and grabbed the shaft of the arrow. She heaved and pulled the arrow out, blood spraying as the barbed head was pulled free. The fae woman looked at the arrow in her hand and then up at Scout. She snarled and crushed the arrow, breaking it in half. The pieces dropped to the ground, and the woman voice went cold with rage, "You dare attack the Morrígan? Your death will be at my hands." Scout reached for another arrow.

She looked at Oude Rode Ogen, who was standing, frozen in place. "I told you I saw death in this place. It will not be yours, today. Flee." Old Red Eyes turned and sprinted away from the Morrígan. Three steps into his run, he shifted into a huge black wolf and quickly disappeared into the woods.

The Morrígan turned and stalked toward Scout and Boomer. A feral grin crossed her lips and her hair blew in the wind behind her. Scout drew and loosed arrow after arrow, and each one she knocked aside, the enchanted projectiles breaking in two. Relentlessly she closed the distance. When she was within forty feet of the DHS agents, Boomer stepped in front of Scout and stood, barring the woman's path.

The Morrígan did not break stride, "Little half-dead creature. Do you think you can stop the Phantom Queen?" Contempt dripped from her words.

"Bring it, bitch."

Boomer felt her vision shift and the fangs grow in her mouth. She leapt at the Morrígan, claws outstretched, reaching for the woman who claimed to be a goddess.

The Morrígan slapped Boomer aside with a wave of her hand without breaking stride. The vampire was airborne for ten feet until she crashed into the trunk of an oak tree. She felt something in her back snap, and she lost all feeling in her legs. The vampire succumbed to the blackness edging around her vision.

The Morrígan stood before Scout. He dropped the bow and tried to draw his knife. The Irish goddess was faster. She reached out and grabbed Scout by the throat, her delicate hands seemingly made of steel as he began to choke. She lifted the archer off of his feet and held him impossibly high, dangling eighteen inches from the ground.

She looked at the young agent for a few seconds, taking measure of who he was. Scout's eyes were wide with fear as the oxygen was cut off to his lungs. With one last desperate measure, he drew an arrow from the quiver and physically jabbed it toward his captor.

Her free hand was fast, intercepting his thrust and viciously twisting the wrist until it snapped. He cried out and dropped the arrow. The Morrígan looked down and spotted the half-full quiver attached to the fed's belt. She smiled cruelly, coldly, and walked the young fed over to the truck of a large oak tree.

Boomer slowly regained her senses and watched as the Irish goddess slammed Scout against the tree trunk, hard enough to bruise him, but soft enough to leave him conscious. Pinning him against the trunk, she reached down and grabbed one of the arrows. She slammed it through his shoulder and into the tree, pinning Scout to the trunk.

"Now you know how it feels. I believe we need to teach your companions not to interfere in my affairs. And you will be the perfect object lesson today."

She slowly drew another arrow from the quiver and slammed this one through his other shoulder. The Morrígan methodically repeated the process until there were four arrows in Scout's torso and one each in his arms and legs.

When she released Scout's neck, his body hung, pinned to the tree like a giant trophy for an entomologist. He gave a few shuddering breaths as his airway was released and then spasmed.

The Morrígan turned to the look at the slowly moving vampire agent. "Warn your companions. This is what happens when you attack a goddess."

The Irish goddess turned and walked back toward the open meadow in the forest. As she reached the edge, she shifted into a giant crow. Between steps, she turned from beautiful woman to large crow flying away from the ground. In seconds it was up and over the tree line on the far side of the meadow and gone from sight.

Boomer stared in horror at the body of her partner. She felt pain as her back began to heal itself, and her torso straightened involuntarily, her spine aligning back into place as her accelerated healing mended her body. She could tell it would be several minutes before she would be able to really move again. She keyed her microphone, tears choking her words.

"Boomer to Spooky. Scout's down and I'm busted up. We need the rest of the team here."

Twenty-five minutes later, Boomer heard the sirens of Alpha Team's SUV screaming into the park. It cut off abruptly with a chirp, and she could hear Heavy shouting questions. She tried again to rise, and she was able to get up to her feet while leaning on the tree trunk that broke her back. The vampire was sore, and she knew she would need to feed after this, but she could finally stand.

Heavy was the first to burst through the trees and find her. Ghost, Doc and Dancer followed close on the big fed's heels. When Dancer saw her, the young agent rushed to Boomer and embraced her in a tight bear hug. Tears flowed down the young agent's face, and she missed Boomer's wince as she hugged her mentor tightly.

Doc, on the other hand, did not miss the wince. "Are you all right?" She looked concerned.

"I'm fine. Can you help Billy?"

The priest turned and went to the agent pinned to the tree. She reached up and felt for a pulse. After a long minute, she shook her head. "The only way I can help Billy is to provide last rites. I'm sorry. He was going to die the minute he was pinned like this to the trunk." She stepped back after closing the agent's sightless eyes. "What happened?"

Ghost stepped forward, looking around the scene. The pain in his eyes showed for a brief moment before his self-control slammed that gate shut. When he spoke, his words were soft, but cold. "Yes, Rebekah. What the hell happened?"

Boomer sat back down on the ground and put her head in her hands. Then she looked back up, refusing to hide from the results of her choices and actions. She watched for a moment as Heavy broke each arrow that pinned Scout's body to the tree. He was choosing a point just outside the skin and snapping the arrows with his brutish fingers. Little G walked into the scene and held the archer's body while Heavy removed the arrows.

"We found the target. He was talking to a big black crow in the middle of that meadow. The crow was perched in that tree." She indicated the lone tree in the center of the meadow. "We listened for a bit and caught a little of their conversation. The crow was supposedly some harbinger of death, so Billy thought he'd oblige it. He aimed for the target, not the crow."

She grimaced at the memory. "In hindsight, it was pretty stupid, but he took the shot anyway. It was right on target, except that crow shifted into a really pretty redhead. This lady caught his arrow, then looked at us. Before I could stop him, Billy shot two more arrows at this new woman. She caught the first one, but the second slipped through and hit her in the shoulder." Tears flowed again as Heavy and Little G gently pulled the body down from the tree and placed it in the waiting body bag. Heavy made sure to put the Navajo archer's bow and quiver in the bag with him.

Boomer continued her story, "She got pissed, and told our target to run away. She then stalked us. That's how it seemed, anyway. Billy kept shooting arrows at her, but she wasn't letting anything get through again. She claimed she was some goddess. I tried to stop her, but she smacked me with a backhand and I hit this tree here. I think my spine broke, and I passed out."

Finished with Scout's body, Doc approached Boomer and knelt beside her, laying a comforting hand on her shoulder. Boomer gladly accepted the gesture and continued her story, "I woke up just as she was putting Billy against that tree. She rammed the first arrow into his shoulder. Then she just grabbed arrows from his quiver and pinned him to the tree with them. She ran out of arrows.

"That bitch then told me that we shouldn't interfere with goddesses and left. She walked about three strides into the meadow, turned into a crow and flew away. That's when I called for help on the radio."

Ghost stood, looking down at his broken demolitions expert. "Did you catch a name? Who was she?"

"She called herself the 'Morrígan.'"

Ghost let out a string of curses. He looked at Doc and apologized before turning back to his demolitions expert. "I was afraid you would say that. We need a secure line to Smith." The DHS team leader pulled out his SSP and placed a call to his boss.

28

GAUNTLET

I t had been another somber trip back. Before the team had left the park, Heavy and Ghost had taken two portable torches back to the spot and torched the tree and the ground around the tree to get rid of any bloodstains or signs of struggle. They had been careful to only burn the surface, and to not set the park ablaze. After a small, but necessary, use of the handy fire extinguisher, the two men had left the area with a charred spot, but no signs of battle or death.

The team was in the conference room of the MCC, and Smith's face showed up on the wall. Ghost worked his way through a recap of Alpha Team's efforts, including the firefight at the Unseelie safe house. When he was finished, Boomer recounted her tale, trying to leave no detail unsaid. When she was done, Agent Smith leaned back in his chair and steepled his fingers, deep in thought.

Smith leaned forward again. "Let me assure you, Ms. Callahan, that there was nothing you could have done differently in that situation. Even Norbert's special rounds in your lovely shotgun would have only made the Morrígan more upset. I'd have lost both of you, instead of only Mister Buckhorn. How are you feeling, now? Are you operational?"

"I'm fine, boss. I'm still a bit sore, but it sure beats being paralyzed. Who is this 'Morrígan' bitch, anyway?"

"She is the goddess in charge of doom and death in battle, espe-cially battle for the *Tuatha Dé Danann* and their warriors—the Celts." The team recognized a lecture when it started. Smith recited the facts. "The Phantom Queen is also the goddess of sovereignty. She can often appear as three sisters although it is just as much the norm to meet her singular aspect. She is known as a rather temperamental goddess, and mortals tend to turn up dead when she is in one of her moods."

Heavy spoke up from the far end of the table, "That's great and all. But how do you kill a goddess? Does Norbert have some special ammunition for us?"

Smith shook his head. "No, Mister Murphy. Norbert doesn't have anything that will offer that much damage, at least that I know about. In this case, we will have to approach that one carefully. I hope that the Morrígan will not decide to play favorites here, but we won't know that until later. I've had some dealings with her in the past, and I hope we can work past this."

Smith let that sink in momentarily. "As to the present, work with the Seelie Court. If this triggers a war, it will collapse the Accords and humanity will be swept up in it. I've updated this to a Priority Black mission, so you have full access to all resources. I will dedicate a team to standby here, and will gather the remnants of Knightfall and Knightsdawn to have them ready for deployment.

"I cannot stress this enough. Work to solve this one before it becomes a shooting war. If the fae go to war, humanity will lose. I have to go brief the Director. Keep me informed." Smith signed off the conference.

The team looked at each other around the table, dumbfounded. Several long seconds went by before Spooky cleared his throat, "So. Now what?"

Ghost's SSP buzzed in his case. He retrieved it and did not recognize the number. "Special Agent Vanhof."

Ghost nodded as if the caller could see him, and then said, "I understand. We are to be there as Signatories and witnesses, but we are not to offer assistance unless asked. We will be there."

He disconnected and looked around the table. "That was the Seelie Queen. She has proposed a settlement for the Tribunal, and the Unseelie King, the Oracle, and the Praetorian have all accepted. Apparently they are doing something ritual called '*Gliairecht*' to determine the prevailing party." He turned to Gretchen.

She shrugged her shoulders, "I've never heard of it. Let me send a note to the boss." She started poking at her own SSP.

Spooky looked up from typing on his wrist pad. "I've got it. It means 'Gladiatorial Combat' or more loosely translated as a more ritualized combat. Think of a trial by combat. The winner determines the winner of the dispute."

He looked up from reading on his wrist computer, "That's bad, isn't it? What if the Unseelie win?"

Gretchen answered, "Then the Unseelie win. We will still have a mandate for the capture of Oude Rode Ogen, but power will shift to an unfriendly side."

Ghost spoke up, "Everyone gear up. We'll be fully armed and armored when we reach the site. Sling your rifles, but take what you need. If this turns into a shooting war, we will win it here. The trial is in three hours. We leave in two."

At that, the team broke up and prepared for action. Now that they had a plan, the team was distracted from their losses, and they were moving with the efficiency that Gretchen knew. By the appointed time, everyone was ready to go. As they walked down the stairs from the MCC, Gretchen dialed the number for the local DHS SAC and let him know that there may be fireworks from an upcoming op.

The Wunder Buggy pulled into a dirt and gravel drive with the sign out front advertising a local concrete contractor. They were waved to a parking spot in the large lot next to the main building. As they climbed out of the truck, Heavy looked around the gravel and dirt lot. There were a lot of high-end sports cars and luxury cars in the lot. A couple panel vans also sat off to one side, their wide side doors open and empty.

The human guard who parked them walked over and said, "Welcome honored guests. Please proceed down that path to the trial grounds. Refreshments have been provided." The man left their proximity when another vehicle pulled into the lot. The human guard walked over to greet its occupants.

Knightmare walked toward the path they were directed to, and Boomer caught the faint whine of drone engines spinning up to speed. She glanced back to see one fly off the roof. She knew Spooky was monitoring both satellite imagery and the drone footage.

Around a bend in the path, the team came out to a wide expanse of a sand and gravel pit. Across from the path, about a hundred yards away, a blue-green reservoir bordered the far edge. Ghost realized that this entire area was surrounded by strategically placed mounds of dirt. He causally pointed out the highest of such small hills to Little G, and the sniper nodded.

The former HRT sniper split from the rest of the party and climbed the small hill. At the top, Little G took a seat and pulled out a compact pair of binoculars. He carefully laid his rifle across his lap and scanned the growing crowds for threats. He clicked his radio mic, "Little G in position." He received a single click of acknowledgement.

A *khoztak* dwarf approached Ghost, "Welcome Special Agent Vanhof. Is your companion not sitting with you? You do realize that this ritual would be disrupted if your man was to act against one of the participants?" The dwarf's voice was accusatory.

Ghost nodded, an expression of innocence written on his face, "Of course I realize that. He's just up there to make sure that the attacks from the last Tribunal are not repeated."

After losing two of his team members within hours of each other, Ghost decided to twist that barb a little more. "We figured that the Protectors would want the help after the last failure. Of course, if you can guarantee our safety..." The DHS leader let the sentence trail away. He had set that barb pretty deep, and there was no way the Protectors would guarantee his team's safety.

A scowl deepened across the dwarf's eyebrows. Ghost could tell the creature was trying to restrain himself. "Of course we would welcome all the help we can get. We do our very best to ensure the safety of our guests, but you realize that we cannot make the guarantee of safety."

The dwarf pointed to the observation section for the Signatories and the team wandered that way. On the walk, they were greeted by the Seelie Queen and her Knight. The Queen had a full retinue of bodyguards with her, and all of them were either elves or minotaur. All of them were armed with the large exotic handguns and rifles they had seen earlier.

The Queen indicated a seat next to her, and Ghost sat. They talked about the logistics for this trial, and the DHS agent was willingly learning about its history and heritage. As the hour approached, the crowd filled out and the noise of conversation grew quiet.

Ghost estimated that there were about forty or fifty non-human creatures present, including the Unseelie Court in their viewing section, the *Seanachaidh* and their Protectors, and a few unaligned fae. He saw two robed and hooded figures in the Unseelie Court and wondered if the Oude Rode Ogen was among them. He noticed an awful lot of trolls and goblins in the unaligned viewing areas.

Beside him, the Queen rose, and Ghost felt a prickle of magical power. "I am Queen Lishe at Merunaré, Sovereign of the Seelie Court and Bringer of Light. I convene this *Gliaireacht* as a member of the *Tuatha Dé Danann* and Signatory of the *E'Tuatha* Accords." Her soft and reserved voice was magically amplified, echoing through the trial grounds.

"The *Gliaireacht* has been called to settle a blood-dispute between the *Seanachaidh* and the Unseelie Courts. The agreement is for singular combat between the parties. Each party must offer a combatant as their proxy. Praetorian, as the aggrieved party, who will serve your combat?"

All eyes were on the Praetorian. She smiled coldly, "I will be the combatant for the *Seanachaidh*, as the Praetorian, it is my duty and honor to serve." A gasp ran through the crowd. Ghost knew from his briefing from Agent Smith that it was rare for a Court member to actually fight in the trial. According to Section 28 records, these trials were often to the death, as yielding over an important manner was considered dishonorable.

If the King of the Unseelie was disturbed at the announcement, he was showing none of it. He stood and called out, "As King of the Unseelie Court, I, Arkanai t'Nakaót, shall stand as combatant for the Unseelie Court."

If the Praetorian had shocked those that were gathered with her announcement, the King's pronouncement silenced them. In the entire written history of the *Tuatha Dé Danann*, neither the Unseelie King nor the Seelie Queen had ever personally been in the *Gliaireacht*. Only once before had the Seelie Court Knight fought in the trials. The Unseelie Knight had fought four times in the written histories, and every one of those trials was against an unaligned fae. It was unprecedented that the King would engage in the battle.

At first, the Praetorian did not believe she had heard correctly. She began mentally reviewing everything she knew about the King and his training, his weapon work, and his capabilities in the field. She recalled that he had been a fearsome opponent on the battle-field before his rise to power.

The Queen of the Seelie Courts regained her composure quickly. "As the challenged party, King Arkanai t'Nakaót, what will your choice of weapons be for the trial?"

The King was basking in the attention. His smile oozed charm and self-confidence. His voice dripped with syrupy sweetness while thinly veiling a cold edge. "My Queen. I shall choose blades. If the Praetorian would like a trial, I shall see that she gets one."

The Praetorian paled slightly. While the King was to be feared in battle, his prowess with a blade was legendary. The King rose and removed his suit jacket. The Unseelie monarch next removed his tie and his crisp white shirt, revealing intricate tattoos running up his arms and over his shoulders.

Boomer had to admit that the King t'Nakaót looked incredible with his chest bare. His slender frame filled out into a muscular torso and arms. The DHS agent shook herself when she realized that she had missed something that the Praetorian had said.

Queen Merunaré turned to the Praetorian, "Blades have been chosen. Is that acceptable?" With the dwarf's nod, she asked both combatants, "According to the laws, each of you is entitled to a second who you may choose to fight in your stead. Unseelie King, who is your second?"

The King smiled, "My second shall be my new Knight, however, I will still choose to fight." One of the hooded and robed figures stepped forward to stand slightly behind and to the right of the Unseelie King. It threw back the hood there was a gasp from Heavy and Boomer. Their target, the large shapeshifter called Oude Rode Ogen, turned his blazing red eyes toward Knightmare. Turning back to its King, it drew a long rapier from its scabbard and handed it, hilt first, to his liege, the King of the Unseelie.

The Queen turned to the Praetorian, barely contained anger riding beneath her calm exterior. "And Praetorian, whom shall your second be?"

The Praetorian was staring at Oude Rode Ogen and his King. Fury was visible on her face. She turned to survey the crowd, her voice stilled and her thoughts racing. As her gaze met Heavy's, the big man leaped to his feet and cried out, "Choose me!"

She thought about it for a moment, then shook her head slightly. As strong as he was, the Praetorian knew that he would be the wrong choice. Her gaze slid on, past Doc, past Little G, and past Boomer. Her gaze came to rest on the youngest federal agent. *Was that a flicker of power?* The dwarf was torn, her thoughts tumbling.

Dancer made the choice for the Praetorian. She stood, chin thrust defiantly. Before Boomer could lay a warning hand on her arm, she spoke up, subconsciously mimicking one of her movie heroines, "I volunteer for the trials."

The Praetorian nodded once. The young DHS agent made her way out of the crowd and walked to stand by the dwarf who was about fifteen inches shorter than her five-foot, three-inch height. Ghost started to yell in protest but felt a warning hand on his shoulder from the Queen.

The Praetorian turned to her weapons bag and drew out two short swords. She reasoned that the contest is about blades, not a blade. She knew that she would have trouble getting within her opponent's longer reach, but a plan was beginning to form.

The Queen once again amplified her voice and spoke, "Challenges have been accepted. Weapons have been chosen." The monarch of the Seelie Court looked at the two assembled combatants as well as their seconds standing behind them. "I declare this *Gliaireacht* convened."

As the Queen was mouthing the word "convened," the Praetorian shifted slightly, and threw one of her short swords without looking at the King of the Unseelie.

29

BETRAYAL

Gliaireacht, 68th St SE, Caledonia, Michigan

T he short sword arced through the air, spinning like a thrown dagger. The Unseelie King could barely raise his own blade in time. His rapier deflected what surely would have been a killing blow. Instead, the blade sliced along the King's left arm. A long gash on his bicep oozed blood, and the elf grunted in pain.

Drawing himself tall, he grimaced and forced the pain down. "Is that all you have, dwarf?" His tight face and the tightness in his voice betrayed the almost insolent question. He quickly advanced on the Praetorian.

The *khoztak* dwarf set her stance and let the King come to her. The elf arrived and his blade arced in intricate patterns. Thrusts were met with blocks. A parry led to a riposte. It was evident to all around the grounds that these two warriors were masters at their chosen weapons.

The King slowly advanced, causing the Praetorian to retreat, inch-by-inch. Her back to the water, the dwarf was growing worried. She felt more than saw the large pond at her back, and her opponent was forcing her to retreat toward it. The ground beneath her feet grew wetter, and she knew it would only take one misstep and the fight would be over very quickly.

The clanging of swords added to the chorus of grunts and

expletives as the two master swordsmen clashed. Deliberately, the Praetorian moved to her right, focusing her strikes on the King's still-bleeding left arm. She was careful, making sure to block the King's attacks. Her strategy seemed to work, albeit slowly. Small cuts and nicks appeared on the King's left arm and left side of his chest. None of them were deep, debilitating strikes, but the number of small, shallow cuts was beginning to affect her opponent.

The King was weakening, and he knew it. This furious battle had lasted ten minutes already, and he was getting desperate. He took small risks to get through his opponent's defenses, and they started to work. The dwarf's shirt was soon showing several places where his blade had slipped past, and the blood was flowing. He decided to risk a bigger strike.

He drew the Praetorian in with feints and apparent fumbles, only barely blocking her thrusts. This went on for about thirty seconds. Finally, he felt the time was right, and appeared to leave himself open to an attack.

The Praetorian watched as the King kept fumbling and leaving himself open, only to barely block her attacks. She saw that his feints were an attempt to draw her in and realized that he was getting desperate. Cautious, she watched and prepared for his gambit, hoping to flip the trap back on the King.

The Unseelie King's guard dropped, and it appeared that he was open for a killing blow. The Praetorian took the bait and struck. As she expected, the elf King turned his blade and struck at her exposed chest, a blow that would have run his rapier through her heart. Instead, she shifted her attack, letting the blade slide perilously close to her body and spun. As she turned, the dwarf pulled a blade from her belt in a reversed grip and swung, driving the sharp blade across the elf's thigh, splitting pants and skin from the inner thigh, across the meat of his muscle, and through the outside of his thigh.

The elf King crashed to the ground, clutching his leg, his rapier forgotten where it had dropped. The cries and groans from the crowd were a dull roar in the background as the Praetorian fought to catch her breath. She slowly stepped over to the King and pointed the tip of her blade at his throat. "Do you yield?"

The King of the Unseelie was on his back, both hands clutching his wounded thigh and bleeding out into the sand underneath him. He was trying to find a way out of this, without yielding. The monarch shook his head, refusing the dwarf's first question. He was buying precious few seconds, however he could not see an exit.

The Praetorian grunted softly, brought the tip of her blade within a hairsbreadth of the elf's throat, and asked again in a louder voice. Her anger flowed through her words. "You are defeated. Again I ask you. Do you yield?" She kicked him right where her blade had sliced open his thigh.

He cried out with the new torture. He did not know how to lose in battle, but here he had lost. To a dwarf, of all creatures. Before he could answer for the final time, he was surrounded by a black energy. In the mere blink of an eye, his injuries closed and an invigorating wave of energy flowed over, around, and through the Unseelie monarch.

The Praetorian barely had time to recognize what had happened. One minute, the Unseelie King laid broken, on his back, and waiting to be killed. The next, he was surrounded by a faint black glow and his wounds were healed. Then the King threw sand in her face, a blinding cloud of the dust exploding into her eyes.

The deadly elven rapier was in the King's hand before he scrambled to his feet. With his opponent blinded by the dust and sand, he slowly prepared his attack, looking for a vulnerable spot in her armor. He saw one and struck.

The blinded Praetorian was panicking. Without her sight, the King would easily defeat her. He must have cheated. He had not cast the magic, one of his Court must have interfered. The contest was finished. She just had to survive.

Fate was not on her side. The Unseelie King struck with all the anger and rage at this mere dwarf beating a warrior of his station. His blade punched through a small gap in the Praetorian's armor, sliding under her arm, in between her ribs, through her lung, and into her heart.

The Praetorian tried to scream. She tried to say anything. All she could do was gurgle as blood flowed from between her lips. The King withdrew his rapier, and the Praetorian fell to her knees. Her face was frozen in a rictus of pain and shock. She slowly collapsed to the ground, face first.

The stunned silence of the crowd erupted into a roaring chorus of cheers from the Unseelie Court, even as two *khozten* healers ran out onto the field to check on the Praetorian. The *Seanachaidh* sat in stunned silent, and the Seelie Court whispered among themselves. The Seelie Queen stood to announce the obvious conclusion, and Ghost leaned over and got her attention.

"Your Majesty, I thought the combatants could have no outside help during the trial? I understood that to have outside help was to forfeit your victory. Is that not so?"

The Queen nodded, not sure where the human from Section 28 was leading with this train of thought.

"The necromancer in the hooded robe next to the Unseelie Knight is the one that healed the King. He did not heal himself. I witnessed his spell being cast."

The Queen looked closely at the DHS leader. "Are you sure that act is what you witnessed? Are you willing to undergo a test with the *Aidmheil?*"

"Yes, Your Majesty."

The Queen of the Seelie motioned for the Oracle and the lead Protector to join her. Across the grounds, the King was still waiting for his pronouncement of victory. His eyes narrowed when he saw the Oracle and the Protector join the Queen by her station. He saw the quick glances in his direction, and then all three turned to question the human, Special Agent Vanhof.

The Oracle reached out with a yellow cord that the King recognized as *Aidmheil* and placed it around the human's wrist. The elf was wishing he had killed the meddlesome human when they had first met.

The King watched as the Oracle and the Protector both asked several questions of the human agent, and the man answered every one of their questions. At one point, the man pointed to the Unseelie Court, pointing at someone to the King's right. The two dwarves then conferred again with the elf Queen, and they talked for several minutes.

By this time, everyone had noticed that there had been no confirmation of victory from the Queen. Murmurs and questions seemed to float on the air as the time dragged. The crowds were getting restless. The King wondered if he could take the initiative away from whatever was happening with the Queen and the two dwarves. He stepped forward, still bare-chested and covered in blood. He enhanced his voice, "My Queen. I demand to be declared Victor. I won the *Gliaireacht*, and claim my right to the Victory."

The Queen glared at the King, and he smiled graciously. She stood and straightened stiffly, and once again magically enhanced her voice, "As the official Witness to this *Gliaireacht*, I, Queen Lishe at Merunaré, Sovereign of the Seelie Court and Bringer of Light, declare that you have been accused of interference, you have betrayed the *Gliaireacht*, and that your Victory is hereby forfeit."

The Unseelie King roared, "This Victory was mine. By right

and by honor, you shall not take this Victory from me. We will go to war."

The Queen paled, and there was a gasp from the crowd. No one dared to breathe as the tension grew. It was palpable in the air. The Oracle stood tall and said, "You have been accused of cheating. Your Necromancer healed you when you were under the Praetorian's blade. Do you deny this?"

"Of course I deny this." The King sounded insulted. "I healed myself with my own power, as is my right during combat. There was no interference."

The Oracle's smile was cold and grim. "Then you would not object being subjected to the *Aidmheil?* After all, if you are innocent, you will be exonerated."

It was the King's turn to smile. "You know that I, as Unseelie King, am above reproach and cannot be subjected to the *Aidmheil.* It is simply my word against the human's."

The Oracle nodded grimly. "Of course. According to our laws and customs, Your Majesty is unanswerable to the *Aidmheil,* should you so choose. However, your Necromancer is not. He will submit, to prove your innocence."

The King paused, mind reeling. He was desperately trying to puzzle a way out of this. He knew the Necromancer would be forced to reveal the truth, and that he would be exposed. Stalling for time, he turned to look at the Necromancer, standing next to his new Knight. He could not see the creature's eyes beneath the hood, but he knew that his dark mage would know the trouble he would cause.

King t'Nakaót shifted his gaze from his Necromancer to his Knight. Oude Rode Ogen had already served him well, causing disruption and despair among the humans and the *Seanachaidh.* He twisted his hand in a small, imperceptible twitch toward his Knight. His Knight whirled, grasped the head of the Necromancer, and twisted. The snap was audible as the Knight broke the mage's neck, almost twisting the head in a full three hundred and sixty degrees. The mage's body collapsed, the robes billowing.

Anger blossomed across the Oracle's face. With the Necromancer dead, the King was the only witness, and he could not be compelled to answer to the *Aidmheil.* The Oracle could not declare victory for the Unseelie King, as the King's power would be out of balance, and he would never have to answer for the attack on the Seelie club.

If he did not allow the Victory, the King's arrogance and hubris would drive him to declare war on the other Courts. That war would spill over into this realm, and the humans would have to get involved. The last time the fae warred on mankind, the humans had dropped atomic weapons. And their power had only grown.

The Oracle was distracted by movement on the ground behind the Unseelie King. The dwarven healers had used their magic on the Praetorian, and she looked to be stirring. He had feared that her death would cause the Protectors to make rash decisions. Now that she was being helped off the field of battle, the Oracle had a glimmer of an idea.

King t'Nakaót heard movement behind him, and he whirled, rapier whipping up to the ready. He was stunned at the two *khozten* helping, half-carrying the living Praetorian off the field. They were carefully guiding her to the *Seanachaidh*, taking small steps, each one causing the Praetorian to wince and whimper. The King grew angry and took one step toward the defenseless Praetorian. The Oracle's voice brought him up short.

"Since the Victory is in doubt, the *Gliaireacht* shall continue. The Praetorian's Second will step forward to battle in her place. Will you remain on the battle grounds, or will you call on your Second, King t'Nakaót?"

The King was indignant. This dwarf was trying to steal his rightful Victory. He watched, rage on his face and murder in his eyes, as the young human agent stepped out on the proving grounds, with a lone dagger attached to her belt. She moved warily, almost unsure of herself. He knew he could beat her, but killing this young human would cause problems down the line. His Knight, however, would be able to kill this girl just as quickly, and there would be no repercussions. After all, it was the *Gliaireacht*.

"Oracle, as the Praetorian has been forced to rely on her Second, I, too, shall rely on my Second. My Knight will fight in my stead. To be clear, my Second can use any personal power or abilities during the combat, as long as it is not powered by another of my Unseelie, correct?"

The Oracle paused. What was the King trying to cover. He knew the Unseelie Knight was Oude Rode Ogen, a fae creature with razor-sharp claws and fangs, and the ability to transform. The Praetorian's Second was a young human girl. Even though she carried the enchanted blade...

The Oracle spoke, "The weapons for this *Gliaireacht* are blades. By law and custom, that does not preclude any combatant's use of natural abilities, nor does it preclude the use of personal equipment that has been enchanted, as long as that equipment has a blade. Is that clarification enough?"

It was the King's turn to pause at the odd wording. The phrasing was strange, even for a dwarf who clearly likes to hear his own voice. But the important part was that the Oracle had just given his Knight permission to use his abilities to kill this young whelp.

"Thank you for the clarification. I wouldn't want there to be any further question of the outcome of this combat."

The King turned and strode to his Knight. The creature bowed deeply to his liege, and the King returned the bow. The creature then stood and dropped his robe to the ground. This was the first time that any of the team had seen the creature up close. The creature was over seven feet tall and well muscled. He looked like an African native, with a clean-shaven head and a strong, prominent nose. His eyes gave away his fae heritage. Red glowing orbs, like dying embers, burned from the creature's eye sockets, giving him his nickname, Old Red Eyes.

Old Red Eyes strode to the center of the battlefield, large, powerful strides eating up ground. He looked like the preternatural predator that he was. He stopped a dozen feet from Dancer and smiled. "It looks like dinner will come early today. I look forward to tasting your fears." The young federal agent watched as fangs grew long in the creature's mouth, turning the smile into a grinning rictus of death.

Dancer smiled and her voice was as sweet as honey, "I will make you suffer for killing my friends. And then I will kill you for hurting Boomer." The young agent reached up and grasped the hilt of *fionfhuil*. She felt Vellath stir and thought to the dragon consciousness in her sword. *Time to wake up, Vellath. You get to drink blood today.*

It is about time. I was getting bored. Who do we get to kill? Vellath sounded amused.

Dancer told him, *Oude Rode Ogen. Old Red Eyes killed two of my friends and hurt Boomer bad. I want him to suffer.* She could feel the dragon's rage building. She wondered what was getting it so angry.

Vellath grumbled in her mind. *I know that one. This will be a pleasure to cause that one pain.*

Dancer smiled and gripped the sword hilt, holding it out in front of her.

The dragon in her sword spoke up, *I have an idea.*

30

FURY

Gliaireacht, 68th St SE, Caledonia, Michigan

rip the hilt like this. Vellath showed Dancer an image in her mind. She gripped the hilt in both hands, fingers tucked in and knuckles touching on each hand. She felt a burst of energy and the blade split into two fully formed blades. The young agent grinned. A small push with her will, and the blades began to glow gold. *Perfect. Now we shall enjoy this contest.* Vellath gave a deep chuckle in her mind.

There was an audible murmur from the crowd around the trial grounds as two slim, medieval arming swords, also known as knightly swords, appeared in Dancer's hands, each of them showing a visible golden glow. The swords were dual-edged, with the blades about two feet long. The simple silver crossbar protected a short one-handed hilt, with a large pommel on the end. Those with keen eyesight noticed faintly glowing runes running up the center of each blade. The young agent dropped into a casual stance, holding the blades at different heights and angles facing her opponent.

The Unseelie King growled in frustration. He had not noticed the blades wielded by the young human girl, and it was too late to take the fight over from his Knight. For his part, Oude Rode Ogen studied the human girl in front of him with new respect, and a little caution. It took a strong will to wield an enchanted weapon, and Old Red Eyes could not underestimate his opponent.

The Queen once again stood. "Combatants, begin."

The two warriors moved, circling with each other, neither one was eager to make the first move. After their second cautious circuit, Old Red Eyes grew impatient. The creature thought his opponent must be unsure of herself. She might have enchanted weapons, but he had decades of experience. It swiped in with a razor-sharp claw.

Dancer dodged easily, twisting to avoid the claw, and bringing one of her blades up to bat away the creature's claws. Her blade left a cut across the back of her opponent's hand, and the thing snarled at her.

"That was just a taste, fae. I'm going to take you apart one small piece at a time." Dancer smiled, trying to work the creature into a frenzy.

The creature held its hand up so the back of it faced her. She watched as the cut mended itself. "Foolish human," the creature growled. "It is you that will suffer for your insolence."

Dancer's smile faltered. If he could heal like a vampire or were-wolf, she might be in trouble. She kept her guard up as she moved, never remaining in the same spot. The young woman waited for her opponent to come to her.

The monstrous fae attacked, slashing claws a blur as they tried to eviscerate the young human in front of him. Each attack was blocked as the young agent used her swords to block the attacks in a rapid flurry of blows. As fast as she was, the creature was faster. Only her training allowed her to barely block each swipe or slash of claws.

The creature kept pressing forward. Oude Rode Ogen's burning ember eyes bored into Dancer's and she kept retreating under his relentless assault. Old Red Eyes pressed his advantage, forcing the young warrior back toward the quarry pond.

Dancer felt the ground shift under her feet. She was trained to be aware of her surroundings, and she noticed that the ground was getting wet under her feet. The dry, dusty packed earth turned to damp ground at the edge of the pond. She felt her boots threaten to lose their purchase, and she shifted her retreat, gradually edging parallel to the pond's edge.

Another flurry of strikes and one made it through the young woman's defenses. Pain erupted along her stomach as one of the creature's claws ripped through her armor vest and undershirt, scoring a line across her abdomen. She stumbled backward, nearly falling.

Old Red Eyes paused and raised one claw between them.

Dancer could make out a small amount of her blood staining the razor point. "The warrior believes she is invincible." The fae creature licked its claw, his long tongue slowly, sensuously drawing her blood from the extended digit. "Your fear tastes wonderful. I can taste your mortality."

Dancer was worried as the two warriors circled each other. She was struggling to keep up with the vicious attacks, and her opponent was not even breathing hard. She knew she could not defend herself forever. All it would take would be one slip of the foot, or a bit of mud to slow her down, and her life would be forfeit.

If you cannot defend yourself, attack him. Vellath's voice rumbled through her head. *Remember, I chose you for a reason. Now kill this bothersome fae.*

Dancer nodded minutely and readied herself for the fae's next attack.

She did not wait long. The large black creature leaped for her, feet leaving the ground and claws outstretched before it. The young agent reacted as she had trained. She spun, pushing the creature past her while slapping aside the claws with her blade. As he went past, she quickly drew the blades across the creature's back, scoring two long lines.

Old Red Eyes howled in pain and anger, the cuts already beginning to heal. She pressed her attack, drawing closer before the fae could recover. She began her own series of attacks. Her blades whirled and struck, slashes and strikes coming from almost every angle. Her martial arts training allowing her to draw and strike and slash, weaving a complex pattern that the human eye could not follow.

It was Oude Rode Ogen's turn to defend as the blades created a whirlwind of sharp pain and death around Dancer. He struggled to block the enchanted blades, and several strikes got through his defenses, each one scoring long, deep slashes and drawing blood. Soon, the fae creature's chest and arms were a mass of criss-cross slices that were being opened faster than the creature could heal.

Dancer watched the creature's desperate defense and noticed an opening, a vulnerability. She waited, keeping up the onslaught and pressure, making sure that the creature was too busy defending to care about attacking her.

Now. A hole briefly appeared in the fae's defenses, and Dancer struck. She twisted her blade slightly, adjusted the angle, and struck. Her blade cleaved through two of the fingers on her opponents right hand, and the claws dropped to the ground, severed at the first knuckle.

The creature howled and leaped away. Turning back to watch his opponent. The fae looked at his mangled hand, two of the fingers severed, and the black blood flowing freely. Even now, the wounds were healing, but he knew the process would be slow. He snarled at the young woman.

Dancer stepped back, into a ready stance. She looked at the creature, and then at her swords. As she watched, the black blood that was dripping down the edges of her blades disappeared, absorbed into the cold, glowing metal.

Vellath's bass rumble purred in her mind, *It is good to drink of the essence of the fae again. This one has a peculiar flavor that I enjoy very much.*

Dancer looked at the wounded and angry fae in front of her. She smiled, "So, if I chop bits off of you, they don't grow back? That sounds like a lot of fun." Her tone, though winded, was almost jovial.

Old Red Eyes snarled in response. Once again, he leaped at the young human warrior, trying to draw her into the same defense again. He knew he could counter that defense. This time, Dancer dropped to the ground, her swords flashing overhead as she blocked and thrust at the fae flying over her head. A quick roll and she was up and moving again.

Oude Rode Ogen was surprised when the young warrior dropped below him, and her devilish blades opened several new cuts as he flew over her. He rolled on the landing, came up, spun around, and crouched in a stance, waiting for her attack.

Dancer's lips curled in a smile, "You're getting slow. I thought you were supposed to be good."

Old Red Eyes bellowed, rage contorting his face. The embers that were his eyes glowed with a deeper red. The fae rushed forward, arms flailing in a wild slashing attack. The young woman warrior defended herself, her blades once again a spinning vortex of metal death. Sparks flashed where the blades connected with claws, and she halted his forward push.

Taking a glancing slash across her protected shoulder, she switched to actively attacking the creature. The federal agent began to accelerate her attacks, causing more minor wounds across the creature's torso and arms to appear. The large fae creature once again lost ground, Dancer's swordsmanship no match for his supernatural abilities. The young warrior could tell that her opponent was tiring, and that the myriad of wounds was affecting his defenses.

One surge forward; Dancer's blades whirling in a pattern she didn't remember learning. Oude Rode Ogen was driven back further, and her last several blows carved whole chunks of flesh from the creature. Two more fingers and a wedge of flesh from the creature's upper arm dropped into the dust. The creature fell back again, this time landing on his back.

Dancer stopped and did not press the attack. Instead, she backed up a couple paces and grinned. She watched as more of the black blood of the creature was absorbed into her blades. "You seem to be losing pieces faster than they can fall off. Do you need to rest?" The young warrior's light voice grated on the fae creature's nerves, and there was real steel behind her sweet smile.

Repeat aloud after me. Vellath's rumble filled her mind. He rattled through a short string of what sounded like a mix of Enochian and Gaelic. His young warrior dutifully spoke the words. *Now we finish this.* Vellath rumbled contentedly.

A white glow began to envelop the blades of the swords she was holding, covering the warm golden glow she knew. She watched as the glow travelled down the blades, enveloping the hilts and covering her hands. She felt a warmth where the glow touched. It continued up her arms and to her torso.

Oude Rode Ogen watched as his opponent muttered a few magical words of an incantation and a white glow seemed to envelop her body. When it was done, the young warrior was glowing with a soft white light that was visible in the daytime. Her hair seemed to be statically charged, and it started waving around as if blown by an unfelt wind. When she looked up at him, he recoiled. Her eyes had turned white and were glowing. Her gaze seemed to pierce his very soul.

Dancer felt a warmth throughout her body. All of her pains and aches from the fight had faded. She felt rested, full of energy, and full of power. The young warrior spoke up, addressing her opponent, "Oude Rode Ogen." Dancer raised one sword blade and pointed the tip at the fae. "You have caused untold pain and suffering for humans for thousands of years. You have murdered my friend. You directly caused the death of another of my friends, and you were responsible for my mentor's pain. Today, I judge you guilty. Your sentence is death."

The fae was frozen with fear as the young warrior woman stalked toward him. He had never felt fear. When his opponent was within five feet of him, he was finally able to break through his paralysis. He roared again, attacking with every last bit of strength and power he had in a dangerous last gambit to prevent his death.

Dancer was expecting the fae's attack and pivoted away from the first swipe of razor claws. Again her blades appeared to fly into a metal maelstrom of destruction. After the first couple seconds, Oude Rode Ogen was once again thrown into defending his life with all of his energy. Dancer smiled at the fae's desperation and switched tactics.

The first strike that got through his defenses took three of his remaining fingers. The next thrust cleaved between his defenses and ran straight through to his side. When the young warrior pulled back to strike again, the blade ripped a large chunk of the creature out of his abdomen, leaving a gaping wound. The next unblocked swing cleaved through the creature's left arm, severing the forearm about halfway up to the elbow. As the large fae howled in agony, Dancer's next strike severed the creature's right arm between the elbow and the shoulder.

Oude Rode Ogen dropped to his knees both arms bloody with stumps at the ends. Howling with rage and fear, the creature looked wildly about. Dancer stood before it and placed the tips of her blades at his throat. She calmly lifted his chin, so they were staring at each other's eyes.

"You understand now. Your life was forfeit when you struck down my friend. Who can save you from your fate?"

From the Unseelie Court, the King stood to his feet and shouted, voice magically amplified, "Hold!" The cry from the King startled her. She paused and turned slightly, her eyes going to the Unseelie monarch. He visibly flinched at her terrible eyes.

"Why should I hold?"

"My Knight is defeated. He must yield." The King pointed to his champion, bleeding on the ground in front of the young woman. "You can claim Victory. I will not object."

Dancer looked at Ghost and the Seelie Queen. The Queen stood, looking thoughtful. "If your opponent yields, it is your choice to accept the Victory while they yet live."

The young warrior looked at the broken and bleeding creature in front of her. Black blood was still trickling down from the stumps that used to be his arms. Blade tips still wedged firmly under the fae's chin, she asked in a low menacing voice, "Do you yield?"

The creature growled and glared at her. Seconds passed, then the creature nodded slightly, ever aware of the sharp blade at its throat. "I yield." The deep bass voice was low. "I yield Victory to you."

Dancer looked back up at the Queen, and then at her boss, Ghost. In the background, several Protectors were yelling "Finish him. For the Praetorian."

Ghost looked at his youngest agent. He did not know what to tell her. If she let the monster live, the team leader had no doubt it would come after them later. And yet, if she killed the creature after it yielded, what message would that convey about humanity? In the end, Dancer was the Praetorian's Second, and it was ultimately her decision. He made a hand signal for her to decide.

"King Arkanai t'Nakaót, Darkness of the Unseelie Court. Do you yield this *Gliaireacht* and claim responsibility for the attack on the *Seanachaidh* and the Seelie club?" Dancer looked at the King expectantly.

The Unseelie King paused. There was no good solution. If he yielded, he might appear momentarily weak, but his Knight would be returned to him, and he could exact his revenge on this young girl. He nodded, "I yield this *Gliaireacht*, and claim responsibility for those attacks. I will make reparations."

Dancer looked down at the creature in front of her. She knew this creature would pursue her for the humiliation it had suffered. She could be the hero here, be good and not kill a helpless opponent, or she could be cruel, but show strength, and maybe get the fae to leave humanity alone for a while. Her moment of indecision past, she knew what she had to do.

31

FAEBLADE

Gliaireacht, 68th St SE, Caledonia, Michigan

Dancer pulled the tips of her swords away from Old Red Eyes' neck. In one smooth motion, the young warrior brought both blades together in a cross, with Oude Rode Ogen's neck in between the blades. With rage contorting her face, and white light blazing in her eyes, she snarled at the fae, "You will never harm another creature again."

The large creature's face was a mask of shock and horror as the blades came together and sheared through the fae's neck. Black blood fountained as the head bounced down and away from Dancer. The crowd of witnesses sat in stunned silence that was only broken by the sound of the head bouncing away and the thud of the corpse hitting the dirt.

Dancer stood over the corpse, swords clenched in her hands, still glowing with white magical power. As she brought her swords up in a guard position, the entire crowd could see the blood on the blades disappear as it was absorbed by the metal.

The Unseelie King shouted. Dancer turned toward the elf and waited. Their stalemate was broken as the Seelie Queen spoke. "As Witness to this *Gliaireacht*, I declare Victory to Special Agent Hannah Sedano, Champion of the Praetorian. I witness the official yield of His Majesty, King Arkanai t'Nakaót, Darkness of the Unseelie Court, and the official claim of responsibility. The Oracle will determine and declare reparations at a later date. Is there any challenge to this Witness?"

The Unseelie monarch looked like he wanted to contest the results. Dancer just stood and watched the elf, waiting to see if he or his minions wanted to challenge her victory. The King looked away from the young woman and toward the Queen.

"No, Queen Merunaré. I do not challenge the victory of this Fury, or your witness thereof."

The King turned, surrounded himself with his Court, and spoke in a strange language. With the accompanying hand gestures, Ghost figured out that the monarch was casting a spell. Soon, a small black portal rose out of the ground. It was a doorway-shaped hole filled with the same roiling, inky blackness that the team had encountered twice.

The King led the way through the portal and vanished into the darkness. The rest of his Court quickly followed, vanishing one-by-one into the darkness. Dancer did not let her guard down until the entire Court had passed through the gateway and it had closed.

Slowly, the glow faded from Dancer. Starting with the glow around her head, the light seemed to flow back down her body and back into the swords. When the light faded, she put the two blades together, and they seamlessly blended into one blade again, before vanishing from the sight of those around her.

As she placed the now-invisible sword back into her scabbard, she opened her mind to the dragon in the sword, *Vellath? Thank you for lending me your knowledge and power.*

The dragon's sleepy rumble answered her, *You are welcome, little one. I enjoyed that fight, and I was able to feed a little, as well.*

We must talk about your dietary needs some time, thought Dancer.

Ah, but that is a tale for another time, little one. The well-sated dragon trailed off to nothing.

The young federal agent thought to herself that she needed to have that discussion pretty soon with the dragon in her sword.

Dancer walked toward her teammates as they rushed to congratulate the young woman. Boomer was the first to reach her, and she swept the young agent up in a big bear hug. Suddenly, she pulled the young agent back to arms length. "Hannah, what happened to your hair?"

The young warrior glanced down and captured a handful of her hair. Gone were the raven-black locks of hair. Her beautiful hair was pure white. It was not the gray of old age, nor was it the blue-white of an even older vintage. It was a ghostly white, thicker than before, and contained occasional highlights of blue and green flashing through it.

"I... I don't know. Must have been Vellath."

Boomer looked at her, "It looks great on you. Seriously."

The rest of the team gathered around to talk to Dancer, praising the young agent with hugs and pats on the shoulders. The victorious warrior soon forgot about her strange hair.

The Oracle approached, followed by a limping Praetorian, who was being supported by two Protectors. The Oracle bowed and paid his respects to the young agent. Dancer bowed back and then moved to the Praetorian and inquired about her injuries. The Praetorian told Dancer of the healing magic being used on her, and then the dwarf celebrated the young agent's victory with her.

The Seelie Queen appeared next to the Oracle and congratulated the young warrior. She asked Ghost if the team could meet at her Court in the morning as they had some final business to discuss. Ghost agreed, and the rest of the Seelie Court joined in the celebration.

It was over an hour later before Knightmare could slip free from the trial grounds. On their way back to the airport, Ghost called Gretchen to fill her in, and to have her set up a conference call with Agent Smith. The team knew this debriefing would last most of the evening.

THE CLOCK SHOWED 12:32pm when Boomer pulled the Wunder Buggy into the driveway of the Seelie Court the following day. The guard at the gate waved the truck through without stopping them, and, as they pulled into the parking area, the minotaur head of the Court's external security team was waiting for them. Ghost recognized a couple of the expensive cars in the lot as belonging to members of the *Seanachaidh*. He realized that this meeting would be much more than a mere debriefing with the fae.

The minotaur greeted the DHS team leader as he climbed down out of the truck, "Well met, Special Agent Jonas Vanhof. Welcome to the Court of Light."

"Well met, Tar Katel. Will we all be attending the Queen today?"

The big minotaur nodded. "All of your team is welcome in the Court today. There is also a ceremony planned. All are welcome to attend as you wish. You are considered Allies of the Court of Light, and you are invited without condition."

Ghost's eyes widened in surprise. "Thank you for your honor and hospitality. We shall maintain your trust."

Behind him, Heavy leaned over to Spooky and said, "What do you think that means?"

The former NSA analyst was already sending a quick message to Gretchen for clarification. He let out a low whistle when he received the answer. "Gretchen says it means we can wear weapons in the Queen's presence, at her Court. She also said don't abuse the privilege. Section Twenty-Eight has never had that status before."

Heavy grunted in acknowledgement. The big federal agent had not planned on bringing his shotgun to the party, but he had not wished to disarm totally. Now he didn't have to leave his toys behind. He left his khukuris in place across his back, and to leave his sidearm attached to his belt.

Around him, several of his teammates stopped removing pistol holsters or knives, and left the weapons in place. Only Dancer still removed her pistol. She left *fion-fhuil* in its scabbard underneath her leather jacket, but she felt better removing the pistol. Boomer carried no weapons with her as she had more faith in her growing vampiric abilities than any blade.

One-by-one, the team exited the truck, with Boomer locking the doors and chirping the horn with the remote fob. They followed Tar Katel to the main doors of the house which were drawn wide open in greeting.

Standing just inside the main doors, Tó Coferal greeted them all warmly, making it a point to bow. The elf welcomed them into the house and led them back to the formal throne room. Ahead of them, the elves standing guard threw open the double doors. The Queen's Knight stepped to the threshold of the doorway and announced, "Section Twenty-Eight, Signatory to the Accords and Allies of the Court of Light." The elf stepped aside and a smattering of polite applause echoed through the chamber as the team stepped forward into the Court.

The team members were all greeted warmly by those in attendance. As protocol required, Ghost led the team before the Queen first, and they all bowed and greeted the elven monarch. The Queen asked Ghost to remain as she dismissed the others, and the team leader lingered while the others went to mingle.

"Agent Vanhof, I want to extend my sincerest condolences on the loss of your team members. They were brave men, who died with honor fighting evil. Please convey my condolences and my well wishes to Agent Smith as well. I do wish he could have been here. We have worked together to maintain peace for a long time now."

"Thank you, Your Majesty. May I ask a question?" Ghost looked earnestly at the Queen. When she nodded, he continued, making his question as innocent as possible, "How long have you known my boss?"

The Queen gave a light laugh, "Let us just say that it has been a long time. I believe I met your boss when my husband unleashed the Black Death on Europe. But that is a tale for him to tell."

Ghost stammered, "Uh. Thank you, Your Majesty. I will have to ask him for that tale."

The Queen softly laughed in amusement at the DHS leader's confusion. "Oh dear. I do hope I have not given away too many of your boss' secrets. But that is not what I wanted to talk to you about."

Ghost brought his attention back to the Queen of the Seelie Court. He filed away the questions for his boss in his mind for a later date. "Yes, Your Majesty. How may I serve you?"

"It is about your youngest agent, Special Agent Sedano. I have a request from the *Seanachaidh* for her. The Oracle would like to test her if at all possible. He believes she may have certain latent powers, or maybe an unknown heritage."

The monster hunter looked at the Queen for a moment. "Will this examination take a long time? Does it have any chance of hurting her?"

"It will only take a few minutes, and I would willingly personally guarantee her safety."

Ghost shrugged, "If she wants to do it, I'm ok with it. But it is her choice."

The Queen nodded, "Thank you. After the testing, we have a ceremony planned for your team, and a special honor planned for Agent Sedano."

Ghost smiled and got Dancer's attention. He waved the young agent over, and the Queen asked her about the test. She looked at Ghost, and he explained that it was her choice, but that the Queen was personally guaranteeing her safety. There was no greater guarantee for a member of the fae and a Signatory of the *E'Tuatha* Accords.

The young agent agreed, and the Queen led them both over to the Oracle who was standing by the Praetorian. The latter had her arm in a sling, and was visibly limping, but otherwise seemed ok.

The Oracle's eyes lit up and his loud, braying laughter filled the room. "Come, Agent Sedano. Let us retire to another, less crowded room. Agent Vanhof, you are welcome to join us, if you are concerned."

Ghost looked at his youngest agent, and the seventeen-year-old's eyes were asking him to stand by her. "I believe that will be a good idea. Lead the way."

The group left together, seeking a suitable room at the other end of the house. In the throne room, Heavy and Spooky were sampling the exotic foods spread across multiple tables around the room. They were comparing notes about the tastes and guessing the origin of each morsel. Doc was deep in a conversation with Tó Coferal about the fae religious beliefs, especially when it came to their gods and goddesses. Little G and Boomer were talking with a late-arriving Tar Katel about the various makes and models of firearms available to the minotaur. The sniper and the demolitions expert accepted an invitation to tour the armory and maybe even test some of the more exotic weapons.

Ten minutes later, Ghost, Dancer, and the rest of the small group re-entered the room. Ghost and Dancer were lost in conversation and barely noticed anyone as they stood, talking. Boomer noticed the deep conversation, the worried look on Dancer's face, and the unsettled look on her leader's face, and wandered over to her protégé.

The conversation finished before she could hear anything with her vampire sense of hearing. She walked up to the two agents and asked, "Hannah? Jonas? What's wrong?"

Hannah turned to her mentor and wiped a tear from her eye. "I just found out some weird news about my heritage." She hugged Boomer, wrapping her arms tightly. "I don't know how Agent Smith will react. Jonas thinks it'll be okay, but I think Agent Smith is gonna lock me in a lab somewhere."

"What? What do you mean heritage?"

Ghost spoke up, "The Oracle and the Queen worked some magic. There was a remark made after the combat last night, and they wanted to follow up. Their suspicions were confirmed."

"Dammit, Jonas. What's going on? Is Hannah part fae, or something?" Boomer was getting concerned.

Ghost shook his head, "Nope. It's actually worse. They believe she has the blood of the *Erinyes* in her. She is part Fury—Greek goddess of vengeance."

Boomer shrugged. After getting scratched and becoming a day-

walking vampire, nothing really shocked her any more. The explosives expert patted the young agent on the back and whispered, "No
wonder you kicked that fae's ass. Goddess power rocks." Boomer
reached up and stroked her hair. "Although apparently it comes
with a new hairdo."

Boomer felt her young friend begin to laugh through her fears.
"This doesn't mean that I'm praying to you or anything. You're just
partially a goddess. I can still kick your butt if you deserve it."

The giggles were contagious, and soon all three were laughing,
with an occasional snort from Boomer. This, of course, reignited the
peals of laughter. It only died to minor chuckles when a tone
sounded and the Queen sat upon her throne. The room gradually
fell silent, waiting for the Seelie Court monarch to speak.

"Honored guests, we are here to celebrate the Victory last night
of Special Agent Sedano, and honor the work that the team from
our friends at Section Twenty-Eight has performed. Special Agent
Jonas Vanhof, will you step forward to represent your team?"

Ghost stepped forward, bowing before the Queen. "It was our
honor to serve, Your Majesty."

"Special Agent Jonas Vanhof, please take my warmest greetings
and congratulations back to Agent Smith. The Light Court and the
Seanachaidh consider your team, and your organization as Allies and
Friends. Thank you."

Ghost bowed again and walked back to stand with the rest of his
team.

The Queen of the Seelie looked at Dancer, "Special Agent
Hannah Sedano, will you step forward?"

The young agent nervously stepped forward. She bowed before
the Queen. Taking her cue from her boss, she spoke up, "It was my
pleasure to serve as Second to Praetorian Urteghat Dhorjachen."

"Special Agent Hannah Sedano, it was your Victory at the
Gliaireacht yesterday that ended a dark reign of terror. As you have
discovered, you are a descendant of the *Erinyes*, and were able to
unlock your potential yesterday. It is with great pride and honor that
I bestow on you the title of *Claíomh an Sí*, or Faeblade in the fae
courts in this realm, as well as the courts in *Álfheimer*, the home of
the *Tuatha Dé Dannan*. You truly are a Faeblade, and thus are
welcomed as an Ally of this Court, and of the *Seanachaidh*. As
Faeblade, you are granted this sash to distinguish your title in Court.
Wear it with pride."

Applause broke out across the throne room, and Dancer tilted
forward so the Queen could slip the sash over her head and neck.

The sash was stunning. A deep blue satin background was offset by the silver and gold embroidered sword. The pommel of the hilt was a golden starburst pattern placed right at her collarbone. The rapier-like blade ended at her waist in a very fine point.

The young agent was fighting tears, overflowing with joy at the honor she was just bestowed. She almost missed the words as the Queen continued.

"Special Agent Jonas Vanhof, would you step forward again?" Ghost complied quickly. "As Signatory of the *E'Tuatha* Accords, bear witness that Special Agent Hannah Sedano is hereby given status as *Cainteoir*. She is now a Speaker to the Court of Light, and a recognized Emissary to the fae courts. Please convey to Agent Smith that Special Agent Sedano is a new Emissary to our court."

Ghost was shocked. The seventeen year old agent was, by the Queen's selection, the official Emissary to the Seelie courts. Smith was going to be apoplectic. "I will certainly convey that message, Your Majesty."

The Queen nodded. "Thank you Agent Vanhof. And thank you *Cainteoir* Sedano." The elven monarch looked over the rest of the crowd, "With that, I conclude the official duties of this conclave." A smile lit her face as if the weight of ruling was suddenly lighter. "Now is the time for celebration. Eat, drink, and be merry, for the day is young."

EPILOGUE

It was 3:05pm, and Agent Frederick Tremblay was once again working the duty desk in the operations center. He sat down seven minutes ago, relieving the first shift alarm monitor two minutes early. Since his first alarm a week ago, it had been relatively quiet. Two minor zombie attacks and a UFO sighting had all been handled on his watch. He felt like he was finally getting used to this gig.

The rookie agent raised his coffee cup to his lips and was about to take a drink when the alarms in front of him started alerting. He reached over and silenced the audible indicator and read the screen. The technician set his mug down, not realizing that it was only partly on the desk surface. As the mug full of coffee shattered on the floor, Tremblay was already pulling the reference binder out to read the code reference.

Looking at the code, he swallowed. He waved to get his supervisor's attention, panic edging into his consciousness. He highlighted the code for his supervisor and then began the process of tracing the location. When his supervisor reached his desk, Tremblay pointed at the reference code. His supervisor paled and pulled out his phone. He called the number at the top of contact list. It was answered on the first ring. The supervisor began talking.

"Yes, sir, Donaldson here. We've got a code Zulu-X-ray. Yes, sir. Zulu-X-ray. Tracking it now." The supervisor looked to see his technician go pale. Donaldson's eyes followed Tremblay's shaking finger, and it was the supervisor's turn to blanch.

"Uh, sir. The Zulu-X-ray is here, sir. Yessir. Within three hundred yards. Yessir, I'm activating the alarm right now."

Donaldson reached over and flipped a plastic cover up and out of the way. It covered a large red button surrounded by yellow and black stripes and had the words, "GENERAL ALARM" above the button, on the desk. He mashed the button down with his thumb. Suddenly, yellow emergency lights began flashing, and a loud wailing siren sounded three long blasts. Ten seconds later, the siren sounded again. Everyone in the operations room scrambled to their feet and ran for the door.

OUTSIDE THE MAIN BUILDING, the security guards in the guard shack watched a roiling mass of blackness form into a large circle about fifty feet above the ground, and about a couple hundred yards away from the building. The guard who was just coming on duty reached into the shack and unlocked the rifle cabinet. He quickly pulled out one of the assault rifles in the cabinet, slammed a magazine into the well, and pulled the charging handle.

The guard handed the now loaded rifle to the other guard, who was supposed to be leaving, and reached for the second one in the cabinet. He quickly made it ready, then grabbed several extra magazines, handing half to the other guard. He leaned back in to shack and raised his hand over the general attack alarm button. He hesitated momentarily and was surprised when the alarm sounded without him hitting the button.

Realizing it had been triggered from the control room, he stepped out of the shack and stood ready, loosely cradling the rifle. He heard the rocket launchers on the roof uncover and swivel into position. He next heard the metal exterior door slam open and the sounds of boots running on the pavement.

The S.W.A.T. Captain halted next to the guards. "What's happening Mike? Where's the threat..." The captain trailed off as he saw the fifty-foot diameter circle of blackness. All the men at the gate raised their rifles as a creature poked its massive head out of the inky black. Bill heard the rocket launchers whine as they tracked the incursion, ready to engage the creature.

GHOST WAS deep in a conversation with the Oracle. They talked about the history of the Accords, and the DHS leader recounted some of his personal history as well. The Oracle had just made a connection between the man in front of him, and the storied lineage of his family, when Ghost's SSP rang. Before the Oracle could say anything, about his family, Ghost looked at the phone, and saw it was Gretchen's number. Reluctantly, he answered it.

"Hi, Gretchen. I don't know when we'll be back to the MMC. The Queen is throwing a serious party." He was cut off by her words abruptly.

"Yes. I understand. We'll be there in ten minutes. Prep the jet for takeoff."

Ghost turned to the Oracle and said, "I apologize. We have to leave now. We've been recalled for an emergency."

The Oracle nodded his understanding even as the monster hunter turned and began grabbing his team. He found everyone throughout the room, and politely, but firmly, interrupted every conversation they were having. Most of them did not want to leave, and at the first sign of resistance, he told them that they had a new Priority Black mission.

In two minutes, they were all gathered at the van, and Ghost said an abbreviated farewell to the fae around the truck. Boomer fired up the engine and eased the Wunder Buggy down the drive-way. She spoke up even as Ghost turned to address the team. "So boss, what's the big deal? Have aliens landed on the White House lawn?"

The laughter died when the team saw the face of their leader. He said, "I don't have much information, only what Gretchen told me."

He was interrupted by Spooky, who was banging away at his keyboard. "Uh, boss? You maybe want to see this? It says there's been a massive terror attack at a business park in Langley. And I'll be damned if it doesn't look like our building."

Ghost looked at the monitor, then back at his team. "That's what I've been trying to tell you. Section Twenty-Eight is under attack. Most of the security forces are dead, and the HRT got wiped out when they responded. Worst of all, the Director's dead and a lot of agents are missing, including Agent Smith."

Grand Rapids, Michigan, Saturday, 9/3/2016

BRYAN DONIHUE

INCURSION: DRAGONFIRE

THE KNIGHT'S BANE TRILOGY–BOOK 3

KICKSTARTER SUPPORTERS

For this novel, I ran a crowdfunding campaign to pay for some of the (rather minor) expenses incurred in self-publishing. In this campaign, I had a group of incredible backers in the campaign. Their support made the campaign successful, and I cannot thank them enough!

Campaign Contributors

Senior Field Agent
Retnuh
Jeremy Sampsell

Field Agent
Eddie Bramble

Veteran Monster Hunter
Agent Stormraider
The Kalafut Family
Pete McCarthy

Experienced Monster Hunter
David Cassiday
Matt Eastman

Eulene Freeland
Troye Gerard
Andrew Guastella
Craig Kramer
Jessie Stevenson
Valerie Wilcox
Joel Wilkinson
Kenneth Zwaggerman

Apprentice Monster Hunter

A Challis

PROLOGUE

The man slowly became aware of the flames around him as they crackled and roared. Groaning, he tried to move, realizing quickly that his legs were pinned beneath something large. Moving his arm to push up, the battered and bruised man screamed in agony, his shattered radius grinding and refusing to support his weight.

Agent Frederick Tremblay winced and moaned again as he shifted and rolled around, trying to wriggle his legs out from under the support beam pinning him to the floor. Giving one massive heave, he felt his knee pop as he yanked his legs free from beneath the beam. He screamed in renewed agony, and his cries ground down into a hacking cough from the smoke and ash swirling in the air. He blacked out.

He opened his eyes again. It may have been a few seconds, or it may have been several minutes. The ash and smoke were still heavy, and he gave a wracking cough as he drew more air into his tortured lungs. As his coughing fit petered out, he heard the moans and cries of those also trapped around him.

Agent Tremblay levered himself into a sitting position, leaning heavily against what remained of his desk. Once the dizziness faded, he looked around at the devastation that surrounded him. The command center had been in a windowless room in the basement of the complex. There had been two full stories above the command center. Now he could see daylight filtering down through the gaping holes overhead.

He could hear the wailing of sirens in the distance as the local first responders made their way to the scene. Off in the distance, he heard the deep "whump-whump-whump" of inbound helicopters - likely the FBI's Blackhawk helicopters sitting over at Quantico. Then he heard the growling behind him.

The Section 28 agent froze. He slowly turned his body around, wincing as he shifted his broken arm and mangled knee. He was nose-to-snout with a giant black and dark green reptilian head. Dragon. It had to be a dragon. The creature opened its mouth and let out a "chuff", almost knocking Tremblay over as it blew a rancid, fetid breath into the young agent's face.

The creature's head was about the size of a Mini Cooper, and the gaping maw was bristling with sword-length, razor-sharp teeth. The outside was layered with rough scales, almost armor-like, and short spines bristled from various boney ridges.

The massive head was attached to a long, scaled neck, which connected to a large body covered with thicker scales. Two massive bat-like wings sprouted from the creature's back, flanking a complex harness, and a rider in the harness.

Agent Tremblay felt the evil in the gaze of the dragon rider. Clad in ornate armor, the figure sat straight in the saddle. Its armor was a matte black metal with silver and gold filigree and exquisitely inlaid with intricate scrollwork. The helm had a horsehair plume as a top-knot, and the t-shaped eye and nose-opening was dark with shadows. The agent's eyes locked onto the two bright red sparks in the shadows of the helm.

A rumbling, rasping voice sounded from the helmeted rider, "Little man, do you know Agent Smith?"

Tremblay shuddered. The rasping voice washed over the young agent, and his voice quavered as he responded. "Um... Yes?"

The cold of the dark rider's oily laugh made the young agent shiver. "Tell your Agent Smith that I now know where he lives. And I shall return to finish our feud."

The dragon rider slapped his mount's neck, "Up, Argohast. We will take our leave." The rider pointed a gauntleted fist at Tremblay, "Remember my message, worm. Tell Agent Smith that I will have his head."

Tremblay was nodding as the rider slapped his mount one more time, and the dragon's wings beat a powerful draft and the creature leapt into the air. The battered and bruised agent watched as a dark rip appeared in the sky, the line crackling and thundering like a black lightning. The rip split the air, and the hole that opened filled with an inky roiling mass. The dragon gave two massive thrusts of its wings and the creature dove into the gaping maw. The tear in the sky disappeared with a loud pop and the crash of inrushing air.

The roaring flames were soon drowned out by the "whump-whump-whump" of the helicopters arriving overhead. A Blackhawk came to a hover directly over Agent Tremblay, and four weighted ropes dropped from the open doors. Four heavily armed and armored figures appeared on the lines and fast-rappelled down the ropes, landing with jarring thumps in the debris around the injured agent. Four more armored figures soon joined the first four, all of them spreading out around the ropes. The ropes dropped free, and the Blackhawk moved off to take up a station a few hundred yards away.

Another Blackhawk appeared overhead, disgorging eight more heavily armed and armored figures in the same manner. In less than sixty-seconds, sixteen members of the FBI's elite Hostage Rescue Team were fanned out around the rubble, and started checking for hostiles and survivors. The leader of the team approached Tremblay and looked at him carefully. As the HRT leader bent over to check on the young agent, the Section 28 agent passed out and collapsed back into the rubble.

IN A DOWNTOWN SEATTLE OFFICE, the man sitting behind the desk reached for his mobile phone. He thumbed the screen to answer the call, "Agent Browning." The man listened for a few moments, nodding absently, as if the caller could see him. His face screwed into a frown, and he covered his mobile device with his hand to muffle his voice. He yelled out into the cubicle warren outside his office, "Someone find out what is happening outside DC. Get on the news feeds."

He pulled his hand away from the cellphone and spoke into it again, "I understand. We'll cover for you here. You're going to owe Karen another dinner."

Special Agent Browning disconnected the call and listened to the rising voices from outside his office. He rose from his desk and strode across the room. He leaned through his door and waived Special Agent Karen Rixon to him, "I've got some bad news. Looks like you're going to have to cover for Agent Black for a while."

I

HOMECOMING

1

AFTERMATH

"Roger, Control. Cleared on runway twenty, winds at ten knots, at two-two-five. Beginning our descent."

The pilot of the massive C-17 Globemaster III gently banked his plane and keyed the internal intercom, "We are beginning our approach. We'll be down in about twelve minutes." He flipped the switch off and nodded to his copilot as they began working through the landing checklist.

The roar of the massive engines powering the Air Force transport grew steadily louder just before the wheels touched down. As the nose wheels touched, the pilot and copilot both stood on the brakes to slow the monster plane. The pilot quickly reached over and reversed the thrust of the engines, causing the massive turbines to roar louder as they fought speed and inertia in the battle of physics and willpower. The crew won the battle again as the plane slowed until it could turn off the main runway and trail the "Follow Me" truck as it guided the way to the plane's parking spot.

As soon as the plane touched down and had slowed to taxi, the men and women in the lavishly decorated passenger area began unbuckling their seat-belts and standing. All but one woman grabbed their small personal kits and headed toward the back door of the passenger cabin. That woman stood and stretched. She picked up her attaché and walked toward the front of the cabin. As the plane came to a gentle halt, she heard the engines wind down and then spin down to a stop.

The Air Force pilot opened the cockpit door, and leaned down the steps, "We're all secure, ma'am. We've got a welcome party coming to greet us. Anything else I can do?"

"No, Captain Kenney. I think we can take it from here." The young black woman paused thoughtfully. She continued, "I don't know what's going to happen to us, or even if you'll have this assignment for much longer. I'll call you with the details once we figure out what happened."

"Thank you, Agent Massey. Let the team know that we're here for them, and you."

Special Agent Massey gave a small smile. "Thank you, Bill. I'll let them know." Giving a half wave, the DHS Agent turned and opened the side hatch on the airplane. She extended the stairs and stepped down to the hot tarmac, to be greeted by a Marine Corps Captain, and a man in black BDUs with the acronym "FBI" emblazoned across his cap.

At just over five feet tall, DHS Special Agent Gretchen Massey was often described as "stunning" by those who have just met her. Gretchen's light mocha skin was offset by her jet black hair, which she usually kept pulled back. It was not unusual for a few of the tight curls to escape her severe hairstyle, all of which enhanced her beauty. As a former gymnast, her training at Section 28 kept her in top fighting shape, even though the most fighting she did now was battling paperwork and requisitions to smooth the path for Team Knightmare. Special Agent Massey was the on-site liaison and administrator assigned to Team Knightmare, and she was very good at her job.

"Special Agent Massey?" The FBI agent raised an eyebrow with the question. Seeing her nod, he reached out a hand to shake hers. "Special Agent Frank Chanthala. Call me Frank. I've been sent to take you to the site. I have transport waiting for us." He motioned towards two black SUVs idling about two hundred feet away.

Gretchen looked at the trucks and then turned as she heard the hydraulic whine as the rear cargo ramp of the C-17 began to lower. The FBI agent followed her gaze, and they both watched as the ramp finished its ponderous journey to the tarmac. She turned back to the agent, "We won't be needing your trucks for the trip over to the base. I'll ride with the team. Although I do need transportation for our casualties. We lost two agents on our last mission and have them in cold storage on the jet. Can you detail men to escort the remains to our holding morgue? I'll give you the address, as well as the codes needed to get in."

The DHS agent heard the familiar rumble of the Wunder Buggy's engine roar to life. A small smile graced her lips. She dug a small radio out of her coat pocket and raised it to her lips. "Boomer, this is Gretchen. Confirm that the Buggy is configured for official duty before you make your appearance."

There was an uncomfortably long pause before the radio crackled to life again. "Gretchen, this is Boomer. Configured. Exiting ramp now."

A large black truck rumbled down the rear cargo ramp of the giant Air Force jet. It looked like a standard panel truck with matte black paint and a blackened steel push guard protecting the grill. A closer look showed that the truck seemed to ride slightly higher than a standard truck, with larger tires and wheels. The seal of the Department of Homeland Security was about a foot across and in the middle of each of the front doors, and white block letters about six inches high proclaimed the same on the sides and rear ramp.

Agent Chanthala stood with a slack jaw as the truck rumbled to a stop a couple feet from Gretchen. He looked up to see a young woman in black BDUs and armor sitting behind the rather large wheel of the behemoth. She just flashed a quick grin as the truck idled. The door on the far side of the truck slid open with a slight hiss, and a tall, lanky man in a black button-down shirt and wearing what appeared to be some sort of leather duster-like jacket clambered out of the passenger's seat. His black gaucho hat was perched atop his head as he waved to Gretchen.

"All set Gretchen. Everyone is on board, except for you. Have you arranged for Do-Right and Scout?"

The beautiful DHS agent looked at Agent Chanthala, "Have you arranged for our fallen agents remains?"

The FBI agent nodded, "We'll take care of it. I'll transport them and make sure they're taken care of."

"Thank you, Agent Chanthala. I'll send you the details." She turned and walked over to the passenger side of the Wunder Buggy, and climbed up, crossing over the passenger's seat to crouch between the two seats. The hard-looking young man swung up into the truck and the door hissed as it slid closed. The muted rumble of the idling engine turned into a roar as the driver slammed the truck into gear and it surged forward, heading for the exit gate. As it approached the gate, red and blue flashing lights lit up along the back of the truck and a siren started to wail.

Forty-five minutes later, Boomer killed the siren and lights. She braked hard to a stop outside a checkpoint manned by local law enforcement about a three blocks from the compound. The older officer waved her to a stop and wandered to her window.

Boomer's door slid open with a hiss, and she looked at the officer as he told her the area was closed to all traffic. Her glare cut off his bored explanation mid-sentence, and he visibly gulped.

She spoke softly, but her words were laced with threats, "Homeland Security. Let us through. Now."

"Yes, ma'am," came the stuttered reply.

The officer's arm was shaking as he waved to the younger officers manning the barricades to move them aside. He retreated to his cruiser as fast as he could without breaking into a cold run.

As soon as the barricades were far enough apart, Boomer slammed her door and goosed the throttle. The truck roared as it leapt forward. As they passed the barricades, Ghost looked at his young driver and quirked an eyebrow, "Laid it on a little thick there, didn't you?"

Rebekah "Boomer" Callahan flicked her eyes toward her boss briefly, before turning them back to the road. The twenty-six-year-old demolitions expert had been recruited to join the team just a few short months ago. She had been a Petty Officer in the Navy, and one of the Navy's two female EOD technicians. Having trained and qualified with the Special Forces, her EOD career was on a meteoric path until the young woman saw the Loch Ness Monster on a diving trip in Scotland.

After she went public with her story, Navy command had recalled the young Petty Officer and send her to teach new EOD tech applicants until she retired. The day she was told of her summary banishment from the field, she was approached by an agent from a small, top-secret division of Homeland Security, called Section 28. Special Agent James Smith had offered her a job and opened a way out of the dreary career of teaching young EOD techs. Rebekah had jumped at the offer.

On her first mission, the new DHS Special Agent had been infected by a genetically modified variant of the vampire virus. That simple scratch had manifested certain vampiric powers in the young woman and had burdened her with the cravings that accompanied the new powers. She had been training hard for the last couple months to control the monster inside her and had proven herself on the last mission. She was starting to enjoy being a living vampire.

Boomer grinned, "Yeah. I probably turned it on too much. But it worked, didn't it?" She caught her boss' bemused nodding out of the corner of her eye.

Ghost smiled at his demolitions specialist. Underneath that young woman's soft exterior hid a monster he knew very well. After all, he had been hunting them for years.

Jonas "Ghost" Vanhof was the only surviving member of a family that had been hunting monsters for generations. Raised by his aunt to hunt monsters from a young age, his parents had been killed before he could crawl, and his aunt just before he turned eighteen. After his aunt was murdered by a lycanthrope, young Jonas had willingly, gladly, picked up the mantle of being a monster hunter, and had hunted the pack until there were no more creatures left.

Revenge complete, he continued hunting monsters of all types, specializing in were-creatures, as well as vampires and their kin. Not aligning with any of the private organizations directly allowed him to take contracts from many of them, building a network to provide information and resources while he chased down creatures.

It was on one of these hunts in Norfolk, Virginia, that Jonas got caught by the local police after he had killed a werewolf and the infected man's wife, who had just been bitten. Resigned to a life in prison, he was surprised when a DHS agent had met him in jail. Special Agent James Smith had offered a simple choice, go to prison for murder, or join his top-secret agency and have access to more resources and information than he had ever dreamed.

Jonas took the offered second chance and quickly became the second-in-command of the newest monster hunting team. This had turned into one of the most difficult vampire hunts he had ever attended. In the end, a master vampire he had chased for years was dead, but so was the team's original leader, Six. Jonas had been leading the team ever since that fateful day.

Ghost looked around as Boomer maneuvered the large truck through the spread of police cruisers and other emergency vehicles from local, state, and federal agencies. She passed a squat, black armored personnel carrier with FBI and DHS markings and pulled up to another set of barricades. Boomer stopped the truck and shut off the engine. Ghost opened his door and stepped out as a man in combat fatigues and heavy armor walked up to the truck.

The man held up a hand in the universal gesture of "stop." His mirrored sunglasses reflected Ghost's image, and his face showed contempt as the DHS agent stood before him. "Sorry, sir. National security incident. I can't let you pass."

Ghost drew out his credentials and held them up in front of the soldier's face. He forced a touch of his willpower into the credentials and watched as the slight green glow reflected off the man's glasses. "Special Agent Jonas Vanhof, Homeland Security. What's your name, soldier?"

"Haywood, sir. Pfc. Brian Haywood."

"Private Haywood, this is OUR incident. You will let me and my team pass. Am I clear?"

Ghost could tell when the suggestion took hold of the soldier. He staggered slightly, shook his head, and then stepped back and to attention. The soldier snapped a quick salute. "Yes, sir. Sorry for the interruption, sir."

The DHS team leader snapped a quick response to the salute. "Thank you, Private Haywood. You're doing a good job here. Keep up the good work."

Ghost turned and waved to Boomer and Gretchen in the front of the truck. He heard the hiss of Boomer's door as it slid open, and the subtle hydraulic whine as the back ramp lowered. He turned back to the young private as his team disembarked.

"Who's in charge right now, private?"

"That would be the FBI, sir. They set up the command post over there." The soldier pointed to a mobile command truck parked about half a block down the street.

Ghost thanked the man and waved his gathered team over to him. He counted heads quickly and realized that someone was missing. He touched his throat mic, "Spooky, this is Ghost. Launch a drone. Give me eyes in the sky until we can get satellite coverage overhead." He looked up at the four helicopters circling the area. He counted three different news logos and a police Bell Ranger.

The DHS leader continued, "Spooky, call the FAA and make this area a no-fly for civilian aircraft, including low flying drones. Section Twenty-Eight Authority. My authority. If you see any other drones, let me know, we'll take care of it."

John Q. "Spooky" Smith was an Irishman from Boston, who looked much younger than his thirty years of age. Graduating from the top of his class at MIT, Smith was recruited straight out of college for his cryptanalysis training by the National Security Agency. There the young man had served for three years before he was chosen to be the liaison to Homeland Security, all while managing the PRISM and ECHELON algorithms. He was one of the NSA's top analysts, and on the fast track for a management spot in SigInt. Then his life had turned upside down.

While working on a coded intercept, he had submitted a summary containing information about a secret group that was hunting monsters. His supervisor would have laughed the report off, but Smith had already forwarded a copy to the Homeland Security supervisor he worked with as a liaison. That weekend, while Smith spent time as an amateur paranormal "ghost hunter," the report landed on the Director of Homeland Security's desk. By Monday morning Smith had lost his liaison role, and his work as a lead analyst for ECHELON.

Fortunately for the young NSA agent, his report was flagged for review by Section 28, the very team that his report had "outed." A DHS supervising agent named James Smith had made a special offer for the young computer analyst, and the NSA agent had accepted the new position. Now he sat at his station in the truck known as the Wunder Buggy, getting ready to launch a drone while dialing his emergency contact to the FAA.

"Copy that, Ghost. Calling the FAA now."

The DHS team leader motioned and walked toward the FBI Command Center. The rest of Team Knightmare fell in behind him while Gretchen stepped up and walked beside the tall agent.

Gretchen lowered her voice so that only the team leader could hear. "Be careful about the authority you are throwing around. We don't know who is actually in charge yet."

Ghost abruptly stopped and faced his team's administrator and headquarters liaison. "We know that our headquarters was deliberately attacked. We have no communications with anyone who was in headquarters, including Agent Smith. We have no communication with the Director, or any of the other team leaders. Until we find someone alive, that puts me in charge, according to the org chart. Listen, I need your help, but if we don't get control of this situation soon, we will never be able to get control again."

Gretchen looked into the monster hunter's eyes for a few tense seconds, searching for... something. She found it and nodded slowly. "You have my support. Just don't write any checks we can't cash."

Ghost nodded and turned to resume walking. They reached the mobile command truck quickly. Standing outside the truck were two more soldiers in Army uniforms and an FBI agent in black BDUs, wearing a heavy armor vest and cradling an M4 rifle.

The army soldiers became more alert as Ghost's heavily armed and armored team approached the truck, and once again, the DHS leader was met with the upturned hand telling him to stop.

The tall monster hunter was quick to raise his credentials as he spoke. "Special Agent Jonas Vanhof, Homeland Security. Who is in charge of this mess?"

The FBI Agent lifted his chin and indicated the truck, "SAC Mulder is in the command truck. But I can't let you go in there. She's in a meeting."

Ghost's eyes tightened, betraying the slight bit of willpower he was using on his credentials. He spoke evenly and slowly, making sure to enunciate each word. "You will let me in to see her. This was a DHS facility, and I am assuming temporary command of the search and rescue and cleanup operations. Now... Let. Me. Pass." The last line was delivered through gritted teeth, and the FBI agent before him blanched.

The agent stepped out of the monster hunter's way and reached for the truck's door to open it. Ghost turned to the rest of the team, "Gretchen? Doc? You two are with me. The rest of you, wait out here."

The three DHS agents entered the FBI's Mobile Command Center.

2

QUESTIONS

Ruins of Section 28 Headquarters, Langley, Virginia

The FBI's Mobile Command Center appeared to be two or three bread trucks mashed together, into a stretch version of the venerable commercial delivery vehicle. Antennae and satellite dishes sprouted from the roof of the truck, pointing in every direction. Painted a dark blue, the exterior of the truck proclaimed, "Federal Bureau of Investigation" and, "Mobile Command Center" in large white letters.

The interior of the truck was already cramped when the three DHS agents walked through the door. Ghost counted eight other people sitting at various consoles. At the far end of the truck was a small area empty of consoles. In the center of that area was a lit glass table with changing electronic readouts flashing on the men and women surrounding it.

All four of the people standing around the table looked up as Ghost and the two women entered the truck. Two of the men were in Army combat fatigues, one with the insignia of a colonel on his collar. The two women were in dark gray suits and white blouses. Each had an FBI ID card clipped to her lapel, and one was leaning heavily on the table and pointing at a particular display. She spoke up, her voice cutting thru the air and silencing any of the background chatter from the other operators.

"Who are you and what the hell are you doing on my truck?"

Ghost smiled his most charming and disarming smile and held up his credentials, "Special Agent Jonas Vanhof, ma'am. Homeland Security. Are you, by chance, Special Agent Mulder?"

Ghost could feel the snarl in her reply, "Yes. Special Agent in Charge Tressa Mulder. This is my scene right now, so you can wait until I'm ready to talk to you. Until then, get out of my truck."

Ghost's smile remained in place, but his eyes hardened slightly. He took a deep breath and exhaled audibly. "Ma'am. I need to talk to you right now, in private, before we both say or do something we'll regret later."

It was silent in the vehicle as her incident command team waited for the coming explosion. The FBI SAC was not used to being addressed with such insubordination, and she took a long couple seconds to react. Her scowl turned into a snarl, and her voice dropped lower. "Let me get one thing straight, Agent Vanhof. This is an FBI operation. Homeland Security can clean up after we clear the scene. In fact, I doubt you are even cleared to be on site, let alone know what installation was attacked."

Special Agent Mulder gritted her teeth, "Now, get off my truck. Before I have you arrested for obstruction."

Ghost's smile dropped, and he felt Gretchen's hand on his arm as a caution. He consciously refrained from using the ethereal power in his credentials as he extended them for the recalcitrant agent to see. His eyes narrowed and his voice grew deep and cold.

"I will say again, I am Special Agent Jonas Vanhof from the Department of Homeland Security. I am the lead agent for one of the teams based in this facility. As of now, you have two choices, you step aside and meet with me briefly, or I exert every available bit of my authority, and you lose. Your choice."

The army colonel looked back and forth between the FBI agent and the DHS monster hunter. Just as he was about to intervene, Mulder let out a small huff. "Fine, Agent Vanhof. I'll meet with you in my office." Her look was cool and professional, and Ghost walked past the small table, through a doorway, and into a cramped office.

When Ghost closed the doorway to the office, Special Agent Tressa Mulder rounded on him, barely holding in her fury at the treatment in front of her incident command team. Mulder was just over five feet tall, with brown hair pulled back into a severe bun. The lines of her face were a little too severe to be called a classical beauty, but she was certainly attractive. The FBI SAC had been forced to work twice as hard as the men in her training class just to overcome the subtle "old boys club" that still seemed to have roots in the venerable law enforcement organization.

Her dedication and hard work quickly propelled her through the ranks of the Bureau until she was granted a coveted SAC title for northern Virginia. Even though she personally hated the political game, she realized that she would be forced to play while she was a SAC in the DC area. And she was good at it. Mulder had encountered the secretive DHS teams led by James Smith three times in her career and hated being steamrolled by all of them. She had also met with their supervising agent, and she had genuinely liked the southern gentleman, despite her interactions with his teams. The FBI SAC had never met this "Agent Vanhof" before, but the name sounded familiar.

Before she could verbal flay the DHS agent, Ghost held up his hands and started speaking, "SAC Mulder, I'm sorry that I was so rough on you in front of your team. The fact is, I need to get a handle on what's happening. To my knowledge, my team was the only one out in the field when the attack happened. I've not been able to get in touch with Agent Smith, or the Director, or any of the other team leaders. Until I do, and until I find someone with more seniority than me, I have to assume authority in this operation."

The FBI agent shook her head and opened her mouth to protest. Again, Ghost held up his hand to stop her. "From your statement to me, you have at least some information about the special nature of the installation that was attacked. You know that most of what it does is classified so far above your pay grade that it doesn't exist to you. My department must take charge of this cleanup.

"I also know it was such a bad attack that we will need the help of your Bureau. I want to cooperate with you because right now we need each other. But I must take the authority in the incident until relieved. Can you at least agree to that?"

The FBI agent considered her options. The DHS agent was right about the technicalities. And maybe, just maybe, if she cooperated with his department, she might learn enough to understand why they were given the latitude they seemingly had available.

Ghost watched her carefully, and felt relieved when she nodded, "I think I can do that Agent Vanhof. As of now, you will be in charge of operations, and my team and the Army units that were called out will support you."

"Thank you, ma'am." Ghost smiled. "And please, call me Jonas."

She shook his proffered hand, "Thank you, Jonas, and please, call me Tressa. That 'ma'am' crap makes me feel old."

The two emerged from the office and there was a collective relaxation from all who were in the main area. Gretchen and Doc were talking with the Army colonel and the SAC Mulder's assistant. Gretchen looked sharply from Ghost to the FBI agent and back again, taking in the more relaxed posture. The experienced Section 28 agent looked for signs of magically enforced coercion and saw none of the usual indicators. She broke off her discussion and walked to Ghost.

The tall monster hunter introduced Gretchen and Doc to SAC Mulder. "Special Agent in Charge Tressa Mulder, may I introduce you to Special Agent Gretchen Massey, my team liaison, and Doctor Noelle Sorenson, my second-in-command."

Dr. Noelle "Doc" Sorenson was the team's esoteric research specialist, and faith-based representative from the Vatican. Not only was she a classically trained combat-exorcist, she also served as a medical doctor, and the team's combat medic. Noelle's journey to join the team was extraordinary and started as a Master's graduate in Sociology returning to attend the University of Notre Dame for pre-med. It was during her many years in South Bend, Indiana that she attended one of the local Catholic parishes, and eventually chose the Catholic faith as her way of life.

Her grades and hard work earned her a coveted spot at the University of Michigan Medical School where she excelled in all her studies. Her work brought her to the attention of Doctors Without Borders, and she served a term with them in several far-off places. It was her work across the ocean that changed her life forever.

Dr. Sorenson had seen strange animal attacks and helped heal them, better than any of the other doctors could. When she confided this to her priest in her hometown, he notified the Vatican. The Vatican had recruited her for a special order of the priesthood that fought what she considered to be mythical creatures. She accepted the appointment and trained hard for just over a year to be ordained into the special, hidden priesthood. After her ordination, she was sent to join team Knightmare as their Vatican representative, where she had excelled at hunting and banishing the undead.

Doc shook the FBI agent's hand and smiled, "It's a pleasure, Agent Mulder. Please, call me Noelle."

"And I'm Tressa." The FBI SAC turned and introduced everyone else around the table. This is my second-in-command, Special Agent Valerie Wilcox. Her specialty is Forensics. And this is Colonel Spenser from the Army's 911th Engineer Company. They are assisting with search and rescue operations. We have about two blocks of devastation, plus all the special oddities that your department possesses. His Adjutant is Command Sergeant Major Ryan."

After the introductions finished, Ghost looked at the table in front of him. The multi-touch electronic display was only slightly less sophisticated than the one that had adorned the conference room at Section 28 headquarters. He saw a large satellite map of the area projection that covered about two-thirds of the surface. The rest was covered with zoomed in areas focusing on trouble spots. As he watched, one area blinked out, only to be replaced with another view by one of the technicians at the workstations.

The DHS hunter looked at Colonel Spenser and SAC Mulder, "Is this real-time? Is it Keyhole?"

Special Agent Mulder shook her head. The colonel spoke up, "Negative. We don't have the priority for the access. We've sent the request to the NSA, but are waiting on authorization."

Ghost pulled a slim USB thumb drive from one of his pockets and turned to hand it to the nearest technician. He handed the technician the USB drive and said out loud, "This does not exist. It is still classified. Just plug it in."

The technician looked at his boss, and SAC Mulder hesitated. She looked at Ghost, then shrugged and nodded at the technician. "You're in charge, Agent Vanhof. This better not fry our systems."

Ghost didn't respond. Instead, the monster hunter keyed his throat mic, "Spooky, this is Ghost, activate Demon Protocol. Drive one."

In less than a second the displays around the truck flickered, and Spooky's disembodied voice floated from one of the speakers. "I'm in, boss. What do you need?"

Mulder's eyes grew wide and a look of terror flashed across her face. "What have you done? You've compromised our systems. And who is on the other end?"

Ghost spoke loud enough to be picked up by any of the microphones around the room. "That's Special Agent John Smith, and he's my tech guy, and is in our mobile command truck. Spooky, say hello to Special Agent in Charge Mulder from the FBI. She's running the Bureau side of things on this site."

The monitor nearest the command planning table winked as Spooky's face appeared on screen. He gave a little wave. "Hello, Agent Mulder. Sorry to startle you." With a mischievous grin, the former analyst addressed the FBI SAC, "I gotta ask, is Agent Scully in the truck?" Seeing the annoyance flash across Mulder's face, Spooky quickly turned toward Ghost, "What do you need, boss?"

"Transfer the feed from the Keyhole satellite to this command table. Allow access for minor control to the technicians in this vehicle, so they can bring relevant info to the table." He paused for a moment, thinking through the process, "Did you get through to the FAA? Are they playing ball?"

Spooky was nodding as his fingers flew over the keyboard. "Roger that, boss. The FAA decided that they would play ball once I talked to the director on his home phone line. He was not happy, I think I interrupted a bar-b-que, or something." The young analyst's fingers were clattering away, and then they stopped. "There you go, control and download established."

The picture on the table transformed. The resolution difference was remarkable, and Mulder and Colonel Spenser studied the table more carefully. Ghost looked at the image of Spooky on the screen, "That's good, Spooky. You can give these technicians their monitors and microphones back. I'll contact you by radio if we need you again."

Spooky winked, and the monitor reverted to the data stream it was pulling before the former NSA analyst had hijacked it. Ghost looked at the lead FBI agent, "Sorry. Agent Smith gets a little... weird. But he's the best at what he does. Now what do we have going on?"

Thirty minutes later, the three Section 28 agents left the Mobile Command Center and stopped to talk to their teammates. Ghost gathered his team around him and they discussed their next actions. "Gretchen, you and Doc go help with any wounded. I would like you guys to interview anyone who is able to talk. See if you can interview the kid who talked to the dragon rider, Agent Tremblay, I think." The women nodded and walked toward the medical triage tent.

The tall monster hunter looked at the rest of the team, sizing them up, "The rest of you will work the scene, pairing up with the Army engineering teams. Boomer and Dancer, work the east quadrant. Heavy and Little G, you guys have the west quadrant. Stay safe. Look for survivors, bodies, and artifacts. Remember, everything on this site is Classified Top Secret. We are primary on this site, so don't let the other agencies box you out. Holler if you find something."

Boomer looked at her team leader, "Anything, or anyone, special that we're looking for?"

"Yes. The Director. Agent Smith. The other team leads. Hell, I'd even give Norbert a hug right now. Also, watch for artifacts. They will need to be stored before they wander off."

"So what are you going to be doing?"

Ghost thought a moment, "I'm going to go to the morgue area, and try to help identify the bodies."

The agents split up, and Ghost worked his way over to the warehouse they were temporarily using as a morgue. He walked up to the front of the warehouse, and the guard saluted before letting him into the building. *Looks like Mulder got the word out. Good.*

The subtle stench of decay and roasted flesh hit him as he walked through the double door. Even with the air conditioning running at full capacity, the large area was losing a battle with the sun beating on the metal roof of the building. A man in scrubs and a surgical mask stopped him inside the door, demanding to know why he was there. A quick flash of his credentials, and the medical examiner handed the monster hunter a surgical mask and gloves.

Ghost walked down the rows of stainless steel tables topped with body bags. There were several men and women dressed in surgical garb gathered in pairs and small groups around several of the cadavers. He walked down the rows, examining the tags attached to the body bags. Each tag had a space for the name, sex, age, location found, and an index number for the records. The first several tags that Ghost read showed him names he barely recognized, some of them from the support services, while others were on site security personnel.

He looked up and found a man with a tablet scanning in tags and making notes on the screen. The tall monster hunter walked over to the man and held up his credentials. "Special Agent Jonas Vanhof, Department of Homeland Security. I need to look up some names to see if they've been identified yet."

"I don't care who you are." The man in scrubs glared at him over the top of the tablet. "I'm Doctor Austin Muratori, the Chief Medical Examiner, and this is my area. When I'm done, I'll search for you. Until that time, you need to leave this facility."

It's always the M.E. that gives me the most trouble. Ghost shook his head and forced a bit of willpower again into credentials, and the script along the edges glowed. He held the wallet up in front of the doctor one more time and watched the doctor's eyes go glassy for a moment. "You are misinformed, Doctor. I'm the one in charge right now. I expect full compliance and utmost confidentiality here. Do you understand me?"

The doctor nodded and the glow from the credentials died. The doctor shook his head, "What the hell? Fine. What names are you looking for?"

Ghost started reciting the most important names he could think of, pausing to allow the doctor respond after each one. "Director Clifton Day?" A nod that the Director's body was in the morgue. "Special Agent James Smith?" A negative shake—still missing. "Special Agent Amanda Watkins?" A nod that she was also a casualty. "Special Agent David Cassiday?" A shake, a pause, and then a nod. Several names later, Ghost learned that several others veterans of Section 28 were still missing.

The DHS monster hunter let out a long sigh of breath. The doctor explained that there were still over thirty bodies that had not been identified yet, and most of those had been identified by their wallet or ID card. "And the list includes none of the wounded. They were all taken to triage, or directly to the hospital. The medics will have a list over there." The doctor's hands shook in fear as the anger and disappointment radiated from the tall agent.

"Fine. I'll be back later." Ghost turned and strode out of the warehouse. As he hit fresh air, he keyed his microphone. He needed some good news, "Gretchen, this is Ghost. Any luck over there? Is Agent Smith there?"

"Negative on Agent Smith, although I need you over here immediately. You will want to hear this."

"Copy that. On my way."

Ghost walked across the debris field to the medic tent. As he did so, he dialed Agent Smith's SSP again, hoping beyond hope that his boss answered.

The Section 28 agent halted. There was a familiar ringtone playing nearby. His head swiveled around, searching for the source. He heard the click of the voicemail system and the ringing stopped. Desperately, he dialed again. Again, the ringing from the rubble. There. It was over by that corner of a building. Ghost clambered across the rubble, searching for the errant phone.

Again, the voicemail clicked in again. He frantically mashed the speed dial, and the couple seconds of dead air as the phone made the connection lasted an eternity. There. Under that pile of rubble. Ghost dropped his still-dialing phone and scrambled in the bricks and lumber to find the device. He found it, lying face down under the debris. The screen was even intact. He let out a cry for help and began clearing more of the rubble.

When he hit unbroken pavement, he sat back, shoulders slumped. His cries had drawn Army and FBI searchers to his area, and they had helped dig through the rubble. As he looked up to thank the rescuers who had helped him clear the rubble from this spot, he realized what was so familiar about that partially standing wall. Framed in the center of the crumbled wall were the monstrous doors to the Warehouse. Completely unscathed.

3

PRODIGAL

"S on of a..." Ghost trailed off, as he peered at the free-standing doorway. He keyed his mic, "Ghost to Knightmare. I need everyone except Spooky at my location. I'm about...." The DHS monster hunter looked around and continued, "A hundred yards from the morgue. Gretchen, I need you at my location."

The tall hunter stood and looked around at the destruction. He noticed all of his teammates, except for Spooky, running toward him. Boomer was the first to reach him as her enhanced unnatural abilities gave her an edge in speed and agility that no mere human could match.

Dancer arrived a couple seconds after Boomer, barely panting as she slowed to a stop. The young woman let out a sigh as she stood in front of her team leader. She addressed her friend and mentor, "Dang it, Boomer. You only beat me because you could leap over that retaining wall."

You weren't trying little one. A deep voice rumbled in the young woman's head. *If you had tapped into your power, you could have easily outpaced her.*

I don't recall asking for feedback from my sword, Dancer smiled as she thought back to the voice in her head.

Hannah "Dancer" Sedano was shockingly young for a field

agent who worked for DHS. The seventeen-year-old stood just a hair shorter than Boomer, and her long white hair was pulled into a loose ponytail. The young Latina was wearing a smaller, customized version of the combat armor that the team wore, with a black leather jacket covering the scabbard on her back. Her black jeans and small combat boots made her look like she was from the Seattle grunge scene, but her eyes were far too old and had lost their innocence.

Hannah had been a resident at a youth summer camp in Colorado just a few short months ago. One of the oldest surviving master vampires on record had made the camp his nest, recruiting a mad geneticist to weaponize the vampire virus. During the fight to destroy that vampire and all of his newly turned "children," Hannah had been rescued by Boomer, surviving to be recruited to Section 28.

When she was training at Section 28, she was chosen by an artifact that hadn't been active in many years. Called *fion-fhuil*, the ancient sword was possessed by the spirit and power of an ancient dragon. Vellath had become her confidante and support as she learned about her heritage. Her bond was at the mercy of the dragon, but Vellath genuinely seemed to like his young wielder.

Her first mission was the previous Knightmare assignment in western Michigan. There she discovered that she carried the blood of the Furies in her veins, which manifested as she fought to defeat an enemy that threatened her team and a fae treaty with humanity. The power coursing through her mythological blood gave her a prowess she would not have otherwise.

Dancer immediately realized what Ghost was looking at, "Hey, that looks like the Warehouse. At least the doors survived."

A giant black man trotted up to the group, asking "What survived? Oh. Wow. Those doors don't even looked scratched."

Arthur "Heavy" Murphy was a giant of a man. Standing over six and a half feet tall and weighing a touch under three hundred pounds, the former special forces sergeant served with the 82nd Airborne until a few short months ago. Arthur had been in Washington DC to visit his parents when a couple men broke into their house and slaughtered them.

When he defended his parents, he found out that the men were much more than their appearance showed. Beaten and desperate, Arthur had grabbed a couple ceremonial Khukuri knives from the wall. The knives had been presented to him by a Nepalese shaman and, unknown to the big man, contained a sacred power to harm the undead. The glowing Khukuri sliced through the creatures necks with supernatural accuracy, finishing the fight quickly. As the bodies had faded to vapor, the police arrived to find Arthur standing over the mangled corpses of his parents with large fighting blades.

Agent Smith had intervened before the big Army sergeant could be charged with the crimes. Arthur was given an ultimatum, join the secret agency designed to fight monsters, or go to jail for the murder of his family. The special forces soldier accepted the job with Section 28 and had been given the call sign "Heavy" for his ability to wield heavy machine guns as common rifles in the field.

"So are they still locked?" Heavy knocked on the door with his meaty fist. The sound that came back was odd. He knocked again and turned to look at the rest of the group.

"Sounds hollow," quipped Little G, joining the group.

Jesús "Little G" Rivera stood slightly taller than six feet and was very thin underneath his armor. The former FBI sniper had grown up near Denver, Colorado in a heavily latino suburb. His parents had been killed by what was described as a wolf when he was fifteen. The distraught young man had sought help and healing at his local Catholic parish. Unfortunately, the priest was more interested in affection than comforting Jesús, and the young man angrily left the church.

Using his inheritance to leave the state, Jesús attended Harvard for their Pre-Law program, graduating in the top two percent. Leaving a promising future at Harvard Law, the young latino applied to the FBI, and was quickly accepted. His career at the FBI reflected his personal work ethic. Driven hard to excel, Jesús was quickly promoted, and eventually accepted to the elite Hostage Rescue Team. As an HRT member, his background skills in hunting and shooting earned him a spot as one of the snipers on the team.

Throughout his young life, Jesús had been plagued by the memory of the "wolf" that had killed his parents. The original investigation had produced no answers about why a lone she-wolf would attack two humans at night, let alone why the remains had been so thoroughly torn and ragged. After a successful mission with the HRT, he had been recruited by Agent Smith to join Section 28. Jesús had made up his mind when Smith had told the FBI agent that it was not a wolf that had killed his parents. Instead, it was a were-wolf who had left her pack.

With his eyes opened to the truth, the HRT sniper had willingly joined Section 28. He had been assigned the radio call sign of "God"—much to the chagrin of the team's resident priest, Doc. The priest had corrected him one day on the radio as "Little G," and the good-natured nickname had stuck.

Little G looked around the area where the doors stood. "So this means that the Warehouse was here. Which means that this was the main corridor to the complex..." He trailed off, mentally calculating distances and directions.

As he pointed slightly away from the group down what used to be a corridor, the team's liaison arrived. She quickly took in the appearance of the doors, and then closely examined the concrete supporting the doors, and all the edges around the doors themselves.

Gretchen looked at Ghost, "This needs to be moved. Now. We need to get the Warehouse into a secured storage facility where our own people can guard it."

"What do you mean?" Ghost looked at their team liaison, surprised at her vehemence. "Why do we need to move this thing? It's just a doorway that's not attached to the building anymore."

Gretchen looked around, checking to make sure that Section 28 personnel were the only ones in earshot. She lowered her voice, "It's not just any doorway. It's the gateway to the warehouse." The woman's gaze drifted over the doors and the archway. Carefully scrutinizing each inch. "And if the gateway is intact, we still have access to the Warehouse behind the gateway." The team's liaison turned back to Ghost, "And that, Mister Vanhof, is why we have to move this gateway to a secure location."

The silence grew as the team members looked at Gretchen and at each other, occasionally glancing at the massive set of doors.

"Damn." Ghost looked back at Gretchen, "Any chance that someone is still alive in there?"

"Absolutely. The gateway seals off the Warehouse from the outside world. If the gateway survives the attack, whoever is inside the Warehouse is just fine."

"If someone is in there, why haven't they come out yet?" Ghost was again looking at the now dormant gateway.

Gretchen pointed to two faint markings that ran along the outer edges. The pattern was dim, visible even in the daylight. "This is the security seal. It's an automatic failsafe if headquarters was ever breached. The moment the walls came down, it sealed itself. We will have to work the ritual to unbind the lock, and it will take a couple of us some time to do so."

"Can we just leave it in place? Cover it and open the gateway here - just to see who's in there?"

Gretchen thought about it. "It's possible. We could set up some sort of temporary structure around the gateway and get some guards to man the perimeter. It would be easier than moving it." She went through some records on the tablet she carried. "It would definitely be easier to open it here. The arch is anchored about ten feet down into solid bedrock."

Ghost looked at the team arrayed around him, and then back at his liaison, "Gretchen, you said we have survivors in the triage tent? And some that have already been taken to the hospital?" Seeing her nod, the monster hunter keyed his radio, "Spooky, this is Ghost. Verify where our personnel have been taken, then ask the FBI to send a few agents to guard them for the immediate future."

"Copy that Ghost. What did you find?"

Ghost took a deep breath and let it out, "We found the entrance to the Warehouse. Contact Colonel Spenser. Have him figure out how to build a temporary warehouse space on this spot within twelve hours. I'm not worried about a physical building, but it must be...." The monster hunter thought about the dimensions needed, "At least thirty feet by forty feet, and at least thirty-five feet tall. As secure as possible, but time is the most important factor here."

"I got it boss." The former NSA analyst signed off and began working.

The tall monster hunter turned to his group and outlined his plans.

HEAVY WATCHED as the massive bulldozer cleared a path through the debris around the gateway. It had been three hours, and there was a flurry of activity. Colonel Spenser had shown up three minutes after Ghost had finished telling the team how they were going to secure the gateway. The commander of the 911th Engineer Company was apoplectic at the orders he had just received and was looking for answers. SAC Mulder was with him, more curious than anything about the developments.

Ghost had pressed the colonel into action, and in thirty minutes there were over a hundred men and women searching through every inch of the immediate area surrounding the gateway for survivors or bodies. Two hours later, Colonel Spenser had figured that every inch was searched visually and electronically at least twice. His survey crew had plotted the position of the new temporary structure and a massive bulldozer, backhoe, and several dump trucks had arrived to clear away the debris. Ghost had covered the design and layout of the new structure and had planned on rigging lighting inside the portable building.

The monster hunter had pulled SAC Mulder aside and asked that she provide eight armed and armored FBI Agents as immediate guards around the structure once it was built. Once that was arranged, he had wandered over to the triage tent with Gretchen and Doc while the rest of Knightmare were staying close to the gateway, making sure that nothing jeopardized the Warehouse.

As Gretchen led Ghost over to the triage area, she and Doc explained that they had found several of their missing coworkers and Section 28 Agents in various sections of the rubble. Most of the people who had been on the ground floor of the office section were crushed in the collapse of the building. Those who had been on upper floors, or who had been in the residential section, had mostly been injured, most with lesser injuries—cuts, scrapes, and broken bones. The guards had not been so lucky.

When the attack had happened, the guards at the shack were obliterated, burned with an extremely hot flame. The ready-alert guards in their barracks were mostly slaughtered as they exited the building. Although a few of them had returned fire, it was the rooftop automated emplacements that were responsible for most of the enemy casualties. The automated machine gun nests and rocket launchers had counted for two of the large casualties and seven of the more human ones.

Ghost was just about to ask who had attacked the facility when he stopped, bent over, and retrieved something from the ground. It was a long bone-like blade. About two feet long, it was thicker at one end, tapering to a point along its curved length. "Dragons." The suddenly pale monster hunter looked at his team's liaison and combat priest. "It was 'effing dragons, wasn't it?"

Gretchen nodded. "We have reports of at least four over the complex, each with a rider, and they were leading a squad of other humanoid soldiers. The remains we've found have been human, or at least human-looking enough that they won't be a problem." She pointed to the large dragon tooth in Ghost's hand, "But dragon corpses? That's going to require some serious coverup."

Ghost nodded and keyed his radio, "Spooky, this is Ghost."

"You must be psychic boss, I was just about to call you. You won't believe what was released on the internet about the attack. Several videos have been posted, and you won't believe what they show in the air."

The monster hunter looked at the women with him and sighed, "Dragons, Spooky. They show dragons. Here in Virginia."

There was a long pause from the former NSA analyst. "Um. Yeah? This 'Wubba' character got about thirty minutes of unedited footage up, and it's got a hundred thousand hits and climbing. So, what do you want me to do?"

Ghost pinched the bridge of his nose with a couple fingers, trying to stave off the headache that was coming. "Do your magic. Make the footage go away, or discredit it. This cannot be public knowledge."

"Gotcha. Already working my magic." The former analyst signed off the radio.

Ghost dropped the two foot long tooth into one of the outer pockets of his leather duster, which swallowed it without showing. Doc watched the tooth disappear into the coat pocket and looked closer. She realized that there was no sign of the dragon's tooth at all. She looked back at the monster hunter, "That's a neat trick. Just how deep is that pocket?"

Ghost looked at the pocket in question and smiled, "Honestly? I'm not sure. It's bottomless, as far as I can tell. Better yet, I've never been gutsy enough to find the bottom. It's actually a gateway to another dimension. Anything that fits through the opening of the pocket will fit."

"How do you find anything in there?"

"Simple. I will it to be in my hand, and it's there."

Doc looked closer at the monster hunter's jacket for a few long seconds, "At some point, you and I need to have a discussion about that jacket."

Ghost chuckled, "At some point we will. Until then, shall we figure out who survived?"

The three walked again toward triage and Spooky called out on the radio, "Ghost, this is Spooky on the private channel. You need to get your butt up to the Wunder Buggy ASAP. Someone just pulled up in a police cruiser, and you need to greet him. Before Boomer or Heavy see him."

Ghost clicked his mic twice and jogged to the truck. He saw a figure step up to the front steps of the FBI's command trailer as the police cruiser reversed, then sped away.

Ghost reached the command truck as the man walked back out of the Mobile Command Center. He drew up short, not believing his eyes. The man standing in front of him was a little paler than the monster hunter last saw him. A couple inches shy of six feet tall, the man's brown hair was clipped to a short military-style flattop. The man's rugged and scarred face told a tale of a hard life, and his brown eyes were as hard as diamonds.

The two men stared at each other for a couple long seconds, and Ghost finally broke the silence, "I do believe I'm seeing a ghost."

The other man cracked a slight smile, "If I recall, you're Ghost. I'm Six."

4

WAREHOUSE

Ruins of Section 28 Headquarters, Langley, Virginia

G host reached, proffering his hand for the former leader of Knightmare. The hard looking former mercenary gladly grasped his hand, shaking it, greeting his former teammate.

Burt "Six" Holstein was the first person recruited for the then-new Knightmare team by Agent Smith. Holstein had left a promising career with the Los Angeles Special Weapons and Tactics team to fight in the Iraq war. After joining and distinguishing himself with Force Recon, he opted for retirement and the lucrative private security contracts available in that country.

Having been recruited by Academi, Holstein became the head of a team that worked for the State Department in theater. Agent Smith found Holstein leading a civilian contractor VIP security team in Baghdad for the Diplomatic Security Service corps. Smith was able to lure Holstein away from Academi with a large paycheck and a hint at finding answers to a childhood UFO sighting.

While on their first mission, the new team Knightmare had chased vampires and other undead across Colorado, tracing the source and infection back to an old master vampire who was hiding at a youth summer camp in the Rocky Mountains. In the ensuing battle, Six had made the ultimate sacrifice for his team members, saving one and distracting the master vampire long enough to allow his teammates to triumph.

"But you died in that youth camp?" Ghost was looking at the man in front of him. "We buried you. Spooky saw your file. You were marked deceased."

"I know. Technically, Burt Holstein died that day, and you buried him. My current name is John Black, Special Agent for Section Twenty-Eight."

Both men turned their head in unison as they heard a feral growl and the sound of running. Six had enough time to tense as he was hit by a flying tackle. His training and reflexes kicked in, pivoting and using his attacker's momentum as the force necessary to throw the person past him. The young woman landed in the dust and debris, rolling to a crouch, while facing the two men.

"Get away from him, fiend. Watch out boss, he's a vampire." Boomer bared her teeth, which now showed two elongated fangs in place of her regular canines."

Six brushed off his jacket, "Hello to you too, Boomer. Isn't that the pot calling the kettle black?" His smile echoed the slight amusement in his voice.

The shock on the young demolitions specialist's face wiped away the growl, and she abruptly stood. "Six? But you're dead. Well, I guess undead? How?"

The taller vampire reached out and accepted a hug from his young teammate, "It's a long story. Which I'm sure I'm going to have to tell everyone, so how 'bout we wait 'til then. You must have turned from that scratch you picked up in the bunker?" He turned the last sentence into a question.

Six turned as Heavy, Little G, and Dancer all arrived, having followed Boomer's headlong run across the ruins. Heavy drew his Khukuri blades, and they glowed green. The big man pointed one of them at Six, "You're dead. Maybe undead. What are you doing here, and why shouldn't I just kill you for being a vamp?"

Ghost stepped between the two men and put a hand up to gently deflect Heavy's blade. "Heavy, stand down. Six says he's still Section Twenty-Eight. You remember what Smith said the Oath does to someone who attacks agents? I can't afford to lose you. So stand down."

Boomer joined Ghost between the two men. "Calm down, big guy. The Oath keeps us under control. Trust me, if Six screws up, he becomes ash, just like me.

"Look at me, you big ox." When Boomer had his attention, she continued, "I'm a vampire too. Just because we're infected does not mean we're evil, right?"

Heavy grudgingly put the blades away. The green glow dying as they were slid back into the scabbards on his back. The big heavy weapons specialist grunted, "Sorry, Six," and stuck out his hand.

"No problem big guy. I wouldn't have expected anything else." Six shook the proffered hand, greeted the sniper, and then turned his attention to the young woman who stood beside Boomer, "You look familiar to me. Have we met before?"

The young woman, really a teenager, shook Six's proffered hand. "I don't think so. I'm Hannah Sedano. I just joined Section Twenty-Eight before all this happened."

Boomer smiled, "Dancer is the girl we rescued from the camp. Remember the one that told me about the vampires?"

The former mercenary snapped his fingers, "Yeah. That's where I recognize you from. Obviously you made it out, too. What about that other guy? The Indian guy that was hiding in the woods? And where's Do-Right? Is he working another scene?" Six locked over and around the shoulders for the former Colorado deputy sheriff.

Ghost shook his head, "We lost Do-Right and Scout on the last mission. I'll fill you in later. Spooky's still with us, he's in the truck, as usual."

"Shame about Do-Right and the other guy, but good to hear Spooky is still being Spooky." Six turned and waved at the Wunder Buggy's windshield. He turned back around and the group walked toward the temporary building that was starting to cover the gateway. "Is Doc still hanging around? I'm guessing she was able to work her magic on the vampire."

Ghost nodded, "She's my second-in-command. She'll be glad to see you."

"Is Agent Smith running around? I'm surprised that I haven't seen him yet. Do we have any idea what happened, or who is responsible?"

Ghost again shook his head, "We haven't seen Agent Smith, and he's not in the morgue. Although apparently the Director and the other team leaders are bagged up there. I'm not sure really who is still active and available, Gretchen is compiling a list for me now."

The tall monster hunter suddenly stopped and turned to face his former team leader. "I've gotta clear something up, right now. There were no senior agents present, or at least in an available capacity. I took over control of this site from the FBI as senior DHS and

Section Twenty-Eight agent available. Are we going to have any issues with that?"

The former team leader paused, looking Ghost in the eyes. The big monster hunter did not flinch, nor did he look away. Six realized that the tall fed's experience and training hunting vampires, bolstered by the Oath of Binding they signed in blood, made him immune to any of his persuasive powers.

"I have absolutely no problem with that arrangement. I'm no longer part of the team." Six paused, and then continued, "I'll back any play you make, at least until we find Agent Smith or another senior field agent."

"Fair enough." Ghost spun and walked toward the structure again. As he was walking, he keyed his mic, "Doc, this is Ghost. I need you and Gretchen to meet me at the gateway. We have a surprise guest."

"Copy, Ghost. We are on our way."

DOC AND GRETCHEN had both been surprised to see Six standing with the rest of the team. Questions flew from all sides, and Six could no longer put off telling his tale.

"I woke up a couple days after I died. I don't know how long I was down, because that time is a little fuzzy, even now. Smith told me that I had apparently ingested enough of that vampire's blood as he was dying. If I understand the process, he intended to turn me, if nothing else, as a giant f-you.

"I guess I was in the lab for several weeks. The scientists experimented on me. They tried to figure out how to sustain me, what my limits were, and even if the Oath still held." The former mercenary looked at Boomer, "I think they were trying to figure out if you could be trusted. Obviously, it worked."

He turned back to the rest of the group, "So I was given an ultimatum. Either I survive as an experiment until they got tired of me, or I continue working for Smith. I chose the latter." The man paused as if considering his next words.

"Smith didn't want me going back to the team. I don't think he ever intended we would cross paths again. He gave me a new identity and a new job, sitting in an office all the way across the country."

Ghost spoke up, "Did anyone else know you were out there?"

"Timothy, for sure. I think Norbert and Russell also knew about me, but I can't be sure. Timothy was my only contact. Did any of them make it?"

Ghost shrugged, and Gretchen spoke up, "Timothy Wilson was identified as a casualty in the morgue, but I haven't had a chance to verify yet. No one has seen any signs of Norbert or Russell. That's why we need to open this gateway to the Warehouse."

Ghost looked at Gretchen, "We will. Did you have time to interview anyone? Especially the Tremblay kid?"

Doc nodded, "We talked to Tremblay, as well as Watkins and Cassiday. Amanda and David had nothing to add, other than they were training with their new teams when the attack happened. The entire training facility collapsed on them." Dancer let out a gasp.

"The team leaders were both lucky." The team's resident priest continued, "They were pinned under a partially collapsed bunker, and only suffered minor wounds, including a broken wrist for Amanda, and a shattered femur for David. They are in triage, waiting for an x-ray machine to open up so their bones can be set."

"What about their teams?" Ghost looked over at the triage area. As he watched, more ambulances were pulling away from the site, heading to whichever local hospitals were taking the wounded. He looked back at the women, "Any casualties?"

Doc nodded, "Amanda's team has one survivor, Theran Nordstrom, who should be going into surgery as we speak. He was crushed under a falling column. David lost his entire team. They survived the initial collapse, but were burned to death by one of the dragons." A solitary tear coursed down her cheek.

Ghost patted his priest on the shoulder, commiserating with her pain. He looked at everyone else, then zeroed on Gretchen. "The morgue has Watkins and Cassiday listed as deceased. After we open this gateway, I may need you to corroborate the lists between triage and the morgue. Now what did Tremblay have to say?"

The team liaison pulled a small notebook out of her pocket and flipped through the pages. "He said he saw the initial incursion, and hit the panic button. The automated defenses lit up about the same time the gate guards responded as well. It was definitely dragons. At least a couple. The leader was fully covered in armor, and mentioned Agent Smith by name. He called his dragon 'Argohast,' or something like that."

Dancer cocked her head to one side, as if listening to something, or someone. She looked at Gretchen, "You said Argohast? Vellath knows of her. Calls her a... 'soulless worm who will partner with any disease-riddled mind.' That was a direct quote."

Ghost looked at his youngest team member, "Any idea who is riding her? Does Vellath know anything else?"

Six looked back and forth between the two of them. "Who the hell is Vellath? And how does he know this dragon personally?"

Dancer flashed the former mercenary her most innocent smile, "Vellath is the ancient dragon who lives in my sword." Her bubbly expression turned into laughter at Six's frown and grumbled return. "Seriously. I wield an artifact called *fion-fhuil*, and Vellath is literally an ancient dragon whose soul was transferred into the sword. And he chose me to wield the sword."

Six shrugged, "Yeah, like that answer helps at all. Whatever."

"Anyways." Ghost interrupted the exchange, "Anything else, Gretchen? Dancer?" They both shook their heads.

Before he could continue, a worker in Army fatigues stepped up to the group, "Agent Vanhof? Corporal Tsevensin, sir. Your temp shelter is ready to go. Anything else we can do? If not, we'll get back to our SAR operations." The corporal handed Ghost a set of keys and spun on his heels, not waiting for his response.

As Gretchen led the way into the temporary shelter, Ghost keyed is mic, "Spooky, this is Ghost. Patch me through to SAC Mulder."

When he reached the FBI agent, the monster hunter asked her to get a half dozen agents available as guards for the temporary shelter. He let her know he would brief her later, but that her people were not to enter the structure without explicit instructions. As he walked through the double doors into the temporary structure, it started to rain.

He stopped as he entered, seeing the massive gateway taking up the entire center of the structure, stretching nearly to the ceiling, and most of the way across the middle. The rain picked up, becoming a constant drum against the plastic and metal paneling that made up the structure, including the roof.

Gretchen had already pulled a piece of chalk out of her shoulder bag, and had started sketching symbols on the floor surrounding the gateway, as well as on the door itself.

Ghost stood next to Six as Gretchen completed the complex layout of symbols. She motioned both of them over to stand in two smaller circles next to her larger one, and said, "All I need from you guys is your willpower. Just concentrate on reinforcing what I'm saying. Even if you don't understand the language, just concentrate on what I'm saying." Both men nodded.

Gretchen stood in her circle and raised her palm. She intoned a litany in a very foreign language. The faint runes on the gateway doors and arch glowed, starting out an angry red glow, and turning to a yellow, then white, then disappearing altogether. She slumped, barely standing after nearly five minutes of harnessing the power to open the seals on the Warehouse.

Ghost and Six both stumbled a little as they left their circles to catch Gretchen. Each of them was feeling the effects of the energy drain required to open the Warehouse. The team liaison refused their help, instead moving to the massive doors and placing her palms on a small black metal plate set into each door at the seam.

Nothing happened.

Gretchen stared at the doors. She removed her hands, then pressed them to the metal squares again.

Nothing.

Gretchen leaned forward, her forehead hitting the roughhewn wood of the doors. She kicked the door in frustration. "Why aren't you opening, dammit?" Her voice quaked, and a tear rolled down her cheek.

Ghost gently took her shoulders and pulled her away. He had never seen their team liaison break down so thoroughly. She had always been calm and cool, even when arranging the details of the burial of Six, or the transport and burial of Do-Right or Scout. She turned and buried her head in his shoulder. Letting the sobs come out.

It was a few minutes of stunned silence before Gretchen stopped sobbing and pulled out of the monster hunter's loose embrace. She stepped back, wiped away her tears, and said, "Sorry. I guess the last couple days have finally caught up with me. I... I'm ok. Thank you."

"No problem. Any idea what's wrong?"

"I may have drained what power I have just clearing the wards. I may not be able to open it until I rest."

Ghost looked at her, "Who has authority to open the Warehouse? Does it require certain staff privileges, or can any Agent open it?"

Gretchen just looked at him. "Of course. Anyone who is an actual Special Agent here at Section Twenty-Eight can open the Warehouse for mission support materials. It's built into the Oath. Place your hands on each plate and just will it to open. It's designed to read you and open at your command."

Ghost let her go. He stepped up and placed his hands on the panels. He felt a mild shock and then was in an empty void. It was pitch black all around him. He could not see his hands. What hands? He could not feel... anything.

Who are you?

The thought beat at him. Startled, Ghost thought back, *Special Agent Jonas Vanhof. Ghost.*

There was an interminable pause.

Accepted.

Ghost was back, leaning against the doors, hands on the metal plates. "What the ever-loving-hell was that?" He looked at Gretchen.

She gave a hint of a smile. "The gateway."

"How long was I... away?"

"Literally? No time." Her smile was back, "Unless you aren't authorized to enter. Then you never come back."

The doors began a slow, ponderous crawl backwards, into the Warehouse. Time seemed to stretch forever as the massive doors took a full minute to make their transition. Gretchen put a hand out to hold the team back. Beyond the doorway was an empty blackness.

"The Gateway has to reconnect. Let's hope it does so."

There was a blinding blue-white flash, and the Warehouse interior suddenly filled the doorway.

Agent James Smith stood at the entrance in his impeccable medium gray pinstripe suit. Arms folded, his calm, cultured voice carried, "I was wondering when you would show up. What have I missed?"

5

FOUND

G host stepped forward and shook Smith's hand. The monster hunter stepped back, asking, "Who else is in here with you? Were you able to get anyone else to safety?"

Smith waved toward the Warehouse. "Most of the Warehouse team is here. They were already in here when the gateway sealed itself. I was just returning from a meeting with Norbert when the Warehouse sensed the attack and locked itself down. I'm assuming we were attacked? Any idea who?"

Ghost paused, "Yes, sir. Three or four dragons and their riders as well as a few soldiers. Their leader specifically asked for you by name. Any idea who it would be?"

Smith frowned and shook his head. "I know of no dragon riders searching for me. A few of the fae would be possible, but not dragons or their riders." He paused, searching for any hints, "I cannot think of anyone who would be so brazen. I assume young Mister Smith is already working to cover up the footage?"

"Yeah, boss. Spooky's working on it."

Six chose that moment to step up beside Ghost and stick out his hand. His boss frowned slightly, "Mister Black, I believe I told you to stay in the shadows. And yet here you are."

Six nodded, "After I saw the news about the attack, I covered things with my boss back in Seattle and caught the first flight. Right now, you need me more than you need to keep my secret."

Smith thought about it and then mused out loud, "You may be right, Mister Black. You may be right. What did the Director say about you coming home?"

Gretchen stepped forward, "The Director was killed in the attack. I believe that makes you acting Director of Section Twenty-Eight, sir."

"Yes, Miss Massey. I do believe it would. So fill me in on what is happening."

As Ghost and Gretchen relayed their pieces of the story, the rest of the team crowded into the Warehouse. As Smith greeted them all, he was told about the attack and also given the current casualty list by Gretchen. Gretchen and Doc explained who was in triage as well as who was already at an area hospital.

Six waved Boomer closer, "While they are working with him, why don't you and I take advantage of our unique abilities, and help the SAR team recover people and bodies." The former mercenary waved at the doors leading out of the temporary shelter.

Boomer looked at Ghost, and he nodded at her. She turned back to her former team leader, "Sure thing." They moved away from the group, Dancer following her mentor to help search for bodies.

Spooky took that moment to chime in on the radio, "Ghost, this is Spooky. Did you get the Warehouse open? I'm getting all sorts of strange energies from there?"

"Yes, we did Spooky. Agent Smith was in there with Norbert, Russell, and the rest of the Warehouse staff. Speaking of which, contact Agent Mulder and ask her to meet me at the temporary building entrance in a couple minutes. Ask her if Colonel Spenser can meet with us as well. Ghost out."

"Copy that, boss."

Ghost looked at the Acting Director and asked him, "Anything we can do for everyone in the Warehouse? We've got FBI guarding this temporary building until we can get some of our own people in place."

Smith shook his head. "They have enough living space in there that they are fine. We will need to bring provisions in, because they'll soon tire of the stored MREs. But I will have them stay in the Warehouse until we get it into a more secure shelter."

Ghost turned to Heavy and Little G, "I want you guys on guard duty, at least temporarily. We can't move the Warehouse easily, so we have to make sure it is secure."

The two men nodded and left, each unslinging their chosen long guns to cradle in their arms as they walked the perimeter. After they passed through the double doors to the temporary warehouse, Agent Mulder and Colonel Spenser walked into the open space, followed by their two assistants.

Colonel Spenser and his aide stopped in their tracks at the sight of the gaping Warehouse that opened into another dimension. Agent Mulder made it a few more steps before she, too, stumbled to a halt. Her aide was absorbed in the screen of her tablet and stumbled into her boss, causing her to drop her tablet and let out a mild curse. The words died on her lips as she finally saw the hulking Warehouse gateway.

Gretchen was as quick as ever. She stepped forward, holding her credentials up so that the four newcomers could see them well. They began to glow green as she loudly proclaimed, "By order of Homeland Security and by the Signatory-status of Section Twenty-Eight of the *E'Tuatha* Accords, I hereby bind you from mentioning this aspect and technology to anyone who is not currently present or cleared to know."

The team liaison snapped her credentials shut with an audible snap and then walked over to the small huddle of very confused people. "Now that you are bound from telling anyone what you see in this building, you probably have quite a few questions. We can answer some of them. But first I would like to introduce you to the acting Director of Section Twenty-Eight, Director James Smith."

Smith walked over to the small group. As he passed the boundary of the Warehouse, he gave an almost imperceptible shudder. When he reached the newcomers, he stretched out his hand, "Special Agent Mulder, it is good to see you again. I believe you are still the current SAC for this region, correct? And your aide is Special Agent Wilcox if I remember correctly." He shifted his hand to shake her assistant's hand.

He then switched to address the Army officer. "If I remember right, you are Colonel Spenser of the 911th. Good to meet you, sir." The colonel's handshake was strong. Smith quickly read the insignia on the collar, shoulders, and chest of the colonel's aide. "Command Sergeant Major Ryan, right? Good to meet you sir." Smith's voice was cultured, but commanding. With its slight hint of a southern drawl, he exuded calm and breeding, and would fit in perfectly at a plantation down south in the late 1800's.

"Director Smith," Mulder started, "Just what was that crap that

Agent Massey was spouting about being bound? We all understand Classified information."

"I'm sorry, ma'am. But you have no idea how deeply this installation and its personnel are classified. As an example, I recall that this installation was listed as a simple support office for DHS. It wasn't listed as strategic on any map or listing that your agency maintains. It's not like Langley or NSA headquarters, which are officially not there, but you maintain a list for strategic response and importance. Am I correct so far?"

Mulder nodded and opened her mouth to speak.

Smith continued, "Then why was it protected by a CIWS system and an anti-aircraft missile launcher? And why was your protocol to launch every HRT team that was currently in house to defend this lowly support office? Are you starting to get the picture, yet?"

Mulder was thinking about those exact questions. As her face wrinkled and her brows furrowed, Smith turned to Colonel Spenser. "And you, Colonel? Why on earth would your highly trained and specialized unit be told to drop every other operation in your purview and support this operation? When was the last time a simple support office attracted the attention of the 911th?"

It was the colonel's turn to think. He and Mulder kept looking at each other and then back at Smith.

Mulder was the first to speak, "Ok, I accept your premise. There is obviously more to this installation than meets the eye. I have cleaned up after a couple of your teams, and I've also never seen a support office with its own runway. But what the hell was all the mumbo jumbo about being bound?"

Smith sighed. "Magic is real. Mostly. There are a lot of weird creatures that occasionally show up in our world, and Section Twenty-Eight is tasked with two missions. First, we track, contain, and kill non earth-based creatures. Our second mission is much harder. It is our job to contain the fallout from any of these reality incursions. That often means requiring an even higher authority than normal law enforcement or federal agents have. We use a touch of magic to control the flow of information."

"What happens if we talk?" This was the colonel.

"It's actually quite simple," replied Smith. "If you can get through the controls bound on you to spill the classified information beyond those who may know, you will spontaneously combust. Unfortunately, the burning is from the inside to the outside. In short, you will burn to death in an excruciating, awful pain."

The colonel was speechless. Mulder laughed uneasily, "Surely you can't expect us to believe you. How will some little speech your agent gave know what we are doing? Like I said, I understand the penalties for leaking classified information. But, c'mon. Magic? Nice scare tactic."

Smith looked at the FBI agent. Calmly, his voice never raising, he said, "If you don't believe me, conduct an experiment. This *geas* works incrementally and gives you plenty of warning. It's a failsafe feature. For the experiment, simply think about detailing all that you see here, including the *geas* itself, in your report. Think about writing that up and submitting it to the Director of the FBI."

Mulder gave a half smile and then concentrated on what her report would say. She started to feel warm. Dismissing that as psychosomatic suggestion, she imagined detailing the words that Agent Massey used in her report, and sending it to her direct boss and then to the Director. She broke out in a cold sweat and felt what had to be the worst case of heartburn she had ever had.

Smith saw her obvious distress and gently put a hand on her shoulder. He gently spoke, "Agent Mulder, that's enough. Don't push the *geas* any more, or you might end up with some permanent effects."

Mulder stopped, convinced that something would prevent her from talking. And that was... magic? She didn't believe magic was real, but something had affected her when she even thought about leaking the details of this site—even to her own bosses in DC.

Colonel Spenser was angry. After seeing what the FBI SAC had gone through, he would take out his ire on this sanctimonious bureaucrat from some DHS office he never knew existed. As the thoughts flashed through his mind, he started getting warm. Sweat rolling down his forehead, he pointed one of his big, meaty fingers at Director Smith, "Listen up, you self-righteous prick. Whatever you did to us, you will undo, or I will bring down the weight of the US Army on your little department, crushing you like the cockroach you are." Ghost's hand drifted toward his holstered Webley. He hoped that the Army colonel did nothing foolish, but the man seemed outraged.

Smith's countenance did not change, his cool gaze stayed on the sputtering Army officer. The head of Section 28 watched as the colonel worked himself into a rage, and he could tell by the flushed face and sweat on the officer's forehead that the man was feeling the effects of the *geas*. "Colonel Spenser, might I suggest that you pause to think about a few things. I understand that you are upset, but you really do have no choice in the matter. Even now you are feeling the effects of the binding, and the more that you think about actively hurting or destroying me or my agency, the more the *geas* will harm you."

The colonel stopped ranting. He finally realized that he was, indeed, being affected by the magic in the binding. It took him a few moments to suppress his anger enough to slow his breathing and heart rate. Finally, the Army Colonel spoke, "I believe you. Now."

Smith smile was gracious and warm. "I'm glad. And to answer your original questions, I want to show you what is important about this work. But before I do, I need to quickly take care of one item.

"Agent Mulder, you need to warn your guards to do a better job of keeping everyone out. I do not want to have to impress anyone else until we can properly move the Warehouse to a secure facility. Tell your guards they are not allowed to let anyone into this temporary facility unless they are my personnel, or are accompanied by my personnel. It's currently limited to the team that you have met, including Agent Black and Agent Massey. This directive includes members of Congress and even the President. Am I clear?"

The FBI agent nodded, "I don't want any of my people to have to go through what we just did, either. Let me step outside now." Mulder walked to the doors and went out into the night air.

As she walked out the second set of double doors, Mulder nodded to Heavy and Little G who were standing guard at the entrance. She called out, "Kyler! Stewart! Come here for a second."

Two members of the HRT trotted over, M4 carbines loosely cradled in their arms. Mulder introduced them to the Section 28 agents. "Gentlemen, this is Special Agent Kyler Joel, and Special Agent Stewart Kralikoski, with HRT. They will be assigned to guard the doors to this shelter."

Heavy shook the men's hands, "Agent Murphy. My friends call me Heavy."

Little G smiled, "Kyler, Stewart. Long time no see. How's the team?"

Mulder looked critically at the Section 28 agent, "You've met?"

The sniper grinned, "Ma'am, until a couple months ago, I was HRT. I helped train Kyler, and Stewart's wife makes amazing brownies."

Mulder shook her head, "Should have figured he poached you guys from other departments. And you Agent Murphy? You also from HRT?" She looked at Heavy expectantly.

"No, ma'am. Eighty-second Airborne. I only jumped out of perfectly good planes. I'm not crazy like the HRT guys." He laughed as he clapped one of the HRT guys on the shoulder. The big man's laughter was infectious, and soon the group was laughing, the tension vanishing rapidly.

When the laughter finally died down, Mulder looked at Heavy and Little G. "So what do you guys do, really? Director Smith fed me a line about a mile long, but what's the skinny?"

Heavy looked at the two HRT guys standing next to him, then back at Mulder. "Ma'am, whatever Director Smith has told you, I'm sure it's accurate. Although he understates things a bit. Ain't that right, Rivera?" He nodded at Little G.

"Yeah. Any other questions you have, you might want to ask the Director. But I might recommend that you wait until we're not around anyone who isn't cleared."

Mulder nodded, thinking about the burning she felt when simply imagining herself spilling the classified information. "I think I'm going to go back in there. Now that HRT understands their orders, are you guys coming in?" Both Section 28 agents followed the FBI SAC through the outer doors.

Inside the temporary building, Smith was leading Colonel Spenser, his aide, and Agent Mulder's assistant around the Warehouse gateway. The colonel and his aide were awestruck as they looked around the back of the structure, then looked through the gateway from the front. Agent Wilcox, on the other hand, was asking Gretchen questions in a rapid-fire staccato, without letting the Section 28 agent answer any of them.

Mulder walked over to the wide open gateway, looking through and seeing the inside of the Warehouse. A caged off area spread off to the left. Lounging in a chair in front of the cage was a big burly man smoking a cigar. His combat boots were kicked up on a footstool made of munition crates, and the FBI agent could see the grip of a stainless steel 1911 with pearl grip panels sticking out of a drop-leg holster.

Little G and Heavy brushed past the FBI SAC and strode toward the man in the chair. He jumped up and shouted, "Well, shit. Looks like you guys found your way back. How are you guys?"

Little G grabbed the big man's hand, "Damn, Russell. I thought I'd never see your ugly mug again. Figures you'd find a way to survive."

Heavy slapped the other man on his back, nearly causing Russell to stumble. The big hunter rumbled, "Good to see you, Sarge. I'm glad you were in here when the attack happened."

Russell Garner, former Master Sergeant in the US Army and

the current armorer for Section 28, just grinned. "Man it's good to see you guys. Everyone else make it? You guys were really in it up to your eyeballs in Michigan."

Heavy shook his head, "Nah, man. We lost Do-Right and Scout."

"Damn." The armorer was silent a moment. "What happened?"

Little G answered, "Scout was killed by the Morrigán, and Do-Right made the ultimate sacrifice to save a fae."

Garner frowned. He then looked back up at the two, "How's Boomer?"

"She kicked ass and is still under control."

"Well, at least there is some good news." Russell looked past the two men, "Who's yer friend?"

Little G waved the FBI agent over to them. "Russell, I'd like to introduce you to Special Agent Tressa Mulder. She's the FBI SAC in this area. Agent Mulder, this is Russell Garner. He's the armorer for our little department."

Mulder shook the big man's hands, her smaller one being swallowed whole by Russell's huge paws. "Nice to meet you, Mr. Garner."

"Nice to meet you, ma'am."

Little G and Heavy both halted suddenly and put their hands to their ears, a near universal sign they were listening on their radios. Heavy spoke up first, "Russ, we gotta go. Can you grab a crate of my ammo and a crate for the M4s? Full-scale event. Looking for Norbert rounds." Russell turned and unlocked the cage.

As he was rummaging inside, Little G turned to Agent Mulder, "Ma'am, we have to go. We need to meet with the rest of the team."

Russell returned, straining to lift both crates of heavy ammunition. Mulder saw that the first crate was marked, "5.56mm, Silver, Banishing." The second was marked, "12GA, Silver, Fin-Stabilized Sabot."

"Just what the hell is a 'Banishing' round, Agent Rivera?"

The sniper grinned, "Well, for starters, hell would be a good place to use them." He accepted Heavy's AA-12 from the big hunter, and Heavy grabbed both crates of ammo. He walked out to where Ghost and Six were standing with Director Smith and the outside visitors.

As they walked up, Heavy put the crates of ammunition on the ground. At Ghost's raised eyebrow, the big man rumbled, "Gifts from Russell. I figure it'll come in handy."

Ghost nodded and turned his attention back to the Director.

Smith said, "Mister Smith has received two alerts from our main-frame. One of them is a Zulu X-ray, and the other is a Tango X-ray. He did a quick analysis, and I agree with his assessment of both.

"The Zulu X-ray is in South Carolina, and is a priority at this point, classified as Priority Red. Mister Vanhof will lead Miss Calla-han, Mister Rivera, and Mister Smith. I will be joining the team for that mission although Mister Vanhof retains mission leadership. We will take the Wunder Buggy and the C-17. I'm not sure what we will run into, but we will need to leave immediately."

The director looked at Heavy, "Mister Murphy, you are to stay here to coordinate defense and security for Gretchen. She will be my authority on this site, at least until we can get the Warehouse and operations moved to a secure facility. The War Wagon is in storage and is at your disposal as a mobile command."

Director Smith finally looked at Six, Doc, and Dancer, "Mister Black, you and Miss Sedano will cover the Tango X-Ray, joined by Doctor Sorenson. There has been either a lycanthrope or some other creature killed in Michigan, and you'll need her expertise for that. The local DNR do not have a clue what it is, so they called in for outside assistance. Gretchen will place a call to the local law enforcement and the regional SAC and let them know that you are coming."

The Director paused and consulted some notes, "Because it's a possible lycanthropy outbreak, I've classified it as Priority Orange. Questions?"

Six spoke up, "Where are we going?"

Director Smith could not keep the smile from his lips, "You are going to Grand Rapids."

6

REMAINS

For the second time in as many days, Noelle Sorenson and Hannah Sedano were in an Air Force plane that touched down on runway 26-L at Gerald R. Ford International Airport. The muted roar of the turbines was a dull rumble in the cabin, and as soon as the sleek Cessna Citation X decelerated and moved from the runway to the taxiway, Hannah unbuckled her seatbelt, strapped on her custom armor, and made the motion of putting an invisible sword into a sheath on her back. A black leather jacket covered the armor.

Beside the young woman, the agent she knew as Six awoke from a short catnap. He unbuckled his belt and grabbed a black suit jacket from the plush seat next to him. The vampire agent checked the Beretta M9 that was cradled in a shoulder holster under his left arm. He double checked the magazines in the holster under his right arm and stood to slide on the jacket. The taciturn agent reached into the overhead bin and withdrew a large black tactical rifle case. He grabbed the rugged black handgun case also nestled in the bin and handed it to his partner for this mission.

"Are you sure you don't need a rifle for this?" The former team leader studied the young woman, "I'd feel more comfortable if you had a long gun, especially if we run into lycanthropes."

"Trust me. I can shoot a rifle if needed, but I'm pretty sure I'm better off without one." Dancer batted her eyelashes, giving her best impression of being innocent. "Besides, it would likely slow me down. I'm kinda surprised you use one, yourself. Boomer gave up using hers. She takes advantage of her less-than-natural talents."

Six flashed a smile with a hint of fang, "I'm not as used to using them in the field as Rebecca is, and I want to at least appear human if stuff goes pear-shaped." He shook his head, "I still don't understand how you came to be part Greek goddess."

She smiled, the genuine smile reflected in her eyes. "I don't know either. But between being a Fury, and having Vellath, I have no fear of lycanthropes. Or any other 'thropes for that matter."

Rising from her seat behind Six, Doc stood and stretched. She pulled her own black jacket off of the back of her seat and put it on over her customary gray shirt. She smiled at Six, "It's great to be back in the field with you, Burt. I mean John. Sorry." The former mercenary waved away the apology. "I would love to really talk with you, especially about your... changes. I've talked a lot with Rebecca, but she's only one perspective."

Six nodded, "I'd enjoy that. It's good to be working with you as well, Doc. Do you need any help with your case?" He nodded toward the overhead storage, where her black satchel rested.

"No, but thanks anyway." The priest reached up to pull her valise down from the bin. She pulled down a second, smaller laptop case. "I've got these."

The cockpit door opened and an Air Force Captain Katy Arnouts stepped out, "We're parked on the ramp, and the airport truck is coming to meet us. You are free to disembark. Open the hatch when you are ready. Anything else we can do for you?"

Six shook his head. "No thanks, Captain. I'm going to open the hatch in a moment. Get refueled and file a flight plan back home. I'm hoping to wrap this one up in a couple hours. We still have a mess to clean up back in Langley."

"Will do. We'll have her ready when you need it."

Six opened the hatch and let the bright morning sunshine flood into the cabin. It had been roughly nine hours since they got the Priority Orange, and an hour and a half of that had been spent flying. The DHS agent watched as the stairs unfolded down to the ground.

Before stepping down, the former mercenary turned to Doc, "Who did Gretchen say we were supposed to meet?"

Doc looked at a small notebook, "DNR Lieutenant Lemaire. She should meet us here at the airport. Gretchen said she would be bringing the carcass with her. Said to make sure we got enough data before we burned it."

"How did they get this body again? Some hunter?" Six was looking at the approaching airport ramp worker. He was speaking into a radio as he climbed out of his truck.

Doc looked at her notes, "It was apparently tearing up some guy's chicken coop, and he stepped out and shot it."

Six looked at her sharply, "With regular ammo? I've never heard of non-silver ammo taking down a 'thrope, unless he took its head off."

The team's resident cryptozoologist shrugged as the ramp agent stood at the bottom of the stairs. The young man spoke up, "Got DNR officers at the gate for you, sir? Do you want to meet them out there, or do you want us to escort them in here?"

Ghost looked down at the man, "Have them escorted in here. Pull them up to this side of the plane."

The ramp worker flashed him a thumbs up and spoke into his radio. He walked to his truck, climbed in, and drove off across the tarmac to the gated access.

Moments later, the ramp agent's truck was pulling alongside, closely followed by a green Chevy Suburban with the logo of the Michigan Department of Natural Resources plastered on the doors, and "Police" across the rear quarter panels. The Suburban rocked to a stop and a woman in a green uniform climbed out of the passenger seat. As she walked up, she pushed her sunglasses up to the top of her head. Lieutenant Lemaire was just over five feet tall, and pretty, in that girl-next-door way. Her long brown hair was pulled back into a pony tail, and her uniform and bulletproof vest failed to hide that she was in very good shape.

Six approached, drawing his credentials, "Special Agent Black, Homeland Security. You must be Lieutenant Lemaire. Nice to meet you, Lieutenant." A warm smile appeared on his face.

The DNR officer clasped his outstretched hand, "Glad to meet you Agent Black. Please, call me Robin."

Six's smile deepened, "Thank you Robin, call me John. These are my colleagues, Doctor Noelle Sorenson and Special Agent Hannah Sedano."

After the DNR lieutenant greeted the women, she said, "So, I guess you want to see whatever was killed, right?"

She walked around the back of the truck and opened the split rear doors. Her driver joined her as they both pulled a sliding game cart out of the back of the Suburban, rolling until a whole body bag was visible. As she unzipped the body bag and flipped it open, she glanced at Six and gestured to her driver, "This is my assistant, Matt Gelderloos." The DNR officer gave a half wave.

The federal agent looked at the creature. He had studied everything that Section 28 had on were-creatures. This wasn't a lycanthrope, or any other type of 'thrope for that matter. It had the face and muzzle of a very large dog or wolf. Long muzzle with lips frozen in the rictus of death, showing a line of razor sharp teeth, including two-inch long canines. The coarse hair was black and gray. The neck was thinner than a lycanthrope's, although still covered in longer fur. The body was a weird combination of canine and human forms, with the rear legs much more dog-like, and the arms mostly fur-covered human.

He turned to Doc, "What do you think?"

The team's medic was examining the body. She found the gunshot wound, and asked the DNR officer, "Is this the only wound?"

Lemaire answered, "He said he fired three to five rounds, but it's the only one we can find. It was a clean shot through the heart."

Six was curious, "What kind of gun did the guy use?"

"He had an old AK-47. Russian import, firing seven point sixty-two by fifty-four."

"Anything special about the ammunition?" Doc looked up as she asked the question.

The DNR lieutenant thought for a moment. She shook her head, "Not that I can think of. Standard target ammo, really. Wasn't even hollowpoint."

Doc pursed her lips, deep in thought. As she examined the body, it was obvious that this was not actually a lycanthrope. One of the few things that one of the latest teenage girl monster movies got right is that lycanthropes change to full wolf-form when they change. Although their mass makes them stand out from a standard wild wolf, most of them were never able to control the change enough to make a bipedal wolf-form. The same was true of all the other 'thrope monster types.

The priest thought through the other indicators of lycanthropy. One of the other key indicators against this being a 'thrope was that this body still looked like some sort of wolf-man hybrid. When any 'thrope is killed, it assumes the form of the human that was originally bitten. This is a slow process, taking a couple hours, but it certainly would have happened by now.

The team doctor took a few pictures with her Secure Smart

Phone and sent the images to Spooky and Director Smith. She looked at Six and sent a sidelong glance at the DNR lieutenant. "I just sent the images to Spooky to reference."

Lemaire looked between the two federal agents. She finally settled on the rougher gentleman in the black suit, "So is this some sort of werewolf? I mean, I don't believe in such things, but it kinda fits the bill, doesn't it?"

Six's smile oozed with charm and sincerity. "I can honestly say that this is not a werewolf, Robin. I'm not sure what it is."

Lemaire knew the fed was not telling her everything, she sorted through his reply, and then looked at the fed carefully, "That's because werewolves don't exist, right John?"

"This is not a werewolf." The former mercenary's smile lost a little of its charm as Six tried to keep it in place.

As the DNR officer started to speak, he held a hand up and raised a now-ringing phone to his ear. He said, "Pardon me. My researcher has some information."

On the phone, Spooky began talking. The NSA analyst had taken the images sent by Doc and had compared them to other known file photos. As expected, the information proved that the carcass in the back of the DNR truck was not a werewolf, or any other known type of 'thrope.

"So, what is it?" Six was listening while staring at the carcass.

Six could hear the smile in Spooky's voice. "I think the guy who killed this thing just proved the existence of something that even our records don't have. I think this is what they call a 'Michigan Dogman.' It's the only thing that fits."

"What the hell is a dogman?" Six saw the DNR officer startle at that.

The analyst's voice was giddy. "It's just what it sounds. These are local cryptozoological myths that no one has taken seriously. Ever."

"Does Section Twenty-Eight have anything at all in their records?"

Spooky paused, then spoke, "No. There is a small footnote stating that this is a myth and has never been verified. So we don't have any information." He paused again as if listening to someone else. "Director Smith said he wants you to take possession of the body and bring it back to HQ. There should be cold storage in the Citation."

"Gotcha. We'll make it go away." Six hung up and walked over to the carcass. He looked up into the DNR Lieutenant's face and could easily read her suspicion.

She blasted him. "Dogman? Are you crazy? There is no such thing, regardless of what the locals tell the outsiders."

Six didn't answer her. Instead, he leaned over and began zipping up the body bag. The DNR Lieutenant was immediately in his face, anger flashing in her eyes. "What do you think you're doing? You guys just got here, and now you are seizing the carcass? You don't have the authority."

The DHS agent looked at Lt. Lemaire, calmly. He sighed and reached into his inner jacket pocket to draw out his credentials. He held them up one more time, this time pushing a bit of his willpower into them. The letters glowed, and he said, "By order of Homeland Security and by the Signatory-status of Section Twenty-Eight of the *E'Tuatha* Accords, I hereby bind you from mentioning this incident or creature to anyone who is not currently present or cleared to know." He turned to officer Gelderloos and repeated the phrase.

He calmly put his credentials away and apologized, "I'm sorry I had to do that, Robin. But I'm afraid I'm running short of time, and I don't have any time to be subtle and convince you. You are bound. You will amend the current report to declare that the animal was a nuisance wolf, and neither you nor your department will pursue any follow up with the gentleman who shot the creature. I need a copy of your current, non-redacted report."

Her eyes smoldered with anger as she stalked over to her truck, opened the door, and pulled out a manilla file folder. She silently handed it to Six, who thanked her. He spent a few seconds reading the report and then looked up at the officer. "Lieutenant, I would like you to amend this report to include what I mentioned. Also state that you met federal Fish and Wildlife officers, who confiscated the remains to take back to their labs. I'm sorry, but that will have to appease your supervisors."

"Why am I being forced to follow your orders? Why can't I arrest you?"

"I told you I was sorry. You are bound from doing many of the things you want to do to me right now. I'd explain it, but that would make your life even more complicated. Right now, I just need to complete my mission."

Six grabbed the carcass and hefted the three hundred pound body bag over one shoulder. He told the DNR officer, "Wait here a sec, I need to take care of this." As he glanced back, he could see two black SUVs speeding across the tarmac, red and blue LEDs flashing. They were screeching to a halt when Six climbed back down from the Citation.

A tall African American man climbed down out of the passenger side of the nearest Chevy Suburban. Doc immediately recognized him and waved, "Good to see you again, Agent Lewis."

Six turned to tell the DNR officers goodbye, but they were already in their SUV and Gelderloos was turning over the big V8. The former mercenary waved and turned to meet the man who was approaching him.

Agent Lewis walked wearily over to the Section 28 agents, ignoring the DNR vehicle as it sped back toward the gate. He stretched out his hand to shake Doc's. "I would love to say that it's good to see you again, Doctor Sorenson, but I have a feeling you are here to stir up more trouble."

"I sincerely hope not." The priest introduced Six, "Special Agent Stephen Lewis, Detroit SAC, this is Special Agent John Black, from our department." She turned to Six as the men shook hands, "John, Stephen helped us clean up from the mission we just completed."

"Agent Lewis, I reiterate Doc's statement. I hope we won't cause you any heartache, except for borrowing one of your SUVs while we are here."

The Detroit SAC nodded. "Please, call me Stephen. That's why I brought a spare. I'll admit, I was surprised you didn't bring your own truck, Agent Black."

Six laughed and shook his head. "We didn't bring the driver. She's off on another mission, and she took it. So we have to bum a ride from you. And please call me John."

Agent Lewis laughed, his deep voice booming. Once he had himself under control, he waved for his driver and the driver of the other Suburban to join them. He motioned at the two men, "Special Agents Tessa Miller and Brad Bishop."

After the two exchanged greetings all around, SAC Lewis spoke up, "Brad, you're going to ride with us while these agents use your truck. Grab your gear out of it." The agent walked to the very back of his SUV and pulled a large black duffel out of it. He left the tailgate open as Dancer began putting bags into the truck.

"Anything else you guys need?" Agent Lewis looked at Doc and Six.

"No. Thanks again." Six shook his hand one last time. "I'd love to stand here and talk, but we have a mission we need to take care of. Doc'll call when we're heading back to the airport so you can get your truck."

The former mercenary climbed into the driver's seat, and Doc joined him in the front. Dancer sprawled out in the large back bench, pulling out her tablet to study satellite images of their destination. Six dropped the truck into gear and they roared toward the gate, and the city beyond.

By the time they exited I-96 at Walker Road, Doc had reviewed everything that they knew. Six told the women that he hoped to handle this situation more delicately than they did with the DNR officer. Dancer and Doc's job was to collect as much evidence as they could, while Six talked to the witnesses.

Doc cleared her throat. She was staring at her tablet. "John, I have an updated casualty list. The Director you already knew about. A Search and Rescue team found his body, and his secretary's body early on. They finally recovered all the bodies from David Cassiday's team, and all but the one survivor from Amanda Watkin's team. In total, we lost eighty-three Special Agents, including those who worked Security Services. We lost forty-six support agents, including almost the entire operations planning team. And Gretchen confirmed that Tim Wilson was among the casualties." Dancer gasped and let out a quiet sob in the back.

The priest continued, "Right now, Director Smith has exactly twenty-two support staff available, including the twelve that are in the Warehouse. Gretchen said she was tapped to be Smith's new aide until he can find a replacement for Tim."

Doc thought about Heavy and Gretchen working the disaster site in Langley. "With only Heavy standing guard, I hope no one decides this is a good time to hit us while we're down." Six nodded.

The GPS announced that they had arrived, and Six looked up and saw a white single story home and a large yard with the front and north side of the house fenced in with chain link. To the south of the house was a sand volleyball court. He pulled into a circular gravel driveway with an RV trailer sitting at the apex of the curve, nearest the house. Turning the key to "off," Six could hear some muted "pops" from outside the house. He threw open the door on his side and was greeted by the distinctive sound of a Kalashnikov rifle barking from behind the house. He signaled the others and quickly stepped out of the truck, drawing his credentials in his left hand and his Beretta pistol in his right.

7

DEBRIS

Six cautiously walked around the south side of the house, followed by Dancer. The former mercenary clutched his Beretta in his right hand, held in a low-ready position with the barrel pointed down at a forty-five degree angle. Dancer held no weapons in her hands, deciding to rely on her unnatural abilities. Doc broke away from the two and walked toward the front door of the house.

As Six rounded the corner, he saw a man standing about thirty feet away, firing at a series of small targets about twenty- or twenty-five yards further away. Realizing that this was merely target practice, the federal agent holstered his pistol and glanced back at Dancer. "Go back around to Doc." She nodded and turned around, going to the join the priest at the front door.

As Six turned back around, the man in front of him stopped shooting long enough to switch magazines. Hearing the voice behind him, he spun slightly, raising the muzzle of the rifle to point at the sky, and leaving the new magazine in his hand—making sure the rifle was unloaded. Six noticed that the man immediately indexed his trigger finger off of the trigger, and laid it along the side of the frame, showing at least some prior training.

"Can I help you?"

Six looked more closely at the man. He stood just over five-and-a-half feet tall. At first, the former agent thought he looked stocky, but closer examination revealed that the man was built like a fire-plug—solid. His short-cut brown hair and intense look spoke of some sort of law enforcement or military background, and his entire demeanor reinforced that impression.

The DHS agent held up his credentials, "Ryan DeBoer? I'm Special Agent John Black from the Department of Homeland Security. Can I chat with you for a few minutes?"

DeBoer looked skeptical. "Yeah, that's me. What do you want to talk about?"

Six smiled disarmingly and pushed a little bit of his willpower into his vampire charm. "We're here to ask about a strange creature you killed a couple days ago."

"Yesterday. And I don't have the carcass. You'd have to talk to the DNR about that. They took it away."

Six tucked his credentials away and stood in a loose, parade rest stance learned from years of service. "I've already seen the creature. I just wanted to get the story from you in person."

The man motioned to Dancer as she went around the corner of the house, "Why in the hell is DHS even interested in this thing? The only thing that would make this more creepy would be if Tommy Lee Jones and Will Smith walk around the corner. No. Something doesn't smell right, and it ain't the gunpowder. I was in the army. I know government bullshit when I smell it."

"To be perfectly honest, Mister DeBoer, I have two other agents with me, but they are not Mister Jones or Mister Smith. They are around the front of the house and should be knocking on the front door. I thought if I approached you by myself, you might listen."

The man's eyes tightened. It was clear that Six was not gaining the man's trust, but the federal agent needed more information. Six began to speak, but was interrupted by Ryan, "Ask your questions. Then get off my land. I've dealt with enough crap from the DNR folks. They wanted to lock me up before they figured it wasn't some asshole in a monkey suit."

Six looked at the man, letting several seconds go by before talking. "Walk me through what happened. What were you doing?"

"I was up on the porch, just relaxing. I heard this awful sound coming from my grandma's house over there." The man pointed at the tall house just north of his house. Six saw a barn and a caged in chicken area in the back yard. The chicken cage was torn apart, and there were feathers and pieces of the birds everywhere. "I saw this big dog tearing up my grandma's chickens, so I yelled. It looked up at me, then looked back down and kept eating. I went inside to grab my rifle."

DeBoer motioned to the AK-47 in his hands. "I loaded a mag in it, cycled the bolt, and stepped back out on the porch. The dog-thing was chewing up the last of her chickens. I popped a shot into the berm over there, trying to scare it out of the pen, but it didn't run away."

"Go on, Mister DeBoer."

"The damn thing growled at me, and ran at me." Ryan looked at the federal agent in his perfect black suit, and then read the lines on his face. He could tell that the federal agent had been through some-thing, probably military. "I shot the thing. It wasn't easy, but I got it about thirty feet from the porch. I gotta admit, I about crapped my pants when it was that close."

Six was making notes as DeBoer was talking. He looked up and asked, "How many rounds did you shoot? Was it a single shot?"

The man shook his head, "I darn near emptied the mag. There were only a couple left in it, so that's what? Twenty-six or twenty-seven shots? The damn thing bounced around and dodged more than any natural dog or wolf would. I would lay odds that this thing was smart and knew that I was trying to shoot it. The stupid thing looked like it was actively trying to dodge out of the way."

Six stopped writing and looked at Ryan. "You ever hunt, Mister DeBoer?"

"Of course. This is Michigan. I've hunted everything from rabbits and squirrels to deer. Anything being shot at runs away from the hunter. And any dog that's pissed enough to attack runs straight at you, not dodging out of the way of bullets."

Six nodded slowly and put his notebook away. "Can you show me where you brought the thing down? I'd also like to take a look at your grandmother's chicken coop."

DeBoer nodded. "Let me set this inside." He unloaded the magazine from the rifle and turned to walk up the steps on the porch. He turned back around, "Come on up. You were probably gonna ask anyways. I'm just gonna lean this inside the door and let my wife know you guys are here."

He opened the sliding door and saw that there were two women inside the kitchen talking to his wife already. Both women tensed when he walked in with a rifle in his hands, but relaxed slightly when they saw Six standing behind him, just outside the door.

Ryan watched his wife hand the younger woman a glass of water. He spoke up, "I suppose you guys are also with Homeland

Security? You aren't the goons I expected." He caught his wife's eye, "Everything ok, Tif?"

His wife smiled and nodded, "Everything's fine, I was just telling them about last night."

Ryan nodded, set the rifle down, and turned. He stepped back out the door, walked past the federal agent, down the stairs, and off the deck. He walked over to a spot about thirty feet beyond the deck, which was surrounded by police caution tape attached to small wooden stakes. "Here is where that thing finally collapsed."

Six knelt down and inhaled. The blood was not human. Not quite. It was not quite lycanthrope, either. There was some human, but more canine that tinged the air. He could also smell a pungent, but faint, musk, as if the animal was wet or marking its territory. The federal agent pulled a small petri dish sample kit from his pocket and gently collected some of the blood and grass for the lab to study.

It looked like the creature had tumbled head first when it had been hit. Six could see the impact of where the heavy creature landed, digging a small divot with its snout. There was the depression where the body hit. And there was where the creature breathed its last.

Six stood slowly and looked at the man standing next to him. He indicated the barn a hundred yards away, "Is that where the coop is located?"

"Was."

That single word weighed as much as the entire conversation with the man prior. "Was." Six corrected his thought process. "Can we take a look?"

DeBoer nodded and walked across the yard. As Six followed him, he glanced to his left. There, the yard ended abruptly and overlooked some type of excavation site. The federal agent spoke up, "Mister DeBoer, what kind of excavation are they doing over there." He gestured to the pit.

"Oh, that's a sand pit. That company leases the land from my grandmother—she owns all of that."

Six nodded and turned back to look at the ruins of a chicken coop in front of him. As they walked up, Ryan absently stepped over some feathers and a bit of wood and wire. Surrounding the main pen, DNR officers had put up their yellow caution tape, and the DHS agent saw bits of yellow ribbon inside the barn itself.

The one large overhead door was physically torn off of its hinges and lay ten feet past the entrance to the barn. Six could see large gaping claw marks splintering the edges. Six knelt down and gently tugged on the corner of the door, feeling its massive weight.

"Agent Black? That door weighs about four hundred pounds. I'm waiting on clearance from the DNR to move the door, and even then I couldn't do it all by myself." DeBoer was looking at the door as if figuring out how to lift the heavy door and put it into position on the barn.

Six nodded and stood. He turned around and walked over to the mangled remains of a chicken coop and yard. About ten foot by fifteen foot, the small yard space for the chickens was covered with debris from the coop and fencing, as well as the mangled and half-eaten corpses of several chickens. The flies and other vermin were already working on the carnage, and the midday sun was creating a perfect environment for decay. The stench was becoming overpowering to the federal agent's heightened sense of smell.

Kneeling down again, he saw the tracks and markings of the creature, his enhanced vision catching small details and allowing Six to see every bit of evidence. There was a tuft of fur clinging to the chicken wire. Another was over there on that ragged hole. A small bit of the creature's blood was left on one of the holes, testament to the durability of the chicken wire. And there, among the scattered bodies of the chickens, the carcass of a cat lay broken and mangled. The coop looked like a whirlwind of death had buzzed through it, and Six remembered the wild and ferocious creature that was on Bugs bunny. *What was that thing called? Some kind of devil?*

Standing back up, Six looked over his shoulder to DeBoer, "This thing really tore up your grandmother's chickens. I've seen everything I need to see here. Let's go back to your house for a few minutes, shall we?"

Ryan nodded. "Sure. Any idea when I can clean this place up? We don't want to leave this crap out here too long. And I'd like to put Grandma's barn back together."

The two men walked toward the back of DeBoer's house. Six nodded, "You can clear away the tape. I've seen everything I need to about this scene. I'll inform the DNR that they don't have to come back out here."

"Thanks."

The men reached the back porch, and DeBoer led the way up the stairs and into the house. As Ryan opened the back slider, Six looked once more toward the initial scene next door. He then swept his gaze across the back yard and down over the back hill, into the sand pit. He saw a couple brown shapes moving along the tree line on the far side of the pit. They were gone before he could tell what they were. Staring momentarily at the spot where they disappeared, he concentrated, focusing his senses. Nothing. He shrugged and followed DeBoer into the house.

Inside, the three women were sitting around the table. Doc and Dancer both had a glass of ice water in front of them, and they were getting the statement from Ryan's wife. They all looked up as Ryan opened the sliding door, and the man walked over to rest his hands gently on his wife's shoulders. He introduced his wife to Six, "Agent Black, this is my wife, Tiffany. She was inside during most of it." He turned, looking at the two federal agents still sitting at his table.

Doc got up and made the introductions. "Mister DeBoer. It's nice to meet you. I'm Doctor Noelle Sorenson, and this is Special Agent Hannah Sedano. You wife has been keeping a welcome company. What a beautiful home you have."

DeBoer shook her hand as Six walked through the slider behind him, closing it. The man looked back and forth between the federal agents. "Is there anything else we can help you with?"

Six opened his mouth to speak and then startled as his phone buzzed. He made a motion for Ryan to wait a moment and raised the phone to his ear. "What's up Spooky?"

As the team's analyst spoke, he walked back out the slider, opened it, stepped through and closed the door behind him to provide some sound muffling. "Hey, uh, boss." There was a question buried deep in that simple greeting. "I just had a similar case pop up about forty-five minutes from you. According to the local sheriff and DNR report, some guy came home to find a couple more of these creatures in his house."

"What happened to him?"

"Wait one sec while the report downloads. Ouch. I think they picked the wrong house. Seems this guy killed at least one and wounded a couple more. You might want to talk to him about working for us."

Six paused, his mind racing. "Does the guy have any family? Any human casualties?"

Spooky grew quiet. "Yes to both. Well, had family. The report says the creatures killed his wife and daughter. Wait one sec. This guy is almost like Do-Right. Hell, he was even in Trinidad while we were there, and he moved up to Michigan after we left."

Six stopped paying attention to the information when he caught a flash of movement out of the corner of his eye. He looked in that direction and saw a large furry shape cross an open stretch of sand pit before it went out of his sight. He watched a second one cross and realized the thing was running on all fours.

"Spooky, I gotta let you go." Six hung up even as the analyst was still talking. He reached for the Beretta on his side as he felt back behind him for the handle of the door. He heard a low growl, and an answering "chuff," and slid the door open.

Without looking, the federal monster hunter called over his shoulder, "Hannah, you are with me. Doc, stay inside and protect the civilians. It looks like we have company."

8

PACK

S ix held his Beretta M9 in a low ready as he stepped aside to let Dancer out the sliding door. As she stepped out onto the porch, she drew her Walther P99. It, too was loaded with some of Norbert's special hunting rounds. Her eyes scanned all around, looking for whatever had spooked her team leader.

"What's going on, Six?"

The burly ex-mercenary never let his eyes stop scanning the grounds. "I think I just spotted a few of those creatures coming this way."

Dancer's eyes tightened as she thought about the implications of that short statement. "Any idea how many?"

"I saw at least two." Six inhaled and paused, then continued, "I think there's more. Damn things are fast and quiet. No special response unless it's needed. We have witnesses."

Behind him, he heard the distinct "click, thwack" of a magazine being inserted into a rifle, and the bolt slamming forward on a Kalashnikov variant. "You don't have witnesses. You have backup."

"Mister DeBoer," Six sighed. "Let us take care of this. This is our job."

"But it's my land. And if there are more than one of those things, you're going to need all the firepower you can get."

Six had reviewed the file on the way to the house, and he knew the man had retired from the Army with excellent marksmanship while serving. Making a snap decision, the federal agent answered, "Fine. But for this op, you are under my command. Period." Six risked a quick glance at the man. "You follow my orders. Even if they don't make sense."

Ryan nodded, "Understood."

Six looked back at the yard, straining to hear the creatures coming. "Done. Stay close to Agent Sedano. If you see one of those creatures' heads pop up in the yard, pull the trigger. You have right flank. I'll cover center. Hannah, you have left."

The next ten seconds stretched into an eternity. Just as Six was about to say something, the head of a dog popped over the ridge, coming from the sand pit. Six realized quickly that it wasn't an ordinary dog, and his trigger finger smoothly drew toward the back of the guard. His pistol barked once, then twice more, rapidly putting three rounds into a tiny space. But the dog's head wasn't there.

"Son of a bitch. Damn things are fast."

Another creature crashed around the corner of the barn at a full run, zigging and zagging across the lawn. Ryan began shooting. Seven shots later, the creature tumbled end-over-end, and came to a rest at the edge of the yard. It flipped around to launch itself at the porch again, but DeBoer was faster. His trigger squeezed twice, and two more 7.62mm projectiles slammed into the creature. One of them struck the head, blowing out the back of the head in a shower of gore and blood.

The man shifted the aim of his rifle and shot at another creature that bounded around the corner of the barn. Another seven rounds were launched downrange, again the final one causing the creature to tumble. Two final rounds put that creature down permanently.

Next to the Grand Rapids man, Six emptied half of his seventeen rounds of ammunition before finally dispatching one of the creatures as they came over the ridge. Six noted that even Norbert's special rounds wouldn't work when they couldn't hit the target. As the next one leapt over the ridge, the federal agent felt his gun "click" as a jam caused the gun not to fire. Realizing that he did not have the time to fix the malfunction, he dropped the gun and hurled himself at the oncoming creature. With one leap, he vaulted up over the railing of the porch and over the small above ground pool beyond, meeting the incoming creature in midair.

As he was leaping, the federal agent's fingernails lengthened and sharpened. As he collided with the hairy beast in the air, his fingers punched through the thick hide of the creature and into its chest cavity. Grabbing onto most of the malformed ribs on each side of the creature's chest, Six ripped his hands away, tearing the creature's ribcage apart. The creature's howl abruptly died as the vampire federal agent reached through one of the gaping holes and tore its beating heart out of its chest. Six looked up and leapt as another of the beasts cleared the ridge.

Dancer was frustrated. She had emptied her first magazine to bring down one creature and was in the middle of her second when Six flew off the porch. Realizing that she, too, needed her particular advantage, she dropped her pistol and reached for *fion-fhuil*. Vellath sighed with contentment as she drew the invisible blade from the sheath on her back. *Time to play?* The dragon's voice purred in her head.

Time to play, you big lizard. Dancer grinned as she leapt from the porch. As a mortal with the blood of a Fury singing through her veins, Dancer was impressive when she let the power flow. With Vellath in her hand, she was nearly unstoppable.

The creature that attacked her did not understand how her empty hand had just provided a deep cut across the shoulder as she swung past the beast. It did not understand the agony and pain in its back as a wound appeared to stab down through the heart and out the front. The beast ceased to care when Dancer removed the creature's head with a mighty blow from Vellath. It was far beyond any mortal cares at that point.

Dancer used the momentum from her decapitating swing to spin a full circle and cleave her sword into the side of another beast that had lunged past her to attack the civilian behind her. The creature howled in pain, startling the man with the rifle. The howl abruptly ended as Dancer drove the tip of her sword through the crown of its head.

Ryan was startled by the sudden howl of a creature behind him, and he missed the beast in front of him. That creature reached the steps leading up to the porch before he centered it in his sights again. The Grand Rapids man felt the bolt click back on his last shot as the beast finally crashed to a halt. He reflexively dropped the magazine and then realized that he didn't have a replacement. DeBoer looked up in time to see another one of the creatures leaping from twenty feet away.

Ryan raised his AK-47 across his body in a vain attempt to block the beast's attack. The creature never landed on him. Instead, the beast crashed to the porch with Six on top of it, hands stuck deep in the creature's chest. Ryan watched as the federal agent literally ripped the creature's ribcage apart, pulling the still beating heart out of the beast. Six glanced over at DeBoer, and the Grand Rapids man realized that the federal agent had jet black eyes.

One final anguished roar came from Ryan's left. He turned and watched as the young, white-haired federal agent slammed a hand down into the back of one of the creatures, making gouts of blood fly. She swung her hand up and in an arc, and the Grand Rapids man saw a blue-tinged outline of a sword, covered with the creature's blood. The translucent sword swung down and cleaved through the neck of the final creature, and the snarling head dropped to the deck with a resounding thump.

The three warriors paused to look around, making sure that no other creatures were attacking the group. After a few seconds, they all stood, and DeBoer looked at the two federal agents.

"What the hell kind of federal agents are you?" The Grand Rapids man watched as Six's fingernails retracted and then as the young woman pantomimed putting a sword into a sheath on her back. "And what the hell are these things?"

Six reached down and picked up his dropped Beretta. After clearing the stovepipe malfunction in his Beretta, the fed holstered the auto and straightened his tie, leaving bloody finger marks on his shirt and tie. Looking at the Grand Rapids man, he smiled a wry smile, and said, "As I said, we work for Homeland Security. Can we talk about this inside while I call a cleanup crew?"

Ryan frowned, nodded and let Dancer walk inside before him. He followed and wearily pulled a chair out from the dining table and sat heavily. Outside, Six placed a call on his SSP to SAC Lewis. "Agent Lewis, this is John Black. I need you and a couple of your close-lipped agents to come to my location with a load of body bags." Six nodded to himself as he listened to the response. "No. No human casualties. We need you to collect the animal carcasses and take them back to our jet." He listened a few more seconds, and then concluded, "Great. I'll see you in about 15 minutes. When you get here, run interference with the neighbors, first. We'll help with cleanup." The federal agent disconnected and walked inside the house.

DeBoer was holding his wife's hand and had just drained a bottle of water. Six looked at Dancer and said, "Agent Sedano, would you go to the front and wait for Agent Lewis. And if any nosy neighbors or local law enforcement drops by, deal with them appropriately." Dancer nodded and walked out the front door.

"Mister DeBoer, I assure you that we are from Homeland Security." He held up his hands to forestall the looming questions from the Grand Rapids man. "We are from a top secret division that is specifically empowered to handle the more difficult or strange cases. That is our charter."

"Like on the 'X-files?'"

Six smiled and gave a slight shake of his head. "Although we don't work for the FBI, it is something like that. In truth, this case has become a lot more complicated with the dogman attack a few minutes ago."

Ryan startled. "Dogman? Are you telling me that I killed a Michigan dogman earlier? And that its... pack attacked us a couple minutes ago? Seriously, when does Mulder and Scully show up?"

The big federal agent again wore a bemused look. "While we do have some backup coming to help us clean up, neither Mulder nor Scully are among them. As it is, I want to formally thank you, from my department, for your help during that attack. I'm not sure Agent Sedano and I would have been able to manage it on our own. You really showed a solid ability to handle yourself, both with a weapon, and when strange things were happening around you. You were in the service, right?"

Ryan nodded, "Yeah. Did a couple tours in the middle east. But I saw you guys out there, What the hell? You ripped those dogmen in half with your own hands. And she killed them with an invisible sword." Ryan waved at the front door, beyond which Dancer was waiting for the local sheriff to arrive.

Six gave another half grin. "Yeah... about that. You're just going to have to forget what you saw. Any impression you got that I might, or might not, be able to rip creatures in half did not actually happen. It was a trick of the light, or swamp gas, or a weather balloon. And that invisible sword? It was invisible. So you didn't see it. Right?"

Ryan spent enough time in the Army to understand when something was being covered up and hidden from the public. He knew exactly what the fed was talking about, and he nodded. "You're right. I apparently was distracted by the swamp gas on the weather balloon. Or something."

Six sat for a long minute, looking at the man and his wife. He looked at Doc, and she nodded, seeming to read his intentions. He reached into his jacket and produced his credentials. His actual credentials. "This is the point when I would normally threaten you and your wife with a long stay at Gitmo if you ever talked about this to anyone not here during the incident. I would also mutter a phrase that would bind your will and twist you up inside if you actually tried to talk to someone about it." He looked down at his still-closed credentials.

The DHS agent looked back up at DeBoer, and then at his wife. "I'm not going to do that this time." He opened his credentials, drew a business card from within, and closed them again, putting it back in his pocket. Six handed the card to the Grand Rapids man. "Instead, I'm going to give you my card. If you decide that you would like to talk to my boss about a job with my agency, I might be able to arrange something."

Ryan looked at the card in his hands. It was a jet black card that seemed to absorb the light. On it, there was a red, angled-box logo, with the typeset symbol for the legal word "Section" surrounded by the numbers "2" and "8." This, in turn was surrounded by a box. Next to this, in white, was the agent's name and a phone number.

Ryan looked up directly into Six's eyes. For the first time in a long time, the ex-mercenary saw a kindred soul deep in the eyes of the Grand Rapids man. Giving a slight nod, Six said, "It's worth it. Give me a call in a couple days."

Six raised his head as he heard sirens in the distance. Realizing that Dancer would likely need some help with the locals, he told the DeBoers, "You guys stay in here until I call you out. Doc, you stay here with them. I'm going out to help Sedano deal with the locals. At least until Agent Lewis is here." He turned and strode out the front door.

It was two hours before the sheriff deputies finally opened both ends of the road and left. Homeland Security SAC Lewis had arrived ten minutes after the sheriff deputies, pulling up in the middle of a tense confrontation between the Lieutenant and Six. It took several minutes and a call to Agent Smith to get the deputies to stand down and go block off the road at both ends.

After they were off the property, Agent Lewis and his crew helped the agents from Section 28 bag all the bodies and various parts. The bags of the various carcasses and pieces filled the backs of Agent Lewis' SUV and were heavy enough to weigh down the heavy duty shocks and struts. Six and Ryan did a final walk through on the property to make sure that they had not missed anything.

Finished with their last sweep, the two men walked around the corner to the waiting SUVs. Doc and Dancer were saying their goodbyes to Tiffany, and Six suddenly stopped and stuck out his hand for Ryan to take. "Mister DeBoer, I'd like to issue you a formal thank you from the United States government, and from me personally. You were instrumental in helping us take care of the attack, and, for that, I can't thank you enough. It was sincerely a pleasure to fight alongside you, and I hope you call me before too long."

Ryan's grip was firm as the two men shook hands. "Thank you, Agent Black. I'll probably do that. What if the press or sheriff shows up again? How do I handle it?"

"Your answer should be 'No Comment.' And then your next phone call should be to me, so I can deal with it."

"I guess this is it, then."

"Thank you, Mister DeBoer. I'll get these nonexistent carcasses out of here before anyone else comes along. If you have any issues, call me."

Ryan wished Doc and Dancer well and then walked into his house with his wife. Six approached Agent Lewis and shook his hand.

"Thank you for the assist. I would appreciate it if you take those animal carcasses back to our jet. I'll call the pilot and have her open the storage area for you to stow them. Unfortunately, my team has to go to a scene in Muskegon. We'll meet you back at the plane as soon as we can."

The senior DHS agent looked at the Section 28 agent, "I hope we don't have to clean up your mess in Muskegon."

Six shook his head, "That's not my intention. This one is a cold scene. Just talking to a witness."

Agent Lewis raised his eyebrows quizzically. "That's what you said about this one."

The former mercenary laughed, "Let's hope this one actually stays cold. I'll see you at the plane, Agent Lewis."

The big DHS SAC nodded and walked to his SUV.

The two Suburbans pulled out of the driveway and went their separate ways, with Agent Lewis' heading across town to the airport and the waiting Citation. There they were waved through the perimeter gate and followed a ramp technician over to the team's jet. It was short work to stow the bags in the refrigerated hold of the aircraft.

Just over two hours later, the SUV driven by the Section 28 team arrived at the airport gates and were quickly let through to the waiting Air Force Citation. Pulling up next to Agent Lewis' SUV, the team disembarked. As Six grabbed the bags out of the back of the truck, Doc walked over to the waiting DHS SAC. She greeted Agent Lewis warmly, shaking his hand.

Six dropped the bags at the foot of the stairs and walked over to

Agent Lewis as Doc and Dancer turned to board the jet. He reached out to shake the DHS agent's hand. "I told you this last one would be a quiet one. Just a simple witness interview."

Agent Lewis grinned, "It's nice to see one of your interviews not need any paperwork from my office."

"Thank you for the assist, Stephen. Doc told me how you were... briefed on our team. I'm trusting you to impress upon your team that they did not officially bag any weird bodies today. I don't want to have to come have a chat with them, especially with all the crap happening in Langley."

The big DHS SAC chuckled, "Hell, John. I don't want to have Agent Massey come back out here. You are scary. She's terrifying."

Six laughed out loud, startling Doc and Dancer, who were climbing the steps into the plane. "For the record, I absolutely agree with you. Thanks again. I hope I don't have to play on your playground too much in the future."

When the Section 28 agent climbed the aircraft stairs, he turned and pulled them up after him. After sealing the door, he nodded at the pilot, "All set, Captain. Back to Langley. We have a hold full of bodies that need refrigerated."

The engines were already starting to wind up when Six took his seat and buckled his seatbelt. They were on the taxiway in two minutes and climbing into the air in less than five minutes. Six was already asleep when the pilot turned off the seatbelt sign.

9

BEFORE

For the second time in as many days, the specially modified Air Force C-17 Globemaster III touched down on a runway other than the Section 28 runway in Langley. This time, the big Air Force jet landed on runway 15 at Charleston International Airport. The familiar roar of the massive engines was a dull rumble in the cabin, and as soon as the airplane was decelerated and moved from the runway to the taxiway, team Knightmare began unbuckling their seatbelts and putting on their armor.

Captain Kenney's voice came over the intercom, "Welcome to Charleston, ladies and gentlemen. It's a nice eighty-two degrees on the tarmac. We'll be parking at Joint Command Base Charleston right next to a bunch of other C-17s. You'll be met on the tarmac by a loadmaster and a support truck."

When the aircraft finally came to a rest on the parking ramp, the pilot activated the intercom a final time, "We're parked on the ramp. You are free to disembark. Open the hatch and the rear ramp when you are ready."

Ghost motioned to Boomer and Spooky, and they walked through the hatchway to the back of the plane where they prepped the Wunder Buggy. The rest of the team stood stiffly and grabbed the gear they brought with them.

Little G picked up his rifle case, having spent the trip cleaning and prepping his rifle. There was an M4 in the Wunder Buggy in his weapon locker, but he figured that he would spend more time with the rifle in the case. It was a lovingly cared for M24-A3 sniper rifle. Based on the Remington 700, the rifle was the weapon system of choice for US Army and law enforcement snipers, including the FBI Hostage Rescue Team. Chambered in a .338 Lapua Magnum, Little G figured that the big bore rifle would stop any critter in its tracks.

Ghost stood, drew on his long leather duster, and picked up a white cane. He reached out to grab Director Smith's worn leather satchel as the man stood and straightened his tie. The director checked his SSP one final time and then tucked it away into his coat pocket. He accepted his satchel back from the tall monster hunter, and slung the well-worn strap over one shoulder.

The captain of the air force jet climbed down from the cockpit and said, "Anything else we can do for you?"

Smith shook his head. "No thanks, Captain. We're going to open the doors in a moment. Get refueled, and file a flight plan back to Langley. We'll deal with this and then return to the chaos back home."

"Yes, sir. We'll have her ready when you need it."

Ghost opened the hatch and let the bright morning sunshine flood into the cabin. It had been roughly eight and a half hours since they got the Priority Red, and an hour-and-a-half of that had been spent in the air.

The team leader turned to the director, "Who did Gretchen say we were supposed to meet?"

The man's calm and cultured voice carried over the whine of other engines on the airport. "We will be meeting Special Agent Kenneth Zwagerman, the local SAC. He will introduce us to the local sheriff, who will escort us out to the site.

Ghost nodded as an Air Force humvee drove across the parking ramp, followed by a black Chevy Suburban. Ghost looked over his shoulder, "Looks like the locals have arrived. You want to meet him, boss?" He let Smith exit the plane first.

Director Smith walked down the stairs, followed by the rest of the team still in the main cabin. The Air force truck slowed to a halt, and the SUV pulled up beside it, about fifteen feet from the stair-well. As he walked down the last few steps, a short man with black curly hair and aviator sunglasses, wearing a rumpled shirt and straight black tie, climbed out of the driver's seat. The small badge on his belt and the sidearm holstered on his side showed that he was a federal agent. He walked toward the Section 28 Director and stretched out his hand.

"Special Agent Zwagerman. Call me Kenneth. You must be the folks from Langley?" His soft southern drawl matched the easy smile on his face.

Smith shook the proffered hand, a slight smile answering the local agent's. "Division Director James Smith. And James is fine. I don't think we've met."

"No, sir. I don't think we have, either. So what brings you folks down to my neck of the woods?"

Smith looked at the man, calmly stating, "Unfortunately Kenneth, I'm not at liberty to tell you. You are not cleared for the operation." He watched the smile fade from the man. "I'm sorry, but this one has to stay classified. We shouldn't be in your... woods for too long."

Both men looked toward the back of the jet as the rear ramp whined down to the ground. The roar of the big engine in the Wunder Buggy followed, and the Air Force loadmaster directed Boomer on the ramp as she backed the big truck down to the tarmac. Once down, she pulled forward to where the team was waiting. Little G climbed up in the truck to stow his gear. Ghost looked at Smith, who motioned for the lanky agent to join him.

"Agent Zwagerman, this is Agent Vanhof. He is leading this particular op, and I'm just along for the ride." Ghost shook the DHS agent's hand.

"I've got the lieutenant from the sheriff's office waiting in the parking lot for you." The DHS SAC appraised the matte black armored hide of the Wunder Buggy, "I see you have your own transport.

Ghost smiled, "It makes things a whole lot easier when we bring our own truck. Shall we get going?"

Smith climbed aboard the truck, sitting in a jump seat next to Spooky and leaving the front seat open for Ghost. Once they had met the deputy and were leaving base, Smith leaned back and closed his eyes, thinking about the last time he was in Charleston.

IT HAD BEEN A LONG WAR. They had to be nearing the end. The soldier called Warren McLeod was tired. After a long forced march, they were approaching Charleston and their colonel had every intention of raiding the British fort. The word came down the line to halt, and the soldiers wearily found a place to sit. McLeod shook off his rucksack and set it carefully on the ground, hearing the clink of his canteen knocking against his precious cargo. The private sat gingerly, easing his aching feet.

McLeod had gone by a number of different names over the years, and this one had been his for less than three. As a name goes, it fit in with his slight Scottish accent and was vague enough that people would recognize it, but not note it. He had been with Colonel Hampton's South Carolina First Regiment, State Dragoons, for the month and a half that the regiment had been formed.

As he sat and ate a bit of hardtack out of his belt pouch, he heard the thunder of hooves announcing at least two riders coming at a full gallop toward the regiment. Warren was one of the first to scramble to his feet, putting his rucksack back on, and grasping his Brown Bess rifle at the ready. He relaxed slightly as he recognized the colonel's dappled horse rounding the corner with his adjutant's stallion following close behind the colonel.

A cry of "Redcoats" buzzed in the air, and the colonel drew his horse up short in front of his captains. The horses whirled, and the cavalry was off like a shot. Three of the captains stayed behind to guide the men, while the horsemen rode back down the lane. Soon, Warren's unit was given the order to make haste after the horsemen.

McLeod's unit arrived at the clearing for the Lewisfield Plantation. The captain split the men into three groups, two larger groups to search the surrounding fields, and a smaller group to search the house. Around the back of the house, McLeod could hear the crack and pop of rifles, and the screams of the wounded. Confused shouts turned into contrary orders and the men milled in confusion. And then he stumbled over a Redcoat loyalist hiding in the field. Startled, he almost killed the man, but he quickly realized that the man had already laid down his rifle. Warren McLeod shouted out, "Found one!"

His cry was repeated across the fields, as the members of the Dragoons found British soldiers hiding. McLeod guided his prisoner to the back of the plantation house, where the group of captured Redcoats was growing quickly. As he prodded his prisoner around the corner, he glanced toward the river and saw two bodies in red coats being hauled out of a pair of small boats. There were already four bodies on the ground, and none of them wore the continental blue or militia brown.

Colonel Hampton had dismounted from his horse and was directing the operation. His captains were busy with their own units, organizing food and medical care for the couple militia soldiers who needed it. One entire unit was drawn aside and directed to guard the prisoners, surrounding them with bayonets fixed in place.

Warren's unit was directed to make another sweep of the fields, looking for stragglers or injured. He walked into the thigh-high cornfield and waded through the stalks. Searching for about a half hour, he stumbled upon a row of rough-hewn blocks and rocks that formed a low circular wall about eight feet across to the other side. Mounted over the top of the well was a rope and pulley system attached to a bucket for drawing water. The wood was old and cracked, weathered from the hot South Carolina summers. With half of one side of the circle crumbling, the well was apparently disused.

Warren McLeod looked around, seeing no one closer than three or four hundred yards. The man knelt to the ground and pulled off his rucksack. He reached inside his pack and brought out a cylindrical object. About a foot and a half long, and about eight inches in diameter, the object was wrapped in rough cotton linens and tied with a simple leather thong.

Warren unwrapped the object to take one final look at it. It was an ancient Greek *pithos*. The urn appeared to be made of solid bronze, although the actual materials were far tougher. Decorated with vibrant reliefs depicting catastrophic scenes, the metal glowed when the sunlight hit it and the vibrant colors of the relief scenes came alive. The lid appeared to be a simple jar top, but Warren knew it was sealed tight. After all, he had sealed it with his blood. As he stared at it, the malevolence was palpable, and seemed to draw him into its grasp.

The soldier shook his head, as if clearing away cobwebs, and snarled at it, "Not today. Not ever. You will remain sealed."

McLeod quickly wrapped it up in its rough linens again, and securely tied the leather thong around it. He held the ends of the cord and muttered a few words in a language that was long dead. A slight blue glow touched the brown leather, and then was absorbed deep into the cord. He looked around again to see if anyone had noticed the glow or the object, and was again happy to see that his actions had gone unnoticed. Warren simply tossed the bundle into the well.

What seemed like an eternity later, there was a dull thump as the urn hit the bottom. The soldier smiled. *Dry, just as I thought. Time to fill it in.*

Warren sat on the ground and placed his back against part of the wall still standing. He dug his heels in and gave a push, feeling the old bricks and rocks shift and move. He continued working like that until a portion of the wall caved into the well. The soldier shifted position and worked on another section.

Fifteen minutes later, he had knocked the last of the wall into the well. The urn now lay buried under hundreds of pounds of rock and brick, in a dry, abandoned well, in a small plantation outside Charleston. It would not be found or dug out, and therefore had no chance to be opened.

Warren heard a booming voice call for the troops to rally, and he calmly climbed to his feet. He picked up his now-lighter pack, and placed it on his shoulders. As he walked to meet up with the rest of his unit, his steps were lighter than they had been in a long time. His pack was lighter, and the weight of his burden was suddenly lifted after hundreds of years of carrying the cursed urn.

ACTING Director of Section 28 James Smith awoke with a start when Spooky nudged him. He looked at the former NSA analyst and asked, "Yes?"

"Sorry to wake you, but we're pulling onto the road to the plantation. I've been doing some digging, and the only thing I found was a report from the Revolutionary War about a minor battle taking place here because some colonel wanted to get lucky." The analyst thought for a moment more, and then continued, "It's not even on a ley line. There ain't nothing out here."

Smith realized that he had been lost in his memories of his first trip to this area. He quickly organized his thoughts, and then looked over Spooky's shoulders at the screens. "Yes, Mister Smith. The only thing special about this place was that small skirmish that we fought in the war. There is something else on that property that you will not even find in the Section Twenty-Eight archives. It is an artifact that I truly hope remains undisturbed."

Smith leaned forward and caught Ghost's attention. "Mister Vanhof, is the officer going to stop at the end of the drive as we had requested?"

Ghost nodded, "The house is currently unoccupied, waiting for some renovation work." As he spoke, the patrol car stopped at the end of the driveway and waited for the Wunder Buggy to pass. Once the DHS truck passed him, the deputy parked the car across the end of the drive, blocking off any further traffic.

Ghost looked at his boss, "So what are we looking for out here? Spooky said there's nothing here, except from some Revolutionary War skirmish site." Smith was concentrating on the fields around them as Boomer drove the truck slowly down the winding lane. He looked to his left, and what he saw made his blood run cold. Off in the field, there were a couple of bulldozers and a backhoe, all of them unoccupied.

Smith thought about the placement. It seemed to be about the right area. And then he saw the first body. The pit that sat in Smith's stomach was cold and growing. *No. It was protected.*

Smith grasped Boomer's shoulder and pointed. The truck gently rocked to a stop, and the team piled out. Smith was the second one to hit the ground, and he looked around for any signs of the people who had committed this massacre. Now that he was out, he could smell the decaying bodies, and hear the flies buzzing around what had to be six or seven bodies.

Smith did not hear Ghost order Boomer and Little G to take up positions on the truck while they waited for him to move. The DHS director's eyes were darting all around, trying to take in every bit of information. He stepped forward to walk toward the mound and Ghost laid a restraining hand on him.

"Wait one second, boss. Let us check this out first." Ghost pointed to Little G and motioned him toward the excavation equipment. The monster hunter pointed at their resident vampire, "Boomer, you're on VIP detail. Director Smith goes home with all of his parts. Understood?" Boomer nodded and moved closer to Smith.

Ghost bent down and picked up something from the crushed gravel drive. He held it up and showed it to Smith, "Is this something, boss? Looks like a leather cord or shoelace." Ghost watched as his boss, the most feared agent in Section 28, and the scariest man that Ghost knew, went pale. The monster hunter watched the color drain from his boss' face and was suddenly very nervous.

Smith reached out for the broken leather thong. Yes, it was the same cord he had tied around the urn to protect it. There should have been no one able to defeat the magic bound in that cord. He looked up suddenly. This was a message, a trap.

"Call Little G back. Now." Smith's tone brooked no argument, and Ghost reached for his throat mic.

It was then that the ground exploded underneath Little G's feet.

10

AMBUSH

One moment, Little G was approaching the excavating equipment cautiously, rifle shouldered and ready. The next moment, he was flying through the air as a massive figure rose out of the ground directly underneath him. The giant creature stood nine feet tall, had rough greenish-gray skin and two massive lower canines sticking out of its misshapen head. Dressed in black combat armor, the creature bellowed a challenge to the DHS team.

"Chikara." Boomer hissed.

Before even her substantial reflexes could intervene, the giant monster reached into the pit it had dug and brought out a gargantuan weapon. The shaft of this massive warhammer measured eight feet long and was at least six inches across. The head of the weapon was double-sided. One side had the flattened end of a sledge hammer adorned with several spikes varying from six to ten inches long. The other side of the warhammer had a crescent-shaped blade that arced with a three foot long blade and narrowing to a razor point.

Little G had landed with a thud about ten feet from the creature and had crumpled to the ground, limp. Seeing the man a scant ten feet away, the big creature lunged a couple steps and swung the hammer. Little G screamed as the monstrous weapon slammed into his back, crushing him between his steel armor plates and sending massive spikes through his backside and the base of his spine. The massive creature raised the hammer again, this time reversing it and aiming the three foot curved blade at the battered sniper.

The creature staggered and missed as a shrieking mass about the size of their demolitions expert hit the Chikara in the side. Boomer tried to sink her now pointed nails into the creature's side, but her claws were bouncing off the hardened armor. She was flung sideways and crashed into the bulldozer hard enough to dent the massive steel blade. Smith watched her slump to the ground, unconscious or dead.

The creature had dropped its hammer when it was hit by Boomer. It looked at the two men still standing outside the truck and gave a barking laugh. The creature spoke in a booming guttural English, "Who dares to stand against Kranak, hunter prime of the Blooddrinkers?"

As Ghost drew his ancestral blade, Smith laid a hand on the team leader's arm. A quick glance told him that Boomer was at least moving, although she was down for this fight. Smith spoke up, "I am James Smith, warden of this sovereign land and Knight of the Realm. I formally accept your challenge to single combat."

Smith unbuttoned his jacket and removed it, handing it to the tall monster hunter dressed in black. Ghost had never seen the man without his suit jacket. His crisp white shirt and black tie looked perfect, even in the wilting heat and humidity. Then Smith did something that Ghost had never thought would happen, the DHS agent loosened his tie and unbuttoned the top button. Turning back to Ghost, Smith reached into his folded jacket and into an inner pocket.

As he drew his hand out, a longsword filled his hand. As the sword emerged into the sunlight, the blade flared so bright it seemed to brighten the sun-drenched day. After the flare died down, Smith was left holding a long sword of shiny steel in his right hand. The handle was a brass and wood combination designed to be wielded with both hands, with an ornate brass crossbar at the blade, and a brass and jeweled pommel at the bottom of the hilt. Smith faced the massive creature and stood in a two-handed stance ready to strike with a mighty blow.

The creature frowned, deep ridges and wrinkles forming as it tried to comprehend the small human before him. "Are you not afraid, little man? What can your metal trinket do to me, the mightiest of warriors?"

Smith gave a small smile, "Do you not recognize *Kaledvoulc'h?* Even a young pup like you must have listened to the legends."

"Bah. Legends and myths. That sword was lost centuries ago. And when I kill you, I will have the trophy."

Smith's smile shifted into a sneer, "Then come try to take it, whelp."

The Chikara roared at the insult and charged forward, raising the hammer above its head to bring it down in a crushing blow. Smith waited to the last minute and then dodged, raising the sword to swat across the haft of the massive warhammer. The head of the massive hammer flew through the air, burying itself blade-first in the ground fifty yards away. The startled creature was left with a light-weight metal shaft in its hands.

Snarling, the beast turned and swung the haft at Smith, who parried with the flat of his blade and was driven back for his efforts. In a deft move, Smith turned the blade edgewise across the haft and again lopped a piece of it off, the blade slicing through the metal like it wasn't there. Smith danced back twenty feet to get out of the way of the now-raging Chikara.

Smith put every ounce of authority in his voice, "Do you yield, Kranak? I will spare your life."

The answering snarl was expected, and Smith ducked out of the trajectory of the now useless length of hammer shaft. The Chikara lunged at the DHS agent attempting to get his massive paws on the insolent human. Again, Smith darted out of the way, this time swatting the creature's backside with the flat of his blade.

"Yield, Chikara. But for your arrogance, your line does not have to end today."

The roar from the beast was deafening and the creature's eyes were wide with insanity. Smith knew he had to end this if there was any hope of getting treatment for his sniper. With a resolute sigh, Smith sidestepped one last time as the monster charged, this time running the edge of the blade across the stomach of the beast, and following up with slices across the hamstrings of both legs. The howling creature crashed to the ground, shaking the area.

"I am truly sorry it came to this, Kranak. Your bloodline did not have to end today." As the creature tried to turn itself over, Smith reversed his grip and slammed the blade down through the armor on the beast's back, through the chest in front, and into the ground beneath the orc. The creature gave one convulsive shudder and went still.

Smith bowed his head and then drew the sword out of the creature. Ghost noticed that none of the blood of the creature remained on the blade. The director carried his sword over to Ghost and moved to retrieve his jacket. The sword disappeared back into the jacket, and Smith put the jacket back on. He then buttoned the last button and straightened his tie.

Ghost ignored his boss and ran over to Little G's still form. The whimpers and cries had faded during the fight, and when Ghost checked on his teammate, the man had already died. Up close, the monster hunter saw the indentations of the massive spikes on the metal armor plating, and realized that the sniper's backside and tail-bone had both been crushed, broken, and pierced in multiple places. Boomer unsteadily walked over to the broken body and fell to her knees, sobbing.

Spooky suddenly announced over the radio, "I've got ambulance and DHS inbound. How is he?"

Ghost looked up and shook his head at the windshield of the truck. Activating his microphone, he said, "Tell ambulance and DHS to hold at the end of the driveway. This scene is not cleared yet." The monster hunter reached over and grabbed the fallen sniper's rifle. Picking it up, he muttered to himself, "But it will be."

Boomer nodded, "Amen."

It took the two of them another fifteen minutes to call the site clear. With Spooky's drones up, and Boomer's extra-human senses, they could quickly cover the rest of the area, concentrating around the dig site. In that time, Smith never moved from his spot by the front of the truck.

Ghost was getting angry at his boss, who didn't seem to care about their loss. *It wasn't right. The man was so damn stoic. And what the hell was that sword he used? While we're at it, what the hell was a Chikara left to guard?*

When they wrapped up their search, Ghost reported to Smith. He let the questions burning in his mind spill out into the humid air. "All clear. This was the only bad guy. Now what was so goddamn important that was worth Little G's life?" Ghost felt his anger threaten to release, and he worked to tamp it back down into his gut.

Smith looked tired. This was the first time that Ghost had ever seen his boss looking tired or hurt or anything negative. The director of their department opened his mouth, closed it, and shook his head.

"I'm sorry. Let's get the scene cleared first. Get the Chikara covered and into the truck, as well as Mister Rivera's remains. I will tell you as much as I can when we are cleared from this place and on our way back to Langley." Smith leaned into the truck, "Mister Smith, as soon as your compatriots have moved the creature, you can let the others come into the plantation. I'm afraid it's going to be cramped in the truck until we get back to transport."

Another two hours had passed before the team could clear the scene. There were many questions from the local DHS SAC and from the local law enforcement. It took Smith a lot of time and a few threats of Guantanamo Bay before the locals would relinquish the scene to DHS. Eventually, the DHS crew was able to start cleanup and sanitization of the area, and no one questioned it when Boomer brought the hundred pound hammer head back to the truck.

The relatively short trip to the airport was silent, and the tension hung in the air while the team stowed the Wunder Buggy and the bodies. Once everything was ready, the pilot called and received priority clearance for takeoff. A couple minutes later, they were passing through 10,000 feet and climbing for the short hop to Langley.

Ghost could not take the tension any more. "All right, boss. We've waited to be alone. Now what was so goddamn important that it cost the life of Little G?"

Spooky chimed in as he ticked off points on his fingers. "You were looking for whatever they found. You had been out there before. That was clearly a trap laid for us. And there is absolutely nothing in that area that should concern us, yet you placed a monitoring station there."

Smith held up his hands in surrender to the barrage. "Yes, I knew what was there. And there was something there; that's why the monitoring station."

Spooky cried out, "Frak me! You said, 'we fought a battle there.' I figured you were talking about the collective 'we' of Americans. But no—you were actually at that battle. That's the only explanation. Shit. How old are you?"

The director's head dropped and he sighed. The weary man was suddenly feeling his advanced age. He looked up, searching the eyes of every agent in front of him. He turned back to address the analyst, "Yes, Mister Smith, I was actually in the battle for Lewisfield Plantation. Although it was only a minor skirmish. I was a member of the South Carolina First Regiment of the State Dragoons. In other words, I was state militia, fighting for the rebellion."

"So what was there?" This was from Ghost.

"I had carried a very special burden with me for a long time, and I was already old at that point. I found an abandoned, dried-up well on a little property out in the middle of nowhere. And I buried my burden where no one would find it."

Just then, the cockpit door opened and the copilot leaned out, "Director Smith? We've been diverted into a holding pattern, so it will add about forty-five minutes to our flight time. Also, there's a call on the secure communications array up here. Agent Massey demanded that we get you to connect with her."

"Thank you Captain. I'll be right there." Smith stood. "I promise to finish when I get done talking to Miss Massey."

As he brushed by the copilot, he read her name tag—Amelia Jenks. "Thank you Captain Jenks. Where do I sit?"

In the team cabin, Spooky was clattering away on his various systems. With a permanent secure link at any atmospheric altitude, he always had a stream of data processing. He suddenly stopped and looked at his team leader. "Hey, Ghost? Do you remember what Director Smith called his sword?"

"Something like Kal-id-volk? Maybe?"

"Does *Kaledvoulc'h* sound about right?"

Ghost played with the pronunciation in his head. "Yeah, that might be it. Why?"

Before Spooky could answer, Smith walked back out of the cockpit, face troubled. Ghost turned to his boss, "What did Gretchen want?"

Smith looked at some notes he had taken on his SSP. "It seems that I've been called before a joint session with the House and Senate homeland security committees. Thankfully, it will be behind closed doors, but only a handful of those members even know that we exist. That means I have to see if I can stall, or if I have to mass hold the room."

"Who's going with you?"

Smith considered that, "I believe I will bring Miss Massey with me. That means you, Mister Vanhof, will have to coordinate with the FBI and the Army." He smiled slightly at the sour look on Ghost's face.

Spooky piped up, "Before you tell us what you buried, I have a question."

"Yes, Mister Smith?"

"Do you really carry Excalibur in your coat pocket?"

Ghost looked back and forth between the two, and even Boomer looked askance at the NSA analyst. Smith smiled, "Yes, Mister

Smith. That is the name of the sword I carry in my left breast pocket."

Ghost looked at his boss, his jaw hanging slightly open, "But that sword is a myth. Excalibur was just part of the Arthurian legends."

"No, Mister Vanhof. I'm afraid that Excalibur is very much fact, and she rests with me."

Spooky piped up, "Holy Crap! You're King Arthur!" His eyes went distant as his imagination ran away with him.

Smith was still smiling as he shook his head, "No, Mister Smith. I am not now, nor have I ever been, Arthur Pendragon. And who I was in the past is not relevant to any of the current problems."

"So if you won't tell us who you actually used to be," Ghost chimed in, "Then at least tell us what you buried in Lewisfield."

Smith nodded, "As I stated, I had carried this burden for a real long time. So when I found this well, I could think of no better place for it. I wrapped it in some armored and enhanced cloth to protect it and tied it with an enchanted leather thong so that even the wraps could not be removed. It was that scrap of leather that you found."

"What needed all that protecting?" Ghost was almost beside himself.

"It's the most powerful, and most foul, artifact since creation. I was carrying the *Pithos* of Pandora. Pandora's legendary box. And now someone else has it."

II

SURROUNDED

11

PLANNING

27,000 Feet Over Virginia

James Smith, acting director of Section 28, could hear the muted whine of the massive engines competing with the roar of the air flowing past the cabin as the C-17 Globemaster III circled in a holding pattern outside Dulles airspace. The rest of the people in the cabin sat in stunned silence at his revelation. The Section 28 agents around him were used to dealing with earth-shaking revelations, but none of them expected Pandora's Box to be real. Let alone for it to have been in the possession of their boss.

Even Spooky had stopped working on his laptop. The analyst sat, mouth slightly agape, as he absorbed the information. Among the agents, Ghost was the first to break the silence.

"You're telling us that Section Twenty-Eight had, in their possession, the legendary box that would literally destroy the world, and they buried it in a field in South Carolina?"

Smith shook his head, "Section Twenty-Eight never had the box in their inventory. I had the artifact long before Section Twenty-Eight was conceived. I buried it there precisely because there was no other way to safeguard it, other than anonymity."

"Why not stick it in the warehouse?" Spooky spoke up, "It's not even in this universe."

"That's precisely why I couldn't place it there. The dimension that the warehouse operates in has a certain... resonance." Smith and chose his words very carefully, "And the artifact would have amplified that, allowing other interested parties to track it."

"What other interested parties?"

"Pretty much anyone who wants to destroy the world, Mister Vanhof." Smith thought for a while and then continued. "I don't have a current list of top suspects. Mister Smith, can you work on that?"

Spooky nodded, "Sure. But I'll need access to the archives. I only have clearance level x-ray."

Smith looked at the analyst, "Yes. It is about time we upgrade your clearance, or your attempts to gain access through other means will eventually trigger an Audit. And you don't want to have their attention."

The former NSA analyst smiled sheepishly, "Should have known you would track that. Do we have to wait until we land to shift my clearance?"

"No, Mister Smith. Log in to central admin. I know you have the backdoor for that far. Find your credentials and upgrade them to zulu. Let me know when you are asked for the code."

Spooky typed for a few seconds and then spun the laptop around to face Smith. "All set boss."

"Type the following alpha-numeric." Smith told Spooky, who turned his laptop around again. "Delta-Lima-Zulu-Six-Three-Echo-Echo-Foxtrot. And hit enter. The response code is all caps, all one word, 'knight of the realm.' And yes, that is a onetime authorization —so don't play with it or I won't be able to save your soul."

Spooky stopped typing and looked at his boss, "Did you say my soul?" His normal easy smile had disappeared.

"Yes, Mister Smith. What do you think the Auditors audit?"

Spooky swallowed visibly and said, "Noted. No more poking the sleeping Auditors."

"Good choice." Smith smiled slightly, "It is always better to let the sleeping Auditors lie. Go ahead and run that search. Do your magic in the database. Just don't poke in any records that are marked 'Indigo,' you won't have access to those files."

Spooky nodded and worked on his laptop. Boomer spoke up, "So what does Pandora's Box do?"

Smith redirected his attention to the demolitions specialist. "It is a container that binds the destruction of our world inside. It is technically not a box. That was a poor translation of the Greek to Latin from the 1500's. I've always thought the mistake was convenient. If people are looking for a box, they will overlook the pretty Grecian urn. The original Greek is *pithos*, which means urn, not box."

"What kind of destruction?" Asked the vampire.

Smith again paused, "It can be virtually anything. Plagues, war, asteroids, the usual apocalypse suspects. Maybe zombies. That would make a few preppers happy, I'm sure."

Ghost looked at his boss, "Has the artifact ever been opened?"

"Yes, twice. Once at the beginning of time, and then once in the late 1300's. Both resulted in major disasters."

"The 1300s? You're talking about the black death? The Bubonic Plague? The Seelie queen said something about that, too. What's the story there?"

Before Smith could answer, the pilot called out over the intercom, "We've been cleared for landing, and we'll be down in about five minutes. Everyone strap in, please."

As the acting director took his seat, he said, "We'll talk about this later. When the other team gets back, we'll debrief together. I also need to gather a great deal more information available before my testimony."

SOME TIME LATER, Smith looked up from his phone to see the team sitting around him. They had landed and driven to the rubble of the Section 28 complex. Once there, Ghost had gone to coordinate with Gretchen and the FBI, and the rest of the team took Little G's body to the morgue holding area. Smith had immediately gone to see Norbert about some special gear he had in mind. After that, he had taken a seat in the rough conference area set up in the temporary building.

Soon, Gretchen and Ghost had cleared operations with SAC Mulder and had arranged for transport with an escort for their boss. They walked across the rubble to the temporary building. As Ghost and Gretchen walked past the HRT sentries outside the door, they were deep in discussion about the realities of working on an active investigation site.

Walking through the entry, they heard Spooky pipe up over the radio, "Ghost, this is Spooky. Do you have eyes on the Director?"

Ghost keyed his mic, "Affirmative, Spooky. Just walked in."

"You guys need to come to the Wunder Buggy. I need to show you something. Probably you, the boss, and Gretchen."

The tall monster hunter arched an eyebrow at Gretchen. She shrugged, then nodded. "Copy that, Spooky. We'll be there ASAP."

Ghost spoke up and addressed his boss, "Spooky has a situation in the Wunder Buggy, and wants you and Gretchen to join us."

Smith stood, and the three of them left, walking across a short span of rubble and up into the back of the converted bread truck. Spooky looked up from his screen array with a frown on his face. "Boss, we got trouble."

Smith walked over and looked at a screen that Spooky indicated. Spooky explained, "It looks like we've got several attempts to dig into Section Twenty-Eight servers."

The analyst looked at his boss, "Speaking of which, where are the servers? Most of this complex was destroyed, and we still have server access. How is that possible?"

Smith smiled. "We house our servers off-site in a very secure location. You and I will discuss the details later. As of right now, rest assured that the database is secure." His smile disappeared. "Can you tell where the attempts are coming from?"

Spooky hit a key sequence, and the screen changed. He pointed to several lines on the screen. "This one here is from the CIA, routed through fourteen different proxies. I recognize his fingerprints from my work at the NSA. I believe his handle is Nightmask." The analyst pointed to a different line. "This guy here is also from the CIA. He's better, and I had to trace him through twenty proxies. What's funny, is he pretends to be part of 'Anonymous', but is actually a plant from the CIA. His handle is either Song Blade or Cyborg Dragon, depending on which profile he's using."

Spooky pointed to another couple lines. "These are the interesting ones. I know these folks. This one is L Wray. She was my direct supervisor at the NSA, and a hell of an analyst. She'd make a great recruit for the new headquarters. This one is Lost Judi, and she worked in my group over there, as well. They tried using my own backdoor systems against me. Kind of amusing that they thought they could get through my own trapdoors. I may have to send them a note."

"What were they looking for, Mister Smith?" The Director's cultured voice was low.

"You, boss. They were trying to dig into our own systems to figure out who exactly you are."

Smith shook his head, "Keep me apprised, Mister Smith. If they actually get close, you can respond. Until then, let them poke around. I may even have some juicy bait for them."

Smith looked at Ghost and Gretchen. "Mister Vanhof, Miss Massey. We need to meet for a few minutes. We need to set up contingencies for a shift in operations. I've got about half an hour before I'm due in front of the National Security Council and the intelligence community for a briefing. Miss Massey, while we are walking, would you have Agent Mulder arrange transport to the city?"

"Already done, sir." Gretchen explained the arrangements as the three Section 28 agents walked back across the rubble to the temporary building. Inside, they walked into the Warehouse, and found a small conference room in the back that was not being used as temporary housing. The three of them sat down and Gretchen pulled out her phone to take notes.

Smith opened up, "We have to come up with a new temporary headquarters location. It has to be a physical building so that we can ward it and protect it properly. We also need to plan for a backup location, in case the mood in Washington shifts too far. We cannot afford to be caught flat-footed again. When I get back from my meeting with the NSC, I would like to have a plan already started."

Gretchen looked up, "What do we need for a new temporary HQ?"

"A permanent building we can mount defenses on." Smith thought out loud, "Has to be big enough inside to house the Warehouse gate, and any other gates we need. Decent access to communications."

Ghost spoke up, "Friendly locals. I think we've about worn out our welcome in this area."

"Somewhere not as close to civilian collateral damage," Gretchen said.

"Near enough to civilization that we can respond, but not in a population center." This was from Smith.

Ghost asked, "What other facilities does Section Twenty-Eight currently have? This can't have been the only site."

Smith thought for a moment and then called up a list on his SSP. "Mostly a variety of safe houses in various cities. Nothing as extensive or as well defended. We have a blank checkbook, but we also have to maintain operational secrecy."

Ghost jumped as if startled, "That brings up another question. What other personnel assets are in the field? Obviously Burt came back in from somewhere else. Are there any other agents or teams unaccounted for?"

"No. Almost everyone was here when the attack happened. The

only reason you weren't caught up in it, was because you were on an assignment. I have no other full assets in the field, neither fully human nor some monster variant. Mister Black was the only one in the field."

Ghost thought for a moment longer, but Gretchen interrupted him, "Sir, any chance we could contact one of our Signatory allies for assistance? There are a couple here in the states."

Smith nodded, "Mister Vanhof, have Miss Sedano contact Queen Lishe ta Merunaré, and the Praetorian. One of them might have something we could use. If nothing else, they might make a good backup until we find something permanent."

Smith glanced at his SSP, "It is time for me to leave for the Capitol." He looked at Gretchen, "Will the FBI be providing transport, Miss Massey?"

"Yes, sir. SAC Mulder will have an agent waiting by the command post with one of their SUVs."

"Thank you. I'll go meet them now." Smith stood. "I'll leave you to work out the details. Let's make the move as soon as possible."

"Yes, sir." Gretchen and Ghost chorused.

A few minutes after Smith left, Spooky again called over the radio, "Ghost, this is Spooky. We have another incursion alarm, and this one's fairly close."

"Copy that Spooky. Gretchen and I will be there in a second."

The two Section 28 agents trotted over to the Wunder Buggy, picking up Heavy and Boomer along the way. All four climbed into the truck and Spooky explained.

"We've got an incursion alarm in Philadelphia. Tracking it and local media reports to a new museum that just opened. Small incursions so far, but I'm betting on a big one any moment. This one is kicking off the same type of readings as the one in South Carolina. Even money it's related." Spooky was pulling a graph of the anomaly signatures.

"Philly's two-and-a-half hours from here." Ghost was looking at the map on one of the monitors. He felt Boomer stirring beside him and looked at her. "Call it two if Andretti drives." The team let out a small chuckle.

Boomer slapped his arm, "At least pick a woman race driver. I'd rather be Danica Patrick."

Ghost ignored her. "Status on the other team?"

Spooky checked the FAA net. "They are fifteen minutes out. Have them diverted?"

The lanky monster hunter nodded. "Divert them. Have them

arrange transport to the site. Let them know we'll be about thirty minutes behind them." Ghost turned to Gretchen. "Call the airstrip and get our pilots moving in the C-17, because we're taking the Wunder Buggy for urban camouflage. Have them file a flight plan for... Philadelphia International. Arrange for parking on the FedEx ramp for both planes."

Gretchen was nodding. "Am I joining you?"

Ghost shook his head, "No. I need your expertise to make the move happen. Bring Russell in for logistics if you need it." The man looked at his watch, "We need to leave. If this is related to South Carolina, we need to be in the air right now."

As Gretchen climbed down from the truck, Heavy sprinted past her and ran toward the Warehouse. He was soon back with a couple crates of ammo, including a new series of rounds for his AA-12 that Norbert guaranteed would work against trolls. Boomer had the truck moving as soon as the back door was closed. Five minutes later the massive C-17 Globemaster III that was becoming their second home was clawing for the sky as the pilot and copilot slammed the throttles all the way forward, firewalling the massive engines. This was a priority mission and Spooky had fast-tracked their clearances with the FAA.

On the flight down, Ghost had received a call from Gretchen. "Jonas, this is Gretchen. I called the Director with the latest information about your incursion, and he is calling for a change in the mission parameters."

"What's our new mission, then?"

"This is a retrieval mission. There is a bust that is now on display at that location. He did not give me why it was important, just that it was your new target. Defend and retrieve that bust at all costs." Gretchen paused, then continued, "I'll send the new parameters to Spooky. There's also special intel in case a guardian shows up. The Director's words, not mine. Unfortunately, he is out of contact for now. Good luck."

Ghost hung up and shook his head. He wondered what was so important about a statue. The monster hunter looked around at the agents with him and nodded. They could handle a simple retrieval.

As it turns out, when the throttles were wide open for most of the trip, the hulking beast of an Air Force transport was actually pretty fast. After landing, ground control guided the pilot to the FedEx parking ramp, where they were parked next to the agency's Citation X.

There was a black SUV idling beside the jet, although Six, Doc, and Dancer were all standing around outside, waiting for the rest of the team to arrive.

When the stairs were finally dropped, Ghost was the first one down the stairs, and went to greet everyone. He greeted the three Section 28 agents and waited for Boomer to unload the Wunder Buggy.

Doc was the first to speak, "How was the mission to South Carolina?"

Ghost grimly shook his head. "It was bad. Pandora's Box is gone."

Dancer looked at the other team and noticed someone missing, "Where's Little G?"

12

BUST

Doc broke in before anyone could answer Dancer's question. "What do you mean Pandora's Box is gone?"

Ghost looked at the team from Grand Rapids, "Apparently our new Director had hidden said artifact in South Carolina sometime during the Revolutionary War. Whoever attacked headquarters took the artifact."

Boomer rolled up in the Wunder Buggy and shut it down as Ghost explained about the missing artifact. She climbed down from her driver's seat just as Dancer broke into the team leader's explanation.

"Where's Little G?" The young agent became more insistent.

Boomer reached out and gently touched her young protégé on the shoulder. "I'm sorry, Hanna. Jesús didn't make it back." There was a hitch in her voice as she continued, "Damn Chikara ambushed us and killed him before we could take it out."

The young agent turned away from the group and hugged herself, not letting the others see the single tear roll down her cheek. The rest of the team could only look on in silence, letting her work through her grief. It was a few seconds before the Section 28 agent with Fury in her blood was able to turn back around, face a stoic mask. "Fine. Let's kill the asshole who caused it."

Ghost turned to the DHS agent who had climbed out of the

black SUV and stood patiently by the idling Suburban. He strode over to the woman dressed in the dark gray power suit of a Washington bureaucrat or federal agent. He stretched out his hand. "Special Agent Jonas Vanhof. You must be SAC Lempke?"

The woman smiled and shook the proffered hand, "Please, call me Kari." She pronounced it "Car-ee."

Ghost smiled, "Thank you, Kari. Please, call me Jonas."

"Ok, Jonas. What are you doing in my city?"

Ghost kept the smile on his face, "I'm truly sorry, but I can't tell you why we're here. It's classified with a 'Need to Know' designation, and unfortunately, you aren't cleared for the information."

The Philly SAC frowned. "Then why in the world am I here instead of my office?"

"Because I need your assistance contacting a building downtown and having them evacuate the premises ASAP. We have a credible threat on a new museum called the Museum of the American Revolution, and I need it cleared immediately. Send local police and available agents to meet us down there, but once we arrive, they need to evacuate, as well. I also would like an escort downtown to the building. Once we get there, I need you to coordinate the response with the local police. I can't have any of them get in the way if things get...interesting."

SAC Lempke stared at him as if he had grown horns while he talked. She nodded and pulled out her mobile phone. As she dialed her office, she looked at Ghost and said, "I've heard things about your office, Agent Vanhof. I don't want a mess to cleanup."

"I hope it doesn't come to that. Thank you, Kari."

The Philly agent walked to the passenger side of the SUV and climbed into her seat. She was already on the phone, coordinating the response with her office. Her driver had already started the engine and moved toward the gate, lighting up the emergency lights.

Ghost looked at everyone gathered and said, "Mount up. We don't know what we're going to find, so armor and weapons for a full raid. I don't care what the civilians think."

The team, plus Six, scrambled aboard the Wunder Buggy. As they all found their seats, Boomer fired up the heavily modified bread truck and dropped the transmission into gear. The perimeter guard barely got the gate open before the big black truck with lights flashing and sirens wailing roared through the opening. Boomer barely registered the shock on the guard's face before she was past the gate and accelerating down the access road.

Less than ten minutes later, the Philly DHS Suburban screeched to a halt just outside a large brick and stone monolith of a building, coming to a stop among three police cars. Behind it, the Wunder Buggy stopped quickly, rocking its massive frame on the heavy duty shocks. Boomer threw open her door and jumped down from the driver's side of the truck. Her black combat BDUs were wrinkled and stained with mud from the South Carolina operation. Before she closed the door, Boomer reached back in and grabbed an equipment belt, quickly buckling it in place around her hips. The Beretta handgun was already nestled in its holster. She quickly checked the holster and magazine holders. Satisfied, the demolitions expert-turned vampire slammed the door of the truck.

On the passenger side, Ghost flung open his door and clambered down onto the street. His worn leather duster flapped in the slight breeze, covering his white cotton button-down shirt and faded blue jeans. He adjusted his gaucho hat to protect his eyes from the sun. The lanky monster hunter also reached back into the truck. He withdrew an old white walking stick. Carefully inspecting it, he put it through a special loop on his belt, and then pulled the duster over it, hiding it from view. Ghost slammed the door and looked for SAC Lempke.

The back ramp of the truck released with a hydraulic hiss and lowered to the pavement. Heavy was the first down the ramp. The torn sleeves of his BDUs peeked out from beneath the heavy ballistic vest carrier that wrapped his chest in armor. Strapped to the back of the former Spec Ops warrior were two large Khukuri blades, hanging in a cross pattern for ease of access. As the large black mountain of a man strode down the ramp, he carried an enormous black rifle in each huge hand. As Boomer walked around to the back of the truck, Heavy grinned and handed her one of the rifles. "I figured you wanted your boomstick," the big man rumbled.

Boomer nodded and watched as her young protégé walked down the ramp. Dancer's petite frame looked minuscule next to Heavy, and the young woman patted his massive arm as she walked past. The youngest Section 28 agent pulled a pair of sunglasses out of her jacket's inner pocket. As she put them on, Boomer noticed that her young friend's eyes were faintly glowing white in the irises. The sunglasses covered Dancer's eyes, and the young Fury pulled her long white hair back into a simple ponytail. Her short black jacket covered the Walther pistol strapped to her side, and Boomer knew the young woman's powerful enchanted sword was invisible and hung in a scabbard down her back.

Following Dancer down the ramp, Six had shed his jacket and

tie. Instead, he wore a thin ballistic vest over his white dress shirt. Two Beretta pistols rode on his belt, one on each thigh in a drop-leg holster. He carried no other weapon in his hand, but the former mercenary's walk and stance told all around him that he was a predator, even with empty hands. The relatively stocky man was twisting and turning as he checked the tightness of the straps. Six wanted to make sure the vest would not slow him down if he had to get into combat.

Last down the ramp was Doc. Her black shirt, pants and jacket were offset by the white square of her collar at her neck. Draped over her shoulder was the black silk stole with silver thread inlays. The esoteric combat priest wore her silver and black rosary beads and carried a special silver cross with a hidden dagger. Doc wore a couple containers full of holy water at her waist in place of firearm magazines, which were covered by the drape of her suit jacket. The esoteric combat priest was also carrying a small black bundle of cloth.

As Doc reached the bottom of the ramp, she looked back at their electronics specialist still sitting at his console. With a nod and a wave from Doc, Spooky flipped the switch that raised the ramp back up to seal the truck. The former NSA analyst tapped a sequence on his keyboard and a series of "clicks" and "thunks" echoed around inside of the truck. All the doors and the ramp had just been sealed, and the Wunder Buggy was now fully locked down and secure. The young redhead pushed his glasses up and keyed his microphone. "Ghost this is Spooky. Wunder Buggy secure. Working on the video feeds now. I'll let you know when I get in. Shouldn't take too long."

Ghost keyed his throat mic, "Copy that Spooky. As soon as you have control, we're going in. Send up a drone to cover the outside of the building."

"Copy that, boss. Drone launching... now."

Ghost looked up to see one of Spooky's drones take to the air and race off up and over the building. He turned back to the DHS SAC and said, "Any idea if the building is clear?"

Agent Lempke spoke into a handheld walkie talkie, "Is the building clear?"

A muffled crackle answered after a moment. "We're coming out the doors now."

Both Ghost and Agent Lempke looked up in time to see the glass and bronze double doors open. A man in a thousand-dollar suit walked toward them, followed by six security guards in blazers and slacks. The DHS SAC greeted the administrator of the Museum of the American Revolution. "Mister Battenfield? I'm Special Agent Lempke, we spoke on the phone. And this is Special Agent Vanhof. His team is the quick action team assigned to this threat."

Battenfield shook Agent Lempke's hand, "Cyril Battenfield." He looked at Ghost, "I'm the Curator of this museum. Can I ask what the hurry is? We close in about twenty minutes, anyway. What kind of threat are we facing? Agent Lempke wasn't exactly clear about it."

Ghost gave his most disarming half-smile, "I'm sorry about that. Agent Lempke isn't cleared for this either." The team filed past, and the monster hunter watched as a frown grew on Battenfield's face. The curator was watching all the military hardware walk toward the front of his museum. "Believe me, Mister Battenfield, I sincerely hope we are wrong about this."

"Spooky to Ghost. I have access to all the feeds. No signs of anyone inside. Cleared for entry."

Ghost looked at the curator. "It's time for us to go in. I'll contact Agent Lempke when we are all clear. Keep everyone out of the building until then." The monster hunter turned and walked toward the group lined up at the front doors. He raised a hand to his throat mic and clicked it open. "Ghost to Spooky. Copy that. We're making entry."

Ghost stepped to the front of the line and threw open the doors. As he walked through the main entrance, he stopped and set a small box onto the floor off to the side, out of the way of the incoming team. He clicked his mic again, "The sensor is placed and activated. Where are we going?"

"Stairs in the rotunda to the right. Up the stairs and to your right. It's the 'New Nation' exhibit. The bust should be in there."

Ghost clicked his mic and then pointed up the stairwell. Heavy was already stopping at the foot of the grand circular staircase, pointing his AA-12 full-auto shotgun upward, providing cover for the rest of the team. Six hit the first step and leapt halfway up the winding stairwell, landing and drawing both pistols, aiming them up and across where Heavy could not cover.

Boomer stopped next to Heavy and raised her shotgun to cover his arc. She glanced at him and said, "Go. I'll cover. I can catch up faster."

The big man nodded, lowered his shotgun muzzle, and thundered up the marble staircase. As he passed Six, Heavy realized that Dancer was right behind him, easily keeping pace. The young agent had drawn her Walther pistol and was jogging up the stairs, keeping an eye on the landing above them. As the two agents crested the landing, they both crouched and raised their respective firearms, each covering a separate field of fire.

Ghost strode between his two warriors and looked around the entire second floor. Not seeing any threat, he called out, "Clear." The monster hunter took a couple steps toward the exhibit marked "A New Nation," with Doc coming up the stairs behind him. He turned and addressed the team was on the second floor landing. "Heavy, you stay here and guard the landing. Boomer is downstairs, and Six can provide backup to either of you. Doc and Dancer, you are with me."

The team leader clicked his mic, "Spooky, this is Ghost. No signs of bad guys yet. Getting ready for artifact extraction. What was the passphrase for the protections Smith put into place?"

"The passcode is, 'The Knight of the Realm requires the artifact.' Not sure who you are supposed to say that too, as that wing is clear, and I can see the statue on my monitor right now."

"Copy that. 'The Knight of the Realm requires the artifact.' We're going for retrieval now." Ghost nodded to his teammates and led Doc and Dancer into the exhibit. As he walked in, he saw displays about the founding of the nation, including a display showing the Constitution carved into marble. As they rounded the corner to their right, the monster hunter saw what they were there to retrieve.

Resting in a clear, safety glass case and lit by several subdued spotlights, was the terra-cotta bust of George Washington. The bust was an original casting of an original statue carved out of pine. Only a couple of the statues were ever cast, and one of those resided at this museum. Unfortunately for the museum, this bust held a secret, and the team would take it with them back to Director Smith.

Doc unrolled the black bundle of cloth she was carrying and held the mouth of the peculiar looking sack open. Ghost looked at the glass carefully, seeing the alarm sensors built into the base. He clicked his mic again, "Ghost to Spooky. Found the artifact. I need you to kill the burglar alarm sensors in this building. The glass is alarmed."

The former NSA analyst took a few seconds to respond. "Got it boss. Alarms are down. I'll re-enable them after you are done."

Ghost reached out and placed his hands on either side of the glass box and pulled. The case barely moved. He grunted and tried again. This time it rose about half an inch before it dropped back down again. "Damn. That thing must weigh a couple hundred pounds."

The young agent beside him smiled, "Mind if I try?"

Ghost looked at Dancer and shrugged and stepped back to give her room to work. The young woman with Fury in her blood carefully placed her hands on the outside of the case and lifted. She grunted, but the case lifted away from the base. She carefully lifted it high enough to clear the bust, then turned and put the case on the floor, dropping it the last couple inches to land with a loud thump.

Dancer smiled at her boss innocently as Ghost muttered, "Showoff."

Before anyone could move, a blue pinpoint of light streaked between the Section 28 agents and landed in front of the now-defenseless bust. One moment the bust was unprotected, and the next moment there was a small humanoid creature with dragonfly like wings and full steel and copper armor on a minuscule scale standing in front of the statue, sword raised and pointed straight at Ghost. The figure was about eight inches tall and male. Blond hair peeked out from beneath the full helm, and the thin face was arrogant.

"Halt. This artwork is protected from your thieving hands by I, Robert 'The Perylous.' Stand down before I run you through." The creature's voice was thin, high, and exuded far more authority than any voice that high pitched had the right to display.

Ghost raised his hands placatingly as Doc and Dancer both gasped. The monster hunter recovered from his surprise, "Well met, Robert the Perylous. We are on a sacred mission to retrieve this artifact. Our message to you is that the Knight of the Realm requires this artifact."

The thin, arrogant face broke into a wide smile and the pixie put his sword back into its scabbard. The creatures voice became more sing-song, "Well why didn't you say so? Sir Knight can have his artifact back. He should be pleased that we have protected it for him for all these years. Did he come with you? Will he require our services again?"

Ghost shook his head, "No. Sir Knight could not make this trip. I don't know if he will require your services again. If he does, I'm sure he will contact you. Can my colleague remove the artifact now?"

The pixie fluttered his wings and rose about two feet off the base. "Sorry about that. Just had to make sure the artifact was protected."

Ghost nodded as Doc reached out carefully with a gloved hand and picked up the bust itself. While it felt heavy for a molded bust, it was not too awkward for her. She carefully placed the bust into the black sack and closed it. The bag still looked flat and empty. She rolled the bag back up into a small bundle and tucked it into her belt.

Ghost was just breathing a sigh of relief when he heard the alarm kick in from the sensor suite he had just placed down on the first floor.

Ghost looked at Doc and Dancer. The young Fury was the first to speak, "Damn."

13

CONTACT

Museum of the American Revolution

"Ghost, this is Spooky. We've got incoming."

"Copy that. Where?"

Spooky was quiet for a moment, "According to the sensors, we've got two incursion events forming right now. Can't pinpoint any closer than this block." Spooky let out a curse. "Got a gate opened right in front of me. It's a big one, maybe thirty feet in the air. Dammit. That's a dragon."

Ghost thought quickly, then answered, "Alright. Backup is on the way."

The team leader turned to his gathering team. Six and Boomer had run up the stairs at the first sound of the alarm, and the rest had worked their way back out to the second floor landing. "Heavy, Boomer. You guys are backup for Spooky outside. I hope you brought some grenades for your toys."

Heavy smiled and Boomer nodded. The demolitions specialist turned vampire clanged her barrel against the former spec ops warrior. She grinned and said, "Meet you out there." Her first leap took her to the curve in the stairs, and the second one carried her out of sight before the big warrior could launch himself down the stairs.

Ghost looked at the rest, "We have to assume that the second gate will go after the artifact itself. Doc is the transport. We all make sure she gets to the Wunder Buggy." The team leader got nods from his remaining team.

As Ghost was arranging his team, they all heard a piercing, warbling whistle. Two more blue lights flew toward the group at high speed, blinking to a halt next to Robert, the pixie who was hovering about two feet from Ghost. The new blue lights resolved into two more pixies, both female, and both dressed in the same armor as their companion.

Six flinched, but quickly realized that Ghost was not reacting to a threat, and assumed that the monster hunter had known about the pixies. Ghost bowed slightly to the newcomers and looked back and forth between their new friend "Robert the Perylous" and his new companions. The female on the right was the first to speak in her sing-song voice.

"I am Ziomarya, Warrior of the Branch, and Matriarch of this Family. As you are still in our care, our protection extends to you, guardians of the artifact and representatives of Sir Knight. You have met my eldest son, Perylous. I also introduce you to my eldest daughter Roywyn. We will help protect you and the artifact."

As the other female pixie bowed, Robert looked perturbed at his mother. His voice seemed even higher pitched, "Mother, my warrior name is Robert The Perylous. Not just Perylous."

The matriarch looked at her son and just shook her head. Looking back at Ghost and the rest of the team, she said, "I apologize for my eldest. He is a fine warrior, just sensitive about his given name. Nevertheless, we are here to escort you and the artifact to your vehicle."

Ghost tried to hide his smile, turning to look at his teammates, who were also smirking. He turned back to Ziomarya, "Thank you, Matriarch. We appreciate your assistance and protection. If you would surround and protect Doctor Sorenson, I would appreciate it."

The fair sprite signaled to her offspring, and they floated into position around Doc. Just as Ghost turned to start down the stairs, his radio earpiece crackled with Spooky's voice, "Contact. Full incursion inside the building. A gate just formed in the rotunda and multiple trolls coming through." There was the sound of an explosion outside and the building rocked. "Shit! A dragon just hit the Buggy. You guys need to get out here."

Ghost grunted into his mic, "Copy that Spooky. Boomer and Heavy will keep you safe 'til we get there." The monster hunter pointed to Six and Dancer. "You guys have point. Hit them fast and hard. Dancer, time to bring Vellath out to play."

The young Fury grinned and holstered her sidearm. She reached up with one hand and drew the invisible sword from the sheath on her back. It glowed white as it cleared the scabbard. Dancer smiled and thought at her sword, *Wake up, you big lizard. Looks like we have trolls to kill. Hungry?*

She heard a sleepy voice rumble in her head, *Is it time to come out to play? How wonderful. I haven't eaten in a while. Am I going to split for this, or are you going to give them a chance?*

We don't have time to dawdle. Dancer grabbed the now visible hilt of the sword in both hands the blade split into two identical swords. She looked at Six, her eyes glowing to match her white hair. "Let's play."

The former mercenary looked back through solid black eyes. His fangs gave him a slight lisp, "Ladies and goddesses first." His clawed hands motioned for her to lead, and the young agent leapt into the center of the circular staircase, landing lightly on the ground floor in a combat stance. Six landed in a three point stance and slowly stood to his feet.

Dancer snickered and commented, "Superhero landing."

Six did not look at the young Fury, instead muttering, "Shut up. Not all of us are a goddess."

Both agents looked at the trolls arrayed in front of them. All eight of them were large, at least nine feet tall, and armed with either the large warhammer that the agents had seen before, or a huge claymore-like sword. One of the trolls stepped forward and growled, "Give us the key and your deaths will be swift."

BOOMER HAD BEEN out the main doors first, crashing through fast enough to shatter the glass panes. Raising her full-auto shotgun, she indexed the muzzle on the first dragon she spotted. This one happened to be hovering just over the Wunder Buggy. The demolitions specialist noticed occasional sparks flying from the hide of the scaly beast. She realized the police officers staged outside the museum were firing on the beast with a combination of light patrol rifles and duty sidearms.

She dropped the full magazine of standard 12GA rounds out of her shotgun. As it hit the ground, she was slamming a twenty-round drum full of mini grenade rounds into the receiver and racked the charging handle—stripping the standard shell out of the breech and loading one of the new rounds.

Heavy crashed through the broken doors just as Boomer's slide loaded the mini grenade. She snarled as she raised the muzzle toward the humongous scaly beast hovering over the team's truck. "Use the grenades. The regular shells aren't working."

Heavy nodded as he thumbed the catch to dump the magazine of standard rounds. As the big Army sergeant drew out a drum full of the specialized grenades, Boomer was already pulling the trigger. With her gun set to semi-auto, the first fin-stabilized mini grenade launched from her shotgun and impacted the flank of the winged creature. The explosion was impressive, however the scaly hide was barely scratched.

The grenade drew the attention of the dragon and its rider. As the large head ponderously swung toward the vampire agent, Heavy's bolt slammed home. The big man raised his shotgun, sighting on the snout of the beast, he pulled the trigger. Heavy barely felt the kick of the shotgun as the grenade streaked out and slammed into the now-open mouth of the dragon. Flames blossomed in the mouth and the beast roared in terrible pain as part of its jaw sheared off and flewa dozen feet away.

Boomer let loose with another grenade, this one slamming into the nose of the dragon. The beast's roar cut off with a strangled yelp as the beast's head snapped back. The dragon's armored driver pointed a staff at the two agents and blue lightning burst from the jeweled end. Boomer saw the attack coming and leapt, slamming into her companion, crashing to the ground and rolling, coming to a stop over ten feet away. The lightning scorched the spot where Heavy had been standing milliseconds prior.

Boomer rolled to her feet, raised her shotgun, flipped the switch to full-auto, and pulled the trigger. A short burst of grenades launched from the barrel and slammed into the side and left wing of the hovering beast. Two of the rounds smacked into the scaly side of the creature, exploding into bright bursts of sound and fury, rocking the dragon and causing its rider to scramble to stay on its back. Three more exploded around the base of the giant wing, rending great wounds in the base of the wing, shredding the light scales and the muscles underneath the hide. The large membrane connecting the shoulder to the next finger ripped in several places, further shredding as the light membrane stressed beyond its capacity.

The great beast slammed to the ground, shaking the entire area and setting off car alarms down the block. The dragon roared in agony and struggled to rise. Its rider was less fortunate as the armored warrior was thrown twenty feet to crash against a low concrete decorative pool.

Heavy shook his head as he rolled to his knees, trying to get rid of the ringing in his ears. He watched as Boomer let loose with a burst of grenade fire, bringing down the dragon. Ignoring the wounded beast, the big warrior followed the trajectory of the rider as it came to a stop against the small pool. He stood and aimed his shotgun at the armored figure slowly rising to its feet.

"Stay down. Drop the weapon. Get on the ground or I will kill you." Heavy shouted at the rider.

The armored and helmeted rider ignored Heavy's shouts and raised his staff, pointing it at the Section 28 agent. As Heavy saw a blue glow form around the tip, the former Spec Ops warrior pulled the trigger, launching a mini grenade round into the chest of the rider.

Heavy could not identify the material of the ornate spiked armor, but it could not withstand the impact and ensuing explosion. There was a fireball covering the dragonrider, and then the figure was airborne, slamming into the wall of the museum. Heavy watched the body drop to the ground, a gaping hole where the rider's breastplate originally covered. Ignoring the damaged museum wall and clearly dead corpse, the veteran warrior turned to find his next target.

The wounded dragon thrashed on the ground as Boomer moved to get a better angle. Snapping its massive jaws at the agent, the beast scrambled to turn and face its greatest threat. Suddenly, the beast gave a great keening sound as Boomer heard a grenade round go off about thirty feet behind her. Using the distraction to her advantage, she aimed at the underside of the dragon's neck, right where it joined the larger chest. The vampire agent pulled the trigger, holding the shotgun steady as she burned half of the remaining magazine, bracing herself against the recoil and the ensuing explosions.

Eight high-explosive mini grenades ripped into the softer, less-armored scales at the base of the dragon's neck. The string of rounds opened up the creature's neck and underbelly, blowing apart muscles and tissue, and severing the spine. A thin string of flesh and scales remained to connect the huge neck and head to the now twitching body. The dragon's corpse collapsed, and the head crashed into the top of the Wunder Buggy before being dragged to the ground.The smear of blood and ichor almost blended in with the matte black paint as it streaked and ran down the side of the truck.

Boomer swung her rifle up as she heard a howling roar coming from above and behind her. It was answered by another, then another as the remaining dragons and their riders sounded their fury. She tracked the barrel of her shotgun across the remaining creatures, waiting to see what would happen. Heavy's footsteps echoed beside her as the big warrior stepped forward. Out of the corner of her eye, she watched the barrel of his shotgun track with hers, moving from target to target.

The vampire agent could barely hear Heavy's low voice over the roaring, "Aim for the rider. It seems to distract the things."

Boomer nodded and settled her sights on the closest dragon. As the front blade settled over the ornate breastplate of the creature's rider, her thumb flipped the selector switch back to semi-auto. Her enhanced hearing picked up Heavy's mutter under his breath, "Three. Two. One." Boomer squeezed the trigger. A fraction of a second later she heard Heavy's shotgun bark as he picked the same target. Both rounds hit the rider in the chest, and it disappeared from the waist up.

The riderless creature immediately threw back its head and began that same high-pitched keening whine, dropping to ground, landing heavily and shaking the ground. Both Section 28 Agents opened up with full-auto bursts converging on the now exposed chest and neck of the dragon. As the now flaming corpse settled to the ground, both agents dropped their empty drum magazines and were reaching for new drums. The charging bolts slammed home on the shotguns as the empty drums clanged off the asphalt.

Heavy was slightly faster to raise his rifle than Boomer, and he placed the front sight over the chest of a dragonrider. His eyes widened as he saw the blue glow at the end of the rider's staff. The former Army sergeant shoved Boomer as hard as he could, throwing the smaller agent across the street and past the Wunder Buggy for cover. He turned to dive the other way as the blue lightning bolt slammed into the street, narrowly missing the big man.

The concussion slammed into Heavy, launching him ten feet into the air and forty-five feet across the small plaza in front of the museum. The Spec Ops veteran slammed into the brick wall and dropped limply to the ground.

Boomer rolled to her feet behind the Section 28 truck. She leaned around the corner and looked for her partner. The young vampire saw Heavy's limp form laying sprawled against the muse-um's outer wall and noticed the cracked and broken brick where he hit the wall. The young vampire slid back behind the truck and keyed her throat mic, "Ghost, Boomer. Heavy's down. Two dragons down, two more out here. I need backup."

"Copy, Boomer." She could hear growls and screams from inside the rotunda, mixed with the occasional gunshot. "We've got some trouble of our own. You've got to hold them off for a little longer."

Boomer clicked her mic in response. Her eyes flashed black, and she willed herself to maintain just enough control to finish the job. She gripped the stock of her shotgun and flicked the selector back to semi-auto. She clicked her mic again, "Spooky, Boomer. Where are they?"

"Closest is about seventy-five feet to the northeast, twenty feet off the ground. The other one is behind it."

"Got it." Boomer slowly peeked from behind the truck, finding the closest dragon. She sighted in on the rider, breathing deeply as she lined up the shot. She breathed out about halfway and her finger twitched. The shotgun barked and moments later the mini grenade struck the dragonrider in its shoulder. The armored rider's right arm was missing when the smoke cleared, and the rider slumped in its saddle, clutching its shoulder in a vain attempt to stem the flow of blood.

The dragon suddenly flapped its wings and rose quickly toward the still-open gateway roiling above it. In three flaps of its giant wings, it disappeared into the black hole in the sky. The second rider looked at Boomer behind the truck and shook its gauntleted fist. Two quick flaps of its enormous wings, and the only remaining dragon in the sky disappeared through the massive inky blackness. The gateway folded in on itself, disappearing quickly and leaving a clear view of the sky.

Looking around to make sure there were no other dragons or threats in the immediate area, Boomer emerged from behind the Wunder Buggy, shotgun held at the low ready. Once she was sure there were no other threats, she ran over to the crumpled form of her partner. Slinging the AA-12 over her back, she knelt and felt for a pulse on Heavy's thick neck, ignoring the sounds of battle coming from inside the museum. After searching for a moment, she found a weak pulse, looking at her watch to count the rate. She then ran her hands slowly around his bloodied head. She felt a gash at the back of his head, and a soft spot underneath that indicated a possible skull fracture.

Moving her hands quickly down Heavy's body, she carefully felt around his hips, immediately realizing that his torso was twisted far beyond the normal range for a human. The Spec Ops-trained Petty Officer also noticed that his left leg was jutting at an odd angle, having gained a second joint above the knee. The blood soaking through his pants told her it was a compound fracture, although it did not appear to be an arterial bleed.

She looked at the Wunder Buggy as Spooky opened the passenger door. She activated her throat mic, "Ghost, this is Boomer." She swallowed heavily, holding back her tears, trying to remain calm. "Heavy's down and seriously injured." A brief pause, and more choking down emotion. "Spooky, call for medevac. Let them know the victim is unconscious, with a probable skull fracture and spinal injury. Also compound fracture to left femur. Tell them to get here immediately and have the police escort them into the combat zone for immediate evac. I'll provide cover."

14

BATTLE

Museum of the American Revolution

"Give us the key and your deaths will be swift." The troll in front of Six and Dancer pointed with the tip of his immense claymore. Standing ten feet away, the razor-sharp tip of the sword wavered about ten inches in front of Six's face.

The teenager with the blood of a goddess of vengeance leapt straight at the monstrous beast threatening her partner. Both halves of *fion-fhuil* were pointed at the giant troll, and the blades bit deep as her flying leap swept her past the giant claymore and into his chest. The force of her momentum punched into the beast's chest, driving him backwards, crashing down onto his back. The huge claymore went flying across the rotunda and buried itself three feet deep into the stone and marble wall. Dancer landed gracefully, kneeling on the troll's chest, with her sword blades buried to the hilt in the creature.

As the troll gave its last gasping breaths, the young Fury pulled her blades free of the corpse's chest and gave an impish grin, her soft words seemed to carry in the stunned silence. "Who's next?"

There was a cacophony of roars as the trolls realized that this tiny human female had killed their clansman. The beast to the left of the fallen troll hauled back her warhammer, intending to smash the impudent human who dared defy them. There was a blur across the troll's midsection and the beast howled in pain. Six stopped five feet away and held up a clawed hand dripping black troll blood. Five gaping wounds tore through the troll's armor and opened up great gashes in her midsection. The troll bent over in pain, grabbing at her stomach in a futile effort to keep her internal organs inside her torso.

Six struck again, this time slamming into the creature's skull with an upraised knee. A loud "thwack" and "pop" resounded in the hall, and the vampire agent clutched his knee as the thick skull of the troll dislocated the joint. The beast faired no better, its head rocked back with the blow, snapping the thick, muscular neck as if it was a pencil. The creature's howling stopped, cut short by the vertebrae in its neck shattering. As the beast crumpled to the floor, Six clutched his rapidly healing knee and looked at Dancer, "Remind me not to do that again."

The young agent's answering grin was hidden as she whirled and leapt at the troll swinging its massive warhammer at her. Dancer's blades blocked the immense spiked hammer, but the impact knocked her sideways, throwing her five feet away and driving her to her knees. As she stood to engage the troll, she heard a gunshot ring out, and the troll howled in pain. She looked over to the stairwell and saw Ghost stepping down the stairs. Her boss thumbed the hammer of his ancient revolver back one more time and pulled the trigger, sending the .38 caliber round into her opponent's skull.

The thick skull of the beast would normally shrug off such relatively anemic rounds, but this ammunition had been developed by Section 28's resident esoteric mad scientist, Norbert. These rounds were designed to penetrate the tougher hides and bones of the monsters that the team routinely encountered. The small bit of cold iron in the middle of the round was also there to provide for extra damage against fae creatures - such as the trolls they were fighting. The impact of the custom .38 caliber round shattered the thick frontal plate of the troll's skull and penetrated to the smaller brain of the creature. There the bit of iron hit the exposed brain, and the creature shrieked as it died a brutal, painful death.

Ghost stepped forward and raised his Webley - aiming at the troll in the middle of the five remaining creatures. From behind the wall of creatures, a voice sounded, "Hold!"

The trolls parted and a short, wizened figure stepped forward. Dressed in a long, dark mottled cloak, the figure threw back the hood and revealed a large, bulbous head that was a weird mix of old man and child. The creature smiled, revealing broken, yellowed teeth.

Shit, thought Ghost. *Friggin' spriggan.*

The creature's voice rasped, "You need to release the key to me. I will spare your lives. If not, my companions will kill you and take the key from you."

Ghost pointed his revolver at the spriggan, "My colleagues already gave our answer to your pets." The trolls around the creature rumbled and growled at the insult. The monster hunter continued, "If you want to receive the same answer, that is your choice, spriggan." Ghost could hear the roar of gunfire and explosions from outside the museum and hoped that Boomer and Heavy were holding their own.

"My name is Meneraus Dline. I have dealt with your kind before, monster hunter. You have more than enough bravado for these lesser fae, but pale when compared to my powers." The creature's rasping voice was changing as the spriggan continued, deepening and losing its roughness. "One last chance before I let slip my... 'pets' as you called them. Our master requires that key. Give it to me."

Without lowering his Webley, Ghost turned and looked at Doc and the three pixies that hovered around her. He then turned to look at Six, then Dancer, wondering what they were thinking. Slowly returning his attention to the spriggan before him.

"Meneraus Dline, your reputation precedes you. My family's archives tell of your life and power. I would like to offer an answer for your bargain." Ghost pulled the trigger.

The report of the revolver echoed in the rotunda as the monster hunter pulled the trigger twice more. The first two rounds sparked off of a shimmering field of red light that appeared in front of the creature, ricocheting around the room. The third bullet slammed through the diminished field of red and impacted the spriggan, causing the creature to scream and clutch his wounded shoulder. The creature's voice thundered as it stumbled backwards, "Kill the humans. Bring me that key."

Ghost pulled the trigger twice more, aiming for the backpedaling spriggan. The wizened old creature grabbed a troll to its right and pulled the beast in as a shield. The troll howled in pain as the two custom bullets slammed into the beast's chest, penetrating deep to lodge into one of its lungs and first heart. The beast whimpered as it collapsed to the floor, dying from the iron poisoning its heart.

Ghost pulled the trigger once more, and the hammer fell on a spent shell. Realizing his revolver was empty, the monster hunter dropped it into his jacket pocket, then grasped the end of his cane. A simple twist released the blade from its sheath. Ghost drew the sword and pushed a bit of willpower into it, causing the ancestral blade to blaze with a white glow as it cleared its hard sheath. Ghost pointed the tip of the blade at the spriggan and smiled.

To the monster hunter's left, Six leapt at the nearest troll. As it drew back its oversized claymore to strike, the vampire agent slammed into the beast, digging his clawed hands through the chest armor of the beast, through the thick, leather-like skin, through the wrist-thick bones of the ribs, and into the chest cavity of the unfortunate target. The troll dropped its sword with a floor shaking "clang" and swatted at the vampire agent on its chest.

Six grabbed the creature's heart with both hands and squeezed. He felt the trolls massive hands slam into his back and neck. The impact shook the vampire, and the pain tinged his vision red as he heard several pops and cracks. Six let go of the troll's heart involuntarily, falling back as he blacked out from the shock and pain. As the vampire agent fell backwards, his target succumbed to the loss of its heart and toppled forward, landing on the unconscious agent.

Dancer had stepped forward, closing inside the range of her target's warhammer. Her blades flashed as she whirled a complicated pattern, slicing across the abdomen and chest of her troll. The radio conversation between Ghost and Boomer made the young agent pause. Hearing that her mentor was under attack by dragons angered her.

The troll realized that the young female was momentarily distracted and swung a backhand to try to knock her off her feet. The young Fury flew across the room, slamming into the base of the stairs. Gritting her teeth, she rolled to her feet, ignoring the gash in her shoulder.

The young Fury's eyes blazed in anger. The troll never saw her move, and suddenly the young human with white hair and eyes was launching herself into its chest, and her blades were buried hilt deep, one puncturing each lung. Dancer pulled the blades free and grinned as Vellath spoke to her, *Keep it up young one, you are finally learning who you are.*

Her reply brought a phantom snort from the dragon, *You just like being out of the sheath, you old lizard.*

Dancer pulled her blades free, placed them criss-cross over the neck of the prone troll. The creature's eyes went wide in fear as the

Fury's white orbs stared back. A swift crossing motion, and the beast's massive head bounced when it hit the marble floor of the museum. The young agent looked up as a blue light flew overhead, warbling a high-pitched battle cry.

She watched as Robert the Perylous slammed his pixie-sized sword into the raised claymore of the troll he had targeted. The "clang" rebounded around the rotunda, and the troll was pushed back a few feet, surprise evident on its rough face. The impish pixie smiled, his high voice proclaiming, "Is that all you've got?"

The troll swung his claymore, hoping to swat the impudent creature out of the air. The armored pixie easily dodged the ponderous blow and dove in, slicing his blade along the wrist of the troll, carving neatly through the armored gauntlet into the skin, muscles and tendons below the armor. The troll roared in pain and frustration as its blade dropped from its nerveless fingers.

Two more blue streaks flashed past Dancer, skimming the ground. They flew past the ankles of Robert's target, and the troll redoubled its howling, crashing to the ground as it was neatly hamstrung by Robert's mother and sister. All three pixies floated over the troll and chanted in a strange language that Dancer did not recognize. In a moment, the troll stopped howling and turned to an ashen gray—the color leaching from its skin, features, and even its armor.

Robert the Perylous turned to the other pixies, "I had it handled, mother. It was only a troll." The pixie sulked. "You didn't have to help."

Ziomarya looked at her son and smiled, "Yes, my son. We just decided to help."

Dancer turned her attention from the pixies to the troll who was preparing to swing his warhammer at the back of Ghost. The young Fury stood and asked her companion, *How aerodynamic are you, Vellath?*

She could almost hear the amusement in his voice, *You'll find I'm amazingly well balanced.*

Dancer slammed both blades together in a flash of brilliant white light. She clenched the sword in her right hand, drew her arm back, and let it fly in one smooth motion. The sword rotated as it flew, slamming into the troll with far more force than she put into it. The blade was buried to the hilt in the chest of the beast, and the creature slammed backwards to the floor, warhammer falling from limp, lifeless fingers.

Ghost saw the flash of light and felt the sword fly past him. His singular focus was on the spriggan in front of him. The tip of his glowing blade never wavered. The creature hissed and raised a hand, forming complex gestures with its fingers. Ghost struck before the spell could go off, stabbing, then slicing repeatedly. The spriggan was forced to abandon its magic as it tried to avoid the monster hunter's blade.

Ghost pressed his attack, not daring to let the creature get off any of his dangerous magic. The spriggan was driven backwards, and Ghost guided him, forcing him into a corner where there could be no escape.

The spriggan finally realized that there would be no escape. "Wait," it cried, voice regaining its rasping quality. It lowered its uninjured arm, and cringed, shielding itself from a blow that never landed.

Ghost put the tip of his blade against the creature's throat, "Tell me why I should not end you."

The spriggan that called itself Menerous Dline spoke slowly, "My master demands the key, I am under his command."

"Who is your master? Why does he want the key?"

"I cannot tell you his name. I am bound by him to serve and to protect him." The spriggan shook his head. "He will come for the key."

Ghost looked down his blade at the creature who had attacked and injured his team at the behest of this unknown master. Boomer's voice crackled over his earpiece, reporting that Heavy was down and grievously injured. His eyes hardened, reflecting his soul as he pondered the destruction caused by this creature. A thrust and a swipe later, the spriggan's head landed on the marble tiles next to a crumpling body.

Ghost looked around, searching for any enemies left standing. He took in the carnage, focusing on the blood trailing down Dancer's shoulder. He realized that he had not seen his former team leader. Looking again, he saw one of Six's legs sticking out from underneath the body of a troll. Glancing at the pixies, he nodded and hurried over to the creature lying on top of his agent.

When Dancer realized what Ghost was doing, she hurried over to help, grabbing a massive arm next to Doc, who had hurried forward. The three of them gently rolled the huge creature off of their comrade, and then Dancer threw the massive body across the room once they uncovered the vampire, smashing through the relatively untouched information desk. Doc knelt down to check on the fallen agent and was relieved to find he was breathing. She looked down when she heard the pop and snap of the bones resetting and watched in fascination as his arms straightened. The team's medic looked up at Ghost, "Do we have a supply of blood in the truck? He's going to need to feed."

Ghost nodded, "I believe we still have a full cache. Go outside and check on Heavy. I'll clean up in here."

As Doc stood and headed toward the front doors, the vampire agent in front of Ghost groaned. His eyes slowly opened, and they were completely human again. Six groaned again, "What happened? It feels like an elephant landed on me."

Ghost gave a slight smirk and patted the agents shoulder, "Troll, not an elephant. On the plus side, you killed it before it smashed you."

Six shook his head to clear it as he eased his way into a sitting position. He looked around, taking in the bodies lying around him. "Did we win?"

Ghost shrugged, "Seems like it, but Heavy's down. Time to get your ass up. We have blood in the truck if you need it."

Six clambered to his feet, "Where'd the pixies go?"

"They followed Doc outside. Let's go."

The three Section 28 agents hurried to the front doors and emerged into the damaged and torn concrete plaza outside the museum. Spotting the others kneeling over their fallen agent, Ghost tapped Six on the shoulder, "I'll go see how Heavy is. You get to the truck and take care of your hunger. We don't know if the bad guys are coming back, and you need to feed."

Six nodded and trotted over to the Wunder Buggy, clambering up the ramp in the back and closing it. Ghost and Dancer made their way to Heavy's side, looking down as Doc finished examining the big agent. The team's medic looked up at Ghost, "He's broken in several places. Hips, spine, femur and neck all seem to have fractures or breaks. We might be able to stabilize him when an ambulance gets here, but they need to be here now."

Ghost nodded and keyed his mic, "Spooky, Ghost. ETA on the ambulance? Get in touch with Agent Lempke and have her bring in a cleanup and response team that she can trust. Have her meet me here by Heavy."

"Ambulance three minutes out." There was a brief pause from Spooky. "Agent Lempke is on her way to you."

Ghost looked up to see the Philly SAC trotting over to the assembled group, holding her phone to her ear and talking quickly. She hung up when she reached the Section 28 team. As she walked up she seemed to startle when she saw the pixies hovering defensively over Doc and the wounded agent.

As the DHS SAC watched, one of the small winged creatures motioned to another one, and the second one became a flash of blue light as it sped back into the building. Ghost noticed the movement and raised an eyebrow at Ziomarya, who had sent her daughter back into the building.

The small pixie spoke, her voice lilting and melodious, "I've sent Roywyn to get our healers, maybe they can help your warrior."

"Thank you, Matriarch." Ghost turned to the Philly SAC and introduced the diminutive pixie, "Special Agent Kari Lempke, this is Matriarch Ziomarya, guardian of the artifact we were sent to retrieve. Matriarch, Agent Lempke is the leader of the Homeland Security office that covers Philadelphia. She is an ally."

The Matriarch bowed while the Philly SAC simply stared. Ghost interrupted the DHS agent's stare, "Agent Lempke, do you have a cleanup team on their way?"

The interruption forced the woman to respond, "Umm, yes. I have a team coming. Is she a fairie?"

Ghost smiled, "Technically? Yes, she and her kind are fae, but more specifically, they are wood sprites, or pixies. Fierce warriors and amazing guardians. I shouldn't have to tell you, but they are also classified well above your pay grade."

Lempke was still staring at the pixies, eyes flitting back and forth between Ziomarya and Robert. She was startled when three blue flashes of light streaked from the Museum's doors to their position. The one Ziomarya called Roywyn had returned with two more pixies in tow. The two immediately began flitting all over the fallen warrior, gently touching various spots and then conversing in hushed tones.

Ziomarya turned to Ghost and Lempke, "May I present Atalie and Zanika, two of our best healers. Atalie is in the red tunic, and Zanika in the blue."

Ghost pulled out his SSP to call Director Smith as he watched the two pixies try to save Heavy's life.

15

INQUIRY

Acting Director of Section 28 James Smith sat at one end of a heavy oak conference table. Arrayed down both sides of the table were government officials from the military, national security, and the intelligence communities, as well as four congressional delegates. Ten chairs lined the wall of the large conference room, each occupied by an assistant or staffer of one of the attendees. Smith knew, without looking, that Special Agent Gretchen Massey was sitting behind him, keeping notes on her SSP.

Peering down the table, Smith pulled out his credentials and placed them on the table, open to the room. Pushing a bit of will into the credentials, they gave a slight, almost invisible glow. With the security of his testimony guaranteed, he concentrated on the people around the room. Smith turned to Gretchen, "Does everyone in this room have prior Section Twenty-Eight clearance?"

Gretchen looked around the room and consulted her phone. "All the primaries, except for Mister Chris Nienhuis, from the NSA. His boss has clearance, he does not."

Nienhuis protested, "Hey, my boss sent me here. I've got the clearance for this meeting as his proxy. Hell, I probably have a higher clearance than you, miss."

Smith gave a short laugh, "I very much doubt that, Mister Nienhuis. I would bet that Miss Massey is cleared for far more than you could even dream about. As it is, you do not have clearance. You are dismissed from this meeting."

The NSA man continued his protest, even as he stood, "Wait until my boss hears about this. You are going to have to brief him individually."

Smith nodded, "I'm sure that I will. In the meanwhile, if he wants to send us your information, we'll consider clearing you for future briefings." He turned to Gretchen, utterly dismissing the man, "Anyone else not cleared for this briefing?"

Gretchen again consulted her SSP, "Of the aides and staffers present, only four of them have prior clearance: Hannah Hall, from the Department of Defense; Amy Swallows, from the CIA; Avery Martin, from Representative McKinney's office; and Odell Weaver, from Senator Weaver's office. None of the others are currently vetted and cleared."

Smith looked around the room. "As you heard Miss Massey, If you were not on her very short list, your seat is no longer yours. Please clear the room. I'm sure your senior staff will contact you when we are done." There was grumbling and scraping as chairs were moved and aides and staffers stood to leave. When the last aide left, Gretchen nodded at Smith, and the acting Director of Section 28 turned to the rest of the table.

"Now that everyone here is actually allowed to be here, let's begin this briefing." Smith pulled a thick folder from an attaché case and laid it on the table, opening the cover to the first page. "At approximately three o'clock yesterday, there was an attack on a building complex owned by the Department of Homeland Security and assigned to the subdivision referred to as 'Section Twenty-Eight' within the government. This attack was fast and brutal, killing many employees of Section Twenty-Eight and destroying many of the buildings on the ground." He looked up from the folder, catching the eyes of those seated around the table. "This attack was carried out by a force comprising shock troops and led by commanders who were riding dragons."

Around the table, the men and women murmured to each other. Representative McKinney made herself heard over the confusion, "Surely you don't expect us to believe dragons are real?"

Her fellow House member turned to her, "Shrita, do you remember what this department actually does?"

"Yes, Cory, I know what we've been told. But all I see is a black hole of funding, and now some ridiculous story about dragons."

Representative McKinney turned to Smith, "Next you'll tell us that elves and fairies are real, too."

Smith tried not to smile, "Actually, we believe these dragons and shock troops came from the fae realm. But we're fairly certain that the Seelie elves had no part in it. After all, we are co-signatories in the *E'Tuatha* Accords."

"What the hell? Elves are real?" This time is was the other House member's turn to remark.

"Yes, Representative Veltkamp. Everything that you have been briefed about Section Twenty-Eight is real. This office has never lied to our congressional oversight." Smith looked back at Representative McKinney. "Any other questions about dragons?"

Receiving a dumbfounded shake of the head from the Michigan legislator, Smith forged ahead. "The attack overwhelmed the substantial defenses built into the site, as well as the guards housed on site. We are still coordinating casualty counts and medical evacuation for the wounded, but this was a terrible loss for Section Twenty-Eight, decimating our current staffing. In the attack, the Director of Section Twenty-Eight was a confirmed casualty. Until the position is filled, I've stepped into the operational Director position, per operating protocols."

The Senator from Indiana spoke up, "What is the current casualty count, Director Smith?"

"Senator Weaver, our current casualty count, including support and security personnel, is currently listed as two hundred twenty-three. One hundred and six support personnel were killed or are missing. Seventy-two security personnel are listed as killed or missing. Forty-five administration and field staff were killed." Smith turned to Gretchen, "How many wounded so far?"

Gretchen spoke up, "As of last count, we have over forty wounded. Almost all have been transported to local hospitals while the rest were treated and released from the scene."

Smith nodded and turned back to the group. "We are currently coordinating with the 911th Engineers Corps, as well as the FBI for search and rescue operations in the rubble, hoping for more survivors. Any questions about casualties?"

Senator Weaver's aide spoke up, "Director Smith, any civilian casualties or wounded?"

"No, sir. As of now, I have no reports of civilian casualties in this attack." Smith was shaking his head.

The Senator spoke up, "How did you not see this attack coming, Director?"

"Jen." The Senator's aide chided her, "It's not like they appeared out of thin air, they must have missed the attack coming."

Smith chuckled, "Actually, Mister Weaver, Senator Weaver, the attacking force did literally appear out of nowhere. The leader opened a gateway to this plane of existence and brought his army through. There was no way to predict or prepare for this attack."

"Unfortunately, the attack was recorded on video from several bystanders." The new voice came from the CIA Director of Operations. "What do you intend to do about the leaks? Part of your division's charter is to keep the public in the dark."

Smith gave the man a stern look. The CIA's second-in-command was aptly named Jacob Hacker and had been the CIA's liaison to his division for the last five years. "Director Hacker, my best technical analyst is right now either taking down or discrediting every scrap of footage he can find. Of course, he would be able to accomplish that much faster if your agency and the NSA were not trying to infiltrate our servers."

Hacker blinked rapidly. "I have no idea what you are talking about, Mister Smith. Although I would like to have some other questions answered when we are finished with the discussion at hand."

Smith nodded, and then continued, "The operations complex at Langley is almost totally destroyed. Other than a couple key pieces of infrastructure, the complex will have to be completely rebuilt. It may take months to clear all the rubble to ensure that we have recovered all of our missing and dead. If you will refer to the summary that was provided, you will see projected timeline and costs for replacing the Section Twenty-Eight division headquarters."

There was a rustle of paper as those present referred to the information. Those aides who wanted to see the report were forced to read over their boss' shoulder. The representative from the Department of Defense spoke up, "Director Smith, do you have any idea why your division was attacked?"

"No, Colonel Bower. As of this time, we do not have any credible information to ascribe motive to the attackers."

Colonel April Bower had been in the Army intelligence brach for a long time before posting to the Pentagon. She had dealt with bureaucrats for the last four years, and this intelligence adminis-trator was no different. The Army officer referred to her notes, "According to my reports, one of your agents was a witness to the attack, and the commander of the attacking force named you, specifically, Director Smith. So was this a personal attack? And who are your suspects?"

Smith kept the smile on his face as he looked directly at the colonel. "Colonel Bower, the agent you speak of had just had a building come down around him, had been unconscious for an unknown amount of time, and was suffering a concussion when he went into surgery for other, life threatening, injuries. While we have his statement, we are working to verify that statement. Unlike the armed forces, if we get intel wrong, the world may actually end."

The CIA representative held up his hand, "Do you have any more information you can provide? What can we tell our respective agencies?"

The acting director of Section 28 looked around the room, "That is all the current information I have for this preliminary briefing. I will forward reports to you, individually, as we gather more intel. Again, I must remind you that this is classified Top Secret, with Need To Know clearance required. And no one in this room, other than myself or Miss Massey, has the authority under United States law, or under the *E'Tuatha* Accords, to determine who can be read in. Questions?"

Senator Weaver spoke up, "If I need to have some staffers brought up to speed, can I have them contact you?"

The half smile that had played over Smith's lips was gone, "Senator Weaver, I can confidently say that none of your staffers will need to be read into this briefing." Smith gathered his folder into his satchel, put his credentials back into his pocket, stood, and motioned for Gretchen to lead the way. He followed her out the door.

Halfway down the hallway, his SSP vibrated. Glancing at the screen, he saw it was Ghost. Sliding his finger across the screen to answer the call, he spoke, "Yes, Mister Vanhof. Did you retrieve the package?"

GHOST TOLD Smith about the battle, and the injuries to Heavy. After the brief conversation, Ghost said into the phone, "Got it, boss. I'll let you know about Heavy."

Just as he ended the call, Ghost saw a blue glow envelop his fallen agent. Once the glow dissipated, The monster hunter looked at the pixies who were hovering over the big man. "So what is the diagnosis? Can you help him?"

The older of the two floated higher, fluttering her wings, "We have stabilized him as best we can. Our magic here is limited, and his injuries are too grim. He needs help we cannot provide."

"Who can help him?"

The pixie looked at her partner, who had floated up next to her. She turned back to Ghost, "I believe he would require the help of the Queen of the Seelie, Lishe ta Merunaré. But Her majesty rarely assists mortals from this realm. I fear you may have a difficult time convincing her otherwise."

Dancer looked up when she heard the Seelie Queen's name. She stood and joined the conversation, "Her Majesty will help. She will not deny a request from the *Claíomh an Sí.*"

There was a collective intake of breaths as all the pixie wings stopped for a single heartbeat. Ziomarya flew up to look Dancer in the eyes. After a few seconds, the pixie backed off and bowed in midair. She addressed the young Fury, "My apologies, *Cainteoir.* We did not realize that you were present. You are correct, Her Majesty, the Queen, would never deny your request."

Agent Lempke was trying to keep up with the conversation happening around her. She looked at the teenage agent with white hair again, seeing the deference that these small creatures showed her. Her radio squawked. She answered it, "Lempke, here."

"The bus just arrived. Should we send them through?"

Lempke looked at Ghost, who nodded. She answered, "Affirmative. Send them through. Have the locals get fire and more medical en route. Call the office and tell Carl to roll the response team for cleanup."

The answer from the radio was drowned out as Ghost activated his own microphone, "Spooky, call ahead and get both planes ready for takeoff. The Globemaster will take the Wunder Buggy and Boomer, Dancer, and Heavy to Grand Rapids. Priority flight plan out of Philly and into Grand Rapids. The Citation will take the rest of us back to Langley for debrief and cleanup. Prep the Buggy for transport, we're leaving in three minutes."

"Copy that."

Ghost could feel the eyes of the Philly SAC on him, so he turned and saw a furious DHS Agent. Agent Lempke laid into him, "So let me get this straight. You brought dragons, pixies and God knows what else into my city, trashed a museum, and are just leaving me to clean up? I don't think so. Your team can ride in the ambulance to the hospital with your man, but you are staying around here to clean up your mess."

The monster hunter looked at the fuming DHS agent and then

glanced around to make sure there was no one else within earshot. Ghost pulled out his credentials, opening them in front of Agent Lempke. He spoke in a low tone that only the two of them could hear, "Special Agent Kari Lempke, By order of Homeland Security and by the Signatory-status of Section Twenty-Eight of the *E'Tuatha* Accords, I hereby bind you under *geas*. You are bound from discussing Section Twenty-Eight procedures, or from mentioning classified objects, creatures, or materials with those who are not also bound by the *geas*. You are also bound from interfering with, or harming Section Twenty-Eight operations in accordance with the Wormsall Decision."

Agent Lempke's eyes blanked for a moment, then she shook her head to clear it. "What the hell did you just do to me?"

"I apologize, Kari." Ghost put his credentials away. "I have to leave. My team has to leave, and they will not be taking the ambulance. I will try to come back to town afterwards to talk to you personally, but our mission here is far more important than a museum."

As Lempke was trying to form a response, the ambulance rolled up, lights flashing. When the medics brought the stretcher over, they quickly checked Heavy. Doc filled them in on the big man's injuries, and they carefully slid a backboard underneath his broken body. With the rest of the team's help, they carefully lifted the backboard and strapped it to the wheeled stretcher.

Before they could leave, Doc opened her credentials and said, "Department of Homeland Security. We are going to transport this patient in our truck, and we are going to borrow your equipment to do so." She nodded at SAC Lempke, "Send the bill to Agent Lempke. Her office will coordinate and forward it to mine. I'm sorry about the inconvenience, but you have no choice."

One of the paramedics started to protest and bluster while the other one pulled out her phone to contact the company headquarters. Boomer stepped up, right into the paramedic's personal space. The diminutive vampire agent's voice was low and filled with menace, "You have approximately two seconds to say, 'Yes ma'am' and then move out of the way. Anything else means that you will need an ambulance for yourself. That is my partner and friend. Am I clear?"

Boomer's eyes had turned black, and she felt the growl in her throat. The paramedic backed off hastily, "Yes, ma'am. You guys can have it. We'll get it later." He motioned to his incredulous partner, "C'mon, Billie. We need to get back to our bus."

Less than a minute later, the team was loading the stretcher into the back of the Wunder Buggy. Six sat down and grabbed one of the support bars of the stretcher, "No need to strap it down. I've got it. Let's get to the airport."

Boomer was already climbing into the driver's seat, and as soon as the doors were closed, she fired up the engine, dropped the truck in gear, and slammed the gas pedal down to the floor. The police officer standing in the road was almost too slow to get out of the way, feeling the wind tug at his uniform shirt as the truck blasted past him.

Ten minutes later the Wunder Buggy was pulling onto the parking ramp at the airport. Boomer pulled the truck straight up into the waiting maw of the open cargo area in their Air Force jet. As she shut down the truck, the team began piling out of the Wunder Buggy and Air Force loader crew members were putting the tie-down chains on the overweight truck. Boomer and Dancer carried the gurney into the passenger compartment while the rest of the team walked down the ramp to get to their own aircraft.

Eight minutes later, the Air Force C-17 Globemaster III was airborne, with the throttles wide open. Climbing for altitude, the jet turned to head towards Grand Rapids, Michigan.

16

ANSWERS

33,000 Above Ohio

"Thank you, Tó Coferal. And thank Her Majesty for agreeing to meet with us and to look at Heavy for us. He is stabilized now, but I don't know how long that will be." Dancer looked at the man on the stretcher she was discussing.

The voice on the other end of the phone was deep and rich, "Absolutely, *Claíomh an Sí*. For the *Cainteoir* of Section Twenty-Eight, we would certainly make provisions to meet with you. As *Claíomh an Sí*, the Queen of the *Sidhe* welcomes your presence and will assist if Her Majesty is able. When will you arrive?"

"We are about thirty minutes out of Grand Rapids. I'm sure that Boomer will have us at your door ten minutes after that."

The voice sounded amused, "I have heard of Miss Callahan's driving. I will inform the gate, and Tar Katel will meet you in the driveway."

Dancer nodded as if the elf could see her, "Thank you again, Tó Coferal. I will inform you when we are on the ground." The young agent hung up the phone and asked her mentor, "How is he? Is he still stable?

Boomer looked up from the small instruments that Doc and the paramedics had placed around the giant. "He seems to be ok. I hope the Queen can do something for him. At least those pixies could help."

"So, how far from the airport to the Seelie house?" Dancer asked the team's driver.

The young vampire smiled, "GPS says twelve minutes. I say about seven if we catch the lights. You better hold the stretcher tight."

Twenty-nine minutes later, the Air Force jet was on the ground and taxied to the same parking spot on the tarmac it had left just over five hours earlier. Two minutes later the Wunder Buggy was off the airport property and careening toward the Seelie stronghold.

When Boomer pulled the truck into the driveway, she pulled up as close to the door as the driveway allowed. Shutting down the truck, the vampire agent flipped the switch to lower the rear hatch, unbuckled her own seatbelt and climbed into the back to help Dancer with the stretcher.

At the foot of the ramp stood a large creature with the muscular body of a man, but the horned head of a bull. The smile that graced his lips faltered as he saw Heavy on the stretcher. Boomer called out, "Well met, Tar Katel. Can you assist us with this stretcher when we get it out of the truck. Her majesty is expecting us."

The deep voice of the head of the Queen's guards rumbled, "Of course, Rebecca Callahan. I was informed of your arrival."

The big minotaur wheeled the stretcher into the house, and then into the audience room of the Queen of the *Sidhe*. Tó Coferal, the Queen's Knight met them inside the house, and waved them through the elf and minotaur guards all the way into the audience of his Queen. Once inside the door, he announced them to the room, as was proper custom. The Queen cut him off with a wave of her slender hand,

"We will not stand on formalities in this one instance, my Knight." The soft melodious voice of the Queen interrupted. "Bring Arthur Murphy before me."

THE GRAY CESSNA Citation X with Air Force markings landed at the airfield adjacent to the former Section 28 headquarters. Before the engines were finished spooling down, the door opened and the stairs extended down to the tarmac. The short, twelve minute hop required a longer taxi on both ends than the actual flight time, and the team members wearily deplaned.

The first person down the stairs was Ghost. His gaucho hat

threatened to blow off his head, and his long leather overcoat flapped in the wind. Six followed closely on the monster hunter's heals and quickly caught up to the team leader when he reached the ground. Doc carried her satchel down the stairs, pausing to look back up the stairs as Spooky exited the hatch.

Six caught Ghost's attention, "Wait up, Jonas. I've got a question for you."

The tall hunter slowed until his vampire teammate caught up to him. "What's up?"

"Do you think we're getting the whole story out of the Director? As a team, we've been ambushed twice now, both times while retrieving something he set in motion a long time ago. What's next?"

Ghost walked for several steps while pondering the question. "I don't think we've gotten the whole story from the Director yet. I think we're going to have to pry it out of him." They walked in silence for several seconds, and then the monster hunter continued, "And I have a feeling that whoever took Pandora's box will not give up on whatever this key is so easily."

The monster hunter looked up from his discussion to see Director Smith and Gretchen exiting a black government SUV next to the tarmac. Ghost changed his direction, angling toward Smith, and the team followed. Smith looked the battle-weary team over, seeing the worry and pain etched on their faces.

The Director said, "Let's go talk in the Warehouse where we can be away from prying eyes and ears. As I understand it, Boomer and Dancer should land in Grand Rapids in a couple hours. I've been assured by the Queen that she would take care of Heavy."

The group walked in silence to the temporary structure housing the inter-dimensional Warehouse. Agent Mulder, the FBI's on-site SAC, met the team at the entrance to the structure, reading the pain and loss on their faces. As the now-larger group walked through the doors. As they did so, Russell wandered out of the Warehouse entrance and looked at the disheveled team of agents.

"Where's everyone else?"

Ghost shook his head and pointed deeper into the Warehouse, "Conference room. We've got a lot of shit to discuss. Knightmare and Section Management are debriefing with the Director. That includes you and Norbert. Will you go collect him from whatever experiment he's running?"

Russell nodded and walked back to Norbert's lab. He was able to get the attention of the eccentric scientist without too much effort and was able to drag him away from whatever he was working on at the time. They arrived at the conference room door shortly after everyone else. The members of team Knightmare had stripped out of their combat armor and gear, with Ghost having shed his trademark trench coat and gaucho hat.

Smith waved the latecomers to spare seats at the table. He then held up his hand to draw everyone's attention, quieting the small group of people. The acting Director spoke, "This is an official debrief for the record. Miss Massey will record this session.

"Mister Black, you are first. Debrief on the mission to Grand Rapids, please."

Six spent some time talking about the encounter with the dogmen. He described the pack dynamics, as well as the appearance and the resilience of the creatures. The vampire agent then recounted his followup of a similar incident on the lakeshore in a town called Muskegon. In that incident, a man had killed one dogman and wounded two more before the pack had run away. The former mercenary then talked about recruiting both Ryan DeBoer, from Grand Rapids, and a man named Pete McCarthy from Muskegon as potential new agents for Section 28. The Director perked up at that announcement.

"And you believe these two men would make a positive addition to the agency, Mister Black?" Smith looked directly at the former Knightmare commander.

"Yessir. I believe both men are skilled enough, and would be motivated enough to do what we do."

Smith nodded. "Thank you, Mister Black. I look forward to following up with those two gentlemen. In your opinion, are those dogmen a current threat?"

Six thought for a moment, then answered, "Negative, Director. I believe that they may be an occasional nuisance, but they do not constitute a threat for Section 28."

Smith nodded in agreement. "Thank you, Mister Black." He looked at Ghost, "It is your turn, Mister Vanhof. Please debrief on the Charleston mission."

Ghost sat up and recounted the mission to South Carolina. He talked about the loss of Little G, and the battle with the troll. As the monster hunter talked about Smith's duel with the troll, Six and Doc both looked at their boss with wide eyes. When Ghost mentioned Smith possessing and using the mythic Excalibur, Doc gasped and raised a hand to her mouth. At the other end of the table, Agent Mulder snorted.

Smith looked at the FBI SAC, "Do you have something to add, Agent Mulder?"

"Yeah." Mulder smiled as she talked, "I can maybe accept that something called a 'dogman' is in Michigan. I can accept that you ran into something that you called a troll in Charleston. But you, Director Smith, have, and use, Excalibur as a personal defensive weapon? Seriously? Am I supposed to believe that you are King Arthur, now?"

Smith shook his head. "No, SAC Mulder. Although I currently do wield *Kaledvoulc'h*, I have never claimed to be Arthur Pendragon."

Six spoke up, "Is that where Pandora's Box was taken?"

"Yes, Mister Black. Whoever left the troll also dug up and took the artifact."

"Wait!" Agent Mulder slammed the palm of her hand down on the table. "You guys had Pandora's Box, and you *lost* it?"

Smith turned back to Mulder, "No, Agent Mulder. Section Twenty-Eight never possessed Pandora's Box. I originally possessed the artifact and hid it in a location that should have been very secure. It was discovered and stolen by the same enemy that razed our headquarters here."

Agent Mulder muttered under her breath.

Smith continued, "Mister Vanhof, please brief us on the recent mission to Philadelphia."

Ghost once again gathered his thoughts and recounted the last mission. "When we arrived at the airport, we met with Six, Doc and Dancer. After meeting with the Philly SAC, Boomer drove the Buggy to the museum. Once there, we had the building cleared, and entered to retrieve the bust, as you directed. We did encounter the guardian you warned us about. That pass phrase worked perfectly.

"After we secured the artifact, Spooky announced two incursion alarms, both local to us. Spooky had the first encounter, so I sent Boomer and Heavy out to provide cover fire for the Buggy, and as an advance attack force to clear the path for the rest of the team."

Ghost gave a long pause, his voice growing somber. The monster hunter willed his voice not to crack, "Boomer reported that she and Heavy saw at least four or five dragons with armored riders. They used the mini grenade rounds in their shotguns. They were able to dispatch a couple of the creatures, but Heavy sacrificed himself to get Boomer out of the way of an attack by the leader. After Heavy was wounded, and another one of the dragons and their riders had been killed, they disappeared through a hellgate that appeared in the air."

The veteran monster hunter looked at Smith, and then the rest of the table. "Inside, we had three of the pixies acting as guardians of Doc while the rest of us escorted her downstairs. The gate inside the museum went active, and a whole bunch of trolls came through. The troll leader tried to get us to surrender, but Hannah killed it. Six and I also attacked, trying to drive back the trolls. Toward the end, we had a spriggan step forward as a challenge. I was able to defeat the creature, killing it. At that point, we finished off the troll attack, leaving none alive."

Ghost felt his throat get tight, "Once we exited the building, we found Boomer guarding Heavy. The pixies were able to stabilize Arthur, but even their healers said they couldn't help him. Once Hannah suggested that we contact the Queen, she did so. I immediately dispatched Rebekah and Hannah to Grand Rapids. They took the Buggy and the big transport jet. We left after they took off."

Smith asked, "And the cleanup? What about witnesses?"

The team leader shook his head, "We left a mess for DHS to clean up, including several corpses and lots of damage. As far as witnesses, I would bet we have several hundred, and most of them would have cell phones. I guarantee that at least part of the dragon fight was caught on camera. We were also likely identified."

The Director looked over at their resident hacker, "Mister Smith, have any videos or evidence appeared on the internet?"

"Does Deadpool like chimichangas?" Spooky looked up from his laptop where he was banging away on the keyboard. "Of course the footage has hit the net. I'm working on knocking the footage down, but it's spreading to every conspiracy site on the planet. I'm also seeing the old footage show up again. Wait a second."

The former NSA analyst was rapidly typing and suddenly made a gesture. The screen behind Smith suddenly lit up with a screen full of numbers and letters, several sets highlighted in red. "These bastards are clever. See these names?" Spooky stood and pointed to the various highlighted names. "Not only are the regular people uploading their footage, but CIA and NSA are also uploading their copies of the files, trying to draw me out. That's just rude."

"How do you know it's the CIA and NSA?" Six was looking at the names. "All I see are typical user names."

Spooky nodded, "You have to know what to look for. This one, Twilight Assassin? He's from the CIA. He always sucked at hiding his tracks. And Jade Sky? I worked with him on that project. Cheeky of him to use that name." The former analyst looked around sheepishly. He turned back to the screen, "These final three are all from the NSA. Bear was my supervisor's counterpart in Signals. Better than my old boss, but not as good as he thinks. This girl here, Lumina, she and I dated for a while. Finally Gar Bear is from the NSA, but he must be a new guy, because I don't recognize the style or signature. Either way, he's in on this, too."

"Can you stop the footage from leaking?" The Director asked his electronics specialist directly.

"No, boss. They've got so much going out that I can't stop it. If I tried, I'd lose control of the system, and we'd lose track of the hackers who are trying to get into our systems. I already caught a couple NSA hackers trying to break into our files. Shezera and Wizzy are both on the group responsible for attacking and taking down hacking groups, and both of them are at the top of the food chain." Spooky thought for a moment, "I think Shezera asked me out once. I know her partner, Wizzy, encouraged it."

Ghost spoke up, "What are they digging for, Spooky? Anything specific?"

The former NSA analyst turned to catch Director Smith's eye, "Absolutely. They are trying to figure out why he doesn't exist in any real system. They're still trying to figure out who our new director is. I'll admit, I'm kinda' curious about that myself."

Smith looked down at the table in a rare moment of vulnerability. He looked back up, slowly gazing around the room, catching and holding each person's eyes for a moment. "I do suppose that it is time I told my tale to someone. After all, if I don't share it soon, it will be lost for all posterity."

He paused, then started again, fingers steepled in front of him, with his index fingers resting on his lips for a moment. "As most of you know by now, I've lived a very long life. My personnel file says I will be forty-five years old this October. In truth, I will be 1,523 years old when that day falls. I was born in the kingdom of Guotodin, on the isle of Briton in the year of our Lord 494 AD."

"No goddamn way, Smith." Agent Mulder was shaking her head. "Seriously? Dragons, pixies, and trolls are impossible to believe. You being over fifteen hundred years old? I'm calling bullshit."

Smith smiled his calm half smile and his cultured voice picked up a very faint British accent, "While I am not Arthur Pendragon, I was one of his knights. I am Gawain, the son of King Lot and Morgause, and the rightful heir to the throne in Camelot. I am the last remaining Knight of the Round Table."

17

KNIGHTHOOD

The Warehouse

The cacophony rising from the conference room was heard by the technicians working in Norbert's lab. Smith sat at the head of the table, undisturbed, with that knowing half-smile on his lips. He waited for the initial furor to die down and then addressed the group.

"I understand that you have a lot of questions. I will try to answer them as I can."

"How can you be a Knight of the Round Table and be over fifteen hundred years old?" Agent Mulder was the first to speak. "I thought those were all myths and legends."

Smith gave a slight chuckle. "Agent Mulder, one thing you will find in this business is that myths and legends usually have at least some small grain of truth at the core. Just as dragons and vampires exist, King Arturius Pendragon was a real king in Briton. He created a cadre of knights that served him and unified a kingdom. And Camelot, though not the Eden that modern myth made it out to be, was his capital, and the castle was truly a sight to behold."

"Hold up. What's this about vampires? You were talking about trolls and pixies earlier." Mulder's confusion was growing.

Six guffawed out loud. "Wait, nobody told you?" The former mercenary turned to Smith, "Were you ever planning on telling her?"

Mulder looked back and forth between Smith and Six in confusion. "Nobody told me what? What am I missing?"

Six looked at the FBI SAC and chuckled, "About me and Boomer. We're both vampires."

"Bullshit."

Six changed. His eyes flashed into pure black, his fangs elongated, and his fingernails lengthened and sharpened. The vampire agent flashed a fang-filled smile at Mulder, who recoiled in horror. "No. Reality."

"What the f-." Mulder cursed and scramble backwards. Her chair tipped over, dumping the FBI agent on the ground. Hard. She scrambled to her feet, looking wildly around the room, "Are all of you some sort of monster?"

Smith's voice rang with a steel none of them had heard before, "Sit down, Agent Mulder. Mister Black is a vampire who is controlled by an even harsher *geas* than you are. All of my agents are controlled by the *geas*. Everyone else present in this room, myself excluded, is pure human. Mister Black was human until he had an unfortunate encounter with a pureblood vampire. While I am technically human, I am the product of a magick that is older than Briton herself."

THE MAN in mail armor swung his sword, cleaving into the unprotected stomach of the bandit. Withdrawing the blade, he used his shield to block a knife thrust from the bandit next to him. Spinning, the nobles's sword arced in the sunlight, slamming into the upraised arm, splintering the bones and rending the flesh. As the bandit cried out in pain, the nobleman pulled the sword back and struck again, this time cleaving through the clavicle and ribcage, finding the bandit's right lung.

The bandit's lifeless husk crumpled to the ground, and the man looked around, spotting no other bandits. He grinned and looked at his companions, "Well, lads. It seems we have run out of bandits."

One of his companions sheathed his sword with an answering grin, "Maybe next time they will not choose to rob those in armor. Did you see any escape?"

"No, Lancelot. I was too busy dispatching the fools who challenged us. Did you?"

The companion nodded, "Aye, my friend. Two of the cowards fled toward the tree line. Shall we pursue?"

"No. Let the wolves feast tonight. If we tarry long, we will not make the keep by nightfall." The nobleman sheathed his sword, and mounted his horse. Motioning for the rest of the party to mount, he said, "Let's continue on. We are still over half a day's ride from the keep, and I would like a warm meal and a warm bed tonight."

Lancelot spoke up, "And I know who you hope to warm the bed with, Gawain." Raucous laughter erupted around the party as everyone mounted their horses.

The nobleman blushed and then joined the laughter. "Aye. But that is Prince Gawain, to the likes of you, Lancelot."

With a salute and a laugh, the mildly rebuked Lancelot spurred his horse forward, taking the point position for the party of men on their way to visit a king. The rest of the journey was uneventful and the small party of weary mounted men approached the outskirts of the city. The large, well-guarded gate in the stone wall stood open, as it was not yet time to close for the evening. Originally constructed by the conquering Romans and maintained after their fall, the wall surrounding Camelot helped protect its citizens from bandits and invaders.

As the band of travelers approached the gate, a guard in a mail hauberk and carrying a spear stepped in front of Lancelot. "What is your business?"

Gawain pushed his horse forward, coming to a stop next to Lancelot, "Gawain, son of King Lot, as emissary to King Arthur."

The guard gave a slight bow, "Welcome, milord. I will send a herald before you to announce you at the manor." He pointed to a young boy of about twelve, and the lad ran toward the keep at the center of town.

Gawain nodded at the guard, and his retinue slowly moved through the gate. As they made their way through the cramped streets, the houses and shops lining the roads were of a better quality than most he had seen throughout the countryside. It was evident that Camelot was wealthy, and that Arthur's reign had been good to his subjects.

Arriving at the base of the hill that the manor sat upon, the men dismounted, and Gawain walked forward to the gate where the herald was talking and gesturing to the guard. As the nobleman walked forward, the guard gave a slight bow. "Welcome, milord. My liege is awaiting your presence in the main hall."

The nobleman thanked him and led his party through the gate and into the main house. Led by a household servant, the men arrived at the main hall. Roughly thirty feet wide and well over sixty feet long, the grand hall was lined with linens and tapestries, all of which showed battle or hunting scenes celebrating Arthur and his ancestors. A fire burned in the open hearth on each side wall, and candles and torches lit the hall.

Arthur stood at the other end of the hall and raised a hand to greet the newcomers. Standing at just over six feet tall, the monarch was broad shouldered and dressed in long robes and leathers over spun cotton clothing. His full black beard was mottled with gray, and his ruddy face was open and smiling as he spoke, "Welcome, Gawain, son of Lot. Please come in and warm yourselves. I believe you have met my wife, Guinevere, and my eldest daughter Lissa. Join me at the table for a repast."

Gawain looked at the fabled table of Arthur. To stop bickering among his earls and nobles about who was primary, the king had a table specially constructed. In a time when most tables were long rectangles, this was completely round, leaving no "head" of the table. Arthur pointed to a seat next to his, and Gawain sat down at the table. Arthur's wife and daughter sat to the king's left, and Lancelot and the rest of his retinue took places around the large table. Once they were seated, the servants brought plates of food from the kitchen. The men were enthusiastic as they ate the roast pigs and deer after a long day on the road.

After the dinner, servants cleared the table and the men and women continued talking well into the evening. Later that night, Arthur offered Gawain and his men rooms in the manor, and they accepted. It was a short time later that the gathering broke up, and the men went to their rooms.

Gawain was late to break fast with his men the next morning. As he approached the table, Lancelot had a large grin on his face as he asked, "So, Gawain, was your bed as warm as your meal last night?"

A slight blush and a twinkle in Gawain's eye told the story as he ducked his head and ignored the question. Lancelot continued badgering the young man, "When are you going to settle down and ask her father?"

"Soon, friend. When the time is right." Gawain looked up in time to see Arther, Guinevere, and Lissa walk through the entrance to the hall. Arthur greeted the young man with a hearty slap on the back. Gawain stood and kissed the proffered hand of the monarch's wife. When he bent to kiss the daughter's hand, she giggled and Gawain blushed crimson. He quickly sat down and buried his head in his food.

Lancelot watched the exchange and guffawed, quickly feigning choking on his food to cover his outburst. Gawain kicked his friend under the table hard enough to thump his knee against the underside. Lancelot's choking turned to a moan of pain.

Gawain laughed and slapped his friend on the back, "Careful, my friend. Do not try to swallow the meal whole." He received a glare from Lancelot for his trouble. The rest of the meal went well, and Gawain and his men enjoyed the hospitality of the King.

It was a week later that the attack came. As his men were walking amongst the townfolk, Gawain and Lancelot were meeting with Arthur discussing a possible treaty with Lot, feudal lord of the land to the west. Gawain's father had sent him to explore allying with Arthur. A guard burst into the main hall shouting for his liege.

"Milord! Gaels are attacking the outer farms!"

Arthur stood and called for his armor and sword. Gawain and Lancelot both stood, looked at each other, and ran to their rooms as the rest of their party burst into the hall on their way to get their own arms and armor.

Donning his mail hauberk and strapping on his sword and shield, Gawain hurried to get ready. He almost collided with Lancelot in the hallway. His friend was wearing a smile and called out, "'Tis about time. I was getting bored with the endless talking. And I don't have a warm bed at night to look forward to."

Gawain clapped him on the shoulder, "Yes, my friend. Shall we defend this kingdom?"

The two men entered the great hall and found most of the traveling party waiting. Arthur entered the hall moments later. Full mail hauberk over his shoulders, conical spangenhelm helmet perched atop his head and large two-handed sword strapped to his side. He looked at Gawain and nodded. As the last two of Gawain's retainers entered the hall, Arthur led the way out into the courtyard, down, and out the gate.

The group of men retrieved their horses from the stables. It was a short time later when the group of men arrived at the first farm that had been sacked. The house was on fire. Arthur rode into the unkempt yard and dismounted, followed closely by Gawain. Walking around to the back of the house, the two men found the remains of the farmer and his family. The man had been cut down by a volley of arrows while his sons had been slaughtered by apparent spear and sword attacks. When they found the farmer's wife, she had been assaulted and left for dead. One of Arthur's vassals walked up behind him.

Arthur looked at the man, concern in his eyes. "Did the man have any other sons or daughters?"

"Yes, sire. He has two daughters, both of age and betrothed."

Arthur turned to look at Gawain, and the younger man nodded, answering the unasked questions, "Yes, milord. We shall hunt down the damned invaders and send them to their reward."

A chorus of agreement sounded from the men on horseback. Arthur and Gawain trotted over to their horses and mounted their waiting steeds. One of Arthur's vassals led the war party outward, riding to catch the invading Gael raiding party.

As the sun crested the sky in midday, the war band saw a rising plume of smoke over the next rise. Arthur spurred his horse on, Gawain and the others quickly caught up to the king.

As the farm came into view, Gawain counted about thirty or forty invaders. They were sacking the farm, taking everything of value to put in the back of their two wagons. A handful of the Gaels were in the middle of slaughtering a man, while two others dragged a woman away from the house and toward the wagons.

Arthur let out a war cry and spurred his stallion to a fast gallop. Gawain drew his sword, let out a war cry of his own, and spurred his own warhorse forward, his own band of warriors following closely.

The invaders realized that they were under attack, raising the alarm around the property. Archers quickly raced to the road, drawing their bows and nocking arrows, the bowmen released a volley of arrows, one of which struck a member of the party. Arthur's warrior cried out and fell from his saddle, landing on his wounded arm.

Arthur drew his sword and pointed it at the bowmen, continuing his war cry, he galloped up on the archers, bearing down at a frantic pace. As he passed the clump of archers, he swung his mighty blade, cleaving into the chest of one of them, and throwing that unfortunate man backwards into two of his fellow raiders.

Gawain and Lancelot both rode through the archers, each of them raining destruction on the invaders. Gawain and Lancelot dismounted, stepping up to flank Arthur. The king had a two-handed grip on his sword, and Gawain saw the fabled blade for the first time. It looked like a normal two-handed long sword, although the stories about its power and magick were legendary.

The king stood firm and called out the leader of the band of invaders. As the Gaels took up their arms and spread out, Gawain heard and felt the rest of the war party dismount and approach behind the three leaders. The ringing of steel echoed around them as both parties drew blades and shields.

The leader of the raiders stepped forward, dressed in the leathers and skins of the barbarians. He raised his warhammer and beat it on his shield. His Gaelic dialect was difficult to make out, but he seemed to be challenging Arthur's reign and kingdom.

Arthur raised his sword and answered in the Gaelic tongue. At his answer, the barbarian raiders attacked en masse. Suddenly, Gawain and Lancelot were fighting for their lives and trying to keep Arthur safe as he fought through the horde.

Outnumbered nearly two-to-one, the war party fought the raiding Gaels with ferocity. Gawain swung his sword time and again, slashing his opponents, driving them back from the king. On the other side, Lancelot was doing the same.

Gawain raised his shield to take an axe blow that rattled his arm. He responded with a slash that struck the forearm of his attacker. His following thrust put the tip of his sword through the Gael's chest, sending the sharp steel into the heart. A gout of blood arced out as Gawain yanked his sword free, and the corpse fell to the ground, only to be replaced by another barbarian.

This barbarian wielded two axes, striking at Gawain in a near constant reign of blows. The young man was forced to use his shield and sword in a purely defensive manner, unable to get a moment to strike back. After what seemed like an eternity, the Gael slipped, stumbling over one of his fallen comrades. Gawain seized that moment and struck.

Pushing aside both axes with his shield, a backhand slash with Gawain's sword sliced open the barbarian's leather armor and across his stomach. The man cried out in pain and clutched at his abdomen to try to keep his intestines inside his body. Gawain's reverse and strike was aimed higher, cleaving through the Gael's neck, and removing the man's head.

Gawain turned his attention to Arthur. The king was standing over the Gael leader's body, surrounded by other raider bodies. Lancelot stood next to Arthur, his sword and shield dripping blood and gore. His longtime friend smiled,

"Still alive, old friend?"

Gawain couldn't help but smile, "Aye. And is your worthless carcass still whole?"

Even Arthur guffawed. Lancelot nodded, "Aye, Gawain. Your majesty? What about you?" Lancelot turned to Arthur.

'Aye lad. I am whole enough that Guinevere won't complain.

Thank you both for your service. Let us make our way back to Camelot, where we may mourn our dead and celebrate our victory."

Arthur, Gawain, and Lancelot helped free the women who were held captive in the wagons, along with the spoils from the raids. Those survivors who had a home or family to go home to, were escorted back to their farm or house. Those whose entire family had been killed were taken back to Camelot, where they were offered a position in the manor, or as a worker in a shop or inn. Similarly, any property that could be returned, was returned. What couldn't was given to the women who needed it.

That night, the manor feasted. Arthur celebrated repelling another Gael raiding party, and a new treaty with one of the feudal lords to the north. Gawain celebrated the new treaty, as well as a formal betrothal to Arthur's daughter Lissa. Lancelot celebrated that he would have a warm bed that night.

The following day, Arthur called Gawain and Lancelot before him. Standing, the king spoke, "Yesterday, you and your men rode with me to defend my kingdom from Gael raiders. In doing so you earned the gratitude of this throne and my people. Gawain and Lancelot, not only did you help defend my kingdom from the raiders, but you personally chose to risk your lives to protect mine. You fought with great courage and skill, defending me and defeating my enemies. It is apparent that we will need such defenders in the times ahead as the Gaels and the Celts get bolder."

Arthur drew his sword, "Lancelot du Lac, step forward and kneel." When Lancelot had done so, Arthur continued, "Lancelot du Lac, in service to my kingdom, you have shown great courage and skill. I knight you Sir Lancelot, Defender of my Realm." Arthur touched the flat of Excalibur to both of Lancelot's shoulders and continued, "Arise, Sir Lancelot. Knight of Camelot."

Arthur turned to Gawain, "Gawain, step forward and kneel." The young man did as asked. "Gawain, son of Lot, in service to my kingdom you, too, have shown great courage and skill. I knight you, Sir Gawain, Defender of my Realm." Arthur touched the flat of his blade to both of the man's shoulders. "Arise, Sir Gawain. Knight of Camelot."

18

USURPER

The Warehouse

"I served Arthur Pendragon for years after that." James Smith, the Director of Section 28, was speaking to his top administrative and direct action staff. "In fact, Lancelot and I were merely the first of his Knights to be honored and recruited. We served with King Arthur gladly. As the husband of his eldest daughter, I was naturally close to Arthur, and Lancelot was my best friend."

Ghost spoke up, "When did you pick up Excalibur?"

"It was after the Battle of Camlann." Smith answered Ghost. "Arthur had led a war party to attack Emperor Lucius in Europe. I and most of the Knights had ridden with him and his army. As the campaign was nearing the end, Arthur received word that Mordred had usurped his throne. Furious, Arthur and I gathered a part of the army, left a few of the knights in charge to mop up few remaining skirmishes, and rode back to the kingdom to reclaim the throne." Smith paused, staring at the empty table in front of him.

The Director looked up, "One thing the legends got correctly," Smith continued, "Mordred convinced Guinevere that her husband had died and willed the kingdom to him. After all, Mordred was the King's nephew, so it was natural for him to inherit the throne. It was all a lie, of course, but the lady believed it, and Lancelot was there to provide comfort to the grieving widow.

"When the King found out about Guinevere, it was too late for him to do anything. Arthur never forgave Lancelot or Guinevere for their betrayal. He took that pain of betrayal and turned it against Mordred. His loyal vassals, and myself, rode against the usurper and his army. We met his army at Camlann."

THE COLD MISTS clung to the ground in the valleys and fields in the early English morning. The bank of the River Allen was steep and unforgiving near the junction with the River Firth. The sky was gray and overcast, as was normal for the time of year. Battle had been raging for three days, and casualties were mounting on both sides. Gawain had stayed faithfully by his liege's side as the king had fought the army raised by Mordred. The veteran knight believed that today would end the battle

Sir Gawain fought valiantly, killing anyone who stood against him. He had just dispatched another spearman when he looked up to see the battle between Arthur and Mordred. Gawain shrugged off another glancing blow from a short sword, turning to ram the blade of his sword through the gut of his opponent. He twisted the blade, then gave a mighty yank, splitting the skin further and fountaining a great jet of blood out of the wound. As he looked up again, he saw the duel of Mordred and Arthur as it was coming to a close.

Arthur was clearly beating his foe, driving him back toward the riverbank. Mordred appeared to panic and desperately waving his sword in his defense, and Gawain knew the man was tiring quickly. As Gawain made his way that direction, he was accosted by yet another of Mordred's soldiers. Trading blows with the man was slowing Gawain down, so he swung his shield at the soldier's head, making the man miss his attack and throwing him off balance. A driving slash and a backhand thrust finished Mordred's soldier. Ignoring the gravely wounded warrior, Sir Gawain stepped over the dying man and continued to his king.

Mordred appeared to get desperate, and Gawain saw the look before the man made his move. Mordred stepped back twice and kicked a pile of leaves and sticks at Arthur, blinding the monarch temporarily. Mordred closed for the kill, moving swiftly to thrust his sword directly through the rib cage of King Arthur.

Gawain cried out as he watched his King fall to his knees on the battlefield, the famous Excalibur falling from the monarch's suddenly nerveless hands. Mordred paused to stare at Gawain, who was running at the usurper. Mordred was barely able to shake off his confusion from the suddenness of the attack just in time to raise his blade defensively.

Gawain slashed and struck, trying to penetrate his target's defenses. It seemed like an eternity, but Gawain could tell that Mordred was growing fatigued, but the knight's anger at his king's slaughter drove Gawain to attack with a ferocity he had never felt. Blow after blow and strike upon strike rained down on Mordred, who desperately tried to defend them all.

The outcome was certain, and Gawain was relentless. More slashes and thrusts slipped through Mordred's defense, causing bleeding wounds on his hand, arms, abdomen, and cheek. Gawain again saw the look in the usurper's eyes, and the knight moved quickly, stepping to the side and ramming his sword through Mordred's side, through both lungs, and out the other side of the ribcage.

Mordred stiffened, momentarily spitted as if for a feast. He waved his hands around in a complex spell, but Gawain saw the move coming and pulled the sword from his side. The knight coldly swung his sword one more time, and Mordred's head tilted back too far for normal anatomy. The usurper's throat had been cut from ear to ear.

Gawain ran to his king's side as the monarch was giving his last breaths. Kneeling to grasp his hand, Gawain looked at the wound on Arthur. Seeing it was a deep one, he calmed the king down as best as he was able, knowing this wound would be fatal.

Arthur took Gawain's hand and mumbled through the blood, "Lad, the throne is yours. Take Excalibur. It will serve you well." Gawain could understand no more as the coughing and choking cut off any coherent words. King Arthur died mere seconds later.

As the last skirmishes raged on around him, Gawain sat, numb, while he realized that the monarch he had served for these years was dead. Gawain reached out for Arthur's fallen sword. When his hands touched the hilt, it gave a slight spark. Shocked, Gawain pulled his hand back. The knight reached out again, and this time grasped the hilt and raised it off the ground in one motion. The shock was not nearly as bad as the first one.

All around Gawain, the sounds of the battle faded away. Time seemed to halt, and the landscape around the knight seemed to take an ethereal quality. Gawain saw the surrounding battle in all of its terrible glory. The soldiers next to him were frozen in a violent tableau, with Arthur's soldier unsuccessfully defending against a violent slash from the usurper's soldier, the spray of arterial blood frozen in the air. On the other side of Gawain, a pair of Arthur's footmen had bracketed one of Mordred's soldiers and were attacking him from different sides. The man was not able to defend himself and the frozen sprays of blood were evidence of his failure.

Gawain looked down at his slain monarch and saw that Arthur's face was glowing. As he watched, the glow dissipated, leaving the kings face slowly. Arthur was less vibrant, less ethereal than the rest of the world around the knight. Curiously, Gawain noted that other bodies on the battlefield were also less vibrant than the living soldiers around him.

As he was pondering this strange reality, the knight felt a deep presence around him. Surrounding him. Judging him? Gawain looked around to determine who was around him. He felt more than heard a word in his mind, and it startled him. *Worthy.*

Suddenly, the cacophony and din of battle returned with a rush, almost deafening the knight. The world lost the ethereal vibrance, and life once again moved. The king's soldier on his right fell on the field, clutching the deep slash across his throat. On Gawain's left, Mordred's vassal met a similar fate as the blows from Arthur's soldiers landed.

It was a few minutes later that the battle ended. Arthur's army had routed the enemy, and those who were left of the usurper's forces wisely began to lay down their arms in surrender. The knight who had been by Arthur's side walked among the celebrating soldiers carrying Excalibur in his hand. Gawain found his fellow knights among the battle and summoned them all to the site of their fallen monarch. There they arranged for a wagon to be brought so they could return the king to his manor in Camelot.

The soldiers from Mordred's army were questioned, and the vast majority had believed the word of Mordred, that Arthur was slain in battle, and that the kingdom was given to the usurper. They had been told that another kingdom was invading, and they were simply defending their nation from invaders. Gawain and the knights believed most of them. The few who were lying were summarily executed. The rest were released with a summons to report to Camelot for duty in the true king's army.

The sight of Gawain carrying Arthur's Excalibur was either a terrifying sight or a welcome sight, depending on who you fought for in the recent battle. Only after walking the field several times did one of the other knights approach Gawain.

"Sir Gawain, might I suggest that you find a sheath for that terrible blade? 'Tis causing a stir among the men, and your aura is frightening."

Gawain looked down at the mythic blade in his hands. Nodding to the knight, Gawain retrieved the scabbard for Excalibur and belted it to his waist. Sliding the mythic blade home, he inquired about the wounded from the battle, and about the disposal of the dead. When told of the progress, he recommended a few changes, and then waited for his orders to be carried out.

It was approaching midday when the battle had been cleared and all the wounded had been attended. Knowing Camelot was at least half a day's ride, he formed his fellow knights into an honor guard and the army began a long procession home to Camelot's walls.

The sun was slowly disappearing from the sky as the procession made its way to the gates of Camelot. There at the gates, the procession was met by Lady Guinevere and Sir Lancelot. Her horrified expression at seeing Gawain turned to wailing when she realized that her former king's body was in the wagon. The Lady turned and buried her head in Lancelot's shoulder, then, realizing what she had done, Guinevere recoiled and ran back to the manor.

Lancelot stepped forward in greeting, but a glare from Gawain quickly stopped him. As they passed, Gawain muttered, "We will talk later, brother." Lancelot nodded and walked back to the manor house, looking for comfort of his own.

It was dark and somber in Camelot that evening. Even the moon seemed to find a reason to hide in the sky. Once the rest of the knights were fed and had retired to their rooms in the manor, Lancelot sought out his friend Gawain. He found him in the great hall, sitting by a low fire with a mug of ale in his hand.

"Sir Gawain. Is this a time to speak?"

Gawain turned to see his once-best friend humbly waiting a respectful distance away. With a weary nod, Gawain spoke, "Come, brother. Sit with me as we muse about the past and the future."

Lancelot walked over and took a seat next to Gawain, who had turned to stare into the fire. After a time of silence that seemed to stretch for days, the penitent knight started "It is good to see you alive, brother. When Mordred spoke of Arthur's death, I believed you were slain as well."

"It would have been better had the rumors been truth, instead of the usurpation of the king's throne. I don't know what hurt him more, the treason of Mordred, or the treachery of you and the

Lady." Gawain turned from the fire to stare into Lancelot's eyes. "He was wrathful toward Mordred for his foul treason, but the Lady's treachery broke his heart. And your treachery broke his spirit. I wasn't sure if he would even fight for his throne again."

Lancelot shook with remorse. "I was there when the messenger delivered the news to Lady Guinevere. The cur must have been bought by Mordred. There was no other way to know."

The silence grew thick and heavy. Lancelot once again broke the stillness, "And what of Mordred?"

"Dead by my hand. He tricked Arthur during combat, and it was the usurper who slew the King. I then attacked and slew the usurper. I wish I had been able to leave him alive to reap the discord he sowed, but the man fought viciously, and I was forced to finish him. I left the body to rot and be picked clean by the crows. I reckoned that was fitting for a traitorous usurper."

"Is that when you picked up that?" Lancelot pointed at the sword now attached to Gawain's hip.

Gawain glanced down at Excalibur. He looked back at Lancelot, "I picked the sword up after Arthur was slain. There is strange and powerful magick in this sword."

"What now, Sir Gawain. Will you take the throne as yours?"

Gawain shook his head, "Nay. I must travel to my father's kingdom and inform him of my brother's death. Mordred was evil, but he was family. Will you?"

Lancelot shook his head, "The knights would never accept me. The subjects would never trust me, and I would never trust my vassals. So we leave it to the Round Table?"

Gawain nodded. "I shall announce my intentions tomorrow when the knights are assembled."

That next morning, the knights broke fast together. Gathering as the court at the famous round table, the knights were all present, except for three who were finishing up the battle of Emperor Lucius. When the knights had settled, Gawain stood.

"My fellow knights. This land needs a new king. One that will continue to bring glory to Camelot, and mercy to his subjects. As any progeny that Arthur had are dead, his line dies with him. Therefore, it is up to his court to find the new ruler of Camelot."

"What say you, Sir Gawain?" a knight raised his voice. "He wanted you to inherit the throne. You were the chosen successor."

"Nay, Sir Durnure. It is with a heavy heart that I must depart for my father's kingdom to the north. As bequeathed to me, I will be taking *Kaledvoulc'h* with me, but I will not accept the throne of Camelot."

At that moment, Lancelot entered the room. Hisses and catcalls erupted from the knights who had been with Arthur for the campaign. The couple that had remained in Camelot remained silent, knowing that they, too could be the target of the court's ire.

Lancelot raised his hands, and finally Gawain had to bang his hand on the table to get everyone to get quiet. Gawain stood again, "Brothers. There are several among us who have caused pain to Arthur, and to this land. The only way to heal this land will be to move forward. I have spoken with Sir Lancelot and am convinced of his sincerity. It is my honor, as Sir Gawain, that I recommend that Lancelot be allowed to serve the new king, whomever that is."

There were a lot of murmurs around the table, but the mood gradually lightened, and Lancelot sat in his appointed seat, to the left of where Arthur sat. The discussion went on for days.

"DOES EXCALIBUR HAVE a dragon in it, like *fion-fhuil?*" Spooky was curious now, and had even stopped typing on his keyboard.

"No, Mister Smith. As near as I can tell, the Lady of the Lake was a water sprite or elemental. As such, it is just an artifact without intelligence. The only time I've heard from it was when it called me 'Worthy' and let me keep it." Director Smith looked around the table.

"What does it do?" This time Ghost spoke. "I mean, anything other than being a really good sword?"

Smith looked thoughtful, "I just do not know, Mister Vanhof. I believe it is a pretty powerful artifact, but I've never really taken the time to test its capabilities. I am honestly a little afraid of what would happen if I started using the sword more."

It was Agent Mulder's turn to speak up, "I'm supposed to believe that you are some original Knight of the Round Table from the medieval times, that you knew King Arthur, and that you gave up the throne of England voluntarily? Seriously, every time I think I've hit the ultimate crazy, you say you're from the 1300's or something."

Doc started laughing. Agent Mulder looked at the combat priest, "What's so funny?"

"I'm sorry." Doc was able to get her laughter under control, "The Director is not claiming to be from the 1300's. Arthur died in 537 AD. So he has to be older than that." Mulder crossed her arms.

Ghost spoke up, "I'm going to assume that you are Sir Gawain, whom I recall is often called the 'Perfect Knight' or the 'Knight's Knight' because of his strict adherence to the chivalric code. Hell, I saw Excalibur, so I know at least that part is real. But that doesn't answer why you've been around for so many centuries. According to the myths, you were just a human being with a bit of royal blood in you."

Smith nodded. "I did not realize it at the time, but my immortality was written and formed long before I ever met King Arthur."

19

SACRIFICE

The old crone in the hut looked out her open doorway and saw the rider reign their horse. The older woman wore a simple cotton coat over a layered spun-fabric dress, her white, stringy hair hanging to the middle of her back. She had lived in this hut her entire life, and her mother before her. Even through the covered face and dark robes, the crone knew who was visiting her that afternoon.

The woman on horseback dismounted and walked to the open door. "Oracle?"

The crone cackled and nodded, "Yes, milady. What makes you seek the Oracle of Traprain Law?"

The woman in dark robes and scarves that covered her head looked around the small house's yard very cautiously. After making sure there were no other visitors to the Oracle that afternoon, and that no one was watching from the trees, the woman pulled back her scarf, revealing a beautiful young woman with dark hair and porcelain skin. She looked at the old oracle, "I need a reading, about my eldest son."

The oracle motioned the young woman inside her hovel and into an empty chair set before a small rough table. The older woman sat as well, easing down into her seat. She picked up the pile of scattered bones in front of her. The oracle chanted, and then dropped the bones into a metal pan, watching them scatter. With a practiced eye, the old woman read the signs and portents shown in the bones.

Gasping, she looked up at the woman across from her. "Death awaits your eldest son. He is fated to die young, with no children to carry the name."

The young woman cried out, placing her hand over her mouth. "Can I stop the fates? How do I protect him?"

"There is no protection from this fate without sacrifice. You will have to find a witch to protect your son." The old crone shook her head, making a sign to ward away the evil spirits. "I can do nothing else for you."

"MY MOTHER, Morgause, wife of Lot, King of Guotodin, told me the story of this encounter." Director Smith looked around the table. "She wanted me to know why I would have to participate in the ritual she found."

Doc looked at him, "What ritual can extend the life of a human without making a deal for the eternal soul?"

Smith shook his head, "As it turns out, it is always a deal for the soul. I remember the ritual, well"

MORGAN LE FAY stood before her half-sister and laughed. "You want me to do what for your heir?"

"Help me make the bargain that will save him." Morgause spoke calmly and slowly. "I know you have congress with dark forces. I wish to bargain for my son's safety."

"Why that one? You have others—both from your husband and my brother. Why is that one special?"

Morgause thought for a moment, "Sister, I implore you. Help me find the bargain to protect him."

The enchantress known as Morgan le Fay gave a cruel and thin-lipped smile to her half-sister. "I will do it. But you do not know of what you ask. Bring the boy with you tonight, at midnight, to the clearing in the trees north of town. Remember, you begged this of me."

Later that night, two horses wound their way through the trees and into the darkened clearing. Morgause dismounted, and motioned for her son, a strapping lad of about twelve, to do the same. She looked at him, "Gawain, this is for you tonight. The enchantress will perform the ritual."

Across the clearing, Morgan le Fay walked out from between the trees with a wrapped bundle in her hands and a wineskin or water skin slung over her arm. She motioned the two forward and met them in the middle of the clearing. Seeing the small stone altar in the middle, Morgause could not help but shudder at the thought of what the witch does in her time in this clearing. Morgan placed the bundle on the altar. As the witch unwrapped the black silk surrounding the items, Gawain thought he saw the bushes near the tree line move.

The boy turned to look, but found nothing in view. Thinking it was a small animal, the lad turned his attention back to the altar in front of him. Morgan le Fay had unwrapped a delicate silver chalice marked with runes inlaid all around the rim. In the bundle was also a large knife that seemed to be made out of a very large tooth, possibly a dragon's tooth.

The witch looked at her sister and said, "Are you sure you want to do this? You know who has struck this bargain."

Morgause looked at her son, then back at the enchantress. "I understand and am willing to accept that bargain in exchange for his safety in the future."

The witch nodded and grabbed the neck of the skin. She removed the cap and poured the dark contents of the container into the waiting silver chalice. Morgan was muttering under her breath as she poured. The liquid approached the rim of the chalice and the witch stopped pouring. She placed the stopper back into the neck of the container and laid it on the ground. Her murmuring rose in volume, but Gawain could not make out what the words said.

As the boy and his mother watched, the enchantress waved her hands over the chalice and the knife in slow, complex patterns. The chalice and the knife glowed a faint reddish glow, and the runes along the chalice rim illuminated with a brighter red glow. Gawain could see matching runes appear in red on the handle and blade of the knife and felt terror creep down deep inside of him.

Morgan le Fay reached out and picked up the knife by the handle, dipped it in the liquid in the chalice, and looked at her sister. "Hold out your hand, my sister."

Morgause looked at the boy, then looked at the witch as she held out her hand, palm facing the darkened sky. The enchantress slowly reached out and dragged the tip of the knife along the open palm of the young queen. Gawain saw a thin red line appear on his mother's hand as she winced, but did not move.

Morgan le Fay pulled the knife back and slowly dipped it in the silver cup. The runes on the knife and the cup both lit with an even brighter light, and the red glow eerily lit the surrounding clearing. Gawain's eyes widened in surprise at the power that was flowing around him. Morgan le Fay slowly picked up the cup and lifted it skyward for a few seconds, never stopping her murmuring. She then gave the chalice to Gawain.

As Gawain took the chalice, his hands tingled with the magick that was enveloping the cup. Morgan le Fay said, "Drink this. You must consume it now, before the spell fades."

Gawain sniffed at the cup, it had an acrid, coppery smell, with a touch of sulfur. "What is it?"

"Drink boy." The witch's eyes grew cold and narrow. "This is all for you, lad. Drink the cup."

Gawain looked at the foul smelling liquid and lifted the chalice to his lips. He took a large drink from the cup and almost spit it out. It was blood, but a blood that had a lot of sulfur in it. Seeing his mother's face, he continued to drink. His stomach rolled and it took all his willpower to avoid throwing the blood back up onto the clearing floor. Soon, he was finished with the drink, and handed the now empty chalice back to the witch.

Morgan le Fay smiled at her sister. "It is done. Well and truly bargained." The witch handed the strange looking knife to Morgause. "This is the only weapon that will permanently harm or maim your son. Guard it well."

Morgause and Gawain walked back toward their horses, leaving the enchantress to clean up her altar. Once the boy and his mother had mounted, they rode back through the woods to the town. After putting their horses away, the boy and his mother parted, each to their separate rooms. As the young lad entered his room, he looked around, trying to find a safe place to keep the strange looking dagger. As a temporary measure, he wrapped the oddity in a rabbit fur and stuffed it into his chest of furs. He knew he would have to find a better hiding place on the morrow, but his bed was loudly calling his name.

"DID IT WORK?"

Smith was startled out of his retelling. He looked at Six, "I beg your pardon. What did you say?"

"Did it work? Did it actually protect you from grave danger?" Six looked interested.

"Yes, unfortunately. There is always a price when you bargain with the devil." Smith again gazed at the table. "Literally, in this case."

IT WAS a Christmas feast in Camelot and Gawain and Lancelot were attending the festivities. The king, his family, and the knights were gathered in the great hall for the celebration. The warmth of the fires and the warmth from the ale had everyone in a celebratory mood.

In the middle of the feast, a dark swirling mass of inky blackness appeared next to one of the fires. Backing up rapidly, Arthur called for his guards while the knights drew their swords. As the guards rushed into the room, a green creature stepped through the blackness, and the gateway rapidly collapsed on itself.

The figure stood over seven feet tall, dressed in leathers and a mail hauberk. All of his clothes, his leathers, and his mail were varying shades of green, from deep emerald to light green. Underneath his spangenhelm, and through the gaps where the clothing or armor showed skin, it appeared the creature was naturally colored green. In his right hand, the knight held a massive battle axe as if it weighed nothing. In his left, the giant held a bough of holly, signifying peace during the season.

King Arthur stood and drew Excalibur, while Sir Gawain and Sir Lancelot both drew their own swords, flanking their monarch as was their custom. Arthur spoke, "What knave is this that interrupts our feast?"

The large creature bellowed his laughter, "I am the Green Knight, and I was delivered here to challenge you, King Arthur, and your court. Will you accept my challenge?"

Gawain put a hand on his liege's arm, and answered for his king, "Pray tell. What is your challenge, Sir Knight?"

"My challenge is simple. Blow for blow. You may use my axe to take one undefended blow against me tonight." The Green Knight talked over the rising murmurs. "In one year and one day, the man will meet me at the Green Chapel and receive the same blow from me."

Gawain turned to his king, "Your majesty, Let me accept this challenge in your stead. I do not know what his game is, but I will offer a blow he can never return."

Arthur nodded and Gawain stepped forward, "I accept your challenge, Sir Knight. I am Sir Gawain, son of Lot."

The huge knight nodded solemnly. "I have heard of your bravery, Sir Gawain. I accept you in the stead of King Arthur." The green creature handed the heavy axe to Gawain.

The big knight bent forward and bared his neck to Gawain. Looking at his monarch, he saw Arthur give a small nod, and Gawain hefted the battle axe. Rearing back, he put all of his strength and power into the blow, aiming straight for the creature's exposed neck.

The razor-sharp axe sheared clean through the creature's neck, sweeping down and burying itself into the floor before Gawain could stop its momentum. The massive head dropped to the floor and rolled until it landed with its face looking at Gawain.

The eyes on the severed head opened wide, the mouth grinned, and the knight's massive hand reached over and picked up the severed head. The Green Knight set his own head back on top of his shoulders, and there was a momentary flash that blinded those present. When Gawain could see again, he noticed that the creature's neck was seamless, and the big knight was looking at him.

"I will see you in exactly one year and a day, Sir Gawain," the Green Knight rumbled. It yanked the embedded battle axe out of the floor, turned and walked out of the manor. It disappeared before it reached the city gates.

Gawain looked at a stunned King Arthur. The great hall was eerily silent, aside from the odd squeak of leathers or the rustle of clothing. It was an hour before the assembled court was once again raucous. Gawain never regained his high spirits that night. His worry for the future was all too specific.

DIRECTOR SMITH LOOKED around the conference room. "That next year was one of dread and terror. As the appointed time of my pilgrimage grew closer, I grew more despondent. Until eventually, it was my time to make the pilgrimage to the Green Chapel."

"Why did you go?" Agent Mulder asked what most around the table were thinking. "What was he going to do? Track you down? Screw that. You're still here. You must've run."

Smith looked indignant. "No. I made that pilgrimage willingly. It was my honor as a knight that was at stake. The only authority in knighthood is found in honor. If you have no honor, you are not a knight. My honor demanded that I go—even if it was to my certain doom."

SIR GAWAIN HAD ONLY TAKEN one of his retainers for the trip to the Green Chapel. It was a long journey, and they finally arrived outside the stronghold of Sir Bercilak de Hautedesert, a nobleman whose estate held the Green Chapel. They were welcomed for the night, and their host treated them lavishly.

Later that night, the door to Gawain's room was opened slowly. It creaked loud enough to wake the room's sole occupant, and the knight sat up in bed. "Who is there?"

Sir Gawain heard a soft, sultry voice whisper back, "It is I, Lady Bercilak. I have come to warm your bed, Sir Gawain. After all, this may be your last night on this plane."

Gawain could see the shapely outline of the Lady of the manor, and though tempted, sent her away, "Aye. Might be my last day in this mortal body, but my soul is eternal. I care more for the eternal than any temporal pleasure."

The Lady stormed out of the bedroom, shutting his door with force. Gawain shook his head, frowned, and tried to go back to sleep. The next morning, the Lady acted as if nothing had happened the prior night, and Gawain was happy to let the charade continue. That night was the Christmas feast. The man of the castle, his court, and Gawain all enjoyed the food and ale that was specially prepared for this feast. Gawain seemed to eat and drink as if it was his final night among the living.

The following morning, a disgruntled and hurting Gawain woke to break fast with his hosts. It was just before midday when Gawain put his armor on, had the stable ready his horse, and left for the short ride out of town to the Green Chapel.

Arriving at the small chapel with a vivid green roof, Gawain dismounted. He walked all around the structure before entering. Discovering no other people or creatures waiting in ambush, the knight pushed through the massive oak doors and into the chapel. Inside was the typical arrangement. The chairs and benches in the small cubicle-like boxes were arranged in order of donation to the church. The cleared floor where the commoners stood or sat was kept clean and debris-free. Standing near the podium was the massive Green Knight. This time, the knave was only holding the battle axe—no holly.

His voice bellowed, "Sir Gawain. It is good to see that your honor is intact."

Gawain answered, "Aye, Sir Knight. I am here as promised. Where would you like me to stand?"

The Green Knight pointed to a spot in the middle of the commoner floor and Gawain walked slowly, calmly over to it. When he received the nod from the Green Knight, Gawain removed his spangenhelm and hauberk, leaving his head and neck fully exposed. The Knight of the round Table then bent over at the waist, imitating the Green Knight just over a year ago.

The creature wasted no time. He stepped forward and swung downward, Gawain felt the blade bite into his neck for a brief moment, and then everything went black.

20

SUMMONED

The Warehouse

"I woke up three days later." Smith was looking at his stunned audience.

Spooky chimed in, "But the legends say the Green Knight only gave you, er, Sir Gawain a slight nick on the neck after a couple feints. Nowhere does it talk about actually beheading Sir Gawain."

Smith smiled at his electronics specialist. "In this, the legends are wrong. I awoke on the chapel floor, with the Green Knight patiently standing above me. I was later told that the Green Knight had indeed chopped off my head. He apparently treated my head just like his—he simply stuck it back on my neck. Three days. That was how long it took to wake up that first time. It took less time over the centuries."

Ghost looked like he was going to ask a question, but Smith held up a hand to stall him. "Yes, Mister Vanhof, I have died many times over the centuries. Sometimes by accident, but it was often a mechanism I used to find a new life when my current one got a bit long in the tooth."

"I give up." A very distressed Agent Mulder put her head in her hands, shaking her head. "Dragons and pixies and trolls are real. Sure. DHS hired vampires to hunt monsters. Okay. The Director of the DHS division not only is a Knight of the Round Table, but he's immortal, and he carries Excalibur." She looked up, directly at Smith, "I think my mind is officially broken."

Smith gave a sympathetic smile, "I don't believe it is broken, Tressa. That you are coherent and working with us says more about your resiliency than you realize. You might make a good Section Twenty-Eight agent yet."

"What was the cost, Director?" Doc spoke softly and was barely heard over the background noises. "Every bargain with the devil has a cost. What did Morgan le Fay bargain with?"

Smith grew somber. "You are correct Doctor Sorenson. Unfortunately, every bargain with the devil has a price, and my mother paid the bill. The binding with the dagger bound my mortality to another person, my mother. Lady Morgause was the price for saving my life and cursing me to an eternal life.

"When I found out about her strange death by beheading, I hunted down Morgan le Fay and confronted her about the terrible bargain. I vowed to live my life according to the chivalric code as a true Knight of the Round Table would. That was my penance for the bargain. I would oppose the devil, and any other evil that roamed the Earth, and make him regret leaving me alive."

"So why retrieve this bust, boss?" Six tired easily of any briefing where he considered the information he received to be unimportant. He wanted to bring it back to the present.

Smith looked at the former mercenary, picked up the relatively fragile statue and slammed it on the solid tabletop. The terra cotta bust shattered into thousands of small shards, revealing a bundle of leather-wrapped cloth laying amidst the pieces. Smith picked up the small piece of cloth and examined the cloth and the leather thong that bound it. He looked at the vampire mercenary, "This is the reason, Mister Black. This is one of the two keys needed to unlock Pandora's Box." He then tucked the key into an inner pocket in his suit jacket.

"So where's the other one?"

Smith thought for a moment, then nodded, as if deciding. "It's in a town called Mansfield, Ohio. I buried it in a very safe and secure place, although that may be your next mission."

Ghost spoke up again, the tall monster hunter remembering something that the Seelie Queen had told him after their last mission. "Boss, Queen Lishe ta Merunaré mentioned something about you and the Black Plague in England. Was that Pandora's box?"

Smith shook his head, "Not the first one. The first pandemic was her husband's handiwork. He was trying to rid the Earth of, as he put it, 'meddlesome mortals.' There was one instance I believe was actually the result of the artifact. And I'm afraid that I likely caused it."

LONDON WAS DIRTY. Sir Gawain could not get over how much dirt and filth and soot the city produced. The streets of seventeenth century London were cobblestone, and the cobbles in the poorer districts ran slick with water, animal dung, and slops emptied from windows. Due to the stench of the sewage in the streets and the smoke billowing from the factories, most people wore a handkerchief over their nose and mouth while they walked through town. Gawain had lived for over eleven hundred years, and he found that this city was the dirtiest he had experienced.

Gawain's informants told him of a rare artifact, a Grecian urn, that was for sale in a small antiquities shop. The knight suspected that this was more than a mere urn, and he hurried to reach the store before it closed. The store had a small sign hung over the door that read "Oddities, J. Sampsell, prop." Gawain walked through the front door, hearing a small ring as the chimes above the door sounded his entrance.

Inside, the store was cramped and cluttered. Rough shelving lined the walls, and a lower line of shelves ran down the center of the shop. Each shelf was filled with oddities and antiquities, from the mundane to the arcane. Gawain saw the proprietor of the store, an older man with clean, close-cropped hair and a leather apron over his clothes. The knight walked over to the man and introduced himself, "John Smythe, of Westminster. I was informed that you have an interesting item for sale."

The proprietor smiled and nodded. "Aye, milord. I have many interesting items, and they are all for sale."

Smythe smiled an open and honest smile, "Yes, 'tis true. I was looking for an urn, one of Greek origins. My wife has a fancy for the things."

The older man nodded and smiled. "I do have such an item." He walked over to the urn on a shelf. "It is a valuable item, with some antiquity from the Isle of Crete. The lid seems stuck fast." The proprietor picked up the urn and gently handed it to Smythe.

Looking carefully at the urn, Smythe realized that it was the artifact he wanted. "I believe the lady shall like it. And what price to satisfy her appetites?"

The proprietor saw that the man wanted the worthless urn. He gambled, "For an obvious gentleman such as yourself? Two pounds."

Smythe looked at the man and weighed his options. The price was outrageous for a simple urn, but the proprietor seemed to know that Smythe desired it. He could haggle over a few pence, but it would not matter. In the last eleven hundred years, Gawain had become a very wealthy man. "Fine. But only if you have a way to wrap it so it does not break on the way home."

The old man carefully wrapped the urn in several soft layers of cloth, then placed it in a box, with more cloth padding. Smythe pulled two guineas from his right suit pocket and dropped them on the countertop. The proprietor's eyes got wide as he saw the golden coins hit his counter. The golden guineas had only been in circulation for two years, and he was quick to snatch them off the counter. The old man bent to find a couple shillings for change and Smythe waved it away.

The old man was beside himself, "Thank you, milord. If you need anything else for the lady, just ask old Jeremy. Jeremy Sampsell. Purveyor of oddities."

Smythe nodded and waved as he left the shop, carrying his precious bundle. The knight climbed into his waiting hackney coach. Signaling to the driver, he closed the door, and the coach worked its way toward his manor. It took the coach almost an hour to work its way across the city.

Located near St. James Park, the knight's "family" home had been his for the last century. Once he was home, he dismissed his servants and entered his private sanctum. There Gawain carefully unwrapped the urn. The knight gazed at the beautiful urn for a long time. This was supposedly the terrible Pandora's Box. Sought for centuries by those who would destroy mankind, Sir Gawain had retrieved it first.

He carefully checked the lid to the urn. It seemed tight, which was a good sign. Gawain had tracked down the key that sealed the urn, and now he retrieved it from his desk. The knight known as Smythe also retrieved an ornate locked box from his desk drawer. Unlocking the box, he opened the lid and withdrew the dragon's fang dagger that Morgan le Fay handed him all those centuries ago. After his mother's death from the bargain with the devil, he had called it Knight's Bane.

Bracing himself, he picked up the "key" that unlocked the urn's magically sealed lid. It was a signet ring of heavy gold, with threads of silver and copper worked into an intricate pattern around the band. The flattened top bore a complex Celtic knot in a raised pattern across the flat surface. He placed the raised pattern against the lid of the urn, and there was a small burst of static energy, accompanied by a small green flash. The urn was unlocked.

Gawain hefted Knight's Bane and held it near the lid of the urn. Carefully, and quickly, the knight pulled the lid off of the urn. Before he could do anything, a puff of black smoke drifted up from the mouth of the urn. Quickly thrusting Knight's Bane into the open mouth of the urn, he let go and slammed the lid shut. Placing the ring back into contact with the lid of the urn, Gawain gave a push with a little bit of his willpower and there was another green flash as the lid resealed itself. The knight picked up a towel and wiped the sweat from his face. *Job done, and nothing escaped but a little smoke.*

"IT WAS three days later that people started contracting the Black Death. The bubonic plague swept through London again for over a year." Smith was talking in a flat monotone, staring at the table in front of him. "Eventually, I realized that the urn had used my actions to bring death back to London. I did everything I could to help. I was immune, so I was able to help people who were sick, and to take care of the bodies of those who succumbed to the terrible disease. It was the Great Fire of London in September of 1666 that finally put an end to the plague. All because I was trying to hide a weakness."

"When did you add the second seal?" Ghost was taking notes.

"It was about twenty years after the plague. I realized that the artifact must never be opened again. I added a second seal to the original Celtic seal, and then I searched for years to find the perfect hiding place."

The table sat in silence for several long seconds, everyone trying to absorb what they had just been told. A beep from Spooky's laptop broke the silence, and he tapped a couple keys and then gasped.

"Shit, boss. We are royally screwed."

"What happened, Mister Smith?"

Spooky was pointing at his screen. "Looks like the President just threw us under the bus. Someone in the administration talked to the press about us. It's all over the major news networks. We're getting blamed for the dragon attacks." He flipped on the projector and the wall behind Smith lit up with news articles and websites.

The Director looked over the information, "Can you find out who leaked to the press, Mister Smith? I have my suspicions, but it would be good to have confirmation."

"According to CNN, the leaker was someone from the NSA. Looks like Anthony Barnhart's office." Spooky turned to look at his boss. "I thought he was on your debriefing panel earlier?"

Smith sighed. "Mister Barnhart is on the panel, but failed to show up. He sent his uncleared assistant instead. Miss Massey, make a note that Mister Nienhuis is ineligible for clearance." He turned back to the rest of the table, "Ok. What are the contingency plans? We need to move quickly."

SAC Mulder stood up, "I'm leaving right now. If I don't know your plans, I can't help them take you down."

Smith nodded, "Thank you, Tressa. I'll be in touch."

After the FBI agent was all the way out of the temporary shelter, Smith continued. "Contingency plans for the Warehouse, our wounded personnel, and our current active personnel. Thoughts?"

Six was the first to speak, "The wounded personnel in the hospital are not an issue. They are literally in the hospital and wounded during an attack. Even the FBI will not remove them until they are medically cleared."

Gretchen spoke up, "The Warehouse can be moved. It just needs sealed and then compressed. But where do we go?"

"The *Seanachaidh* have offered us sanctuary at their trial grounds." Ghost looked at his notes. "They have an unused storage building that would work as a temporary housing for the Warehouse until we can build a permanent one. Plus, they are warded and protected lands."

Smith nodded, "The Gray Court is an excellent option; set it up. Now about you who are still active..."

Spooky cut him off as the former NSA analyst highlighted something on the wall, "Sorry boss. We have no time to decide that. DHS has just issued subpoenas for interrogation. They are specifically for you and any currently active Section Twenty-Eight agents."

Smith stood. "Meeting adjourned. Mister Black, as of now you are seconded to Mister Vanhof's team. Knightmare, you are charged with escorting the Warehouse to the new site. Use ground transportation, I have a feeling our air transport is going to be pulled.

Finally, Miss Massey. seal and compress the Warehouse. Accompany Knightmare to the new site."

Gretchen looked at her boss, "And what about you?"

Smith's smile was frigid, "I'm going to show what happens when you mess with the only esoteric practitioners in America. This was a bad power move for Barnhart. I'm going to make him regret it."

The people assembled in the conference room scattered. Russell and Norbert left to tell their teams what was happening, and to prepare for the move. Their respective departments would ride out the move inside the compressed Warehouse, but it would take a little bit of preparation.

Six and Spooky ran across the destroyed complex toward the War Wagon. Six ran ahead to open the Wagon and prep the systems to start it while Spooky clambered up inside and activated his electronics. By the time that the big 9.3L diesel engine was roaring to life, the screens in Spooky's nest and along the dash were lit and processing data. Six put the big truck in gear and slowly drove over the rubble toward the temporary shelter.

Director Smith and Gretchen stopped outside the massive doors of the Warehouse. With Ghost and Doc standing behind them, the two slowly swung the doors closed. As Gretchen began to chant and wave her hands, Doc watched the runes along the door edges light up with an inner glow. Gretchen's chanting got more guttural, as it switched from Enochian to another language that neither Doc nor Ghost knew. Suddenly, Gretchen placed her hands on the closed and sealed doors, and the entire frame shrank.

In a couple minutes, the Warehouse entryway was approximately three feet tall and about a foot wide. Gretchen stopped, staggering for a moment as the energy and adrenaline faded. Ghost quickly supported her by the elbow until she could stand on her own.

As the veteran monster hunter reached down to pick up the much smaller Warehouse entrance, the radio crackled in his ear.

"Ghost, this is Spooky. We gotta move now. ETA for the DHS arrest team is twenty minutes. We need to be long gone."

"Copy that, Spooky. Be out in thirty seconds."

The monster hunter looked at the rest. "The arrest team is about twenty minutes out. We need to leave now. Six and Spooky are in the War Wagon. Are you sure you don't want leave with us, boss?"

Smith shook his head. "You get out of here. I'll deal with this. Call me when you figure out something."

The three agents ran to the waiting War Wagon, and the giant black MRAP was soon driving through neighborhoods and across town on surface, avoiding the highways and the waiting DHS contingent.

It was fifteen minutes later when a convoy of six black SUVs rocked to a halt in the parking lot around the FBI's command trailer. Twelve DHS agents dressed in fatigues and body armor and cradling submachine guns climbed out of the black trucks. They were followed by two men in dark suits, one of whom was holding a folder.

Smith stepped out of the Incident Command Trailer, his suit and tie perfectly straight. Agent Mulder followed on Smith's heels, stepping down the short steps to stand slightly behind Smith. The Director singled out the two bureaucrats immediately and waved.

"Mister Nienhuis. I figured that this was your doing. And Mister Barnhart, I thought you were smarter than this."

Barnhart stepped forward, waving the manilla folder like a talisman, "Agent Smith, I have a subpoena for your immediate appearance before an oversight committee. You and any of your active-duty agents are compelled to appear immediately. Where are they?"

"I honestly have no idea. Besides, it is my neck you want to chop. And I am ready to appear."

"Agent Mulder." Barnhart called out to the FBI SAC. "Where was the team meeting? I need to see this 'Warehouse.'"

The FBI agent pointed to the bright yellow temporary building. "I have two men who are stationed at the entrance who are under strict orders not to let anyone in. Let me clear them away first." She reached for the radio on her hip, and a few seconds later, the guards were ambling back toward the Mobile Command Unit.

Barnhart pointed to Nienhuis and motioned for him to check out the building. The assistant took six of the armed agents with him. He walked through the front doors, and then immediately came back out. He trotted over to an impatient Barnhart.

"It's empty, sir. There is literally nothing in there, sir."

Barnhart went red, "What do you mean that there is nothing there. That's where the Warehouse was located, right Mulder?" The FBI agent nodded. He turned on Smith, "Where is it? We know that's where your precious Warehouse was stored. Where in the hell is it?"

Smith chuckled, "Well, not in hell, for starters. It is currently out of your reach, Anthony. Now, take me in to the committee. After all, I am your prize today."

Barnhart nodded and led Smith to one of the black trucks.

Smith climbed in and sat next to Nienhuis. Barnhart sat up front with the driver.

Smith looked at the man next to him, "Just to let you know, your security clearance request to attend Section Twenty-Eight briefings is hereby denied. We do not clear petulant children for briefings."

"And Mister Barnhart?" The secretary looked at the former knight. "Consider your clearance revoked for briefings. Permanently."

III

KNIGHT

21

ARREST

At eleven o'clock at night, the hearing room was mostly empty. The raised dais in the front of the room held eight seats, each of which was fronted with a heavy oak facade. Sitting on top of each desk was a nameplate and microphone. Each nameplate announced the name of a House member on the Homeland Security oversight committee.

Smith was sitting at another oak table with a microphone on it. Two FBI agents and two uniformed Capitol Police officers stood at parade rest behind him, blocking his view to a nearly empty gallery. While the acting Director of Section 28 was not in handcuffs, he was conscious of the threat of such from behind him.

Four people sat in the gallery made to seat over a hundred. A very smug Chris Nienhuis sat next to his boss from the NSA, Anthony Barnhart. Across the aisle sat a man and a woman that Smith had never before seen. He searched his memory for their faces but came up empty. Smith gave a slight nod in greeting and turned as the door behind the dais opened. The eight men and women of this oversight committee filed out and sat in their respective places.

The chairman of the committee knocked a small gavel on the wooden block made for that purpose. His name placard read, "Hon. Mike Sabo." His amplified voice resonated across the room. "This is an emergency meeting of the House Homeland Security oversight committee. For the record, this is a closed hearing, and the contents of this hearing are Classified Top Secret. Penalties for its disclosure without permission will be to the full extant that the law and congressional rules allow."

The man looked around the room and continued, "Before this committee is Special Agent James Smith from the Department of Homeland Security. Agent Smith is the acting director of a secret division which reports to the Director of Homeland Security and the President of the United States. Agent Smith is with us to provide witness testimony to the violent attacks on a DHS facility in Virginia and a museum in Philadelphia. Agent Smith, do you have an opening statement prepared?"

Smith gave a tight-lipped smile, reached into his coat to retrieve his credentials, and stood, "Yes, Representative Sabo. I do have a statement prepared. Because I can count at least seven people in this room that are not cleared and read into our existence, I must begin by clearing those present to hear about our department."

The Knight opened his credentials and pushed a small amount of his willpower into them. The letters and sigils around the ID glowed a slight green. "By order of Homeland Security and by the Signatory-status of Section Twenty-Eight of the *E'Tuatha* Accords, I hereby bind you under *geas*, and forbid you to speak about our existence or operations to anyone who is not currently present or cleared to know."

A chorus of indrawn breaths and startled noises sounded around the room. Those who had been cleared by Section 28 felt their *geas* reinforce. Those who had not been previously cleared felt something snap around their brains. As suddenly as it had begun, the sensation had withdrawn, leaving several people startled. Both Capitol Police officers reached for their sidearms, only to stop in mid-draw. Their faces contorted as each felt an immediate burning sensation in their hand and arm.

Hearing two grunts of pain, Smith glanced over his shoulder and realized what had happened. He turned fully and said, "Officers, might I recommend that you stop trying to draw your firearms and point them at me. The *geas* I just placed on you will literally burn you if you don't stop quickly."

The officers turned to look at Barnhart, and he nodded. They both put their guns back in their holsters, sighing as they stopped struggling against the *geas*. Smith looked back at the committee members, some of whom were still shaking their heads, trying to get rid of the feelings they just endured.

The Director of Section 28 addressed the Representative who was chairing the meeting, "Now that we have that unpleasantness out of the way, what questions do you have for me?"

The representative on the far right raised his hand slightly, and Sabo acknowledged him. The representative's name placard read, "Hon. Gabe Yskes." The younger looking man spoke into his microphone, "Agent Smith, What did you just do?"

The director's face was serious, "I used a specific binding incantation that we have tied to our credentials that binds the recipient from discussing or attacking Section Twenty-Eight, or its agents, with anyone not physically present." Seeing the blank look on the man's face, Smith said, "In short, I used magic to bind you and keep you from talking to anyone not in this room about my agency."

Yskes responded, "Really, Mister Smith? You expect us to believe that you cast a magic spell over us?"

Smith gave a small shake of his head, "Representative Yskes, it does not matter what you believe. The truth is that the binding incantation was performed. Whether you want to believe it or not, magic is real, it exists, and my department has been tasked, from its inception, to combating the enemies of the United States who attack using more esoteric means. The CIA is charged with overseeing mundane intelligence matters outside our borders. The NSA," he gave a slight wave toward Barnhart and Nienhuis, "is tasked with overseeing intelligence within the borders of the United States."

The former knight paused, then continued, "My organization was chartered and tasked to respond to the areas where the mundane intelligence agencies are not equipped to respond. As I stated before, magic is real, and there are things, creatures, and beings who cross into our world from another plane of existence. My organization is responsible for separating friend from foe, and for making sure that this other plane does not harm our citizens."

Another committee member spoke up, "What is this shit? You don't expect this committee to believe what you are saying? You are just a rogue agency that got caught."

Smith looked at the man whose name placard read, "Hon. Jeff A. Smith." His voice was tinged with exasperation. "Representative Smith, as I said before. I do not particularly care if you believe in magic. I was recounting why my department was originally formed in 1942 as a part of the OSS, the predecessor to the CIA. With the

Homeland Security Act in 2002, our reporting department got moved to DHS. In truth, we've always been a need-to-know executive-level department."

"Agent Smith, regardless of how your agency was formed, we are most interested in the events of the last several days, both in Virginia and in Philadelphia." The speaker was another committee member whose name placard pronounced that she was Representative Theresa Hooper. Smith recalled that she represented a Pennsylvania district that bordered Philly.

The Director of Section 28 shifted to address the Pennsylvania representative, "A couple days ago, the headquarters for my agency was attacked by a group of dragons, with support from a few squads of ground troops. The dragons and their riders utilized a magical gateway to appear over our headquarters with very little warning and proceeded to attack. While our defenses inflicted some loss on the enemy, their firepower was overwhelming. I do not have the final numbers, but our personnel, both support and active duty, were decimated, with a high number of casualties. Those who were wounded are receiving medical care, but the wounds were very traumatic."

"Dragons, Agent Smith?" Hooper responded. "You claim dragons took out your facility in Langley?"

"Yes, ma'am. Dragons and their riders. The firepower from a standard dragon would easily compare to an Apache helicopter gunship, but they are far more maneuverable, and have better armor than the Apache. In a standup fight, it would be a tossup. A whole pack of dragons working together is a fearsome sight."

Hooper gave a slight snort, "Dragons. Next you'll be telling us that fairies and trolls are real, too."

Smith smiled, "You did ask about the Philadelphia mission, ma'am. That was a case of an external dragon attack, and a coordinated attack by trolls inside. Thankfully, the pixies were there to help my agents, or else they might not have survived."

Sabo spoke up, "Really, Mister Smith? Need I remind you that lying to Congress is a serious offense?"

"Of course not, sir. Although, from the news coverage, I would think it a national pastime instead of a crime. But this is your committee, and I assure you I am telling the truth."

"Are you telling us that the news coverage and the videos all over the internet are real?" This was a new committee member.

Smith turned to look and saw he was addressing the "Hon. Laura Kramer." He knew she loved to get in front of the cameras at any opportunity and had made a name for herself by joining every Sunday morning show she could book.

"Representative Kramer, it is my understanding that most of the Philadelphia videos are authentic. However, most of the footage from Virginia has been taken down or debunked by my internal opsec team. It is our standard protocol."

Smith gestured to Barnhart and Nienhuis, "Unfortunately, the NSA has been actively stopping us from our standard protocols for operational security. In fact, I would bet that this emergency meeting was only raised when I refused to brief Mister Nienhuis at the prior meeting. He was not cleared for the information, but his boss insisted that I brief him. According to the law and my own *geas*, I could not legally, or safely, do so."

The room grew quiet, and the silence seemed to stretch. Representative Sabo finally spoke up, "Is there anything further that you wish to say, Agent Smith?"

"Yes, sir. I have a warning for this committee. Forecasting informed us that something big was potentially coming soon. The attacks on the Langley, Philly, and one outside Charleston, all are specifically targeted to enable a much greater disaster to befall this world. If you do not let Section Twenty-Eight do our job, the United States, and potentially the world, will be in jeopardy."

"Theatrics do not work well in Congress, Agent Smith. And threatening this body will see you in prison. You are dismissed as a witness, and this committee will come to a close."

Smith stood and watched as the congressional representatives filed out of the room. He turned to look at the FBI agents behind him, "So, can I at least get a ride back to Langley?"

Barnhart stepped up, followed closely by his subordinate. He pointed at the FBI agents, "Agent Strait, place that man in custody. Charges are lying to Congress and threatening Congress. Book him through the system and drop him in a cell. I'll file the paperwork with your office."

The young FBI agent paused, she knew Barnhart was the head of the NSA, and did not have the authority over her or her partner. She looked at her much more senior partner, and he nodded, "Go ahead, Lizzy. The AG said to follow Barnhart's lead."

Agent Strait turned to Smith, "Sir, can you hold out your hands in front of you?" She was suddenly sweating profusely, and her chest felt hot. She struggled through it, "I must place you in handcuffs to transport you, sir."

Director Smith looked at her sweaty face and took pity on her.

He held out his hands willingly, "Here you go, Lizzy, is it? I'm not resisting."

Suddenly, the young agent felt better, and she could concentrate enough to put the handcuffs on him. Smith turned to Barnhart. His voice was quiet and calm, seeming to chill the very air around him, "Mister Barnhart, this is one of the dumbest mistakes you have made. You have chosen your side. To quote an Indiana Jones movie I'm quite fond of, 'You have chosen, poorly.'"

Barnhart sneered, "I've heard a lot of men say that. I'm still here and you are going to jail. I'll track down your rogue agents as well. I don't know how you do your mass delusions, but they are done, now."

Smith was escorted outside to a waiting black SUV where he sat next to Agent Strait for the short ride to the FBI building. Once there, he was brought into booking, where he was fingerprinted, a mugshot was taken, and was then escorted to a holding cell. Before entering the holding cell, he was stripped of his credentials and SSP. The FBI agent who was processing him found nothing else on him or in his pockets. He was told he would get one phone call, and he was given access to a phone sitting on an old wooden desk.

Dialing a number he had memorized a long time ago, he heard the line go through a series of clicks as it was routed through several different phone servers. Finally a series of beeps indicated that it had been swept and cleared of any electronic listening devices. The phone on the other end rang.

"Hello?"

"Miss Massey, this is Smith. Barnhart had me arrested by the FBI. I am currently working through booking. This is rather inconvenient. You know who to call."

"Yes, sir. I'll place that call immediately. What do you want us to do?"

"Secure the second key and proceed with plans. If you need help, call Mulder. She might help. Be prepared to run. Keep the keys out of anyone else's hands."

"Yes, sir. Good luck."

"Thank you, Miss Massey."

The FBI agent standing over him looked at him quizzically. "You aren't referring to SAC Mulder, are you? I've known Tressa for years, and she would be the last person to help a fugitive."

Smith smiled and shook his head, "I'd never ask her to compromise herself like that. I respect her way too much. She wouldn't be helping a fugitive."

The FBI agent furrowed her brow at that thought. She then shrugged and moved Smith into the holding cell. The agent went back to the desk and worked on the paperwork. While he was waiting to be processed, Smith thought about his arrest. *How had Barnhart been able to resist the geas? He should have been stopped from interfering. That makes this twice, now. I'll have to ask Norbert about that.*

The phone on the desk rang, and the agent picked up the receiver, "Holding." The agent listened for a bit, and then replied, "Yes, Agent Mulder. I have him in custody. No, ma'am. I do not have the current list of charges in front of me. I was told that Mister Barnhart from NSA would arrive in the morning to provide the final list of charges."

There was a long pause as the young agent listened intently to her caller. "Yes, ma'am. According to the list, he is scheduled for arraignment tomorrow at ten-thirty in the morning. I have not put him in one of the other cells because we don't have the charges and paperwork from the NSA, yet." Another pause. "No, ma'am. I'm going to have to leave him in holding for the night. No, ma'am. He's been a model prisoner. I was going to grab a pillow and blanket for him. He'll have to use one of the benches in holding, but at least it's off the floor." A short pause. "Yes, ma'am. I'll let you know, personally. What's your number?"

The agent wrote the information down on a notepad near the phone. She tore the sheet off and stuck it in her pocket as she listened to the person on the other end of the line. "Yes, ma'am. I'll take care of it." A nod of her head, "You too, ma'am. I'll talk to you in the morning."

The agent stood and left the holding area. A few minutes later, she returned with a pillow and blanket in her arms. Looking at the man in the cell, she said, "I have to leave you in this area tonight. I have a pillow and blanket for you if you agree not to try something stupid when I open the cell."

Smith nodded, "I promise." He took two steps back and sat on the bench, folding his hands together in his lap.

The agent opened the cell door and dropped the bundle on the bench nearest the door, about four feet from Smith. She quickly stepped out and closed the cell door. "Thank you for behaving, Mister Smith. I'll see if I can find some food for you." The young FBI agent left the area.

Half an hour later, the agent brought him a bag of food from a chain sandwich shop. As she handed it through the bars, she said, "Sorry, I didn't know what you would eat so I got you a turkey sandwich with cheese and all the veggies. There's chips in there, as well. Would you like something to drink?"

Smith smiled graciously. "Water will do just fine, Agent...?" His question trailed off, waiting for her name.

"Agent Zolen, Mister Smith. I'll get you a bottle of water." She left and returned quickly carrying a couple bottles, handing him one. They sat in silence for a half an hour as Smith ate his sandwich and chips with no complaints. He rolled the trash up neatly, including the water bottle, and slid it through the bars for Zolen to grab.

"Can I ask a question, Agent Zolen?"

She turned to look at him, "Sure."

"Why the extra nice treatment? After all, I was brought here on charges from the head of the NSA." Smith looked genuinely puzzled.

"SAC Mulder seems to like you and trust you. I trust her judgement. I've also met Mister Barnhart in another setting. I didn't like him then, and I don't like him now."

"Fair enough, Agent Zolen. Will there be a specific lights out time, tonight?"

"Call me Heather, at least when there are no other agents around. And I will turn off some of the lights, but at least half will stay on. I'm going off duty soon, but other agents will check on you throughout the night. I'll be back in the morning."

"Thank you Agent Zolen. Heather. I shall bid you good night then." The Section 28 Director leaned his head back and dozed while sitting in the upright position.

22

PURGE

S mith sat in the holding cell for just under eight hours. At
7:30am, the same FBI agent who had booked him in the
night before entered the holding area. It was half an hour
later that the Agent's cell phone rang. The agent answered the call
in a slightly sleepy voice, "Zolen."

She listened for a moment, and then replied, "Yes, ma'am. I was
waiting for Mister Barnhart to bring his paperwork in for the
arraignment today.... Yes, ma'am. He has been in Holding all night."
There was a long moment where the look on the agent's face took
on a confused expression. "But ma'am, the holding paperwork has
the NSA chief's name as the complainant. His statement includes
approval from you and your office for the arrest."

Smith gave a slight smile as he listened to the conversation. Miss
Massey had made the call to the United States Attorney General's
office. In that call, his ever-capable assistant would have reminded
the AG about an operation that her department had fouled up three
months ago. He had to send Knightsdawn to Oregon to clean up a
fae problem that her team had caused. She owed Smith a large debt,
and he had just called on the marker.

Agent Zolen looked more confused, and Smith could almost feel
the lecture from the Attorney General. "Yes, ma'am. I'll cancel the
paperwork and escort him out of the building. Ma'am, what do I tell

Mister Barnhart?" The woman listened and smiled. "Yes, ma'am. I'll convey that sentiment to him when he asks where this guy went."

Zolen handed the phone through the bars to Smith, "The Attorney General would like to talk to you."

Smith held the phone to his ear, "Smith."

"James, this is AG Komondy. As of right now, we are even. Correct?"

"Yes, Lori. Thank you for helping me out."

"James, let me give you a warning. Get out of DC. Barnhart's got a real hard-on for you, and he's got the President's ear. I can no longer protect you or your team. It may be time to call in any other favors people owe you."

"Thank you, Lori. I will reconnect when this blows over. Until then, if you need us to deal with something, call me on my private line."

Smith ended the call and handed the phone back to Agent Zolen. The FBI agent took the paperwork she was working on and theatrically ripped it in half, dumping the pieces into the nearby wastebasket. The agent stood and used the keys to unlock the cell door, handing Smith his credentials and SSP as he stepped out of the cell. In a cool, professional, no-nonsense voice, the agent said, "Sorry about the mixup, sir. The FBI officially regrets any miscommunication or errors that led to your brief arrest." Thinking for a moment, she continued in a slightly warmer tone, "Unofficially, I'm sorry for having to stick you in Holding all night. Thank you for being professional with me."

"Thank you, Agent Zolen. And I appreciate your professionalism as well."

"Director Smith? Can I ask a question?"

Smith nodded, "Sure."

"Is it real, sir? The dragons and trolls and stuff. Is all that stuff in the news something that we need to be worried about?"

Smith looked at the agent. She was in her late twenties or early thirties. Relatively young for a posting to DC, he knew she was fast-tracked for higher positions. *If working with the AG on this doesn't hurt her,* Smith mused.

The former knight looked into the young woman's questioning eyes and answered, "Yes. It's all real. My agency is the one that deals with the weird and esoteric. If you are ever looking for a new position, call me. We are always recruiting those with rather flexible minds." He fished a business card out from his right jacket pocket and handed it to the young agent.

"Thank you, Director. I just might take you up on that offer."

Agent Zolen escorted Smith through the building and out the door. As they reached the foyer, Smith saw NSA chief Anthony Barnhart walking through the metal detectors, trailed by his assistant, Nienhuis. Smith smiled as Barnhart saw him and the NSA chief's face turned bright red.

"Who the hell let you out, Smith?" Barnhart roared across the foyer, stalking closer and shaking his finger at the Section 28 Director.

Smith was about to reply, then Zolen stepped in between the two men, putting a hand up in front of the NSA chief. "Director Smith was released by the Attorney General directly, Mister Barnhart."

"Arrest him again. I want him up on charges of terrorism and lying to Congress." At this point Smith was worried about Barnhart's heart, as the man was crimson with rage. "He runs a rogue agency. And he, or they, need to be stopped. Place him in cuffs right now, or I'll have your badge."

Zolen smiled and replied in the calm bureaucratic voice, "Mister Barnhart, the AG had a message for you if you tried to re-arrest Director Smith. I believe the response was, 'You do not have a high enough clearance for that.'"

Barnhart snarled and Niehuis looked shocked. Barnhart was the first to respond, "That's it. I'll have your badge for that, agent. And you, Smith, I will see you in jail." Barnhart spun and stormed out of the building, almost running a young pregnant woman over in the process. Nienhuis scurried after him.

Zolen sighed and looked at Smith. "Director Smith, about that job you were offering?"

———

THE GIANT BLACK MRAP affectionately referred to as "War Wagon, Version 2.0" sat in the parking lot of a small hotel outside Mansfield, Ohio. Six had driven the large truck up the interstates all the way north from Langley. Occasionally turning on the red and blue lightbars to clear traffic ahead of him and only stopping a couple of brief times for food or rest stops, the team had made good time, arriving in the Mansfield area around four o'clock in the morning.

Gretchen had wearily gone inside the office and rented two connecting rooms. She and Doc had stayed in one, and Six and Ghost had stayed in the other. Spooky had elected to stay in the War

Wagon. At seven o'clock in the morning, Spooky's alarm went off, and he groggily opened his eyes, rubbing the sleep away. He tapped a couple keys and all six monitors lit up, with a series of alert boxes arrayed across his vision.

Groaning, the former NSA analyst opened the alerts. The first one made his eyes bug out a little, and he reached for his Secure Phone, sending a message to both Ghost and Gretchen. He opened more of the alerts, and everyone he opened got worse. After opening the final one, he hung his head and muttered, "Well, shit."

Fifteen minutes later, someone knocked on the hatch, and Spooky looked at the camera in the back of the truck. Recognizing Gretchen, he hit the switch to lower the ramp. A few seconds later Gretchen climbed up next to him and peered over his shoulder.

"What's going on, John?"

"Hey, Gretchen. We are well and truly frakked. According to news reports, the President is holding a press conference in about two hours announcing an arrest has been made for the attacks in Langley and Philly. My guess is that they arrested the Director."

He pointed at another window, "This one is a LEIN BOLO for our War Wagon and the Wunder Buggy. They actually released a BOLO for us, citing 'extreme caution' and 'armed and dangerous' in the notice. I can kill it, but if anyone has already printed it, they'll have that copy."

"Kill that BOLO." Ghost announced from behind Spooky. "How else are they trying to screw us?" The team leader handed his electronics wizard a large mug of coffee.

Spooky took a sip and sighed. "The Philly attack is the lead story everywhere. The media have eyewitnesses, and apparently there was at least one civilian casualty due to the dragon attack." He clicked on a video window and it enlarged.

On the screen, the logo in the corner announced the national news channel, and four experts were discussing the Philadelphia dragon attack, and reviewing footage live on the air. The lower third graphic at the bottom of the screen announced "Dragon Attack in Philadelphia - One Dead." The anchor gravely intoned, "If you are squeamish, you may wish to look away. This next segment is not for younger viewers." There was a pause, and then a cell phone video appeared, with the sound muted. The anchor provided the voice-over, "This video shows the one known victim in this attack. According to police, the victim is David Cato. As you can see from the video, the man stood in the middle of the sidewalk, right underneath where one of the dragons was hovering. Here you see him draw his concealed pistol, which we are told he had a permit for."

The anchor took a breath and continued, "After firing several shots at the thing, you can watch the dragon respond, it just... it just..." On the screen, the giant beast bent his head down and looked at the creature before him. The video showed sparks skipping off the thing's hide—the bullets. Suddenly, in one motion, the head snapped forward and downward. The jaws gaped wide and clamped over the man. The head came away, the upper half of the man in its mouth, and everything from the man's waist on down slowly collapsed. "I'm sorry folks. I just can't explain this." The anchor turned to the experts, "Any of you?"

While most of the experts were quiet, one of them spoke. "I can tell you, Jason. The man who is behind this gruesome attack is in custody right now."

Gretchen muttered, "That arrogant, unadulterated prick. Should have known he'd find a TV gig."

Ghost raised an eyebrow. Reading the name on the graphic, he asked, "So, who is Anthony Barnhart?"

Spooky chimed in, "He's the head of the NSA. My old boss. What's he got to do with this?"

"That asshole is the man who arrested the Director. Apparently he's coming after us now. I thought he was under the *geas*."

The experts talked back and forth. Within a few minutes, the anchor said, "That's all the time we have for this segment. I want to thank my guests for their expertise. My name is Jason Bock, and you've been watching Fastbreak. Coming up next, we interview a couple of witnesses to the attack."

After a commercial break, the anchor came back on the screen. He turned and motioned to three people seated in the studio with him. "With me today are three of the survivors and witnesses from the horrific attack yesterday in Philly. Kevin and Ashley Smiley were visiting the new American Revolution Museum when they were directed to evacuate. Asher Diep was a security guard at the museum, and he will talk to us about the attack." The guests talked about what they saw, and the horrific speed and ferocity of the attacking dragons.

As they were watching the news report, Gretchen's SSP buzzed in her pocket. Pulling it out, she recognized the number. Answering, she said, "Massey."

She listened for a few seconds and then replied, "Yes, sir. I'm glad that worked. We're in Mansfield right now. We're going to retrieve the second key today, but we need to know where it is."

Again, she was silent, but nodding as she listened. She gave a low whistle, "Well, when you want a key to be safe and secure, you don't play around. Yes, sir. We'll find it. Where do you want to meet?" After a few seconds she nodded, "That sounds good, sir. We'll meet you there." Gretchen hung up the phone.

She looked at Ghost, "Smith is out. Let's gather the team in one of the rooms. I'll get Noelle." She turned to Spooky, "John, do you want a shower before we meet?"

Spooky shook his head, "No thanks. I'm going to stay here and monitor the situation. Take one of the mics and place it on a table or something. Once you guys are done, you can have someone spell me in the truck while I get cleaned up."

The other two nodded and left the truck, and Spooky sealed the ramp behind them. Gretchen went to gather Doc as Ghost went in to make sure Six was ready. The vampire agent was sitting in the lone chair, watching a movie channel. He looked up when Ghost entered the room and turned off the tv.

"Team meeting in about two minutes," Ghost announced.

Six grunted, got up, and ambled over to a small cooler in the room with them. He opened it and grabbed a red liquid-filled bag. Flashing a set of fangs, he said, "I'm going to go eat breakfast. I'll be right back." He entered the bathroom and closed the door.

There was a knock at the door, and it was opened by Gretchen. She and Doc walked through, finding seats on one of the beds. A few seconds later, Six walked out of the bathroom, carrying the empty blood bag. He reclaimed his seat in the lone chair. They all looked to Ghost.

"Gretchen? You received a call from the Director. What did he have to say?"

"He was released from custody this morning." Gretchen looked at the relieved team around her. "He's on his way to Grand Rapids, and will meet us at the Queen's residence. He also told me where the second key is stored, and what it looks like. You are not going to believe where it is."

Ghost's phone rang, and he looked at it. He looked at the rest of the team as he answered it, "What do you need Spooky?"

"Turn on the TV. Now. Get it to a news network. You have got to see the President's press conference."

Ghost turned around as he hung up and turned on the TV. Turning to the same news channel they were watching before, he saw the President behind his podium in the White House Briefing Room.

"With the actions of this morning by some elements in this administration, I will be forced to take several actions to bring these rogue actors to justice. Philadelphia was a tragedy perpetrated by a rogue agency, headed by one man. The attack in Virginia was from the same agency. They have sponged off the American taxpayer long enough, and they have become a liability." The President paused, and the Briefing Room was silent, breathless.

"As of ten minutes ago, the Attorney General has been relieved of her duties, pending charges of insubordination and potentially treason. Attorney General Komondy has been taken into custody and is awaiting formal charges in this matter. Unfortunately, she was able to plan and execute the escape of the head of the rogue agency that has caused all the destruction."

The President of the United States held up a picture of Smith, "This man, James Smith, is the acting Director of the rogue agency, and has escaped FBI custody with the help of the Attorney General and a few corrupt FBI agents. This man is a wanted fugitive. The agents in this man's agency are also wanted for questions regarding their actions in these attacks. This information is being spread to law enforcement agencies around the nation, both federal and local. If you have any information, please contact your local law enforcement."

The President put the picture down and looked at the camera directly. "This agency has been allowed to go without any real oversight for years, all while spending vast sums of taxpayer money. That stops here and now. I've issued an Executive Order to temporarily freeze all their accounts, and I am requiring an extensive review of their accounting and operational oversight. I will not let a rogue agency run roughshod over this country. Not on my watch. Not while I'm the President." The President gesticulated.

"Because this agency is a part of the Department of Homeland Security, I am temporarily removing it from serving in that capacity. The head of the National Security Agency will be temporarily assigned control and oversight over the agency, at least until another person can be found. I will introduce Anthony Barnhart later as the head of the NSA, as well as the new oversight for this rogue agency."

The TV exploded in a shower of sparks as Six's right shoe slammed into it and penetrated past the LED screen. Ghost turned to the vampire and gave a frown, "Now we can't hear what's coming. And we have to pay for the TV."

Six stood and walked over to the still sputtering and sparking television and pulled his shoe from the middle of the screen. "Spooky's watching it for us. Hell, I'll pay for the TV, if you need me to. I couldn't stand the lies anymore. And I didn't want to see Barnhart's smug grin."

Ghost chuckled, "Hey I felt like it too, I just had better impulse control."

Six gave a wry grin, "Yup. Still feel better."

"Now that we have that out of the way, Gretchen, where is the second key?"

Gretchen looked at the team around her. "It's in one of the most secure and safe spaces built. It's at the old Ohio State Reformatory, in the cornerstone."

23

BARGAIN

"There you go, Mister Smith. Here is your card back. And if you would wait a few moments, I'll have your tickets and itinerary."

Smith accepted his card back from the impeccably dressed young woman behind the desk. He smiled as he placed it back in his wallet. He was in the office of a charter flight service out of the Washington D.C. area. He looked at the young FBI agent standing next to him, and as the operations manager turned to get the paperwork from her printer, he said, "Are you sure about this? This is your last chance to back out. I'm not sure how much longer my agency's charter will last."

Agent Zolen shook her head. "I was serious about this. I trust SAC Mulder, and she trusts you. I think Washington is going to be very unhealthy for me for the near future."

Smith nodded. "I happen to agree with you. If you are sure about this, then you are welcome to join Section Twenty-Eight."

Smith's SSP rang. He answered it, "Smith. Hello, Agent Mulder. How may I assist you?"

The Director of Section 28 listened to the other end of the phone. When he answered her, he sounded amused, "Hmm. I had not thought Barnhart could work that quickly. I may have to deal with him earlier than I had planned. And what are your plans? Do I need to worry about you and your team?"

He nodded as if the other person can see him, "Yes, and I appreciate that. I'm currently at the Manassas Regional Airport. I got word that our Air Force jets were grounded, and I thought I'd avoid Dulles. I leave in two hours. You are welcome to join me if you can get here on time."

An hour and forty-five minutes later, Special Agent Tressa Mulder walked through the automatic doors and into the waiting area. Two people who were very obviously fellow FBI agents trailed behind the Washington SAC. After spotting Smith and Agent Zolen, she and her entourage walked directly over to him.

Smith stood and held out his hand, "Good to see you, Tressa. I didn't think you would make it."

The FBI agent shook the proffered hand, "I'm glad we got here, I wasn't sure Barnhart's goon, Nienhuis, would let us leave." She looked at Agent Zolen, sitting next to Smith, "I didn't expect to see you here, Heather. Did Smith convince you to tag along?"

Zolen shook her head, "No, ma'am. I asked him if I could join. I kinda pissed off Barnhart and figured that this might be a better job opportunity."

Mulder nodded, "It might just be, especially after the President's press conference a half hour ago." She turned to her companions. "Director Smith, this is Special Agent Rick Stratton. He's a member of my personal team and was on the short list for HRT." Smith shook Stratton's hand. Mulder continued, "And this is Special Agent Chris Swanson. You might recognize her from my Mobile Command Center. She's one of my electronics and intel specialists."

The Director indeed recognized the young woman in front of him and greeted her with a handshake. She said, "Most people call me Spooks." Her Australian accent was light and musical to Smith's ears.

'I do indeed remember you, Spooks. I'll have to introduce you to a young fellow we call Spooky. In fact, I believe you have at least seen his face on a monitor or two."

The young agent faked a groan, "Great. It figures his nickname is Spooky, too."

The operations manager for the charter service approached the group and got the Director's attention. "Mister Smith? Your plane is ready to board. If you and your companion would follow me...."

"Yes, ma'am. Would it be a problem if we add another person or two to our manifest? My friends just arrived and are looking forward to the trip." Smith gestured at the new arrivals.

The young woman looked them over, "No, Mister Smith. Your charter pays for a flight regardless of how many people take the trip, up to the maximum capacity of the plane. Your flight would certainly hold your friends as well. I will just need to get identification from all of them for the FAA records. I can take care of that at my desk."

The three newcomers followed the ops manager. Agent Zolen stood and followed Director Smith across the waiting room to the woman's office door. In a few short minutes, the paperwork was done, and the party followed the operations manager out through the rear of the building and onto the parking ramp. There was a gleaming white Cessna Citation X, outwardly identical to the agency's Air Force jet, except for the color and civilian markings.

Mulder gave a small whistle, "You guys are way better funded than the Bureau. How do you guys afford this?"

Smith gave a small smile, "It helps when the budget is a single line item and is classified far above even the President's pay grade. Besides, this was not funded by the government. I have access to certain... discretionary funds that receive no oversight from any human government. You can thank the elves for this one."

The FBI SAC shook her head and mumbled, "Great, now elves are real." Smith laughed.

The group walked up the stairs and boarded the plane. Smith and Mulder sat next to each other so they could talk on the way out of town. The other three agents sat close to them. The cabin was spacious, appointed with leather and mahogany. All the FBI agents stretched out and relaxed as the comfortable executive seating enveloped them. Smith had specifically requested no steward on the flight, so the copilot raised the stairs and secured the door. Once the pilot and copilot were seated in the cockpit, the cockpit door closed and the copilot gave an abbreviated version of the standard flight safety information. The copilot also announced that the galley would be available once they were in the air and cruising.

The muted roar of the engines grew louder as they spun up to operational capacity. The jet moved from its spot, and Smith watched the parking ramp workers direct the jet toward the runway. The charter flight received almost instantaneous approval for take-off, and fourteen minutes later the jet was at cruising altitude and the speed was quickly climbing toward nine-tenths of the speed of sound.

Once the pilot announced that they were free to move around the cabin, Smith relaxed. He was moving very rapidly away from Washington DC. Mulder tapped him on the shoulder, and he turned to look at her.

"By the way, where are we going? I realized that I never asked where you were setting up your new headquarters." The FBI SAC sounded bemused.

"Grand Rapids, Michigan. I'll brief everyone once I bind the newcomers with the security *geas*."

Smith unbuckled his seatbelt and stood. He turned and addressed the rest of the party. "For those of you who do not completely understand who I am, I am Special Agent James Smith, the Acting Director of Section Twenty-Eight. We are a small, mostly independent agency within the Department of Homeland Security. Our charter is to protect the United States, and the world, by dealing with beings and powers from outside our plane of existence. We also handle those humans or former humans who work with, or conspire with, those beings."

Spooks raised her hand slightly and spoke, "What do you mean beings from outside our world? Are you talking about aliens?"

"In a way, yes. What most people do not realize is that there is a wall, a separation, or a barrier that separates our world from other planes of existence. Sometimes, that barrier gets thin, and energy from another plane leaks through. That energy may manifest in the form of a creature or being from society's collective subconscious. This is originally how vampires, were-creatures, and such creatures were formed. Sometimes the energy directly affects a human, and transforms them. This was how Vlad Țepeș was changed into Vlad Dracul. Or you may know him as Dracula."

"Wait!" Agent Stratton spoke up, "Are you telling us that Dracula was really a vampire, and not just some bloodthirsty tyrant?"

Smith smiled, "I assure you, Agent Stratton, Vlad was very bloodthirsty. His infection triggered his change. Sometimes, those same areas let beings from those other planes through into our world. Most of human folklore has at least a grain of truth about the creatures coming through—at least from an uneducated human-ity's perspective. Sometimes, those creatures are powerful enough to force open gates between realities. My agency is charged with find-ing, tracking down, monitoring, and sometimes killing non-human beings. To answer a question, that everyone has been asking, yes, the dragon footage is real, and they appear to be attacking my teams directly, hunting for me."

Stunned silence greeted him. Smith looked at the three FBI agents in front of him. "Now that you know who I am and what we do. Does anyone wish to back out? If so, this may be your last chance. I don't normally recruit this way, but you all volunteered for various reasons. Now is the time to, shall we say, un-volunteer yourself."

Mulder stepped up next to the Director, "I know you all joined me in moving to Section Twenty-Eight out of a sense of personal loyalty or trust. I appreciate that, but this has to be your decision. I've been working with Director Smith for a short time, and in that time I've seen evidence that what he says is real, and I've grown to trust him. I've made my choice. You have to make your own. There are no hard feelings either way, but it has to be your own choice."

Agent Stratton looked up, "I'm in. I've seen what demons can do. I'd love to be able to fight them and creatures like them."

Spooks hung her head, shaking with silent laughter. She looked up with a large grin on her face and addressed Mulder, "You know, boss, I always thought you got too much flak for your last name, but damn. I think you might just live up to it. I'm in."

Agent Zolen nodded, "I already said I'm in. What's next?"

Smith nodded, "I'll have the contracts written for you sometime in the near future. Until then, I'm going to administer an oath that will bind you to the office." He raised his credentials and pushed a small amount of willpower into them, "By order of Homeland Security and by the Signatory-status of Section Twenty-Eight of the *E'Tuatha* Accords, I hereby bind you under *geas*, and forbid you to speak about our existence or operations to anyone who is not currently present or cleared to know."

The expected momentary flash and stunned look on their faces registered with Agent Mulder. This was her first time seeing the geas placed after her initial read-in, and she admitted that it looked odd.

Smith tucked away his credentials and spoke, "Now that you are bound to the office, I can tell you where we are going. We are flying to meet my last remaining active duty team in Grand Rapids, Michigan. There, we will set up a temporary headquarters on the grounds provided by the Gray Court. They are one of the three fae courts, and they are neutral toward humanity. At that point, we will decide what our next move is."

Smith looked around the plane's cabin. "I would recommend that all of you get some rest. I don't know when we'll next be able to relax." Smith turned and sat down, thinking about Knightmare and the retrieval of the second signet ring. That turned his thoughts to the moment so long ago when he hid the ring.

THE RICHLAND SHIELD & Banner paper proclaimed that it was "Mansfield's Greatest Day" as the cornerstone for the new prison was carefully laid. The local dignitaries and officials stood about in the blustery winds as the workers muscled the heavy marble stone into place. It was November 4, 1886, and Smith stood next to his boss, smiling as the heavy block was levered into place.

Smith had worked for his boss, Friedrich Ferdinand Schnitzer, for over ten years. Having starting working for the man shortly after Schnitzer started his company, Smith had become the man's assistant and secretary. He helped his boss design and build massive projects. This was the latest of his projects, the Intermediate Penitentiary. While the design of the project fell to Levi Schofield from Cleveland, Schnitzer had secured the bid to build the prison for the state of Ohio. After two years of work, they had raised enough funds to begin construction, and today was the day that the cornerstone would be laid.

"Be prepared to fetch the cab, Samuels. This infernal wind is numbing my hands and feet." Schnitzer spoke low enough that only Smith could hear.

"Yes, sir, Mister Schnitzer. I'll have Harry bring it around as soon as the photographers have taken their pictures." Smith was using the name Richard Samuels and had grown accustomed to his boss' gruff manner.

It was later that evening, under a partial waxing moon, Smith traveled back out to the site. Light clouds dimmed what light the moon provided, but Smith knew exactly where he needed to be. He stopped by the cornerstone and laid a hand on the cool marble. Taking a bit of chalk from his pocket, the man sketched a small, complex diagram of runes on the side of the block. He muttered a few words and lightly touched one of the chalk lines.

The chalk glowed green briefly, and then the glow vanished. A small, high-pitched voice sounded behind the man. "You called, human?"

Smith turned and came face to face with a small pixie. Rather face to body. The small fae hovered about ten inches away and looked impatient. The small female creature tapped its foot in midair as its wings blurred in a soft blue glow, "Well?"

Smith spoke, "I am Sir Gawain, Knight of the Round Table and Defender of the Realm. I ask that you hear my request, fae warrior."

The pixie looked startled. She recovered quickly, saying, "Well met, Sir Gawain. I am Aurora Plicci, Matriarch of the Family. As you have the ear of my queen, I shall grant you the boon of listening to your request. What do you have to request, Sir Knight?"

"I ask that you and your Family guard this block until I come to retrieve it, or until my representatives do. That may be many human years."

"And what boon will you grant to I and my Family, Sir Knight?"

Smith had been thinking about this very question. Fae were shrewd bargainers and never granted a favor without recompense. As the smallest fae, pixies did not often get to travel outside their small area. But they craved information and entertainment. "I shall tell you stories of my travels. You recognize my name. I have lived on this Earth for over fourteen hundred human years. I have stories that would entertain your entire Family for generations. I will sit with you for at least two nights per week for the next year, telling you my stories, so you may entertain your own Family."

The Matriarch seemed to think about the offer. Smith hoped fourteen hundred years of stories would be worth the favor he was requesting. She made her decision.

"I will grant you this favor, in exchange for the favor you offer. I expect many nights of storytelling from you, Sir Knight."

"Yes, Matriarch. I will begin with a tale tonight and then tell you my stories as often as I possibly can. Is this acceptable?"

"It is a bargain, well and done." Smith felt a wave of energy cascade over them, and knew the fae bargain was sealed. He settled down and recounted a tale from his time before Arthur. Smith visited the job site at least twice a week, always at night, to regale the sprite with tales from his life. This continued until the prison opened almost ten years later, on September 15, 1896.

Smith could not return to the building until after the reformatory closed in 1990. The Matriarch met him upon his return in 1991, and was happy to see "Sir Knight." Smith intentionally stayed behind the tour, and was able to spend the night telling more stories of the last hundred years of his life. It was that night that Smith learned that the haunted nature of the old reformatory was due to the Matriarch and her family. Aurora let the knight know her offspring had made it a sport to produce the haunting effects for the humans who visited, and they both laughed long into the night.

The former Knight of the Round Table made an effort to return to the reformatory at least once a month to talk with the Matriarch and tell tales of his life. He also enjoyed hearing the stories of the haunted reformatory from the pixies in the building. Unfortunately, Smith's work forced him to stop the visits about ten years later, shortly after 9/11.

As he drifted off to a light nap, he realized he missed being able to talk with the Matriarch.

24

CORNERSTONE

Ohio State Reformatory, Mansfield, Ohio

The big government MRAP pulled up and parked in the lot outside the historic reformatory. As Spooky launched a drone, Ghost called his boss, hoping for more information. The monster hunter engaged the speakerphone function so they could all hear, and Smith answered on the second ring.

"Good morning, Mister Vanhof. How can I help you?"

"Hey, boss. I have you on speakerphone here. We are at the old prison, trying to figure out where the key is. Where in the prison is it? And are there any guardians like last time that we need to be worried about?"

"The key is buried in a solid block of marble used as the cornerstone of the building. Like any other cornerstone, the block has an inscription on it, dedicating the Intermediate Penitentiary. The large stone is set into the walls and building itself. On the bottom of the stone is a hole about the size of an apple. There is a marble plug in it, but you should be able to remove that. Inside the block is a cavity that contains the key. It is a gold and silver signet ring wrapped in oiled leather and cloth."

Ghost looked at Gretchen, who was frantically taking notes. She spoke up, "Where is the cornerstone, Director?"

There was a slight pause from Smith, "If I recall correctly, it is on the front facade, on a corner near the main entrance. Ask one of the guides, and they will point it out. As to a guardian, there is a Family of pixies guarding this on as well. The passphrase is the same phrase as the last time: The Knight of the Realm requires the artifact. That should get you past the pixies."

Ghost again spoke up, "Anything else we need to know about the reformatory, boss?"

"No, Mister Vanhof. I was on good terms with the Matriarch, so you should have no trouble. And hopefully the dragonrider does not make an appearance again. Get in, get out, and get to Grand Rapids with the key."

"That sounds good." Ghost paused and then asked a question he had been dreading, "So what are we going to do, boss? The President just declared duck season and we are the pesky waterfowl. How safe are you?"

"I'm currently cruising at about forty-thousand feet on my way to Grand Rapids. I believe we got out before the net could close. When you get the second key to Grand Rapids, we will discuss our strategy. Until then, do not call local DHS offices, or any federal offices. You might get away with contacting local law enforcement, but it will be risky at best."

"Gotcha, boss. I kind of figured about the DHS offices. Didn't think about the FBI or other cops. We'll be careful."

"That sounds good. I need to get off the phone, the pilot has announced that we are beginning our descent into Grand Rapids. Take care." Smith hung up the phone.

Ghost put away his phone and was about to begin the plan when Doc's SSP rang. Startled, she glanced at the number and gasped. "I have to take this. It's the Vatican."

The team's combat priest answered her phone, "Doctor Sorenson."

After a short pause, "Yes, Archbishop Ferrer. It is good to hear your voice." As she listened to the archbishop, her face grew dark. Frowning, she shook her head. Finally, she could no longer stop herself.

"Father, I believe you are wrong. This is the worst course of action. Director Smith and this organization have done nothing wrong. I'm willing to Witness to their work, and I believe that the order does need to have a representative with the agency."

The War Wagon became silent, and the team could hear the archbishop on the other end. His voice was rising and his tone grew menacing, even through the phone. Doc's face grew bright red as her anger won over her confusion.

"No, Archbishop Ferrer. It is a mistake to recall me. I will not leave in the middle of this important mission. These incidents have consequences that may affect the whole world. It is the Church's duty to protect people, and it is the Order's holy mandate to save the world from the forces that are gathering."

Doc took a deep breath and looked Ghost directly in the eyes. "Yes, Archbishop Ferrer. I understand that I may be excommunicated. Yes, I understand that my status in the Order and in the Church is a direct reflection of my spiritual state. I understand that I am risking my soul to remain with the team. I have to ask you one question: If I am risking my soul because I am trying to protect the world, aren't you risking yours by threatening me with excommunication *because* I am trying to save the world from a fate that would cost millions of lives?" The priest disconnected and glared at her phone.

"What the frak, Doc?"

"Thank you, John." Doc looked up and smiled at the electronics specialist. "I believe that about covers it."

Ghost cleared his throat, "Uh, Doc. Are they serious about excommunicating you?"

Doc shrugged. "I don't honestly know. I think they were bluffing when he first talked about it, but my comments at the end may push him over the edge. It's up to him and the pope if they want to knock me out of the Order, or excommunicate me."

"What happens to your power?" Ghost gesticulated, "I mean you turned an entire lake into Holy Water and zapped a camp full of vampires with a massive miracle. Will that go away?"

"I don't know, Jonas. I've never talked to an excommunicated member of the Order. I still have my faith in God, and the training. But I don't know if I still need the ordination to work the rites."

"Fair enough. Let's hope we don't have to find out." Ghost turned to the rest of the team, "So, with no real DHS authority, we have to find and gain access to the cornerstone, rip it out of the wall, and get the key from it, all without getting arrested. And before the bad guys show up. Any thoughts?"

Six looked around from the driver's seat, "We punt. Go in and use our credentials to gain access. Assuming they still have the magic power, we use it to delay any response until we get the stone out. We need tools. Find the nearest hardware store, buy the crap we need, and take it out in broad daylight."

Spooky pointed to an overhead shot he had from the drone. "That is the current prison. About a couple hundred yards away from the old one. Which means lots of cops and quick response. Should we wait for nightfall?"

Ghost shook his head. "This truck stands out too much. We cannot sit around all day waiting to be investigated by a beat cop. I won't have another Do-Right on my hands. Six, fire up the Wagon. Spooky, find us the nearest hardware store. Hopefully they have big enough tools."

Spooky quickly recovered his drone, and Six turned the ignition over and slowly crept out of the parking lot, following Spooky's directions from the back.

THE CHARTERED CESSNA Citation X descended into Gerald R. Ford International Airport. Once it touched down, the jet taxied to the smaller ramp designed for private planes and charter flights. As they taxied, Smith saw the huge C-17 Globemaster III that had been originally assigned to Section 28. It had several parking ramp attendants waving their batons. It looked like the plane was preparing to taxi and takeoff.

On a whim, the former knight dialed the cell number he had for the pilot of the plane. The call was answered on its third ring, "Captain Kenney."

Smith smiled and spoke, "Captain. This is Agent Smith, currently Acting Director Smith. I see you are in Grand Rapids again."

"Yes, Director. Although we won't be here for long. We've been directed to break off the secondment to your agency and return to our home airbase in Charlotte. I'm glad you called. It's been a pleasure working with your agency. Once the current flap blows over, let me know if you want to use us again. I'll see if I can get the same crew for you."

"Thank you, Captain. It has been a real pleasure working with you and your crew as well. Let them know I said that, please. Do you happen to know if the Citation we were using has also been mysteriously recalled from duty as well?"

"Officially, sir, I have no idea. Unofficially? I would bet good money on it. Our charter got pulled by someone from the NSA, working directly on behalf of the President. I would bet that your other transport has been pulled as well. My copilot just informed me that the preflight is done. I have to let you go. Good luck, sir."

Smith nodded to himself, "Good luck to you, too, Captain. Safe flight."

Mulder was listening in to his side of the conversation. "Lost your transport aircraft?"

"Both of them. Barnhart will have to answer for this vendetta of his."

She looked thoughtful, "Good thing they hadn't cancelled the government credit cards yet. Although I bet they are all cancelled now."

Smith gave a low chuckle, "That would not have stopped us. As I implied before, one of the benefits of working for Section Twenty-Eight—our funding does not rely on the government budget." At her raised eyebrows, he explained, "Oh, we still have a substantial budget because we are a black agency. But the majority of our funding comes from sources that are far more... esoteric in nature. When the Unseelie court is mandated to provide twenty-five percent of their assets to you by the Gray Court, twenty-five percent of immortal fae holdings works out to be a very large sum of assets.In fact, if we had applied it to the government's budget, it would have made a sizable dent in our current national debt. But what they don't know will not hurt us."

The plane taxied to a halt outside a small building, and the pilot exited the cockpit and released the doors and stairs. As Smith walked past him, the pilot said, "It was a pleasure to fly you, sir. If we can be of any help in the future, please let us know. The passenger lounge is through those doors, and they can arrange for ground transportation if you have not already done so."

Smith shook the man's hand, "Thank you, Captain. I will certainly keep you in mind for my travels." Smith disembarked and was followed by the rest of the group.

As the group walked through the doors, Smith knew there would be a wrinkle in his plans. Standing just inside the doors were four uniformed law enforcement officers in blue shirts and darker trousers, and a man and a woman in suits that identified them as law enforcement, possibly FBI.

Smith walked to the front of the group and held his hands up, palms raised. All four of the uniformed officers drew their sidearms, although they kept them held at a low-ready position instead of at Smith. One of the suits stepped forward and held up handcuffs.

"James Smith? I'm Special Agent Simon Verburg, FBI. You are under arrest. Please turn around and place your hands behind your back."

Without turning around, Smith asked, "Who signed the warrant, Agent Verburg?"

Verburg's eyes tightened, "Mister Smith, I'm under direct orders to effect your arrest. Please do not resist."

"Special Agent-in-Charge Tressa Mulder." The female agent stepped forward, displaying her own set of credentials. "Who is your supervisor, Agent Verburg?"

Verburg was taken aback at this turn of events. He glanced at his partner, but she shrugged. He answered Mulder, "SAC Rees, ma'am. He couldn't get out of Detroit in time to meet the plane."

"I know Scott, Agent Verburg. Wait one while I give him a call."

Mulder pulled out her phone and walked past the waiting officers while she dialed the other agent's number. Verburg looked at the three people behind Smith, "Who the hell are you?"

All three of them pulled their own credentials and introduced themselves. Verburg and his partner were getting more uncomfortable at the situation by the second. Taking a lone rogue agent into custody at the behest of the President was a great assignment. Confronting a supposedly rogue agent who was actually surrounded by FBI agents, including the Washington SAC sounded like it may be a career-ending assignment. Seeing the confusion among the FBI agents, the Michigan State Police officers all holstered their firearms and stood at parade rest, watching the entertainment.

Mulder said, "Thanks, Scott. I'll tell him." She hung up the phone and told Verburg, "He'll be calling you in a couple seconds."

Verburg's phone rang. He answered it, "Agent Verburg... Yes, sir... But, sir..." There was a longer pause as the man listened to his boss. "Yes, sir. I understand. We'll clear from here and head across the state to meet you at your office." He hung up and looked dumbfounded at Mulder and Smith.

"Whatever you said to my boss got his attention, Agent Mulder. Mister Smith, you are free to go. For now."

Verburg turned on his heel and looked at the MSP officers. "Sorry guys. I'll call your post and let them know what happened. Thanks for backing us up." He shook hands with the officers as they walked out the door. Smith saw the FBI agent and his partner start talking as they walked to their government sedan.

The Acting Director turned to Mulder, "And what did you tell his boss, Agent Mulder?"

The Washington SAC blushed slightly. "I asked him who had signed the warrants, and he told me it was Barnhart. I reminded him that one of Barnhart's operations almost cost Scott his career. That man sure has pissed off a lot of people over the years."

Smith raised one eyebrow. "Remind me never to piss you off, Agent Mulder. Thank you, again, for sticking your neck out for me. Now, we need to rent a vehicle and introduce you to the Queen of the Seelie fae."

IT TOOK the team half an hour to find a hardware store that had heavy excavating tools. Six bought several types of tools, and more than one of each. He bought four twenty-pound sledgehammers, a variety of pry bars, and an assortment of other tools. The person manning the counter looked at the DHS agent strangely, but rang everything up and offered some help to take it to his car. Six declined and rolled the loaded cart out to the War Wagon.

As they pulled into the reformatory's parking lot, Six's phone rang. He glanced at the number and groaned. Dreading this call, he parked the behemoth MRAP and answered, "Hey, boss."

"Yes, sir. That is what the tv is saying. And the internal memo is probably weighing on your mind as well, right? Yes, I know that I'm still officially assigned to your office. Yes, sir. If I happen to meet with Agent Smith, I'll be sure to handle the meeting appropriately. Yes, sir. Appropriately."

The rest of the crew heard the loud, "God dammit!" from the tiny speaker near Six's ear.

The former mercenary smiled and said, "Yes, sir. I'm sure the big guy already has. I will contact you once this current crisis is over with. Goodbye, sir."

When he hung up, the vampire merc hung his head and muttered, "Shit."

Ghost laughed, "Yup. That about sums it up. Ok who is going to contact the tour crew and let them know what we are doing? Gretchen?"

The team's liaison nodded. "Doc, why don't you join me? We'll be less threatening. Once we find it and let them know what we will do to it, you guys can come knock it out."

Gretchen and Doc grabbed radios and dismounted out the back, leaving the hatch open as Six and Ghost sorted their gear. They would not take their heavy weapons with them, but they would carry the tools to remove the cornerstone. Six grabbed all four sledgehammers while Ghost took two of the larger pry bars.

Gretchen and Doc walked up to the front of the reformatory, following the signs for the tour office. Walking inside, there was a woman in her thirties standing behind the counter. Dressed in an Ohio State Reformatory polo shirt and jeans, her curly black hair was cut fairly short, and her glasses added to her librarian look. The name tag under the OSR logo said "H. Kalafut."

The woman smiled, "Hi folks. How can we help you today? We have a tour that will be going through the reformatory in about thirty minutes."

Gretchen smiled disarmingly and held up her credentials, "Special Agent Gretchen Massey, Homeland Security. Can I speak with the manager, please?"

The woman looked puzzled, then worried. "I'm the manager. My name is Heather. What can I do for Homeland Security?"

Gretchen nodded, "I'm afraid we've got a situation that is classified, so I can't tell you exactly why I need to know, but can you show me the cornerstone for the reformatory?"

Heather looked puzzled and then nodded. "Is there something dangerous in the building? I have a tour group in there now, and we have two more scheduled today and this evening."

Doc shook her head, "We don't believe it will require any disruption to your schedule. We need to see the cornerstone first."

Heather placed a small sign in the doorway that proclaimed someone would be back within a couple minutes. After locking the door, Heather motioned for Gretchen and Doc to follow her as she led them to the main entrance of the reformatory. There, in one of the corners formed by the architecture, the cornerstone was built into the wall. Approximately three feet wide and eighteen inches tall, the beautiful marble block dedicated the "Intermediate Penitentiary" and listed the names of the first prison board, the architect and the construction engineer.

Gretchen and Doc looked at the stone and nodded to themselves. Gretchen turned back to the manager, "Heather, I hate to ruin your day, but we have to bring in a crew to remove part, or all, of this cornerstone. Today. It is a national security matter."

Heather protested, and Gretchen began to answer her protests as Doc grabbed her radio off her belt. Holding the transmit key, she said, "Ghost, this is Doc. It's here. It's about three feet by a foot and a half. We've got about half an hour before the next tour shows up."

"Copy, Doc. We're on our way. Ghost out."

25

REFORMATORY

Ohio State Reformatory, Mansfield, Ohio

Heather, the reformatory tour and gift shop manager, trailed off her protestations as two men carrying sledgehammers and pry bars walked toward the front of the reformatory. They had emerged from behind the large black military tank-like vehicle and walked with a purpose toward the two Homeland Security agents standing with her. She finally got her wits together enough to ask Gretchen, "What are you going to do?"

Gretchen looked at the woman. She realized that this woman was in charge of preserving the historic site of the reformatory and that she would have to explain to her boss that someone from Homeland Security had just broken open the cornerstone for the building, without a warrant or court order. The federal agent put a gentle hand on the woman's shoulder, "I'm sorry. But as I said, we have to take apart at least part of the cornerstone. Why don't you call the tour guide in the reformatory and tell her to delay coming out for a while? It will be easier for them."

The tour manager raised her radio to her lips as Six and Ghost stepped up to join the group. Six dropped two of the giant sledges he was carrying. He looked at the cornerstone and then back at Gretchen. "This looks like the one Smith described. Should we carefully work it out, or are we in a hurry, today?"

Ghost looked at Gretchen, then back at the vampire. "Normally, I'd say we carefully pull it out, but I don't know how long we'll have before the police show up once we start breaking it open. I'd say we're in a hurry. Gretchen?"

The team's liaison nodded, and Six took a step closer to the cornerstone. Grasping a sledge in each hand, he raised his right arm to smash into the stone and brilliant flash of blue went off in his face. When his eyes cleared, he was staring at the minuscule point of a tiny sword wielded by a pixie in full battle armor. As he stared at the little pixie, he saw a second blue flash and a second pixie appeared in front of Ghost, holding the tip of her sword about three inches from the monster hunter's left eye.

Heather gasped and dropped her radio from nerveless fingers. Gretchen startled and then realized that these were the guardians that Smith had left so long ago. Ghost did not move any muscles, except to slowly drop the pry bars in his hands.

The female pixie in golden armor spoke in the high, trilling voice of a pixie warrior, "Stop your desecration, or you shall feel the wrath of our Family. By what right to you lay claim to this stone?"

Ghost thought back to the pass phrase, "The Knight of the Realm requires the artifact. I am Special Agent Jonas Vanhof, in service to Sir Knight, and my companions are retrieving the artifact to present it to him."

In a blink, the pixie was two feet from Ghost, her sword safely in its scabbard, and hovering at eye level to the tall monster hunter. The little sprite bowed, "Aurora Plicci. Matriarch of the Family and Guardian of this artifact. Well met, Jonas Vanhof."

The pixie in front of Six glowered at the Matriarch, "Mother. How do we know they were sent by Sir Knight? And this one is not human. He is far darker, possibly Unseelie."

Six growled, "Shut your mouth, pixie. I'm not Unseelie. And if you don't want to meet what I am, you'll put away that toothpick."

The Matriarch sighed, "I apologize for my youngest son." She glared at the wayward pixie, "He is headstrong and does not yet know when to mind his manners." She turned back to Ghost, "May I present Enitza Colluzo, my youngest son who is still learning maturity. These first hundred years are the roughest."

Ghost chuckled, then gave a slight bow to the younger pixie, "Well met, Enitza Colluzo."

The young faerie sheathed his sword with a flaring gesture and made a bow to Ghost, "Well met, Special Agent Jonas Vanhof. I serve Sir Knight and jealously guard his artifact."

Six could not hold back a grunt of laughter, and the pixie whirled on the Six with a speed that even the vampire could not follow. Once again, the pixie's sword was pointed at Six's eye.

Six clamped down his laughter, apologizing, "Pardon, Enitza Colluzo. I mean no offense and do not doubt that you make a mighty guardian of the artifact."

The Matriarch trilled something in a high-pitched and sing-song language that Ghost could not follow. The young pixie once again put away his sword, glaring at Six the whole time.

"Again, my apologies for my offspring, Jonas Vanhof. He shall be taught manners at another time."

"It is nothing," said Ghost. "We understand and appreciate the eagerness and bravery of your offspring as he guards the artifact. May we retrieve the artifact now?"

"What the hell are those things?" Heather's quivering voice from behind the agents and pixies startled them all. "And what the hell are they doing here? In daylight?"

Gretchen turned to talk to the manager and pull her away from the cornerstone. The Matriarch watched them go, "Oh dear. We have never revealed ourselves to her, or anyone else directly. I fear this may cause you trouble among other humans."

Ghost looked at the pixie and shook his head, "Gretchen will work with her. Although, you might consider vanishing until she is gone, or until we need your help."

The Matriarch nodded, "We will do so. Call my name if you wish our assistance. Farewell, Jonas Vanhof." The two pixies faded from view.

Six looked around to make sure there were no more pixies around, then he swung his right arm with a large amount of his prodigious strength and landed the hammer on the marble face of the cornerstone. The sledge rang against the stone, and a large crack appeared, spreading about seven inches out from the center of the impact. He followed with his left, soon developing a rhythm with the hammer blows that almost sounded like the beating of a giant steel heart. It took Six about thirty seconds before the head of one of his hammers knocked a large piece out and Ghost could see a hollow spot behind it.

The monster hunter held up a hand for Six to stop and then stuck his hand into the small cavity in the solid marble. He grasped a small leather-wrapped bundle and smiled. The bundle came out of the hole easily and he held the bundle up in his outstretched hand. Six bent down to peer into the hole and indicated that there was nothing left in there.

The manager was apoplectic and struck dumb at the destruction to the polished marble of the cornerstone. She pulled out her cell phone and dialed a number with tears in her eyes. "It's Heather. They've destroyed the cornerstone." She turned away and walked back toward the tour office.

All the agent's radios sounded, and Spooky's voice had risen in pitch due to excitement. "Ghost, this is Spooky. We have two incursion events in this area. Like Philly."

Ghost cursed, and Doc quietly murmured, "Amen."

The monster hunter snatched his radio off his belt, "Copy that Spooky, we're heading back to the Wagon." He let go of the transmit button. Looking at his companions, he pointed to Gretchen and Doc with his hand that still held the radio. "Gretchen and Doc, take cover in the tour office. If this is more dragons and trolls or Chikaran orcs, you will do better to keep everyone else safe. Have that manager tell the tour folks to go to solitary. They should be safe there."

He nodded at Six, "Let's get back to the truck and gear up. We may only have a couple seconds." The team split, Gretchen and Doc sprinting for the tour office, with Six and Ghost making the dash for the War Wagon. Ghost shouted out, "Aurora Plicci, I summon you."

Suddenly there were two blue-tinged pixies flying along and pacing the men. The Matriarch said, "You called, Jonas Vanhof?"

Breathlessly, Ghost nodded. As they reached the truck, Six jumped up inside to grab some armor and firepower. Ghost looked at the two pixies, "Yes, Matriarch. There are two gates opening in this area, and I believe whoever is coming will be trying to take the artifact. I would ask for your help in defending the artifact, my team, and the other humans here."

Six leapt out of the truck. Having donned some of his armor, the vampire had one of Heavy's AA-12 shotguns on a single-point sling across his chest. Clenched in his right hand, he still held the two sledgehammers. In his left, he held Ghosts's long coat and cane. Those he tossed to the monster hunter with a casual indifference. "I figured you might want these."

The pixie known as Enitza Colluzo stared with wide eyes at Six, "What are you? You are not fully human." Six flashed his fangs and his vision changed as his eyes went black. The pixie recoiled in horror, "A nightwalker!"

Ghost got the young pixie's attention and tried to calm the fairy.

"But he is our nightwalker. And the enemy won't see him coming." The pixie nodded as if reassured, but he noticed that the small sprite glided away from Six, putting Ghost between the vampire and the pixie.

The air pressure changed and Ghost and Six whirled around to see what was coming. A large black gate formed in the sky, about twenty feet over the parking lot. In one smooth motion, Six dropped the hammers to the ground and shouldered the AA-12. He flipped the safety off with his thumb and pointed the sights at the inky black hole.

The first dragon's snout that poked out of the hole got three mini-grenades across its nose and one even up it's flaring nostril. The explosions rocked the dragon's head and great gouts of blood and ichor rained down. The dragon's momentum caused it to tumble forward out of the gate, crashing onto its back and throwing the armored rider to the pavement in a heap of arms and legs.

Six adjusted his aim and placed two shots in rapid succession into the chest of the rider as it shakily climbed to its feet. The grenades exploded on contact, ripping through the armor and the flesh hiding underneath the protection. The armored rider was torn in two by the twin blasts. A blast of energy slammed into the pavement about two feet away from Six, throwing him to the ground as two more dragons flew through the gate.

Ghost slapped the panic button on the inside of the hatch and then got out of the way as it levered into place, sealing with a pneumatic hiss. Hastily donning his jacket, he looked at the dragons exiting the portal and realized that he was not carrying enough gun for this fight.

The hairs on the back of his neck stood up as he felt another gate opening. Looking around to locate it, he heard screams coming from inside the tour office. *Shit.* The monster hunter ran toward the office, hoping Six would be able to defend himself against the pair of dragons.

The gate had opened just outside the tour office. Drawing her sidearm, Gretchen stood in a low-ready position, waiting for a target to come through the door. Doc grabbed Heather and pulled her behind the desk. Shoving the manager roughly down, the combat priest waited to see what was being sent this time.

They did not have long to wait. The door crashed open, splintering as it bounced off the interior wall, and crashing to the floor. Heather screamed in terror and a large troll stepped through the opening. Gretchen pulled the trigger rapidly, carefully starting at center mass and walking her rounds up the target to its head.

The 9mm rounds would normally have bounced off the creature's armor and hide, but these were special rounds that Norbert had loaded. Every round flashed as it hit the creature. The center of each hollowpoint consisted of a small primer and a tiny amount of a very energetic explosive. When the round struck something, the primer detonated the explosive, shaping and driving the energy in a tiny super-heated ball of plasma. The plasma cut through armor and the tough troll hide before coming to a very painful rest inside the troll. The final round into the creature's skull penetrated through the thick bone and liquified the creature's small brain.

The massive body fell with a thud that shook the floor. An enraged roar came from the hallway and a pair of trolls smashed through the doorframe, entering at the same time. The one nearest to Gretchen got four quick rounds to its neck and head before it could even comprehend the threat. The giant troll next to it back-handed Gretchen, throwing her across the office to land in a crumpled heap against the far wall. Heather screamed as she saw Gretchen land. The DHS agent groaned and was moving very slowly.

Doc stood and held up her large cross. Saying a liturgy in Latin, the troll seemed puzzled at first. It then laughed, "Silly human. Your god has no sway over me." It casually stepped closer to the priest, laughing. Standing over the still chanting priest, the troll spoke again, "If your god is powerful, have him smite me. Your god is weak and has no power over my kind."

Doc kept chanting, although she gripped her cross slightly differently. The troll towered two feet over her, and its rancid breath was causing her to lose concentration. Sensing the creature had utterly dismissed her, she pulled the hidden dagger from the sheath in the cross and plunged eight inches of blessed silver upward, through the underside of its chin, and into its tiny brain.

The creature's laughter died, as did the rest of its body. Doc sidestepped neatly as the tall, heavy corpse slammed into the floor at her feet. She looked at the doorway again as a Chikara stepped through the open portal. It saw the naked blade in her hand, and she knew she would meet her Savior that day.

Hearing the screams, Ghost ran as fast as he could toward the tour office. On the way, he drew the sword from his cane, and it glowed blue. As he rounded the corner, he came face to chest with a large Chikaran orc. Slamming his enchanted blade into the crea-

ture's guts, he stepped back and yanked. Blood flew from the puncture wound in its chest, and the beast crumpled to the ground. The
creature's roar of agony turned to a burble as blood and ichor
bubbled out of its mouth. The troll behind the Chikara raised its
warhammer to strike down the human in front of it when two blue
streaks slammed into the creature's chest, making it stagger back.

The pixies split up, each going after one of the troll's upraised
arms. They danced around the massive wrists, drawing blood as
their razor sharp blades cut deep into the hide and bone. In the
blink of an eye, both of the creature's wrists were severed, and the
massive upraised warhammer was crashing down on its own skull.
The pixies giggled as the troll's cranium was mangled by its own
weapon, and Ghost felt a chuckle come from his mouth as well.
Nodding to the pixies, the monster hunter said, "Thanks. You may
need to help my colleague outside."

Both pixies shot down the hall toward the parking lot, and Ghost
stepped through the gaping doorway. He watched as the Chikara in
front of him backhanded Doc, driving her across the room and into
a bookcase. As he watched their priest land on the floor, the monster
hunter shouted, "Hey, asshole. Not brave enough to attack a man?
Have to attack women? You must be a cub fresh from its mother's
teat."

The Chikara whirled, eyes glowing red in anger. "You dare insult
me, puny human? I will rip your limbs from your body and use
them to beat these females to death."

Four loud shots rang out, and the orc got a strange look on its
face. The red eyes extinguished to coal black, and the creature's
head tilted up, as if looking at the sky. As the creature slowly fell
forward, Ghost sidestepped to avoid being crushed. As the creature
landed with enough force to shake the floor, the monster hunter saw
the holes in the creature's armored back.

Stunned, he looked up and saw Heather, the tour manager,
holding Gretchen's service pistol, with the slide locked back on an
empty chamber and magazine. He slowly reached out and took
ahold of the weapon. Once he had it in his grasp, he looked at the
woman. He said, "Thanks for that. Nice shooting."

She turned to him with wide eyes, and in a low, shaking voice,
said, "What... the fuck... was that?" Realizing what she had said, she
blushed and covered her mouth with her hand.

Ghost shook his head, "That was a troll." Ghost trailed off as he
strode over to Doc. He knelt by her and looked at how she had
fallen. She was on her side, with several books lying on top of her.

Gretchen moaned and stood, holding her wrist and arm. Ghost handed the gun to Gretchen, and she worked with one hand to release the magazine, slide another one into the receiver, and drop the slide. She reholstered and looked down at "Doc. Is she...?"

Ghost felt for the pulse in Doc's neck.

26

VICTORY

Six rolled to his feet and raised the shotgun to his shoulder. Remembering what Boomer had told him, he aimed at one of the riders and stroked the trigger three times. All three shots missed, and the rider threw his hand out toward Six, slamming him to the ground again with some kind of invisible force.

So you want to do it the hard way, huh? My pleasure. Six unhooked the shotgun and dropped it to the pavement. As he sprang forward, he scooped up the two sledgehammers at a dead sprint. He bounded up the hood and roof of a small pickup truck in front of the dragon and leapt into the air.

Using the momentum from his leap, he carried past the side of the dragon and landed on the back in front of the rider. The federal agent-turned-vampire swung from both shoulders, timing the swing so that the sledges slammed into the shoulders of the dragonrider at the same time. The force required to break marble will also break the bones of most living creatures. This rider was no exception. The back and chest were shattered underneath the crushing armor, and both arms hung useless. The rider gave a single cry before Six swung one of the hammers and slammed it into the crown of the helmet. Blood fountained from beneath the helmet and the rider slumped in his saddle. The dragon gave a high keening sound as its rider was taken from it and then dropped the last ten feet to the ground.

Six managed to stay on his feet and he turned toward the head of the great beast on which he was standing. The vampire agent tossed one of the hammers to the ground where it landed with a clang. The other he gripped like a baseball bat and wound up, the sledge over his right shoulder, prepared to strike. He whistled to get the beast's attention, "Hey, you overgrown lizard!" Six roared. "Missing your buddy?"

The dragon's great head roared and swiveled to approach the creature who taunted him and killed his bonded rider. As the massive head approached, Six swung with all of his might. The sledgehammer slammed into the side of the dragon's skull with all the force of a wrecking ball. Bones shattered. Blood and ichor sprayed, and the dragon's brain was pulped. The massive head dropped to the ground, taking Six and his sledgehammer with it.

The vampire rolled to his feet and gave a mighty heave to pull the hammer free from inside the skull of the dragon. Behind him, a rider shouted in an unfamiliar language, and Six instinctually dove to the right, diving over and rolling behind the head and neck of the dragon he just killed. The agent's instincts saved his life as a white hot ball of flame landed and exploded on the spot where he had just been standing.

As the agent was contemplating another reckless sprint at the dragon, he saw two blue light trails blur past and head straight toward the big beast. The dragon roared at its new challengers. Six looked up over the neck of the dead beast. One of the pixies was buzzing around the dragon's mouth, and the beast was snapping at it, trying to snatch it from the air. The other pixie was diving on the rider. The pixie with the golden armor, who Six assumed was the Matriarch, slashed and stabbed at every joint in the complex armor.

Seeing that both the dragon and the rider were occupied, Six rushed out from behind the dragon corpse and ran at the head of the beast where Enitza Colluzo was harassing the giant lizard. Winding up as he ran, the vampire covered the distance in a mere blink of an eye. Just before he reached the lowered head of the dragon, he yelled out, "Out of the way!"

The young male faerie heard the warning and shot straight up about ten feet. The dragon also heard the warning and turned his massive head just in time to catch the full brunt of the sledge-hammer being swung by a vampire. The fiberglass shaft shattered and the now loose hammer head slammed down through the head and continued through to exit out of the bottom of the skull covered in brains and ichor.

The dragon dropped suddenly, and the rider was thrown from the saddle to crash on the pavement. As the shaken dragon rider got to its feet, Six slashed out with clawed talons and sliced through the armor and skin of the neck. The next swipe ripped out a large portion of the rider's trachea and jugular vein. The rider collapsed and convulsed on the ground for a few seconds before succumbing to death.

The vampire federal agent looked up at the remaining rider. This one had more ornate armor and weaponry. Six snarled, "You're next, asshole."

The rider turned his dragon in mid hover and flew it back through the already closing gate. After the dragon disappeared through the inky blackness, the gate spun down and disappeared. Six turned to the pixies and said, "Thanks. Let's go see what happened to Ghost."

Six jogged toward the tour office, followed by the pixies. As he entered the building, he came across the bodies of the trolls and orcs laying in the hallways. Jogging past the corpses, he came to a halt inside the shattered doorway.

"She has a pulse. It's weak, but it's there." Ghost said to Gretchen before seeing Six. "Everything taken care of, John?"

Six nodded. "The dragons and riders are dead or gone. How can I help?" He indicated Doc's prone form.

The Matriarch floated forward, sinking down to float at Ghost's level, "Perhaps I can assist?"

Ghost bowed his head slightly, "I would be in debt to you, Matriarch." The monster hunter scooted back, letting the pixie into the small circle of humans.

Six walked over to the stunned manager, "Heather, is it? Do you have a first aid kit, Heather? Also, can you check with the other staff and visitors on site? Make sure no critters got away from us?"

Heather started, then cringed away from the agent. Six realized that he must still be showing his creature, and he had a giant automatic shotgun strapped across his chest. He closed his eyes and took a deep breath. When he reopened them, they were back to human colors, and he felt the canines retract into his jaws. He smiled a now-fangless smile. "Heather?"

She slowly nodded, eyes wide. "But you're a.... And those creatures.... I had to shoot it."

"Yes, Heather. Those creatures were real, but they're dead now."

Six tried to soften his voice. He tried to remember that she had just been attacked by trolls and orcs. "I need you to check in with the other tour leader. Find out if they are ok."

She nodded, slowly, shakily grabbing the radio hanging off her belt. As she called to the tour guide, Six turned back to Doc and the Matriarch. He saw that the priest was enveloped in a soft blue glow that intensified around her head.

The pixie was speaking in her high-pitched melodic voice. Six could not understand what she was saying. Doc suddenly coughed and opened her eyes. The priest tried to sit up and winced in pain. Her voice was a quiet rasp, "What happened?"

Ghost knelt next to her, "You picked a fight with a Chikara." He gave a small smile, "by the way, you lost."

Doc gave a small laugh and then groaned in pain. "Don't make me laugh, it hurts too much." She looked around, and saw Six and Gretchen, "Are you ok, Gretchen? I saw you hit the wall."

The team liaison nodded, cradling her arm. "Just a banged up arm. Do we need to get you to the hospital?"

Doc looked at the pixie floating above her. The Matriarch shook her head, "Just some rest. I believe I have repaired the damage, but your body needs to help the healing process. You need to let your body rest and recuperate."

Doc slowly sat up, wincing at the pain in her back and ribs. Her head swam for a moment and she closed her eyes. Once she opened them, she motioned for Ghost and Six to help her get to her feet. Standing was painful, but she looked at the wall where she impacted, and realized that she was lucky to be alive.

The priest looked at Heather, who was staring at her. No, she was staring at the pixie that was hovering behind her right shoulder. "Are you ok, Heather?"

"I'm fine. But I think I'm having a mental breakdown. First it was giant trolls, and now tiny pixies. I don't understand any of this. Why would they attack here?"

Ghost spoke up, "Because of the artifact we were retrieving. We'll be taking it with us, so they won't be bothering you again."

"Bothering? You call this 'bothering?'" The woman gestured at the ruined office around her. "I don't know what your definition is, but this is way beyond bothered to me!" Heather's voice shifted from fear to anger. "How are we going to repair all the damage you've done?"

Ghost's radio crackled, interrupting the woman's tirade. "Ghost, this is Spooky. You guys gotta get out of there. Police inbound, and it sounds like locals, sheriff, and state police. The prison next door is locking down, and I expect choppers overhead soon."

"Copy that, Spooky. We're on our way. Pop the hatch and recall your drone." Ghost looked at the others and said, "You heard him. Time to go." The monster hunter turned to the Matriarch, "Aurora Plicci, I thank you for your protection and help. You are welcome to join us, for we are headed to the Queen's throne."

The Matriarch bowed, "Thank you, Jonas Vanhof. We shall accompany you and help keep the artifact safe for Sir Knight. It would be good to converse with Sir Gawain again." Her youngest son enthusiastically nodded. The elder pixie moved and spoke over her shoulder, "We will join you in a few moments. We must gather our possessions."

As Ghost turned to walk out, the tour manager stood right in front of him, hands balled into fists and planted firmly on her hips. The woman raised one hand and pointed her finger at Ghost. "No, sir. You are not leaving here before the police show up. How am I going to explain the presence of these creatures? Besides, your agency better cover the repair bill for this office and anything you damaged outside. Especially the cornerstone. No. You are not leaving me here to talk to the police alone!" Her voice raised an octave toward the end of her ranting.

The monster hunter looked the woman over critically. She had just encountered Chikaran orcs, and she had even killed one. And now she was standing up to heavily armed federal agents. She might just make a good addition to the agency. Ghost looked at Gretchen, then back at Heather, a bemused smile on his face. "Fine. Come with us, then. If you don't want to explain all this to the police, you had better be on our truck. If you are not on the truck, you will be left behind."

Six and Gretchen were helping Doc shuffle past the angry tour manager. Once they were out the door, Ghost lowered his voice held his hands out to try to placate the angry woman. "Look, Heather. You showed incredible courage when you attacked that orc. You haven't freaked out with Agent Black's vampirism. And you even accepted the pixie Matriarch in your office without having a mental break."

Ghost was counting points on his fingers, "You are plenty tough, and have shown yourself to be flexible enough. Why don't you consider at least applying to my agency? I can guarantee an interview with the Director if you come with us, and the pay and benefits are far beyond what you might make here. What do you say?"

Heather stared at the federal agent with a slack-jawed expression. She paused, considering how crazy this federal agent's offer seemed. But she just killed that orc-thing, right? With no family to tie her to Mansfield, and not even a pet at home, she decided to try it.

"Okay. Let me grab my purse, and I'll go out with you." She reached behind her trashed desk and found her purse. Miraculously, it had not spilled when Doc had bounced into the desk and bookcase surrounding it. She quickly followed this strange federal agent out the mangled doorway, down the hall, and out of the reformatory doors, carefully stepping over or around more creature bodies.

As they hit the sidewalk, Ghost broke into a jog, and Heather kept up with him. She slowed a bit when she saw the massive dragon carcasses in the parking lot. She quickly caught up to Ghost. Breathless, she asked, "Are those?"

"Yes. We need to leave now. Questions on the road." The federal monster hunter heard sirens in the background, and they were getting closer. He gently held the woman's elbow, encouraging her to move a bit faster.

When they reached the back of the War Wagon, Heather's eyes went wide. Ghost coaxed her up the rear steps and hit the hatch button when they were both inside the truck. Six was already throwing the massive MRAP in gear before the hatch sealed itself shut. Heather hastily found a padded seat and buckled her seatbelt just as Six took a hard left out of the parking lot and onto the access road. Ignoring the stop sign, a hard right put the truck on South Olivesburg Road, and another quick right put the truck on US 30. Six flipped on the lights and sirens and mashed the pedal to the floor. The massive vehicle accelerated at the top of the ramp and the team was soon on their way through the city of Mansfield and heading towards Michigan.

As Heather caught her breath, she looked around the back of the MRAP. There was another federal agent in front of several computer screens. Sitting next to him was the priest they called Doc, and Gretchen, both of them cradling parts of their body. The team leader, called Jonas something by the pixies, had climbed up into the passenger seat by the scary vampire driver. Resting on the bench beside Heather was the pixie Jonas had called the matriarch and sitting on the gun rack behind her head was the other pixie. She closed her eyes wondering what she had just gotten herself into.

About fifteen minutes later, Six turned off the lights and sirens. The relative silence startled Heather, and she sat up straight. The young agent in front of the computer screens called out, "No pursuit from law enforcement. They still are trying to figure out what happened and what all those creatures are. We can go back to highway speeds." Heather saw the driver nod, and the vehicle felt like it slowed.

The young man behind the computers turned to look at Heather and the pixies. He bowed slightly to the older pixie, "Well met, Aurora Plicci, Matriarch of the Family. I am Special Agent John Smith."

The pixie returned the greeting in her melodious voice, "Well met, John Smith. This is my youngest son, Enitza Colluzo. We thank you for your hospitality."

The young agent then turned and stuck out his hand to Heather, "Hi, Special Agent John Smith. You can call me 'Spooky.' Everyone else does." His grin was infectious.

Heather smiled, "Heather Kalafut. You must have been the voice on the other end of the radio. Nice to meet you, Spooky."

"As an amateur paranormal investigator, I have to ask. Is the reformatory really as haunted as they claim? I've seen the shows, and the evidence looks pretty convincing."

Heather nodded. "The official answer is always, 'We don't know.' But the unofficial answer from anyone who worked there or investigated there will be a resounding yes. Frankly, I've had enough shit happen to me that I won't close up at night by myself."

"Sorry about that." The high-pitched voice was filled with laughter and came from somewhere to Heather's right.

Heather turned to look at the pixie who was sitting on the gun rack. He was laughing, rocking back and forth, and holding his stomach. Heather glanced down, and even the Matriarch was trying to suppress a smile. Heather frowned, "What's so funny?"

The younger pixie's laughter redoubled, and the tiny creature fell off the gun rack. Landing on its backside, the creature winced, "Ouch." The pixie stood, still giggling. "I actually am apologizing for scaring you. I didn't know you at the time."

"Wait! You mean to tell me that you were behind the ghost stuff?" Heather was getting perturbed. "For all those years since the building closed?"

The Matriarch smiled and spoke for her offspring, "Yes, Heather Kalafut. I and my family have been the cause of the supernatural occurrences. You can hardly blame us though. After all, protecting a building for over a hundred years does get boring."

Spooky muttered a soft curse. "Well, that's one place that gets removed from the bucket list. I'll have to tell the team when I see them. They're gonna be crushed."

Twenty-two miles behind the War Wagon, a tour guide and several tourists were being led out of the Ohio State Reformatory by police officers. While not in custody, the small group was being questioned about the bodies of the creatures in the main hall and the tour office. As they were led outside, the group gasped or screamed at the sight of the giant dragon carcasses. The tour guide was almost to the back of the police cruiser when he turned to the police officer and asked, "Where's Heather?"

27

RECRUITS

Seelie Court, Grand Rapids, Michigan

The rental SUV pulled up to the gate at the end of the drive, and a tall, thin man with long blond hair stepped out of the guard shack. He approached the side of the truck and the driver lowered the window. He stepped closer and looked in, "Good afternoon, ma'am. May I help you?"

"Director James Smith from Section Twenty-Eight to see the Queen." Agent Mulder looked at the man. He was different in a way that was slightly odd. *Maybe it was the purple eyes,* she thought.

The man leaned down and looked inside the truck. Recognizing Smith in the passenger seat, he bowed his head, "Well met, Sir Gawain. It is good to see you again."

Smith smiled and bowed his head slightly, "Well met, Alexis Darkcinder. It is good to see you as well my friend. Is Her Majesty able to meet with me?"

"I do not doubt it, but I will call ahead. Your wounded warrior is currently under her care."

After a few moments on the radio, the man leaned back down and said, "Your visit has been approved, Sir Gawain. Your companions will wait in the courtyard with the vehicle."

The gate opened and Mulder drove up the drive. She glanced sideways at Smith, "That man was odd. And where do you get a name like Alexis Darkcinder? Sounds like a thirty-two-year-old gamer who lives in his mom's basement."

Smith gave a slight smile, "I am sure he got the name from the same people he got his looks, his elven parents."

"Wait, you mean he was an elf? Dammit, I wish you'd warn me of these things."

From the back, Stratton leaned forward and piped up, "He called you Sir Gawain. Like the knight? Is that a title, or something?"

Smith shook his head, "It's not a title. It is my name. Agent Mulder can tell you some of my story while you wait, but the short version is that I actually am Sir Gawain, Knight of the Round Table and Defender of the Realm."

Stratton slumped back in his seat, mouth agape. Spooks shook her head, "No way. How are you still alive?"

Smith looked over his shoulder, "That is another tale. We shall have to discuss it later." Mulder brought the SUV to a halt next to a large black panel truck with DHS markings. "For now, you may exit the vehicle, but stay in this direct area. Do not go where you are not explicitly invited. This is the Seelie Court, and I do not want you to make an interplanar incident."

All four doors of the SUV opened, and five people stepped out. Smith turned to see a familiar face approaching from the main house. He bowed slightly, straightened, smiled, and loudly proclaimed, "Well met, Tar Katel. It is good to see you are still serving Her Majesty."

The creature approaching the truck was tall. Mulder noticed the powerful physical build and the large horns that came from the side of its head and wrapped around to almost touch in the front. She did not recognize the make or model of the pistol on its hip, but she noticed the sword that hung in a scabbard from the other side of the creature's waist. It boomed a greeting.

"Well met, Sir Gawain, Knight of the Round Table and Defender of the Realm. It has been entirely too many years since we have shared a meal. Her Majesty is eagerly awaiting your arrival in the Council Chamber where she attends your fallen warrior. Your other warrior and the *Claíomh an Sí* also await you in the chamber. My guards will keep your companions company while you attend the Queen."

"Thank you, Tar Katel. I am looking forward to our meeting. Shall we go?"

With a glance back and a silent warning to relax, Smith followed the large creature into the house. As he disappeared inside, Mulder and the other FBI agents looked around at the compound. It was a large house set back in the woods with a copper-colored metal roof that had a patina of blues and light greens. The sprawling ranch-style house had a circular parking area in front of the main entrance, and a brick walkway and patio area leading to the front door. Four large creatures similar to the one that had greeted Smith stood in various locations, all within several yards of the front door.

Inside, the minotaur led Smith through the hallway to the doors outside the Council Chamber. Tó Coferal was standing and waiting at the open doorway. Reaching out to Smith, the Queen's Knight said, "Well met, Sir Gawain. It is my honor to welcome you, friend."

Smith reached forward and clasped the forearm of the elf while the elf's hand clasped his own forearm. "Well met, Tó Coferal. It has been far to long, my friend."

"Her Majesty is working the final weaving to help heal your warrior. Please join us in the Chamber."

Smith followed the elf inside the room. Looking around the large room, Smith noticed the wall of windows that let in the light and looked out upon the forest beyond the window. The room was rich with dark woods and dark green colors, and several chairs were against the wall ringing the room. In the center of the room stood a platform around which everyone stood. Heavy lay stretched out on the platform, with the Seelie Queen standing over him muttering phrases and chanting in the ancient elvish language of magic and power.

His warrior was enveloped by a soft green and white glow, pulsing with energy and concentrating around the big warrior's head and chest. Four pixies hovered opposite the queen with their backs to the doorway , all of them with upraised hands and chanting in their melodious harmonies. Even the Queen's Hand-maidens were unusually still. Each of the specially chosen pixies that guarded the Queen were almost stationary, slowly letting themselves drift a few inches before slowly drifting back to their position.

He nodded to Boomer and Dancer across the room as he entered, and he slowly made his way over to them. He shook hands with Boomer, but Dancer wrapped her arms around him and hugged him. Not comfortable with a hug from a Fury, but recognizing the inner turmoil of a seventeen-year-old, he patted her on the back a couple of times before he gently disengaged her. They stood silently as the Queen and the pixies worked on Heavy.

It was a few minutes later when the Queen finally let her arms drop. She bowed her head, exhausted, as she stopped chanting. The pixies also dropped their arms, and the green and white glow around Heavy seemed to sink into the big warrior. His breathing seemed to ease, and his skin slowly went from gray-ish to his normal dark color.

Tó Coferal stepped up to his Queen's side and gently took her elbow, allowing her to use him as a crutch or prop. She looked up and saw Smith for the first time, smiling. "Sir Gawain, it is good of you to return to the Court of Light."

Smith bowed at the waist, "Your Majesty. It is good to be able to return to the Court of Light. It has been far too long."

The Queen waved her hand at the doorway, "Let us retire to the throne room where I may welcome you properly, Sir Knight." Smith nodded and the Seelie Queen led the way, leaning heavily on her knight as she walked. Boomer and Dancer trailed behind their boss, glancing at each other. Boomer silently mouthed the question, *"Sir Gawain?"* Her protégé shrugged.

Silently, Dancer questioned Vellath, *Hey, Big Guy. The Seelie Queen just called Director Smith "Sir Gawain." He can't be that knight, can he?*

She heard another one of the dragon's chuckles in her mind, *'Tis not for me to tell his stories, Little One. You will have to ask him yourself.*

You big lizard, Dancer complained. *When are you going to give me a straight answer?*

This time she knew the dragon was amused. She could hear it in his tone, *When are you going to ask the right question, Little One?*

Dancer pursed her lips and went silent. She felt the amusement as the dragon contained in her sword fell back into his slumber. She shook her head at Boomer. They would have to ask him directly.

In the throne room, the Queen settled onto her throne. An elven servant brought a goblet to her Queen and left just as quickly. Once she drank from the chalice, she straightened a little and nodded at her Knight.

The elven guardian stood straight and cleared his throat. Projecting his voice, he proclaimed, "Sir Gawain, Knight of the round Table and Defender of the Realm. Signatory to the *E'Tuatha* Accords."

The Queen said, "Well met, Sir Gawain."

Smith gave a short bow and said, "Well met, Your Majesty. May the Light ever shine on this Court and on your Reign."

The Queen nodded and smiled, "Now that we have observed the court formalities Sir Knight, how can I be of service to you?"

Smith smiled and visibly relaxed. "Your Majesty, I am here to inquire about my warrior, Arthur Murphy. Will he survive his terrible injuries?"

The Queen nodded, "Yes. I believe we have repaired all of his internal injuries, including the broken neck and back. He should be able to recover well, although there may be some minor impairment. He will need to rest for days until he can regain the energy that his body used to repair itself. However, he is no longer in any danger of dying."

Smith looked relieved, and he heard a sigh and a murmured "Thank god" behind him. The Section 28 Director could not keep the relief out of his voice, "I and Section Twenty-Eight thank Your Majesty for your generous help. How may we repay the debt to you and your Court?"

The Queen shook her head, "There is no debt. The *Cainteoir* requested our assistance, and we willingly gave it. This Court is pleased that we could assist your warrior. As to the other matter that was asked, we have contacted Praetorian Urteghat Dhorjachen, and she was glad to be of assistance. When they are needed, my warriors will be there."

Smith nodded and thought for a moment, "Your Majesty, may I ask a question?" When the Queen nodded, he asked, "May I meet with my warriors here. I have need of their services before my other team arrives at the Gray Court. Once I send them on their way, I would stay and converse with Her Majesty for a time, if it pleases you, Your Majesty."

The Seelie Queen nodded, "It would please me much, Sir Gawain. Send your warriors out, and then join me for a repast in my dining area."

Smith turned and motioned for Boomer and Dancer to follow him out the door. With Tar Katel as their escort, they made their way back to the courtyard. Once there, Smith motioned for the FBI agents to join them by the Wunder Buggy. Once the introductions were made, Smith outlined what he needed them to do.

"Miss Callahan will be driving. Miss Sedano has both addresses. I would like all of you to go in the Wunder Buggy to recruit two people." He looked at Boomer directly, "This is a recruiting mission, not a kidnapping." He addressed everyone again, "I would like you to recruit this Ryan DeBoer and Pete McCarthy for assistance for at least a short while. You can promise funds and equipment. We will not know about our status with Homeland Security for a while, however, I am confidant we will come out of this okay."

He looked at all the agents surrounding him, "We will square everything away with human resources and get the contracts signed later, but as of right now, you FBI agents are part of the agency. For the purposes of this mission, Miss Callahan is the team leader, as she has the most experience with the agency. Agent Mulder, you are her second-in-command. Your experience at the FBI may help in certain areas. Miss Callahan, you would do well to listen to her, she has a long career at the FBI. Any questions?"

"Yes." Boomer looked at her boss, "Are you really a Knight of the Round Table? Or was that a title like Hannah's Faeblade?"

Smith looked at her and smiled. "I am Sir Gawain, born in 494 AD, and I am a Knight of King Arthur's Court. Agent Mulder can fill you in on the drive to recruit the two men. Any other questions?" Getting shakes of the head, the Director said, "Good luck. Mount up."

As Boomer climbed into the driver's seat, Smith called out, "Miss Callahan? As we are now on the run from our own government, might I recommend you change the looks of the truck? Something not so official-looking?"

"Yes, sir." Boomer hit the switch to unlock and lower the back ramp. As the others were climbing up into the truck, Mulder opened the passenger door and climbed up into the back. Once everyone was on board, Boomer closed the hatch and fired up the engine. She punched in a code on one of the keypads in front of her and flipped another switch. The truck's black paint rippled and changed. In thirty seconds, the Wunder Buggy was white and wore the decals of a local energy company. Two minutes later they were down the driveway and heading toward the north side of Grand Rapids.

"Hannah, can you call Mister DeBoer and see if he's home?"

"Sure, Becca." Dancer pulled out her SSP and dialed the man from her contact notes.

Spooks spoke up from the electronic warfare seat, "Hey, um, Agent Callahan? Do you have the login for this terminal?"

The demolitions expert smiled and shook her head, "Sorry, Spooks... right? Spooky has that locked out. You and he should get along just fine. By the way, call me Boomer. Everyone else does."

Fifteen minutes later, Boomer was pulling the Wunder Buggy into the driveway at the DeBoer residence. She shut the engine down and slid open her door. After hitting the rear hatch release, she climbed down and stretched. Dancer joined her by the driver's side door. A slightly paler Mulder joined the two Section 28 agents.

"Do you always drive like that?"

Boomer smiled and Dancer laughed, replying, "You'll get used to it. She hasn't killed us yet."

The three women walked toward the front door. On the drive over, Mulder recommended that the other FBI agents stay with the truck, and they agreed. Having been called, DeBoer met them at the front door. As he welcomed them in, he motioned to the truck, "The electric company? Isn't that a bit clichéd?"

Dancer laughed, "Yes, but some of the best tricks are the oldest."

After Boomer and Mulder were introduced to DeBoer's wife, Tiffany, they all sat at the dining room table. Ryan finally broke the ice, "Ok, I give up. Why are you back so soon? I haven't talked to anyone."

Dancer shook her head, "It's not that. I know Agent Black gave you his business card about possibly coming to work for our agency. Have you thought about the offer at all?"

Ryan looked at his wife, then back at the agents, "Yeah. A little. I have a whole lotta questions, though. Why do you ask?"

Dancer looked at Boomer, and the older agent took over, "Because we have a straight up job offer for you. It is a definite temporary job that will, if you want it to, turn into a permanent job. Think of it as a really high paying temp job that you get to choose if it goes permanent."

"What is high paying? I was in the Army. I know what government work pays outside the armed forces, and federal law enforcement doesn't pay that much."

"Six figures. Starting. Plus expenses, travel, and equipment." Boomer saw the look in the man's eyes. "Agent Sedano said you did really well in your incident. You have a flexible mind and skills that would be useful. The truth is, we had a major catastrophe and we desperately need agents right now."

DeBoer sat back and looked at his wife. "Where would I be stationed? And when would I leave? I don't want Tiff to be a military wife with her husband constantly deployed. I did that once. It sucks."

Boomer shook her head, "For the near future, you would be stationed here in Grand Rapids. Home at night, at work in the morning. Generally. You would start today. Now. We'll figure out the HR stuff soon, but you know we're a black budget agency. And you know what that means."

"I need to talk it over with my wife. Can you excuse us?"

"The clock is ticking on this one, Mister DeBoer. We'll step outside and wait by our truck. Come out and let me know what your decision is. If you are coming with us, dress for training or guard duty. Fatigues if you have them, or even BDUs, but don't worry about weapons. We'll take care of that."

Fifteen minutes passed and Boomer had decided to go knock on the door. As she climbed out of the truck, the front door opened and Ryan walked out the door. He was wearing a pair of fatigue pants, combat boots, and a fitted t-shirt. He had a light jacket in his hand. He kissed his wife and jogged to the waiting Wunder Buggy. As he reached the truck, he gave a low whistle, "Nice ride."

Boomer smiled and jerked her thumb toward the rear hatch. "Wait til you see the inside. Welcome aboard."

Five minutes later the Wunder Buggy was on the entrance ramp to I-96 westbound toward Muskegon. In the back, Ryan was introduced to the team. Seeing and hearing that almost everyone in the truck was only recently recruited, or had volunteered, Ryan leaned back and wondered what he had just gotten himself into.

Forty-seven minutes later, the DHS truck was pulling up in front of a house outside Muskegon. Boomer saw the truck in the driveway and noticed the scrap of police tape still tied to the front porch rail. Like the DeBoer house, Boomer, Dancer, and Mulder approached the front door, with Dancer in the lead as the familiar face.

The man that answered the door stood just over six feet tall and easily weighed about two hundred eighty pounds. The dirty blond hair on his head was unkempt, but short. He wore a flannel shirt over blue jeans and work boots. Boomer noticed the 1911 pistol in the holster on the man's hip.

Dancer spoke up, "Mister McCarthy? This is Agents Callahan and Mulder. Can we get just a minute of your time?"

The man crossed his arms and leaned against the doorframe. "Speak your piece."

Boomer spoke, "I'm going to make this simple. We would like to offer you a job."

28

SANCTUARY

Interstate I-96, East of Muskegon, Michigan

It had taken over half an hour to convince Pete McCarthy, but he eventually joined the team. When told that Section 28 would supply his weapons, he shook his head. "All of my gear is custom, competition-proven. I trust it implicitly, and it is far more accurate than any government-issued gun. I'll bring my own gear."

Boomer had shrugged and let him bring his gear. She thought if Russell approved of the gear, she would have no problem with it. And if not, she'd let Pete and Russell settle the issue. Once he got to the truck Pete was introduced to the rest of the team and sat next to Ryan for the trip back to Grand Rapids. After seeing everyone else buckle their seatbelts and make sure they were tight, he had shrugged and had done the same. About ten minutes into the trip, McCarthy was glad he was strapped into his seat.

Just outside a town called Coopersville, Mulder received a call on her phone. She didn't recognize the number, but she answered it anyway, "Mulder."

"Agent Mulder, this is Smith. Please tell Miss Callahan that the other team will arrive at the Gray Court Trial Grounds in about an hour, and I would like her to divert there. You all need to be there, anyway. I will join you this evening."

Smith paused and then asked, "Was your mission successful?"

"Yes, sir. Both men have agreed to join us. At least temporarily. They are coming back with us."

"Excellent. I shall meet them at the Warehouse."

"Yes, sir." Mulder disconnected the call and turned to Boomer. "Director Smith says the other team will arrive within an hour at the Gray Court Trial Grounds. He wants us to divert there and assist that team. Do you know where you are going?"

Boomer smiled and nodded and pushed the pedal a little closer to the floor. The occasional flash of her headlights gave some warning to the cars that were in her way that her multi-ton behemoth would run them over if they didn't move.

Twenty-five minutes later the huge black panel van pulled off of 68th Street and into the driveway of a cement contractor. It was also the cover industry of the Gray Court of the fae. At the end of the driveway a very short man in a hard hat and yellow safety vest waved Boomer to a stop. She threw open the door and showed her credentials. "Special Agent Rebekah Callahan, Homeland Security. We should be expected."

The short man nodded and spoke with a surprisingly deep and gruff voice, "Well met, Special Agent Rebekah Callahan. I am Gryffin LeKroz. I am in charge of the special security for the Court and the Praetorian. She is expecting you. If you would allow me to ride along, I will guide you back to the building."

Boomer nodded and indicated the door sill. Leaving the driver's door slid open so that the dwarf could lean out and see where they were going, she eased forward slowly. Gryffin LeKroz took her back behind the main storage warehouse and showed her a spot in front of an apparently unused outbuilding. Boomer shut down the truck and flipped the switch to lower the rear hatch.

The dwarf jumped down and pointed to the doorway at the near end of the building. "The Praetorian is waiting inside for you and your agents. I must go back up front to meet your other team. Well met, Rebekah Callahan."

"Thank you, and well met, Gryffin LeKroz." The dwarf turned and jogged toward the front entrance. Rebekah climbed down and stretched. The rest of the team met her as she waited. When everyone was present, she turned and led the way to the front door of the building. Boomer turned and motioned for Dancer to enter first, "You are the *Cainteoir*, after all. And the Praetorian genuinely likes you."

Hannah good-naturedly grumbled, but opened the door and entered the building. Seeing the Praetorian lounging in a chair, she smiled and ran over to the head of the Khoztak faction of dwarves. The Praetorian smiled and stood to greet the exuberant young woman.

SIX PULLED the War Wagon into the driveway of the Gray Court Trial Grounds under the direction of Ghost. He stopped when he was waved down by the same short man with the hardhat and yellow vest. Putting the truck in park quieted the massive engine enough to have a conversation. He opened his door and held up his credentials. "Special Agent John Black, Homeland Security. Director Smith sent us."

"Well met, Special Agent John Black. I am Gryffin LeKroz, Special Security for the Court and for the Praetorian. You are expected. If you will allow me to climb aboard, I will guide you to the building."

With a nod from Six, the dwarf scaled the massive armored hide of the truck and clung to the now-closed front driver door. The vampire followed the dwarf's directions, and the War Wagon pulled up right next to the cooling Wunder Buggy.

The team dismounted, including the pixies. Ghost even convinced Spooky that he should come inside to meet the new agents that Smith had recruited. Spooky reluctantly agreed and closed down his terminal.

Gretchen was the first through the door, and entered a large lounge or rec room with a couple dining sets, pool and ping pong tables, and a lounge area with recliners and a large screen tv. She looked around at the crowd and eventually spotted the Praetorian and Dancer huddled in a corner, deep in a conversation.

Boomer greeted her as she came in, followed by the rest of the Knightmare team. Dancer saw the team enter and broke off her conversation with the Praetorian. Both of them worked their way over to Gretchen and Ghost. After greetings were exchanged, Ghost called out, and called everyone to gather. When they had gathered in the lounge area, Ghost and Gretchen stood in front of the group and addressed them.

"I hate to be the bearer of bad news, but we have a lot of work ahead of us. First, I want everyone to introduce themselves. There are many new faces in this crowd, and we need to know who we are working with. I will start. I am Jonas Vanhof, callsign Ghost. I am the team leader, and that currently includes everyone here except our friends from the Gray Court and the Matriarch and her Family. Gretchen?"

The entire group introduced themselves, and included the reasoning why they had joined, if they were brand new. The introductions took about forty-five minutes, but everyone had some idea of who was on the team. After everyone was introduced, Ghost once again took charge.

"By now, you all know, or should know that we are currently under attack from two sides. First, our own President is trying to shut us down. Fed some lies by the NSA, the President is working with Congress to rescind our authority. But that is only funding and cooperation. There is also a rogue group that is actively trying to kill Director Smith and anyone else who gets in their way. They already succeeded with the attack on our headquarters in Langley. The numbers are bad, and we lost a lot of good women and men during that attack."

The monster hunter looked around the now somber room. "Some of you are warriors. You were recruited for your skills, or you are currently on an active team for Section Twenty-Eight. Some of you are not warriors. You may become support personnel, or you may find that you have a warrior hiding inside. Gretchen and I will work with each of you individually to find your best fit. But understand this, there may come a time in the near future when the support has to become the warrior. Prepare yourself mentally now."

Ghost picked out a couple of the people, "For now, Boomer and Six, I want you to arm and check out Mister DeBoer and Mister McCarthy. Kit them out with armor and weapons from the trucks until we get the Warehouse open." All four people nodded. "Spooky, I want you to get Spooks up to speed. Get her a login to our system and get her logged into one of the trucks. As of right now, you two are the entire electronic warfare team. Agent Mulder, you are with Gretchen and I, as we work to get the Warehouse set. The rest of you can relax and get a bite to eat. As of this point, no phone calls home unless they are cleared through myself or Gretchen. Director Smith will be here in a little while, and may change things up. But until then, you have your operational orders."

Six, Boomer, and Spooky took Ryan, Pete, and Spooks outside the building. Spooky and Spooks climbed up into the Wunder Buggy, which had slightly more room inside than the War Wagon. The former NSA analyst looked at the Aussie FBI agent and said, "I remember you. You were in the Command Center, weren't you?"

"And you were the guy who rooted our system to get control of it."

"That was me, in the, err, electrons? Anyways, you were good. I saw what you were doing. Let me get you onto this system."

Spooky fired up the terminal and logged into the back-end servers. Using his new Zulu-level access, he was able to add Spooks as a user, and provided some of the access and tools he had in his own personal tool chest. In five minutes, she was added and ready to get active on the Section 28 servers and systems. As he was showing her around the systems, he got an alert.

"Son of a bitch."

Spooks looked over his shoulder and saw the alert. Looking at his screen, she, too, saw the intrusion attempt. "Looks like a government server. NSA, maybe, with those identifiers. Do you know this 'Dorian Ad Astra' character?"

"Yeah. Frakkin' NSA is still at it. I'll work to keep him out from this end. You jump on the other system and burn him. If he sees you and fights back, I'll hit him from another blind side. Let's see how good you are, Aussie."

Spooks smiled a wide grin, "As good as, if not better than, you, Yank."

The NSA analyst gave her the access credentials and handed her a radio with a throat mic. Once they were both mic'd up, he showed her how to switch from the main channel to a private channel between the two of them. She ran to the truck next door and booted up her system. The NSA intruder was in for a very rude awakening.

In the back of the War Wagon, Six was handing armor out to Ryan and Pete. Ryan just shrugged and strapped on the armor. Pete watched and then followed his example. Six looked them over and asked, "What do you have in mind for weapons, gentlemen?"

Ryan spoke first, "Got a Beretta? I carried an M9 and the SAW in the Army. Good with both of them, plus the M4."

Six smiled, "A man after my own heart." He rummaged in the weapons bins of the teammates who were not currently with them. He came up with a Beretta M9 in a drop-leg holster and several magazines filled with Norbert's ammunition. Digging in Heavy's bin, he found the SAW and a couple cans of linked ammunition. He also found a scoped M4 in Little G's bin. He grabbed several magazines filled with ammo. The vampire agent addressed the man, "Choose one of the long guns to carry now. Stow the other in this bin marked 'Little G.' If you want to switch out, swap out of that bin."

Ryan nodded and grabbed the M4. Placing several magazines in the pouches on his vest, he slung the rifle and grabbed the handgun, which he quickly strapped into place. He stepped aside so Pete could talk to the agent.

"Pete, right? What's your preferred setup?"

"I've got my own gear. Custom STI 2011 on my hip and an AR-15 in the case. I also have a Benelli twelve gauge in the case, but I figured the rifle was better. Unfortunately, I didn't bring a lot of ammo."

Six rummaged in Do-Right's bin for more AR magazines with Norbert's anti-fae ammo. As he did so, he asked over his shoulder, "Forty-five auto in the handgun?"

"No, sir. High-capacity nine millimeter."

Six paused and looked over his shoulder. He shrugged and pulled out several long MP5 magazines from Scout's bin. He placed those on top of the pile of M4/AR magazines. "The AR mags you can use straight away. Do yourself a favor and swap out your ammo for the ones in the MP5 mags. They are a very different ammo, and your standard match or defensive rounds won't work against our enemies."

He then pulled out four radios with throat mics and earpieces for the four of them. He also had Boomer run four additional sets inside, handing them to Ghost, Gretchen, Dancer, and Doc. While Boomer ran off, He showed the two new recruits how to wear and use their new radios. After testing them, Six looked at both men, "Questions?" Both men shook their heads.

"Ryan, you pair up with Boomer. She's like me, so watch her back. You guys patrol this side of the compound. Stay within a hundred and fifty yards of this building. Pete, you're with me. We'll patrol that side and stay within a hundred and fifty as well. Good luck, and holler if you see anything."

Inside the building, Ghost, Gretchen, Mulder, and the Praetorian had been very busy. The dwarf had led them through a door and into a cavernous warehouse space. It had a semi-sized roll-up door at the far end. The worn concrete floor was clean and did not have cracks. The walls were apparently insulated, as they were at least double thick, and the ceiling was over thirty feet high at its peak.

The Praetorian pointed to a mark on the floor in the center of the room. "That is the center of the room. It also happens to be on a ley line and the strongest point in the floor. I would recommend that you put the entrance to the Warehouse there. We will position guards around the building once the Warehouse is set up. As you can see, there is ample parking for your vehicles, and the door at the far end will accommodate even your monstrous trucks."

"This building is warded, isn't it? I can feel them?" Ghost held out his hands and closed his eyes.

"Yes, Jonas Vanhof. The wards are powerful anti-detection and shielding wards. They are fed by the ley line directly for their power. That is why we have offered this building as a sanctuary for the Warehouse."

Ghost looked at Gretchen, and she nodded. He turned to look at the Praetorian, "I agree. This is perfect, at least for temporary storage and access. Now, if you will excuse us, we will call it out."

The Praetorian nodded and bowed, "I am pleased that we can be of assistance. I will be in the main office arranging for the security details."

"Thank you, Praetorian. Please feel free to ask Agent Sedano to accompany you. I do not want to interrupt your conversations."

"Thank you, again, Jonas Vanhof. I believe I will do so."

After the Praetorian left, Ghost reached into his pocket and brought out the small, scale model of the Warehouse. Mulder looked at it, and then looked from Ghost to Gretchen, "Is that a replica? And how in the hell did that fit in your pocket?"

Ghost shook his head and smiled. "This is the actual Warehouse gateway. We shrank it so it was portable. And my pocket is a whole lot bigger on the inside. Gamers call it a 'portable hole.' I call it convenient."

Gretchen and Ghost went through the reverse of the ritual that shrank the Warehouse gateway. Setting it down, they both intoned the proper words, and the Warehouse began to glow. It sank roots into the concrete floor without cracking it. The gateway then extended up and out, eventually growing to the full size.

Ghost and Gretchen then both used their power to open the sealed doors once again. In all, the process took a little over half an hour, and the two Section 28 agents were exhausted by the end of it.

After they finished and the massive doors opened, Ghost's radio crackled. "Ghost, Gretchen, this is Boomer. We have a Gray SUV heading down the road and making the turn into the Trials Area. I believe it's the same one Smith was driving, but I'm not sure."

"Copy that, Boomer. All guards get into position just in case. The Warehouse is open in our building. Protection of the Warehouse is number one priority. I will join you outside."

Gretchen entered the Warehouse while Ghost and Mulder left

through the lounge door, gathering Agent Stratton as they went. Stratton and Mulder had their firearms drawn when the Gray SUV drove around the other building and into sight. Hanging from the running board was the same dwarf that had led each truck into the compound. Ghost keyed his mic.

"This is Ghost. Stand down. It's the Director. Go back to your patrol unless you are called in."

As the SUV came to a stop, the driver door's door opened and a man in a perfectly tailored pin stripe suit stepped out. Director Smith smiled and went to greet his agents.

29

INCURSION

As Smith walked over to greet Ghost, the two rear doors to the SUV opened. Two large minotaur unfolded as they emerged from the back of the SUV. The truck's heavy duty shocks and struts eased and the truck lifted several inches as the heavy creatures exited the vehicle. Both creatures walked around to the rear hatch. Once opened, they retrieved long black rifles and large handguns. Once their gear was properly settled about them, they walked up to join Smith.

Smith had already greeted and shaken hands with the three agents who were standing outside the new building. When the minotaur walked up, he introduced them, "Agents, this is Bearkinos Feralson and his mate Azriandra Darkshade."

The two minotaur bowed, and the first one rumbled, "Well met, Jonas Vanhof. I am Bearkinos Feralson, Seelie High Guard. Sir Gawain speaks very highly of you. We are at your service to defend your Sanctuary, compliments of Her Majesty."

The second minotaur, the female, stepped forward and bowed, "Well met. I am Azriandra Darkshade, Seelie High Guard. I serve your Sanctuary at Her Majesty's pleasure."

Ghost bowed to the two warriors before him. "Well met. I am honored to have the Seelie High Guard protecting our... Sanctuary." He turned back to Smith, "Shall we head inside, sir? We need to plan for defenses, and I'm sure the Praetorian is looking forward to seeing you, again."

As they turned to enter the building, Spooky popped his head out of the War Wagon, "We've got incursions. Lots of them forming right now."

Ghost looked at Smith, and the Director nodded, "You've got command, Mister Vanhof."

Ghost keyed his mic, "Ghost to Knightmare. Incoming incursions. Multiple gates. If you don't have gear, get it from the Warehouse or trucks now. Assignments are as follows."

A brief pause, "Gretchen, you are in the Wunder Buggy with Spooky. Spooky, you and Spooks are our eyes and ears. Get those drones up now. Button up the trucks when the lead starts flying."

"Copy." That was Gretchen.

"Boomer, Six, DeBoer, and McCarthy, maintain your current teams." Looking around, he saw Boomer and Ryan jogging across the parking lot. As they reached the trucks, Ghost pointed to his demolitions expert. "Boomer, your team is west flank. Six, You have east flank." He watched as Boomer reached into the back of the Wunder Buggy to grab her AA-12 and a vest from her locker, Ryan slung the rifle over his shoulder, grabbed Heavy's SAW and a box of ammunition, and the two of them jogged out to a stack of crates and an old water tank that Ryan could use as an emplacement for the SAW.

"Doc, you are medical and triage. Heather, will back you up. Get her up to speed. Dancer, you and the Praetorian are south side. Between the two of you, defend the building and vehicles. Ask the Praetorian to get us some backup."

Ghost paused, mentally running through the list of who was on site. "Spooky says this is a big one. Be ready."

The monster hunter pointed at Stratton, "Rick, grab a rifle from the back of one of the trucks. Look for something you are familiar with. Get ammunition. Armor if possible. Once you are loaded, grab a spare rifle and take it inside to Gryffin LeKroz. Ask him to guard the entrance to the Warehouse while you guard out here." The FBI agent nodded and went to the back of the War Wagon to rummage for gear.

Ghost looked at the two minotaur standing in front of him. "Bearkinos Feralson and Azriandra Darkshade. You will be on the north of the building. The drones will let us know if you need assistance." Both creatures bowed at the same time and jogged toward the north side of the Sanctuary building.

Ghost turned to face Mulder and Smith. "Boss, Mulder and I are your personal bodyguards today. I know you can handle yourself, but we'll watch your back. Tressa, let's see if any of Boomer's armor fits you. You can also grab a rifle if you want."

As the team and their Seelie allies prepared for battle, Spooky and Spooks were inside the two command trucks, each of them wrestling with inputs and drone controls. Spooks selected Spooky's private channel and then keyed her mic. "Spooky, one of us should pilot the drones, and one of us needs to monitor all the radio and air traffic in the area. Also, we're in the flight path for the airport, and I don't want to see a 737 hit a dragon."

Spooky nodded to himself and thought quickly. "Spooks, you take over the drones. All of them have a limited autopilot, so work them as you want. I'll monitor traffic and call the FAA to get the airport shut down when the gates start popping."

"Call them now, Spooky. I'm showing a signature of an active gate. I've got the drones."

Spooky clicked twice and then dialed the Federal Aviation Administration's local office. He gave them a codeword shutdown order that originated at Homeland Security. Within two minutes, anything not already on final approach or on fumes was diverted away from Grand Rapids. The skies would be clear.

Spooks moved to the general channel and announced, "There are eight active gate signatures, spread around Sanctuary. All are close-in. I repeat, there are eight active gate signatures, cardinal and ordinal points on the compass, and we are the epicenter. Pucker up people." Her Australian accent was thick but understandable over the radio. She reached up and toggled the hatch switch. The rear hatch motored up and sealed with a hiss. "Check that. Three more just popped open, all of them airborne. Airborne gates are Southwest, Northwest, and Northeast."

The gate in front of Six and Pete solidified into an inky blackness that rippled in disturbing ways. Six raised an AA-12 shotgun to his shoulder, and Pete raised his AR to a low ready. The gate erupted with... things. Mutated insect forms gone terribly wrong swarmed and scurried through the gate, sometimes pushing over or through each other. Pete froze in terror.

The cacophony of the full-auto shotgun next to him shook Pete out of his catatonia. Raising the sights to the gateway, he starting pulling the trigger on the incoming flood. Between the shotgun and the rifle rounds, the creatures swarming through the front were shredded, pieces falling everywhere.

The bolt locked back on Pete's rifle, and he automatically dropped the magazine with one finger, and slammed a new one into the receiver, and dropped the bolt back into place. McCarthy's practice and shooting matches paid off as the exchange took less than a second before he was shouldering the rifle to shoot more of the creatures coming through the portal. As he started firing again, the rattle of the shotgun next to him stopped. He kept shooting the creatures as they emerged.

The flood of creatures slowed to a trickle as the shotgun being used by Six opened up, scattering bugs and parts. Seeing the trickle come to a stop, Pete concentrated on putting down the survivors. He put two or three shots into any moving body, or body part, still active among the collection of carcasses. Agent Black tapped him on the shoulder and pointed to his right. Pete saw the other gate disgorging trolls. Nodding absently, Pete swung his rifle around and aimed at the first troll he crossed. Placing the reticle from his sight over the creature's chest, he pulled the trigger. Twice.

The troll fell, clutching its chest. Pete shifted to another, ignoring the gunfire, screams, and roars around the compound. He missed the first two shots, but his third one tagged the shoulder of one of the creatures. The things stumbled and let out a roar. It and its fellow trolls turned and ran toward Pete and the agent with him. As he resettled the reticle on the troll he just wounded, the marksman felt something grab his leg, and then he felt a terrible pain as the creature's mandibles bit down into his flesh.

Six spent an entire drum magazine of the shotgun shells on the black mutant insects pouring through the gateway. On semi-automatic the drum lasted perhaps thirty seconds. The carapaces of the insects were no match for Norbert's specialty 12GA ammunition. The rounds penetrated easily, scattering chunks of mutant insect and viscera everywhere. McCarthy had frozen for a moment, but had snapped out of it when Six started killing the critters.

As he reloaded the drum, he saw movement out of the corner of his eye. Seeing the gate to their right disgorge trolls, he quickly swung the AA-12 around and targeted the trolls. When Pete's shots slowed, Six reached over and tapped him on the shoulder, pointing to the trolls. Pete immediately switched targets. Before the vampire got his shotgun up, Pete cried out and fell to the ground.

On the west side of the building, Boomer and Ryan had opened up when the black bug-like creatures swarmed. Boomer hated bugs, and a four foot roach-like creature really grossed her out. The rapid-fire bursts from Ryan's Squad Automatic Weapon ripped through the creatures as if they were made of paper. The M249 was humming along, with DeBoer using short bursts so the barrel did not melt.

With the hammering of the machine gun, the swarm was bottle-necked right at the opening of the gate. Boomer concentrated her fire into the creatures that were still moving or getting through the fusillade. The chittering of the creatures and their high pitched whine as they died was grating on the young vampire's nerve. She plucked a grenade from her vest, pulled the pin, and let it sail, right to the mouth of the gate. The grenade exploded amidst the pile of bodies, and bits of insect flew outward in a wide arc. Ichor and pieces of shell landed on and around Boomer and Ryan.

DeBoer was smiling as the emplacement he had created blew up with a shower of blinding yellow energy. Hurled backward, the Army veteran landed about five feet from the pile of now-kindling. He looked to his left and saw an orc-like thing raise a glowing staff again. While sitting, he unslung the rifle he was wearing, pulled it to his shoulder and pulled the trigger multiple times. The line of impacts stitched the orc from his torso to his neck, with the final round flying square through the creature's throat.

The massive creature danced as the rounds landed, and then fell over, clutching its ruined neck until it bled out. Boomer sat up and dropped the drum magazine out of her shotgun. Grumbling under breath, the young vampire slammed an eight-round magazine of explosive grenade rounds into the breech. "Want to play rough?" Boomer muttered, "Then I'll play rough."

Shouldering the stock, she rattled off a three-round burst into the emerging orcs. Three thumps followed by three minor explosions told the young warrior that her rounds hit the mark. She shifted her aim to another Chikara, she pulled the trigger three more times, then heard Ryan scream.

She looked over and one of the hideous black mutant insects was on top of Ryan, and the Army vet had jammed his rifle side-ways into the thing's jaws to avoid being eaten. In a flash, Boomer dropped her AA-12 and sprang, letting her claws come out and watching her vision spectrum shift. Boomer landed beside the crea-ture and kicked, cracking its carapace.

The thing squealed and swung its jaws at the vampire. She grabbed the jaws and pulled, ripping them apart and away from the body. A final kick to the thing's side sent it back and over on its back. Boomer looked down and groaned. She had insect ichor all over her boots.

Boomer turned to offer Ryan a hand up and crashed to the ground, another creature landing on her back. Ryan grunted and drew his Beretta. He pulled the trigger four times, each shot hitting the head of the creature. The five foot stag beetle slumped and slid off of the vampire. It was her turn to mutter thanks. As she bent to pick up her shotgun, she flew sideways and crashed to the ground, blood and ichor leaking from the massive gunshot wound in her side.

On the south side of the building the Praetorian had drawn two wicked looking blades when the portal opened. Dancer had reached back and drawn *fion-fhuil*, thinking *Wake up Vellath. Time to feed.*

The young Fury concentrated and placed her hands on the hilt. The sword glowed a visible white light, and then it split. The mystical sword had split into two blades, one half ending in each hand. Vellath almost purred, *I see you are serious this time, Little One. I am glad.*

It was then that the wave of chitinous black mutant insects rolled out of the gateway. Dancer looked at the Praetorian, who smiled and leapt. Keeping up, Dancer landed among the black creatures, scattering them like bowling pins. Her escrima training, combined with her innate power, and Vellath's instincts, made her a whirling dervish.

Slashes, thrusts, kicks, and stabs flew in all directions. Her grace from dancing shown in the deadly beauty that was her swordfight. A slash moved fluidly to a stab, which moved fluidly to a kick, and back to a slashing motion. The Praetorian watched in awe as this beautiful Fury became the Faeblade.

The trailing edges of her sword took on a blue tinge as her power built. Energy crackled from the tips of her hair, and her eyes grew a white glow. Vellath was overjoyed at her dance, *Keep it up, Little One.*

Shut. Up. Vellath. I'm trying to concentrate.

Dancer whirled and turned, making a royal mess of the creatures. Soon, she had killed the last one, and she slowed to a stop amidst the carnage. The young Fury cried out as the massive spear landed in the small of her back, cutting through the armor and almost hitting her spine. The Fury dropped to the ground.

The Praetorian whirled on the Chikaran orc that had thrown the spear. Though not a demi-god, the Praetorian had years of practice, and knew the terrain better. She rushed the creature who drew a sword and readied it. As the Praetorian reached the orc, it swung downward to crush the dwarf. She neatly sidestepped the attack, slammed the flat of her blade against its wrists to break one of them, and then gave a backhand swing that cut through the orc's guts with a single blow.

The dwarf turned on another orc and caught it off guard, slamming her sword through its stomach. An upward slash ripped a gash in the creature's guts, and it slowly collapsed. The final orc in the line was cut down where it stood. It didn't have time to raise its defenses. The Praetorian rushed to Dancer's side to help her.

On the north side of the building, the two minotaur were in the thick of it. When the black insects came boiling out of the gate, the two Seelie High guard opened up with their large automatic rifles. The insects were chewed apart, forming a bottleneck in the gate entrance. As the two mates were finishing off the shiny black creatures, Azriandra Darkshade noticed the Chikaran orcs coming out of the northeast gate.

The minotaur fired a short burst, and then her rifle locked shut. She looked at the jammed shell and simply dropped her rifle. Drawing her strange-looking pistol, she fired at the orcs. The massive handgun was louder than her mate's rifle. Bullets flew past her as the orcs returned fire. She heard a grunt behind her. Looking back, she saw that Bearkinos Feralson had caught one of the rounds in his shoulder, and he was spun around from the force.

Growling in anger, Azriandra Darkshade spun and barreled toward the orcs. Lifting her pistol, she fired at the orc in front of her, emptying half of the magazine into the creature. Reaching the falling corpse, she pushed off of it and slammed into the orc next to it. Her pistol gripped in her hand, she shoved the massive blade that ran underneath the frame and slide into the orc's throat and slashed sideways. Great gouts of blood flew from the dying Chikara. The minotaur was already shoving the orc out of the way when she was shot three times in the chest by the last remaining Chikara.

Bearkinos Feralson watched his mate crumple, and he roared. The massive minotaur covered the distance very quickly, his feet digging up great divots and ruts as he ran. The minotaur dropped his rifle and slammed headfirst into the orc. The crunch and grunts echoed across the lot. The Seelie High Guard minotaur wrapped his massive hands around the neck of the orc. Growling and grunting, Bearkinos Feralson crushed the creature's neck as hard as he could, crushing cartilage, bone, and blood vessels. The orc's death took over a minute, but the minotaur would not wait. Satisfied with his revenge, he rushed to his mate's side.

Standing at the door to the Sanctuary, FBI Agent Rick Stratton was wondering what the hell he was doing there. He watched as Boomer and Ryan destroyed the giant mutant insects. A flash of movement caught his eye on the roof of the building next to theirs. He looked up and saw a large creature pop out of a gate that was on the roof. When the creature aimed a rifle at Agent Mulder and Director Smith, Rick raised his own rifle and sighted through the reticle on the red dot optic mounted to the top of the M4. He pulled the trigger twice, putting both rounds through the creature's chest.

As he aimed for the next ugly creature that appeared, a howling scream echoed around and he missed wide to the right as he jerked the rifle. Settling back onto target, two more rounds hit the creature's chest, and it collapsed. He saw more movement from the gate that was in the air, right over the creature gate. When the dragon's head popped through, he felt a great weight hit the bottom of his stomach and his bowels quiver. He shakily grabbed the radio mic and transmitted, "This is Stratton. We have dragons coming through the gate."

"Shit," Ghost muttered to himself.

"My sentiments exactly, Mister Vanhof." Smith watched as the portal in the air directly in front of them filled with dragons. Three of them emerged. Looking around, the Section 28 Director saw that three had emerged from each gate. Nine dragons.

One final dragon came out of the gate in front of Smith. The rider was dressed in an ornate black plate armor with silver and gold filigree. The plumed helm and glowing red eyes swiveled and settled on Smith and the agents with him.

Smith looked up calmly, staring into the face of the dragon and rider that had killed his people and caused him so much trouble. "Demius Sayevuud, I presume? It is about time you come to face me. I can't abide cowards who attack the innocent and then slink away. I have one question though, who are you?"

30

CHALLENGE

A raspy, breathy laughter sounded from the dragon rider. "I am surprised that you do not know me. I have been chasing you for years, Agent Smith. Or should I say Sir Gawain? I have an army of dragons around you and your precious agents. I will finally have my revenge. Yield."

Smith looked at his agents around him. He saw the Praetorian dragging Dancer toward the door into the building. Boomer was helping Ryan toward the building as well. On the other side, Smith watched the male minotaur lean over his mate and administer aid. The Director turned back to his adversary. Smith knew he had to stall, to protect his agents until the Queen's warriors arrived.

"I challenge you to combat. You, Demius Sayevuud. If you defeat me, you will have your prize. If I defeat you, your dragon riders will leave. What say you?"

Laughter again. "You. Against me and Argohast? You are getting foolish in your old age, Sir Gawain. Bargained well and done."

Smith felt the familiar shiver as the power of a fae bargain washed over him. He nodded and removed his jacket. Turning to Ghost, he handed the monster hunter his jacket. "Whatever happens, do not interfere. Trial by single combat. We are on the

Trial Grounds. Spread the word to everyone, including the new recruits."

The Knight then removed his tie, unbuttoned two buttons on his shirt, and rolled up his sleeves. Handing the tie to Ghost, he reached into his jacket's inner pocket and came out with Excalibur. Again, the sword blazed light as it saw open air. Ready for battle, Sir Gawain turned to face his enemy.

The armored dragon fighter sat motionless as his dragon flapped its wings and hovered a few scant feet off the ground. Landing his dragon, the rider stayed on the creature's back. Smith looked at the massive creature before him.

The dragon's dark green scales transitioned to a lighter tan on its underside. The creature stood ten feet tall at the shoulder, with a rough, scaly hide adorned with spines and hard chitinous plating. The head of the dragon was the size of a small car, and the mouth was filled with razor sharp teeth. But now that it was on the ground, it did not have some of the protections and maneuverability that flying provides. The dragon roared its own challenge, echoing across the lot and down the street.

Gawain took a stance with Excalibur and nodded at the dragon rider. "When you are ready to meet your fate, you may begin."

The dragon struck. It was far faster than Gawain had ever seen, and he almost did not move in time to avoid the long teeth. Barely ducking out of the way, he had the presence of mind to slash across the jawline of the scaly beast. A line opened on the face, laying open the cheek from near the horns almost to the snout. The dragon screamed in agony. So did the rider.

Dancing back, Gawain thought he understood his adversary. The dragon and rider were linked. If the Knight hurt the dragon enough, he might cause the rider to yield. Dancing back out of reach of those claws, he studied how the dragon moved.

The beast reared back and opened its maw, inhaling. Gawain danced out of the way just as the fiery breath weapon spewed out. The breath weapon came out in a tight line of fire, scorching the packed earth where Gawain had stood. Noticing the Knight's movement, the dragon swept a wing out and hit Gawain in the chest, sending him flying back into a pile of fifty-five gallon drums.

Gawain quickly scrambled to his feet, Excalibur held ready. The next breath weapon attack was already on its way, and the Knight leapt over a couple barrels, rolling and spinning to get away from the flames.

Seeing his opportunity, he ran straight at the dragon. The beast opened it mouth and inhaled right as Gawain ran under it. The Knight slashed upwards with his sword, slicing through the tough dragon hide as if it was cotton. He dragged the blade down the throat and across the belly, running out beneath the dragon's left shoulder.

Great gouts of flame exploded out of the dragon where the blade had pierced the hide. The dragon screamed in agony as its own internal flames ignited with the fresh oxygen entering through the wounds. Dragon blood and ichor splashed as the creature thrashed around, throwing the dragon rider thirty feet through the air, only to have him land in a heap of armor.

Gawain stepped forward once more and swung upward with the blade, neatly severing the three-foot-diameter neck on the beast. The dragon's body crashed to the ground, shaking the buildings in the compound. The head dropped in front of Gawain, bouncing and rolling, ending up on its side.

Breathing heavily, Gawain turned to face the rider. As the armored figure climbed to his feet, he reached for a sword on his hip. Drawing the blade, he held it up to show the Knight what he held. The blade itself was polished metal with a fuller down the center of it. Darkened metal formed the crossbar which was angled upwards as a sword catcher. The hilt was wrapped with black leather, and the pommel was a darker gold.

"Recognize this blade, betrayer?" The adversary hissed and rasped.

Gawain flushed and pointed Excalibur at the adversary. "How did you come by *Tanlladwyr*, fiend?"

A dark chuckle sounded from beneath the armored rider's helmet. "I took it from the owner when he had no further use for it. After I ran him through."

Gawain shook his head, "Lancelot du Lac died of heartbreak, in his castle."

The Knight could hear the sneer in the thing's voice, "Just like you only got nicked by the Green Knight, no? He wanted to die. I merely helped him along."

"You killed Lancelot? You will see justice."

"What justice? You? You are a betrayer and are incapable of passing judgement on me." The armored rider pointed a gauntleted hand at Gawain.

The Knight crouched, preparing for an attack, "I am no betrayer, fiend."

Demius Sayevuud tensed and attacked, slashing at Gawain with the famed "Bright Killer". As he attacked, the armored rider punctuated each sentence with a grunt as he brought the sword down, only to be blocked by Excalibur, "You betrayed your family over position." Crash. "You chose your friend over your family." Crash. "You betrayed your own brother as a sop to your king." Crash.

Shocked, Gawain was not as quick to parry the next attack, and *Tanlladwyr* struck a glancing blow, slicing across the Knight's left shoulder. Gawain danced back, out of the range of the next strike. His opponent laughed and rasped, "I have struck a nerve, among other things."

The armored rider swung again, and Gawain was able to parry the blow. His riposte sliced across the rider's left bicep, and Excalibur sliced through the ornate armor, biting deep. The rider cried out and then lunged again, trying to drive off Gawain.

The duel raged on as both opponents used their considerable skill against each other. Gawain twisted behind a stack of pallets as the rider's sword slammed into the wood, splintering several of them. Gawain's strike was countered, and his opponent shoved a splintered pallet at the Knight, causing him to stumble, giving the rider time to recover.

The rider moved behind a stack of steel fifty-five gallon drums, some of which were scattered from Gawain's fight with the dragon. Instead of going around them, the Knight rammed into the barrels, causing them to topple onto the armored rider, and the adversary landed hard on its side. Gawain's strike was not quick enough, and the rider was able to block Excalibur's strike while rolling away and to his feet.

Gawain noticed something as the duel went on. The fighting style was familiar. Every person has their own unique style and tells, and he was sure he had seen this style used by someone else. Every strike. Every counterstrike. That twist of the blade as the rider parried his blow. That particular movement of the adversary's elbow before a strike. Where had he seen it?

The sword fight had gone for nearly ten minutes, and neither opponent had shown any sign of fatigue. Gawain was starting to tire, and the myriad of small cuts had scored his back and arms. One cut had marked a line across his chest after a close call that nearly saw him run through. Each cut had healed, although his once-immaculate shirt was tattered and bloodstained.

His opponent was not faring any better. Gawain had opened many gashes and tears in the metal armor with Excalibur's enchanted blade. Several small pieces of the armor had been cut away and lay discarded on the field. Everywhere that skin was exposed, the flesh was a pale gray color. Gawain knew he had to end this battle. And soon.

Summoning every bit of energy he had, the Knight of the Round Table lunged forward, and started a flurry of blows against his opponent. The whirlwind of attacks were overhead strikes, cross-body slashes, and thrusts with the tip, each strike, slash, or thrust flowing from one to the next in a fluid dance. His opponent tried desperately to block the blows, but too many were getting through his defenses.

Finally, his opponent stepped on a piece of cut-away armor and lost his balance. Crying out, the armored rider fell back, landing hard and losing his grip on *Tanlladwyr*. Seeing the opportunity, Sir Gawain thrusts forward with Excalibur, driving it through the breast plate and into the heart of Demius Sayevuud.

The rider gave a piercing scream and crashed back. Leaving Excalibur in place to pin the creature to the ground, Gawain leaned over and gently kicked the helmet off the armored figure. The face underneath was pale gray and sweating profusely. The blood-red mouth was leaking blood out of the corners, and the long violet hair was scattered and stringy. The creature's slightly pointed ears hinted at fae blood, while the eyes lost their red glow and became coal black.

Gawain watched as the creature coughed up more blood in a racking, gasping, burbling cough. The Knight drew his sword from within the creature's chest and pointed it at the crooked nose of the defenseless rider. "Your wound is mortal, but it need not have to be. Who are you, fiend?"

The breathy rasp was hard to hear. The dying creature gasped, "Do you not yet know, brother?"

"My brothers are long dead. I have no kin as you should know. I ask again, who are you? If you do not answer, I will run you through, and no one will know your name."

"But, brother, you are wrong. Your kin has survived to this day."

Gawain could feel his anger building. He had no relation to this fiend. His kin was long dead. And then the thought struck him. The style of the swordsman. It was familiar because it was his brother's style. The weight of his actions crashed onto him like a great burden from the heavens above.

The rider saw the change. He watched as the anger turned to puzzlement. Then the Knight realized the truth. "Yes," the voice rasped. "Now you understand, brother."

Gawain's face turned pale, "Mordred? How is that possible?"

The rider cackled, "Yes, Gawain. I am your brother, in the flesh. Your pathetic attempt to finish me in Camlann failed. Your betrayal was never as complete as you had wished for."

"But I killed you in battle. You were dead. How?"

"How are you still alive, brother?" Mordred hacked as more blood burbled to his mouth. "I was part of the bargain, as well. Although I would say you received the better part of the bargain." Mordred remembered that night vividly.

MORDRED HID in the woods as he was instructed. He watched as his mother, Morgause, and his brother, Gawain, walked across the moonlit clearing. Morgan le Fay was already standing in the middle of the clearing waiting for them. He watched as the sorceress worked her magic over the chalice and knife. When the witch sliced open his mother's hand and dripped it into the full chalice, he blanched.

Mordred watched as his brother drank from the chalice, and he noticed a slight red glow that permeated the air around his rival. He knew his mother would never have performed the ritual to save his life from the fates. Gawain was always the favorite of his mother. And no matter what Mordred learned to do, his brother learned it faster and better than the young man. He knew Morgause had consulted the Oracle and had heard his mother discussing the prophecy with his father late one night.

Once he realized that his mother cared more for her favorite than for him, he vowed to undo whatever his mother did to protect Gawain. After learning that his mother had consulted Morgan le Fay, he had gone to his aunt and begged her help. The smile that had crossed her lips at the time had driven chills down the young man's spine.

So he waited in the woods outside the clearing, watching the ritual take place. As it concluded, he saw Morgause and Gawain leave the clearing, listening to their horses ride back to the manor.

After a few minutes his aunt motioned for him to join her in the clearing. He walked out to the middle, standing on the opposite side of the stump from his aunt. She had refilled the same chalice that Gawain had used. The sorceress spent time working a slightly different enchantment over the chalice. Again, the rim and runes glowed a diffuse red.

Morgan le Fay lifted the cup, "Drink, my nephew. Drink it all."

Mordred drank from the chalice. The wine was acrid and smelled slightly of sulfur and copper. Once the chalice was drained, he set it down on the stump. His aunt looked him over, satisfied with what she saw.

Morgan le Fay watched the glow appear over the boy, then gently sink into him. She spoke, her voice breaking slightly, "Well and truly bargained."

The breeze ruffled her hair and sounded like words in her ear, "Well and truly bargained, daughter."

Mordred stepped back in alarm as a blue and white fire consumed the wineskin and chalice on the stump. His aunt looked at the young man, "Go, boy. There is no further business for you here."

The brother of Gawain turned and ran. Reaching his horse, the young man leapt onto the back of his stallion and left the woods at a gallop. He would make it back to his quarters without waking the servants. It would be years before he would become the Usurper.

MORDRED WAS SNAPPED BACK to the present when Gawain stepped on his hand. The Usurper howled in pain and cursed his brother. The Knight looked at his trapped adversary and said, "I will only ask one more time. How did you survive our battle?"

Mordred laughed in spite of the pain. The rasping, gurgling laughter turned into a choking fit as the blood spilling from the man's chest found its way to his lungs. "I have already told you, brother. I am just like you. I was preserved for battle, cursed to walk the planet." Racking coughs forced him to pause.

"My one solace was that I would be able to find you and to take my revenge." Another coughing fit. "How are your agents, brother? Their numbers seem to be dwindling."

Gawain grew red again and placed the tip of Excalibur to the right and just above the creature's breastbone. "Speak not of them. They died in service to a greater cause, and will be remembered for it."

"And of your lovely wife, Annabelle? She was very pretty. She was surprised when my minions captured her. You had not warned her of magic, of the fae." Another coughing fit. They seemed to be getting worse. "Not that she would have been able to prevent what they did to her. Did you ever find the body?"

"You may have been my brother, but you are no longer human.

You are not fit to linger on this plane. And as the Defender of the realm, I hereby send you to whatever god will accept you."

Sir Gawain raised Excalibur above his head in a two handed grip, with the tip pointed down to pierce the Usurper. He slammed the sword down, through the breastplate of the armor, and through the chest of Mordred. It sank over a foot into the ground beneath the vile Usurper.

Mordred cried out, shuddered and lay still. Gawain knelt down to one knee next to the body. He bowed his head and placed his right hand over his heart in a closed fist. He payed his respects to his brother's deformed body for over a minute, then slowly, wearily rose to his feet. He took the hilt of Excalibur and pulled, removing the sword from Mordred's chest.

The Knight turned to see the dragons and riders staring at him and at the body of their fallen leader. Gawain spoke, "Your liege made a bargain. It is fulfilled. You will be leaving."

Gawain heard a creaking behind him, that of steel armor plates grinding together. He heard his brother's voice, now clear and without the breathy rasp, "I think not, brother. The terms have not been fulfilled."

31

DRAGONFIRE

S ir Gawain spun, hands to his side and defenses lowered, to stare at his brother. The man stood, his armor clanging and rasping together. Mordred sneered, "I told you, brother. I am alive because you are alive today."

The wind suddenly picked up across the compound and then died down just as suddenly. Gawain and Mordred both looked around the compound. They heard a distinctly feminine voice from the shadows say, "I may have had something to do with it." Her Irish accent was thick.

A woman stepped out of the shadows. Long red hair fell in curly waves across her shoulders. Her exquisite porcelain skin was accented with the ethereal beauty of a goddess. A forest green vest covered her white peasant blouse, and the blouse was tucked neatly into her tan breeches. Brown calf-length boots completed her look. She had a small brown satchel slung across her body, hanging low across her right hip.

Boomer was about twenty feet away and she snapped her AA-12 to her shoulder, leveling the shotgun at the woman. The vampire hissed through clenched teeth, "Morrígan."

The Celtic goddess of war and the battlefield turned to look at Boomer, "Now, dear. Remember the last time you tried this? It did not end well for you. Or your friend."

Sir Gawain barked out a command, "Stand down, Miss Callahan. This is not your fight."

"Yes, deary." The goddess' voice dripped with sarcasm. "Stay out of this and let the grownups talk." A flick of her finger, and the AA-12 fell apart in Boomer's hands.

"Morrígan." The vehemence in Gawain's voice drew her attention back to him. "What do you mean that you helped?"

The goddess of the battlefield laughed. "Who do you think struck the bargain, Sir Knight? Morgan le Fay came to me for the bargain, and I arranged it. Unfortunately for her, she also asked for her favorite nephew's good fortune as well."

Mordred looked at the Morrígan, "Morgan le Fay was the reason that I drank the chalice that night?"

"Yes, little man. She wanted protection for the lad she would install on the throne. The lad who would overthrow her brother. Unfortunately, she was not willing to curse herself to save you. So she left the bargain to me." The Morrígan looked at both of them. "In all truth, you both owe your lives to me."

"What was the bargain? She did not die the first time I did."

"Have you looked in the mirror, Mordred? Your vanity was your price. Every time you die, every time you get a grievous wound, every time you suffer physical damage, your body becomes more fae. More of mine." The Morrígan looked at him and licked her lips, "You are mine."

The Usurper shouted at the goddess, "No! I am not yours to claim. I am my own. My revenge is my own, not yours."

The goddess laughed, a bright laugh sounding around the compound. "My dearest lad, you have no choice in the matter. It was bargained, well and truly. You are bound to me for as long as I keep you around."

Gawain watched the exchange, desperately searching for a solution. He knew Mordred was insane, and that he would continue to hurt the people around him, his people, until he was stopped. But how do you kill an immortal who cannot die?

The Morrígan looked at Gawain, "Sir Knight, what are you pondering right now? How to kill your brother? How to end his madness? Would you like the solution to your problem?"

Gawain held Excalibur out in front, waiting to block the anticipated strike. "Yes, Morrígan. What is the solution to my problem?"

She smiled. Without taking her eyes off of his, the goddess reached into her satchel and came up with a leather and cloth wrapped bundle. Unwrapping the bundle, she withdrew a beautiful Grecian-style urn. Gawain's eyes widened, and Mordred howled in frustration. The goddess held it out to the Knight of the Round Table and moved closer to him.

"It is yours, Sir Knight. Inside is the only weapon that can truly kill your brother and save your world. Take it." She held the urn in her hands, within arm reach of Gawain.

The Knight's eyes narrowed, and he spoke through clenched teeth, "It was you who led my brother to the urn. It was you who led him to the keys. Can he open his own gates, or did you do that for him as well?"

The mischievous smile crossed her lips but never reached her eyes. "He is powerful enough for one short gate. For this power?" The goddess gestured around her, "For this, he needed my help. Just another of his bargains."

"All those deaths? All that destruction? All those good people? Gone at your whim? What is your game, Morrígan? You are usually not this capricious." Gawain's eyes narrowed and his hand tightened on Excalibur's hilt.

The Morrígan's eyes narrowed. "You presume too much, Sir Knight. I do not answer to you, nor to anyone else. I grow tired of him, and of you. It is time to end this charade of life." She still held the urn out, "Now take the artifact, before I give it to your brother."

Gawain accepted Pandora's Box. Tucking it under his arm, he stepped back a few paces from the Morrígan and Mordred. The Knight looked back and forth at the goddess and his brother. Neither could be trusted, yet he had all the pieces. He had the power to end this feud.

With the Knight's Bane Dagger held in this artifact, he could kill Mordred. The attacks and hatred would stop, and he would be able to make things right with the fae. Is it worth the risk of re-opening Pandora's Box and possibly triggering another disaster? What would be acceptable? A minor plague might be handled by modern medicine. Natural disasters bring out the best in humanity. He could be open the urn, grab the dagger, and then close it quickly, only letting a little of the legendary curse loose.

"Open it, Sir Knight." The Morrígan purred in his ear. "End this feud with your kin once and for all time."

Gawain shook his head. The Morrígan wanted him to open the artifact. What did she get out of it? She only ever acted in her favor. He looked at the goddess, "Why?"

She stared at the Knight, not saying a word. The goddess of the battlefield was staring at Gawain and not talking. He shivered at the implications. Once more, he looked at the artifact in his hands. Both keys were in his pant pockets. It was so tempting to finally end this fight.

Gawain decided, he nodded to the Morrígan and stuck Excalibur into the hard-packed dirt of the compound. The blade sank to about a foot, and the Knight knelt to one knee.

"No!" The shout from Mordred startled Gawain. The Knight looked up and his brother, the Usurper, was running at him, intent on getting ahold of the urn. Gawain pulled back before he heard a single command from the Morrígan.

"Hold." Her voice was calm, almost bored, but the effect was instantaneous. Mordred froze in position. No, that was not right. Gawain could see his brother moving ever so slightly. It looked like the goddess had slowed time for his brother, making him move at a glacial pace while the rest of the world moved in normal time.

The goddess of the battlefield looked at Gawain. Her voice was soft, almost fragile, but there was a slight command to it, "Finish what you started. Finish your brother's time on this plane."

Gawain reached into his pockets and withdrew two small, well wrapped bundles. He peeled the layers off the first one and laid the ornate ring in the dust at the base of the artifact. The second one came unwrapped as easily, and now there were two ornate gold signet rings laying in the dirt and dust next to the artifact.

Looking around, he saw Ghost. The monster hunter was frantically shaking his head, "no." His gaze slid on, seeing Doc and Heather treating the wounded warriors. His warriors. His responsibility was to avenge those who had been killed, and to stop the attacks from ever happening again.

Gawain reached down and grabbed one of the signet rings. The Knight placed it on his index finger and lifted it to the lid and rim of the urn. He muttered a few command words in Enochian and pressed the top of the ring to the corresponding spot on the lid of the urn. There was a bright flash, showering green and blue sparks in a wide arc. Once the light cleared, the seal was gone, and the ring was just another signet ring.

The Knight dropped that signet ring into the dust. He bowed his head, praying and raising the courage to do what had to be done. Gawain carefully reached out and picked up the second ring. He paused for a moment. He was really going to unseal Pandora's Box and let evil loose on humanity. All to kill his brother with the knife inside the ancient artifact. The knife. Inside the artifact. The Knight paused, puzzling through some comments that the Morrígan had said.

The Morrígan was the key. What was in it for the goddess? Can the Knight's Bane dagger, meant for his life, really kill his brother? Gawain knew the knife would kill him. Would it remove the same immortality from another? The Morrígan said they were tied together. That their life force was each tied to the Knight's Bane. That was the catch. Neither bargain could be broken by the Morrígan directly. The goddess was deceiving him. He saw it now.

Stabbing his brother with the Knight's Bane would not affect him in the slightest. Mordred was, and is, the Morrígan's champion. Attacking Mordred would leave him vulnerable to a counter attack. The Usurper would move, and he would horribly maim or harm Gawain. Battle over, Mordred would seek to destroy the world, and all that Sir Gawain ever held dear. He saw his only option. Both Gawain and Mordred were tied to the Knight's Bane. There was only one solution.

The Morrígan could not see this coming. Gawain bowed his head one more time and asked for the strength to do what he knew must be done. The Knight touched the signet ring to the proper spot on the top of the urn and there was another blinding flash of light that sent sparks arcing out. The goddess grinned an evil, hungry grin.

Gawain dropped the now useless second key into the dust beside the first one. He paused, putting both hands on the lid of the urn. The Morrígan licked her lips. The Knight saw the gesture and gave a slight grin. "I know what you want, Morrígan. You'll not get it today."

A quick turn of his wrists and the lid was released. He shoved his hand inside Pandora's Box to grab the Knight's Bane. His hand looked older, withered, when it emerged gripping the hilt of the dragon tooth dagger. His other hand slammed the lid of the artifact back onto the urn, quickly spinning it closed. Inhaling one final breath, his other hand grabbed the hilt of the Knight's Bane. Red runes lit up around the handle and blazed brightly in a spiral up to the tip of the dagger. Sir Gawain thrust the dragon's tooth blade, point first, into his own chest, underneath the sternum. He pulled hard, the pain immense, as the curved point of the dagger rode under the breastbone to pierce his heart.

The Morrígan's cry of fury was drowned out by the screams from Boomer and Mulder. Howls of agony also roared as the nine remaining dragons and riders blazed a bright red and then collapsed, shaking the earth as they landed. Boomer was the first to reach her boss, who lay dying on the hard-packed dirt of the compound. As she ran to him, she watched Mordred collapse as well, sprawling on his face, and landing hard.

Gawain was rapidly dying. Blood started to pour out of his mouth as he tried to talk. "Miss Callahan."

Boomer could barely see through her tears as she cradled her boss' head in her arms. "Hang in there, boss. Doc'll be here soon. Hang in there."

"It has been a long life, dear." A coughing spasm hit Gawain. "I believe it is time I earned some rest."

"No, boss. Stay here. Stay with me. We need you." The tears were flowing freely down the vampire's face. She looked up and watched as Doc ran across the compound to get to them. Boomer had seen enough death to know the priest would not make it in time.

The dying Knight smiled through the pain and blood, "Tell Miss Massey that I wish I could have said goodbye." He was racked with coughing spasms, and when they ended he had passed on. His blank eyes stared at the sky, all the light extinguished.

As she gently reached up and closed Sir Gawain's lifeless eyes, the young vampire whispered, "Don't worry, boss, we'll keep the world safe." The world around her was in a slow motion fog. She watched Doc and Mulder come to a stop and hit their knees.

Doc put a finger to the Knight's neck to feel for a pulse. Finding none, she also felt his wrist. As she tried to find a pulse, she examined the gaping wound. She pulled the now burnt and blackened dragon's tooth blade out of the wound and blood barely seeped out. Seeing the angle and curvature of the blade, the priest knew the dagger had driven deep into Gawain's heart.

Ghost stood in stunned silence as he watched the one man who knew his family's history fall and hit the ground. Through a haze of shock, he stumbled toward the gathering group of agents. Looking down at the body in Boomer's arms, he could not believe that the Knight that he had known as Agent Smith was dead. The man's jacket and tie were dropped and forgotten as the monster hunter stared down in mute shock.

Gretchen crashed to a stop when she reached the group. Tears flowing freely, the young agent who had been working directly for

Agent Smith the longest was devastated. Smith was her father figure, her mentor, and her confidante. He was her boss, and then some. Weeping openly, she gently took his head and shoulders into her arms; Boomer let her grieve.

The rest of the human agents slowly gathered around the fallen hero in shock. The silence was only broken by the sounds of grief.

EPILOGUE

I t had been six months since the incident at Sanctuary. The new Section 28 headquarters was currently being constructed around the building. The Gray Court had graciously parted with some of their land for certain concessions from the United States Government, and the bureaucrats had reluctantly agreed. Sanctuary was the official designation for the headquarters, and the agency could not be happier.

When the DHS and FBI teams had shown up, there had been mass confusion, and Boomer had almost attacked the agents in her rage and pain. Cooler heads had prevailed when Mulder and Ghost had stepped forward. It had taken hours, but eventually a call to the Vice President had turned into cancelled orders. The Morrígan had disappeared by the time anyone remembered to look for her.

Videos of the incident, especially that of dragons, the gates, and the terrible creatures that spewed forth had forced the President to stop ignoring the remnants of Section 28. Media pressure had steadily grown until even Barnhart fell out of the President's favor. Neither Barnhart, nor his aide Nienhuis, ever attended another briefing.

Barnhart had his own problems, as Spooky and Spooks, working in tandem, dumped hundreds of incriminating and scandalous documents from the NSA director onto the internet. It took three days before Barnhart was fired, and only one more for his lacky, Nienhuis, to join him. A rumor went around that Barnhart had been assaulted by a couple street thugs about two months after he was fired. Although nothing was ever said, Boomer had appeared exceptionally happy that next morning.

The pressure from the media and the internet had driven the existence of creatures into the country's collective consciousness, and it was a very short time before Section 28 had been officially reinstated. The new Director was confirmed very quickly, and the teams, although severely lacking in manpower, began to deal with the increasing frequency of activity.

"TRESSA?" The voice came from the Director's office.

"Yes, boss?" Assistant Director of Section 28, Tressa Mulder, leaned her head into the door of her boss' office. "What do you need?"

"Did you see this new plan that the President is proposing?"

Mulder walked into the room and leaned against the doorway. "I've looked at it. I don't know if I like it, but at least we won't be hidden away. The paperwork I've read says this will be Cabinet-level, like NSA or DHS. What do you think?"

Gretchen Massey, the youngest Director of a governmental agency looked at her Assistant Director. "Yeah, but the name kinda sucks, doesn't it?"

The former FBI SAC agreed, "Sounds like something right out of the comic books. Office of Transhuman Affairs. Sounds like we'll be dealing with mutants, or something." Mulder smiled.

The Director nodded her head, "On the flip side, it sure sounds like a government name."

At that moment, both Mulder and her boss got a message on their phones. Mulder looked at hers first, "Incursion alarm. Ops briefing in five. They think this one is at least a Category Red." Massey nodded, skimming the message on her phone.

Director Massey locked her computer and stood, "We need to figure out who's up to speed. At least we have time for coffee on the way down."

THE RATTLE of fully automatic shotgun fire drowned out all other sound. Even the snarls of the creatures were blessedly muffled. Automatic rifle fire from an M4 carbine picked up as Six reloaded his AA-12. When the last creature landed on its back, Six slammed the drum into his shotgun's receiver, released the bolt, and rattled out a short burst, killing the horse-sized beast.

Special Agent Ryan DeBoer looked at his partner, weariness etched on his face. "The next time I want to volunteer for a 'simple' mission, just slap me."

Special Agent John Black grinned, a hint of fang showing. "It's about time you learned that lesson, Roach."

DeBoer shook his head, "I'm never going to get used to that call-sign. Just because I almost got eaten by a six foot long cockroach. I swear." His partner was laughing, and soon the rookie agent joined him.

AGENT HEATHER KALAFUT stood in front of the conference room. As a member of the monitoring and planning team, it was her turn to present the incursion alarm, and the recommended response. Director Massey and AD Mulder both walked through the door, making the meeting complete. She motioned for someone to shut and ward the door, then started her presentation.

"As of 10:28am, we received an incursion alarm from the detectors placed at a place called Blue Mountain Camp, in Florissant, Colorado. Sensor readings indicated a gate activation near there. Nothing else is showing, but we don't think it's random. According to the records, there was an incident there about nine or ten months ago? Is that why we have hardware in the area?"

The Director nodded, "Yes. That was Knightmare's first mission. It was bad enough that this becomes a priority. Who's available?"

Kalafut looked at her notes, "Knightfall is still in certification. Amanda is trying to get her team up to speed, and Heavy is helping to work the new recruits through as fast as he can. Knightsdawn is still waiting on warm bodies. David is working on more recruiting, but it's been slow getting the clearances." Kalafut looked up at her boss, "Looks like Knightmare or a couple independents, ma'am."

Massey thought and then consulted her own notes. "Send Ghost and Boomer. See if Dancer is available. Get them wheels up in an hour, and contact the local DHS office. I believe Special Agent Sonja Hart is still the SAC in that area. Have her provide support."

PETE MCCARTHY KNELT DOWN and looked at the body at his feet. He noted the claw marks running all over the upper torso. They were not quite human, but not animal. The young girl's throat was torn out, and she had died with anguish and terror on her face.

The man looked around the body for footprints or other signs. He was confused. This kill was fresh, but not devoured. This was not a vampire or revenant attack, the claw marks weren't correct.

Something non-human had killed this young girl and the State Police who caught the case contacted him directly. McCarthy had worked with officers from this particular post a couple times in the past, and they had quickly realized they were once again out of their depth.

Pete had decided not to stay with Section 28 after the fight. Instead, Gretchen had convinced him he should become an independent contractor, occasionally working with Section 28 as they needed. His injuries from the Sanctuary battle had not helped his state of mind, but they were now healing nicely.

Pete pulled out his work phone and dialed the only number programmed into device. After one ring, a woman answered. "Sanctuary Cleaning Services. How may I direct your call?"

"This is Paladin. I have a probable incursion activity at my location. I need assistance with identification and elimination. I could use a couple agents on this one."

———

TANLLADWYR WENT into secure storage with Norbert in the Warehouse, hanging alongside the Knight's Bane dagger. The signet rings were wrapped up separately and were safely placed in their own containment fields.

———

EXCALIBUR CHOSE ITS NEW KNIGHT.

———

THE *PITHOS* of Pandora was never recovered.

———

FINISHED 11/07/17, Grand Rapids, Michigan

SPECIAL AGENTS MEMORIAL WALL

I have the best fans on the planet. Period. Several of them became a Section 28 Special Agent while I was writing this book. My Special Agent fan club has many perks, and one of them is to get your name in print. These awesome folks are the newest Special Agents for Section 28.

Without further ado, in order of appearance, here are the Special Agents for *INCURSION: Dragonfire*.

Chapter 1

- Bill Kenney - pg. 8
- Frank Chanthala - pg. 8
- Brian Haywood - pg. 12
- Tressa Mulder - pg. 15

Chapter 2

- Spenser - pg. 20
- Ryan - pg. 20
- Valerie Wilcox - pg. 20
- Austin Muratori - pg. 23

Chapter 22

Chapter 23

Chapter 24

Chapter 25

Chapter 27

Chapter 28

Chapter 29

- Azriandra Darkshade - pg. 265
- Bearkinos Feralson - pg. 265

To learn more about becoming a Special Agent, find Bryan at a local comic/pop culture convention. Watch the website and facebook page for schedules.

IncursionLegends.com

Incursion Legends Facebook Page

Thank You!

Thank you so much for reading The Knight's Bane Trilogy. I appreciate your time and hope you enjoyed it.

If you enjoyed this book, please take the time to add a review on the website of the retailer where you purchased this book.

This trilogy is part of the larger series exploring the Hidden Worlds, called the World of Incursion. More information about the World of Incursion series and the Hidden Worlds can be found online and on Facebook.

Online: IncursionLegends.com
Facebook: facebook.com/incursionlegends

Sign up for my World of Incursion newsletter and receive an exclusive short story about a mysterious delivery that threatens Section 28.

Go to: https://bookhip.com/PPJKFG

PREVIEW OF SIX FEET UNDER

Prologue

Darkness. I love the darkness. It hides all kinds of sins.

The light from the overhead streetlamp formed a small pool in the midst of the darkness cloaking the street—it was the only streetlamp still glowing on this block. This neighborhood was old, and what few businesses remained hid behind steel roll-down barricades for the evening. It was just past midnight, the fabled witching hour, and the streets were almost empty. Any residents who were left in the tenement buildings were sleeping behind locked doors and barred windows.

Three blocks away, another neighborhood was in the middle of an "urban revitalization," which meant that hipsters had decided that the neighborhood contained the requisite charm of old chic and they were steadily moving in to create new, trendy cafes and nightclubs among the row houses that had suddenly quadrupled in value. In that neighborhood, every street light worked, and the area teemed with life.

But not here. If anyone happened to drive through this neighborhood after sunset, they were surely lost. And if they got lost in this neighborhood, I guarantee that their doors would be locked and their windows would be rolled up.

I looked out of the small dormer window in the apartment I currently occupied. I visually searched the block, looking for occupied cars, pedestrians, or neighbors looking out the windows. I found no signs of life. Even Mrs. Parkesian seemed to be huddled inside her own apartment. That nosy old biddy had almost seen me several times, and I knew I would have to be more careful.

Her curtains, like the rest of the curtains I could see, were all closed against the night. I stopped and closed my eyes, listening for the sounds of life around me. I could hear the faint noise of the crowds in the new neighborhood drifting on the still night. Several loud, expensive sounding engines idled and roared from that direction, but no engine noises around here. Listening with my senses wide open, I heard some scurrying in the alley below my perch. It sounded like rats. Maybe two? Three? Not enough to get excited about.

Hearing nothing larger than a rat close to me, I decided it was probably safe to emerge. I grasped the upper windowsill and swung, vaulting up and out of the window, and swinging up onto the roof of the building. I landed in a crouch and paused to make sure my exit went unnoticed. I then stood, slowly, to gaze over the neighborhood. My neighborhood.

I turned toward the newer neighborhood and made my way from rooftop to rooftop. The spans between the buildings were seldom more than fifteen or twenty feet across, and I knew this route well. This was my neighborhood. I knew where I could land from a jump without crashing through into the apartment below, which roofs were strewn with debris where I might trip, and which rooftops were favorite make-out locations for young people.

It was a dark, moonless night, and an overcast sky kept the stars invisible as well. The low overcast did faintly reflect the lights of the bustling city below, and I could see just fine as I silently loped across the skyline. I could not see in full darkness, my eyes weren't that good. But if I had even the faintest hint of light, my eyes adapted, and I could see well. It was basically the same principle as a night vision camera system, and I still required a small amount of illumination to work with. With tonight's illumination, I could see well, albeit in a monochromatic spectrum. As with a night vision camera, I stopped seeing colors, and everything was a shade of gray in low levels of light.

I was almost two blocks away from what I considered my home when furtive movement caught my eye. I slowed to a halt and squatted. I peered over the edge of the rooftop and looked into the alley below.

Hidden behind a dumpster, a man fidgeted with something in

his hands, nervously waving it about himself in small motions. He kept glancing back around the corner of the dumpster toward the street. I could see his lips moving. I knelt and concentrated until I could make out his words.

"No. I don't wanna do it. But if I do, I can get some. Johnny said I needed cash. I can't get green. But they might. I need it, but Johnny's a real dick. He won't give it to me."

I waited. The man's conversation seemed to drift along those lines for a while, so I inspected the man. He was… scruffy. He wore a military surplus Army jacket that was threadbare and worn. It was filthy and stained with several rather dubious looking spots. Underneath the jacket, his dirty t-shirt was stained a dark brown and gray. His pants were long and hung on his gaunt frame, with holes in the knees and worn thin on the thighs. He wore dirty sneakers that looked as if they might have been red at one time. His drawn frame spoke of hard street living, probably helped by the hard narcotics he was currently arguing with himself about.

What caught my attention was the small revolver clutched in his shaking hands. From my vantage point, it looked like a cheap brand that was "chrome plated." If it sold in a gun store for over two hundred dollars, I'd be shocked. Even at Seattle's inflated prices it was a real piece of junk. He kept caressing the gun as if it was his security blanket. And it likely was. After all, it helped this petty thief steal enough to buy his chosen narcotic poison.

He suddenly went still as he saw something that interested him around the edge of the dumpster. I followed his gaze in time to watch two well-dressed young women walk past the end of the alley. As they walked, the one on the left stumbled, almost overbalancing her girlfriend on her other arm. From the stumbling and loud whispering, I noticed that they both were too drunk to be walking alone at night, especially through this neighborhood.

The man below witnessed the same actions, and I looked back at him in time to see a look of hunger and cunning wash across his face. He licked his lips as if he could taste the drugs he would buy once he rolled these two girls. He stood up and began slowly walking to the end of the alley. I rose and stepped off the rooftop.

The ground was about fifty feet below and seemed to rush up at me. I bent my knees to absorb the impact and felt my feet hit the asphalt. I landed and bent further to absorb the shock, crouched with my hand out on the pavement for support. Any superhero would be proud of that landing. And through it all, the loudest sound I made was the soft rubber soles of my shoes making a dull thud against the pavement. I had landed less than five feet behind the addict.

Even through the haze of desire and addiction, the man heard my landing. He turned around in time to see me rise from my crouch. Seeing the look in my eyes, he hastily raised the revolver and pointed it at my face.

I doubt he had loaded silver bullets in the gun. I could almost guarantee that there were not any of Norbert's special vampire killing rounds in the revolver. And I cannot imagine that he had his bullets bathed in holy water. With that being said, I still did not feel like getting shot tonight. It hurt, and the gunfire would draw too much attention to the area. Besides, I would have to find more new clothes. So I did not get shot.

Even if he were not an addict going through withdrawal, my reflexes would still be faster than his. I lashed out and grabbed the revolver, ripping it out of the guy's hand before he could even register that I had moved. As a followup, I decked him. Hard. I didn't put all my strength into the blow, but I used my boosted strength to give the man an uppercut that rattled his teeth, slammed his skull against the dumpster, and knocked him out cold.

I pocketed the revolver and picked the man up. I tossed him into the dumpster, where he landed on several bags of trash. I dusted myself off, and stepped out of the alley behind the two very drunk, and very oblivious, young women. From twenty feet away, I could smell the odor of expensive booze, arousal, frustration, and... despair. I'm sure a human could have at least smelled the booze.

"Ahem." I cleared my throat.

The young women whirled around, unsteady on her feet. I held my hands up in the universal gesture of peace.

"Ladies, you seem to have wandered far from the club. Are you lost?"

The slightly less inebriated woman slurred, "Nope. I'm sure my car is around here, somewhere. Now back off pal. I'm not looking for a hookup."

I looked around the quiet, empty street and frowned. "Listen, I'm sure you are fine, but your car isn't on this block. I think you took a wrong turn, and should go back to get a cab from the club." I took the time to catch her eyes, concentrated, and fought her willpower through her alcohol induced-haze. Finally, I felt her will slip, and become mine.

I softened my voice and spoke with her, "You know that you went the wrong way. You know that you need to go back to the club and get a cab. And you know that I can be trusted to point you in the right direction."

The young woman was nodding as I spoke. And just because I found it funny I ended with, "These are not the droids you are looking for."

The enthralled woman spoke up, "These are not the droids I'm looking for, and I can trust you to show me how to get back to the club."

I smiled and pointed the way back to the street filled with clubs and cafes, "Go back that direction, until you find the club you were in. There, you will have the bouncer call you a cab."

She beamed a huge smile at me and nodded enthusiastically. She grabbed her friend, and they began to stumble back the way they had come, toward the life and action. As they left, I turned back to the alley and made my way over to the dumpster and the unconscious addict.

I hauled the man out of the dumpster and got my bearings. There was an abandoned factory about two blocks east, and I began heading in that direction. I stuck to the darkened alleys the whole way, carrying the addict over my shoulder in a fireman's carry. When I had to cross streets, I waited in the shadows until I was sure that there were no vehicles or pedestrians about, then sprinted across the street. It was only a few minutes before I arrived at the factory.

I tossed the man over the chain-link fence surrounding the building and followed him with a leap. I picked up his unconscious form in a fireman's carry again and carried him into the heart of the factory, into a special room that hid from all but the most deter-mined searchers. From the outside, the metal door was rusted and stained, with a simple pull handle attached. Affixed to the wall next to the rusted door was a placard that read, "Storage Closet." I took a moment to look around and made sure that I was still alone in this abandoned factory before I grabbed the handle and pushed the door inward.

Although it seemed rusty and decrepit from the outside, the well-oiled hinges swung the door silently open into the awaiting darkness. I stepped through and tossed the man onto the cold cement floor. I turned back around and swung the door closed, pushing a three-inch-thick steel bar into place to lock it. Although I could see perfectly in the pitch black, I enjoyed the terror that usually accom-panied my prey when they saw my fangs, so I reached out for the stack of chemlights that I kept on the shelf next to the door and grabbed one, snapping it and shaking to make the chemicals inside react to each other. The sickly green glow lighted the room.

Roughly fifteen feet square, the walls and ceiling were cinder block construction, and the floor was a smooth, polished cement. In the middle of the floor sat a massive sewer drain with the inch-thick bars deep set into the floor, the cross-hatched bars forming a grid with two-inch openings. Through the grate, I could hear the sound of rushing water—one of the larger sewer drains in this section of town.

I heard a moan from the addict as he stirred. Once he pried his eyes open, panic dawned across his face as he took in the solid walls around him. His darting glances finally landed on me. I was crouched down, staring at him. Waiting for him to speak.

He started babbling, "What the... where am I? How did I get here? Who the hell are you?"

I smiled, it was a dark, unsettling smile with just the tips of my fangs showing, and he blanched, his face going white. "You are my dinner guest this evening."

"Wha? Whaddya mean, 'dinner?'"

I leaned forward slowly, motioning as if to tell him a secret. He hesitantly leaned forward, and I reached up and grabbed the back of his head. I grimaced slightly, smelling his fetid breath as I leaned in and whispered in his ear, my voice soft and low, "You."

My fangs elongated. I tilted slightly down and then ripped out his throat before he could even scream. I fed.

After I finished feeding, I looked at the mangled corpse in front of me. The throat was missing, the wrists were shredded, and there was a fist-sized hole in its chest. It would not take an autopsy to notice that the heart was missing. I licked my lips, sated. I would not be hungry for another few days, and my body was already neutralizing the toxins that were in his bloodstream from his long history of drug abuse. I looked at the grate in the floor. The bars were set into a square metal box set in the floor. I tugged at the grate, and it rose up and aside. I looked down into the darkness below and saw water glinting in the harsh green glow of the chemlight.

I grasped the corpse and dropped it into the rushing water below. This line of the sewer was a continually running main trunk that fed beneath the industrial plants in this area. The fast moving water was about three feet deep, and would carry anything dropped into it over three miles away and deposit it in one of the larger trunk lines that fed out to the bay, and then to the sea. Along the way, the body would be battered and beaten by the walls and grates, torn apart by the currents, and eventually end up in the sea, behind a large grate. If anything remained, the crabs would feed on it. I knew that there were other creatures that lived in the sewers further down the stream that would make that entirely unlikely.

I leaped down into the murky water and held my ground against the current. I took the time to clean any trace of the blood from my face and hands, and to wash out my clothes. I knew that I could not go back up top with any trace of the addict on me. I would have to change into the spare suit in my truck before I went into work.

I finished washing myself off and looked at my watch. I had allowed myself to forget about time. It was almost dawn. I hoped that it was raining up above, or I would be the only one walking around in wet clothes.

Yes, I can walk around in daylight, although I do get sunburned easily. In fact, I had a job that I needed to attend. I had let myself be too distracted by hunting, and my boss would not be pleased. This was the second time this month that I was going to be late, and I would probably be reprimanded.

My name is Burt Holstein, but you can call me, "Six." I work for the Department of Homeland Security in a top secret division called Section 28. And I am a vampire.

WE HOPE that you have enjoyed this preview of *Six Feet Under*. If you want to find out how Six became a vampire and learned to like the Northwest, you can find the novella in ebook or print at IncursionLegends.com or your favorite online retailer.

ALSO BY BRYAN DONIHUE

INCURSION: Knightmare

The Knight's Bane Trilogy–Book 1

Sometimes the barrier that separates our world from others gets thin, and nightmares come through to our world. Team Knightmare is the latest special response team from Section 28 designed to control or eliminate threats from other planes. Their first mission is a vampire hunt. Will it be their last?

INCURSION: Faeblade

The Knight's Bane Trilogy–Book 2

A massacre at a fae nightclub drives the Seelie Court to blame humans. Team Knightmare is sent to Michigan to investigate the horrors, and their job is about to get very difficult. With skepticism from the fae on one side and a group of human monster hunters on the other, Knightmare is trying to stop a war between the fae courts and humanity.

INCURSION: Dragonfire

The Knight's Bane Trilogy–Book 3

Section 28 is the secret agency that is tasked with hunting monsters and with controlling mystical forces that live on our plane. The agency is under attack from forces from Smith's past and from within the United States Government. Can Section 28 survive the attacks? Can Smith?

Pick up ebooks and signed copies of the books at:

IncursionLegends.com/shop

or at Amazon, iBooks, and your favorite retailer.

You can read short stories from the World of Incursion at:

IncursionLegends.com

ABOUT THE AUTHOR

Early in his life, Bryan decided that he would try as many different jobs as possible. Well, it was his high curiosity and low attention span that decided for him. He started in fast food and has worked in sales (retail, used car, business-to-business, door-to-door, credit card processing, vacuum cleaner, and firearms). Bryan has also been a security guard, police officer, and armored car vault manager. And he was a youth pastor.

Eventually, he decided he'd take the "easy path" and become a writer. He was an idiot. Writing is not easy, but it turned out, he was pretty good at it. People seemed to like his stories, so he kept telling them.

Bryan is a published author (fiction and non-fiction), game designer, graphic artist, web designer, consultant, trainer, ministry leader, and multiple-business owner. He is also happily married to his wife of over 20 years, Christina, and father to six or seven kids, depending on the day. He even sleeps occasionally.

Bryan is currently writing from a hidden bunker in Grand Rapids, Michigan. At least that's what he claims. We know he sits in a home office with a brass plaque that reads "Dungeon" affixed over the door.

To read more of the World of Incursion:
IncursionLegends.com
bryan@incursionlegends.com

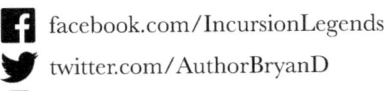

facebook.com/IncursionLegends
twitter.com/AuthorBryanD
instagram.com/bryandonihue

ABOUT SECTION 28 PUBLISHING

Helping Authors Find Their Voice...

Section 28 Publishing is a small, independent press created by author Bryan Donihue to publish his dark paranormal fiction. The fiction published by Section 28 is typically urban fantasy. Currently, Section 28 only publishes works from Bryan, but we are looking forward to working with other authors.

Why "Section 28"?

Originally, the name "Section 28" was created by Troye Gerard, and he graciously allowed Bryan to use the name as a secret government agency in the world that Bryan was creating. The first book set in that world was INCURSION: Knightmare. In that book, "Section 28" is the name of the secret division of Homeland Security that is charged with monitoring and controlling the paranormal in the United States. Bryan chose to use the name as his publishing imprint in homage to that organization, and his first published fiction.

The Mission of Section 28 Publishing

Section 28 Publishing's mission is to help authors figure out the labyrinth that can be independent publishing. From cover design and layout to marketing and sales, Bryan loves to help authors go from a manuscript to a published book that readers want to buy. For an author, nothing is better than having that first fan approach them at a venue, and Bryan wants every author to get that chance.